I0579964

August of Deliverance

August of Deliverance

Michael Cameron

Published by Deeds Publishing in Athens, GA
www. deedspublishing. com

Printed in The United States of America

Cover design by Mark Babcock

ISBN 978-1-947309-20-3

Books are available in quantity for promotional or premium use. For information, email info@deedspublishing. com.

Second Printing, 2019

10 9 8 7 6 5 4 3 2 1

to my Father and my Mother

1

DINGY CHOCOLATE SMOKE CASCADED HASTILY SKYWARD, AS if trying to escape from itself, through the rusted metal chimneys of the dark and dank downtown tire factory. Under thick billowing layers of EPA-be-damned pollutants, along the bleak avenue on both sides of the street, were smaller but similarly dilapidated archaic buildings, many of which once housed thriving businesses that had long ago become defunct. There they sat, unoccupied and decaying. Sundry shades of grays, blacks, and browns melded together, yielding an oppidan landscape that seemed to almost frown at the sun.

A few small manufacturing plants and parts-supply stores still survived, crammed tightly together behind cracked, sagging sidewalks acceding to occasional splashes of nature's verdant color of hope. Grass stems and weeds sprouted a foot high in some places from uneven sections of concrete, forcing the harsh ambience to accept an un-manicured but soothing touch of defiant green. This blighted, smog-soaked scenery, home to the homeless as well as a destination for those who sought the proverbial walk on the wild side, repeated itself for several blocks in either direction; another aging urban industrial community continued to exist in aesthetic competition, on summer days like this, with the divine cerulean canopy above.

Such was the scene offered, this Wednesday, August 1, 2018, by a routine workday on Miracle Boulevard in the Drollman district of Detroit, Michigan.

"Shit down here, pretty up there. We got some serious atmosphere goin' on in da 'hood, baby. Oh well, what da hell? It's a life," Smilin' Al said to some local passersby as he carried an armload of rubber refuse from Spinoza Tire Company to the dumpster at the edge of the parking lot. "I got a job; I ain't complainin'. We be rollin' in the Motor City."

Smilin' Al, at the age of seventy-eight and a 41-year employee of Spinoza, kept on working hard with no intentions of retiring anytime soon. "What would I do? Besides the money I make—it ain't much but it's good enough for my bills I pay—work keeps my mind alive. I don't care if it is the same damn thing I keep doin' over and over again," he explained to a coworker. "I'll keep doin' it over. Work is good. I work my black ass off here, but Spinoza needs me. Yeah, man, dey needs me. Dey needs me haulin' dem tires. I'm a badass worker and dey know dat's true. Had to slow down the past few years, though…had to slow down a bit…probably need to slow down some more."

****

Across the street from Spinoza, another crumbling edifice featured a stark sign which injudiciously identified its commerce in mockingly paradoxical terms. "Downtown Secrets" was printed in oversized, slashing letters with gaudy mauve paint on an 8' by 2' heavy, tan, wooden board supported by only two twisted thick wires running through holes in the wood and attached to the semi-rotted awning. A single red, low-wattage limelight affixed below and aimed upward illuminated the seedy designation.

This unstable and equally unsubtle signage hung menacingly over the entrance to the blasphemous blues club, dangling about 11 feet from the walkway below and precariously over the heads of entrants who ventured inside to "dance." Pictured on either side of the title were caricatures of nicely dressed couples dancing to the blues. The club promoted itself as a place where despondent revelers could "use the Blues to beat the Blues."

Everyone familiar with the community knew the overarching lure for most patrons of Downtown Secrets had little to do with dancing, unless it was lap-dancing in the VIP Room, where interactions typically advanced from dancing to debauchery. Strangers in the dark, whose physical closeness ensured their emotional distance, furnished the intimacies of their bodies while locking their hearts. But there were exceptions.

Lonely men with the blues in their souls came to Downtown Secrets for some red-light diversion. However transitory and ultimately unfulfilling such short-lived soothing might prove in terms of enduring bliss, for many of the men who came, fugacious pleasures of the flesh and a feminine caress trumped the coldness of sterile isolation.

****

Kristi Lou, one of the "dance instructors," was standing outside with a few other working girls, including her work-friend, Dark Rochelle—the cognomen thirty-eight-year-old Yolanda Simmons, genetically infertile and childless, had chosen for her on-duty name. Kristi Lou was intentionally soaking in some early-evening sunshine. She did not want to develop what she termed as "that prostitute paleness," though she also feared contracting a melanoma, especially from tanning beds.

There was no name obfuscation for Kristi Lou; her choice was to use her real name in all circles, including when she posted comments on blogs and message boards as well as on social media.

Kristi Lou waved and congenially shouted, with her delicate lilt,

"Hey, Smilin' Al," as he slowly strolled toward the back gate of Spinoza. Al cordially returned her gesture, with his trademark wide, ivory smile framed against a pitch ebony face, then yelled across the street, "You still got yo head in the clouds, babydoll?" He then receded into the comforting toils of his rote labor.

"Yes, I'm still a skyscraper. I can't help it. But I don't look down on anyone."

Kristi Lou propelled her melodic voice with as much projection as she could muster, but was unsure whether Al heard her affable replies as he drifted away with his slow stroll, vanishing beyond a mound of tires.

****

Caucasian, flawlessly symmetrical with striking Teutonic features, including soft, unblemished skin, highly-arched cheekbones, B-34-size firm breasts, a blatantly bubbled butt, and Amazon-like toned and cut 44-inch legs which virtually appeared to rise to her neck, the lovely-beyond-rational-dispute Kristi Lou Jones, perhaps showcasing God's blueprint for the classic blue-eyed blonde, unfurled to reveal an athletic, sylphlike frame of 147 pounds proportioned with genetic artistry throughout her height of 6'1" or, as she preferred to say, 5'13".

Kristi Lou, reared in a pleasant suburb of Little Rock, Arkansas, sometimes wondered whether she should have eschewed basketball in high school back in her hometown, where she politely spurned the pleadings of Ms. Hermine, the longstanding coach/chemistry teacher at Central Arkansas High. Rather than follow in the footsteps of her parents, both of whom had been accomplished hoops stars at the high school level, Kristi Lou declined, having housed diametrically opposite concerns: it would have perhaps been too easy to dominate the other teams' players and she may've embarrassed them—or, she may've, despite her high-top advantage, failed.

Instead of basketball, she opted for track and cross-country, excelling at both, particularly the latter. She had immensely enjoyed the courses that were long and winding through the woods; she would leap over crevices and high bumps swimmingly, like an insouciant impala.

****

Almost three months prior to this mildly humid August evening, back in May, Kristi Lou had completed her junior year at Wayne State University in midtown Detroit. She carried a 3.8 GPA, with a declared major in education and a minor in English.

She had waitressed for two-and-a-half years at The Potato Place, an on-campus eatery on W. Warren Avenue. Kristi Lou consistently saved most of her tips. Every other week, upon finishing her Friday day shift, she would walk a short distance from the restaurant to the almost-next-door Bank of America branch to deposit her gratuities into her savings account.

Kristi Lou had not dated anyone since February, having engineered an amicable parting of the ways with a young man, Andrew, of age twenty-three, with whom she had gone out four times. She had realized that, although he was well-mannered and considered quite good-looking by most females, she didn't feel mutual chemistry sufficient to sustain a long-term romance. She didn't want to string him along and have his feelings for her become too deep; the sooner she broke away the less he would be hurt. She let him down gently, telling him that he could still call her and that they could get together now and then if he wanted to, and provided him with the de rigueur assurance given in such breakups: they could "still be friends."

As of April 1, she had finally reached the milestone of twenty-one years of living.

I'm a legal beagle. What do I do with myself now?

On that very birthday, after conversing intently with herself, she decided to *quit studying for a while and earn some major-league funds … check out another style of life … cross over to the other side … see how it feels.*

She had passed by Downtown Secrets, located about three miles from the WSU campus, on several occasions while riding in cars driven by college friends or dates. After reviewing her initial decision of April 1 and re-contemplating the possible consequences, a contemplation in which she immersed herself on and off for several days, Kristi Lou took the plunge and stepped over the ethereal border and fit herself into one of civilized society's darker crevasses.

Kristi Lou was interviewed April 15 by the sixty-seven-year-old owner, Samuel Beneventi, who, at 6'6" and 275 pounds, was known as Big Sam. She was accepted on the spot. A few weeks remained till the end of the spring semester, but she wasted no time in delving into her lifestyle permutation, beginning work at Secrets that very night.

Now I'm officially a Lady of the Evening, she had thought to herself as she rode home in a taxi following her first shift.

In the back of her mind, she wondered whether hers was the immature decision of an impetuous knave.

Maybe I'm an April Fool for real.

Kristi Lou had attended Mass at Sweetest Heart of Mary Roman Catholic Church on Russell Street since soon after beginning her freshman year at WSU almost three years earlier, in fall semester of 2015.

She stopped going to church.

I can't go to church anymore … too incongruent … no, I just can't … I wonder if I know what I'm doing … I don't know whether I know … am I trying to reincarnate Mary Magdalene? … actually, there are no verses in the Bible that clearly say she was a … but now you are …

She didn't slink into one of the backrooms to sleep with a customer till mid-May, the day after completing her spring semester at WSU.

Why do they call it "sleeping"? I was awake the whole time. I know; it's a euphemism.

The girls were allowed the option of discretion, but management at Secrets had become concerned over the length of time Kristi Lou had spent with no known congress for pay. However, she was always careful to provide courteous explanations that were delivered with such charismatic charm and seeming sincerity that not a single patron had complained about her in-house celibacy.

****

Kristi Lou had continued her listing with a reputable modeling agency, but had modeled sparingly as of late—which was fine with her—having fallen out of favor with both the owner and her booking agent over the past year due to refusing numerous auditions. She had claimed that her studies took precedence and often conflicted with the model assignments, which, in part, was true. Chiefly, though, she had simply become weary of the work, which, she felt, did not pay enough for the time she invested.

Nevertheless, occasional hassles and insufficient compensation notwithstanding, Kristi Lou appreciated particular aspects of the modeling industry and liked most of the models and clients with whom she had worked. She was not one of those ungrateful models who take pride in sneering at modeling as essentially subtle slavery for airheads from which they had broken away because the toil of beauty—which had originally flattered their egos, as well as earned them some livelihood and strengthened their self-concept—had at some point fallen beneath their intellectual and occupational dignity.

She resented such models for their resentment.

****

Above her defense of the modeling industry, though, was Kristi Lou's signature philosophical calling card:

Men are not villains because they are sexually attracted to women they find physically appealing.

Kristi Lou, fundamentally rebellious against this societal convention, neither relished nor participated in the customary vilification of heterosexual males who sought carnal gratification from women in general as well as from her and her contemporaries in the sexual entertainment industry, as long as these men did not manifest their desires in disrespectfully crude demonstrations. However, she did not deem all crudeness to be disrespectful, as mutually agreed upon dirty talk was quite palatable to her—albeit sometimes embarrassing—as long as such dialogue fell within the context of role-playing and was thus not intended as seriously dehumanizing.

As she had told one of her girlfriends about a year earlier as they strolled across campus, "They can't help it. They've got to be attracted to attractive females, especially of reproductive age; it's ingrained in them from zillions of centuries of evolutionary instincts. That attraction is precisely the antithesis of perversion—of which men are often ridiculously accused here—because such heterosexual allure is staggeringly natural, regardless of society's legal or cultural rules, or the age, appearance, or financial status of the aroused male. I'm pretty darn sure those nature-driven arousals have a lot to do with why we're all here today."

Her loving parents, living back in Kristi Lou's hometown of Little Rock, knew she was taking a hiatus from school. But, as is typical with the families of most college-age women who enter the sex industry, Mom and Dad did not know the deeper nature of their enterprising daughter's employment endeavors. They thought she really did teach dance. And they were right about that; she did provide dancing lessons in Downtown Secrets. They just didn't know what else she provided.

Besides, as Kristi Lou would assure herself, *it's just sort of a white lie, and it's to protect them, and I really don't do it… not, you know, not all the way, anyway… with most of these men; I mostly mainly just dance with them or for them. And I do really instruct some of them on dancing techniques; well, sometimes I do. So that's teaching. Yes, I realize that with working in this place and being with these guys that I'm compromising my rectum, uh, I mean, my rectitude, but, still, I mainly just help them dance better. That's really mainly what I really do, really; I'm really a dancer and a dance instructor, so that's… that's actually what I primarily am.*

And this assessment, replete with her self-comforting rationalizations, was technically veracious; she had copulation with only a small fraction of her total clientele, that being no more, usually, than about two or three per month. And she was always careful to size them up for probable "disease-freeness," as she tagged her precaution. She was ever-cognizant of her commitment to not stay in the world's oldest profession too long; she had a healthy fear of Human Immunodeficiency Virus as well as other STDs, hence her intransigent policy of *no condom-less coitus.*

Kristi Lou was not going to permit herself to sink too deeply into the sometimes-fabled hooker lifestyle, with the wild and reckless daily living and often crawling off the bed beyond the break of noon with raccoon circles surrounding eyelids, and with the dependence on addictive narcotics, whether illegal or not. No crack whore would she become—not even in appearance.

She forbade herself to develop that hardened, unyieldingly cynical facial countenance that she felt typified many of the "veterans."

Concerning epidermal ink-art, ne'er on Kristi Lou would be found a tattoo.

And she would avoid acquiring that raspy voice, which she concluded was usually induced by cigarettes. She once took a pen and notepaper and wrote a memo to herself asseverating that she would avoid that "grating, cough-laced spew of discordant oral noise." Those "scratchy inflections" spoken by such women was "a cacophony that is stridently unfeminine. Regardless of however severely stressed I feel, I will not placate *any* stress with the unhealthy habit of tobacco. No! I won't do it!"

Regarding the pervasiveness of illicit recreational drugs throughout the sex industry, Kristi Lou was certain she was the only entertainer in the history of Downtown Secrets to never have used, at a minimum, the ever-heralded "drug that should be legalized." She was offered marijuana on multiple occasions when she began working at Secrets in April, though by August all other dancers had long since abandoned their efforts to persuade Kristi Lou to do weed.

She had turned down pot while in high school as well as rejecting it over the past three years up the road on the university campus, though she came close to accepting an offer from one of her college roomies. She had the reefer in her hand and was already a little high from the other girl's smoke pervading the dorm room. Some trigger in her compelled her to "just say no" to this girl, albeit politely, and to get up and leave.

As she once recalled during one of her frequent self-analyses, *I may have been channeling Nancy Reagan. I think I maybe felt like the First Lady from back in the '80s was hovering over my shoulder saying to me what she said on TV—"Just say no!"*

To her coworkers with whom she discussed the subject, she made her commitment to abstain as clear as her libertarian perspective that usage of all feel-good drugs should be legalized for people of adult age, as long as they didn't drive under the influence, operate a boat, fly a plane, perform a medical procedure, or engage in any activity that their drug-induced impairment would cause to be an endangerment of anyone else.

Notwithstanding her tolerance for other people of sound and adequately mature mind deciding for themselves whether they would or would not use such mind-altering concoctions, there would be no drugs of consequence in Kristi Lou's body that were not medicinal.

Kristi Lou knew some of the women at Secrets, as well as some of the male staff, snorted cocaine and/or smoked crack, and at least one shot up heroin; she once saw the woman's track marks under bright lighting, a sight so disturbing to Kristi Lou that she was made to shiver violently.

As she told other women working at Secrets, including her friend Dark Rochelle one night back in April during her first week at work: "I don't want to do drugs. I am not going to do drugs. That's all there is to it. Anyone here will be wasting his or her time trying to get me to do drugs. I will not do drugs. Period."

And she promised herself she would *never, ever* allow herself to develop that coarse, perpetually hostile personality that settles into the dispositions of many girls after they remain a *pro* in the sex industry for longer than they arguably should.

****

On this August evening, Kristi Lou and Rochelle were gum-bumping with idle prattle about whether it's still socially cool to leave shoelaces untied in public, while Hokey Washington, the fifty-six-year-old, 6'9", 345-pound bouncer—euphemistically called the "floor manager"—stood about fifteen yards away guarding the entrance to Downtown Secrets. Kristi Lou suddenly switched conversational gears to offer her views on the personas of what she saw as the meaner version of modern, radically liberated women.

"I'm not going to become a brittle B termagant always looking for a confrontation. I'm not going to become a shrew against men. I'm not going to become a bigoted man-hater harridan. I'm not going to become that kind of venomous feminist," she assured Rochelle.

"I've observed that many younger women about my age, in their 20s, or those in their 30s or 40s, like to put down older feminists who were young radicals in the 1960s or '70s as 'irrelevant' along with other insipid insults of that nature. They're wrong. The influence of those '60s and '70s feminist types, as obnoxious as their anti-male chauvinism often was and is, continues on today, whether or not these younger women who dismiss them realize it. The younger women who are feminists comprise what's called third-wave feminism."

Kristi Lou paused her audio to aggressively scratch a sudden sharp itch at the top of her forehead.

"And, I should like to point out that there are countless numbers of these older feminists, who brought about second-wave feminism, who are still quite alive. And many of them go to the polls and vote and therefore directly impact social patterns and the actual laws that govern us. And also, these older women feminists are just as much a part of the population known as 'women' as these arrogant, in-denial younger women critics who denounce old-school feminists and claim that 'women' these days don't care about these feminists' issues. They can't commandeer the word 'women' and they can't rationally apply it only to themselves. And, when it comes to younger feminists, they are, in some real ways, worse—in my opinion—than the older ones when it comes to their strident bigotry that comes from their anti-straight-male sexuality feelings and attitudes. And most of them will deny it and many of them don't even seem to realize they think and feel that way."

Dark Rochelle, an eighth-grade dropout who both liked and admired Kristi Lou, stood nodding, offering an occasional verbal affirmation such as "oh yeah" or "uh-huh."

"And, there's one more thing I want to say," added Kristi Lou.

"Oh, I doubt dat," said Rochelle. "Probably mo than one mo."

"I know I've been criticizing feminists, myself. But those younger women in my age bracket who denounce all feminists, bunching them all together in the same category—that is the extremist man-haters lumped in with the reasonable feminists—are making a mistake. We all really do owe a debt of gratitude to the more moderate but still assertive feminists of years gone by. That includes the first-wave feminists who battled for and won the women's suffrage movement back in the early 1900s so we all can vote nowadays. And that includes the reasonable feminists of the '60s and '70s who valiantly fought for causes and effected positive changes that many of these same insulters take for granted today. That includes the achievements made in the fight for, as they say, 'equal pay for comparable work' so women these days can and usually do earn the same salaries for the same jobs that men earn.

"OK, according to some reports there might still be improvements left to be made in that area—that is, the equal pay thing. But, you know what? More men get educated and trained for the higher-paying careers and more women get educated and trained for the lower-paying careers. More men pursue STEM degrees—that abbreviates science, technology, engineering, and math. Those jobs pay more. And, frankly, men are, I think, just naturally better—with exceptions, of course—than we are at those things. When I say better, I mean genetically better, more predisposed toward excelling in those fields of endeavor. I know that's sexist, but I believe there's too much evidence over the centuries to deny.

"As an outgrowth of what I call betterness, anti-malesim is rife with bitterness. Males, overall, are better at numerous enterprises. Relatedly, look at the dissection of anti-male versus anti-female attitudes. The former is much more widespread. The anti factor may total about the same numbers re overreactions to being spurned/burned by the opposite sex over romantic disappointment. However, the *aggregate* carriers of *all* anti feelings are very unequal. More members of one side harbor bitter envy toward the other for possessing superiority anent life-enhancing inventions such as indoor running water and electricity, businesses, technology, governmental/economic systems, and infrastructure vital to civilization. Imagine a magic eraser that erased all female contributions to those entities. Then, imagine that eraser erasing all male contributions. One of those erasures would likely make all of us neighbors of the Flintstones. Overall, men are doers while women are sayers. Sexist? Yes. Factual? Yes. The contraposition of the poppycock sexistly opined by the otherwise estimable Margaret Thatcher? Yes. Sexistly? Did I just say 'sexistly'? Yes.

"But, anyway, yes—many of the second-wave feminists were indeed bigoted against straight-male sexuality and were bigots against men, in general. An example of that bigotry is a rabies-froth, somewhat-suf-fused-with-silliness, anti-male novel, first published in 1977, titled *The Women's Room*. The book-cover title serves as a placard presaging the linchpin theme that can be found within the interior pages of the book: The patriarchy is oppressive. Why? Because of its imposition of traditional gender-specific and allegedly female-suppressing roles. And, from the book, here's a see-it-daily example of the exhaustive cultural deconstruction that is sorely needed: You must designate any public restroom for females as a *women's room* rather than a *ladies' room* because the latter nomenclature supposedly carries with it a long-established, shameful stigma imposed by the raunchy and execrable patriarchal op-pressors, which is this—a mere *lady* is weak and un-hear-me-roaring. Nope. Pure unreality. Some of the mentally strongest women anywhere are tradition-drenched ladies.

"One of the book's pivotal thematics is the vacuous tosh that men can't really know women because we're allegedly too unfathomably mysterious for them and therefore intellectually impenetrable—and being radical feminists, such females are surely not fan-girls of dick-stick physical penetration, either. Anyhow, that 'we're-an-intricate-mys-tery' formula is designed to lead to this most convenient ruling about men's outlook toward women: 'Since you don't know 'em, you can't criticize 'em.' Right. Congrats girls—you're unknowable! Thus, you should henceforward be able to sweet-step through life while being revered by guys as immune from reproof and exempt from reproach!

"There's a nonsensical blurb on the front cover of some versions of the book avowing that *The Women's Room* is beneficial 'For every man who thought he knew a woman,' blah, blah, blah. That oft-propagandized 'women-are-incomprehensibly-enigmatic' notion, if it's going to possess any merit, requires epic miscommunication such that women must be total verbal and nonverbal failures at expressing themselves; or that men—the population of people who've been brainy enough to invent practically every useful thing we women utilize in our daily lives—are too blockheaded to understand what women say or do; or that women are thoroughbred liars with their words and actions, inveterately portraying themselves mendaciously and with little or no integrity. The author, who is now lamentably deceased—and may she rest in peace—was a second-wave rad-fem who seemed deeply into anti-maleism. She might've otherwise been a sensible-minded lady … oops … woman—sorry, unintentional slip-up, really. But, she had—and some of her myrmidons still have—the gall to contend that such clairvoyant feminists are somehow able to *know* other women they haven't even met better than men know their own female loved ones in whose presence they've consistently lived for a long time—for years, for decades, for generations, for lifetimes.

"Arguing with wacko-ish people while applying rationalism is challenging. But, still though, the levelheaded, non-lunatic feminists—we are indebted to them."

"Buncha big words jumpin' offa yo tongue, again. But, yeah," agreed Rochelle, "we does owe 'em somethin' for what dey done."

"Yeah, yes we do," said Kristi Lou with a firm smile and one of those half-inch chin dips that people use to show emphasis. She breathed deeply and, whirling around while standing about two feet away from

Rochelle, kicked her right foot and sleek black pump playfully in the air as she spun.

****

Rochelle, remembering that Kristi Lou had announced back in April, during her first week at Secrets, her commitment to vegetarianism, asked her about her dietary choices.

"If you still a vegetarian, you don't eat no meat. Whatch you eat?"

"Vegetables."

"Dat's all you eat?"

"No. I eat fruit, too, and grains, and sugar-sinner candy, and bread—with gluten; I'm not gluten-intolerant, so …"

"Oh yeah, I hear all dis and dat 'bout not eatin' no gluten—gluten dis and gluten dat, and …"

"I know, right? But gluten is good 'cause it makes bread tastier and gives it a more-gooder, chewy texture. So, I'm glad I can have it.

"Oh, I also love ice cream, but I despise the cruelty inflicted upon cows by the dairy industry. Hence, I will no longer eat it. I choose the non-dairy version of ice cream, typically called frozen dessert on the cartons. I like the So Delicious brand, made with cashew milk, soy milk, coconut milk, almond milk, or oat milk.

"OK, Rochelle. Gird yourself. Here comes a data-packed rant.

"Based on my research, I doubt there are many happy cows, especially on factory farms. The dairy marketers show on their websites cows masticating mirthfully and seemingly happy while being treated kindly. But those cows are the minority. Dairy hides from the buying public what goes on behind the scenes of the money-milk industry. It's hard to be happy when you're stuffed into a cage called a rape rack—that's what some dairy workers call the mini-dungeon where they shove a gloved hand holding an insemination tube containing semen taken from a bull up your anus and inject sperm into your cervix—and forced to be constantly pregnant throughout a life span reduced from a normal two decades for cows to about five years due to your body breaking down from perpetual pregnancy and your teats being mercilessly milked by milking machines; your screaming babies ripped away from you soon after birth while your milk that both you and nature intend for your calves gets stolen to go to humans who don't need a drop of it; and with your neck with a rope around it for hours on end while you're restrained in a tie-stall; and your swinging tail cut off—euphemistically known as docking—so you won't slap feces in the face of some human crouching under you to hook you up to mechanized hoses; and your udder so distended from injections of rBGH—recombinant bovine growth hormone—that it drags on the ground; and then when you're no longer able to produce money milk, your reward for your service is that you're sent to an abattoir and hung upside down causing level-10 pain from hip dislocation before your throat is cut so your blood will drain away 'cause humans don't want too much liquid crimson in their prettily packaged dead-flesh meat meals.

"And that burger meal looks quite un-brutal, with no plaintive screaking to be heard or messy slaughterhouse to be seen by anyone who bites into that neat-meat slab clustered with condiments between two unmenacing buns. Many meat-eaters will react to a preachy conveyor of these cruel realities—someone like me—with shoot-the-messenger reactions, claiming higher moral ground based on the critic being rude, and protesting that they resent such rudeness and disrespect forced upon them via being upbraided for spending their dollars on meat and hence financing the ongoing production of death-food for alimentary extravagance. Their attitudes boil down to: 'Don't inform me. I prefer to be blissfully ignorant.' Or, for the already-informed: 'I do know about food-animal suffering. However, I wish to turn two blind eyes to it and ignore it and not be bothered with it because the meat tastes too good and I'm angered by your reminding me because when you remind me or inform me, you're shoving your views down my throat. You're so inconsiderate!'

"Meanwhile, they continue to shove inessential-for-healthy-nutrition dead body parts down their throats for no reason other than selfishly enjoying the flavor they relish during those in-the-mouth moments we all have while eating.

"'You're flavorful. So, I'm going to eat you.'

"Any inconsideration there? Of course, most meat-eaters don't speak to the meat. The meat is just a tasty thing to eat. The meat is nameless and, by the time it arrives in a human's mouth, it is—with the horrifying exception of some fish entrées—faceless and eyeless.

"Regarding idiomatical throat-shoving, I would ask all of them if they've ever considered an issue important enough to openly express a disagreement about it to other people. I'm certain of the true answer.

"Some meat-eaters who are resentful of someone who's outspoken against the cruelty that stems from consumption of dead flesh seem to have the decency to feel guilty, which is greatly why they become offended when criticized and which reveals that at least they are not uncaring. They know they're monetizing the infliction of brutal bondage and premature death. They are chafed and unsettled by such troubling reminders. The other people are just taking offense at receiving criticism. Impervious to the anguish endured by these animals, they don't care an incy-wincy jot about how their eating behavior for which they're criticized causes sentience-filled beings to needlessly suffer and prematurely perish.

"To augment blood-money profits, factory-farm bovines and other animals are beaten to be eaten as they are hurried to move faster, faster, faster to their deaths by being fist-bashed, foot-kicked, and shocked with electric prods to ruthlessly hasten them along the kill lines when it's their turn to meet the Grim Reaper and see their heretofore forsaken lives ended.

"'You're just things we workers need to rush to your slaughter; don't dither 'cause my shift-super is watching how fast I'm able to herd you to your demise. Your plangent cries of terror and agony fall on deaf ears 'cause we've gotta give the flesh-gobbler folks who seek you in stores and restaurants the decadence-food they want and are willing to pay for.'

"OK, I've gotta tell you, Rochelle, that I never—unless confronted by persons coming directly at me with their pro-meat commentaries—speak my remarks in an up-close, personalized conversation to anyone who would take serious umbrage, especially my harsher remarks or my satirical remarks. For instance, I knew that you, Rochelle, even though you eat meat, would not wrongly conclude that I'm personally attacking you; I dislike what you do, but I still like you for how you otherwise are. Anyway, for those people who become miffed and piqued over the challenging of their eating habits, what do they have to put up with? They have to put up with feeling offended by being criticized with words. By comparison, what do farmed animals have to put up with? They have to put up with the results of what the criticized people are being criticized about—lifelong enslavement in wretched conditions and then heartless liquidation. Who has the worst thing to put up with?

"Consider the male calf, who is not drainable for money milk. Unless he's among the few lucky boys kept alive to be raised as breeding bulls, he's often killed right away or made to wear a spiked nose plate to prevent him from nursing with his mom, or he's simply separated from her—all so he'll conveniently starve to death. Or, he's sold as a future veal meal and thus crammed into an impossibly narrow crate for his entire sad, short life to prevent him from moving so his muscles won't harden from exercise so he'll yield soft-flesh body parts on the end of some human's fork. He endures a miserable existence, after which he's brutally slaughtered. Some boys are kept alive for maybe 10 months and sold as beef cattle. Most boy bovines never make it to their first birthday.

"Anyway, I belong to this anti-cruelty organization called Mercy for Animals. They have these remarkably brave undercover investigators who get themselves hired to work in these hellacious hellholes. They're equipped with these secretly worn cameras, and they take videos for evidence of the monstrosities that go on—to show to the citizenry and to submit to prosecutors. I can't watch most of those stomach-turning videos through to the ending. I can't. But they're incredibly valuable for documenting the carnage, the bloodletting, the screaming, the trembling fear, the look in their eyes before they go dim that seems to cry 'Dear God, will somebody please save me?'

"It's…it's…the cruel treatment of the poor cows—and other animals like pigs and chickens and fish on factory farms—it's…it's unconscionable and turns the videos into real-life horror movies.

"Fish? Yes, fish. I referenced fish several moments ago. They constitute the only animal type to which many people have become insensitive as far as seeing their suffering and deaths on TV, in movies, etcetera. But fish can't breathe when they're pulled out of water, and they writhe while trammeled in nets or have a hook in their faces—sometimes through their eyes—and they suffer as much as anyone else.

"People get hooked when they're children on consuming dead flesh, and the meat companies pour on the advertising and keep that addiction going for billion-dollar profits; meat is luxury food—not survival food—for people in all but a few places on the planet.

"An inane claim is that consuming tomatoes and potatoes mimics the consumption of animals 'cause plants are also lifeforms. Baloney. No mater or tater has a central nervous system. No plantlike food can possess a CNS. A fruit, a vegetable, a grain can't feel pain. Or fear. Or loneliness. Treat plants with reasonable respect. But, plants' consciousness and capacity to suffer is not remotely near that of our non-human-animal brethren.

"Meat production in first-world countries such as the U.S. and the U.K. should be limited to producing sustenance for our pets, namely cats and dogs; unlike humans, they are carnivores who must have meat. Ideally, when cows, pigs, chickens, and other current food animals near the end of their cruelty-free lives and become elderly, they, as needed for canine and feline food, could be euthanized as gently as possible to feed our four-legged loved ones.

"If only more mainstream people in the general public could see these videos, such exposure would soon spawn legions of vegetarians—and vegans. And, on television, they will unhesitatingly show the reaping of an innocuous food harvest. They show apples picked off trees. They show potatoes pulled from the ground. They show rice lifted from water. Why don't they show, as the saying goes, 'how the sausage is made'? Yeah. That's a rhetorical question. Anyhow, recently, I've actually permutated from vegetarian to full-force vegan.

"And don't get me started on the heinousness of hunting, whereby animal murderers, euphemistically known as hunters, go into the forested homes of beasts while toting guns or bows and arrows with the express intent of killing fully sentient beings for the pleasure of the kill. Unlike olden times, or nowadays in a small number of isolated populations, killing animals for food is completely unnecessary for human subsistence; humans are omnivores and hence do not nutritionally require the consumption of meat. However, such hunts as those I just referenced were and are sadly necessary, and thus justified, simply because people residing in these locations don't have adequate access to enough nonmeat food. Everyone else is hunting for the joy of killing. Hunters enjoy stalking, and then stealing lives—violently. Why go to the store and buy neatly packaged dead flesh that is courtesy of the hidden-away-from-the-public barbarity of factory farming when you yourself can directly experience the thrill of the kill?

"Hunters—many of whom are otherwise good people—oblige themselves to reject reality by viewing the animals they maim-murder as mere their-lives-and-suffering-don't-matter playthings. Some of these recreational killers will say that God put the beasts here to be used however mankind pleases, including as kill-'em-and-mount-'em toys. Hunters sometimes aver that they're actually doing their victims a favor because, if they're hunt-killed, there's no risk of them starving. I can tell you that all animals would reply, if they could, to that offer by saying, 'I'll take my chances on finding food.'

"Plus, as an added hunter-gift bonus, animals, while being pursued and shot at, are filled with anti-ennui excitement. So, by trying to kill them, hunters are graciously preventing animals from being bored. Animals would say, 'My days and nights are very unboring, please know. But were they not, I wouldn't want my boredom relieved by your bullet or bow.'

"In addition to relieving animals of listlessness, hunters may deny that animals suffer too much before perishing and then claim that animals expect to die, anyway. Such deniability is a self-coaxing rationale needed by hunters to hide themselves from any moral liability for their coldhearted inhumanity. Although they're inflicting needless and cruel doom, they enable themselves to avoid charring self-reproach as well as self-recognition of their cruelty-fueled immorality.

"'Itification'—that's how I classify this avoidance-of-inner-guilt mechanism. Hunters, as well as laboratory researchers, factory farmers, some but not all dead-flesh swallowers, and other causers or inflictors of such butchery, perceive non-human and non-pet animals—other than their worthwhileness as things to be used—as insignificant 'its.' Via itifying and thus disavowing the integral value of animals, these brutes conveniently cloak themselves in rationalized, mind-fix insurance policies against culpability for not feeling remorseful. To indemnify, they itify.

"Hunters inflict upon animals horrible final moments, replete with writhing and gasping and bulging of eyes and gushing of blood—and desperate cries, as the victims of hunting realize they're dying but still want to somehow continue living. Hunters are not shooting inanimate objects; they are butchering something—someone—who is no different what-so-freakin'-ever from any human anywhere as far as the ability to feel pain, fear, desperation, and an instinctive desire to live. That's why they try to get away.

"Hunters smile proudly for photographs in which they're seen holding up the lifeless head of a deer they're proud to have killed or the limp head of a bird they've shot out of the sky. They mount dead heads on walls of death. They keep taxidermists in business. They unfeelingly feel no remorse. Rather, they hunt their victims joyously because hunting is, for them, a form of entertainment. Hunters are often called sportsmen. But, a real sport is a competition in which all parties understand the sport and agree beforehand to participate in a game. Hunting is not such a sport, as no beast endorses terms that say, in effect, 'please try to kill me so I can see if I can avoid getting killed.' No, hunters hunt animals for … here it comes … for … for … for … fun. That's right. It's fun-time. Seeking animals to kill and then killing them is fun. Yippee!

"Oh, switching gears asudden but on a related note, I'll toss this in—I deplore the flaunted-in-plain-sight, subtle viciousness of fur coats. Wearing fur for fashion or because it feels lush to the touch or because it looks aristocratically stylish or because of any non-survival reason is, to me, just about the Mt. Everest of narcissism. That is my judgmental judgment. I presume many fashionista fur-wearers block from their minds what they know happens before they drape their swanky garments onto their backs—the screaming and killing from electrical shock or clubbing or other death inflictors utilized by trappers and furriers—so they can avoid confronting themselves about their cruelty-for-ritz. At least they have some feelings about the animals whose lives they poach. Other fur-flaunters are, of course, portraits of apathy and could not care less. Fashion-plate fur is heartbreaking.

"OK, I'm done," said Kristi Lou, visibly quaking while exhaling lustily as her eyes glistened with a vivid combination of anger and sadness.

"Well," said Rochelle, "dat rant started out 'bout how you still a vegetarian—'cause I axed you 'bout it—and then you blew it up ta rantin' 'bout how all deez animals dat we use for meat and milk and so forth are treated real bad. I ain't never thought too much 'bout dat, but …"

"Please do. Please give it some serious thought, Rochelle. Please."

"OK. I will."

"Here, Rochelle, I want to give you this."

Kristi Lou removed from her purse one of many small pieces of paper upon each of which she had written the same information for on-the-spot distribution whenever she encountered anyone who might be interested in the welfare of abused animals. She handed the note to Rochelle. In faultlessly legible print, four Web addresses appeared: www.mercyforanimals.org; www.safehavenfarmsanctuary. org/learn-more/cows; www.nationalreview.com/2013/10/pro-life-pro-animal-matthew-scully; and www.nationalreview.com/2016/12/animal-welfare-standards-animal-cruelty-abolition-morality-factory-farming-animal-use-industries.

"Please use your smartphone to visit these websites."

"OK baby, I'll do dat," said Rochelle.

"But, you know what? You got deez real liberal 'pinions and you got deez real conservative 'pinions. You all over da place wit' yo 'pinions."

"I know. I'm the strangest person I've ever known."

"Dat's all right, babydoll. You juzz be you."

Rochelle checked a text message on her phone and snickered.

"My sister be askin' me for mo money."

"Well, I know she does that a lot. I can help with that if you need for me to."

"I know, but no," replied Rochelle. "Dat's real sweet of you, but no."

"OK. Just let me know if you change your mind."

"Thank you, Kristi Lou."

2

WHILE ROCHELLE TEXTED HER SISTER BACK, KRISTI LOU moseyed up the sidewalk. She began to reflect on what she had just articulated to Rochelle and then pondered her own personality and her carefully thought-out views about the opposite sex.

She actually liked men, and, as a *professional*, offered her clients a caressing fantasy that had in recent years become known in the business as GFE—the Girl Friend Experience. If Kristi Lou felt he was "nice to me, and he brushes his teeth," she would, if he so desired, kiss her patron on his mouth and hold hands with him, as if she were his girlfriend. And she would also "cuddle," which was one of her pet words as well as favorite pursuits when she was being intimate.

She walked briskly back to Rochelle, noting Rochelle had impatiently stuffed her cellphone back into her purse.

"I've got some more things I want to say about what I was talking about," proclaimed Kristi Lou with restrained excitement.

"Well, I'm shocked as shit to hear dat."

Kristi Lou grinned and then immediately resumed her aberrant, on-the-sidewalk jeremiad.

"I'm unconditionally not going to morph into one of those hypocritical women who despise men or are hostile toward men just because men are sexually turned on to females they find physically alluring. That's rank hypocrisy; all straight women—of any age—are instantly attracted to men they feel are handsome, without knowing a thing about their personality or anything. It's especially contradictory for women who are in our line of work to loathe men who seek sex, because, for goodness' sake, we're out here luring and tempting them—knowing full-well we're trying to take advantage of those urges they have that they can't stop any more than the need to breathe—so we can get their money.

"Perverts? Flumadiddle! I scrupulously demur. We're the ones who are the pervs more than they are. Oh my goodness! Perversion implies extreme deviation from the norm, and they're trying to get sex based on their nature while we're trying to get their money based on their nature. We're the ones out here selling ourselves. How normal is that? Who's more normal here? And some sex-industry workers irrationally feel they have to hate the men they tempt in order to maintain some form of self-respect and that this hostility enables them to hold on to more dignity. That's not reality; that's irreality. And it's just cow droppings."

"Hey Hoke, Kristi done got up on her soapbox again and she still ain't sayin' 'bullshit.' She don't say dat word. She juzz went talkin' on bout 'cow drippings.'"

Rochelle and Hokey began spinning and snorting on the sidewalk.

"Droppings. I said 'droppings.'"

"Oh, droppings? Well, whatever then. Droppings or drippings—it's still shit," said Rochelle.

Kristi Lou playfully wheeled herself around in a circle and recommenced.

"Yeah, I know. But, anyway, all the guys are basically doing is trying to satisfy that normal craving that we know darn well they can't help but have. And we females darn well have it, too."

"'Darn'? And a minute ago you said 'my goodness.' You burnin' my ears with dat ghetto mouth. Girl, you nasty. I'm so embarrassed," whimpered Rochelle, dropping her gaze and tucking her chin against her left shoulder.

"Sorry," replied Kristi Lou as she re-launched her diatribe. "But I've got more to say."

"No—I kaint believe dat," rejoined Dark Rochelle.

"Yes you can. Anyway, another thing, you see, is that many of these men—even if they're too proud to admit it—are lonelier than they can bear and just want a woman's touch as well as sex. When it comes to being perverted—like I said—we're closer to it in the first place because of what we're doing, but we're double perverts because of hypocritically condemning *them* for being perverts. It's not them; it's us. We have one finger pointed out and three back at ourselves. And our thumbs. The guys could rightfully tell us that that's like being called ugly by a snail, or being called impotent by a eunuch. OK? Yes, the guys who are after S&M and domination/submission, and similar indelicacies are, technically, pursuing some type of perversion just because what they want deviates significantly far outside the lines of society's majority sexual behavior patterns. So, yeah, I guess they are perverted, theoretically, in that regard. But a lot of women like that sort of racy thing, too, right?"

"Whaz race gotta do wit' it?" inquired Rochelle.

"No, not that kind of race. I'm not talking about skin color. But I am talking about showing skin, and the onlooker being very glad about that skin on display. I said 'racy,' which, for our purposes, means sexually stimulating and maybe a bit scandalous. My point here is that men aren't the only ones who enjoy kinky, racy sex."

"Yeah, dat's true. I think more men'r into kink than women is but yeah, dere's definitely women who get inta dat, too—bein' uh, racy, like you sayin' wit' yo vocabulary and all. I mean, I juzz heard you doin' dat talkin' 'bout 'deviates significantly' or whatever dat high-shit talk was. But, anyways, yeah, dere is kinky women around, too."

"Absolutely. And if it's all an agreed-upon game between consenting adults then it's not so bad for either gender. So, it's wrong to have a double standard whereby you vilify one group—men—and give the other a free pass or even a thumbs up. It's just not right and I'm against it."

"All right, yeah. I see whatch you sayin'.'"

Kristi Lou, with earnest exasperation still draining from her face, nodded at Rochelle and breathed deeply to recover her full stamina. Both women, as well as Hokey, silently relaxed, casually looking around their neighborhood that had become decorated in the red-yellow hue of a sunny gloaming, with nightfall rapidly approaching.

****

Kristi Lou was well aware of how odd she seemed to others and also to herself when she worked herself into a metaphoric lather because of her heartfelt conviction, as a twenty-one-year-old attractive female and man-magnet, to the cause of defending men and their sexual attraction to women. *Were I to have a Greek God as my boyfriend, he'd have to be Priapus.*

She knew how unusual she was for choosing this particular perceived inequity as her cause célèbre of social injustice, whereas other young adults her age, she observed, were more likely to base their protests on popular issues to rail against such as racism—as long as those portrayed as victims were non-white—or environmental insensitivities such as global warming and/or climate change or supposed economic unfairness with *the rich* cast as selfish, tax-hating, capitalistic demons who want to keep as much of their own money as possible and, of course, the ever-popular movement to promote *a celebration* of diversity.

Kristi Lou felt those causes warranted attention, but her principal focus was locked on to opposing what she considered to be the dogma of virulent feminism and discrimination against straight-male sexuality.

She would sometimes query herself: *Some launch-trigger caused me to get on this kick. What was the causal embryo? I don't know the etiology. And, timewise, although I don't know the incunabula, I've been devotedly on it for a long time and I'm gonna stay on it 'cause I believe in it.*

****

Hokey, who had listened to only a scintilla of Kristi Lou's latest eristical asseverations, decided to snap the silence.

"Oh, baby, did you just say 'sexual behavior patterns' a few minutes ago wit' all dat other educated shit you was spoutin'?" inquired a cordially smirking Hokey.

"Damn straight she said dat shit," confirmed Rochelle.

"Yes. I believe I did. Thank you for tuning me in. I need to restart my pontification."

"Is dat like fornication?" asked Rochelle.

"No. It means I'm sorta preaching here."

"I know dat's true. Ain't no sorta to it, though. You preach on, baby. We be yo congregation."

"Yes, I'm preaching outside of a juke house where I work. But that's all right."

"Juke house? I think I heard dat before somewheres, but …"

"Way down South in Dixieland 'juke house' is one of our names for a brothel," clarified Kristi Lou. "But it's not regular language."

"So, it's a slang thang," said Rochelle.

"Yeah, it is. But, anyhow, let me get myself back to preaching about anti-male sexual discrimination."

"You get right back on dat pulpit, girl."

Kristi Lou was now full throttle into one of her earnestly felt tirades, as she caught her breath again and resumed her proclamations with ardor.

"OK, so from a religious standpoint, though, I can see how it might not be too virtuous, because God may not like people pursuing those feelings. Maybe that's the big test, just as advertised: 'I, God, make you have these powerful natural urges but you must resist satisfying them as a tribute to me unless you engage in holy matrimony, and if you don't show this loyalty it's a sin and you'll be punished in the afterlife.'

"I don't know if the preachers are right about that. But guys just wanting to have straight-up sex are not perverted—sinful, maybe, but not perverted—any more than women who have and enjoy, or would like to have and enjoy, casual sex, which many millions of women for centuries all over the world have had and continue to have. I think it's blameless to enjoy pleasurable things, including sex, so far as no one is harmed or inexcusably deceived.

"Speaking of excusable deception, yes, some men whisper insincere sweet-nothings into our ears, such as falsely claiming love, to get into our pants. It's a prerequisite—a form of foreplay we foist upon them; we make them do it before we let them do what they want to do. But, we girls typically compel them to be deceptive to have the smallest shot at enjoying casual sex. And, as I said, many women often pursue casual, informal sex, whether or not they own up to it. Studies confirm that.

"Sure, true love is better—it's the best, really—and people should be faithful, but people can't typically just walk out the door one fine and dandy day and find true love whenever they want it. And even if they have true love, the desire for sexual enjoyment is still urgently compelling. We should resist temptation if we have someone to be faithful to, but sometimes our wife or husband or significant other is abusive or strays first or turns not-just-a-little-bit cold, or whatever. And why should we be taught to feel such shame because of our bodies, anyway? And now I'm really rambling, but I don't mind. Do you?"

"'Urgently compelling'—did you just say dat?" inquired Hokey.

"I did."

"Good gawd."

"Well, Kristi Lou, I guess you …" Rochelle was unable to finish her answer, as Kristi Lou was off and dogmatizing again.

"Anyhow, women—and not just us working girls—entice guys with all of our makeup and lipstick and toning our bodies and pushup bras and whatever sexy clothes and then get mad or act disgusted and roll our eyes like unscrupulous Bs when they want it and express wanting it even decently and non-crudely. We have a right to be offended if they're seriously crude, that is, expressing truly mean crudeness outside of mutually enjoyable dirty talk that he has reason to believe that we like, as in explicitly declared—or implicitly understood—role-playing; that's where we could fairly draw the line and be justified in seeing them as scurrilous and maybe vile. Otherwise, though, when guys are just showing regular attraction to us after we get dolled up and we get all huffy-puffy or even overtly aggressive, it's tantamount to inviting somebody in and then slamming the door in his face, right Rochelle?"

"Yeah, I think…"

"Good. That's what I think, too. I'm glad you do think the same way I think about that. Anyway, I'm not going to do men that way like too many of the women do, who do what we do, do—or do to them. Well, I do think I just said a lot of do's. But, I do hope you do know what I mean when I do say what I won't do. Do you?"

"Damn, baby, dat's a shit-load of do's."

"Or a doo-doo load of do's. Sorry. I know that was corny. I couldn't resist. Well, I suppose maybe I could have. So, I should've said I didn't resist. But, anyway, I do think that was a respectable rant I just made and I was totally sincere with every syllable. Do you agree with me? You don't have to agree, but you do agree, don't you? Do you?"

"I *do*," agreed Rochelle with hyperbolized sincerity. "You as right as you is white—not dat those things always go together, but…"

"You two gettin' married?" inquired Hokey.

"Yeah, we gettin' married, Joke, I mean Hoke. And you ain't invited to da weddin' unless you get yo toolshed ass fixed up and dress better," said firebrand Rochelle.

"Ain't nothin' matter wit' my clothes, you little dummy. Sheeeet." Hokey laughed and picked his jeans out of his butt while Rochelle raised her right hand and waved him off as if to dismiss his relevance.

"OK, y'all, we'll get married later," said Kristi Lou. "But listen. I wish to also add that I've often wondered how many women look at little boys of elementary school age, maybe their own sons, and think to themselves with a warped disgust something like 'When he gets older he's going to be one of those male oinkers who's sexually attracted to women's bodies. He's going to be disgusting.' I mean, can you imagine that? Some of the more radical femifascists, AKA feminazis, might hope that their little boys will turn out gay—so they won't be turned on by the anatomies of girls they find curvy or somehow sexy. There are few worse things than the insidious femifascist manifesto."

Kristi Lou paused for four seconds to draw a deep breath.

Rochelle and Hoke looked on in amazement as did two other working girls who had ventured outside into the warm August night.

Kristi Lou reloaded.

"On the other hand, another side of these anti-straight-male-sex women really wants more heterosexual men in society so there are more guys to hate on for treating women like sexually attractive people. We get to unify for the cause of standing against these wicked hetero males. It's so empowering!

"It's as if straight women don't see men as sexually attractive people when they are gazing lustfully at some guy's shoulders, or butt, or biceps, or back, or legs or whatever male body parts they like. What do you think FGM—female genital mutilation—is about, as practiced by some oppressors over in Africa? They mutilate females' genitalia to reduce or eliminate their sexual urges generated by the sight of physically appealing men. An altered girl theoretically won't stray and be unfaithful to the man to whom she's supposed to belong. As I was saying before, I think some of these females start resenting guys really young, when they're still little girls who get trained by the anti-male-sex culture, and their parents, like the FODs—Fathers of Daughters—when they stop and anticipate that one day God or Mother Nature will mobilize, which, of course, guys can't help any more than the need to breathe. Have I already said that?"

"Probably," answered Rochelle.

"'Need to breathe'? Yeah, I said that just a few blabbings ago. Anyway, they conveniently ignore the fact that heterosexual women, which are most of us girls, are attracted to some men on-sight, without knowing anything about their minds or personalities. Oh my, I've said all this already, too. But, anyhow, even if they are acquainted with him they aren't thinking of his views on politics or his personal history of behavior or how much money he's given to charity when they're ogling his pectoral muscles or his hiney-quarters—the exact same thing that they roll their eyes about or verbally snap about or physically slap about when they blab and bluster about being seen as or treated as, as, as—OK, get ready for it. Here it comes now—as 'sex objects!'

"When's the last time you heard women chastised for 'objectifying' men? What a silly word—'objectify.' Of course people are sex objects—we're *supposed to be* sex objects if somebody is sexually attracted to us. I mean, during the moments when someone is staring at us or thinking about us as sexually attractive, we are indeed objects of sexual desire, just like when someone feels affection for us we are objects of affection. And that works both ways, both ways—I say again—both ways, I say."

"Both ways—dat's true," agreed Rochelle.

"Oh, and I just mentioned objects of affection. When did you last hear or read about some female being upset over being seen as an *object* of affection? Doesn't that make us affection objects? In other words, if the part about which they're so disgusted and indignant is whether they're seen or treated as objects, then they should be offended by being seen or treated as affection objects—because those women are still objectified and they are objects of those feelings, regardless of what type of objects they are seen as being."

Hokey leaned forward in his heavy metal chair on the sidewalk in front of the entrance to Downtown Secrets, and checked his email on his smartphone. He looked up and sensed that Kristi Lou was staring at him for confirmation that he was at least listening now and then, which he barely was.

"Oh yeah, I *heard* dat. I know dat's right. You right. Dat's real right—what you just said. Dat shit is right."

"I say it's wrong or shallow or whatever only if the turned-on person—male *or* female—sees the object of sexual desire exclusively, in an overall way, as a sex object. And just because some man is, during the moments he's heated up over her pulchritude, focusing on her body with lust, doesn't mean he doesn't realize or appreciate that she's a human with a mind. Have I already said that?

"Anyway, you don't have to listen to griping about being 'an object of affection' or the 'apple in someone's eye' because with those sayings and concepts the sex-object complainers suddenly don't care about the literal application of the word *object* because it's hard to denounce someone for feeling affectionate—that's socially cromulent and, in fact, desirable. But we're trained by society to routinely accept—without hesitation, and I mean automatic acceptance—put-downs of men for being sexually attracted to women so we throw in an emphasis on the literalness of *objects* because it grants permission to punish men by making them feel dirty and somehow disrespectful of her dignity, which they claim he has done just for feeling that completely natural sexual attraction to women's bodies and accusing men—even if they're not wrongfully crude—of such rudeness or even degeneracy if they dare manifest said attraction."

"Make sure you keep breathin' while you talkin'. But you tell it, baby. You preach it," said Rochelle, who had become somewhat zoned out of Kristi Lou's discourse, as had the two dancers standing several yards away.

"That's why men have to worry about getting quote caught unquote looking at a girl's boobs or butt or legs for more than a nanosecond. She makes him feel guilty with her embarrassment or discomfort and she gets to supposedly be some sort of victim due to her dignity somehow being assailed, a status which won't take long for her to enjoy. Thus, she has the power to make him feel as if he's a dirty-minded jerk for expressing what he can't help but feel and the precise thing she also feels and hypocritically expresses for people whose bodies she's turned on by, and so she gets the control at his expense.

"I realize I've already made some of these points, but, anyway, for many of us, seemingly, there exists a don't-you-dare-hanker-covetously reaction—sometimes jealousy-based—to what we think is a fervid desire by someone to obtain something. The sought-after thing could be almost anything that provides her or him with high-level pleasure—a boatload of money, a marvelous house at the lake, a luxury car or whatever whatnot, you know, such as simply getting overall further ahead in life than we are. 'Hey you! If it feels good, *don't* do it!' Well, that resentment-reactive mindset is ratcheted sky-high toward males who seek sex from females. The more enthusiastically a male wants sex from a female—outside of a she's-got-him-wrapped-up commitment relationship—the more he's seen as transgressing, e.g., sinning or objectifying. Typically, when a male is perceived as desiring—or especially if he's actually trying—to attain non-commitment sex from a female on a given occasion, there's an iron-solid cultural correlation between *how much* he's seen as wanting it and *how much* the targeted female or a typical onlooker feels adversarial toward his wanting it. 'The more he wants it, the badder he is! The more he wants it, the less of it he should get!' As I was just talking about, that's greatly the reason a guy seeking sexual pleasure has to lie and pretend that sex is the furthest thing from his mind until she perhaps relents after forcing him to perform as a jump-through-the-hoops game player—or until they fall in love and he commits to her. But sometimes both individuals in a pairing are better off limiting themselves to casual sex. That's because, as I was saying, even though sex within love is, in my opinion, the most wonderful form of human sex, there are many people who can enjoy pleasurable and respectful sex together but are terminally unsuited for the long haul.

"Dignity? My sense of dignity is sufficiently strong for me to not feel it's diminished one driblet just because a guy manifests sexual attraction to my anatomy. Is a woman's dignity supposed to be that pathetically fragile and weak? I haven't exactly seen a plethora of male drama kings who react hysterically with: 'Oh God, she touched my breasts or my butt or made a catcall or a whistle or stared for a few seconds at my body! She has disrespected and debased my dignity! She's a perv, a lech, a creep! I need to cry! And maybe file a lawsuit! I'll feel better after I get paid.'

"And, most of us just go on OKing this ridiculous double standard, with some FODs—again, Fathers of Daughters—being among the most fraudulently self-contradictory, as in 'If you're anything like me, stay away from my daughter,' while he continues to be attracted to and often pursue other men's daughters, cousins, sisters, moms, wives, girl-friends and whatever females have the curves he likes. But, accepting their own daughters' sexuality, especially when their female progeny are young, can be knotty for FODs because of how they're societally trained. If they actually discuss it, she can try to appease him by falsely claiming she's still a virgin. He won't know otherwise—unless he learns she's pregnant. Pregnancy is proof. While caring about her well-being, he may initially be more distressed that her condition confirms that a bogeyman has tampered with her hymen.

"'I don't trust any-damn-body packing a penis who wants to do to my daughter what I did to her mother,' proclaims the feelings of the FOD.

"If the FOD has a youthful male offspring, the FOD will often find himself eagerly anticipating his young son's loss of virginity—while absolutely dreading his young daughter's loss of virginity. FOD, pointing to a girl in a swimsuit, speaking to his son: 'How'd you like to get ahold of that?' FOD, pointing to a boy in a swimsuit, speaking to his daughter: 'Don't let that get ahold of you!'"

"Yeah, I know dat's …"

"Do you grasp my meaning?"

"Ooh yeah, I be graspin' dat," agreed Rochelle.

"Let me interject this qualifier. Of course, if a woman—or a man—makes it clear that she or he is uncomfortable with or is offended by or upset by a grope or a touch or a catcall or whatever—even if we feel she or he is badly overreacting or wrongfully reacting—then, as a matter of respect and consideration for her or him, we should cooperatively compliantly discontinue those behaviors. Cooperatively compliantly?

"Anyway, so I read this article on the Internet—it was actually a reprint of an old magazine article from maybe 15 years or so ago—that said women are almost as prolific at watching porn as guys are. The article had an interview with video store owners who said that female shoppers, although many of them seemed a bit uncomfortable when walking amongst the shelves with the skin flicks, still came into the stores and made purchases of DVDs and VHS tapes, and that they constituted an appreciable percentage of the shoppers.

"And, the article also quoted this older guy who used to own an X-rated movie theater back in the '70s—before those types of theaters were driven out of business by the proliferation of porn stores and ordering and/or watching movies over the Internet—and he said there were many nights when he saw almost as many quote horny gals unquote in his theater as there were quote horny guys unquote."

"Yeah—whatch you just said dat old dude said—you gotta watch out for dem horny gals," offered Hokey.

"Absolutely, you do" said Kristi Lou. "Girls really are frequently just as concupiscent as are guys."

"They are?" asked Hokey. "Yeah, well, I'm glad to know dat 'cause I'm all the time feelin' con-coop-uh-whatever-the-fuck you just said."

"I said concupiscent. It's from the root word concupiscence, meaning ardent lustful desire."

"Oh, dat's it—yeah. I just forgot it for a second. Dat's one of my best words dat I know," said Hokey.

"You don't know shit," chided Rochelle.

"What-the-fuck-ever," said Hokey, who turned to walk into Secrets. "I'll be back."

"Anyhow—and here I go again about to repeat myself for the sake of emphasis—untold millions of women routinely view men as sex objects during those moments of lust, and this goes on throughout the world every second of every day of every year. And lesbian and bi women love to be turned on by the sight of and the thought of other women they find physically appealing. But you don't hear—or at least I don't hear—any moaning and groaning about women seeing women as sex objects, although they indubitably do.

"Indubi…"

"But the ultimate hypocrisy is women seeing men as sex objects and then hypocritically getting offended—though I guarantee they keep the compliment—by men doing the same thing toward them, and saying 'oh, it's different for women.' No, it's identical. There's not a trace, a speck, an iota of difference. It's the perception that's different—mind-benumbingly so—and that's what I'm complaining about. And no, perception is not reality, other than the perception, itself. Something is real if it's real, and not if it's not, regardless of how any people might perceive it."

Hokey reappeared on the sidewalk and approached Rochelle, shoving a chair under her while grabbing her shoulders and easing her down into the seat.

"I thought you might could use dis since you listenin' to a speech. You-know-what-I-mean?" said Hokey to Rochelle as he nodded and grinned at Kristi Lou.

"Well, thank you for dat," conceded Rochelle. "I'm glad you finally made yo-self useful. Now go get me some popcorn."

"Oh yeah, you know I be right back wit' dat."

"Ha-ha. That's funny, you'all," said Kristi Lou. "Anyway, I need to finish diatribing. Diatribing? Yes, diatribing."

"Oh shit; I knew dat was comin'," exclaimed Hokey.

Kristi Lou glanced down at the now-seated Rochelle, who sat about three feet away with her arms crossed and her purse clutched in her right hand while silently gazing way up at Kristi Lou, who laughed for about two seconds.

"Well, bless your heart. Are you comfortable?"

"Oh yeah, baby, I'm feelin' right. I'm ready for mo of yo crazy-ass sermon on the sidewalk."

"OK. Cool. Regarding how only females can be biologically tasked with enduring nine months of difficulty and even danger, yeah, that's true. But although that's probably at the root of the discrimination against men, going back centuries, that's not what—pregnancy, that is—that's not what women are getting offended about. They're not usually worried about getting pregnant. No, because of social brainwashing, they're offended by the expression of male sexuality. When we get whistled at or receive some type of sexual-attraction comment, are we physically harmed? Is our skin cut? Does our hair fall out? Do we incur any compound fractures or snapped cartilages or contract any diseases? No. It's the sex itself to which these women react with vexation. But, when men are on the receiving end of such compliments, it's 'Hey, no problem!' And most all of us have been, over time, culturally conditioned to blindly accept this unfair-to-men and irrational double standard.

"And no, if women began to act accepting of such expressions of attraction, that acceptance would not lead to an outbreak of men stalking and raping women in some massive breakdown of social order and self-restraint.

"These females take offense at just his sexual attraction to them, and say high and mighty and often hypocritical things like 'So we're so supposed to accept these catcalls as compliments, huh?' Yes, you are, and yes, you do. All these females with their being so upset and offended, they—and because of how they are raised they often are truly upset and offended, though not always because sometimes it's a put-on—they file away that leer, that whistle, that looking her over, despite her outward eye-rolling or outright hostility.

"And, if she reacts *discriminately*—based on a *man's* looks—to *his* expression of sexual attraction to *her* looks, whether it's catcalling, wolf-whistling, or a direct approach to try to finagle sex out of her, she is emphasizing physical appearance—the same thing that men are routinely blasted for placing emphasis upon. On other occasions, she may emphasize his known or perceived financial or class hierarchy status. So, sometimes, if a woman finds the catcaller/whistler/approacher—what? approacher? I think I'm birthing a word—to be visually unappealing or of insufficient rank, she will insult his looks or his social position. She responds to his affirmation of her attractiveness with a denouncement of his. Toad! Pig! Loser! Creeper!

"She may use—as in being a user—unattractive males, who somewhat brashly convey attraction to her with catcalls, etcetera, via censuring them scornfully or aggressively as a way of supposedly defending her dignity. If a whistling man does not strike her fancy, and he whistles at her in public, she may reject him and his compliment rudely in order to assure any onlookers—and reassure herself—that this non-status or non-handsome or non-monied or non-prestigious male is too beneath her dignity to be allowed to catcall her or wolf-whistle her or hit on her. 'What a creep! What was he thinking? He really thought he had a shot at me?' In reality, the complimentary element of whatever is said or done is wholly independent of the attractiveness, ranking, authority, or prestige of the complimenter; viewed logically, it's still a compliment whether he looks like a Chippendales studmuffin or a male Medusa, or whether he's a mega-millions CEO or a minimum-wage ditch digger.

"However, if she feels the guy is hot enough, she may be magically less concerned about her dignity, and then accommodate his catcalling or even pursue him—it happens all the time. For instance, who's been buying—for decades—those millions-of-sold copies of bodice-ripper novels, replete with their beefcake-sexual-assaulter-turned-lover handsome heroes? Women, that's who. In these steamy stories, virgins are deflowered and all lovely ladies are hence despoiled and taken like chattel by romantic rapists, with whom, as the pages turn, they often live blissfully ever after. Those fictitious men overpower the distressed damsels, blasting past melodramatic remonstrations of 'No! No! No!' But—those men are embodied with muscle-packed bodies. They have unflawed, square-jawed faces. They are genetic Porsche 911 Turbos. Furthermore, they are confidence-filled alphas—the type of males who are publicly debased by militant feminist ideologues. I realize that, of course, just because someone fantasizes about something doesn't mean she'd want it to happen in actuality. Still, the fact that so many women around the world enjoy these eroticized fantasies raises the question as to whether some of that appeal would indeed spill over into their attitudes and actions in, as they say, real life. Hmm, I wonder how many rad-fems are secretly avid readers of bodice-ripper fairyland stimulators. Could there be any cognitive-dissonance perplexities there?

"Anyway," said Kristi Lou, "feminist or not, the woman…she…she's going to emphasize desirability in a man when responding to his expression of attraction to her, no less than a man emphasizes desirability in a woman—though he is typically not nasty while rejecting unwanted advances. Sadly, she often is…unnecessarily.

"Her natural-selection neurons, passed on through millions of years and embedded deep within her genetic survival programming, may be subconsciously notifying her that what the catcaller or pass-maker wants to do to her could result in nine months of steadily increasing unpleasantness, including body-bloating, child-birth agony, and possible medical complications, plus the introduction of another human for whom she'd be the primary caregiver for about two decades and whose life thereafter would unceasingly affect hers. Therefore, such an instinct might compel her to feel inclined to—and entitled to—an expression of ward-him-off revulsion when the male who shows he's sexually enthusiastic about her fails to meet her standards of worthiness."

He'd stick that sperm spewer in me if I'd let him. So, if he expects me to tolerate his manifestation of a desire to do that to me, he'd better be worthy of me taking that risk by having the best baby-maker genes nature has to offer or I'll justifiably castigate him as a defiler, a creep, an assaulter, or a failure. I'll be warranted in inflicting some type of punishment.

"Wrong. That instinct would not give her any such God-given or biology-based entitlement. That instinct would justify caution when making a selection. That instinct would not justify asperity when making a rejection.

"You know, non-hot-and-handsome men have to have a lure-hook other than sexy-on-sight optic appeal. Men who use their talents or luck or intelligence or aggressive drive to ascend to positions of power utilize status, not looks, to try to get sex from women to whom they're attracted. That type of man uses status-power rather than hunk-power to leverage for carnal pleasures. But, he's often disparaged as a creepy predator. What? Non-handsome men who push themselves into positions of power should not be rewarded for their success with sex from women they'd like to seduce or be seduced by?

"OK, if he's unquestionably degrading or abusive or violent, or he regularly threatens damage to women's jobs or career pursuits or promises definite advancement in exchange for sex but then doesn't make an effort to deliver, then he's an abuser and a serial liar and should be considered as sleazy and sexually predatory. However, if he does not make such promises, but instead says, to the effect, that, although he guarantees nothing, he'll put in a good word for these women—and it's true that his position is indeed powerful enough for him to have a realistic prospect of delivering—and he does try to open the opportunity doors for them as he indicated he would, he's not a predator; he's using his status/position power as would a handsome charmer use his handsomeness power. What's the difference? Both are forms of power.

"The high-status man who gets sex from an array of women may be accurately viewed as a lady-killer who uses position power the way a stud-looker uses looks power. Why is the position-power man a predator while the looks-power man is not? Have you heard of all these actors and athletes and rockers whose fame includes their alleged multiple thousands of sexual conquests of females? Some of those men are good-looking, but plenty are not. And, whether they're handsome or not, you can be sure their status power is a ginormous factor in obtaining copious nookie. Are they predators for their consensual sex episodes? I don't recall hearing or reading about many of those guys being labeled 'predators.'

"Also, how about women who are sexually aggressive? Yes, we all know of the SWT contumelies: slut, whore, tramp. But, why aren't these women also derided as predators? Why is a man who uses his status power to pursue lower-status females automatically a predator—especially if he's demonstrably unattractive—but a woman who uses her pulchritude power to pursue higher-status males automatically not a predator? If such pursuits by her are successful, then she, as she has known all along, is contributing to imperilment of his career via possible company reprimands, dismissal, damaged employment reputation, sexual harassment suits—filed by her even though she came on to him—and threats to his personal relationships, such as if he's engaged or married.

"With a catcall or a whistle or a leer-look or actually hitting on her, he isn't saying that she's puke-ugly. That is, he isn't saying she is *not* attractive. He's saying she *is* attractive. Hello? Other than times when she feels particularly awful, such as illness, pain, depression, anger, or grief, unless he's unduly vulgar or crass—even if she doesn't reciprocate the attraction—why not just agreeably accept the compliment … and, under the right circumstances, even thank him for it?

"On the other hand, I can understand her not responding cheerfully—but I think this circumstance is fairly rare—to being approached exclusively for or primarily for sex if she's in a stretch whereby she's truly looking for love but there's been a recent ongoing onslaught, so she believes, of many men coming on to her for sex only. But, even then, she can tell them 'no' without taking offense over the fact that they're non-abusively seeking sex. She's simply tired. She can tell them briefly that she's still flattered by their attraction to her body, and ordinarily she enjoys being objectified, but that nowadays she's weary of too much of that because she's been actively seeking long-term romance. In other words, she's not conventionally hostile toward the men's sex-seeking efforts and/or expressions of attraction to her physique. Rather, she's just weary. She's become weary from too many sex-only passes when she wants to send out signals conveying that she's on the lookout for romantic commitment to go along with the pleasures of sex.

"There've been incalculable millions of not-so-attractive girls and women throughout the world since the dawn of female-male interactions who would've loved to have been tastefully catcalled or wolf-whistled. Many have doubtless been deprived of such compliments they otherwise would've received from guys who were scared off from proffering such flattery by the societal repudiation enforced by harshly/coldly-reacting women. In my view, genuinely down-to-earth, warm-spirited, male-sex-positive females—including some who are notably pretty—appreciate a decently expressed seal of approval of that successful weight-loss, or of those workouts and resultant toned curves, or of that carefully applied makeup and lipstick, or of those figure-hugging threads.

"Additionally, I suspect that, for a lot of looks-challenged flaming feminists, their virulence in demonizing males for the supposed piece-of-meating and so-called objectification of females stems from a deep-seated case of wishful-thinking syndrome: they wish they could be accosted by some decent catcalls or guy-gazes. And, for some ladies who've significantly improved their appearance, they feel they've truly arrived when they can join the 'I-hate-being-objectified!' sisterhood.

"The reactions to receiving nonviolent expressions of sexual attraction from men should, ideally, in my opinion, be basically the same on the outside of a sex-themed club as they are on the inside, where standards of typical societal restraint are, of course, considerably relaxed. Some degree of increased strictness would seem appropriate, but not too much. Inside the nightclub, maintenance of her dignity is significantly based upon receiving money in exchange for greenlighting overt sexual attraction from men. Secondly, the location, as is accepted by everyone, gives the cover-charge-paying man understood permission to pay and play. While inside, she A/ gets paid and B/ has the power of granting permission to men to go for it: 'If you're here, have a beer and a leer. If there's pay, it's OK.'

"When they thus pay, we are the commodification of sex. The pay goes to permission which goes to control which goes to power.

"Modern extremist-feminist ideology is greatly predicated upon furious resentment of male power and a parallel coveting of said power, and this obsession with you-got-it-I-want-it power has, over time, wormed its way, while attached subtly to sex, into the minds of many mainstream females—and males—to insidiously suggest that each instance of non-approved-beforehand exhibition of sexual attraction, such as catcalls, wolf whistles, lustfully looking at her, and verbal compliments about her curves, are all, on some level, connected to, and hence a non-contact form of, rape. Therefore, the man is a perpetrator of not only supposed disrespect but is also a virtual rapist, indictable for mind-rape.

"But, you know what? For men, anywhere they go, they—excepting male stripteasers and gigolos and such—get no pay and have no control over catcalls, wolf-whistles, or leers from women. And yes, as I often say, there are frisky women who do engage in those, uh, *objectifying* behaviors. Such rules are neither applied to nor pursued by men and, in fact, don't really even exist. Women and girls, I think, should duplicate the men's way of responding to non-vulgar and non-threatening displays of such attention: take it in stride and as flattery. Thankfully, some females—down-to-earth, sex-positive females—already do.

"The reality is that, on the inside of nightclubs such as strip-clubs or clubs like Secrets, regardless of cash storms and having control via providing permission, we females are nonetheless catcalled or wolf-whistled or sexually stared at and so on. But, almost all of us, when we walk out of the club at the finale of our shift, do not feel a deletion of or a devastation of our dignity and self-esteem. I know that, despite some occasional culture-induced serious misgivings, I don't lose my feeling of self-worth. That truth proves that a female—not only a sex-industry female but a conventional female as well—can receive overtly manifested sexual approval from men and go right on with her life still intact. She could routinely say: 'At work today, men I don't know from Adam gawked at me and catcalled at me and whistled at me and told me I have a nice ass … for the past 10 hours—again. And now, just after getting off the day shift, I'm going to the store, or to the mall, or to a friend's place, or to the movies, or to a concert, or to the library, or going to be with my boyfriend or my husband, or I'm going home.'

"And, many extremist-feminists tend to harp fanatically about how a man will dehumanize a woman by openly displaying a sexual attraction to her physical assets. Well, dwelling within him is the feeling of being turned on by her body, whether or not he manifests that sensation outwardly. So, applying this line of logic, all straight men are essentially urge-rapists and ceaseless, beneath-the-surface dehumanizers of women.

"Meanwhile, in other news, we continue to await the complaints from rad-fems about females committing urge-rape and dehumanizing males by being attracted to masculine body parts. Oh. Yes. They. Are.

"So, anyhow, here's another of my takes on this flapdoodle. By feeling—and showing—an attraction for a woman's anatomy, he's actually doing the polar opposite of dehumanizing her. Unless he's bestial, he is not attracted to the body of a female rabbit or a female cat or a female dog or a female horse … or to a desk or to a vacuum cleaner or to a wheelbarrow or any inanimate thing. Rather, he's showing an attraction to a female person. Is he attracted to any of those other female animals of different species or to any garden tools? No, I don't think so. Therefore, if anything, he's solidifying a humanization of her because she's, well, you know, a human.

"It's incontestably natural for men to be attracted to us. Feminism, quite deliberately, runs counter to nature and uses this anti-nature mindset to demonize men for being men.

"For many culturally preprogrammed ladies, the psychological adjustment required to stop taking offense upon the reception of feisty male sexual approval of their bodies may seem to be a bridge too far. But, they can try. However, some women might not want to cross it, because they'll have to relinquish something—a hefty hunk of their censure-shame power. But, I say trying to get there is worthwhile, because—why respond to someone *praising* you by *deprecating* him?"

About 10 minutes earlier, three other dance instructors had come outside onto the sidewalk at about the same time that two male patrons had arrived near the front door. All five had stopped to listen to Kristi Lou, who had glanced quickly at and away from them to acknowledge their presence while simultaneously continuing her impassioned lecture without skipping a beat.

One of the dancers was puzzled by the level of fluidity with which Kristi Lou spoke.

"Kristi Lou, how can you say all these things, these sentences, so articulately, with all these, you know, points you make and all the proper phrases and all? It's like you memorized it."

"Thanks. I did. In my private moments, memorizing my viewpoints is something I do."

"Oh, OK."

"So, no—these women, typically, aren't truly concerned about getting pregnant and usually, in most situations, they're not worried about getting raped, either. They're mad—but still flattered—just because of the fact that men are showing an attraction to their curves and naturally have an urge to do the reproductive act or at least some intimate touching or at the very least obtain some visual entertainment and pleasure from being able to ogle us and gaze at us without being hypocritically condemned as perverts, lechers, sleazeballs, or shallow or disgusting or whatever type of degenerate they're supposed to be—but women magically aren't villains when they artlessly view or say out loud that a guy is hot. That's right—hot. The operative word is 'hot.' Girls like to refer, without fear of reprisal, to 'hot guys'—hot, hot, hot.

"There are, tragically, over 50 million abortions worldwide, annually, according to a pro-choice outfit called the Guttmacher Institute. I'm Catholic, so I consider abortions to be tragic, though I think that, despite the tragedy, they should be safe and legal during the first trimester. Anyway, we can safely presume—not assume—that only a comparatively small-scale segment of these aborted fetuses comprises pregnancies that resulted from rape. Thus, most of these unwanted pregnancies are birthed by WLS—willing leg spreading. Then, we can use extrapolation to envisage the unknowable number of all the WLS intercoursisodes—what? I think I'm combining 'intercourse' with 'episodes'—that, uh, that did not make anybody pregnant. I'm also presuming that just a relatively small percentage of abortions come from within marriages from conjugal-rights and mutual-desire-intercourse pregnancies that are accidental and not wanted. Yes, I realize there are other factors such as personality, desperation, money, etcetera. But, largely, here is the utmost veridical and accuracy-i-tized conclusion: there's lots of female WLS going on because of girls and women being physically-sexually attracted to the bods of guys the ladies feel are hot.

"Whew…OK, let me breathe for a moment. OK, I'm back. OK. As I was saying, just because a guy is turned on by a woman's curvaceous body doesn't mean he's denying she has a distinct personality or character or intelligence. It's truly absurd and totally anti-fair that men, unless they're in a strip club or someplace like Secrets here, are almost always socially forced to be in a perpetual state of apology for being physically attracted to women while women are never admonished for being turned on by men's physical asses, uh, assets. It's almost as if society makes men act as if they're always saying 'I'm a real Neanderthal for being physically attracted to you nice-looking women and my sexual feelings make me a low-grade person.'"

Kristi Lou quickly gulped a swig from her water bottle and then returned it to inside her purse, which she left open with the top half of the bottle protruding above the zipper. She exhaled audibly, puffing out her collagen-less full lips, and then resumed her unbridled sermonizing.

"Yes, these women are often otherwise, uh, well, quite divergent in their social stances. Look at right-wing, church-going women. Very conservative, religious women, who are typically at odds with radical feminists, come together with rad-fems to make strange bedfellows—double-entendre pun intended. And these ladies are joined by the I-won't-admit-it-or-even-realize-it-but-in-the-name-of-defending-my-daughter-against-male-sex-I'm-really-defending-my-own-ego FODs.

"Actually, well … umm … I believe my own beloved FOD, if he knew what I'm … when and if he learns what I'm … uh … I believe … I believe he'd struggle with it somewhat but then be more OK with it than most FODS are. In fact, I'm sure of it. Yes. I am. Well …

"Anyway, because of this combination of nature and systematic indoctrination, these bigoted—and it is bigotry—women get to use men as the perfect victims for their irrational and vicious venom."

Kristi Lou drank some more water.

"And if people, especially men, criticize such women by saying things like what I've been saying here, then they get hammered by the extremists as hating women. That's neither fair nor reasonable. The population known as women does not equal the population known as radical women. Some men hate all women, yes, but many men hate—or at least strongly dislike—radical women. They hate feminazis and femicommies. That doesn't mean they hate women; it means they hate those versions of women. And the reality is that such men hate these women directly because these women hate them; the latter precedes and precipitates the former. I don't hate these radical anti-male or anti-male-sexuality women. I just hate their views and I often hate how they manifest their views by being unjustly mean to men.

"For being sexually attracted to women's bodies—and especially for *expressing* said attraction—a man must somehow be made to pay … and pay … and pay. He must pay with money or he must pay by being punished, whether overtly or subtly. Of course, it's even better, so says rad-fem gospel, if he pays with both.

"He can pay via verbal debasement with objurgatory insults such as sleaze, pig, pervert, perv, lecher, lech, creep, or other mordancies.

"He can pay via the modern-day office-based anti-maleism of punishment based on false or unfair charges of sexual harassment in the workplace—yes, sometimes quite justified but often not—whereby he gets shamed and ostracized and demoted or fired whereas she gets victim status and she gets ego-strokes in that her body she supposedly doesn't want any male to show attraction toward must be really attractive, and she maybe gets a promotion to avert a lawsuit for failing to provide a work environment that is, uh, safe from the awful evils of expression of male sexuality, and if she quits and sues she gets settlement moolah.

"He can pay via physical violence, such as slaps in the face or kicks in the balls or some hero-inclined other male rushing to the rescue to defend her honor—which many such white knights hope will lead to her rewarding him with what he attacked the first guy for wanting from her.

"He can pay via paying for most of the female's expenses while dating, courting, or just getting together, such as in a restaurant or at a concert or at a ballgame or at a dance nightclub or whatever entertainment place.

"He can pay when in a strip club, or a joint like Secrets, via tips.

"He can pay via—and here are two vertex-level, judiciarily sanctioned, fleece-the-men cozeners—1, not-reasonable-but-*excessive* child-support reparations, and 2, marriage. In either case, his dirty instincts were slaked. If married, he likely received sex from her often. Hence, he owes her for his prior vagina-access privileges for the rest of his lecherous life. Emolument is collected by her per the all-time flimflam champion: divorce and its partner in pillaging—here it comes—alimony, or, as I alternatively sometimes call it: **all**hismoney. Do you know what percentage of alimony in the U.S. goes to women, Rochelle? Do you?"

"No," said Rochelle. "I kaint say dat I do, but I guess it's most of it. And what was dat about e-mol-u-whatever and ob-jurg-a ..."

"It's freakin' 97 percent!"

"Dat much?"

"Yes! It's 97! What does that tell you? It's an astonishing 97 percent! It should tell everyone that not all but much of **all**hismoney is a thoroughgoing racket—a feed-at-the-trough arrangement that almost retrenches husbands to 'I-Do'-to-Grave meal tickets. It's very lucrative for us females—and for **all**hismoney attorneys lavishly prospering in the divorce industrial complex. If you're a man entering marriage, don't forgo the prenuptial agreement. Prenups! Prenups! Prenups!"

"Damn," said Rochelle. "I didn't know it was no 97 percent. Dat is sho'nuff lopsided."

"Yes, it is. And let me slip this in here: I love and support the wonderful, traditional institution of marriage, of holy matrimony. I know there's a movement ongoing now called MGTOW, which is an acronym for 'men going their own way.' I don't blame many of them, especially the ones who've been burned, for feeling like that. But I believe that's going too far. There are goodhearted, non-**all**hismoney-targeting women out there; the guys just have to find them.

"If rad-fems verily believe that 'a woman without a man is like a fish without a bicycle,' then they should view alimony as patronizingly demeaning, 'cause, after all, since women who are left to their own devices are naturally powerful enough to be wontedly found roaring with independence, they shouldn't need men—or their iniquitous patriarchal dollars. Right?

"Oh, and on the topic of marriage in conjunction with how men are societally required to pay, in some way, for enjoying sex with women, here's a thing that fits right into that equation: consummation. A marriage is considered by law as consummated—that is, the marriage is formally finalized as a legally binding contract, which opens the door for hereafter alimony payouts—after a certain action is taken. That action, according to the female-favoring law, completes the marital union. And what is that action? It's intercourse, of course! It's sex! Yes, again, sex is the thing for which he must pay—even including setting him up for potential *future* sex-triggered payments.

"And here is a societally cleansed reality: Those women around the world who marry mainly for money are doing what we're doing, without the honesty. Those money-grubbers, known as gold-diggers, are under-the-radar prostitutes who don't work the corner."

"They won't look at it dat way. They ain't goan admit it," said Rochelle.

"Of course they won't. But, skirt-wearing Lotharios who plot their money-procurement divorce settlements prior to their marriages are hooking as are we—but doing it subtly; they just have fewer clients, whom they service for longer periods, as they shrewdly convert their husbands into unwitting johns."

"I know dat's right," said Rochelle.

"I say use the male reaction model for both sexes; if a sex-based behavior arising from a female to a male doesn't offend the male, then females should be mentally reconditioned so that the same or corresponding sex-based behavior arising from a male to a female doesn't offend the female. It can't be done? Sure, it can. It is. That's proved by a certain type of female who does exist and does, indeed, follow that approach. I'm one of them, living proof. And I'm not alone. But, implementing that mindset society-wide would require a cultural paradigm shift that would result in loss of…something described by a word that starts with the letter P. And that leads me to tell you this:

"The whole anti-straight-male-sexuality thing is, in great part, a centuries-old, well-designed, societal power play. Power. Power. Power. If you're a sexy gal—make 'em pay. Hey hey hey, you guys must pay! Try to get some money out of it, and then, of course, deny that money was what you were after at the beginning. But, if you can't get money, then at least force them to suffer shame, embarrassment or some type of defeat. Power—get some, girls. Right?"

Kristi Lou scanned her audience, most of whom had become riveted by her sheer audacity in voicing such a strident pro-straight-male position even though they lacked a thorough comprehension of all her points.

"What we have with malevolent feminazis and femifascists and femicommies is the ever-continuing vilification of straight-male sexuality."

Kristi Lou stood erect, all 6'1" of her standing 6'5" with her four-inch high heels, breathing heavily, and looked around at everyone as if prepared to field challenges. There were none.

Four other dancers had joined the group for the final minute of Kristi Lou's oration. No one knew what to say. Finally, after about eight seconds of silence, Hoke spoke.

"Well, as one of dem discriminated-against males, I say I agree wit' everything Kristi had to say. Kristi—you da man!"

"Thanks, I think."

"OK—you da woman!"

"That's more like it. Thanks, Hoke."

Rochelle weighed in, swinging her head in a shoulder-to-shoulder jest while leaning forward in her chair and pointing at Kristi Lou with the four fingers of her left hand held together.

"Oooohhh babydoll, you been out here makin' a street-corner speech on Miracle Boulevard. You dealin' some radical 'pinions. But I think you just 'bout wound down. You been bustin' yo sisters' balls 'cause dey wanna put a shame-down on men for wantin' sex. Dat's one of dem ole time-honored traditions, Kristi-baby. You know dat's right."

Kristi Lou paused for a moment to consider what Rochelle said, turning her head left, then right, and then formed her retort.

"Yeah, it's right as far as your being correct about how many women do that, but it's dead wrong as far as wrongness when they do it. Get it? Because it's unfair and stupid and a form of anti-straight-male-sexuality bigotry that is frankly as pitiful as it is abusive. And, I know I'm being a heretic, an agitator. But even though I'm basically a traditionalist 'cause I love most traditions, that's a wrong tradition."

"I gotcha, baby; I'm wit'-chu on dat," assured Rochelle.

"All right. I'm feeling considerably calmer, now that I've vented part of my conspectus, but, well, I think I'm going to repeat myself here, on purpose. I want to emphasize, again, what I was saying."

"But-chu don't need ta say too much of it no mo, though. Right? You know, 'cause you done said it all, hadn't you?" asked Rochelle.

"Yeah, but still, just to wrap up … and I know I just feel obsessively compelled to do it, but …"

"I know; straight dudes gettin' discriminated against when it comes to showin' bein' turned on and all."

"Look, women and society, in general, have devised different disguised ways to punish men for being sexually attracted to women's bodies. As I was saying a minute ago, what do you think alimony is based on, at least to a considerable extent? The courts say to men, without plainly saying it, that 'if you marry a pretty, sexy girl and *she* divorces *you, with no abuse or infidelity on your part*—she still gets to squeeze you for major money.' Yeah, being a dreamboat is not mandatory for scoring alimony, but perhaps a typical judge tends to award a heftier alimony settlement to a pulchritudinous female 'cause, after all, her ex-husband might've been more sexually stimulated by her while using her for sexual gratification than he would've been by a not-so-sexy wife. And, straight men need to be forced to punitively pay for trying to enjoy sex, and maybe that payment should be, the judge may think, roughly commensurate with his perceived level of enjoyment. Even if she planned it all along, which many of them do, he still pays. He pays. Yeah, there is reverse alimony with the guy getting compensation if his ex-wife is loaded, but those situations are the overwhelming exceptions."

"Yeah, I guess dat's true," said Rochelle.

"It is true. I assure you it's true. As I told you, 97 percent of all **all**hismoney payments in the U.S. go from ex-husbands to ex-wives. Ninety-freakin'-seven percent! For alimony, it's a ball-busting 97!"

"Dat don't leave much alimony for divorced dudes," said Rochelle.

"Prenuptials! Cognately, if you've got a tallywhacker in your undershorts and you're a straighty hombre, you may even need to become a prenupter when you realize you've settled into a long-term relationship with a live-in girlfriend 'cause alimony's got a satanic, kissin'-kinfolk—a money-vacuum known as palimony. Although far less common than alimony, palimony does happen. A guy is just living with her and she supposedly makes sacrifices as would a wife, as if the man doesn't do any sacrificing, and so on. And there are attorneys, with the abetment of former-attorney judges, ready to cash in. Male entertainment-industry bigwigs are particularly vulnerable to palimony money-grabbers. Prenupter? Yes, prenupter. If you're a getting-married male, you need to be a prenupter to guard against alimoniers. If you're a longtime boyfriend with a live-in, money-mining girlfriend, you might need to be a prenupter to guard against palimoniers. Alimoniers? Palimoniers? Yes, alimoniers and palimoniers.

"You're a guy? You're conveying physical attraction to a female's body? Again, in some way, you must pay. Yeah, as I was saying, it can be getting verbally condemned and shamed, but if we can somehow get some money, then that's really a sugar-sweet grab and a great get. They've got it then we get it. And furthermore, this virulent hostility toward straight men outwardly expressing—with even a reasonably tactful expression—any sexual attraction toward a female's body has become so culturally ingrained into the minds of people over the years that it has become a definite meme."

"A what?" inquired Rochelle.

"A meme."

"Mean what? I don't know whatch you mean."

"No. Not what I mean; I said meme. Oh, OK, that word is…"

Hokey grinned and pointed at Kristi Lou. He gestured at the gathered audience outside the club.

"Oh, here we go with another one of Kristi Lou's highfalutin words she likes to throw at us."

"Yes, that's correct. I am. Anyway, the word is meme, and it's spelled m-e-m-e. Most all younger people my age know it."

One of the customers, an older-looking gentleman whom Kristi Lou did not recognize—*he must be a newbie*—spoke up.

"So, what does meme mean?"

"I'll tell you. And thank you, sir, for asking. Meme means, basically, a concept or behavior that has been repeated so much in a society's popular culture that this way of thinking or behaving has become accepted as OK, even if it doesn't necessarily make good sense. A meme is transmitted through massive repetition so much that it's passed on from one generation to the next almost like the transmission of a gene. And meme rhymes with gene."

"Ooh, I know'd a Jean who useta work here," said Rochelle. "She transmitted lotsa stuff 'fore she got let go."

"That's cute, Rochelle. Of course, my gene here is g-e-n-e. It has nothing to do with herpes or whatnot."

"Oh, I know what genes are," said Hokey. "Dat's what gives us traits we inherit and all dat."

"Yes, that's right," said Kristi Lou. "Anyhow, the etymology for meme is…"

"Eta what? You may as well tell us dat one, too, while you at it," said Rochelle.

"Etymology refers to the historical origin of words—where words came from. Oh, I just said 'historical origins.' That may be redundant, because all origins are histori…never mind. But, anyway, memes are now part of the zeitgeist."

"Oh, lord. OK, go on and dee-fine zeitgeist, you know, while you got yo vocabulary on," said Hokey. "Other girls here get their freak on; Kristi Lou gets her vocabulary on."

"Zeitgeist essentially means the currently prevailing trends and moods in a society—what's popular and dominant during any current period. It's kind of like the spirit of the times."

"Oh, dat's some good shit to know and I'm so glad I know it," said Rochelle. "Dat's what's been missin' from my life. I always like to get useful information."

Hokey chuckled while one of three dancers who were standing together off to the side snickered something to the other two girls, eliciting muted laughter.

"So, as I started to say, the etymology of meme is that the word was coined in 1976 by a scientist named Richard Hawkins, who is an evolutionary biologist. He introduced the word meme to make it sound like the word gene. He described a meme as being 'the selfish gene.'"

"Dawkins. The gentleman's last name is Dawkins, not Hawkins," said a voice from the sidewalk.

Kristi Lou, along with the other people assembled under the August full moon, turned and saw a man whose arrival in a dimly lit area none of them had noticed a few minutes earlier.

"Oh my goodness. You're right. His name is Dawkins. Sorry about that. Thank you, though."

"Somebody done caught Kristi Lou makin' a mistake. You must be slippin', baby," said Rochelle with a loud laugh.

"I make plenty of mistakes," replied a smiling Kristi Lou, humbly dropping the aim of her eyes toward the pavement.

3

JUST AS KRISTI LOU GLIMPSED THE DIRTY SIDEWALK IN FRONT of Secrets, an ambulance with lights flashing and siren blaring ripped around the corner of the intersection 45 yards up the street, turning onto Miracle Boulevard and momentarily tilting slightly on its right-side wheels, which screeched with the classic sound of burning tire rubber. The driver had not switched on the alarm features until a moment before he entered Miracle, causing everyone outside Secrets to be momentarily jolted away from Kristi Lou's declamation.

About 40 seconds after the ambulance had sped by the club, Kristi Lou positioned herself below the luminance of a streetlight and then reached into the oversized but inconspicuous side pocket of her skirt and removed multiple sheets of printer paper stapled together.

"OK, everyone. Before I return to my harangue about discrimination against straight-male sexuality, I, I, well I, uh…I realize I'm gobsmackingly aberrational but I just happen to have with me one of my theme papers from school. Why would I bring such a college-type thing—this detail-loaded monograph—to work tonight? I don't know; sometimes I just, I…I just feel compulsions."

Rochelle looked over at some of the other dancers on the sidewalk.

"Oh, lord, here she go. She goan go off on another Sermon on the Mount. Watch at her. She be like Jesus in a miniskirt."

"Yeah, Rochelle. Kristi Lou's a thinking-man's harlot," said one of the dancers.

"Thinking? Well, OK, maybe sometimes," offered another dancer. "But look at these guys standing around. They're not thinking about what she's preaching. They're watching her preach."

Kristi Lou had taken several seconds to review her material. Then she commenced.

"Coincidentally, what we were just talking about before the ambulance came along—and I pray that whoever's in it, or will be in it, will be all right—relates to what I just pulled out of my pocket. So here goes.

"I want to say that the scientist Richard Dawkins—not Hawkins—is wrong, and blatantly wrong, with another of his views. He is wrong, along with his contemporaries, with his un-provable concept that there is—as they advocate with absolute or near certainty—no God. Atheists are wrong even if it turns out they're right. That is, if there is no God, they are still wrong. Why? They're wrong because they claim, essentially, to *know*. They can't know. They aren't capable of knowing. They're not wrong for believing—although I believe their belief is wrong. Rather, they are wrong for irrationally claiming—ironically under the banner of rationality—and falsely believing that they absolutely know. Or that they so strongly *believe* that there is no God that their belief is of such a degree of assuredness that they are virtually certain that they know. They don't. They can't. With an IQ of 1,000, they still can't know.

"Infallible knowledge that God does not exist is unknowable."

Kristi Lou took four steps and noticed the high-rise hemline of her skirt had hiked over her left thigh even higher than it already was, having bunched up by about two inches. She pulled it down.

"Verification of the non-existence of an omniscient being is unattainable.

"Atheism, regardless of the highest education level or the advanced intellect of the atheist, is one of the most profoundly unsubstantiatable and therefore fatuous beliefs that could ever be believed. Are there implausible and seemingly absurd religions? Yes, I think there are. All religions, just like all scientists, are—as they say—not created equal. Believing in God—and any associated religion—is, by definition, based on faith.

"Again, the word is *faith*. There is faith in something that can't be seen, unless God decides to physically show himself. If he did, on a wide-scale basis—say on TV or the Internet—then there would be little or no need for faith because everyone would automatically believe based on 'seeing is believing' rather than on faith based upon documented teachings handed down to us in information sources such as scriptures, like the Bible. In that scenario, most people, motivated by inarguable proof of God's existence—he tangibly reveals himself coming down from heaven now and then—might be so scared to not resist the temptations of what he has deemed as sin that, in order to ascend to heaven and to avert descending into hell, they might easily conform in lock-step obedience. They would not have any faith-based tests to pass. Thus, the hallowed tenant of faith, the very bedrock on which belief in God hinges, would be rendered almost moot and null.

"God, if he does exist—and, although I can't literally prove it, I believe he does—probably wants entry into heaven, or at least its higher echelons, if there are levels, with perhaps the empyrean as the top-floor penthouse, to be attained only by those whom he considers worthy based on their life choices, actions, thoughts, feelings, and/or faith.

"I also believe that God is a just and fair god and hence accepts into heaven—with a free pass, you might say—very young children, the mentally retarded, reality-in-absentia psychotics and—wait for this—animals. Non-human beings may have different places in heaven;

I don't claim to know how it all works. But what I am saying is that I feel he takes in those who are innocent of unfairly harbored malice, calculated selfishness, ruthless cruelty, and treachery. The populations I just referenced have spirits and souls, no matter how violent their bodies may behave, void of premeditated and/or nourished meanness, and are incapable of spiritual non-innocence.

"A long-voiced protestation against God and/or his existence avers that a spiritual creator who is morally honorable, anti-evil, and the lifeblood of what is good would not permit all the suffering that has inundated the world for eternities, including agonies that afflict exemplars-of-innocence newborns, cherubs, and prey animals. My reconciliation is that the answer lies within the conceptualization of God as a universal and omnipotent master who does not always intercede in Earth's mortal affairs, but, for those who are heaven-worthy, especially those who are as innocent as freshly fallen snow, God ensures their earthly Gehenna yields this ascent: Their reward is great in heaven.

"I once read a quote that I can't find on the Internet or recall exactly—neither the verbatim wording nor the philosopher, though I believe he was German—that stated, to the effect, that a god who often revealed himself would not be a deity; he would be a celebrity.

"There is a principle known as Occam's Razor, which principally avows that, in the absence of absolute proof, the best hypothesis to accept among competing postulates is usually the simplest one that carries the fewest assumptions. Some atheists foolishly try to use Occam's Razor to disprove the validity of all religion and a belief in God. In reality, Occam's Razor is anything but the atheist's friend; it is the atheist's enemy. The idea that there was a "Big Bang" can be scientifically determined to likely have happened, but there is no simplicity and no shortage of assumptions involved when one looks at the expanse of space and tries to scientifically explain away—in supposedly simple terms—the creation of multiple universes beyond ours. Lots of other big bangs? Who or what instigated these bangs? Did these bangs create themselves out of nothing?

"Plus, the principle of Occam's Razor is just that; it is a *principle*, not an always, every-single-time applicable truth. In other words, sometimes the belief that carries with it the greater number of assumptions and is the more complicated to evaluate is eventually proven to be the belief that is accurate.

"Next, no scientist, after systematically proving the big bang or similar science-friendly theory, is capable of proving that God did not actually create that big bang. That's right; the big bang may have happened, but God may have made it happen. If there is a god, and God is indeed omnipotent, then he could choose, if he wanted, to use a super-megaton explosion as his way of bringing the universe and its planets into literal existence.

"Prehistoric outer-space aliens whose flying vessels and advanced technology persuaded ancient Earthlings that they, the visitors to Earth, were gods? Is our entire foundation of religion based upon visits centuries ago from extraterrestrial guests who seemed god-like and were accordingly written about as God, with the legend passed down through the ages in documentation such as the Bible? If ETs, seen descending mightily from or back into the sky and whose intelligence would've been millenniums ahead of that of our ancestors, were here, they would surely have been feared, respected, and could've been easily accepted and worshiped as gods.

"Such brilliant Martians or Venusians or Saturnians or owners of other planetary demonyms may have indeed acted as engineers directing labor provided by early-era humans to build the Great Pyramids, using technologically unheard-of machines similar to today's gigantic cranes. If these aliens were here, and then were legendarily described in religious chronicles as gods, leading to an eventual belief that they were sent from Thee God, could not that circumstance be entirely true?

"Paralleling God's possible use of a big bang event, even if super-superior aliens were here and left cryptic edifices and geometric figures on land that can be seen these days only from the air, and even if our primitive relatives did mistake them as being gods when they were actually advanced mortal beings, such a fact would not and could not dismiss the possibility that the real God sent these aliens to Earth to do whatever work he wanted done.

"If God did use aliens to establish something on Earth, did he pay them well-above minimum wage? That would be another intriguing enema. Stop. Make that enigma.

"God directing space aliens? Crazy? A huge leap of faith? Maybe, but—though this is an imperfect analogy—the Wright brothers, speaking of aircraft, were mocked as fools.

"Again, the alpha phenomenon that dominates here is faith. You cannot use science to factually dismiss, in an absolute or near-absolute way, an entity that is not physically testable via testing devices. Faith does not yield to instruments or scientific logic.

"Interestingly and very ironically, because faith-based belief systems defy conclusive, evidence-driven, logic-based analysis, it is logical to accept the possibility that God in some form does exist, regardless of whether his existence can be concretely proven, while it is thus illogical to presume that he cannot exist—just because you can't see him—due to the reality that his existence cannot be concretely disproven.

"A hallmark of pseudointellectual and pseudoscientific arrogance and deception is the false notion that you can prove an unseen negative. In fact, you indeed cannot—with absoluteness—prove an unseen negative. Yes, you can come close to proving a highly implausible unseen negative, with that semi-proof based on logical reasoning and historical evidence.

"What is this so-called negative? It's the idea that I just talked about. It's essentially an argument that says no one can absolutely prove with certainty that something unseen does not or did not exist in any location anywhere. The positive refers to positive proof that can be observed, i.e., evidence. The negative refers to a negation of positive proof, i.e., no evidence. The negative in this case equals proving that an un-seeable or unseen entity, such as God, does not exist because, in essence, there is no hard, tangible evidence that it/he does exist. Atheists will go beyond 'absence of evidence' by reversing the keywords and creating a clever-sounding apothegm that proclaims 'evidence of absence.' God, you see, is evidently absent from reality because no one has any, uh, scientifically authenticatable proof of him being or having been around—like a YouTube video or perhaps traces of Divine DNA.

"These people, fooling themselves times two, are desperate to disprove the existence of a holy almighty and they fool themselves and others who are hoping to seem/feel intellectual by getting lost in, among other things, semantics, such as twisting and interpolating the meaning of 'you can't prove a negative' to claim that the concept that you can't prove a negative is itself a type of negative. So what? That's mere semantical gymnastics, promulgated by atheistic types, which are designed to confuse congregants and allow an escape route from logic while pretending that their position is logical. Regardless of their verbal window dressing disguised as reason, you cannot prove, with absolutism, that an entity based upon faith is non-existent. You cannot.

"Typically, these cynical contemplators, while trying to exalt their alleged intellectualism as well as sometimes embarrass believers in God via ridicule, will lump God into the same facetious sentences in which they reference Santa Claus, the tooth fairy, the Loch Ness Monster, the Easter Bunny and—an all-time favorite of theirs—unicorns. Yep, if you believe in God it's the same as believing in the tooth fairy and unicorns."

Kristi Lou, disheveling the clearly numbered papers from which she had already read but keeping them in order, looked up and saw that her audience on and around the sidewalk had not changed. She inhaled/exhaled deeply, looking at winding concrete cracks and frowning slightly, as she was ablaze with internal recognition of her seeming inability to stifle her desire to obsessively rave.

The two male customers were still there, watching her in awe. Of Kristi Lou's seven coworker acquaintances, five remained attentive, at least ostensibly; two had zoned her out. Hokey spun around and strolled back into Secrets. Rochelle sat quietly, mesmerized, not by the content of Kristi Lou's decrees against atheism but by the fathomless bulk of her verbiage and the intensity with which she spoke at length without tiring. None of the girls would dare tell her to shut up. They knew Big Sam allowed her ravings. They knew that Hokey and Rochelle liked and safeguarded her. They knew that if you messed with Kristi Lou you were messing with Hokey and nary a one of them wished to clash with such a formidable protector.

She and her homily reignited.

"Yes, the Bible does reference single-horned animals. The Hebrew version of the Bible refers to a creature known as a reem—that's r-e-e-m and sometimes spelled with an apostrophe between the two e's—and a reem is transliterated by some translators as referring directly to what is today called a unicorn. But many scholars of religion believe that reems mentioned in the Hebrew Bible refer not to equines—that is, horses—with a single horn, but rather to now-extinct aurochs—that's a-u-r-o-c-h-s—who were the progenitors of bovines, i.e., cattle, and that the Old Testament verse is probably about powerful, undomesticated oxen.

"Moving to The King James Christian Bible, unicorns are identified by name nine times. Unicorns in the Christian Bible could possibly refer to rhinoceroses, who as we know are always parading their single horns. Indeed, the genus for rhinos native to India is Rhinoceros unicornis. And yeah, if you do the research, you can discover that the rhinoceros is an odd-toed ungulate—as are horses and zebras, making them the kissin'-cousins and closest kin of the rhino.

"I suspect that most scholarly researchers don't claim that the Bible is claiming that Earth was once graced by magical, bright-white, horn-headed horses. Rather than horses, they likely conclude that unicorns as referenced by the writers of the Good Book were wild oxen or early-age rhinoceroses. But ridiculers are gonna be ridiculing, so, regardless of the more probable link with oxen or rhinos, let's look further—kinda-sorta for the heck of it—at the possible prior existence of horsey-type unicorns.

"Consider the tactic, sometimes bedizened with ad hominem ridicule, positing that belief in God imitates belief in unicorns. Yeah—unicorns. A scientist or philosophy professor might claim the syllogistic series of conclusions goes like this: 'paleontologists have plentiful fossil records for dinosaurs as having traversed the planet but have no fossil records for unicorns. Therefore, we can know with certainty that unicorns did not ever exist.' That conclusion is, of course, prima facie absurd, regardless of how many doctorate degrees are owned by the concluder. Unicorn fossils may exist without having yet been discovered. For generations, there have been new discoveries by geologists, oceanographers, archaeologists, and paleontologists who have unearthed findings both on land and under the ocean, including animal remains that have been assigned new phylum classifications. Perhaps ancient or primitive written records of unicorns did exist but were destroyed. Maybe unicorn fossils still exist but are buried or somehow hidden away somewhere.

"I'm not claiming that unicorns exist or that they used to exist. I don't believe they did exist. But, scientists not having records of unicorns does not equal the nonexistence of unicorns. Not every inch of Earth has been excavated. If a tree crashes in a forest and no person hears it, the crash still made a sound. Similarly, the presence of records in the possession of educated humans is not required for an entity's existence.

"Finally, here's another thought regarding their pet fallback animal, unicorns, as related to Biblical teachings and belief in God. Unicorns—regardless of whether unicorn fossils are out there yet to be discovered and will one day be added to the fossil records—would be earth-bound creatures. God is not. Do scientists and philosophers aver that lack of fossil records for God's bones on Earth prove that he doesn't exist? Just because mentionings of unicorns appear seriously in the Bible but are presented fancifully in writings of fiction whose authors intend that the unicorn should be viewed as a fictional character does not mean that God should be viewed as a fictional character; in the most serious literature, primarily the Bible, the writers irrefutably intend to portray God as profoundly real.

"Elitist intellectuals, who devolve into atheistic pseudointellectuals on this matter via their false belief that they can somehow prove all negatives beyond a reasonable doubt in order to achieve what they're really after—claiming that they can disprove the existence of God—have another trick up their sleeves: the good ole strawman strategy. In an effort to discredit and even scorn religious people, they try to attach to these folks some bizarre or fantastically silly hypothetical that most believers in God would never believe, and then say that the attached ludicrous notion is equal to belief in God.

"For example, the scientist or self-proclaimed rational reasoner could say that claiming you can't prove the nonexistence of God is akin to claiming that, despite voluminous evidence from oceanographers that coral reefs form from larva, that maybe coral reefs are the work of industrious, undersea little amphibious blue/green algae men who live beneath the lost continent of Atlantis. Well, no. You can make that kind of case—invoking absurdity as an attempt to inflict discreditation—against anything that, frustratingly, can't be disproven. If strategizing absurdifyingly is your proof against the existence of God, then you have nothing but illogical, non-reason on your side. Absurdifyingly? Yes, absurdifyingly.

"Here is the clincher for these people. They use the term I just used a minute ago—'reasonable doubt.' Note the use of the adjective 'reasonable' in front of the noun 'doubt.' Define 'reasonable.' Their definition? Any doubt that they have—and usually desire to have so as to satisfy their atheistic agenda—that is based on absence of records of fossils, rocks, etcetera, as if all discoveries that are possible have already been made in a certain genre and are all recorded, based on test tubes, based on chemicals in beakers, and based on the hard physical evidence that they worship as their own infallible god.

"They always can, and they always do, claim that doubts associated with their 100 percent absence of proof of nonexistence are not reasonable, and thus they attempt to rationalize away any further discussion.

"Their failsafe default position to try to shut down believers in God is a combination of mixing absurdity-analogy with strawman stratagems plus closeminded usage of the word 'reasonable.' You cannot rationally extrapolate out a disbelief in the existence of unicorns to equate to a disbelief in an omnipotent being of universal presence. The perhaps likely nonexistence of one exceptional phenomenon—unicorns—does not cancel the reasonable possibility of existence of another exceptional phenomenon—God.

"I can prove the nonexistence of a washing machine in my bedroom. I can see what is and isn't in the room. But I can't, nor can anyone else, regardless of education, prove the nonexistence of a divine supernatural being, i.e., God. Such disproof simply cannot be achieved—beyond a reasonable doubt.

"We have belief versus belief. One belief is no more or no less a belief—as opposed to a knowable fact—than the other. That is, belief in God is just that—a belief. Likewise, notwithstanding the impudent and impotent temerity of some scientists and some philosophers, belief in the nonexistence of God is just that—a belief. A believer, unless he or she has actually observed God, is wrong when he proclaims that he *knows* that God exists. Rather, in reality, he fervently *believes*—a priori—that God exists, and is the uttermost entelechy. Analogously, a nonbeliever is wrong when he asseverates that he *knows* that God does not exist. Rather, in reality, he fervently *believes* that God does not exist.

"Another term that applies to the debate pitting God versus atheists is 'logical fallacy.' Many of the people who misuse logical fallacy attempt to apply the logic only one way and thus torpedo their integrity. Regarding burden of proof, it's no more incumbent upon the believer who advocates for the existence of God to prove existence than it is incumbent upon the nonbeliever to prove nonexistence. Often, the nonbeliever/skeptic complains about the believer requiring the nonbeliever to prove nonexistence. But he fails to acknowledge or even recognize the indefensibility of the double standard that manifests when he conversely requires the believer to prove existence.

"Using his one-sided, obtuse thinking, the nonbeliever presents the following scenario, replete with a glaring misattribution: 'I, the believer, can't prove to you, the nonbeliever, with tangible evidence that meets your satisfaction, that God does exist. You prove that he does not. If you can't, then he *does* exist.' Well, no.

"First, unbeknownst to this confused thinker, the believer does not base his belief or its continuation on the inability of the denier/nonbeliever to provide proof of *non*existence. Rather, his belief is based on what he, the believer, thinks/feels is proof of *existence*. He or she is guided by what he considers to be compelling evidence, usually religious scripture such as the Bible and teachings, combined with his faith.

"Second, the denier/nonbeliever may refuse, unless forced, to input a reverse application of his own logic, which, if applied, would effectuate a non sequitur that would look like this: 'I, the nonbeliever, can't prove to you, the believer, with tangible evidence that meets your satisfaction, that God does not exist. You prove that he does. If you can't, then he does *not* exist.' Well, no.

"Inability of the believer to produce physical evidence or verifiable documentation thereof to the satisfaction of the nonbeliever that a spiritual entity exists does not logically preclude the existence of said spiritual entity.

"The misguided skeptic, fueled by his own nebulous deductions, may then further misconstrue the thinking of the believer, and unwittingly refute his own argument while advancing it, via this illogical syllogistic conclusion: 'There may be good reasons to believe that God is real, but continuing to believe he exists just because his existence can't be literally disproven is not one of those reasons.' Well, no—and yes. Actually, yes, it is indeed a *very* good reason to…continue.

"Here is yet another logical fallacy emanating from skeptics who believe they're somehow logically refuting a logical fallacy. They are perpetrating a logical fallacy based on false attribution. The illogical and fallacious concept here is refuted, once again, by the fact that the average God-believer is not, not, repeat not, basing his spiritual belief system on what he sees as paucity of proof that God does *not* exist. He/she bases his belief system on what he sees as the abundance of proof that God *does* exist. Videlicet, that evidence is, as I just said, religious scriptures and teachings, plus marveling at the splendors of nature, the patterns of birth, life, and death, contemplating in awe the perfectly orchestrated changes of seasons—all interwoven harmoniously by and with faith. Those entities are, for him/her, quite proof enough.

"Yes, the believer will continue believing unless you can produce evidence that will convince him to unbelieve. That mindset, however, goes to *continuation* of a belief—until there are persuasive evidentiary reasons to stop believing—but does not go to the reasons for the *origin* of his belief, a differentiation misapprehended by many nonbelievers.

"This sophrosyne-deficient cynic surpasses temperately claiming that *doubts* about the existence of supernatural entities such as God are reasonable; he/she hubristically claims that he does not just doubt the existence of God, but that he can *prove* that God does not exist. That's his word: 'prove.' He believes he can prove, beyond the heralded reasonable doubt, that God is nonexistent. He can't. He can think, speculate, believe, but he is impotent to prove for a split second that there is no reasonable doubt that God doesn't exist. God choosing to not show himself readily does not prove that he isn't there somewhere. He's God; he can hide in exaltation if he for-God's-sake wants to.

"Think? All right, think of how unreasonable it is to believe that a chipmunk could speak English, or any human language, plus record songs in a music studio. Alvin, I'm looking at you. Then think of how equally unreasonable it is to put belief in a fantastical singing chipmunk in the same category of feasibility as that of an omniscient, all-powerful, exalted human-type being capable of creating and managing universes without physically revealing himself. By definition, a being who is supernaturally omnipotent could pull this off, whereas a chipmunk, based on commonsense reasoning and presence of mountainous evidence about chipmunk abilities, is, beyond any doubt that is reasonable, incapable of this status.

"An omnipotent chipmunk? Or a toaster that can calculate your taxes? Or a flying magic carpet upon which you can sit, hang out with Aladdin, and travel through the sky? Yes, while possible in a blatantly phantasmagoric sense, those are likely things that sane persons with sound reasoning and discernment would reject as unbelievable beyond a reasonable doubt. However, lumping a belief in God into that mixture of absurdities—to shame the believer as ignorantly superstitious and farcical—is unreasonable. An all-powerful god would be, as an essentiality of his stature and being, fully singular. Belief in polytheism, such as pluralistic Greek gods, seems to me much more of a stretch than belief in one commander-in-chief god. He would, by necessity, be at the apex of uniqueness. Hence, *of course* he—or she, if you insist—could possess spectacular abilities that transcend the wherewithal of science and humanistic logic to disprove them.

"You can advance what appears to be a logic-based supposition, e.g., that there is no evidence that so-and-such, including God, has been or is in existence. But, absence of evidence verifying that something not seeable does exist cannot amount to proof that it does not. Rejecting what should be seen as the incontrovertible truth of this dictate constitutes a classic logical fallacy. I can see the nihility of a bathtub in my fireplace but I can't see that God is not visiting in my backyard. Put another way, when considering unseen or un-seeable phenomenon, absence of evidence to prove does not equal presence of evidence to disprove. Failure to refute this reality is a damnatory lacuna, an AWOL element, in atheism's illogical argument.

"Notably, William of Ockham was, according to accepted literature regarding his career, a believer in God. He was not an atheist. He was an avowed theist. Mr. Ockham advocated strongly that while science was based on discovery, religion/theology was based on, on, on what? Faith. Mr. Ockham has been quoted as saying: 'Only faith gives us access to theological truths. The ways of God are not open to reason, for God has freely chosen to create a world and establish a way of salvation within it apart from any necessary laws that human logic or rationality can uncover.' God's existence is not scientific; rather, it is unfalsifiable.

"Atheism, when examined rationally, is ripped open by irony; atheism, when accepted as absolute or near-absolute truth, is irrational.

"While it's theoretically possible to prove the existence of God, e.g., somehow convincing God to reveal himself for millions of people to witness and in front of TV cameras recording his extraterrestrial appearance and maybe generating a miracle such as lifting a building and setting it back in place with all the plumbing immediately intact, no individual—scientist or not—can prove the opposite: that God does not exist. You can't—ever, under any circumstances—sensibly claim that just because any clearly mysterious figure doesn't show himself that he *absolutely* isn't there. A hermit-like way of life, for a being who is all-powerful and who wishes to impose a trial-by-resistance-to-temptation obstacle course that we must navigate successfully in order to earn the blessing of living eternally with him, is, without a reasonable doubt, an existence that, while far beyond the range of mortal normalcy, very doable. That is, if he's God, he can do what he pleases.

"So, it is literally impossible—that is, not even remotely possible—to disprove the existence of God using test tubes or beakers or laboratories or quantum physics or logic-based theorems. Science, in the form of erudite humans known in the English language as scientists, is 100 percent impotent to construct, much less verify, such a disproval. Science can't get it done because science is simply out of its league in this matter. God, religion, hell, heaven cannot be tested in a lab. It's something we believe, a miraculous, non-scientific phenomenon that, by its nature, is beyond the boundaries of physical entities such as those things that scientists are restricted to using in order to analyze things. Science is quite simply constrained by the natural world.

"God is beyond the scope and reach of science. Resentful, imperious scientists, while wanting to procure grant money and promote their intellectualism and ridicule anything they can't refute with testing procedures, dislike their intellectual impotence in being unable to prove the non-existence of God; they really enjoy proving things. So, lashing inwardly and then outwardly, they persist implacably with their denouncements of something—a belief in a warm, rewarding, misery-free afterlife—that brings so much joy and comfort to people who suffer mortally here on Earth, for instance those suffering from terminal illness, or those who lie bleeding or gutted on the battlefield with war wounds and sense they are about to perish, or the fears of the elderly as they confront the inevitable conclusion of advanced age. You see, these are people who have celestially reassuring hopes of realizing heaven's promise of no more agony and of being reunited with beloved loved ones in the Heavenly Kingdom someday.

"I say this: Atheistic scientists and other educated atheists should know better, as a matter of morality and human decency based on kindness, than to try to poison people's hoping and yearning, which is at once non-harmful to them but does absolutely provide them with immense comfort and peace of mind while living temporally here on our planet."

Kristi Lou pulled her papers to her chest, and then looked around to check her audience, which seemed to her to have grown by one or two attendees. Satisfied with the attention, her haranguing resumed.

"And, what happens to the souls of beings, if God and religion are true, whom atheism convinced to reject divinity? What blameworthiness does atheism and its advocates share for the afterlife destination of those it has recruited? Has atheism, and its ally known as science, led those people into eternal damnation? I don't know. I hope God will be forgiving as much as he can see fit to do so.

"Absolutism is the pseudointellectual parasite that is the bane of atheism, whether or not atheists realize that realness. Delusional? Belief in God is *not*; the unfounded absolute belief that God can't exist *is*. Atheism's bum-steer Weltanschauung is the antithesis of apodictic certainty.

"Atheism, because of its inherent cruelty, is the unconquered champion of unethicality.

"As I said earlier, not all religions are the same; some are historically and conventionally negative in their ideology, as they are guilty of promoting unjustified violence, domestic oppression, and meanness, while other religions, such as Christianity, Judaism, and Hinduism are substantially the opposite. The animal-sacrifice fiendishness of Kapparot and the Gadhimai Festival are disowned by most Jews and Hindus, respectively, the latter adhering to Ahimsa, a doctrine of nonviolence. Practitioners of these religions are primarily positive in their worldview missions, as most of their acolytes usually want to promote peace—favoring violence only when essential for short-term or long-term survival. Good-hearted believers within these religions mostly seek to foster goodwill, respect, philanthropy, as well as fair and functional laws, such as the Old Testament's Ten Commandments and what they contributed to our legislated statutes based on such Ten Commandment moralities as 'Thou shalt not kill,' interpreted in some scriptures as 'You shall not murder,' meaning don't kill unless it's justified, and 'Thou shall not steal.'

"As contrasted against the fairness of *agnosticism*, which intelligently, reasonably, and Kantian-noumenally declares that 'I don't know,' *atheism*, steeped in its hubris, idiotically fulminates that 'I do know … I do know that belief in God is dumb and I do know that God isn't real even though I can't prove it with my scientific toolbox.' Atheism is at once the epitome of ignorance and a universal social demon—a destroyer of hope. So what if God is not real? Belief in a mostly benevolent god, a good god, a decent god, including within the framework of a creed based upon sacrifice and comity, does not hurt anyone but, in fact, helps so many people and animals through promoting acts of kindness while discouraging and often preventing bad behaviors, including crimes such as beatings or stealing or rape or homicide. Kind-hearted religions, even if we don't agree with all of their ideals, generally favor treating others with considerateness and sacrifice and generosity and kind words and deeds such as giving money and food and clothes and time to charities and to those in need.

"Atheism, contrastingly, yells at believers and scorns them as stupid for believing they'll be reunited with their loved ones again. Atheism's scornful sacrilege hollers at them: 'Reunion? Forget it. No, you'll never see them again. I must disabuse you of religion so that you have no hope. It's all hopeless. You'll just fade to black and enter into nothingness. I want to crush the warmth of reassurance that you cherish. Everything is empty, your faith is folly, and you're a fool for believing otherwise.'

"Regarding unkindness, atheists may inform you that, unlike some religions, atheism won't warn you that you might agonize with stopless rotting inside an interminable inferno. Non-consciousness is better, they'll say, than infinite wretchedness. Yes, non-existence and thus non-awareness would bring no hellfire after mortal life has ended. But, it could not bring the unending joy found in heaven. Also—maybe there is no hell. And, despite a lifetime that a dying transgressor and his or her condemners might view as sin-soaked in evildoing, he/she can be comforted by believing that God may grant atonement and hence heaven-worthiness via saved-by-Jesus redemption, via last-rites expiation, or via the penitent having led a more spiritual, God-pleasing life than he/she realizes. Atheism, belligerently manifested, attempts to snuff—to chillingly demolish—all hope."

Kristi Lou, as if she were standing behind an imaginary lectern, was no longer glancing back and forth from her audience to her notes but was exclusively reading from her paperwork with pressured speech and lunatical focus.

"Atheism, as well as deep, anti-religion secularism, lodges amid its quasi-nihilistic disciples the following genocidaires:

"1. Adolf Hitler—yes, he participated in paganism, but it was not religious paganism, but rather secular paganism. Dinesh D'Souza, respected author and political commentator, using information gleaned from historians Allan Bullock, Richard Evans, and Richard Weikart, writes that Hitler and many of his Nazi topmost cadre—Bormann, Goebbels, Heydrich, and Himmler, all of whom were atheists and detested religion—'relied on ancient myths in the modern form given to them by Nietzsche and Wagner…because they could give depth and significance to a secular racial conception of the world.' Neither Nietzsche nor Wagner actually believed those mystical gods were real, and neither did Hitler; they just acknowledged their acceptance by many ancient Germanic peoples. Hitler made references to these anagogical gods to infuse a 'mystical aura' into his vision of a master race populated by

German Übermenschen—that is, supermen—and his statement 'By defending myself against the Jew, I am fighting for the work of the Lord' was directly designed for public consumption by the German citizenry, including Bavarian Catholics and Prussian Lutherans. As part of his effort to whip up a frenzied hostility against Jews among rank-and-file non-Jewish Germans, whose support he coveted during his ascension to power, Hitler combined extremist depictions of Jews as dangerous demons with occasional usage of phrases such as 'doing the Lord's work.' In other words, his pro-religion message was consummate perfidious propaganda. Hitler and his prime chieftains were quintessential mendacity-style propagandists. Hitler not only wasn't a Christian—as some anti-religion zealots falsely claim—he loathed Christianity and thought that the Christian tenets of compassion and forgiveness were elements of weakness. He was, according to some disputed accounts, an off-the-battlefield murderer of more Christians than Jews during the infamous Holocaust. Estimates garnered from the U.S. Holocaust Memorial Museum tabulate about six million slaughtered Jews versus about eleven million slaughtered non-Jews, scads of whom were Christians, including about 5.7 million non-Jewish Soviet civilians, inclusive of many Russian Orthodox congregants; about three million Soviet POWs, inclusive of many servicemen Orthodoxian congregants; about 1.8 million non-Jewish Poles, inclusive of many Polish Catholics; about 312,000 Serb civilians, inclusive of many Serbian Orthodox congregants; and about 1,900 Jehovah's Witnesses.

"2. Hitler's World War II adversary, Joseph Stalin, the Butcher of Moscow and killer of about 20 million people, including the Katyn massacre and the under-publicized Holodomor of 1932-33 during which scores of rural Ukrainian farming families were systematically starved via a government-orchestrated famine, plus countless more people whom Stalin and his NKVD caused to just disappear. Regarding the Holodomor, there were three apposite elements, each of profound gravity. First, both Stalin and his activist henchmen—foremost among them the Second Secretary of the Communist Party of the Soviet Union from late 1930 through early 1939, Lazar Kaganovich—considered the country folks known as Kulaks, who were relatively affluent peasant farmers, to be culturally inadequate and of a grossly inferior and very expendable social class. Second, the paranoid Stalin harbored a suspicion that, were an insurrection to ensue against him, such an attempted usurpation would likely be helmed by the Kulaks. Third, Stalin appointed Kaganovich, a Ukrainian Jew whose birthplace and paideia was in Radomyshl, Kyiv Governorate, as his steward to oversee what Stalin viewed as the must-not-fail-at-any-cost construction of Moscow's impending modern subway system. Stalin's ego dictated he be forever hailed as the grand modernizer. Tens of thousands of subway constructionists required food. Stalin, knowing the USSR was not purely autarkic, needed a commodity with which to purchase imported foreign technology and equipment for the subway and other industrialization projects. Consequently, he and Kaganovich instituted a cultural cleansing campaign known as *dekulakization*, about which they had no reservations combining with the deplorable governmental policy known as *collectivization*—the political principle that a nation's products, services, and industries must be collectively owned by the entire citizenry altogether, with distribution of ensuing benefits to the at-large public controlled by a few government authorities who comprise *the state*. That's what socialists and communists do. The antipodean economic philosophy is capitalism, which emphasizes individual ownership and personal responsibility. That's what capitalists do. As applied to the horrors of the Holodomor and its seven million or more murders by starvation, collectivist ideology resulted in the rapacious confiscating—i.e., stealing—of all grain from Ukrainian farmers. Kulaks were mere low-class, bucolic bums—according to the twisted propaganda with which Stalin inculcated Muscovites and other city-dwellers.

According to Stanford historian Norman Naimark, the Kulaks were publicly denounced by Stalinists as 'enemies of the people'; 'scum'; 'vermin'; 'filth'; 'garbage'; and 'cockroaches,' along with other niceties that were employed to foment dehumanization of the Kulaks in the minds of urbanites—the class of people of whom Stalin generally approved as the prototype of acceptable Soviet citizenry—and thus incite wholesale detestation of such supposedly reprehensible peasantry while removing moral concerns about extinguishing them. Plus, writes Naimark, there were prominent displays of agitative slogans, such as 'We will make soap of the Kulaks' and 'Our class enemies must be wiped off the face of the earth.' Yes, *class*. Hitler's race-based bigotry had nothing on Stalin's class-based bigotry—and the genocide that resulted. AAMOF, fascism and communism, as to oppression, subjugation, violence, and mass murder, are two sides of the same coin;

"3. Saloth Sar, better known as Pol Pot, of Cambodia, who authored the deaths of multiple millions while inflicting his grossly oppressive communist regime;

"4. Genghis Kahn, with countless victims spanning across much of Asia and Europe;

"5. Napoleon Bonaparte, the egotistical French conqueror who terminated about six million Europeans;

"6. Kim II-sung, 7/ Kim Jong-il, and 8/ Kim Jong-un, North Korean communist cult-of-personality dictators in order of inherited succession of father, son, and grandson, respectively, have collectively—thus far—reportedly killed more than 4 million Koreans;

"9. Benito Mussolini, Italian self-avowed atheist, anti-Semite, Axis Power comrade of Hitler and invader of Ethiopia in 1935 who used poison gas and bombed hospitals in an effort to extinguish Ethiopians, whom he deemed too inferior to continue to exist;

"10. Slobodan Milosevic, ex-Yugoslavian president and genocidaire who authored the Srebrenica massacre;

"11. Fidel Castro, of Cuba, yet another communist atheist dictator—see the pattern?—and one who appears responsible not only for typical communist societal oppression, but also for killing, over time, about a million Cubans;

"12. and finally—although there are more atheistic mass murderers than the ones I've listed here—the unconscionably sub-animal hominid and genocidaire who was the Chairman of the Communist Party of China from 1943–1976, Mao Zedong, AKA Mao Tse-tung, another anti-religion communist whose brutality, especially during his Cultural Revolution and his famine-inducing purge of people known as The Great Leap Forward, fast-forwarded to a premature finality, according to various documented historical accounts, at least a staggering 45 million lives. This arbitrary and colder-than-ice despot thereby earned what currently remains as the world record for killing more humans than any single individual in recorded history. He wanted to oblige China to become more modern, and to do so posthaste. Echoing Stalin's perspective regarding Soviet farmers, rural citizens in China, conjectured Mao, were just too backward and old-fashioned. Because they were not adequately progressive, they were an inconvenient impediment to the national modernity for which he wished to be credited and then receive everlasting encomium. If he were to enjoy such laudation within his mortal lifetime, patience could not be his virtue; those backwater pastoral peasants were in the way and had to be liquidated with promptitude. Some historians believe the fatality total of Mao's magnum opus of murder surpassed 70 million sacrifices to modernization.

"Note that, although not homicidal lunatics themselves, German economist Karl Marx, who authored The Communist Manifesto, and his ideological adherent, Vladimir Lenin, whose Soviet reign and secularist philosophy immediately preceded and profoundly influenced the brutal atheistic rule of Stalin, combined to craft a dedicated anti-religion secularism that has greatly contributed to the sadism and Machiavellianism inherently ineradicable in many communist societies. It was Marx who declared that: 'Die Religion … ist das Opium des Volkes,' which translates into 'Religion … is the opium of the people.' Stalin, at the time of his arcane death on March 5, 1953, was purportedly planning yet another pogrom, this one dubbed the Doctor's Plot, which entailed falsely accusing Russian physicians, predominantly Jews, of plotting assassinations of Soviet Party officials, thus supposedly justifying their extermination.

"Just stand back and take a historical look at the bloodbaths inflicted over the years by the anti-theist, communist dictatorships wherever they have existed in the world."

Kristi Lou by now was reading with an obsessive anger, fuming and snarling with the enunciation of many of her words. A few of the dancers had become concerned about her well-being, and, to a point, about their own safety in her presence. Rochelle was on the verge of intervening, but held back. Kristi Lou saw Rochelle's worried expression.

"I'll be done soon, Rochelle. I promise."

"OK baby. I hope so, 'cause dis'un is different. You way too wound up, like you crazy, you know?"

"Yeah, but now that I've gone this far, I've gotta get it all out."

Hokey, who a few minutes earlier had stepped outside through a seldom-used door on the side of Downtown Secrets, called to Kristi Lou.

"Hey Kristi. You all right? Dis time, dis uh, you know, dis carryin' on of yours … it's way worse than usual. It's just dat … I don't know, but …"

"Thanks, Hoke, but yeah, I'm OK. But I've gotta get done. I've … I must finish."

"OK. Unless somethin' happens and I gotta rush back in, I'm stayin' out here till you done."

"OK. Thanks."

Kristi Lou rubbed her face, and then readied her papers. She raised her voice back to speech volume and resumed her outburst.

"There is one religion that unfortunately does share a commonality of violence with its anti-religion atheistic counterparts, and that is Islam, in its radicalized form. Islamic extremists, known fairly as Islamofascists, are Muslim jihadists who are hell-bent on bloodthirstiness and Hitler-style or Stalin-style domination or elimination of those they consider to be infidels, with their typical targets being Christians, Jews, or fellow Muslims who they feel have betrayed Islam or whose Islamism is not sufficiently hardline. Often, they will also go murderously after non-Muslims, whom they call kafirs—that's k-a-f-i-r-s—who just so much as comment disrespectfully about their prophet Muhammad. They are willing to resort to medieval barbarity here in the 21st century while trying to establish a so-called caliphate.

"A despicable and absurd tendency is for atheists to make the witless mistake of dumping all religions into the same category as fanatical Islam. When Muslim jihadists behead, bomb, or otherwise murder innocent victims in the name of their Allah, typical atheists pontificators will spew disparagement to the effect of blaming religion for inspiring the violence—all the while conveniently ignoring or irrationally trying to rationalize away the grotesquely violent behavior of atheist dictators, as already referenced. The problem isn't *religion*, per se. The problem is with that particular religion—Islam—in its radical, terroristic state. Think of slaughterers Osama bin Laden and Idi Amin Dada.

"How can Muslims think like that? What type of god would advocate butchering someone just because he/she doesn't believe in him a certain way, or just because he/she criticizes or ridicules his alleged prophet?

"Christians don't kill to proselyte, punish, or dominate; Jews don't; Hindus don't; most other religions don't. Only Islamic extremists or their type do. Such malignity is likely instilled in them in madrasah seminaries.

"The Christian Crusades? Besides occurring a long, long, long time ago, as in 1095–1291, there are ample and credible historical accounts that aver that the Crusades comprised a highly justifiable military campaign by Christians to defend themselves against massive marauding violence that had been perpetrated by Muslims.

"The Catholic Inquisition? That also happened a long time ago, and ended in the early 1800s. It was tragic and wrong-minded, but the cumulative death toll from executions in Spain and Portugal, according to historians, was about 3,000–4,000, having occurred during a period spanning about three-and-a-half centuries. While each murder and torture was a tragedy, those numbers pale alongside the multiple millions of victims who have perished under the savagery of secular genocide.

"Some deluded Islamofascist killers apparently believe they'll be recompensed for slaughtering non-Muslims on Earth by getting to enjoy sexual bliss for eternity with 72 beautiful vestal virgins as wives in Paradise, whereas some deluded atheistic killers believe they know with certainty that there is no life after mortality and thus no punishment can await them as retribution for their atrocities.

"Irony can be very intriguing, as it's amazing to see how Islamofascists and atheist murderers who are ideologically and sometimes physically at each other's throats can inadvertently have so much in common.

"Murdering religionists—usually Islamofascist, terrorist types—kill, in great part, because they're inspired by the idea of reward in an afterlife. Murdering atheists—usually Stalinist and/or Mao types—kill, in great part, because they're comforted by the idea of no retributive consequence in an afterlife.

"The true believers—who worship a sometimes punitive but still primarily kind and righteous God, who seeks to bestow benevolence upon his earthly children if they are worthy, owing to their own kindness—are not the fools. Atheism is a false liberation, as in being liberated from the freedom of real happiness, which can be found by believing in something good and strong and beyond the sometimes baseness of our natural selves; it's akin to Orwellian doublethink, such as avowing that *war is peace* or *freedom is slavery* or *ignorance is strength* or *2+2=5.*

"Now, consider this: What entity other than God could have the power to create itself? What else could have always existed? Name something—anything—that wasn't created by the actions of some other thing or things, whether it's biological animal reproduction or packaged foods or buildings or boats or colliding planets and big bangs.

"Please—for those of you who want to be edified—go to the library or go online and read The Quinque viæ, which, translated from Latin, means The Five Ways. These are the renowned five reason-based arguments to logically advocate for belief in the existence of God, as proffered by 13th-century Italian theologian and philosopher St. Thomas Aquinas, who—despite his irrational, coldly immoral, and unsaintly dismissal of animals as mere usable things allegedly meant by God to be used with callous impunity in the service of mankind, and whose suffering somehow doesn't matter merely because they supposedly aren't capable of rational reasoning—presents credos for accepting the reality of God that are solidly cogent.

"I want to say earnestly that there are decent-hearted atheists who are not hubristic, with some stating that they value the community-strengthening presence of churches and synagogues in their towns. I harbor no disdain for them but, in fact, appreciate such agreeableness.

"However, for the blackhearted and brutal atheists, and for atheism itself, I say this:

"Atheism is a sinister enslaver and a would-be destroyer of kindness in times when munificence of spirit is the only soothing medicine. Atheism is ice-cold. Atheism is winter 365. Atheism is mean. Atheism is mean-spirited. Atheism is an archenemy of ethics. Atheism is a bottomless nadir. Atheism is a monster!"

Kristi Lou, as she dropped both arms simultaneously, spilled several pages of note papers from her right hand onto the sidewalk, where she left them for eight seconds before squatting down to retrieve them. She noticed that not even the weakest of winds were present to scatter them.

Emotionally frothing within herself and unashamedly in tears, Kristi Lou knew she had produced not only an articulate oral presentation of her anti-atheism philosophy, but that she would necessarily be seen by this audience standing on concrete outside a whorehouse as a—perhaps *the*—archetype of incongruity: a street-corner, sex-industry professional championing God.

As Kristi Lou, panting, stood and peered straight down at nothing in particular, a teardrop gently splashed eight inches above her slightly bent-forward right knee upon her bare thigh, entirely exposed due to the salacious shortness of her skirt. She was again compelled to momentarily consider the oddity of her personal ethos, framed against the ingrained ethos of the culture that surrounded her: Her ethos encompassed her moral code, which included one of her basal creeds: God is good; sex should be shameless.

Of what had snowballed into a group of about 20 spectators, all were stunned into silence, not from boredom or contempt, but from respect for Kristi Lou's stirring dithyramb and the precision and passion with which she had adduced her points. All remained speechless.

All but one.

"I agree with every syllable you just spoke while you were so fiercely perorating," avouched the man in the darkened area who had corrected her regarding the scientist's last name. "Well done," said the gentleman, as he turned away from Secrets and disappeared into the darkness.

"Thank you, sir."

Kristi Lou removed a tissue from her purse and dabbed it onto her face.

"I swear—even though I had these papers stuffed in my pocket—I had no idea I'd be ranting tonight from them…all these papers…about the follies and hope-assaulting coldness of atheism. Then why would I even bring these papers here? But, well…I don't know why things happen, and I don't know why I am the way I am, but…I don't know."

4

AS MOST OF THE GIRLS AND CUSTOMERS, STILL SOMEWHAT DAZED by Kristi Lou's street-side, term-paper screed against atheism, began to disperse in silence and head toward the front door, Kristi Lou's volcanic obsessiveness caused her to feel compelled to try to recapture their attention. But she refrained. A few people lingered and stared with bewilderment at Kristi Lou, but then they, along with Hokey, also strolled into Secrets.

Kristi Lou looked down at Rochelle, still seated in the chair Hokey had brought to her.

"Well, but anyway, to backtrack to my original argument and to close it out the way I want to I …"

Rochelle interrupted, sternly, with sincere concern etched on her face.

"Kristi Lou, you goan keel over and die if you don't rest. I know you young and healthy and all, but you fixin' ta drain yo battery. You need ta take a break from dem rants. Also, Big Sam is here tonight and he might come out here and want you ta get back in the club. He gives you a lotta leeway, but come on, girl."

"I know. You're right. But…"

"No buts…"

"But let me get this said, just to you, OK? Everybody else is back inside now, anyway. Well, here comes Hoke back outside, though."

"All right," conceded Rochelle, "I'll listen. But you need ta seriously take it easy. Drink some mo water. You got dat bottle there in yo purse."

"OK."

Kristi Lou downed the remainder of her water in two large gulps.

"All right, girl," said Rochelle, rising from her chair. "You be still awhile 'fore you take off again. Don't say nothin'. Chill. You be chillin' and stillin'."

"OK."

Kristi Lou stood motionless and silent for just beyond two minutes.

"Thanks. OK. Here goes. I want to repeat what I was saying before, that heterosexual males are so very often routinely and wrongly discriminated against, as if they're all barely restrained rapists, just because they have and display—at all, in any way—sexual attraction to females' physical assets. There are lots of memes in social interaction, even if we don't always know it's going on, and that includes me. Here a meme, there a meme, everywhere a meme—meme, meme, meme. But this patently anti-male meme is a very bad meme, and is profoundly prejudicial against men and should be viewed as insulting to everyone's intelligence. Quite frankly, it's both grossly discriminatory and entirely indefensible."

"Oh yeah, I know dat's right," concurred a supportive Rochelle, moving her chin up and down.

"The evaluation is right; the unreasonableness is wrong. It's bovine manure."

"What?"

"Another way of saying 'cow droppings.'"

Rochelle's mood lightened as she saw that Kristi Lou's vitality was more than stable.

"Oh, really? OK. You suburban white girl, you crackin' my ass up again. Next thing you goan say is 'gee whiz' or some shit like dat."

"Gee whiz."

"Thank you," said Rochelle.

"You're welcome, you urban black girl."

"Oh, OK. You done got me back on the racial thing. I know dat."

"Yeah, but anyway, as I was about to say, men who hate all women have a derogatory word aimed at them—misogynist. Well, I learned a new word the other day when I was reading the dictionary on my computer, and it's …"

Kristi Lou was abruptly interrupted. Rochelle produced a bulge-eyed, facetious scowl and bent herself forward with laughter.

"Say what? Girlfriend, you—you what? Oh no, no, no! You been readin' da *dictionary*? Readin'? Not lookin' up some words, but readin' it—like a book? We *gotta* get you a life. I mean—*damn*, girl!"

"Well," said Kristi Lou, now a hyper-energetic whrilwind, "I guess I could use a semblance of a life. But anyway, as I was saying, there's the flip side to misogynist. It's the reverse discrimination equivalent."

"The reverse discrim …" Rochelle, while regurgitating what she had just heard, was interrupted by Kristi Lou, whose energy was full-on.

"You know these men-hating women who paint all or most guys with a wide brush but hypocritically squawk about men negatively stereotyping women? Hmm, OK, here I'll interrupt myself to say that such people gladly accept positive, pro-female stereotypes with which they agree while—of course—duly avoiding usage of the oh-so-trendy-to-disavow word *stereotypes* to describe those stereotypes—or any other stereotypes they like. But, anti-stereotype balderdash permeates society, regardless of subject: 'If I approve, it's the truth! If I disapprove, it's a stereotype!' Nope. Umm, uh, sorry about my digressive self-interruption intended to extol the naturalness and necessity of accurate and fair stereotypes, be they complimentary or critical. Anyhow, to end my divagation and reclaim my antecedent focal point, I say that those wide-brush-painting, male-basher women can correctly be called *misandrists*."

"Dive-uh-what-shun? Anti-see-what-unt? Miss-what-ists?"

"Misandrists. Hmm … a misandrist can be a man-hating man, I suppose. But, for the purpose of my forensicality and debate principles, these are anti-male chick bigots who lump and dump on all straight guys by lumping and dumping them into the same all-encompassing, disparaging category."

Kristi Lou, with a quick grin, stamped one high heel on the sidewalk to emphasize her declaration.

"I will not become a misandrist."

Rochelle filled her cheeks with air. "My face be 'bout ta splode if I say too many of dem fat-ass words."

"So," Kristi Lou continued unabated, "just because some women are jerks doesn't make it so that all women are jerks. And, by the same token, just because some men are jerks doesn't cause all men to be jerks."

"You ain't done yet, is you?" predicted Rochelle.

"Not quite. There's another phenomenon in play. If people, especially men, criticize any genre of women in an intense way, just as I'm doing now, many females will try, knowingly or unknowingly, to intimidate them into shutting up by branding them as misogynists. In their minds, if you admonish women as a population about … anything … then that makes you automatically guilty of misogyny—even if you're complaining about and exposing misandry.

"And, if a guy tries to explain his male viewpoint and why he disagrees, nowadays he's denounced for *mansplaining*. But, conversely, if a girl tries to explain her female viewpoint, she's somehow magically not guilty of *womansplaining*. In fact, I don't think womansplaining officially exists yet as a word."

"Yeah, I know 'bout mansplainin'. Hokey does dat shit. But, yeah, 'fore you say it—I know dat's a both-ways thing."

"Yes, it is. If a guy asserts that 'some women, as a group, are unfair toward men' in this or that way, and his protests are impassioned, then he's often branded as a misogynistic mansplainer. 'He hates women! He's a misogynist! He's a woman-hater!' But many of those same critics will let women unfairly and negatively stereotype men half to death without blasting them for unfair negative stereotyping and without labeling them as misandrists."

Seeing Rochelle grinning from ear-to-ear, Kristi Lou jutted her jaw, stood at military attention and heralded her conviction with bemused piety.

"And, as I emphatically stated a few moments ago, I am not going to permit myself to become a misandrist."

Rochelle, tilting her head back and forth while jovially feigning a state of being impressed, asked for further scholarly info.

"So, I know you goan spell mis—mis—og—nist or whatever and mis—and—drips or whatever. I just know you goan be spellin' dem fine-fuck words."

"Sure," as Kristi Lou recited the correct spelling she acted out the role of erudite effete snob, aiming her nose toward the rooftops and speaking each letter in that affected droning intonation that comedians choose when satirically impersonating a wealthy elitist.

"I have deigned to amply correct your solecism," droned Kristi Lou while displaying stern-faced, hyperbolic condescension.

Rochelle gave a half bend-over with her hands on her waist and chortled. "You done corrected my what? You a stuck-up, snooty slut. Girlfriend, you a high-class hoe. You is a hofessional."

"Hofessional? Ha-ha. I guess that's like saying 'the S-word' instead of 'slut' or 'the W-word' instead of 'whore.' Or 'the H-word' in your parlance."

"In my par-what? Parlance? I didn't know I had one of dem. 'Nother one of yo forty-dollar college words. Hey Hokey, come here. I wanna tell you I got me some parlance; I don't know what the fuck it is but Kristi say I got some!"

"That's cool, baby," said Hokey. "I wonder if I got any parlance in me. Hey, Kristi, how 'bout it? What about me? I got some parlance? Maybe I ain't got none. If I don't, I best get me some of dat."

"Please? Please? Pretty-please?" Kristi Lou ignored the teasing banter between her two coworkers. "Will you please consider my views on these issues? I'd like to know that my ranting wasn't wasted."

"Oh, you such a fussy hussy. Oh, OK, OK. You so sensitive, girl. But, OK. I know. I'm sorry, sweetie-pie, if we don't look like we take yo crazy rants—I mean yo passionate rants—seriously," reassured Rochelle.

"That was a dandy-fine and *intellectual* rant," offered Hokey, strongly accenting "intellectual."

Rochelle walked casually toward the Walk/Don't Walk sign and called back over her shoulder. "You know we all look out for you."

"I know, and I appreciate it a whole bunch." Kristi Lou ran and caught up with Rochelle, giving Rochelle a hug on the top of her head, as Kristi Lou didn't feel inclined to bend down for hugging her 5'3" colleague.

"Hey, don't be messin' with my weave, baby girl. I got it fixed just right."

"Well, all righty, then. Excussssseeee me!"

"But what was dat word you was runnin' out at me—parlance? You still ain't told me what kinda parlance I got."

"Well, it's basically your idiom … well, I, uh, that's, that's not really the word I meant to …"

"Oh, now I'm an idiot. It ain't enough dat I got parlance. I gotta be an idiot, too."

Hokey was leaning against the doorframe of the front entrance, with the partially open door resting on his chest.

"Hey, Hoke, did you know I'm an idiot?"

"Oh yeah. I knew dat; everybody know dat."

"Wrong answer. Fuck off and blow yo-self."

"No, no, no," chimed Kristi Lou. "This word situation is getting really zonkers tonight. I didn't say 'idiot'; I said 'idiom.' Idiom is like parlance. It's your way of speaking—how you usually express your-self—your style of talking."

"Brains and stems up to yo neck. You lethal, baby."

"Oh, thanks."

"But you told me da other night yo shoe size is only 8. How you get such dainty little feet instead of boat paddles like you supposta have wit' bein' 12 feet tall and all? You even got tiny toenails."

"I can't know. They just didn't get big."

They both were laughing as they began to scan the streets around Downtown Secrets for any approaching Wednesday-night regulars. Seeing none, they reentered the brothel.

****

During the course of the evening, Kristi Lou welcomed two men whom she considered regulars, including one named Leonard. She danced to blues music with them, garnering generous tips, as well as with several strangers who were less unstinting. But, as usual, she did not go to the back rooms.

Kristi Lou observed that the deejay, who billed himself as DJ YoCrunk, repeated certain songs this night more frequently than he normally did. His blues musical selection included repeat plays of Muddy Waters's "Mannish Boy," "Tik Tok Blues," "I Can't Be Satisfied," and "Got My Mojo Working."

She spoke to herself, in her thoughts, as she often did while counting her share of the tip-out money that each girl paid to the disc jockey for his approximated percentage of her music-boosted earnings.

He really likes Bo Diddley and Ronnie Wood, but I know he loves Muddy Waters songs the best. I guess he was just in a Muddy mood tonight. DJ YoCrunk is the guy who told me Muddy's real name was McKinley Morganfield.

"You were in the mood for Muddy tonight, weren't you," asked Kristi Lou with a big smile, as she handed a wad of cash to the flamboyant disc jockey, attired in a red silk shirt tucked inside yellow, ultra-tight, wool trousers.

"You know it, baby. Muddy was just flowin', so I had to go with him."

"That's cool. No one objected that I know of; everyone seemed to like it. You always do a good job."

"Yeah, thanks for that, Kristi Lou. You get yo pretty, white-girl ass home safe."

"OK. I will. You get your cute, black-boy buns home safe, too."

While gathering from her locker things she wanted to take home this night, Kristi Lou dropped a clump of Benjamins next to her feet. Upon retrieving her money, she was led to think about an issue that was mildly troubling to her but that she had never discussed with Big Sam. *Hmm, tax-wise, I might be a Lawless Lucy. Taxes are deducted from dancers' salaries, but I think I'm maybe supposed to be keeping track of my tip earnings, which is by far most of what I make, and then sending some of it to the feds. Jeez, I don't wanna be immoral by not paying what I owe, and I don't want the IRS to get me. But nobody around here seems to do tip-tax payments, so I … I'll … I might look into it sometime.*

She departed from Secrets a few minutes after the club's closing time for this night, at 4:30 a.m., walking out with Leonard, whom she trusted. Kristi Lou commented that she didn't see her usual cab. Leonard offered her a ride home. She amiably accepted.

Leonard is like Big Sam and Hokey; none of them ever tries to sleep with me—or any of the other girls here. Leonard just likes to talk with me. He's lonely and sad, but he's nice. I like him a lot. Not that he would not have niceness if he did try to sleep with me, but, anyhow…

5

LEONARD LET KRISTI LOU OUT AT HER APARTMENT COM-
plex—Moonbeam Landing. Built in the 1960s during the apex of the
Bohemian hippie movement, Moonbeam Landing had been reasonably well-maintained over the decades, especially compared to many
of Detroit's buildings. "The Moonbeam" featured exterior and interior
architecture that reflected a quasi-Boho-Chic style.

After walking into the street-level living room of her townhouse-type,
double-decker, furniture-furnished apartment, Kristi Lou plopped down
on her sofa with a graceless, sprawling collapse. She was immediately
joined by her tomcat, Mr. Dooflotcher, who sprang from behind the
coffee table to claim his customary spot in her lap and commenced
to purr boisterously while squinting his emerald eyes in blissful con-
tentment as if to say, "Mommy's home."

"I've got C-I-L.," she said to Mr. Dooflotcher, a remark she was
quite fond of making to him. "Cat In Lap, C-I-L. You're not *on*; you're
in, 'cause I spread the top of my legs just enough to give you your own
personal gappy slot to snuggle down into and get comfy. All is well
with C-I-L. We make a fabulous team, don't we, Dooflotch?"

Kristi Lou would often gush unabashed baby talk to her kitty-cat,
whom she had rescued from the alley behind the apartment building

in April, four days after moving in. He was then a rough-but-sociable stray. After enduring plenteous bites and claw-slaps from her prototypal gray-mackerel tabby with black stripes, Kristi Lou eventually assuaged his quasi-feral aggression, effecting a reasonably domesticated one-person cat. She paid $125 on Monday, April 30 to a nearby veterinarian to geld him. She also had him vaccinated against rabies, FIV, and FeLV.

"Oh man, Dooflotch, you should've heard me tonight at work. Holy guacamole! I dove headfirst into one of my most lunatic-ish rants yet. I couldn't stop myself. Oh my god."

Kristi Lou gently sat her kitty on the taupe carpet and climbed out of the soft, deep, couch cushion and began to trek toward the kitchen. She was, however, halted by Mr. Dooflotcher's aggressive maneuvers, as he felt he'd not been petted enough and hence darted relentlessly around and between her feet. She bent over and cupped her right hand under Mr. Dooflotcher's forelegs, scooping him off his paws in one fell swoop and then transferring him to the inside of her left forearm, holding him upside down against her midsection as she walked. He once again blissfully squinted the way cats do when they feel content and safe, making his eyelids form thin, fur-lined fissures.

"Here him is—my sweet boy. Him's so sweet; yeth him is. Him's my innocent wittle furry and purry baby. Him's my sweet wittle sweetie. You're always glad to see me and I'm always glad to see you. Yeth I am. You like me no matter what. Yeth you do. And this isn't my lap; it's our lap…'cause my lap is also your lap which we share so it's really our lap. And I give you scritches, which are gentle scratches, on your chinny, chinny, chinny. I wuv you, my sweet wittle Mr. Dooflotcher. Yeth I do."

As she gingerly placed Mr. Dooflotcher on the kitchen floor and fixed his dinner, she thought about the possible unspoken reactions of some people were they to hear her deliver such sugary professions of adoration to her feline child. She rebutted the imaginary throng as if her scorners were in her kitchen.

"I guess some of you might think I sound sickeningly saccharine and too mushy-gushy. I don't care. I'm a sappy girl and I like me that way."

****

Before going to bed, Kristi Lou lay supine on the bedroom floor, her head partly submerged in a plush pink pillow, quietly meditating for more than 20 minutes. With a curled-up ball of fur purring nonstop on her chest below her chin, she stoically pondered her self-chosen station in life. She thought of how she had put on hold most normal social pursuits, including the quest for starry-eyed courtship summiting in wedlock—the shameless, banal bliss of romantic love and its marital consummation for which she inwardly lusted.

Reflecting on how she had no shortage of dates nowadays, she realized that her liaisons were understandably brief and distinctly lacking in the tenderness of romance. She blurted her fears to Mr. Dooflotcher.

"Who wants to fall in love with a…?"

Kristi Lou did what she would often do; she blocked a certain word from fully surfacing in her self-critique.

When in this mode of filtering her self-assessments, she would seldom allow herself to think of that word more than a second beyond its original emergence. However, there were moments such as these during which she would be frank with herself, including the inward acknowledgement that, in a strictly technical, precise application, that defamatory word was like the ugly pair of shoes someone gave you that fit so well they just had to be worn.

Still lolling on her back on the floor, she stretched her arms and legs sideways with a sudden burst, and just uncaged it.

Here I am—a whore on the floor. I am a whore who rationalizes about her whoring. I am a whore, but only at this juncture of my life. One day, I'll be a whore no more, and find my amaranthine love to last forevermore.

Such introspection continued to occupy Kristi Lou's mind this late Wednesday night/early Thursday morning as she uprooted herself from the floor, outened the lights, and slid beneath her bedsheet, followed by Mr. Dooflotcher who burrowed under the sheet and scooted to his spot a few inches outside her right foot.

Reclining supinely, Kristi Lou, weary from obsessing, quickly dozed off while watching the barely illuminated ceiling fan's blades spin hypnotically. After about 15 seconds of dreamless sleep, a crystal-clear dream had her happy-stepping jauntily through an unknown town. She saw a small shop. As she beheld the signage above the storefront door, the appellation changed from "Community Store" to "Community Whore."

Kristi Lou's somnolent illusion swiftly shifted. Now in her car at nighttime, her dreamworld thrust her into the parking lot of a giant orange warehouse. She felt driven to purchase a big bag of screws and locknuts. She drove toward the store and looked o'er the door. As she eyed "Home Depot," the m flickered and then burned out.

She snapped awake. She did not move a muscle.

"No! Dear God, don't let it be so!"

Thinking of her protective mechanism in which she would occasionally criticize but then reassure herself with vocalized, self-critiquing comments while alone in her apartment, Kristi Lou decided she needed to thus comfort herself now.

"I yearn for my troubadour to sing me a love song or recite a romantic poem he wrote for only me. I wanna get married in a traditional white gown on a warm, sunny spring morning on a beach at low tide with calm waves washing gently ashore with his family and mine and a recording of Petula Clark singing 'There Is Love'—minus the unkind, superfluous lyric about a man leaving his mother upon marriage. That frigidity will be edited out; my betrothed's mom shan't hear it. I wanna sing to him the 1970 song 'For the Love of Him,' by Bobbi Martin. Can I be so young and have already thrown away a chance for love? No, no, no!"

Scaring more than reassuring herself with her cerebration, she turned abruptly over, harmlessly grazing Mr. Dooflotcher's chin with her left-foot instep.

"Just take it easy. Relax. You're all right. You still have so much living ahead of you; you have yet to do all that you're going to do, and you're going to do a lot. Always remember—nil desperandum!"

Although the dark usually comforted Kristi Lou, this darkness found her unusually restless. She became too tired to sleep, lying in bed awake, tossing and turning while thinking about her body, her clothing, her choices at work in Secrets as well as other sundry aspects of her daily life.

I'm so tall but I wear high heels but that's OK but … I don't know, but …

Without trying any longer to form sentences in her head, she let her thoughts roll freely, in spurts of broken phrases.

Yeah … mighty tall I am, but, you know … heels … gotta wear 'em …heels mandatory, even though tall 'cause, uh, havta fit in with the other ladies …

Kristi Lou thought about how, with her 44-inch stems, despite natural athleticism—she recalled the accolades she received in high school, being named all-conference as a cross-country runner and as a high-jumper, with the old newspaper clippings saved in a photo album—she sometimes wobbled on the spiked four-inch heels that she did not need but felt obligated to wear in order to blend in with the women with whom she worked. Besides, pumps were part of the trade and were expected by men, and made her look all that much more appealing, she surmised.

Also, as she reminded herself while jouncing herself back to alertness and stroking Mr. Dooflotcher's ears with her toes, she at least didn't wear those eight-inch stilettos; those extra few inches just might miscarry and push her conspicuous height above many men's psychological line of demarcation.

Too much artificial elevation could backfire and cause me to become less, not more, alluring to guys because of being too intimidating. If I'm too high I might seem too mighty. Of course, it's just the opposite with my masochistic, femdom clients who want me to govern them.

Kristi Lou casually watched a small moth fluttering frantically upon the ceiling above her bed, navigating in and out of the narrow swaths of dull light that radiated from a nearby street lamp and that always leaked upwardly through her closed venetian blinds.

He's a nervous bug. I wonder if moths are always scared during their few hours of life. I hope he's all right up there and has enough light in here. Moths like light. I wish he'd land himself and be still inside one of those streaks of light. Maybe I should switch on a lamp for him. I hope he doesn't get thumped by the ceiling fan. Moths never live long as it is, so ... I guess he's OK, though.

She thought about how she did not wish to utterly dwarf any of her smaller, normal patrons and thus cause them to suffer some form of visual enfeeblement.

My motto is "stimulate, not emasculate."

Kristi Lou did not want to repel most of the "normys," as she called them, the men who were anchored in relative normality, and thereby leave only the fetish buffs, such as the sadist/masochist types; she felt ill-at-ease playing the role of dominatrix. She didn't relish making them feel like, well, one of her former educators who had happened to be painfully short. But she comforted herself by realizing that very few of her clients were non-normys, and that her domination was a facet of role-playing, in which she and the man acted the parts in a fantasy.

It's not the real me or the real him; but it's real pleasure. We don't truly see each other as really that way and that non-realness makes all the difference.

After nearly two hours of reviewing whom she perceived herself to be, Kristi Lou finally fell asleep near sunrise and slept later than usual, till almost 11:30.

****

Awakening with what she recognized as a slight tinge of depression, she looked onto the bedside table at her small turquoise alarm clock on which she never set the alarm. She welcomed Thursday, August 2, and then looked at Mr. Dooflotcher, who had chosen to sprawl languidly on the other pillow, splooting and staring silently at her.

She felt compelled to gaze for a few moments at the old alarm clock, whose color was now faded, hailing from her childhood days in Arkansas—the same clock she used to occasionally set to wake herself up starting in the fifth grade through her senior year in high school. Her Aunt Charlene had given the clock to her one long-ago Christmas. Kristi Lou thought back to how she used to take pride in being independent and adult-ish via awakening herself with her own alarm clock, but other times she let Mom or Dad awaken her just to enjoy the reassuring warmth of being awoken by her parents—warmth for her and warmth for them.

Mr. Dooflotcher sat up. He reached forward and gently pawed Kristi Lou on her nose.

"Your breakfast? I'm late feeding it to you? Oh, OK. Why didn't you wake me up? You know I sometimes don't set the music alarm on our smartphone and that I don't ever set the alarm on this old alarm clock. You know that. Then again, perhaps you were just being considerate by letting me sleep in. But cats don't do that. And you always want to eat on time. In fact, you always want to eat, period. So, are you all right? Oh well…"

After feeding Mr. Dooflotcher, Kristi Lou spent most of the day reading through her abundant stack of magazines and surfing the Internet.

She also expended about 45 minutes watching the Weather Channel on her 32-inch LED television. Having been fascinated by and frightened of tornadoes since she was a child, Kristi Lou noted in her thoughts that tornadoes were featured in many of the discussions imparted by on-air reporters. While lounging on the sofa this afternoon, she heard one meteorologist say that August is historically the fifth-most torna-do-producing month of the year.

I'm not astraphobic; thunder and lightning don't frighten me too much. But tornadoes … I'm lilapsophobic, for sure. There aren't many tornadoes that come through Michigan, but my home state of Arkansas is smack-dab in a tor-nado alley, prevailingly along I-30 and Highway 67. Oh my goodness. Aunt Charlene told me I was not quite two years old when 56 of those nasties roiled up outta hell on those roadways during just two days, on January 21 and 22 back in '99. Multiple deaths and injuries. God, such a heartbreaker. Now I'm lying here worried about Aunt Charlene, my parents, my whole family, my friends back home as well as all the animals that could be endangered. I have to worry about them; that's good in that it's part of caring, but I hope I don't get too obsessed about them getting blown away. That's not going to happen, is it? Is it? No, it isn't. Jeezakerrs … me and my lilapsophobia …

Kristi Lou was sometimes haunted by visions of imaginary tornadoes. She was often horror-stricken by videos of actual tornadoes. At times, after seeing a tornado on TV, she would obsess for hours on end, unable to clear her brain of such images; her mind would intermittently create exaggerated panoramas of merciless funnels of violent wind sweeping up people, creatures, and buildings, hurling them hither and thither.

I'm inarguably lilapsophobic. Since I am so lilapsophobic, why do I watch tornadoes if I know they're going to scare me the rest of the day? Am I mas-ochistic, like some of my non-normys? I might be. I totalistically doubt there are too many twenty-one-year-olds who'r still terrified of the flying-house scene in The Wizard of Oz. But I am. Yikes!

Around midafternoon, after taking a brief nap, Kristi Lou pushed herself to exercise, performing a shortened version of her self-scripted calisthenics workout.

6

THURSDAY NIGHT FOUND HER BACK LOITERING IN HER FA-vorite area of the sidewalk outside Downtown Secrets, about 25 feet to the right of the old sign hanging over the foreboding entrance. But, on this occasion, she was alone, as everyone else—besides Hokey—was busy inside.

Rochelle, standing near the front door a couple of minutes earlier, had cheerily greeted a regular, with whom she entered Downtown Secrets together, leaving Kristi Lou to her oft-wandering mind. She knew Hokey always kept a watchful and protective eye on her when her feet followed her thoughts. Seeking solitude away from any audience whose presence might tempt her to preach and pontificate, Kristi Lou wandered off farther to ensure that *I will be only with me.*

Always aware that she was quite the dreamer and meditator, Kristi Lou propped her left shoulder against a light pole and let her mind roam. She sometimes dreamed of what the future might offer, while other times she drifted into her yesteryear, with this occasion taking her en route to the latter sentimental destination.

She wanted—she needed—to reminisce.

As she began ruminating, Kristi Lou suppressed, as she usually did, an inveterate discomfort, an occasionally recurring anxiety whose roots had emerged during the segment of her life she termed "the year of Gorgonian growth," that of her grisly self-consciousness of how she was frequently a human tower looming monstrously over the top of male domes; as a twelve-year-old, she often knew more about how much dandruff an adult man had than did he.

Yeah, it's here again; it's the same thing as always. I love being so tall nowadays since I'm grown up, but I still feel that old permeation of pain during any given reminiscence when I first remember what I'm remembering right now—how painful it was back then, in 2009 and 2010. But it's OK 'cause, these days, that bad feeling goes away after a few seconds, but…

Kristi Lou pondered how her historical distress was traceable to her experience with her homeroom teacher during a certain hormonally angst-infested school year—that of grade number seven. Now, almost a decade later, she had not experienced a single day since early winter of her harrowing seventh-grade year without at least one instance of thought directed toward the Napoleonic 5'1" Mr. Bud Battle.

Standing in self-imposed isolation, she considered what she was doing. That is, she was once again doing what she would occasionally do: delve into remembrances of Sky Man, which was one of the monikers by which kids used to call Mr. Battle behind his back. Kristi Lou smiled as she thought of how he was also surreptitiously known as Big-Stud Bud, and Bad Bud Battle.

Golly, perhaps even crueler than those facetious ironies were the almost literally accurate slurs they used to call him, like Itty Bitty Bud, Bud the Spud, and Bud Very Light. Why do I like to think of Mr. Battle and those times in school? It seems to give me some feeling of reassurance. I don't always understand myself, but oh well.

Kristi Lou remembered how she had already ascended to 5'10" by age 12. She recalled how unwelcoming was Mr. Battle's bizarre attitude of enmity toward her, which was not understood by her at first, in September, but which she intuitively grasped by November. She had, from early childhood, been more perspicacious than most children, often sensing, accurately, what was transpiring around her, even if she did not or could not formulate the right descriptive words. Soon before Thanksgiving of that year, she came to more clearly comprehend Mr. Battle's anxiety, aided by talks with her lanky parents, both of whom had towered above their own seventh-grade classmates.

As she stood unaccompanied in relative darkness on Miracle Boulevard, Kristi Lou's aberrative-level nonlinear life-thoughts bred her reflections, which drifted without direction. She recalled some of the "Mr. Battle episodes," as she termed her recollections of events involving Bud Battle, whom she had come to know at Mary Our Lady of Mercy Catholic School for Gifted Pupils of Little Rock, Arkansas—an aged campus still soldiering on after its construction in the 1950s.

****

Short-legged with a longer-than-normal torso, while appearing ano-rexic everywhere except his corpulent potbelly, the pale-complexioned and pear-shaped Bud Battle was vociferously denigrated one afternoon in September of Kristi Lou's seventh-grade year by Wilma Wilson, social studies teacher, with whom he had harshly argued over politics, as resembling a "pasty, pregnant, cocktail fork."

Some students, including Kristi Lou, who happened to be pass-ing by the teachers' lounge near the beginning of the tit-for-tat, animus-swapping altercation, to which they chose to stealthily listen, heard Ms. Wilson proceed to offer her view that Bud also looked like "a bead of water that can't quite fall off the spigot." Mr. Battle flamed back against this boorishness from his adversary, deeming Ms. Wilson to be an "overt and unmitigated imbecile."

"You couldn't teach a school of fish how to swim," chided Bud.

"Originality?" Wilma Wilson retaliated with a lip-curled smirk.

"Originality? What originality? Would you know how unoriginal that put-down probably is? No, I suppose you wouldn't."

Wilma, who stood 5'11" and weighed over 230 pounds, and Bud had become locked into a verbal fight with their mutual goal being to out-berate each other, not unlike a duel between two of the kids whom they were charged with teaching.

Wilma further countered Bud's invective by ridiculing him over the never-published educational pamphlets Bud had made known he wanted to circulate, with middle school students such as those in his classes as the designated reading audience. Thinking that he could benefit kids nationally and even internationally if his publication became critically acclaimed, Bud had presented four transcripts and their respective titles to his compatriots at Our Lady for critique. Catechetical in their pedagogical technique, Bud's pamphlets posed questions then supplied answers. He had sought peer affirmation as a reassuring precursor to mailing his work to publishing companies.

Ms. Wilson was one colleague who was not about to let him—or anyone else on the school staff—forget what he was eventually dissuaded from submitting to any publishers.

"I'm a bad teacher?" exclaimed Wilma Wilson. "That's what you're saying about me? As I recall from last year, you are the preeminent author of the following pamphlets that you wrote to middle school kids. Yeah—middle school kids! You were going to market this claptrap to middle school kids!"

Wilma reached into her purse. She pulled out a crumpled piece of paper, unfolded it and began to reference it as a source of information to bolster her argument.

"Let's see now; oh, yes, you named your lovely leaflets as follows: Hemorrhoids—The Future of Your Anus; Yeast Infections—What Every Girl Should Know; The Wet Dream—A Boy's New Friend; and Journey of Internal Discovery—You and Your Uterus."

"What? You, you, you actually keep a record of what I was going to name my pamphlets—in your pocketbook—a year after the fact?"

"It sure looks that way, doesn't it? You should thank your lucky stars that some of the other teachers here talked you out of going forward with that stupid gibberish—just embarrassing. I mean, really, what do you know about yeast infections and uteruses?"

"Yeah," rebutted Bud Battle, "well, yeast infections and uteruses may not be my main bailiwick, but I teach school kids, don't I?"

"No, not really; you just hang out in the classroom and get paid for it."

"Bullshit! That would be you. Unlike you, I am a *real* teacher. And I thought I might help them, the kids, prepare for what may come along later in their lives and yes, be a bit clever with it, too. So what? And I don't need you to be embarrassed for me. And if you suffered embarrassment because, I guess, of association with me because you're also a teacher—well, technically, by title, you are, supposedly—then, then, then you can just get the holy-heck over it. And regarding my knowledge of yeast infections and uteruses, I can honestly say that you don't have to have 'em to know 'em. I can read medical journals and newspaper articles and magazine articles and Internet articles and listen to discussions on TV and on the radio. I learned from those sources."

Bud raised his forefinger and shook it aggressively at Wilma.

"I know yeast infections!"

"What?" gasped Wilma.

"I know uteruses!"

Bud realized in an instant that his outburst may've caused him to sound like a buffoon.

"Oh? How many uteruses do you know?" inquired Wilma. "What are their names?"

"Huh? I wasn't saying I'm personally acquainted with specific uteruses. I was saying that I'm uterus literate."

"You're uterus literate?"

Wilma looked at Bud with incredulity, hands on hips, smiling derisively. She then burst into spiteful laughter.

Several other teachers standing or sitting in the breakroom also chuckled at Bud's proclamation. Some teachers, however, whether or not they laughed at Bud, sensed—despite his peculiar choice of topics for his pamphlets—his sincerity in wanting to educate, beyond standard classroom edification, those students who were grappling with their mushrooming adolescence.

Wilma practically snorted while delivering her next defamation.

"You're a comical little fool. A laugh-out-loudable runt-wussy. A peewee shrimp-wimp. A poster-boy for heightism. A man manqué."

Bud glared at Wilma for about six seconds while trying to conjure up his retaliation, and then began what he hoped to be a searing counterstrike. He thought about saying what he really wanted to say: *you wear so much perfume you smell like a French strumpet on military payday! And the way you wear your hair makes you look like a plump hedgehog with a permanent!*

But, he ascertained that, being a male teacher, he would likely be fired for unleashing such indelicate and sexist invectives. So he discharged a deluge of polemics that he deemed somewhat less in-the-gutter but still scathing.

"You think you can just insult me with your *pregnant fork* and *water spigot droplets* or what-the-hell-ever you said and get away scot-free with it? You're making depreciatory remarks about my physical appearance. You know, I could—since you have an obvious weight problem—publically call you things like Wide Load Wilma or the Obeser-Teacher or say 'Hey 501! You know you're a fatty when you have your own area code!' But I actually don't say things like that—about how you look. So where do you get off saying those types of ugly things about me about how I look? Blubber-butt!"

Instantly, Bud realized that, with the obloquial philippic he had just finished administering to Wilma, he had done the very thing he had cautioned himself against doing before he opened his mouth. One of the kids covertly listening in from the hall was highly entertained by hearing two grownups—teachers, no less—blasting each other.

"Oh man—they're throwin' down!" he exclaimed, while tantalized teachers in the room looked on shamefacedly as if they were in a grocery line reading through the cover of a tabloid newspaper they deemed as beneath them but from which they could not look away.

"And you, you," stammered Bud as he resumed his retaliation while the glowering Wilma stood unnaturally apoplectic, "you are the one who grades tests with discussion questions by just skimming over the answers; you barely even read them. You said as much that day last year when you were talking in this very lounge with Mary Lynn. If she still taught here she'd back me up on that."

"I did not tell her that!"

"Like hell you didn't! Yes, you did! I heard you, or, I should say, I overheard you … not trying to listen in but I walked in here to get a Coke and I couldn't help overhearing what you were saying, what with that cankerous loud mouth of yours spewing forth. You were sorta snickering about it, about how you just 'hit the highlights' and all that when you grade those tests. That's not ethical to grade tests like that; you can give inaccurate grades and that's unfair to the students. You should be ashamed of that and I could report you for it. So, watch your step with your blabbermouth disrespect or I might have something to say to our esteemed principal, Daniel Alexander, or maybe to the next session of the school board."

"Oh, so that's a threat?"

"Darn tootin'! You should be reported. You shouldn't even be working here. You should be … well, I don't know what you should be but you shouldn't be a teacher. Realistically, you aren't a teacher. That's because teachers teach and you don't!"

"Listen, you little shit-sack! I'm a damn good teacher!" defended Wilma, standing toe to toe with Bud while glaring down at him.

"No, you aren't!" proclaimed Bud, looking up at Wilma and hoping to not be shoved to the floor or punched unconscious.

"Oh. Yes. I. Am." Wilma Wilson tilted her chin minaciously to about two inches above Bud's bald head and lowered her voice while deepening her tone, achieving a masculine-sounding, menacing, bass inflection that Bud instantly admired but resented her for possessing.

Then, fear set in, as Bud knew Wilma could likely pulverize him.

Wilma enunciated each syllable slowly, with deliberate accentuation.

"And I'm a better teacher than you, Spud, I mean, Bud, although that's obviously not saying too much. Everyone knows you doze off in the classroom—a lot. You might be asleep more than you are awake, which, since you can't teach a lick, might be a blessing for the students. You probably dream about turning into an actual man. You're an abysmal excuse for a teacher; for one thing, you can't see over your desk to observe what the kids are doing."

Wilma Wilson grinned wickedly.

"Eat you-know-what, you gorgon!" fumed Bud.

"Gorgon?"

"Yes—gorgon!"

Bud and Wilma escalated into a loud yell-fest, yelling over each other with sometimes barely coherent sentences that became so intertwined that onlookers could not understand what either said.

Claire Mumford, the elderly, ectomorphic matriarch and English teacher whose tenure at Our Lady exceeded that of most of the other teachers combined, entered the room. Mrs. Mumford, as she wanted to be known, stepped slowly between the inflamed combatants and imposed a taut adult intervention.

"If you two don't stop, I'm going to have to go get Mr. Alexander.

It'll be a real shame if I actually have to report fighting teachers rather than fighting pupils to the principal's office. Don't you both agree?"

Upon being properly admonished by someone whom they both respected, Wilma and Bud disengaged. At Mrs. Mumford's implicit behest, they submissively turned away from each other though their corralled emotions continued to run rampant.

Although he wouldn't say it even to himself, Bud was thankful that he hadn't been decked.

Bud was tempted to fire one more parting torrent but thought the better of it and resisted the temptation. He looked at his watch and announced, veraciously, that "I've gotta get to class; it starts in two minutes."

As he grabbed the doorknob, Bud's resistance waned. Without looking back at Wilma as he stepped into the doorway, Bud launched one last blast.

"A certain teacher could, whether she's in class or out of class, try to, for a change, conduct herself *with* class—if that's possible. In the meantime, pardon me while I depart from someone's presence and consequently climb several notches back up the evolutionary ladder."

"You should stand on a ladder whenever possible so your students won't step on you," said Wilma.

Bud churned his squatty legs and bolted past the door.

Wilma seethed for a moment and then started to go after Bud. But she was halted, as if she were suddenly frozen in place, by a single, firm word from the physically delicate but overpowering Mrs. Mumford. She looked at Wilma and issued a command saturated with sternness.

"No."

****

Kristi Lou and the other kids who had been mesmerized as they listened in on the unexpected theater had quickly dispersed away from the teachers' breakroom doorway upon hearing Mr. Battle's stated plan to depart from the room, giggling as they scattered.

"Teachers gone wild!"

"Yeah. That was wayyyy too cool."

"I hope I'm around when they go at it again."

"Did anyone get that on video?"

"Oh shit—I forgot to pull out my phone."

"So did I. Fornicate me."

"We coulda put it on YouTube. Oh maaannnnnn…"

"I know, right? Double-downer, man. What a wasted opportunity."

****

Kristi Lou snapped out of her reminiscence long enough to look back at Secrets, where about a dozen patrons, carousing together, were exiting onto the street. She noticed more than half the men were drunk. She saw one man emerge from the pack and heard him say, in a clear, steady voice, "I'll get the car," as he strode confidently toward the public parking lot a half-block away.

Oh good—one of the sober guys is driving.

                                  7

NONLINEARLY QUIRKY IN HER THOUGHT PATTERNS SINCE
childhood, she returned to her memories, thinking—though she wasn't
entirely sure why—about Mr. Battle and her eternal connection with
him and how things were between them during her seventh-grade year.

Kristi Lou recalled that she'd comprehended, even as a first-semester
seventh grader, that Bud's shortage of height was not merely a minor
annoyance, but hovered in his mind during every waking moment like
a scorning ghoul.

Eventually, her intuition received definitive validation.

I was right.

                                ****

Bud Battle was sometimes haunted by sudden daydreamed visions, invading
his consciousness with no warning, of what he saw as the Greek God of
Vertical Manhood peering down upon him with disdain, shaking his trident
pitchfork, sniggering loudly and thundering his disdainful condemnations.

"You are so much shorter than you should be. Your penis resembles
a cherry stem. It also looks like a worm, which is why you should never
be nude in the presence of foraging birds."

Mr. Battle, under siege by such neurosis, had conveyed from the opening day of class his resentment toward Kristi Lou via his verbal modulations and facial expressions. He had long felt unfairly deprived by nature's gene pool, a bitterness rooted in his own adolescence, and Kristi Lou's accident of anatomy screamed this unfairness at him every Monday through Friday. Why should this broomstick female of only a dozen years of existence get to enjoy being a freak of the natural order and have what he should have been entitled to have had all along?

A man is supposed to be taller than a woman, but especially a damn twelve-year-old girl.

As if to gruesomely sensationalize this genetic injustice, she had the audacity to be one of his students.

Compounding the daily distress of feeling perpendicularly impotent, Mr. Battle's pathology of social consternation was exacerbated by his alopecia, his baldness having afflicted him before he turned twenty-three. He combed his lone swath of meager hair horizontally across the middle of his wide head and plastered his crucial strand immovably in place with a copious mountain of mousse, giving the top of his noggin the appearance of a shiny plastic pink Easter egg ready to be twisted open.

Bud Battle's classic Napoleon Complex had led him to feel his masculinity threatened by Kristi Lou as much as she fretted that her femininity was diminished by him; his sagging bellybutton could almost greet her knees and they both virtually hated one another for this incongruous U-turn of normality.

Why does he have to be so squat? Kristi Lou used to ask herself such questions, including one mid-October day during her seventh-grade year.

Why does he have to be my teacher? Why can't he grow? Aren't there some medications or some bottled get-tall potions or some holistic herbs he could take?

During the same stretch of autumn, the forty-seven-year-old unmarried Mr. Battle would sometimes inwardly yell disingenuous disclaimers at Kristi Lou as he pitifully tried to assuage his self-loathing.

The little perpendicular bitch thinks she's hot stuff because she got genetically lucky, but that means nothing to me! I don't care, I don't care, I tell you—I don't care!

Once, in late October, while he absentmindedly stood beside his desk as Kristi Lou entered the classroom, he unleashed in his mind a silent scream of denial. *She's flaunting it like a vamp. Look at her sashay. I won't grant her permission to look down on me. No—don't you go looking this way! Oh hell! But—so what? You think I care? I don't—damn you!*

Bud was blasted by the awareness of what he avowed he would not permit her to figuratively do is exactly what she literally did do every single second she looked at him—unless she was sitting. He cherished the minutes she sat at her desk, which was when he felt most like standing. During these blessed intervals, he was taller than everyone, including Kristi Lou. And the world, at least for a while, was righted and as it should be.

****

Kristi Lou returned again to the present tense, glancing at Hokey. Although he was directing his gaze away from her, she knew that Hokey was watching over her, protectively.

Yeah, Mr. Battle and I both could perceptively feel the mutual bitterness, adult and child, but we managed to co-exist. We did. He gave me a somewhat charitable B+ in general science.

She realized that, despite his awareness of the juvenile whinnying from kids that seemed endlessly ongoing just beyond his earshot, Mr. Battle had mustered the integrity to grade her fairly—and perhaps with a little extra fairness.

He was fair. But, oh my god, there was that, that time that he … oh my god.

Tacitly understood by Kristi Lou and Bud Battle, with no words ever exchanged, had been the admonition that they would always, without fail, avoid being juxtaposed standing side-by-side after what came to be known as *The Incident*.

Eight years later, *The Incident* remains a legend of lore at Kristi Lou's middle school alma mater.

OMG, it'll be forever with me, seared unremovably in my retrospection. I can't forget it.

****

During a chilly Friday morning in January, the rapidly burgeoning Kristi Lou, no longer prepubescent, shed her thick coat and left it at her table in the laboratory, revealing a rather unseasonably thin T-shirt to cover her blossoming thoracic endowments. She ventured to the water fountain in the hallway.

After bending to have a drink, she rose quickly to her starboard side to return to her botany studies in the lab. At that precise moment, the diminutive Mr. Battle, who had un-fortuitously removed his eyeglasses and had been waiting a few feet away to quench his own thirst, broke from his conversation with six other teachers, turning abruptly leftward. Upon this gruesome instance, the cosmos yielded a ruthlessly star-crossed confluence between student and teacher.

The hard point of Kristi Lou's brassiere, with embarrassing force, jammed poor Mr. Battle directly in his left eye, sending him sprawling ignominiously backward into the well-muscled and zaftig Mrs. Bulloch, phys ed instructor extraordinaire, from whose sturdy body he haplessly ricocheted face first like a pinball onto the old-school wall radiator. During the fracas, one of his tiny testicles was jarred out of his zipper door, which the forgetful teacher had failed to securely seal upon leaving the restroom earlier. Bud's dangling manhood became stuck between the radiator's burning-hot heating pipes. He impulsively emitted a shameless primordial shriek.

His normally beady eyes bulged bulbously, making him resemble an indignant grouper. Amidst the sudden agony and mortification, Mr. Battle was just as suddenly swept over by a fatalistic feeling of morbid resignation that seemed to mockingly assure him that he was deserving of such peril, with the physical pain less painful than the humiliation.

This may as well be happening to me. Why not? I must deserve it.

While his genitalia were being desecrated by the ruthless radiator, Bud Battle felt that his misfortunes were perhaps punitive measures imposed from above and were thus ineluctably fated; he must have lived as a scoundrel in a pre-mortal spiritual dimension somewhere.

Holy shit. I must've been an asshole in my pre-life.

Unlike the riotous kids, observing teachers, upon comprehending the grotesque discomfiture that had godlessly enmeshed their comrade but seeing no imminent plausibility of beholding his extinction, all valiantly repressed a near-explosion of delectably wicked laughter— holding it inside akin to suppressing a violent urge to urinate.

No adult laughed—with one exception. Bud, without looking, knew the lone laughter, blasting unashamedly like a cacophonous screech from perdition's abyss, belonged to his bête noire, the wretched Wilma Wilson.

"I hope your vagina gets caught in a sewing machine, bitch!"

Wilma kept on laughing, her hooting guffaws sounding to Bud as if they emanated from the bowels of Beelzebub.

But most of Bud's contemporaries in academia felt genuine concern, while not entirely wanting this playfully malicious hilarity to end. They were morally and ethically obliged to determine what to do to free the seized vigor of the humiliatingly contorted Mr. Battle from the clutches of the sizzling radiator, putatively inanimate but which somehow seemed reluctant to let go.

Someone summoned old Frank Earlie, the ancient 6'7" maintenance man who seldom spoke and about whom some of the kids weaved smart-aleck Frankenstein stories, calling him Franken-Janitor. Frank, using screwdrivers, wrenches, pliers and a hammer from his toolbox, managed to unscrew parts of the radiator, which had not been touched by a tool in eons, allowing the pipes to widen just enough to permit Big Bud Battle's besieged burning balls to hastily retreat into his britches.

****

His timbres were merged with higher-than-normal tonality to begin with, and, in the aftermath of the even higher pitches that manifested during *The Incident*, the jokes abounded, leading many kids to increase their vocabularies by learning a word—"falsetto"—that otherwise may have eluded them.

Furthermore, in addition to continuing to be known sardonically as Sky Man, the luckless Mr. Battle came to also be denominated by some teachers and many kids with an updated, more savage sobriquet, germane to the school's Arkansas location, as he was clandestinely renamed Mr. Little Rocks.

Kristi Lou was no less horror-struck than Mr. Battle, realizing that her tallness had coalesced with his shortness to birth an insuperable event from which neither of them, she prophesied, could possibly ever recover; their mutual dignity had been jointly lost through all eternity and beyond. She and he would be irrevocably intertwined forever throughout the time/space continuum. News of this tragedy, she feared, would span the globe in a gushing burst, what with the Internet and social media, and she would be the ultimate worldwide laughingstock all the way into purgatory, from which she could not have hope of graduating to heaven. Such ascendance could not happen, not after one of her *terrible titties*, as she termed her breasts, was ultimately responsible for Mr. Battle's family jewels getting grabbed by the radiator, causing him to stagger away to the principal's car in which he had been rushed to the doctor for the mending of his toasted nuts.

****

Kristi Lou spent most of her weekend in self-imposed exile, alone in her room obsessing ad nauseam about *The Incident*, avoiding everyone, including Mom and Dad.

Although not in an ecclesiastical mindstate, she did, dutifully, go to church. Sitting quietly between Mr. and Mrs. Jones during Mass on Sunday morning at Cathedral of St. Andrew, Kristi Lou heard the voice of the priest during the liturgical service but listened to nothing he said. She received Holy Communion, swallowing the wine-drenched hostia wafer more quickly than usual. She barely budged throughout the entire Eucharist, and afterward spoke only when spoken to. She was silent in the car while riding home.

Kristi Lou's parents attempted to comfort themselves by reassuring each other that her diminished appetite, which they knew befell her from time-to-time, was probably attributable to nothing more than garden-variety adolescent angst. However, they sensed their daughter's sullen seclusion was likely reflective of abnormal stress. They had carefully read articles and watched television shows that addressed depression among ten- to thirteen-year-olds and whose aptly educated participants explored how numerous kids feel reluctant, because of abashment, to talk about their heartache or don't quite know how.

Mr. and Mrs. Jones realized that Kristi Lou was disenchanted with her skyward assurgency, which they knew they had surely given to her. However, their tall little girl had succeeded in veiling the deepness of the despair she felt stemming from the disturbing biology of what seemed to her to be unceasing growth.

For gut-wrenched Kristi Lou, the ungodliness of the next school day had to come; there was nothing she could do to prevent Father Time and his scythe from cutting through the impermanent shelter of Sunday evening and delivering her into the kindless clutches of Monday morning. This tyrannous ineluctability meant returning to the seemingly unmerciful Our Lady of Mercy, to the place of emotional carnage—to the site of *The Incident*.

8

After getting into bed Sunday night, Kristi Lou rolled over and set her turquoise, bedside-table, alarm clock on low ringer volume for 6:10 a.m., wanting to escape quietly from the house before Mom or Dad, who typically arose at seven o'clock, could spot her.

Mr. and Mrs. Jones, blue-chip environmental-compliance lawyers representing several discrete private firms around Little Rock via floating assignments, enjoyed flexible work hours. They often did not arrive for their first on-site visit at a client's building until late morning and performed many of their functions online in their home office.

Upon the direful arrival of Monday, Kristi Lou dragged herself from under the protective covers of her bed. She glanced with a frown at the depressing sunlight streaming through her window and kindling her room. She got up and forced herself to use the privy, almost forgetting to flush, not flushing, to her, being an abomination. She slipped into her purple-with-gold-striping bathrobe she kept on the bathroom door apparel hook. Moving with the stealth of a jaguar prowling through a rainforest, she exited the bathroom. She tiptoed into the kitchen and to the refrigerator. She made herself sip an ounce of orange juice from the carton bearing her name, and then returned to the bathroom to brush her teeth. She then lugged herself back into her bedroom to get dressed.

Donning her only pair of designer blue jeans, which her paternal grandmother had bought for her and mailed just seven months prior, Kristi Lou observed that about a half-foot of legs were showing below the cuffs, which, the last time she recalled wearing the jeans, covered most of her ankles.

Kristi Lou was rarely subject to tantrums. She became unhinged.

Still mindful of not wanting to wake her parents, she exclaimed her distress within a muted cri de coeur and then rebuked herself rancorously.

"Oh … my … god! No! I've outgrown these clothes, too! They weren't too short a few months ago. These jeans weren't. They weren't. They weren't then but they are now. Why? What am I—eight feet tall? When will my mile-long legs ever stop growing? Never! I punched out Mr. Battle with my boob! I'm a walking freak show! Why should I keep on living?"

Consciously struggling to hinder her conniption from owning her, she snatched her pillow off her bed and threw it violently across the room.

"I see other people's dandruff while it's still on their heads."

Babbling furiously while seeking relief via lambasting herself, she shoved word-salad yammer from her mouth to expel massive frustration and thus alleviate her self-loathing by describing herself self-loathingly.

"I'm justa dandruff-seeing-on-top-of-heads disgusting dandruff seer unfeminine dandruff-flake watcher tall gross dandruff-spotter thing! Justa … justa … justa taller-than-everybody, taller-than-any-girl-in-history, taller-than-God piece of stupid dandruff-head-expert no-count nothing!"

Kristi Lou, sinking deeper into her morass, stared brutishly at her reflection in her dresser mirror, looking herself over from head to toe. Then, in a frenzy, back and forth she went, kicking one leg with the other, trying to chop herself down to her vision of a normal feminine stature.

She placed her hands atop her head and pressed downward with all her might, but could not reduce her precipitous height.

Suddenly still, she peered at herself with repulsion, monotonously speaking her next self-assessment with a coldly calm, uninflected delivery.

"I hate myself. I'm too tall to live. I should die."

Crestfallen, she plopped her posterior down in a heap of despondency into her old seat-near-the-floor chair that she seldom used but into which she could still fit less than a year ago. However, on this crash-landing, both of her knees bolted up and popped her under her chin, jolting her head backward into the bookcase and dislodging one of her pigtails from under its bobby pin. Overwhelmed by hopelessness, she began crying, less from pain than from anger and sadness. But she steadied herself, fueled by the pride she marshaled, hurriedly halting her tears rather than granting herself further release.

****

Still wearing the too-short blue jeans but now with knee-high, same-shade blue socks, Kristi Lou fulfilled her plan for early departure. Successfully sidestepping her parents, she absconded from the house, sneaking through the den door into the backyard. After petting her sweet-natured family dog, she walked up to and opened the chain-link fence's gate. She coasted noieslessly through the opening, then quietly lowered the U-shaped fork latch back onto the metal gatepost, sans the slightest clanging sound. She had left a note addressed to "My dearest Mom and Dad" explaining that they "shouldn't worry" about her "skimpy eating," that she was "not developing anorexia nervosa or bulimia or whatever" and that she was sorry if she seemed rude by avoiding them but that "it was nothing personal." She wrote to Mrs. Jones an affirmation that she cooks "the best homemade vegetable fried rice in the annals of Earth."

Kristi Lou began dolefully trudging the three-quarter-mile walk back to Our Lady of Mercy. She had been too distraught since Friday to eat more than a few bites. She had skipped Monday breakfast altogether, aside from the tiny gulp of OJ. Regardless of hunger pangs, she recognized her inappetence and knew she would be unable to swallow any solid food; she felt as if her throat had declared: "You got away with gulping a few drops of orange juice. Forget about putting anything else in here."

As she approached the gateway of the Our Lady campus, Kristi Lou sniffed her right hand, which still retained the soothing, musty smell of Buster Brown, her eleven-year-old chocolate-colored Poodle/Labrador mix, with whom she had been growing up. She had petted and hugged him for an extra-long time in the backyard after he had bolted from his doghouse to greet her. She felt she needed Buster Brown's succoring, unqualified approval of her before embarking on her dreaded excursion.

"We've really grown up—as in way, way, way up—with Buster Brown," she said to her legs. "Poodle and Lab—what a kooky combination; I guess he *should* be my dog. At least he stopped growing."

As she continued walking, she remembered her dad's gentle quizzing of her on Saturday evening. Mr. Jones, naturally low-key, had said, in his easygoing manner, "We had to call you four times to come down here to the table, and now you're just piddling with your vegetable fried rice. That's your favorite. I know last night we had meatloaf, which you don't care too much for, but not going for your fried rice? Something must be wrong. What is it, sweetie?"

Kristi Lou recalled the note she'd left for her mom praising her fried rice, and then thought of her elusive reply to her dad.

"Oh, it's nothing much, Dad. It's just that I'm kinda tired; that's all."

Kristi Lou strolled about 20 yards onto the school grounds, then, snapping loose from her daydream, became acutely aware of the stares from her schoolmates.

The little toad-frogs better not say anything about what happened Friday.

She stared at the ground as her thoughts raced.

I can barely see the ants. That's because my eyes are 30 miles away from where they're crawling.

She felt, more than heard, the muffled snickers. She made a beeline to where she hoped to find at least a momentary respite, where she could focus in and steel herself for her impending day of reckoning. She quick-stepped into what was supposed to be an asylum, the girls' restroom adjacent to the biology wing, as she knew that, typically, not many kids were in or around this room at this time of the morning.

"Why? How could he? How could God make me so *tall?*" Kristi Lou bellowed while smushing her nose onto the 10-foot-wide mirror.

Nasty Nate, all 5'0" of him, stuck his smirking face into the doorway and shattered the sanctity of Kristi Lou's refuge.

Nate Perkins rather enjoyed being known as "nasty" and he prized the consequent nom de guerre of "Nasty Nate" as bestowed upon him in the sixth grade by a timid boy on whom he had picked. The further his reputation for unloading at-the-drop-of-a-hat maliciousness spread, the tougher he thought he'd be seen. But, Nasty Nate knew he was the antithesis of tough, a vacuity that chagrined him into being even nastier.

"Skyscraper Tree, Skyscraper Tree—there she is—the Skyscraper Tree," taunted craven Nate, relishing the chance to immiserate.

Kristi Lou instantly thought of how Mr. Battle appeared to enjoy standing next to Nate whenever she happened to see them near each other.

"Shut up, Nate, you vulgarian! You puny punk! You dork-butt! Beat it, you butthead butthole! You, you, you little scuzzy, sawed-off runt! I'll kick your smartass, dumbass ass!" Kristi Lou, morphing instantly into a kinetic fireball, charged like a lioness toward the door, yelling at the top of her lungs—"I'll get you!"—with nostrils flaring and irises flashing.

Nate withdrew posthaste. He skedaddled a dozen yards down the hall.

Kristi Lou grabbed the doorframe and halted herself.

Almost in tears, she yelled out another defensive salvo.

"Yeah, I'm tall but you're small. At least I'm not a smidgy-midgy little Twinkie! You're just mad 'cause you're so little. You try to cut everybody else down to build yourself up. Hey! It isn't working. You're still little!

And even worse, you're just plain mean! And that makes you a little boy in more than just your size…you, you…you whatever you are!"

"King Kong! Kristi Lou's King Kong's kid. The kid of Kong. The long Kong kid. She's long and her daddy's Kong. Longy Kong, Kongy Long!"

"I have a real daddy and he's wonderful; you leave my family out of this, you…you watermelon piss-head. You're the one last year who made that short and shy sixth-grade boy cry by scaring him when you told him the watermelon seed he swallowed was gonna grow into a watermelon-bomb in his tummy that'd burst him open and make him dead. You're such a slimy little jerk."

"At least I'm not some girl who looks like a tree somebody pulled out of the ground! Ha! Ha! Ha! Ha!"

Nate exultantly phonated each "ha." He barked over his shoulder while escaping down the hall lest Kristi Lou decide to retaliate by materializing her threat, which he knew she could easily fulfill. He felt there was greater prudence in conducting his badgering from afar. If she chased him she could quickly catch him, her strides being more than twice his.

Her rangy body jiggling with self-restrained fury, she bated her infuriation again while she held open the restroom door. She let him go.

Kristi Lou, in the middle of weathering torment from Nate Perkins, spoke inwardly to herself, with a new word, "anguish," which she had learned the day before from overhearing her dad's favorite Sunday radio show while adopting the entire phrase in which she'd heard it encapsulated.

I'm at the height of my anguish. What? What did I just say? Oh, even my anguish has too much height. I can't get away from myself.

Nate, belaboring Kristi Lou demoniacally, stood near the end of the hall and unloaded another acerbic, arboreal-themed obloquy.

"Skyscraper Tree, Skyscraper Tree—Mr. Battle's head comes to her knee!" shouted the opprobrious poltroon.

Nate was waylaid by an invasion of fear. Sensing that Kristi Lou might explode, he froze. He saw her move with purposeful slowness and step 18 inches outside the girls' restroom where she released the slowly closing door. Nate observed that she became rigidly still. Her long arms hanging motionless and straight down, Kristi Lou aimed at Nate a glare that seemed to personify death. Nate felt that she resembled an enraged zombie preparing to unleash itself—like a killer under decrescent control.

Five seconds passed without any utterances from anyone, including passerby students in the hall who had stopped and formed an audience. The quasi-homicidal expression that had materialized upon Kristi Lou's face having registered viscerally with Nate, he was ready to run again. But, feeling flush with the power to injuriously impact someone's feelings and the attention he was garnering from his spectators, the vituperative bully-boy couldn't resist one more fusillade of hectoring. Nate, his voice trembling, pushed from his mouth one more contumely.

"How'd it feel to whack Mr. Battle in the eye with your goofy booby? There she is—the super-tall whacker boober! You're such a freakin' freak show! You should be in some circus! You could be The Hundred-Foot Freak Girl! I bet you're gonna grow to be…"

Kristi Lou interrupted but did not yell. The other kids standing near her in the hall were already motionless. They—all of them—were briefly traumatized by what they saw in Kristi Lou's eyes. Her visage was such that they had never seen from any person but somehow innately recognized and then understood primordially. She reacted against Nate with a guttural, jungle-predator growl and then spoke her words just loudly enough for Nate to hear, evoking seriousness far beyond the ordinary margins of a seventh-grade girl.

"I'll kill you."

Nate Perkins fell silent as a gust of phobia surged through his system that caused the color to drain from his wanning, pallor-stricken face.

Kristi Lou turned around rapidly in her own private circle, and then spoke out loud so she could be heard by the other kids, though her eyes were aimed at the floor.

"No, I…I shouldn't have said that. I know. I know I shouldn't have said…I'm sorry," she said, quite deprecatorily.

Everybody stared. Many snicker-laughed impishly, but did so cautiously, worried that Kristi Lou might note their indiscretion with louring chagrin.

Although the majority of her classmates were fond of her, and some knew of and were sensitive to her woe over being exceedingly tall, they were still wary of antagonizing her.

Kristi Lou unleashed a quick scan of all eyes watching her, as if to say, "watch it or else." Everyone got the message. All grinning faces lost their grins. All non-walking feet began walking.

Kristi Lou stepped back into the doorframe of the restroom, holding the door open with her shoulder.

Nate, having retreated a healthy distance away, thus mollifying his terror, saw Guinevere Lindsay approach the restroom. Despite what seemed an impending threat of expiry, his compulsion to bully again overrode his concerns about mortality. Nate, for emphasis, sang to Guinevere his latest foul admonition:

"Don't stannnddd under Kristi Looouuu. She's so tallll she might wet on yooouuu!" warned Nate with fear-diminished musical merriment.

"Oh, Nate, you're such a jejune and contemptuous child," softly retorted the eye-rolling Guinevere, who stopped and looked at Kristi Lou.

Guinevere, who, in appearance, was a consummately nondescript girl, began walking at a slow pace straight toward Kristi Lou, exuding a mien of composure and purpose.

Kristi Lou momentarily shifted her focus to the approaching girl and realized that, although she was not well-acquainted with Guinevere, she felt that Guinevere was abnormally normal in almost every sense, excepting her precocious maturity and grasp of the importance of fairness and respect. Kristi Lou would soon learn that Guinevere, of Scottish lineage, was a rare intellectual prodigy who had never scored below an A in any class, a polyglot fluent in French and Spanish as well as English, maturationally sui juris at age 12, and whose parents had declined an offer from school officials allowing her to skip from the sixth to the eleventh grade. Mr. and Mrs. Lindsay were trepidatious about causing Guinevere to be bereft of age-appropriate personal pleasures and the social development supplied by growing up with her preponderant network of socialization constituted by kids her own age.

Kristi Lou, who envied Guinevere for what, ostensibly, was her prominence as the instantiation of normalness, sensed that somehow Guinevere was coming calmly to rescue her from what Nate was doing to her and from the consequences of what she might do to Nate.

But Kristi Lou, after looking at Nate again, felt a resurgence of fury toward her recreant tormentor and knew she needed to finish her current dealings with Nasty Nate by independently asserting herself. She refocused her attention on the runty tyrant, her anger surging once more.

"I'll get you, Nate Perkins. You know I'll get you for this, you wormy little pisspot!" Kristi Lou hollered as she thrust her upper torso into the hallway, seeing Nate disappear beyond the eighth-grade lockers and into another hall.

****

Kristi Lou glared intensely for about three seconds at the open space Nate had vacated. Wishing to recapture her composure and decorum, she attempted to slide slowly back into what she hoped would, from then on, prove to actually be the emotionally safe confines of the girls' restroom, uninfringed upon by rancid mini-ogres such as Nasty Nate.

I need to get into the ladies' room.

But her right breast became hung, just momentarily, on the doorframe.

"I hate these things!" Kristi Lou growled as she sought to reenter the restroom. A few kids glanced at her, but then quickly looked away.

As the door closed behind her, she put both hands on her breasts, and, for a moment, tried to literally push the unwanted protrusions back into her chest. "Get off me! Go away! Go away! Go away! I want to be flat-chested!"

Guinevere methodically soft-stepped into the restroom, smiling pleasantly at the frazzled and gangly girl, while discreetly ignoring Kristi Lou's eldritch rant. Although the two seventh graders had heretofore been no more than friendly acquaintances, Guinevere's calming aura instantly filled the stark, gray-brick lavatory with a permeating mellowness that wafted gently into her lofty classmate's inflamed senses.

Kristi Lou felt a sudden bond.

"Don't worry about what Nate says." Guinevere spoke slowly, with a Mona Lisa smile. "He's not worth it. You know how he is. He's just a teeny-weeny meanie who likely fears his weeny will always be teeny. If he doesn't adjust his personality, he may grow up to be a professional armpit sniffer. That'd be the ideal job for a nincompoop such as Nate."

Rather than speaking these caustic ripostes with the hyper giddiness that would typify an average seventh grader, Guinevere delivered her commentary with meticulous precision, reminding Kristi Lou of her slow-talking and kindly but spirited Aunt Charlene in Fayetteville.

"Ha-ha. OK, well yeah, I know you're right. I shouldn't be worried about whatever he says. Thanks, Guinevere." Kristi Lou raked her hair back from her face and smiled warmly, feeling very gladdened to receive such soothing support.

"You're nice to me."

"Of course. You're just as nice to me, Kristi Lou. We've never really talked that much before but I can tell you're a nice person. You weren't nice to Nate just then, but he manifestly deserved it. You had a right to retaliate. Though you really shouldn't threaten violence and you certainly shouldn't actually do it. I know you won't. And don't go on worrying anymore about the, well, you know, *The Incident*."

"Thank you. But..."

Kristi Lou affixed her gaze downward onto a housefly crawling along the baseboard below the sink.

"...I overheard Timmy Burton talking to Jamie Davis last Wednesday in the lunchroom and you know what Timmy called me?"

"No. What?"

"Elongated."

Both girls paused and looked at each other for an extended moment. Guinevere smiled softly and slightly tilted her head, as if to say *I know they say those things, but it's all right.*

"Timmy told Jamie that 'Kristi Lou is *so* elongated.' I know what it means. He was trying to show off his vocabulary because he'd just learned that word and all and, well, he called me *that*; he called me *elongated*. How can somebody call another person such a horrible thing? It wouldn't have been so bad if he'd just called me a bitch or a slut or a whore. I wouldn't have exactly liked being called a bitch slut whore, but being called a bitch slut whore is nothing compared to being called elongated. Guinevere, he called me elongated! It was so horrible. It was horrible, just horrible. Elongated...he was saying I'm...that I'm, I'm...luh, luh, luh...long...that I'm all longish and unfeminine and weird-looking, like what Nate was just saying when he was insulting me. But when Timmy called me that, that...that word, in like a non-insulting, serious, that's-just-how-she-is sorta way, it...it was even worse than Nate's nastiness. It hurts so much to hear that. I don't want to be elongated."

Kristi Lou became unable to block her need to cry. Her prideful restraint, which she had mustered earlier in the morning after her accident in her bedroom chair, surrendered to soft sobs. Three wet streams cascaded downward, gushing so fast that they startled Guinevere.

"Kristi Lou, listen to me when I tell you that..."

Guinevere was interrupted by another outpouring of melancholia. Gazing upon poor, effusive, addled Kristi Lou while listening sensitively to her self-assaulting strictures, Guinevere visualized a dam bursting into pieces and releasing a manmade tsunami.

"And last year in September, just after school started, some of us were standing around the flagpole hanging out and David Darnell was talking to me and he called me a giraffe. He's kinda tall himself and he's not mean and he didn't mean to be mean; he thought I would like it, but…"

"Kristi Lou, listen. Look at me when I tell you…"

"He called me a giraffe, Guinevere. He saw I was sad and then he apologized. And the other kids, they didn't say anything, but it was so embarrassing, but I wasn't mad at David but…I don't know…It's just that it's…I hate being so gross and tall. I'm ugly."

"Ugly? You're anything but…"

"Well, at least no one's called me a stalagmite—yet. Not yet. Not yet, they haven't. But I know someday somebody will," whimpered Kristi Lou. "Stalagmite. I'm so tall that somebody somewhere someday is going to call me a stalagmite. Oh no, oh no, oh no—I don't want that to happen. I don't want to be called that and be seen like that. I don't want to be an ugly, tall stalagmite. Kids like Nate Perkins just haven't learned that word. It means a piece of rock or something in a cave that grows up from the floor really, really, really high—like tall and ugly me."

"Now listen, Kristi Lou…"

"I have to accept reality."

Surmounted barbarously by her dysmorphophobia, Kristi Lou could not stifle her impending detonation, delivered with a piercing scream.

"I'm a stalagmite!"

Two eighth-grade girls entering the restroom saw and heard Kristi Lou's somatopsychic self-deprecation, glimpsed at each other, then turned around and walked out immediately.

"Listen carefully." Guinevere, with a firm but gentle grip, took Kristi Lou's arm as the door closed behind the exiting thirteen-year-olds.

"You're not a stalagmite; you're a human being and a very pretty girl. And you're a really feminine girl. Do you know how many girls in this school would give anything to have just half of your height?"

"Well, maybe they'd like half of it. But…"

"OK, let me reword that. Ignore the 'half' part."

Guinevere smiled and, at 5'2", looked straight up at her beleaguered new friend, tilting her head as far back as she could and feeling a minor strain in her neck muscles. Reaching upward at a sharp angle, she used her delicate hands to gently remove two long side-bangs that had become plastered to Kristi Lou's moist cheeks.

"Many of us, myself included, I assure you, would love to be tall like you. It's great for girls to be tall; it's been considered desirable, and, I might add, sexy, for a really long time in our society. Look at all the models, which you'll probably be someday. You should already be a model. Most all of us would jump at the chance to look like you. And, do you ever pay any focused attention to your face? God knows you're anything but ugly. You're a truly beautiful girl. Not that looks are everything; they aren't. But if you've got them, which you do, you may as well be modestly glad for it and feel good about it. Here you are thinking and feeling you're unattractive when you are exactly the opposite. Yes, you're tall—and you're pretty and sweet and kind and intelligent and very, very, very feminine. And, that's the truth, Miss Future Model; believe you me!" said Guinevere, emblazoning Kristi Lou's muliebrity.

"Well, that's really kind and nice of you to say, but, well, I just have trouble believing it. I so much want to be feminine. And, I know you don't want to lie, but you're trying to be nice, and you are nice, but…"

"Kristi Lou—I would love to be tall like you! There—I said it again. I said it and I meant it. You don't want to make me out to be a liar, do you? That would be hurtful to me."

"Oh no! Oh my goodness. Of course not. I don't want to…I would never want to do anything that hurt you. Thank you, Guinevere."

Kristi Lou accepted a pink tissue from her newfound friend's purse and dried her saturated face.

"Trust me. Before you know it, even though right now it seems like forever, there will be a lot of boys taller than you—or, well, there will be more boys taller than you than there are these days. After a year or so, some of these or maybe even lots of these same boys that are now shorter than you will be taller than you. I guarantee it. Look at all the tall women when you go to the mall or wherever, and then notice all the men who are even taller than they are. And, right here in school, look at Ms. Wilson, the social studies teacher; she's taller than you. Then, look at Mr. Earlie, our janitor; he's taller than she. It kinda evens out after the seventh-grade year and the boys catch up with the puberty situation and have their growth spurts. Just watch it happen."

"OK."

Kristi Lou left the restroom, with Guinevere at her side, still feeling shaky, but with a conviction she could somehow go on living.

"I'm going to my algebra class now," said Guinevere as she strolled away from Kristi Lou, looking back over her left shoulder as she spoke. "You'll be fine, Kristi Lou. I promise you; you will. I absolutely promise you that you will. I always make good on my promises."

"Thank you, Guinevere. I'll see you later."

"You definitely will," replied Guinevere, still walking. "And you know where that'll be."

"Oh my goodness. That's right; you're in my general science class with Mr. Bat..."

"Yeah, I sit up front and you're like a back-row Baptist—except we're Catholic—with you sitting way in the back. I'll be there and so will you. And, as I said, you'll be fine, just fine."

"Thank you so much. I'll...I'll, uh..."

"Yes, you will."

9

KRISTI LOU, WALKING DOWN THE HALL WHILE IGNORING everyone and forgetting for a few moments where she was going, was delighted with her nascent friendship. She felt hope mingled with a shaky confidence that she would be able to rely often on Guinevere for consolation and bolstering of her waning ego through the impending tumult of her future as a girl tower.

As for this frostbitten day in January, though, she still had to face second-period general science, and that meant coming face to face—*well, my face won't be facing his face unless we're both sitting down*—with Mr. Battle. This was to be their first occasion together since *The Incident* on Friday. Kristi Lou had been dreading the moment of initial eye contact since Friday night; her intestinal region often felt so constricted that mental imageries would flash into her mind of her stomach tied not metaphorically but literally in knots. As the awareness of their reunion being only about an hour away became acute, she felt her abdominal muscles again tighten; she saw an image of her intestines metamorphosing into a boa constrictor and squeezing her other insides. Swallowing became barely possible.

Kristi Lou, who had never before cut even one class, skipped Mr. Battle's homeroom as well as first period U.S. History. Having observed that Mr. Earlie almost always spent Monday mornings toiling in another part of the building, she took a chance and concealed herself in the janitor's closet. Vacillating between sitting on his stool and pacing in the limited space, she obsessed and trembled. Her apprehension was intermittently mitigated by tranquil thoughts of what Guinevere had said to her just minutes earlier, plus the awareness that Guinevere could be counted on for such tender reassurances going forward. Though she calmed herself, to a degree, by recalling Guinevere's cheering speech in the girls' restroom, she still felt compelled to look elsewhere for additional comfort.

Mr. Earlie's cleaning contraptions and other tools surrounded her, and she felt a strange kinship with the broom, which Frank Earlie had left, as usual, propped on its handle end, with the straw whisk pointed up. Although she knew the narrowness of the janitor's closet would seem like claustrophobic environs to many people, Kristi Lou felt somewhat mollified by the closeness of the walls, as if she were barricaded within an architectural womb. Unlike many of the other kids, Kristi Lou had never been afraid of the very-tall-himself Mr. Earlie, would not refer to him as Franken-Janitor and, in fact, actually liked him, albeit from a distance.

While cowering in Mr. Earlie's closet, she called upon her imaginary private friends, of whom only she knew. She saw them, as always, in a large bubble—something akin to the dialogue ovals drawn by cartoonists above their characters in comic strips. They were four choral angels wearing long, flowing dresses made of silk, one wearing red, one wearing orange, one wearing green, and one wearing blue. She called them her Singing Seraphs. Kristi Lou had developed them the year before, during a particularly depressing day in the sixth grade. The Singing Seraphs always wore gentle smiles on their placid faces, and Kristi Lou knew they were permanently on her side, no matter what.

They sang to her soothing, simple lyrics, including their choruses of

"God is with you, dear Kristi Lou…" and "Keep your faith and you'll be happy and safe…"

After more than an hour of hiding and occasionally summoning inspiration from the Singing Seraphs, at 9:48 a.m., Kristi Lou summoned her courage and her reservoir of fortitude.

It's time to go. I've gotta do this. Hi again, God. Please stay with me.

Breathing deeply with her mouth partly open—*Oh my god, now I'm a mouth-breather*—she exited Mr. Earlie's janitorial headquarters. As Kristi Lou opened the door, she quickly realized that she may look outlandish leaving the janitor's closet and speculated as to what people might think: *What was she doing in there?*

She hoped no teachers and especially no kids like Nate Perkins would spot her. Only one person, an eighth grader, noticed her exit and he quickly looked away with no apparent interest, as his head was sandwiched between wireless earbuds while he grooved to his music.

Kristi Lou trod gradually toward general science and her unavoidable get-together with the minute teacher whose already-dubious virility had been felled by her unwanted womanhood.

As she turned to her left into the next hall, Kristi Lou, without intent, glanced to her right. There stood Mr. Frank Earlie, a spray-bottle of glass-cleaning detergent in one hand but no cloth in the other. He was standing perfectly still and looking at her while unveiling what she sensed was the slightest of smiles, but a smile, nonetheless.

Mr. Earlie never smiled.

But, she felt that, as she continued to walk while gazing back at him for two full seconds before dropping her eyes, in the midst of her life-altering journey toward destiny, the 6'7" Mr. Earlie and his weather-beaten face gave her a look which seemed to gently say *you're going to be all right, young lady.*

Kristi Lou wondered if he had seen her go in or come out of his little station. She felt that, even if he did know she had trespassed on his territory, *he's not mad at all.*

And she also felt that maybe, maybe, just maybe, the reticent Mr. Earlie, himself a social outcast enduring the brutally unforgiving environment of a middle school, knew of her gut-twisting insecurities, perhaps identified on some real level with her, and hence quietly extended his sympathy.

Oh my goodness, Mr. Earlie might've maybe needed some tools or something from his closet but let me stay in there without interrupting me or … I don't know, but … he might've—I think he did.

Kristi Lou knew that much communication is unvoiced.

She tried to make her strides as un-long as possible, being even more self-conscious than she usually was about her loping walk.

Before arriving at Bud Battle's general science classroom, Kristi Lou had to pass by Principal Alexander's office. Despite being immersed in her own melodrama, she could not avoid hearing the exchange between a parent, Mr. Coleman, and a kid who was acquainted with the bullies who had been bullying Mr. Coleman's son, Mike, who was in the eighth grade. Mr. Coleman was seated in a chair in the hallway waiting to go in and speak with the assistant principal, Mr. Gaskins, about Mike's oppressors. He and Kristi Lou happened to overhear the kid, who was sitting in a nearby chair, say to a second boy who moments earlier had sat next to him, "Mike Coleman has been picking on them."

The naturally sympathetic Kristi Lou, though racked with her own in-school torment, obsessively felt herself compel herself to stop herself in her tracks, on the other side of the hall, to observe as unobtrusively as possible. After about three seconds, she stepped slowly, shambling on uncomfortably and shuffling her shoes as she walked. She mostly looked down at the floor, occasionally glancing over at Mr. Coleman.

Man, has that kid got that story totally backward. Mike's in the eighth grade so *I don't know him too well but I know he's quiet and nice and that those—at least three of them—boys have been picking on Mike, not vice versa.*

Then, she heard Mr. Coleman angrily respond.

"I'm here to find out who's picking on who! I believe it's the other way around! And I'm going to put a stop to it!"

The boys clammed up immediately.

That must be Mike's dad. Good for him for defending his son. He's probably waiting to talk to Mr. Gaskins, and that should help 'cause Mr. Gaskins is a stand-up guy—very conscientious and a straight shooter. My daddy would come here and fight for me, too, if he knew I needed it. But nobody's been trying to hurt me, physically. And, besides, the average bully around here is afraid of me 'cause I'm such an unfeminine hulk. Anyway, I've gotta get back to what I've gotta finish. I've gotta get there—to Mr. Battle's class. I hope Mike will be OK. I think he will. His dad is going to see to that.

****

Seeing that the controversy there was complete, she pulled herself out of observing someone else's drama that somewhat mirrored her own trauma. She refocused on her nerve-racking objective, with ground zero nigh.

Moving briskly, she arrived outside Mr. Battle's classroom door and halted herself for about five seconds.

Dear God, please give him my height. He doesn't know how lucky he is, never bumping his head on stuff and never punching people in the eyeball with a boob.

She entered the general science lab. To her amazement, some force inside her compelled her to go, slowly but without hesitation, directly toward Mr. Battle, who was not standing. Rather, he was sitting, quite providentially, behind his elevated desk. This fortuity constituted a blessing of immense magnitude and elicited from Kristi Lou a spontaneous internal prayer. Kristi Lou stopped walking about eight feet from Mr. Battle and pretended to look at notes in her book while praying with reverent sincerity.

All glory goes to you, Immaculate Deity, for letting him be sitting in his chair.

Her further supplication was spoken with frenetic rapidity.

He's not standing. He's not standing. That's so outstanding that he's not standing. He's sitting. Oh, you see that God, don't you? He's sitting. When Mr. Battle is sitting it's a beautiful thing to behold. I'm supposed to be higher in the air than he is when he's sitting. This is how life should happen. Please, oh merciful and inimitable Lord, Rock of the Ages, please don't let him stop sitting till I get to my desk, please. You know, Lord, his platform shoes don't really help all that much. Thank you, most kind and gracious Heavenly Father, Lord and Messiah, Hail Mary, Mother of Jesus!

Kristi Lou crossed herself thrice before she knew her arm was moving, and then glanced down at her hand as if to confirm she had actually made the sign of the cross in triplicate.

She resumed walking. She stopped about four feet away from him; despite his not standing, she did not want to push her luck, in case he abruptly arose without warning and unwittingly melodramatized this godless and aberrant contrast, this breach of chromosomal etiquette.

Maybe I shouldn't stop like this; maybe I should just blow on by. It's just that I'm trying to stay away from him. But I've got to get by him to get to my desk. But the longer I stay closer to him the more time there is for him to stand up close to me. I've got to do something. What do I do? Oh look—there's Guinevere at her desk looking at me like she's saying "You can do it."

With stillness rivaling that of a marble statue, she stood sideways next to her teacher, looked up ever-so-slightly from her notepapers and peered at him through the corner of her right eye.

Kristi Lou shocked herself by spontaneously turning to face Mr. Battle.

"Are you OK, sir?"

"Yes, I am. I'm … I'm well. Thank you. Uh … so yeah, I'm OK. Yes. Thank you," stammered Bud Battle while glancing meekly back and forth between his paperwork and Kristi Lou.

Both Mr. Battle and Kristi Lou manufactured quivering smiles, and both were simultaneously aware that their smiles may have made their faces look a bit silly. Bud wondered whether Kristi Lou had noticed his boob-clobbered black eye.

Maybe she didn't notice. But she will notice. Everybody has to notice.

She noticed. But, she was so relieved to have safely endured the initial contact with Mr. Battle that she didn't obsess over the hideous blackness surrounding his swollen orb.

Rather, she smiled at him again, faintly, but devoid of the quiver, and almost ran to her desk in the rear corner of the room. Forgetting her previously self-imposed shorter strides, Kristi Lou, enlivened with momentary insouciance, exchanged a quick smile with Guinevere and then spryly covered the distance like a frolicking antelope.

Bud Battle was likewise taken aback by the mutually pleasant exchange, and he noticed, with surprise, his own feelings were void of antipathy. Even though the atrocity that was *The Incident* had occurred Friday—the most recent school day—and many of the kids, as well as teachers, were gossiping behind his back, he felt a second, maybe even two seconds, of genial warmth toward and from Kristi Lou.

She felt it, too.

I had no idea I was going to ask him if he's OK. OMG. But I'm glad I did.

****

Mr. Battle watched the other kids settle into their desks and, buttressed by the quick but comforting exchange with Kristi Lou, surmised that just maybe life on this day wouldn't unfold with the level of insidiousness inflicted upon him by the previous night's dream.

141

But he couldn't simply let that dream go without going over it—in detail—or else it would, as he knew, surge into the forefront of his mind whenever it wanted to cause mental mayhem, and maybe at the most inopportune times. He had to ponder such dreams to diminish their power.

OK. Things just went well with Kristi Lou. But I've got to go over last night's dream-from-Satan nightmare about her. I know I've got to confront it, what with me remembering the damn thing so vividly and whatnot. All the dreams I have like this have to be dealt with. I've got to do it or I know it'll come back and wreak a shit pile of havoc. There was a good thing this morning; there was a bad thing last night. I've gotta deal with last night to maybe make it as good as this morning.

Bud gave the class a reading assignment, chapter 47 of the textbook, with the falsified warning that there may be a pop quiz near the end of the period. He then braced himself for the minefield of reentering the dark pit of his dream from the previous night, a therapeutic exercise whose subsequent catharsis could be reached only through his enduring a Freudian-like mental reenactment.

****

After opening his teacher's version of the general science book and pretending to read, Bud recalled that before driving to school this Monday morning, he had stood and frowned at his eight-cylinder, solid-black, chrome-stripped-off Crown Victoria, remembering how large, powerful vehicles had appealed to him since childhood. As he had often done in the past, he reaffirmed an urgent denial, averring that big cars were neither a surrogate extension of his height nor his wiener.

Sitting in his garage and listening to Wagner's "Ride of the Valkyries," Bud made himself think manful thoughts. He also had prepared himself by instituting a noiseless warning system if an emergency arose at school Monday or any day thereafter. Fearing one of Kristi Lou's dreaded breasts might swing in his direction, he had coached himself to initiate evasive action by inwardly yelling a warning that he found to be ridiculous but warranted.

Bogey at two o'clock! Make that booby at two o'clock! Whatever.

This plan of self-defense to be in place upon his return to Our Lady was rooted not only in *The Incident*, but in his brutal nightmare of Sunday night from which he had awakened just a few hours earlier. His dreamscape, which unfolded within his sleeping imagination in personalized Technicolor, placed him in the line of fire on a military battlefield. A super-sized Kristi Lou, clad in army-green camouflage, marched toward him, reminiscent of the she-behemoth in *Attack of the 50 Foot Woman*. Bud's head-trip movie, which, after awakening, he remembered in disturbing detail, was far scarier than the 1950s original; his was private cinema from the netherworld of infernal shortness.

Slumping at his desk, Bud's recall of his *she's-12-and-tall-you're-47-and-short dream from the rectal canal of Lucifer* was full-steam-ahead on.

****

While Bud frantically loaded Milk Duds into his slingshot, Kristi Lou's feet pounded down and caused the earth to quake. She uprooted trees and tossed them over his head as if to taunt him before the slaughter. She approached with malice, stalking him with her thunderous footsteps.

Kristi Lou was so high above Bud that her kneecaps blocked and unblocked the sun with each eclipsing stride.

Her booming voice rained down upon him with sneering scorn, each syllable turning into grinning cannon shells that ignited as they exited her mouth, spilling debris upon him.

"I will squash you like the bug you are, my truncated teacher. You are infinitesimal and have no real significance in the arena of humanity.

You should be in Oz with the other Munchkins. I have commandeered your manhood, my petite pedagogue, and now I shall take the rest of you and grind your frail bones into a haute-couture bellybutton ring."

Laser beams shot from her nose, scorching the terrain around Bud's perimeter and setting fire to sagebrush which tumbled toward him with talking flames that burned him with invectives such as "You will die a very short man," and "Randy Newman wrote his song about you."

Instantly, on cue, a full orchestra and chorus comprised of maleficent seventh graders from his classes plus all of his teaching colleagues appeared perched on an ebony cloud and began to sing "Short People." The choir of calumny was conducted by arch-nemesis Wilma Wilson who, gorged with hauteur as she waved her conductor's baton, would intermittently look down over him while flashing an evil grin and chest-thrusting her embroidered shirt that proclaimed, "Fuck you Bud you tiny spud."

Upon completion of the debasing serenade, all singers, led by the scornfully laughing Wilma, flipped off Bud in perfect unison with a synchronized middle-finger tribute. They then evaporated into the dark sky.

Brobdingnagian-sized Kristi Lou, who had been standing aside and singing along with the demeaning chorale, restarted her assault. To Bud's horror, her murderous breasts began morphing into artillery guns, then airborne tanks, then flame-throwers—all firing one volley after another from either side of her deadly thorax, the emasculating explosions smashing him down, down, down into his mud-pit foxhole and making him shorter, shorter, shorter. The wet dirt of shame enveloped him in castrating ignominy as his feminine enemy planted him like a peanut seed.

"You look like a tinier-than-normal, fruit-filled dumpling that I could swallow whole but you might become annoyingly wedged between my biscupids. Before destroying you, you molecule, you undersized scrawny speck of semi-human bread crumb, you shrinking animalcule, I now enjoy the pleasure of informing you that I have sent in a Photoshopped picture of you wearing tight Speedos to an international magazine—*Dwarf Dudes on Parade.*"

Bud, mildly drowsy though not asleep, then curiously experienced the phenomenon of realizing a conscious awareness that one is trapped in a bad dream and wants to wake up—but can't.

But, I'm already awake. What? Why am I ... ?

Kristi Lou's breasts of barbarism converted into rocket-propelled-grenade launchers, with RPGs exploding around him just far enough away to not obliterate him but close enough to splash mounds of greenish, slimy soilage that somehow kept amassing into a cone-shaped hillock above his ears, and then forcing him to wear upon his nearly hairless head a dunce hat made of fodder.

"You are a humpty-dumpty homunculus. Your shortness is such that you are a mere freckle on the ass of life, an apostrophe in a footnote, a lowercase t not high enough to cross. You are too short to vote. You are not allowed on most amusement park rides. Tattoo's shadow would eclipse you on *Fantasy Island.* Women can barely see your penis and they laugh at your erections. You are a small waste of space that must be expunged to purify the planet. You are a frumpy-dumpy fluke of nature, a pint in a world of gallons, a violation of Darwinian selection. Desiderata was written to include everyone but you: You are a chump of the universe; you have no right to be here."

Bud yelled his retort as he began to disappear beneath the mud. He tried to sound daunting while yelling but instead he shrieked.

"Get away from me, you bride of Frankenstein! You stole my genes, beanpole bitch! Mayday! Mayday! I'm outflanked! I need air support! Mayday!"

He awakened in a cold sweat, clutching his pillow. He rolled over and off his king-size mattress. He hit the floor with a thud. He lurched up and banged his head on his Honcho Man bedpost, his strand of hair catching in one of the decorative crevices.

Let go of my hair, idiot bed. I don't have much, and my damn bed isn't going to take it. Betrayed by my bed! Why did you let me have that dream and then grab my hair?

Upon freeing his hair, Bud murmured under his breath with fatalistic resignation. "My life now is like having to eat peas and carrots when I was six."

****

Bud, after reliving the previous night's dream in precise detail, sat at his desk with his chin nestled inside his right palm while his fingers and thumb impulsively massaged his cheeks. Blinking rapidly to aid his effort toward reinstating his focus upon the current day, he took stock of what had actually transpired upon his return to school and realized he was solaced beyond description that, despite the horrors in his dream, no such melodrama had developed this next morning in the classroom.

Fortified by the surprisingly pleasant exchange with Kristi Lou at about ten o'clock, Bud Battle taught his classes without any catastrophic events. All of his students were subdued and behaved well, externally. Inwardly, almost every one of them wanted to erupt with laughter at the thought of what had happened Friday.

****

For this school day, Kristi Lou wanted nothing but boring placidity.

During the latter part of second-period general science, Kristi Lou paid close attention to Mr. Battle's post-dream-recountal lesson, gleaned from chapter 47 and which just happened to be about the composition of the female chamber of flowers, known as pistils, and how they consisted of the ovary, style, and stigma. This subject was preplanned, as were all of Bud Battle's lessons, a week in advance. Although she could have interpolated the meaning of this topic by personalizing it against herself—pistils are *long* stems that rise *high* in the flower—she did not.

Kristi Lou felt temporarily placated by the ostensible normalcy of a classroom lecture. She buttressed herself further with deliberate flashbacks to her palliative conversation with Guinevere earlier in the restroom. She poured herself into the lesson, while intuiting that Mr. Battle did the same. She took copious notes. She remained seated like a rock.

I won't stand next to Mr. Battle today, even if someone says he'll shoot me if I don't.

As Kristi Lou scurried out of the room at the end of general science, she and Mr. Battle happened to glimpse each other at precisely the identic instant, looking through the other kids as if they were translucent ghosts. Before leaving her desk, she had feared that their glances would meet but had discrepantly hoped that they would, as she sensed that the pre-class "niceness," as she termed their mutual feeling, would reprise. Her sentiment proved prescient. They both looked away in synchronized unison, unlocking their eyes in the same split moment. Kristi Lou and Mr. Battle shared one of those seminal trices they would keep through the years as they instantly reached a permanent armistice, lastingly suspending warfare they had fought only within themselves and agreeing to an unspoken, timeless truce over a war about which to each other they had at no time ever spoken.

10

DESPITE THE TENDERHEARTED REASSURANCES FROM Guinevere and a few other kids, Kristi Lou's internalized shame over being so altitudinous continued to intermittently assail her through the remainder of Monday's school day and into that night.

Throughout the week, although Guinevere's perpetual kindness kept Kristi Lou from becoming semi-suicidal, she nonetheless often relapsed into depressive states. Kristi Lou, as she confided in Guinevere, was simply not yet able to complete the break-away from *The Incident* and her progressive disease that she sometimes called "tall-girl-deformititis."

She was the reluctant Amazon of Little Rock. She fantasized about magically becoming a pygmy; if she could find a reputable witch doctor, she'd give the occult a whirl. Or, maybe, she thought, if she or her family struck it rich she could afford a plastic surgeon that could saw off part of her legs—*preferably with anesthesia.*

Could that be the kind of thing an epidural block is for? Like having a baby or getting sawed?

Worsening the humiliation beyond exponential proportions was the fact that her anatomically condensed teacher had been horrifyingly felled by one of those *things* that had started to sprout from in front of her ribs. These protruding growths were assets of which she should be proud, she had heard, but with which she had not yet come to psychological grips, although she had heard remarks that the eighth-grade boys were interested in gripping them.

Gross! Just gross. Boys can be so gross!

Anxiety to the nth degree had forever, so it seemed to her, teemed recklessly within her. And now this unspeakable faux pas had to go and happen.

Tuesday afternoon, although schooltime had unwound unremarkably, found Kristi Lou obsessing alone in her bedroom. Following nearly an hour's worth of pacing between her bed and her chest-of-drawers, she carried herself and her obsessions into the backyard.

"I know we had a nice conversation yesterday and all, but, it's just that…my God! Now I've gone and knocked down Mr. Battle with one of my dadgum boobs! I guess I'll, I'll, I'll…just have to be careful with these things!" screaming the last part of her exclamation. "I hate it how they always go into a room before the rest of me."

She had punched her science teacher in his "wee squinty peeper," as termed by Ms. Delilah Holcombe, geography teacher and vehement gossip-biddy sidekick of Wilma Wilson, who, like Wilma, had always been antipathetic to Bud Battle. As if that reality wasn't sufficiently awful on its own merits, Kristi Lou had accomplished this unfeminine feat—fracturing Mr. Battle's eye socket and dropping him like a wadded sandwich wrapper—without even using her fist.

It's still the same thing with me; I despise being so tall. He got one of his thingies stuck in the heater! I'll never live this down; the whole school will know about it and they'll follow me around the planet and torment me till I'm six feet under!

Kristi Lou refused to talk to her mom and dad about this matter, although she wanted to. She came close Wednesday night, but phoned Guinevere instead. Within seconds after she hung up from receiving reassurance from Guinevere, whose calmative counsel she saw as akin to getting a fix from an addictive drug, she felt placated enough to go to bed and sleep.

I've heard that addicts quit shaking after they get their fixes.

Kristi Lou collapsed onto the bedspread, not bothering to slip under the covers. She fell asleep within a minute, her exhaustion rushing in like a flood to fill the void created after the maturely consolatory Guinevere had temporarily vanquished her desolation.

I'm all the sudden so sleepy. I needed another dose of Guinevere. I know I'm crazy, but I'd go totally crazy without Guinevere. Right now, I'm only partially crazy. I don't want to go total.

****

Guinevere tried to persuade Kristi Lou to speak with the guidance counselor at Our Lady of Mercy, Ms. Gloria Goble. "That's what she's there for, Kristi Lou." But Kristi Lou professed to being too embarrassed to discuss her tallness with grownups, except her parents, and there was discomfort talking with even them about the issue. Besides, as she explained to Guinevere, Ms. Goble "is half a foot shorter than I am."

The enlightening, sagacious-beyond-her-years Guinevere had become Kristi Lou's own personal luminary. She urged Kristi Lou to visit a child psychologist. Guinevere was unsurprised that Kristi Lou, at the outset of Guinevere's urgings, steadfastly refused. Though she was cognizant of not becoming overbearing, Guinevere determined that she would persist in occasionally, with tact, pressing the idea of Kristi Lou seeking professional therapeutic intervention. Guinevere vowed to herself to watch her friend carefully. If Kristi Lou showed signs of severe depression, Guinevere would have to violate Kristi Lou's trust, for the sake of her well-being, by informing the proper adults who could help. Guinevere reassured herself accordingly. *Should such a violation be provisionally required, the performance of that action will be my moral feasance.*

As the post-*Incident* days went by, guffawing erupted periodically around the school. Whenever someone heard a group of people, pupils or staff, trembling with laughter, it was almost assumed that the subject was *The Incident*. Bonded by yet another kindred commonality, both Kristi Lou Jones and Bud Battle became quasi-paranoid when they saw and/or heard anyone laughing in the distance but could not define with certainty the source of the amusement.

They're laughing at something over there. What are they laughing at? I know what they're laughing at.

11

THURSDAY, SIX DAYS AFTER THE INCIDENT, ARRIVED TO FIND Bud and Kristi Lou's communal desire to move beyond this episode further compromised by the glaring reality that Kristi Lou's vicious breaststroke had given the embattled Bud Battle that conspicuous black eye—which, over the previous few days, worsened by an infection, had swollen so that it resembled a miniature helium balloon.

Bud was swept under the tide of obsessive recounting of the details of what transpired and his analysis of implied symbolic meanings. He vacillated from periods of calm to stretches during which he was locked into thinking, thinking, and thinking some more about his infamy. After sadistic fate had stabbed him in his eyeball with an amateur breast, he had bounced off the gym teacher's unforgiving stout chest! He had not been in a fight with another man; he had been defeated by one half of a pair of female protrusions that were attached to one so young she didn't know what to do with them. And she wasn't even trying to inflict harm. For six days running, he carried a stark reminder to all onlookers on the school grounds that he had been busted down by a fledgling mammary.

Though the animosity toward Kristi Lou had abated, there were many waking moments during which Bud Battle felt so minuscule that he wanted to become even smaller—to the point of vanishing altogether.

If he could only bring to reality that presence about which he had fantasized for most of his life: a purveyor of masculine power.

Oh, how he wanted to transform into a mountain of manliness. If he could just trade his extraordinary intellect for the height and body of Schwarzenegger—to be the Terminator! Yes, the Terminator! Now that would be living! What a favorite fantasy—to become the real-life Terminator!

I would be the Teachernator! Yeah—then I'd show 'em. I'd show 'em what a badass man looks like.

Ever the fantast, Mr. Battle's daydreams of testosterone, humongous muscles, and standing anywhere from about 6'5' to 6'10" were rich and varied while always casting him as the untamed conqueror. Some days, especially while the kids were monopolized by taking their tests, he would enter a dream world of machismo sports combatants. He would be the conquering boxer, wrestler, martial artist, or some strain of animated superhero.

****

During second-period general science on this Thursday morning in January, the kids, all of whom, including Kristi Lou and Guinevere, had arrived early and seated themselves quickly, had just begun reading in preparation for their next exam, per Mr. Battle's assignment. Kristi Lou felt the urge to discreetly but frequently glance up from her book to peer over the other students at her teacher's face. She saw what she thought was *that far-away look in his eyes*—one of which she had caused to sink inside a purple and black welt—and she sensed that his mind was likely off somewhere dreaming away.

She was, of course, right.

****

Bud chose as his first indulgence for this dream session a self-directed serenade featuring the poem-song he'd composed almost a year earlier. After numerous revisions covering two days of obsessive creativity, he deleted the document from his computer, having never clicked the floppy disk Save icon, saving his lyrical self-aggrandizement exclusively on a flash drive, which he kept locked in his wall safe. He had committed his song of personal exaltation, featuring his intimidatory mount atop a deep-black steed, to perfect memory. Nearly six weeks had gone by since he last altered the lyrics; he had his song where he wanted it and could enjoy it whenever he had time to himself. He knew that, were he to somehow gain the capability of actualizing what his song described, he would not really do all those things he sang about as being done by his imaginary macho self. But, the general idea of seductiveness and preeminence was still most pleasing.

Bud, feeling the kids were well-occupied, silently sang his song to himself, with the tune patterned roughly after the 1961 Jimmy Dean hit "Big Bad John," and his verse reminiscent of, so he fancied, the prosody of eminent 4th-century-B.C. Greek lyricist Pindar. *No poetaster am I!*

THE BALLAD OF BAD BUD BATTLE
(ODE TO BUD, THE TOUGH-GUY TEACHER)

Some sounds you hear
Cause primal fear
The tiger's roar, the rattlesnake's rattle
The virile voice of Bad Bud Battle

Hey Bud! What-chew got?

I got it all; that's what I got
I'm studly
I'm budly
I ride so high up in the saddle
Kneel and cower; I'm Bad Bud Battle

Bad Bud … Badass Bud

Standing high above at six-foot-ten
A mass of muscle towers over men
He's the wicked saint, the sanctified sinner
Most of all, he's the macho winner

Hey Bud! What-chew got?

I got it all; that's what I got
I'm studly
I'm budly
I ride so high up in the saddle
Kneel and cower; I'm Bad Bud Battle

Bad Bud … Badass Bud

All you menfolk have no chance
He's gonna get in your women's pants
Lock up your daughter, hide your wife
Compared to Bud you're all Barney Fife

Hey Bud! What-chew got?

I got it all; that's what I got

I'm studly
I'm budly
I ride so high up in the saddle
Kneel and cower; I'm Bad Bud Battle

Bad Bud … Badass Bud

His legendary balls drag the floor
Nice-girl virgin turns writhing whore
Mayor gives him the key to the city
Mafia lord cries "Please gimme pity"

Hey Bud! What-chew got?

I got it all; that's what I got
I'm studly
I'm budly
I ride so high up in the saddle
Kneel and cower; I'm Bad Bud Battle

Bad Bud … Badass Bud

****

After inwardly singing his private self-tribute song about his imagined self, and noting the kids were still quiet and paying him no attention, Bud Battle next indulged himself wantonly in another episode of his oneiric escapism. He was the king of professional wrestling, feared not only because of his unparalleled strength and brutal toughness, but also because his integrity was of such a superior eminence that he refused to allow his matches to be fixed; he would compete nobly and with all intentions of winning sans any orchestrated outcomes.

While evoking his standard cover-up strategy of gazing blankly into his teacher's syllabus and pretending to read, Bud Battle fled the emotional dangers of the classroom to enter into his notional, self-created world of 300-pound berserk adversaries with brutish intentions. He felt much safer there.

He was now the testosterone-saturated subjugator of all opponents in the SSWA (Solar System Wrestling Association), and on this occasion was the biggest, baddest, championship-belt-defending, butt-stomping badass in the annual "Wrestle-Egeddon—Battle for Supremacy Throughout The Macrocosm"—televised internationally in primetime.

I'm not just state-wide. I'm not just nationwide. I'm not just worldwide. I'm freakin' universe-wide. Yeah, baby! Sinewy muscle-ripplin' comin' atcha!

The imperial Bud entered the audience area from an entrance situated above the crowd. He majestically appeared as two sumptuous burgundy curtains parted. He stepped forward slowly, staring with menace into the multiple TV cameras, all aimed at him. He stopped for intimidating effect, and then resumed tramping toward the ring, at least 40 yards away to the loud sound of the "Get Ready 4 This" song.

Are they ready? No! Hell no! They're not ready for this. They're not ready for raw power. They're not ready for me. They're not ready for what I've got. And my pitiful opponent most certainly is not ready for Brawny Bud Battle.

Mr. Bud Battle, via the magic of his transcendent dreams, was no longer one of the short people. Standing 6'10" and weighing in with 355 chiseled pounds of ironclad muscle, including bloated biceps and impeccable pectorals, no bantamweight was he. The fantasy-fueled augmentation of the real-world bantam-Bud swaggered through a manly mist of jet-black vapor pumped out by theatrical fog machines that were reserved to melodramatize the entrance of only the most feted wrestlers. With his long, dark, gothic hair flowing in wavy locks beneath his broad-as-a-bridge shoulders, Bud the Teachernator just might be the baddest badass alive.

After stepping for about 25 feet, Bud Battle was joined, in accordance with the rehearsed entrance routine for superstar fighters, by four curve-laden, bikini-clad ring girls, all 20-somethings, whose job was to escort the mighty warrior to ringside. He fashioned a condescending countenance toward these amatory sirens and pretended to barely notice them, intending to foster the impression, for public consumption, that he was quite accustomed to being fawned over by erogenous babes and that they had reason to be more enamored with him than he with them; escorting the mighty Bud was their privilege, for which they should be libidinously grateful.

Bud's dream had chosen the ring girls by precisely variegating the hair-color choices. All athletically slender, pretty in the face and whose curves were proportioned symmetrically, one was a brunette with brown hair; one was a brunette with black hair; one was a redhead; and one was a blonde.

Now, Bud Battle's fecund fantasy was all-out on. As he approached the ring, he looked ahead and simply glimpsed at his soon-to-be-demolished opponent, who was already inside the square circle anxiously awaiting his facile and inevitable annihilation. Bestowing an occasional glance upon the mesmerized crowd of fans below the descending ramp in order to give his throng of rabid and awestruck worshipers a brief personal association with his he-man highness, he was aware of his sensation of feeling that he was doing them a favor by merely glancing their way—parallel to his condescendence toward the ring girls.

Quickly, Bud's delusion had him leaving the sightline of the fans in the arena as well as those watching on television, as he entered into a dimly-lit tunnel. He could still hear the fans cheering, but he knew they could not see him. In Bud's mind, the ring girls were also aware that they and the mouth-watering Bud were temporarily out of sight from the eyes of the fans.

They want me; they've got to have me. Yeah, I could go for some carnal pleasure before I thrash my hapless adversary in that ring down there. Sex and violence—I can do 'em both, one right after the other. I am the conquistador.

****

Bud, as he sat back in his chair while his students continued to study in their books, took a quick survey of the room to ensure no one was observing him closely.

Kristi Lou, who was counter-observing her teacher by recurrently checking his eyes, saw Mr. Battle's scrutiny go initially toward the pupils on the front row, and she quickly looked back into her textbook.

Bud, satisfied that no one was on to him, returned smugly to his escapist pipedream. He felt his upper lip furl just a bit with a conceited satisfaction that, in his dreams, not only was he the almighty conqueror, but he could get away with entering into this realm whenever he felt so inclined—and no one knew about it or could stop him from going there.

His glimpse around the classroom was so fast he was able to return to his dream without diluting either its intensity or its logistics; the arena was still there and so were the ring girls.

Bud was becoming drowsy; he felt a whiff of worriment but mostly contentedness, as the kids were quiet, the bell was 52 minutes away, and Kristi Lou was sitting.

He sank back deep into his chair, his eyelids now sleepy slits. For a moment, he acknowledged his drowsiness and cautioned himself to not doze off. But then he decided that all was well and he would not fall asleep and plop onto the floor.

He reindulged his magnificent dream. Heretofore unexampled, he was Bad Bud Battle, the mighty, the muscular, the mesomorph man.

****

Bud lasciviously homed in on his fetching escorts.

Yes, they've wanted me ever since they saw me step out of the dressing room. Oh yeah.

Bud stopped walking. He looked over all four women individually, scanning them from head to toe. They, his fawning aficionadas, began to swoon from his lustful focus upon their bodies.

Abruptly spouting lust-drenched poetry, they all serenaded Bad Bud in unison:

"Oh Bud, you're so sublime; you're just too fine; you gotta be mine."

Bud confidently assured himself with self-praising thoughts as he reveled in the yearning of the ring girls.

One day, my unprecedented penis, my man-pole, will be displayed in the Icelandic Phallological Museum. Presently, cologne companies that make man-scents wish to extract pheromones from my body to mass reproduce in bottles so other men can simply pour some of me on them. And then they, vir-il-i-tized by my essence, could have such hot women begging to be banged by them. That's right. This is how it is: Women want to be with me. Men want to be me. Those fragrance-makers would make a fortune. And so would I. But, I'm not yet ready to share that much of myself. I recognize the reality that I'm simply too exceptional to become too commercialized; my virility is sacred.

He knew these fertile, nubile women would be thrilled upon looking down at his crotch and witnessing the expansion of his historically colossal power-drill pounder, his phallus rumored in many wrestling magazines to be dangerously abnormal.

Upon Bud's first step, they all began to walk again, trailing him like tail-wagging, obedient puppies, with His Majesty The Bud leading the way.

After advancing another 10 feet, one of the ring girls, the statuesque redhead, about 5'10" in real height but about 6'4" with her six-inch stilettos, could no longer resist the irresistible animal magnetism of Bad Bud Battle.

Amidst the roaring din of the crowd beyond the tunnel's partitions, she stopped all five of them from strolling farther, erupting upon Bud with her impassioned entreaty.

Oh Bud, we're here in this secluded section of the tunnel. We temporarily can't be seen by the crowd. I've got to have you now, now, now—right now! Take me, Bad Bud. Ravish me! Ravish me! Ravish me with righteousness!

****

Bud the teacher, with his squinting eyes closed except for the slightest of cracks that afforded him minimal viewing through the blur caused by looking between his eyelashes, was now in maximum arousal, but, in seeming contradiction, was even sleepier than before. He maintained a vague sense of awareness of his classroom environment while indulging his rising dream by letting it take over his mind and go wherever it wanted to go.

He recalled what he and most people already knew; dreams, by their nature, don't always obey logic, but still carry a meaning.

His dream resumed, and into it he dunked himself deeply.

****

The other three ring girls became lubriciousy intoxicated with Bud, struggling to control themselves. Dropping obsequiously to their knees in the tunnel, the writhing women appeared to form a fellatio consortium.

They requested permission to pursue the wondrous pleasure of sex with Bad Bud Battle, who unselfishly responded to his rapturous serfs' solicitations with royal benignancy.

May we touch you, Bad Bud—please? cried the nymphomaniacs.

Yeah, why not? Sure, go ahead, all of you, if it'll make you feel better. There's enough of me to go around. While you're down there, you might as well give yourselves the satisfaction of providing me with oral pleasure.

Oh, Bad Bud, our phallic-master satisfier, we bow gratefully to thy testes!

As the overheated, fawning lasses fell to the tunnel floor around Bud, fondling his bulging muscles while competing for his zipper and then stroking his magnetism, Bud began to grow…and grow…and grow. But his growing was disproportionate. His already mammoth man-piston, now inspired by the nymphomaniacal onslaught of the Bud-struck ring girls, suddenly dilated to 14 inches in length and three inches in girth; Bud's dream began channeling triple-X legend John C. Holmes.

****

The kids saw that Mr. Battle was about to doze off; they were accustomed to his occasional dozing and they tried to be just quiet enough so as not to fully awaken him. That way, they could get away with antics, if they chose, or just take their own naps.

"Mr. Battle's about to doze off again. See his head bobbing?" whispered Xavier Archibald to Kristi Lou as he leaned back from his desk one spot up from her in the next aisle. "I like to watch his chin bounce off his chest. It's even funnier now because his eye is all black and, oh…sorry, I, uh…"

"It's OK. Yeah, he'll be in La La Land anytime now."

****

Bud, referring to himself as His Muscularness, was almost swimming in his synthetic testosterone while seeing himself as a roguish version of Don Quixote; he was the scalawaggy Bud-Studman of La Mancha.

Flagrantly picaresque Bud Battle, now a cocky, bad-boys-are-sexy rapscallion, immensely enjoyed the unrestrained lechery he had implanted in the covetous ring girls, who had disintegrated into utter delirium.

The exquisite women began to fight over him. Pushing and pulling one another's hair in the tunnel, they all vied for Bud's dynamic virility.

I love catfights, especially when the pussycats are clawing and hissing over me. But, of course, I'm used to it.

These amazons' combativeness, especially since they were fighting for the prize of being his sole sex toy, stimulated him even more.

They're like licentious racecars, battling for pole-position priority in my pants.

His primitive pole swelled to 22 inches in length and four inches in girth.

The ring girls saw, all at once, a gigantic bulge in his boxer trunks. They stopped battling one another and gasped with lustful desire plus a tinge of concern.

Bad Bud, please take me! beseeched the black-haired woman.

No! I beggeth thee to taketh me! supplicated the brown-haired woman.

No! You need me! I'm wild and red-hot, like my hair! Be my ravisher! Ignore these inferior bitches! Take me! enjoined the red-haired woman.

The blonde, desperate to be graced by a pole-pounding penetration from Bud, could no longer contain her eroticism. Entreating Bad Bud for his approval, the buttery-haired nympho damsel boasted of her assets.

No! I'm your real-life stereotype. I'm the kinky-sential blonde. You must take me! Like, look at my ass! I do aerobics and glute training! That's right; I train my caboose—and I'm slutty and loose! I'm the one you want; I fuck better than all of them put together. And I'm like dumb and horny and I even have yellow pubic hair! Oh, Bad Bud, I'll blow anything, just like the old joke says—I've got lipstick on my steering wheel from blowing the horn!

Bud was titillated.

Man, I really like this dream; it's groovy, thought half-asleep Bud, who, as usual, was aware that he was dreaming during the very time he was clenched in that same dream's pleasant grasp.

The girls simultaneously saltated at his crotch. At that instant, his penis mutated to five feet in length and 13 inches in girth, exploding through his boxer trunks like a penile missile. As the girls retreated by stepping backward, Bud's ominous lust log aimed itself back and forth at each of them, oscillating threateningly, as if it were plotting and sizing them up for a strike.

Their prior carnality vanquished and replaced by survival instincts, three of the girls yelped in fear and ran out the back of the tunnel.

Help! Help! Somebody help me! Bud heard one of the escapees scream.

The blonde considered the possibilities.

Oh, oh, I don't know. It might not fit anymore.

What are you worried about? You can stretch, defended Bud.

Really? Like, that much? Are you like sure? I'm like scared it might hurt. But, like, I don't really know, so, hey—it might be OK.

Upon being made abreast of this accommodating outlook from the blonde, Bud's penis felt very happy and mushroomed to 16 feet in length and 15 inches in girth.

Everything above his shoulders shriveled to the size of a grapefruit and his face looked like the anterior portion of a shrunken head mounted on a stick by cannibals in Borneo.

Now flat-out asleep at his desk, with his chin buried between the open collar of his black Polo shirt, Mr. Battle was consumed by his dream.

His penis expanded again. Burgeoning to a turgid torpedo, it was now 22 feet in length and 19 inches in girth.

The blonde ring girl finally concluded that her vagina probably could not cater spatially to those dimensions.

No, I'm sorry; I think that, statistically, it just won't work. Frankly, I think that size seems unnatural. Oh, Bad Bud, you're still such a hottie, so if you could like, get it down like maybe several feet smaller—maybe more— then, maybe we could talk, but, like…I don't know, but…"

Then she saw his head disappear into his neck.

Bud's bad-dream alarm went off in his mind.

Too big! Too big! Too big! Wimble way too big! Get smaller! Get smaller! Overkill! Too much! Too big! Get smaller!

But, Bud's want-to-be-wimbling penis was, like Hal, the mutinous computer in *2001: A Space Odyssey*, now running the show.

Bad Bud's insubordinate penis launched itself into warp expansion, transmuting to 32 yards in length and four feet in girth, and went for the blonde, who at this point seemed to sense noteworthy danger.

Turning away and then screaming with terror, she ran forward through the exit end of the tunnel, directly in front of the crowd of fans still cheering and waiting for Bud's arrival.

Bud's penis dragged what was left of the rest of him along the tunnel, whose walls were pressed outward and were about to break, with the floor shaking from the weight of the Bud-mutation whenever it moved.

His arms had vanished inside his shoulders. His legs were now even shorter than they were in real life, and were crumpled and dragged helplessly underneath his leviathan penis, which immediately learned to move itself by slithering like a snake.

Bud's tyrannical Jurassic penis, now with kinks and bends like a gigantic water hose, continued after the blonde.

His bad-dream warnings jumped into his mind again.

No, no, no, no! We don't do homicidal rape! I want my head back! I want my arms back! Too big! Too much! Get smaller! I'm a gross-a-zoid! Oh shit!

As Bud, who was now almost all penis, emerged from the tunnel, his male member had adapted in the fashion of Darwinian survival of the fittest. His monstrous tool had grown eyes—eight of them—spinning around in wild circular motion.

The fans scattered in affright, as did the theatergoers who saw King Kong break free from his chains in 1933.

Bud pleaded with his dream.

No, damn dream. Make it smaller! Too big! If I ejaculate people will drown!

Drowning in a sea of semen! Disgusting thought! Dick too big! Smaller! Smaller! Smaller!

Bud's penis was still questing for the blonde ring girl, who had filtered herself into the throng of fans. She tried to lose herself among them, all, by now, running scared as well, but she was the only person way less than one-tenth dressed.

She took off her eight-inch spiked high heels so she wouldn't be as easy for the marauding super-penis to spot, just in case it was still looking for her. But she carried them with her as she retreated with the terror-stricken fans.

Speaking to some fans who were momentarily slowed by the pan-icked crowd in front of them battling for access to the doors, she paused from her fright to explain herself.

Like, these are like fashion-forward, expensive shoes but they were like free 'cause I didn't pay for them. They didn't cost anything, either, so I didn't spend any money. The salesman said they make my-already-hot hiney look even hotter. So I boinked him in the stockroom. He said I was paid in full. But I don't want Bad Bud's schlong to boink me 'cause I don't like bad-fitting peckers.

Bud's stalking Frankenpecker, pillaging through the fighters' arena, slithered under the squared circle, raising, flipping over, and then slamming the entire upside-down elevated ring and its ropes onto the concrete floor, thereupon razing the doomed structure, which buckled hideously into an as-if-steamrolled-almost-flat surface, crumpling as would a stomped-on shoebox. Crushed metal, nails, rubber, plastic, foam padding, canvas, dust, and pieces of shattered wood splintered aerially in all directions.

As fans continued stampeding toward the exits, with some get-ting stepped on while others were powerlessly swept along with the terrified tide of humanity bunched together, Bud's pleading with his dream began to yield some success. His penis size suddenly diminished, receding to just 11 feet in length and two-and-a-half feet in girth. His head popped back up and his arms reappeared.

But, six seconds later, it dilated back to enormity—huge and horrific. His head re-submerged, followed by his torso.

Damn you, Bad-Dream Alert, you jerk—you were taunting me! You asshole! Bad-Dream Alert! Bad-Dream Alert! Come on Bad-Dream Alert! Do your job! Smaller! Smaller! I demand a smaller dick!

Bud's dream redirected with inexplicable suddenness. He was surrounded by the same admiring ring girls, but in a calm and private place—he wasn't sure where, but they were all sprawled on a large sofa. They were coming on to him again, as his head had recrudesced and his body had returned to its steroidal magnitudes of 6'10" and 355 pounds. Bud's erectile statistics were at the Holmesian level of just over a foot. The sex-starved nymphets were wickedly thrashing all around and upon him, as he, nearing wakefulness, entered a hypnopompic state.

Yeah, I'm gonna do 'em all right here; I'm gonna drive 'em to raw ecstasy. Uh-huh, I know they're ovulating, which makes 'em crave a ruthless badass. That's right; when women ovulate they gravitate—to a macho man like me. The Village People sang a song about me.

Bud's dream began to sing, serenading him with "Macho Man."

****

Bud's priapic fantasyland was disrupted. Asleep and slouched in his chair while wearing an ever-so-slight grin that none of the kids noticed—except Kristi Lou and Guinevere—he was inopportunely evicted from his Walter-Mitty trance by sweet, demure Marsha, who expedited his awakening and was standing beside his desk with an urgent need to pee.

12

Marsha's parents had indulged their avant-garde sense of humor through the naming of their child. Mr. and Mrs. Mellow had foreseen no prospective injurious consequences.

"Mr. Battle, sir, I have to go to the bathroom," entreated the minute Marsha, whose unimposing crest, topping off at 4'10", allowed even Bud Battle to surpass her uppermost peak.

Bud, still woozy but highly aroused from his gratifying daydream, barely heard Marsha's quiet voice. But she jolted him back to earth just enough that an impulse compelled him to look down at his fastener. He hoped to see what he knew he wouldn't—a foot-long bulging love log remaining from his hallucination of Bud the Conquistador as well as the stretching of his necessarily spandex pants. Rather, he saw a small boner bump in his mundane polyester trousers. Frowning at the real-life extent of his maximum expansion, he rolled his eyes at himself.

"Mr. Battle, sir, Mr. Battle. Uh, I really need to go."

"Huh? Go where?"

"To the bathroom."

"Oh, yes, you said 'the bathroom.' OK, go then."

"May I have a hall pass, please?"

Bud's attention had already drifted away from Marsha, as he was trying to recapture his primal grandeur which the polite little girl had vanquished with her untimely interruption. Marsha began to knock her knees together and sway, because she truly did have to go.

"Mr. Battle, sir, Mr. Battle?"

"Huh? What? Just go ahead and go…oh, the hall pass. Here you go. Thank you."

Marsha froze.

"No, I have to thank *you* by saying 'thank you' to you," said Marsha with authentic pertinacity.

"What?"

"You gave *me* the hall pass, so I'm supposed to thank *you* by saying 'thank you' to you or else it's not right and bad things can happen."

As Bud was well-aware, Marsha Mellow, despite being bashful and soft-spoken, was not always but often intensely precise when conversing, as well as punctiliously redundant so as to underscore her precision.

Marsha, who was utterly void of malice and whose persona was engulfed in innocence, was well beyond being afflicted with moderate obsessive-compulsive disorder; she felt almost defined by OCD, which was her steadfast and governing companion.

"Well, what difference does all that stuff make, Marsha? I was just being cordial," argued the impatient Bud, minus cordiality.

Despite his awareness of Marsha's OCD and her friable emotions, Bud wanted her to go away without delay so he could resume dreaming before the dream and his sensation of virility completely evaporated. He spoke brusquely, thinking that indeed if he rushed back to his castle in the sky within the next few seconds he could perhaps recapture the whole thing while it was still vivid.

"Just go ahead and go."

"OK. But…" She spoke delicately, with her solemn politeness, as she turned back to her angst-ridden teacher after taking a single step toward the door. "I was wondering if you could, please, sir, tell me 'you're welcome.'"

"For what?"

"Because you're letting me go to the bathroom," said Marsha, who was starting to squirm more vigorously.

"If you could please tell me that, Mr. Battle, sir, then I could go to the bathroom, even though 'the bathroom' is, of course, a loosely applied term in our case because there's no tub here at school to take a bath in but bathing is not our present purpose, anyway, but we often call it 'the restroom,' which has some accuracy to it because sometimes people will go in there to just rest awhile, but for most situations including mine as defined by my current needs we could more accurately call it 'the toilet room' but 'the bathroom' is too prevalent everywhere to quickly change the words in the name so there'd be widespread recognition and acceptance, and I should go to the bathroom because I haven't gone there—to the bathroom—since the last time I went to the bathroom and that was a few hours ago and since then I've been drinking a lot of water because I have my water bottle at my desk, and I really have to go there to the bathroom as soon as I can get there, so I'd like to go there now…please."

"OK, then, you're welcome."

"But first I need to say 'thank you.'"

"Look, Marsha, I've already said you could go to the bathroom," said Bud, who was becoming confounded and exasperated. "And we've already said 'thank you' and we've already said 'you're welcome.' So there's really nothing left to say. I've got some papers to grade here and you need to go to the bathroom so just go to the bathroom."

"Mr. Battle?"

"Yes?"

"Are you mad at me?"

"No, I am not mad at you. I just think it would be divine if you'd go to the bathroom before you tinkle on yourself. I think you're about to pop. You're wiggling like a wiggly worm, you know, so, just go—OK?"

"OK."

"Thank you … Oh no," said the tetchy Bud, under his breath.

"For what, sir?"

"For going to the bathroom."

"But I haven't gone yet."

"Now see here, Marsha Mellow, please go to the bathroom."

"OK, I will."

"Thank you."

Oh shit, thought Bud.

"There you go again, Mr. Battle. *I'm* supposed to thank *you*."

"All right, then thank you, I mean, thank me, or … thank whoever should be thanked …"

"I say 'thank you' and you say 'you're welcome.'"

"OK then, say it already!"

"Mr. Battle?"

"What, what?"

"Are you mad at me?

"No! I'm not mad at you, damn it!"

Marsha burst loose wailing. Weeping with a decibel level that seemed too loud to emanate from her diffident facade and fragile 4'10" frame, she continued to jiggle with her hands over her front, bravely battling her bladder.

Marsha blubbered, simultaneously singing and crying.

"I've got OCD, OCD, OCD, OCD."

"Oh dear God, Marsha. Why are you singing about your OCD?"

"Sometimes if I sing about my OCD four times between 2.9 and 4.1 seconds it's not as dangerous and I can maybe stop the terrible things from happening," explained Marsha, whining through her tears.

"Huh? Between 2.9 and 4.1 seconds? How do you count exactly between 2.9 and 4.1 seconds?"

"I can do it. I detest doing it. But I can do it. I've been doing it for years. I'm really good at it. I can do it and I have to do it," gushed Marsha as her cries and singing proliferated.

"I've got OCD, OCD, OCD, OCD."

"No, no, no—please don't cry. I'm sorry, Marsha. Please, I'm so sorry," Bud entreated, as other kids started to snicker.

"My mom says she's sorry, too, 'cause she says she gave it to me," whimpered Marsha. "When we're in the car on the interstate she has to flex her butt cheeks two-and-four-fifth times within six-and-a-half yards of passing a mile marker," Marsha wailed.

"She has to what?" asked Mr. Battle with a grimace.

"This morning on the way to school she did three complete fanny flexes so we had to go back so she could do a proper four-fifth flex."

"What?"

"Mom said 'I flubbed my flex. Number three was a full flex. We've gotta go back.'"

"She, she turned around and went back?" queried Bud. "I'm not even going to ask how to measure butt-cheek flexes."

"She's really good at it."

Marsha's weeping escalated.

Bud looked aghast.

"I've got OCD, OCD, OCD, OCD."

****

Kristi Lou monitored the melodrama with fascination and sympathy. Guinevere observed analytically but with concern. The remaining kids relished the entertainment.

****

I thought I was screwed up, said Bud to himself.

You are, Bud replied to himself. *Just because she is doesn't mean you aren't.*

Bud, still morosely thinking to himself, remembered an old self-help book from the '70s titled *I'm OK—You're OK.*

For me and Marsha that would be retitled to "I'm Fucked Up and So Are You."

Bud forced a strained smile and attempted to pacify the unraveled little girl.

"I'm supremely sorry, Marsha. OK, wait…here it is. I'm going to say it now: You're welcome! You're truly welcome. Marsha Mellow, you are *so* welcome."

"Thank you for telling me I'm welcome," sniveled Marsha.

"You're welcome."

Bud paused. He yearned for Marsha to navigate herself to the bathroom.

I want to exit the Twilight Zone, please.

Marsha wavered to and fro, grasping her tortured crotch. She stared at the floor for about five seconds, finally lifting her eyes.

"But we still have to do it in the right order."

"What, uh…what?"

"I'm going to say 'thank you' and then you say your part."

"But we just *did* that," protested Bud, in a genuine whine, sounding more like Marsha's age than Marsha.

"No, sir, we didn't. We didn't do it right. You said 'you're welcome' after I thanked you for telling me I'm welcome. But you still haven't said 'you're welcome' at the right time for when I thank you for saying I can go to the bathroom. So, we have to do that right, please, so I can block these bad things that my mind says could hap…"

Marsha abruptly interrupted herself with more music—but untimed.

"OCD, I've got to pee-pee, OCD, I've got to wee-wee. OCD lives inside me-me. OCD, OCD, I'm the girl who's got to pee-pee."

"Oh good god," said Bud into his hand which his brain noticed was rubbing his face.

"Why has this situation not come up between us before? I mean, it's January. You've been in this class since the last week of August, and I don't recall…OK, I do remember there were a few times that you…but nothing this, well, extreme and, I don't know…"

"It's just that it's extra bad today—my OCD—and before I haven't always needed to go to the bathroom all this much during your class."

"Oh, thanks for explaining that."

Bud stroked his mouth with the back of his hand.

Why the hell did I backhand my mouth?

"OK, sir? Are you ready? Here goes. I'm about to say it now."

Marsha sobbed as she readied herself to speak her vital expression.

"Thank you," pled Marsha in a beseeching whisper.

Before Bud could respond, Marsha Mellow laid bare her detailed adjuration.

"Now, Mr. Battle, sir, you must realize, if you don't mind, please, that that particular 'thank you' that I just said was the 'thank you'—like the 'thank you' I said to start with a while ago—for you letting me go to the bathroom, even though I still haven't gone to the bathroom because you haven't said what you're supposed to say so I can actually go to the bathroom, which is a place I really need to go to, quite soon. So, you owe me a 'you're welcome.' But it doesn't count as much if I have to keep telling you what you're supposed to say and when you're supposed to say what you're supposed to say. So please try to say it right this time, please. OK?"

Bud looked upon her with astonishment.

"OK. It's your turn, please, Mr. Battle, sir," said Marsha with a whimper as she tried not to bawl again. She erupted with bullet-speed singing.

"I'm the girl with OCD who's got to pee, got to pee;

   it's me, it's me who's got to pee, OCD I bow to thee."

Marsha checked her watch to confirm 2.9 to 4.1.

Bud steeled himself for his pronouncement.

Trying to maintain his poise, Bud breathed deeply, furled and unfurled his lips, clasped and unclasped his hands, and looked around the surface of his desk.

"OK, Marsha, I hate to ask you to wait anymore but please give me just, uh, just…just a few moments to make sure, if, uh…"

"All right, sir."

****

All pupils were mesmerized by their own reality show, as if they were the audience in a TV studio. This captivating and thrilling display was Marsha's most dramatic OCD episode they had yet to witness. They half-heartedly tried, with marginal success, to keep their voice volume down.

"Devastatingly cool," said Xavier Archibald.

"You can say that again," said Robby Losley.

"Devastatingly cool," said Xavier Archibald.

"This is the best Marsha-moment ever," gushed Alison Altoid.

"I betcha she floods the floor right here," forecasted Tanya Watson.

"A dollar bill says she holds it," wagered Gregg Richardson.

"You're on," replied Tanya.

"My lunch money says she tinkles on the floor," crowed Xavier, as he looked around for takers.

"My lunch money says the floor stays dry," said Alison, though not with much confidence in her voice.

"She's gonna make a pee puddle," said Robby. "Bet me on it, Gregg and Alison—a dollar."

"Your bet is placed—a dollar it is," said Gregg.

"Yeah—bet me, too," said Alison. "I'll take your money, Robby—and yours, too, Tanya."

"I want in on that action," whispered Steffani James, seated in the next desk up from Xavier. "My lunch money says she wets the floor. Look at her. She's wiggling like a string in the wind. She's gonna explode any second. Mr. Battle can't get her to go to the bathroom. She's fixin' to pee-pop. Oh, man. This is awesome!"

Alison, feeling more confident, though she did not know why, jumped out of her desk. "I'll wager all you suckers that Marsha takes it with her to the toilet."

Alison quickly completed the bettor's handshake with Robby, Tanya, Steffani, and Xavier. She then hopped back in her seat to continue watching the spellbinding spectacle, chin in palms and elbows propped. "I'm gonna be rich, y'all … if Marsha doesn't blow up."

****

Bud leaned forward on the edge of his chair and barely noticed that he knocked over the empty beef jerky jar where he kept his pencils. He was ready to speak.

"All right, hold on, Marsha. Oh yeah, oh yeah, oh totally yeah. I've got it now."

Bud looked down at poor Marsha with determination and spoke with profundity.

"You're welcome!"

The classroom fell dead silent.

Bud gazed upon Marsha for about three seconds, beyond eager for her approval.

"Did I do it right? Did I? I did, didn't I?"

Marsha emitted an eerie squeak as she replied.

"OK, sir. I think I'm about to go to the bathroom," said Marsha, who tried to walk but could not lift her feet.

As he gawked at Marsha's spastically twisting shoes, an abrupt mesmerization overtook the overwhelmed Bud Battle, rendering him momentarily spellbound. Motionlessly gazing upon Marsha with his mouth open wide, he was only minimally aware of the environment surrounding him.

"No! Spray it, Marsha!" pleaded Steffani in a whisper that was muffled but readily audible around the room.

"Don't spray it," pleaded Gregg.

"Spray it, Marsha!" Steffani chirped, barely whispering. "Spray! Spray! Spray!"

"Don't spray! Don't spray! Don't spray!" said Gregg.

"If she's wearing underwear, how can she spray?" asked Alison. "She'll just do a little trickle."

"No, she's about to have a nuclear explosion. She'll spray right through her underbritches," said Steffani. "Spray it, Marsha!"

"Don't spray it!" repeated Gregg, cheering on Marsha as he went back and forth with Steffani.

"Spray it!"

"Don't spray it!"

"Spray it!"

"Don't spray it!"

Mr. Battle, after snapping loose from his catalepsy and glaring at the insensately verbalizing kids with an expression understood by them as an order to shut their demeritorious mouths, grabbed the front edge of his desk and looked intensely at Marsha Mellow, whose body, while still stuck in place, had begun to shake with visible tremorous vibrations. Marsha looked as if she were shivering in freezing weather.

Marsha muttered softly.

"Umm, as I was saying, I'm gonna go to the bathroom, OK?"

"Yes, Marsha, yes, oh yes, that's so incredibly OK. Bye, and have a good pee … I mean, have a good trip to the …" said Bud, beaming with hope-fueled enthusiasm. "See you when you get back."

"OK, sir. Thank you."

Marsha stood shaking and waiting, watching her teacher with her ears more than with her eyes, listening for the critical reply her harrowed urinary tract achingly craved.

"Oh! Yeah, right. Welcome! I mean, uh, I'm welcome. No. You're welcome. Er, uh…one of us is welcome. That's it! I've really got it now, Marsha Mellow. I am welcome. No, wait. You are welcome. You, Marsha, are so extremely welcome—specifically—for me saying you can go to the bathroom. You are truly the most welcome girl in world history. You are more welcome than I can evidently say. Now, please pee."

"Here?"

"No, hell no! I mean heck no. Of course not here. Where are you going to pee in here? On the floor? You, uh…OK, uh…no, no. I apologize. I didn't mean to sound harsh. I promise I didn't. I, uh, I should've been more precise and I should've said 'please *go* and pee.' I should've said 'go.' So it was my fault. My bad! I did a sin of omission; I should've said the word 'go.' So, just go—go to the bathroom, please, Marsha. It's down that way, around the cor…well, you know where it is. You've still got your hall pass. Just…go…use…the…bathroom…please. And, once you get there, you can pee—in the toilet, which I've found is really the best place for that…just to make sure, so, you know, you can…"

"Mr. Battle?"

"Yes?"

"Are you mad at me?"

"No. No, goodness no…I, I'm, no, I'm not, uh…" Bud forced a smile through his bafflement. "And I want to say that you're really and completely welcome for when you…or I…or one of us…said, uh, that thing that's supposed to be said…oh—it's 'thank you.' Yes, thank you. No, but…it's…it's when you say 'thank you' and I say 'you're welcome.' And you are…welcome."

Bud scratched an imaginary itch on his left earlobe with his right forefinger and then stuck that finger in his nose without realizing at first that he was doing it and then quickly pulled it out.

Why the hell did I stick my finger in my nose?

He felt the onslaught of one of his hammering headaches.

"OK," said Marsha, with meek dissatisfaction, as she sympathetically recognized her teacher's desperation accompanying her own.

Marsha Mellow, compelling herself to be motionless, was now bent forward at a 45-degree angle in frozen fixation, presenting an aggrieved facial expression and crisscrossed hands.

After four seconds of silent paralysis, Marsha's closed thin lips secreted a muted but bloodcurdling high-pitched, squealing utterance that Bud felt could cause wolves in the Ozarks to howl.

Innocent little Marsha, continuing to squeal helplessly, appeared to be ensnared within an Exorcist-like demonic captivity, evidenced by a contorted posture Bud saw as both bizarre and worthy of heartfelt pity—and decisive action. Fearing a civic display of ignominious incontinence in front of jeering seventh-grade peers that could inflict a lifelong psychological scar upon the already fragile child, Bud became desperate for a rescue.

"Guinevere, would you kindly come up here and escort Marsha Mellow to the bathroom, and make sure she gets there and that…that she, uh, relieves herself? But don't thank her for anything. That is, unless you're sure that she's sure you did something good for her. And be sure you tell her 'you're welcome'—but only at the point when you're sure that Marsha's sure that you surely should tell her that—or…uh, whatever I'm trying to say…I'm not really sure."

"Sure," said Guinevere with a calmness that left Bud thunderstruck.

Guinevere smiled with amusement, compassionately stifling an urge to laugh out loud at Mr. Battle's bewilderment, and then looked gently at her OCD-trapped classmate.

"Come on, Marsha, let's go to the bathroom."

"OK. Thank you, Guinevere."

"You're welcome, Marsha."

The bathroom-bound girls embarked on their suddenly unencumbered-by-OCD journey to Marsha's urinary emancipation.

How the hell did Guinevere just do that? wondered Bud. *Why couldn't I fucking do that? I am a fuckwad.*

****

"You guys owe me a buck apiece," said grinning Gregg to Tanya and Robby.

"I hope they're serving something yummy in the cafeteria 'cause I'm gonna have lots of lunches today," boasted Alison with a victor's grin as she scanned the frowning faces of Steffani, Tanya, Robby, and Xavier.

Tanya stuck her tongue out at Alison.

"OK, I'll pay," said Xavier with a frown, "but it's not fair. Guinevere helped. She wasn't supposed to get into this."

"Says who?" rebutted Alison. "Nobody said that rule—that Guinevere or whoever else couldn't help."

"Yeah, whatever. I'm gonna be hungry today, I guess." Xavier reached into his front-right pants pocket and forked over his lunch money.

"I would actually like to have lunch today," said Steffani. "Do I have to pay up now? Will you take a check?"

"No," replied Alison. "Besides, you don't have any checks. You're twelve. Come on, Steffani, pay, pay, pay, please, please, please. A bet is a bet is a bet."

Alison, in full collection mode, waggishly extended her open palm, smiling broadly.

"OK—here," said Steffani, as she paid her gambling debt. "You know we sit next to each other in most classes. I hope my stomach growls the whole afternoon and bothers you bad, bad, bad."

****

Mr. Battle tilted his now-aching head into both hands and rubbed his slick scalp. Bud was long since no longer in the mood for stimulating escapism. He reached into his top-right desk drawer. Fumbling through sundry things while looking at his belt buckle rather than what he was seeking, the would-be Teachernator felt and then grabbed his 300-count, almost-empty bottle of extra-strength acetaminophen. Bud, using the water in his coffee mug, plashed into his gullet the standard adult dosage of two capsules. Three seconds after resealing the cap, he twisted it back open. Choosing to eschew circumspection, Bud scarfed down another 500 milligrams of pain relief.

I'll worry about liver damage some other time.

****

Kristi Lou had been quietly observing from her desk in the rear of the room. She felt empathic toward both Marsha and Mr. Battle, having come to relate with sensitivity to the maladies of other misfits.

As she sat and looked at the frazzled Mr. Battle wiping his eyeglasses with his cleaning cloth, Kristi Lou realized ever more clearly that, as the school year had gone along, her former enmity toward Mr. Battle had yielded to a peculiar commiseration.

Although compassionate regarding the anxiety Mr. Battle and Marsha had just borne, Kristi Lou felt grateful for observing someone else's angst. But she did so without any schadenfreude-ish jubilation. Rather, the travails endured by Mr. Battle and Marsha served to reassure her that *there are other warped people on the planet besides me.*

13

MARSHA AND GUINEVERE TREKKED ALONG TOWARD MARSHA'S requisite rendezvous with the toilet, her urgency momentarily less acute, and her bladder's walls having been partially calmed by the ultra-mature Guinevere's placating intervention.

Upon exiting the girls' lavatory, however, there were Nasty Nate Perkins and equally mean Rudy Kaiser, sans hall passes, strolling along the other side of the hall, having just departed the boys' restroom.

About two seconds later, Nate and Rudy were regrettably, from Marsha's perspective, joined by Jennifer Jackson and Kirsten Williams, two of the meanest girls in school. The snide-faced enfants terribles happened to exit an otherwise empty lab where they had been enjoying some smokes they had easily smuggled into Our Lady; no one inspected girls' purses.

The four converged for what seemed to Marsha Mellow to be the perfect storm of malevolence.

"Oh no, Nate and Rudy are going to start calling me 'packrat,'" whimpered Marsha to Guinevere in a fear-laced whisper. "And Kirsten and Jennifer are going to make fun of my OCD."

As if taking a cue, smirking Rudy chimed away.

"Packrat. Packrat. Packrat. Look at Guiny-Guiny-Guinevere hangin' out with the pukey packrat," Rudy gleefully exclaimed while pointing at the slow-walking girls.

Nate, not wanting to be outdone, quickly added, "That'll help your reputation, Guiny. You hangs with the thangs. You hang with the sky-scraper thang and you hang with the packrat thang. What a joke!"

"Yeah, look what she hangs out with," said Rudy. "Guiny's gonna become a packrat, herself, if she keeps going around with Marsha the packrat."

"Yeah, your friends show who you are," laughed Nate.

"Guiny and Marsha the mushy-mellow packrat—they make a cute gay couple!" jeered Rudy.

"Fags!" said Nate, after which both boy-bullies looked at the two girl-bullies as if to say "You're up."

Jennifer and Kirsten had stopped walking to form an audience for the boys' degradation efforts, awaiting their turn. They both leaned against the wall, sneering, as Guinevere and Marsha walked slowly by.

Jennifer pointed at Marsha's dress and proclaimed. "Oh, the little marshmallow freak is wearing wrinkly clothes so she can, like, count the number of wrinkles which will stop her weird world from falling apart."

Kirsten cackled splenetically and added "Hey, Marsha, baby, it'd be easier to like count the number of boys that are gonna wanna go out with you when you grow up if you don't like stop with all that psycho-shit. And little miss sophisticated Guiny-queer won't help you, either."

Guinevere, having stopped Marsha with a slight touch on the arm, paused for effect, looked back at the tormenters with her trademark self-assurance and, as she and Marsha turned to face their oppugners, inimically but serenely retorted.

"Yes, you are often known by the company you keep. Look at the company the four of you are keeping. All four of you so flawlessly reflect one another—observably imbecilic, repulsive cretins who cele-brate their insecurities by attempting to build themselves up through bullying someone else down. Congratulations on your companionship choices. Perhaps one day you'll consummate your union of significant others by entering into the perfect marriage whereby you can advance to the more intimate associations you solemnly desire. Jennifer and Kirsten and Rudy and Nate will sexually unite themselves in reptilian bliss as they slither through life, squirming together in the everlasting purgatory of eternal classlessness."

"Oh, screw you, Guiny-queer, you pseudointellectual bitch," retaliated Kirsten.

Guinevere, looking placidly at Kirsten, issued another unruffled counteroffensive.

"I would expect you to curse and call names, as you typically cannot produce any coherent or logical points in your arguments. Frankly, I'm somewhat surprised that you know the word 'pseudo' and that you can even pronounce the word 'intellectual.' You must've practiced said pronunciation for several hours. And regarding your denouncement of me as a bitch, I will not respond by averring that you are a bitch because I harbor an aversion to egregious tautology."

"That's just big-word bullshit, Guiny-queer," blurted Jennifer. "Bitch-butt Guinevere the loser! You suck!"

"'You suck'? What an intelligent and mature rejoinder, Jennifer," replied Guinevere. "You certainly display a rapier wit and you proffer statements that are remarkably substantive."

"Rejoin what? Rape what? You, like, don't even make sense, you weird weirdo who goes around with the OCD freakazoid," said the sophomoric and thoroughly stultified Jennifer, frustrated by her inability to match neither Guinevere's intellect nor her unflurried comportment.

"Packrat, packrat—look at the packrat and the Guiny-queer," yelled Rudy.

"Yeah," said Nate, "now Guiny's packrat junior. And she goes around with that really taaaalllllllllll Kristi-giraffe-Lou. Freak-show assholes attract each other."

"Guinevere, may we go now, please?" begged Marsha.

"Yeah, Marsha the marshmallow needs to go sit down with a mirror and like count her nose freckles backward," screeched smirk-smiling Kirsten, who knew full well that Marsha was highly sensitive about her innumerable dapples and wanted all but four of them to magically disappear from her face.

Jennifer began to laugh loudly.

Marsha began to cry softly.

Guinevere, genuinely appalled by Kirsten's insensate acerbity, put her right arm around Marsha's tiny waist.

"Cruelty becomes you, Kirsten," retorted Guinevere. "Ugliness seems impeccably felicitous for you. Being a confirmable dastard, you seem so natural and in your element when being vicious to those who don't deserve your vitriol and who you assume are susceptible to bullying and would struggle to mount any self-defense."

"Eat shit, you little nerd—you *and* the packrat."

"Hmm," said Guinevere, "I'm not sure whether your imbecility engenders your arrogance or vice versa; it's too close to call."

"What? Fuck yourself and die, Guiny-ass."

"No, thank you," calmly answered Guinevere. "You might consider obeying that directive by partaking in coition with yourself, which, in your case, will involve no respect, an entity of which you are not worthy, meaning that you'll share something in common with the many males who will penetrate your dehumanized orifices. Please utilize contraceptives so that you do not breed."

"What? Bitch! I can stomp your nerdy ass. You know that," threatened Kirsten.

Hearing a threat of violence directed toward Guinevere was too much for even mild-mannered Marsha to remain in the background.

"If you hurt Guinevere I'll get Kristi Lou and she'll get you good!" Marsha fumed as she spoke, forcing herself, though still fearful and intimidated, to unleash an aberrant display of pugnacity.

Then, quickly realizing she had left her timidity zone, Marsha recoiled fretfully behind Guinevere.

Guinevere immediately appreciated the reality that she had just been defended by the meek Marsha Mellow. She knew that Marsha, by warning that she would recruit Kristi Lou as a righteous paladin, had forced herself to temporarily leave the relatively safe confines of her pusillanimity to rally a courageous defense of her friend. Guinevere recognized Marsha's uprising, as mild as it was, as an act of bravery. Guinevere knew that Marsha was not made for confrontation, and any such justifiable derring-do meant that Marsha had risen gloriously to the occasion.

"Kristi Lou? Screw her. She's just tall; that's all. You think I'm scared of Kristi Lou?" protested Kirsten with a sneer.

"No…" Guinevere replied as she was interrupted by Kirsten.

"You're friggin' right I'm not."

"…because she's not after you—now."

"I wouldn't be scared of her, anyway."

"Yes, you would. Checkmate. I strongly advise that you never touch me or—especially—Marsha. Kristi Lou looms bigly."

"The bigger they are, the harder they fall," said Kirsten.

"The bigger they are, the harder they hit," said Guinevere.

"Drop dead, you geeky nerd-ass," said Kirsten.

"Oh, by the way," said Guinevere with a slight upturn of her chin and eyebrows, "you may be interested to know that several girls were talking yesterday in my gym class about your menstrual travails."

"What?" said Kirsten, no longer smirking and immediately fearing the worst—that someone had heard about her seeking the assistance of Ms. Bulloch, the phys ed instructor.

Kirsten, it seemed, had somehow struggled to properly apply her tampons, and was fully flummoxed to the point of panic at even the thought of word getting out and smearing her vainly cultivated notoriety.

"What does she mean?" asked Jennifer.

"Nothing. She's just talking her stupid talk. She's just…she doesn't know shit…she's just full of it."

"If you're nice to Marsha from now on, I shall refrain from undue elaboration in your societal circles about your plugging problems," bargained Guinevere. "We all have things that we bungle, don't we?"

Kirsten gave Guinevere and Marsha the dirtiest of looks, presented her left—then her right—middle finger with her arms thrust forward and high above her head, then turned and stormed off, with Jennifer lagging behind somewhat slowly, as if she wasn't quite sure she wanted to catch up.

"Bitch!" exclaimed Kirsten, looking back over her right shoulder at Guinevere—while ignoring Marsha—as she turned the corner halfway up the hall, with Rudy and Nate standing stiffly, the two jackanapeses having been left dumbstruck by Guinevere's it-factor display of commanding odyl force.

"Kirsten aimed her slur only at me, not at you."

"Yes. I'm sorry she called you that name."

"I'm not; I just consider the source. OK. We can go now, Marsha."

"Thank you."

"You're welcome."

The girls, walking in the opposite direction of the two dispatched viragos, began journeying toward their classroom, passing with total disregard the now cowed-into-silence Rudy and Nate.

"Can you teach Mr. Battle to say 'you're welcome' like that?"

"I'll try—yes, I can and I will," said Guinevere with a comforting smile and soft laugh.

****

Nate and Rudy remained in the same place in the hall, continuing to cut class for as long as they could get away with it. Feeling a resurgence of confidence due to Guinevere's departure, the two persecutors stood disdainfully, mannishly wagging their torsos and chattering loudly with false bravado while watching other kids obediently exhibiting their hall passes go by and sneering at their un-tough conformity.

"What was all that stupid-ass stuff Guiny-queer just said?" scoffed Rudy Kaiser.

"Who knows? Who cares? She's just a don't-matter, faggy lezhole. I think she was just using some big words, again," offered Nate Perkins.

"Yeah, she's so dumb," reassured Rudy.

The bullying boys walked off, unsure of all the specifics of what Guinevere had said against them, but feeling they had somehow been verbally disemboweled.

****

Meanwhile, Marsha and Guinevere, having completed their restful sojourn in the restroom and then having withstood an unexpected contentious aftermath, were nearly back to Mr. Battle's classroom. Marsha Mellow sought a locker with the number 4 printed on the door.

"Tar-K-Cap, Tar-K-Cap, Tar-K-Cap, Tar-K-Cap," repeated Marsha while she touched the 4 on a locker door four times with her forefinger.

"OK, Marsha, explain that ritual to me, please," requested Guinevere.

Marsha Mellow instantly answered, with her reply breathlessly rolling off her tongue in a way that told Guinevere that Marsha had memorized each phrase—probably honed with obsessive repetition while speaking to herself.

"When they call me 'packrat,' I must say that turdywordy backward and pronounce it perfectly four times within four seconds and it's better if I can actually see the number 4 and betterer if I can actually touch the number 4 while I say what I must say and betterest if I use my right-hand forefinger to fulfill said touching because it's the fourth finger counting in reverse from right to left starting with the pinkie finger and the word forefinger has a lovely four in it even though it's spelled f-o-r-e because it's still pronounced like the number 4 spelled f-o-u-r.

"Tar-K-Cap. Tar-K-Cap. Tar-K-Cap. Tar-K-Cap."

"Oh," replied Guinevere with a furrowed brow and an ever-so-mildly amused, but understanding, nod.

"I had to say it an extra time because I'm way late saying it because I'm supposed to say it immediately after I hear 'packrat.' I hope I won't get punished for being tardy."

"Who would punish you? God?"

"No, not God. I believe God wants me to be able to stop. Mom and I don't really know who will do the punishment. It's like some OCD emperor out there that might get us and allow bad things to happen to us or Dad or my grandparents and my friends—like you. I can't let anything happen to you. You just protected me and I have to protect you back."

"Oh, well, I think I'll be OK. I doubt the OCD emperor-monster, if I can call him that, will get me," said Guinevere. "As far as protection, that appears to be mutual. You just protected me back there. You protected me by telling Kirsten that you'd sic Kristi Lou on her if she tried to harm me. I am grateful for your looking out for me; I really am."

"You are my friend, aren't you, Guinevere?"

"Yes. I am. I'm definitely your friend. And I'm honored that you are my friend; it's my privilege."

"Thank you."

"You're welcome," replied Guinevere, with the competence in responding that Mr. Battle envied.

****

Fresh from the encounter with their four adversaries, Guinevere and Marsha reentered the classroom. As they passed by Mr. Battle's dais desk, Guinevere looked at him with glee, and then broke away from Marsha and walked back, leaning in toward him so no one else could hear.

"Hi, Mr. Battle. Everything came out just fine," Guinevere said with a muted chortle. "Sorry about the lack of originality in my humor. Anyhow, Marsha did have to do three-and-one-quarter flushes to stop the sky from falling."

"How, exactly, do you do a one-quarter flush? Then again, maybe I don't want to know."

"She pushes the handle down exactly one quarter of the way on the fourth flush. She told me she's measured it before."

"Measured? She's, she's learned how to measure a flush?"

"Yes. I'm afraid she has. She showed me an itty-bitty mark she drew on the wall behind the handle with some paint she got from Mr. Earlie that she had put on the tip end of her pencil. So she squats down on flush number four so she can watch the handle so she can pull it down to just the right spot."

"Oh, heavenly God," said Bud, with a mild but warm laugh. "All right, thank you, Guinevere."

"Why, no, I should thank *you* because you're supposed to say 'you're wel…' I'm just joking, Mr. Battle." Guinevere grinned over her left shoulder as she returned to her desk.

"You're quite a funny girl, Guinevere," replied Bud with a tired grin of his own.

Bud looked at Marsha, who was comfortably seated at her desk, calm at last—at least for the time-being. He had known of Marsha's affliction since the first week of school back in late summer, having been informed by Daniel Alexander, who called Bud into the principal's office to tell him, along with Marsha's other teachers, that Marsha and her mother suffered from a serious case of obsessive-compulsive disorder.

He had seen her fidget and squirm on many days, appearing to go through strange routines, and he'd figured that was her OCD manifesting. But, as he had indicated to Marsha, he had never before beheld such an excruciating eruption of her OCD. He imagined what life must be like for Marsha and her mom and dad at home, and he felt sorry—in a genuine way—for all of them.

Bud bade Marsha to his desk.

"Yes, sir?"

"Marsha, if you don't mind me asking, are you and your mom going and talking to somebody on a regular basis to get help with your, uh, situation?"

"You mean, are we going to therapy?"

"Well…yes."

"Yes, sir, we are, including my dad."

"Oh, your dad, too? Well, does your dad, uh, also have O…"

"He has to live with us."

"Oh, right. Well…good. I'm glad, and, uh, I hope it's helping."

"Yes, it is. And we'll keep going. It's our best hope. It's just that some days and hours and minutes and seconds and milliseconds are worse than others with the racing thoughts like a runaway train. And getting well takes time, like our therapist says."

"Yes. I'm sure that's right, but I'm also sure you'll get there. And you do so well here in school making good grades and being polite to everyone."

"Thank you for caring, Mr. Battle."

Bud paused, and then steeled himself.

"You're welcome, Marsha."

"Well done, Mr. Battle."

"Thank you."

"You're welcome, sir."

Bud Battle accidentally touched his darkened eye and felt a tinge of still-lingering pain. He realized that during the ordeal with Marsha he had not worried even once about the appearance of his eye or gossipy fallout from *The Incident*.

"I'm going back to my desk now, if that's OK with you," caringly replied Marsha, who now felt a degree of concern for her awkward teacher, knowing Bud Battle was fearful of facing another of her OCD episodes, all the while dealing with the social aftermath of his swollen and blackened eye, which she noted was partially adumbrated by what appeared to be amateurishly applied maquillage. While Marsha was feeling concerned about Bud as she stood before him, he recalled that he had searched for and found, buried in the bottom-middle drawer of his dresser, a very old box of multi-colored crayons he knew he had stashed somewhere in his house, and had applied to his eye the stick labeled "flesh." Of course, Marsha Mellow knew about *The Incident*, too.

"Yes. That will be fine."

"Bye."

"Uh, bye—but you're just going across the room."

"I know," Marsha said with a smile, as she exited the conversation and returned to her desk, where Bud watched her open her textbook and commence studying.

Bud re-observed what he had seen throughout Marsha's ordeal; only because they didn't want to get in trouble, all the other kids in the classroom were intensively struggling to suppress grossly insensitive outright laughter—all but two. Guinevere, the rescuer, was her usual unflappable self. And there in the back of the room sat lanky Kristi Lou, wearing an expression, he sensed, of fascination mixed with earnest concern.

****

Mr. Battle did not interfere when he saw Kristi Lou quietly transfer herself to the empty desk behind Marsha Mellow.

Kristi Lou was not surprised that her teacher did not order her back to her seat. She had just observed Mr. Battle's own kindness toward Marsha, and felt that he would appreciate any further support bestowed upon the small, frangible child strapped with OCD.

"Hi, Marsha," whispered Kristi Lou.

"Oh, hi. What are you doing here?"

"I just came over to visit. And, I don't think Mr. Battle minds at all. I saw him sorta smile at me just a moment ago when I sat down. I just, uh, I just wanted to see if you're all right. I mean, I think Guinevere really helped you a lot, didn't she?"

"Yes, she did; she was very sweet and nice to me. And she defended me, too."

"How? What happened?"

Marsha summoned her "finger #4/fourfinger #1," as she had named her left-hand forefinger in collated notes she'd written to herself. She tapped four times on the far left end of the pencil-holder slot at the top of her desk, on which textbooks and notepads were spaced proportionately, with no items positioned askew.

"Well, so, we both got hassled by these hateful kids in the hall, and Guinevere stuck up for me."

"Who? What?"

Marsha tapped her left nostril four times with her right minimus finger, known officially to her, per her private, self-authored guidebook of OCD terminology, as "pinkie #2," which was her eighth finger counting from the left side of her left hand. She did not count her thumbs in her official finger tabulation because "thumbs are thumbs, not fingers," and "although they're very related, they still have their own category."

Kristi Lou looked on with categorical fascination, but also with serene understanding.

"Well, we were walking back here from the tinkle room and, uh, well, it was, uh—Nate Perkins and Rudy Kaiser. And then it was Jennifer Jackson and Kirsten Williams. Actually, it was Jennifer and Kirsten who said some of the meanest things. They all bombarded us with a slew of sequential insult-bombs. And, well, uh…"

"Oh my god. Nate—he's such a jerk. Don't worry, Marsha. He has insecurity issues and acts like a little bully. He needs to put other people down to prop himself up. He calls me names, too."

"He does?"

"Yeah," said Kristi Lou, looking down at her twiddling fingers. "He calls me Skyscraper Tree. He knows, well, speaking of insecurity issues, he knows that I'm, uh…that I'm insecure about being so tall and all. He tries to cut me down to his size. In a way, I wish he could—that is, physically down. Then, I'd look more like a real girl 'cause I wouldn't be so tall and such a gross-looking, quasi-girl thing. But, anyway, I and my problems aren't the subject 'cause I came here to talk about you, so…"

"I wish I could be tall like you. I think you're feminine and beautiful."

Kristi Lou's personage became motionless. Only her eyes moved as she looked into Marsha's face, and Kristi Lou had to stop herself from crying.

"Oh my goodness. Really? Thank you. Uh…thanks, Marsha. You sound like Guinevere. She kinda says kind things like that, and it's nice to hear, but…"

"But it's true when she says it and it's true when I say it."

"Oh, thank you so much. Just, well, thank you."

"You're welcome."

The two girls paused for about five seconds.

"So, what did they do? What did they say?"

"Rudy started calling me what he usually calls me. He called me packrat."

"Oh, that Rudy better leave you alone or I'll…"

Marsha immediately responded to herself.

"Tar-K-Cap. Tar-K-Cap. Tar-K-Cap. Tar-K-Cap."

"Uh…?" Kristi Lou began to inquire.

"I'm really revealing myself today. I told Guinevere back in the hall and now I'm telling you. Whenever someone—and it's usually Rudy, but not always because sometimes other kids call me that—whenever somebody calls me packrat I have to say it backward four times to prevent bad things from happening."

"Oh, all right then. I see." Kristi Lou dropped then quickly raised her eyes to Marsha's eyes while wearing an expression of both absorption and benevolence.

"Hey," said Kristi Lou, "one more thing…you let me know if Kirsten or Jennifer picks on you again, OK?"

"Oh, OK, thanks. I will. And Guinevere, too, right?"

"Of course Guinevere, too. Why? Did one of them do something to Guinevere?"

"Kirsten made a threat to stomp Guinevere's you-know-what. I told her if she did I'd tell you and you'd make her pay."

Kristi Lou's back arched like that of an angry cat. Marsha could see her literally bristle.

"If Kirsten touches Guinevere I'll…I don't know exactly what I'll do but I do know that what'll be left of her will never touch Guinevere again."

Marsha felt a tinge of fear even though she knew that none of Kristi Lou's ire was aimed at her.

"Uh, yeah, I … that's … that's what I thought. I think Kirsten knows that, too. Anyway, thanks for coming over here to be with me."

"You're very welcome."

"Hey, Kristi Lou. Have we just bonded here? I think we have. I hope…"

"Yes. Yes, we have. Yes, we sure have. I'm glad for that."

"Oh, I am, too. And you know what? Mr. Battle hasn't made us hush. He's let us talk," said Marsha.

"Yeah. That's really big-hearted of him."

****

Neither Kristi Lou nor Marsha spoke another word throughout the remaining two-and-half minutes of class, quietly immersing themselves in Mr. Battle's reading assignment. Both girls mutually sensed that they were enjoyable conversationalists for one another and could continue to be trusted, beyond this day, to treat the other's insecurities with sensitivity.

Kristi Lou sat behind Marsha till the bell rang.

Marsha and Kristi Lou walked toward the door together, where they were joined by Guinevere. The three girls, warmly gravid with their newfound triple bond, stepped into the hall together.

Without a word, they, resembling a parade of soldiers turning their heads in unison toward their commander while marching by, looked simultaneously back through the doorway at their teacher. Mr. Battle was already watching them. He gave them the faintest of smiles, but it was a smile that all of them instantly discerned.

14

BUD, ALTHOUGH UPLIFTED BY THE EVENTS OF THE MONDAY
and the Thursday following *The Incident*, sunk intermittently into episodes of despair, usually lasting five to eight hours.

By Saturday, he was seeking comfort on the Web. His condition was unprofessionally diagnosed as a form of "manic-depressive bipolarization" as well as "personality delusional disorder" by a person calling herself Dr. Ex-Depression Patient who had responded to Bud's anonymous plea for help. The blog, called "Been There Felt That," or BTFT, was designed for people struggling with mental illness who wished to discuss their issues with their peers—non-professionals, some of whom were currently in therapy and some of whom were not.

The blogging woman remarked to Bud that "I'm not a real doctor. I just play one on the Internet."

The website proclaimed in bold fonts at the top of the Home page that content was closely monitored and that participants should never pretend to dispense advice or treatments as if they were professionals, although this dictate was not always enforced carefully. Thus, the post from Dr. Ex-Depression Patient was not deleted.

The site's stated emphasis was on empathetic commiserating among those who suffered, with the hope of alleviating sorrow through mutual exchanges of kindness. Participation in this online altruism, however, required a nonrefundable registration fee and monthly membership payments.

Bud, desperate for relief, had gone online to seek precisely such reassurance and guidance. He paid with his American Express account. Beyond his anonymity as far as not providing his real name or location, he was also very careful to avoid any identifying details in his posted remarks that described his ordeal. Of course, he omitted any direct references to *The Incident*.

As of Sunday evening, nine days after *The Incident* and one day on Been There Felt That, he had had enough of BTFT.

I'm sure there are some fine folks on that thing, but I think I probably need an old-fashioned professional helping me. They can keep the subscription money for the rest of January.

Bud politely replied to the six people who had responded to his description of his woes and then cancelled his membership.

****

Bud realized that, in order for him to perform his job through the upcoming week, in lieu of his refusal to take leave time to heal in private—*the staff and kids will talk about me even more if I'm absent*—his demasculinizing disfigurement necessarily had to be paraded in front of middle school students, a cruel populace whose potential for unbridled insensitivity and capacity to be sneeringly obnoxious were seen by Mr. Battle as not yet having been matched within Earth's narration.

While watching—through one normal eye and one still-disfigured eye—his homeroom students trickle in Monday morning, 10 days after *The Incident*, Bud recognized what he viewed as commendable exceptions to this rule of middle school meanness, including Kristi Lou, Guinevere, and Marsha. But, when viewing the population as a whole, Bud surmised that the mannerly graces of lascivious drunken sailors on shore leave in a red-light district after six months at sea were less crass and coldblooded than the collective callousness of seventh and eighth graders.

"The verdure of their youth is dreadfully coupled with their grandiosely exaggerated concept of how much they're *certain* they know of life," opined Bud, sitting in the breakroom early Monday afternoon. Conversing with an assemblage of teachers—notably minus Wilma Wilson, who had walked in and, upon seeing Bud, walked out—Bud waxed philosophically about the proclivity of people in this age group to inflate, in their own minds, their base of knowledge and their self-purported unassailable wisdom.

"The kids who readily admit to their immaturity and to still having a lot to learn are typically the ones who, ironically, are the most mature and learned."

****

Bud, notwithstanding the uplifting partial bonding with Kristi Lou, was still assailed intermittently by episodes of depression and neurosis.

Why is my damn eye not healing?

He was convinced that wearing a patch would look that much more glaring, and he sought to avoid Cyclops jokes. He therefore contemplated alternate methods of escaping from his eye.

Twelve days after *The Incident*, on Wednesday, Bud Battle drove his discolored orb to a department store 40 miles out of town where he felt no one was likely to recognize him. He had decided to resort to makeup, which he purchased at the cosmetics counter. Bud told the clerk that he was buying the product for his wife, whose complexion, he said, just so happened to be about the same as his own. The unconvinced saleslady noticed there was no ring on his finger, and then sold him a tube of cream called "Tender Porcelain," which coated human flesh with a shade of diluted pastel beige, thereby nearly emulating his ashen facial hue, that of grayish eggshell.

The poor man's dark mark of infamy had transmogrified over a week-and-a-half period from a blackish-purple glow to what had over the past two days become a yellowish-green blotch. Unbeknownst to Bud, these colors indicated the culmination of the healing process was near.

Despite his attempt to cover his breast-inflicted blemish with Tender Porcelain, his periorbital hematoma stood out garishly like a painted hooker in Sunday school and often sent him into a self-assailing snit.

Now I've got green and yellow and beige all mushed up. Tender Porcelain, huh? I look like somebody puked on me. When the hell is this thing going to heal?

By Saturday, 15 days after *The Incident*, the discoloration was, bless-edly, gone.

*I guess I wasted 35 damn bucks on that makeup plus a quarter-tank of gas. Shit. I wish I could have hindsight **before** I do something, but …*

****

Sometimes Bud felt OK; other times he felt conspicuously shorter than ever before.

He persisted in his mania of castigating himself as the Lilliputian teacher whose eyeball had been blackened and puffed by a towering twelve-year-old's barbaric breast—a heinous gelding, more so even than the literal version he nearly suffered in the coils of the radiator, that he assumed would surely bedevil him all his lonesome days. This paranoiac fear compelled Mr. Battle to seek therapeutic intervention with a highly regarded Little Rock psychiatrist, Jack Jackerson, M.D.

No more Been There Felt That amateurism; I've gotta go to a pro.

His first session with Dr. Jackerson was Friday, three weeks to the day after *The Incident*. As he drove home from Dr. Jackerson's office, he knew he felt both comfortable with his new therapist and pleased with himself for mobilizing the wherewithal to actually commit to therapy.

It wasn't so bad. In fact, it was good. I've gotta make myself tell him all my embarrassing dreams and things that upset me. That might be hard, but I've gotta do it. Anyway, I've got something in common with Marsha Mellow; we're both aberrations. And now we're both in therapy. Same thing with me and Kristi Lou except I don't know whether she's getting her head shrunk. Anyhow, I wonder if Dr. Jackerson is coincidentally the same shrink Marsha and her family go to. Why am I wondering about that? There must be a zillion headshrinkers in Little Rock. God, it would be embarrassing if I were coming into or out of Dr. Jackerson's office and Marsha and her parents saw me. But, I won't ask Dr. Jackerson. They can't talk to one patient and say the names of their other patients—not without express permission. That's one of their things about protecting patient confidentiality and being ethical. I get that.

****

If *The Incident* held a silver lining for Bud, his faculty peers affirmed, seeking therapy would be it. In their collective view, he had needed to see a therapist for quite a while. But they all concurred that this disgrace was such a rough way for a little teacher to learn a large lesson about watching the directions he chooses.

"Now that Bud is attending therapy, he has a very real chance to work through his insecurity issues and find more happiness and become an even better teacher than he already is. And he is an outstanding, conscientious, and kindhearted teacher," declared Claire Mumford in a confidential conversation with Principal Alexander.

15

AS THE REMAINING MONTHS OF THEIR SEVENTH-GRADE
school year betided, Kristi Lou could be seen daily towering over
Guinevere and Marsha in the schoolyard.

Once, when Mr. Battle happened to descry them standing side by
side in such an arrangement, gabbing merrily outside after lunch, he
had an impulsive thought. *That scene looks like an old picture of the Empire
State Building in New York City before the other skyscrapers were built.*

Because of Kristi Lou's de facto role of enforcer looming ominously
over them, Jennifer, Kirsten, Nate, and Rudy were forced to adapt. They
learned to limit their traducements to nothing more than reveling in
behind-the-back aspersions.

The shared camaraderie between Kristi Lou, Guinevere, and Marsha
continued growing through the winter and spring, as their friendship
reached a depth they all thought was not emotionally known by most
people their age.

****

Kristi Lou had continually observed Mr. Battle's on-and-off battles
with embarrassment and despondency, as manifested in his face, his

tone, and his body language. Always aberrantly introspective, she recognized that her feeling of appreciation for her teacher's perseverance in battling his insecurities had steadily deepened, yielding a warmth-soaked vicissitude: During the second half of her seventh-grade school year, beginning with the events of that Monday after *The Incident*, the former reciprocal rancor dissolved, replaced by a mutual acceptance of the reality of their bodies.

Still, both would have instantly said "yes" had God offered a transposition.

Not lost on Kristi Lou was that the eradication of her acrimony toward Mr. Battle paralleled almost perfectly with the timing of her newfound BFF/Best Friends Forever with Guinevere and Marsha.

****

At last, for Kristi Lou, the end of May was forthcoming. She had endured. Her season of the seventh-grade pilgrimage through the hell of heights was on the cusp of conclusion. She had recently discontinued therapy with George Carlisle, Ph.D., a well-respected adolescent psychologist. Even though Dr. Carlisle advised Kristi Lou and Mrs. Jones that the stoppage might be premature, she, her mom, and Mr. Jones decided that her emotional stability had markedly improved enough to safely stop—and that Kristi Lou could, if necessary, resume her sessions.

****

On this warm Tuesday afternoon during the third week of May, as Kristi Lou was standing alone in the grass yard outside the cafeteria and studying the patterns of interlocking cumulus clouds, she felt someone give her a gentle hip bump.

Guinevere snuck behind Kristi Lou and put an arm around her waist.

"Well, look what we have here. We're almost at the end of the school year."

"We are, indeed, aren't we? And now we're both—drum roll—teenagers; we've reached the advanced age of thirteen," said Kristi Lou. "I feel so antique-ish-ey."

"Yes, we are well-nigh fossilized and decrepit."

"But worldly wise with the astuteness of advanced age."

"Yeah, right," said Guinevere. "And with that wisdom you've come to accept and sort of almost—to use my Mom's word—'embrace,' being tall. At least you're kinda somewhat embracing it."

"Yeah, I'm feeling more OK about it now," agreed Kristi Lou with a cautious but big smile. You see those fluffy white clouds up there?"

"Yes."

"When you bumped me I was just reassuring myself that I'm really not high enough to reach out and touch them—yet. But, yeah, overall I definitely feel better about being, uh … about being …"

"… tall."

"Yeah. That's it. I feel better about being tall."

"I know you do. And I've got to tell you this, again, Kristi Lou. It's what I told you that morning in the restroom back in January when Nate Perkins was giving you grief. It's true, whether or not you want to believe it. All you have to do is look around at some of the eighth-grade boys. Notice how much taller most of them are than the seventh-grade boys? Then, when you're shopping or walking around wherever you see older boys—the ones in high school—just look at how they're even taller. Next, just concentrate on looking at the grown men and how most of them are taller than the grown women.

"What I'm saying is yes, you will always be taller than most girls and grownup women. But many of the guys will catch up with you and pass you. That's part of the puberty thing. We usually get there about a year earlier than they do. And guess what? This is that year.

This is the year for you—the seventh grade—when the tallest girls are often taller than the tallest boys—and some of the boys might feel bad about being shorter than the girls. It can work both ways. But, like I keep telling you, it mostly reverses over the next year or so. It's sort of hard when you're twelve or thirteen to look very far ahead; you feel stuck in the present and you think a few months is forever. But it isn't, Kristi Lou, it isn't."

"Yeah, you're right."

"As I've been saying—and I realize I'm repeating myself but I'm doing that on purpose for the sake of emphasis—in a couple of years, you'll still be taller than a bunch of the boys, but you won't be taller than as many of them as you are now. And after you finish growing up, you might be taller than most men. But there are always going to be grownup men taller than you. And you'll probably marry one of them and have a tall kid like the one your mom and dad had. You'll see."

"Thanks, Guinevere. I really don't know what I'd do without you."

"Well, I think you'd do just fine."

Guinevere paused for a moment, looking away then back at Kristi Lou.

"Unfortunately, you'll get to find out soon."

"What are you talking about?"

"I won't be in Little Rock anymore after next month. We're moving to Ohio in July."

"No!" remonstrated Kristi Lou, instantaneously swamped with suffocating lachrymosity. Her frantic eyes splashed in tears that did not spill.

"My dad got transferred by his company to Toledo, in Ohio. You know—the town they're referencing when they say 'Holy Toledo!'"

"Yeah, I know, but …"

"Anyway, as I told you one day when you were over at the house, my dad's an aerospace engineer. He designs things. He's a genius. When I say he's a genius, I'm not hyperbolizing. He really is, quite literally, a genius. He's been a member of Mensa for many years. And he's one of the smartest Mensa people ever. Mensa keeps records of IQ test scores. You have to get at least 130 on the WAIS—Wechsler Adult Intelligence Scale. Dad obliterated that mark. Anyway, the company is going to have him working at a manufacturing facility in Toledo, designing things for the U.S. Government. His company is one of the government's biggest contractors."

"I don't want you to leave. Please stay here," pleaded Kristi Lou. As the corners of her lips sagged downward while she exhaled hard, she wrung her fingers together and looked at Guinevere's shoes and then into her face.

"I can't stay. I wish I could but I can't. I can't stay because …"

"Ask your dad to get another job here. Can't he do his genius designing here, working for some local company? There are lots of businesses around here. I guess that's selfish; well, no, I know that's selfish. It's selfish. I'm being selfish. I'm sorry. But it just means that I don't want to lose you as my friend."

"I don't want to lose you, either. And we won't stop being friends; we'll just be apart for … I don't know how long, but I know we'll get back together. But when you're our age, you have to go where your parents take you."

Kristi Lou nodded in reluctant agreement to Guinevere's statement of cold realism.

"I remember Dad saying that kids typically say they'll be friends forever," said Kristi Lou with a muted whimper. "But then, after they split away, they stay away. They never see each other again. That makes me feel depressed to just think about it. And it scares me."

"You won't lose me as your friend. It's true that so many people, especially kids like us, have made vows to always be friends, but then they drift away from one another, even when they stay in the same place together, like the same school. They see each other in the halls between classes and they don't even speak or look at each other, or only just a little bit now and then."

"I know."

"What happens is that they get a year or two older and things change when they learn they have developed different interests. And, well, that means they've just grown apart. That's sad to me, too, like it is to you. But you know what? Some friends don't grow apart. You and I are going to be those friends. I think we'll always be friends, even if we don't see each other for years—or never again."

"'Never again'? No. Please don't say that, Guinevere," said Kristi Lou, with more unfalling tears forming afresh in her large azure eyes.

"OK, OK. I won't. I'm sorry. Don't worry. Don't cry. It's OK. I sense that somehow we *will* be back together."

"Yeah, that sounds much better. Yes, I think we can do it; I think we can get back."

"I know we can. Absolutely."

Guinevere checked her glitter-coated silver wristwatch.

"I've gotta go to English Lit. Let's try to do a movie this weekend. I can think of three or four I want to see," said Guinevere, abruptly shifting the topic to protect her friend.

"Yeah, all right," said Kristi Lou, mechanically wiping her domed cheeks as if tears had dripped upon them.

"I'm going to call Marsha and invite her. She'll perform her rituals quietly. I trust her."

"Yeah, that should be funny. I know Marsha can do her favorite number—4—without making noise. I wonder if she'll buy four candy bars and stack them just so … well, I shouldn't make fun …"

"Oh yes you should. Don't worry about it; you're just joking in a good-natured way. Oh, you know, Marsha told me her birthday happens this month, here in May, but she won't say what day … it's an

OCD-fueled inhibition—something about her birthday doesn't have adequate four-ness."

Guinevere looked away from and then back at Kristi Lou.

"I may as well tell you now."

"Oh no. What? Another bad thing? Yes, it is, isn't it? What is it?"

"Marsha is going to do what I'm going to do. She's moving, too."

"No! No. Just no. I'm losing two friends in one summer—my best friends, maybe my only friends in the world."

Kristi Lou again became tearful without fully crying.

"Is Marsha moving to the other side of Earth?"

"No, no, no. My timing is way off. I got you to feel better but now I'm making you feel bad by telling you too much too soon. I apologize."

"No, Guinevere; it's all right. I need to know."

"As a matter of fact, Marsha's just moving across Arkansas a-ways, to the northwest corner of the state, to Fayetteville."

"Fayetteville? Marsha's moving to Fayetteville? That's where my Aunt Charlene lives."

"Yeah, I remember you told me that. Anyhow, Marsha told me a few minutes ago at my locker. She just found out last night. It's happening fast. Her dad's company is transferring him, too. They're moving in about three weeks from now, in mid-June. So she and her family will move in spring, not summer. You know, most of the month of June is in the season of spring. The summer equinox always arrives around June 20, 21, 22 or thereabouts. Many people want to see June as a summer month but it's really mostly a spring month."

Guinevere glanced at the books under her arm as she shifted her grip on them, and then smiled up at Kristi Lou.

"OK, I just threw that factoid in there to try to ease the seriousness of what we're talking about."

"Yeah, I knew that's what you were doing—a little normal talk to take some of the sting out of what, what we're…what we're dealing with. But…so, if she's just moving to Fayetteville, maybe I'll still be able to see her when I'm there to visit Aunt Charlene; I don't know, though. As we were saying, often kids drift apart."

"Yes, but as we were also saying, that unhappy ending doesn't always come to fruition. Some kids drift apart but later get back together. Some kids keep their friendship going, whether they drift apart or not, even into adulthood. Even while they're away from each other, they preserve the feeling. It may fade somewhat sometimes, but it can be rekindled later 'cause it's been preserved. Our friendship is like a jar of jam."

"Are we strawberry preserves or fig preserves or blueberry preserves, or boysenberry preserves or…"

"We're girlsenberry preserves. Anyway, I'll call Marsha and get back to you on the movie."

"Yeah, why can't we have our own berry? OK. The movie thing sounds good," said Kristi Lou. "I'll check with Mom and Dad and let you know soon—before the end of the week. And, uh, speaking of fruits, I like your word 'fruition,' you vocabulary queen."

"I've never been called 'vocabulary queen' before. That's a bunch better than the names Kirsten calls me. OK, then. See ya."

"Oh, one more thing…" said Kristi Lou.

"Sure. What's that?"

"BFF?"

"BFF. I promise," replied Guinevere, who held her gaze upon her gangly friend's eyes for three full seconds, with sincerity in her face and her voice that saturated Kristi Lou with a heartening reassurance.

****

Kristi Lou, Guinevere, and Marsha chummed around for the final few weeks of the school year and the first half of June, often visiting at one another's homes, going out to eat, texting, and orchestrating three-way phone chats. On rare occasions, so as to maximize their joy arising from conversation uninterrupted by OCD incidences, Kristi Lou and Guinevere furtively excluded Marsha from their get-togethers. These exclusions always prompted feelings of guilt; they took strenuous measures to hide such rendezvous from their hypersensitive friend. Marsha never knew.

Marsha's final night before moving from Little Rock was June 17. She had Kristi Lou and Guinevere over at her house. The girls sat among and on loaded boxes sealed with brown tape and talked while Marsha's parents continued busily packing. Kristi Lou was sure that she witnessed at least two instances of Marsha's mom gazing fixedly at a certain white box in the dining room as she approached it, then slowing her pace, followed by the center of the seat of her pants being sucked into her buttocks cleft. Kristi Lou saw what appeared to be an image drawn with a black felt-tip marker pen on the box's side. While Marsha was looking at Guinevere as they chatted, Kristi Lou discreetly zoomed in on the drawing and saw that it resembled a road sign with numerals drawn inside.

Oh my god. Mrs. Mellow drew a mile marker on the box and she's performing her butt-cheek flexes. I remember that day with Mr. Battle, and Marsha once told me more about it. Oh golly; she's fanny flexing with a box. She timed them, too. No wonder Marsha is so screwed—no, quit it. She's a nice mom.

Mr. and Mrs. Mellow were quite cordial, as always, toward Guinevere and Kristi Lou. Mr. Mellow politely told them that Marsha had to go to bed by no later than nine o'clock, as she had to get up the next morning at 5:15. The moving van people were due at the front door at about 6:20, and their departure for Fayetteville was to commence by about 11:00.

Kristi Lou and Guinevere, at the same moment, hugged Marsha

Mellow goodbye in the driveway, forming a triumvirate of huggers. Marsha and Kristi Lou cried softly while embracing.

Marsha hugged Guinevere quickly four times, with a quick pull-back and then another quick hug until four hugs were accomplished.

"We'll be together again, Marsha. And, as they say, we will stay in touch—phone calls, texts—and I mean that."

"I know you do. And we will."

Turning her attention to Kristi Lou, Marsha hugged her with the same four-centric routine, but had to direct her hugs sharply upward. Both girls giggled.

"I'm just moving to Fayetteville, Kristi Lou. So, you can…I hope we can…let's at least see if we can see each other some."

"Oh, I want to do that so much. Maybe our parents can drive us over. But I can definitely look forward to seeing you when we're in Fayetteville to visit Aunt Charlene. I still don't know how close your house will be to her house. But, anyway…I love you, Marsha Mellow."

"Oh my goodness!—as you like to say. I love you, too, Kristi Lou."

"I have an 'I love you, too,' just for you," said Guinevere, smiling at Marsha. "I should've said that a moment ago."

"That's all right. I love you, Guinevere. Thanks for all you've done for me."

"Oh, I haven't…"

"Yes, you have."

With Marsha waving goodbye from her soon-to-be-former front porch, Kristi Lou and Guinevere, now 40 yards away, looked back, in unison, while continuing to walk and gave Marsha one last wave before turning at the street corner and onto the other side of a row of high hedgerow.

16

KRISTI LOU, HAVING ALREADY LOST THE SAME-TOWN NEAR-
ness of Marsha and harboring doubts as to whether they would ever
connect in Fayetteville, knew the abominable day of Guinevere's departure had to come. Kristi Lou and Guinevere watched the movers
begin loading the huge moving van on a hot morning in late July. Mr.
Jones, sympathetic to his daughter's impending sorrow over her friend's
migration, had driven Kristi Lou to what was still—for another few
hours—Guinevere's house, situated only three blocks from the Joneses'
home. She wanted to spend as much of this day with Guinevere as
possible.

Guinevere's parents, despite the hubbub of moving, were glad to
allow her these final hours with her dear friend. Though having had no
more than a dozen conversations with Kristi Lou, they had developed
an abiding affection for her. They knew of her fear of her own height
via Guinevere. Mr. Lindsay, comprehensively educated, was not unfa-
miliar with genetics, and agreed with Guinevere that Kristi Lou was a
very pretty girl who would grow into a stone-cold beauty as an adult.

The two girls, while missing Marsha but realizing they both missed
each other even though Guinevere had not yet left, helped the movers
with things that weren't too heavy by placing such items outside near

the enormous truck. She and Guinevere were sternly cautioned by Mr. Lindsay to steer clear of the movers' pathways, especially when the men were toting the heaviest things, such as larger furniture.

The hours seemed to evaporate. At about three o'clock that afternoon Kristi Lou, moments after she and Guinevere professed their undying friendship-love for one another, stood in what was at that point her friend's ex-driveway, watching as Guinevere rolled away and out of her life.

Kristi Lou, raising both rope-long, slender arms as high as she could lift them, began waving wildly, with overflowing tributaries bucketing down her sculpted cheeks. She was beset with an urge to run after Guinevere's car, but that impulse was instantly quelled by an evanescent resurgence of her prime insecurity; with the north/south longitude of her giraffe-legs, she feared she might catch it.

****

Likewise, Guinevere waved, while twisted around in the backseat, till the sight of long, tall Kristi Lou was abruptly eclipsed by the same two-story house on the corner Guinevere had walked by going to school and other places for the past four years. Guinevere seldom cried. Mrs. Lindsay reached back and gave her a gob of Kleenex.

****

Kristi Lou felt as if her body had sunk inside a sadness that seemed to possess a physical thickness that could almost be touched; she was overrun by a sensation of wanting to peel away layers of heartbreak. Looking downward in a stupor, she walked off the driveway, oblivious to the fact that she had stepped several feet into the street. Kristi Lou heard the sound of rolling tires a safe distance away and, without looking up to see the approaching vehicle, nonchalantly spun around and retreated onto the grass beyond the curb and headed toward the sidewalk. Upon stepping onto the pavement, she noticed that she really wasn't too concerned about much of anything, inclusive of being hit by a car, except the idea that *Guinevere must be about three-fourths of a mile away by now.*

Kristi Lou loped slowly about five yards, and then, on impulse, turned around and went back to Guinevere's old driveway, where she stood still for just over a minute staring at Guinevere's old house, particularly Guinevere's old bedroom window. She dropped her eyes, turned away slowly, and then walked home.

17

During this to-be-remembered summer, Kristi Lou, now reduced to speaking with Guinevere and Marsha over the phone and exchanging email and copious text messages, would occasionally spot Mr. Battle in the grocery store where her parents, especially her mother, usually shopped. For some reason, Mr. Battle, whose house she knew was located about four miles from hers, seemed to have begun shopping in the same store. When they happened to cross paths in the store, she and her ex-teacher would smile and wave pleasantly, but with no conversing, save a "Hi" or "How are you?" and continue along the aisles. She once thought of introducing her mom to him there in the store, but she felt somewhat uneasy, so she declined.

****

One August afternoon, however, Kristi Lou did point out and identify Bud Battle to her mother. He and Kristi Lou had exchanged one of their brief cordial greetings after which he had pushed his buggy sufficiently far away so that she believed that her and her mom's conversation was out of his hearing range.

"That's Mr. Battle. That's him. That's the guy, my teacher, who I've

215

told you so much about—that we went through a lot with him being so short and me being so tall and us wanting to swap heights and being mad at each other for it. And there was that…that *incident* thing that happened that day. And, as you know, much of my therapy kinda had to do with him and what went on in school. But—I know I've told you before—it's OK between us, now. I actually like him pretty well. I think we both, kinda at least, have gotten over it."

"Yes, I believe you have, too," said Mrs. Jones. "Guinevere bolstered your self-esteem. And so did Dr. Carlisle. Anyway, Mr. Battle seems like a nice man. I hope he doesn't have too much more obsession with his own, uh, well…height-based issues. You know, I almost said 'his shortcomings.' I guess that would be a bit unkind, huh?"

"Yeah—funny, Mom. But, Mr. Battle's way across the store over there—see him?—so he can't hear you. He has shortcomings; I have longcomings. Oh well."

****

As her ex-teacher and ex-nemesis wheeled his buggy into the produce section amongst the fruits and vegetables, she continued thinking about him while her mom stood about 10 feet off to her side and perused the refrigerated chip dip. Kristi Lou had a keen awareness that most of her thirteen-year-old peers would not spend many of their summer moments thinking about the past year with a teacher, even one as peculiar as Mr. Battle. But she, as always, was cognizant of her own peculiarity, not only in regard to her height, but also regarding her mind.

She stood and watched Mr. Battle inspect fresh fruit. He seemed to meticulously evaluate each piece for bruises, as if he might either be repulsed by eating any bad spots or was a science teacher delving in pomology.

Why am I looking at Mr. Battle look at fruit?

As Kristi Lou stood unobtrusively watching Bud Battle shop for his groceries, she observed him finally complete his laser-focused inspections. He grabbed four apples, then three pears, and then two limes, bagging each type of fruit separately by gingerly placing them inside the grocery store's tear-off-the-roll, pale-green, transparent plastic bags. Next, he seized a pre-bagged sack of oranges. When she saw him finish neatly scrunching all four bags up against each other in his buggy and then smooth out the bags' wrinkles, something unknown to her about that action seemed to somehow trigger her memory of an impromptu episode she felt she would never forget—an occasion of coincidental overhearing that quickly morphed into deliberate eavesdropping.

She quietly drifted farther away from Mrs. Jones, who was now looking down and perusing salsa and other sauces stacked in their longwise, three-feet-off-the-floor cooler-chests. While standing near the summer squash and about 18 yards away from Bud Battle, sensing he was no longer consciously aware of her presence in the store as he lingered in the fruit section, she reflected back to the previous winter and the unplanned event that yielded certain stunning revelations about her teacher and herself that she was not supposed to learn but had secretly entered her knowledge bank, forever altering her perception of Mr. Battle, herself, and people in general.

****

Upon the insistence of her mother and father, back in late February, she had eventually relented and taken Guinevere's advice: she sought help with her emotional torment over her tallness from the guidance counselor, Ms. Goble.

After a single session, Ms. Goble ascertained that Kristi Lou needed professional intervention and directed her to therapy with George Carlisle, whose office was located on the other side of Little Rock. Her mom drove her there every Friday afternoon after school from the last week of February through most of May.

****

Following a therapy session one chilly Friday in March, while Mrs. Jones carried on what she knew would be a lengthy cellphone conversation with her sister, who was Kristi Lou's Aunt Charlene up in Fayetteville, Kristi Lou was allowed by her mother to leave the car and walk to the discount department store two blocks from Dr. Carlisle's office.

"I'm going to talk with Charlene for about an hour … oh, well, maybe less," said Mrs. Jones as she self-interrupted her chattering with Charlene and then glanced at the two battery bars displaying in the upper right corner of her phone screen. "I thought I charged this thing last night, but apparently I didn't."

"But you've got that car battery charger in the glove box, remember?"

"Oh yeah, that's right; so I do. Oh, and I'll be walking over there across the street to Snappy Mart for a few groceries. So, if I'm not here when you get back, that's where I'll be. Anyway, so, you can go to the store for about 30 minutes or thereabouts. If you buy anything, I advise you to be frugal with your allowance. But be back here by no later than 4:30, OK?"

"OK. I will. Thanks, Mom. See you someday soon, Aunt Charlene," said Kristi Lou as she leaned across the front seat to speak directly into her mom's high-end mobile phone.

"I'll look forward to it," replied Aunt Charlene.

"I love you, Aunt Charlene."

"I love you back, Kristi Lou."

Kristi Lou sat back up and then merrily bounced herself off the seat and out of the car. "Bye, Mom. Back in a jiffy…well, probably not a regular jiffy…maybe a protracted jiffy," she said, and then closed the door.

Kristi Lou strolled down the sidewalk from the two-story, multi-office, brick building where she and her mom had just completed their weekly conference with Dr. Carlisle. She meandered casually up to the Mr. Right Price storefront. After grabbing the handle of the entrance door, she stopped and stood still for about a second, then yielded to an impulse to instead venture toward the high-brow, expensive coffee shop two stores down from Mr. Right Price.

As her hand came within six inches of the door to Coffee Snoots, Kristi Lou thought she caught a glimpse of an animal racing toward the patch of woods behind the café.

Oh my goodness! Was that a kitty-cat? He could be lost. He might need rescuing. I've gotta go check.

Unwaveringly softhearted, Kristi Lou trotted quickly into her potential rescue mission and into Coffee Snoot's small backyard. She entered the cleared-out area, which was about 20 ft. X 25 ft. worth of crisply mowed grass. She saw the same movement again, but only via an unclear peripheral view and just for a split moment. Something darted into the woods. She followed about three yards beyond the landscaped lawn and into wooded thickets, where she spotted a shaggy, twitching tail bolt up a tree, vamoosing frantically away from her.

Oh, that's a squirrel. He belongs out here, so he'll be OK. All right, then. He ran cheetah-fast to get away from me. I know squirrels almost always hightail it, but he went faster—'cause I'm so tall I look like Godzilla to him.

As she turned back toward the grassy section flanking the rear wall of Coffee Snoots, she stood still and continued her conversation with herself.

Of course, I just finished my session with Dr. Carlisle and he said the same reassuring things he always says and what Guinevere says—that lots of people will be around my height when I get a little older and lots of people will even be taller than I am, but … I just … I don't know …

As Kristi Lou was thinking of Dr. Carlisle, while standing behind Coffee Snoots at the edge of the woods, she heard his voice. Startled, she froze in place with her eyes aimed toward the ground while seeing nothing.

Is that Dr. Carlisle? What's he doing here? Did he walk down here after talking with me and Mom?

Flanked by several thick trees that were much taller than her, Kristi Lou was not visible to Dr. Carlisle and another therapist, Helen Harcourt, M.D., a psychiatrist. The two colleagues shared the same office space together. Kristi Lou had seen her on occasions in the small hallway, and had noticed her and Dr. Carlisle briefly exchange greetings.

Here in this impromptu juncture, Kristi Lou leaned privily to her right and peeked soundlessly beyond the lengthwise-grooved, light-gray bark environing the massive oak behind which she was semi-crouching. She saw them walking closer, about 20 feet away, strolling unguardedly through the coppice and between some Arkansas pines. Kristi Lou realized that they thought their conversation was being conducted in total privacy. Both psychotherapists spoke freely, with not the slightest attempt at susurrus. The first articulation she was able to distinguish from garbled wordage was halfway through one of Dr. Carlisle's sentences.

" … bright girl, and she's making real progress toward realizing her tallness is something she'll one day come to embrace. And, also, I can tell you Kristi Lou's doing much better at not feeling so insecure when she's near your short client in the classroom. She's coming around."

"Good. I'm glad she's getting there. As I told you last week, I wasn't sure I could take Bud as a patient from Jack Jackerson after Jack's illness forced him into retirement. But I'm glad I fit him in because I enjoy working with him. Bud is still tormented by his shortness, but the intenseness is subsiding, and he really doesn't carry within him any enmity toward the girl anymore; there's actually some amity there. He still feels threatened by her, but they had that quick-but-nice conversation after what they call *The Incident* and—right there in the classroom they had it, just a pleasant little exchange—and he's more OK with her since then, but he's still got a ways to go with his emotional security. There's still the ongoing rampancy of his dreaminess, but he's not a luftmensch; he works quite diligently at earning a living as a teacher and …"

Both therapists turned their faces away from Kristi Lou's direction, causing her to hear only vague mumblings. During this interval of indiscernible interlocution, she panicked mightily within herself.

Oh my god! OMG, OMG, OMG! That woman is Mr. Battle's therapist! And she … she was, she was talk … they were talking about me! And they were talking about Mr. Battle! I mean, she's … she's right there in the same building and that means that Mr. Battle comes here … there … right there in the same build … OMG! I could have seen Mr. Battle there all these weeks, and I could still see him in there—in that building, and, but … OMG! I mean … I wonder if he's seen me there. OMG, OMG!

The voices once again became audible. As Kristi Lou, heart pounding and wobbly on her feet from intense sudden-onset anxiety, stood mesmerized behind tall trees, she couldn't help herself as she was besieged by racing thoughts, such as this bizarre coincidence—*is it a coincidence or is it not a coincidence?*—combined with the irony that trees—the very plant life to which nemeses such as Nate Perkins sadistically compared her and that she often saw herself as resembling—were concealing her from the view of the man who was the professional trying to guide her toward overcoming her aversion to her tree-like height.

As she continued to listen in feverishly on the therapists' incautious tête-à-tête, with no shame of being an eavesdropper, she came to not care about being caught—except for the likelihood that awareness of her hitherto furtive presence within this womb-ish boscage would likely ruin an unfiltered flow of mind-jolting, staggering information.

After about 15 or 20 seconds of both analysts praising their respective patients, Kristi Lou was stunned at what she heard over the next seven minutes of auditory spying.

Dr. Harcourt related to Dr. Carlisle every detail of Bud Battle's fantasia—Bud's surreal sweven starring Kristi Lou as the conquering 50-foot woman from Bud's personal Hades. While also elaborating, now and then, on some of Bud's other strange obsessions that she believed underscored her diagnosis of him as a borderline schizophrenic, Dr. Harcourt spent most of her remarks describing Bud's dream that night. Kristi Lou heard herself chronicled as the star antagonist.

While most twelve-year-old girls would've found such a revelation to be either a source of embarrassing and/or creepy, frightening confusion or of ammunition for jubilant and ego-fulfilling gossip, Kristi Lou, upon absconding away from the therapists, ventured deeper into the copse where she felt a deep feeling of empathy toward Mr. Battle rush into her chest. After she observed that she was headed the wrong way and quickly reversed her direction, she stepped hastily but cautiously toward her destination of the Coffee Snoots storefront. She did not want to reveal her retreating presence by causing any dry leaves or twigs to crepitate under her clean, snow-white sneakers.

While walking, she realized that of great significance to her was her feeling, itself; Kristi Lou, once again under the spell of what was anomalous introspectiveness for a person of any age, was immediately attuned to the fact that she recognized that she had begot this empathetic feeling, and she was more relieved than pleased that this sensitivity lived within her.

Abandoning her intended stroll while waiting on her mother, Kristi Lou walked straight back to the car, used the spare key her mom let her carry, got in, and stared through the windshield. Not seeing anything in her sights other than a pair of cavorting mockingbirds fluttering about, she fell into a deep meditation about school, Mr. Battle, his shortness, her tallness, and what she thought she should consider important—that is, whether or not she could actually coerce herself to think and feel the thoughts and feelings by which she believed she should be governed.

Like Dr. Carlisle said, those psychological personality tests show I'm way off-the-charts serious for somebody who's not quite thirteen—serious about many things. I'm so serious. Why am I like this? Seriously. I don't know why I am how I am. And now I know that Mr. Battle thinks I look like I'm 50 feet tall. But he can't help it and he hates being so short and I make him feel shorter.

Kristi Lou, after about a quarter-hour of intense obsessing, became emotionally exhausted and fell asleep with her head against the front passenger window. Deep into a few minutes of solid sleep with no dreaming, she was awakened by the sound of her mother opening the trunk into which Mrs. Jones placed five brown-plastic grocery bags.

"Hey," said Mrs. Jones, as she shut her door and reached for her seatbelt. "Did you have a cheery stroll? Do you have any money left?"

"Mom," said Kristi Lou, ignoring her mother's questions, "I've got to tell you…I just, I just overheard Dr. Carlisle talking in the woods to Mr. Battle's therapist and they talked about me and how I'm so tall and he's so short and he's maybe getting better and I'm maybe getting better at not being so freaked out by all that and…"

"What? You think you heard them talking in the woods? You sound like some kind of a nut."

"Gee thanks for that, Mom. I mean, Dr. Carlisle is my therapist and that means I need therapy so, yeah, I guess I might be a nutter—as they say in England. Anyhow, don't drive yet. Just listen, OK?"

Kristi Lou explained, in obsessive detail, what had transpired.

"Well, that's really something else…the timing and everything," said Mrs. Jones.

"I know."

"All right. You should tell Dr. Carlisle about this during next week's session."

"Yeah, I will."

"He'll likely be embarrassed and apologetic, and he should be, somewhat," surmised Mrs. Jones. "But, looking at it logically, he and Mr. Battle's therapist had good reason to believe that no one would be listening in on them out in the woods. They should've been a bit more careful, though. But considering that they were indeed in the darn woods, I'm not angry with them."

"I'm not, either," said Kristi Lou. "Actually, it was quite informative. I think it may have helped me. I think it did help me. Yes, it did help me. But, yeah, I'll tell Dr. Carlisle all about it."

****

Kristi Lou snapped back to the present, there in the supermarket. While she had been remembering her auditory spying on her and Mr. Battle's respective therapists that had occurred in March, she had watched him go from the fruit section over to the bags of bread, which he had begun sifting through, obviously trying to make up his mind whether to buy hot dog or hamburger buns, or whole wheat, multigrain, or white.

My goodness, he takes a long time to decide what he wants. Why am I looking at Mr. Battle look at bread?

Kristi Lou was brain-bombed by another thought.

OMG! I still don't know for sure if Mr. Battle knows that we were having therapy in the same building, till I quit going about three months ago, in May. But he's gotta know, 'cause I told Dr. Carlisle as soon as I saw him again about overhearing him in the woods talking to that lady, Mr. Battle's shrink, and she, she, I mean, Dr. Carlisle surely told her and she, uh, she would've told Mr. Battle but... but maybe she didn't tell him... so... but Dr. Carlisle never would tell me, whenever I would ask him, whether he told her, that woman, Dr. Harcourt, so... I don't really know if Mr. Battle knows that we were so close in that building—the very same building—and talking to our head-shrinkers—about each other! And the shrinks' offices were just a few doors apart on the same hall. And, but... maybe our two therapists fixed the whole thing... scheduled our appointments so we wouldn't be in that building at the same time so we wouldn't cross paths, but... no... Mr. Battle must know, but... oh stop worrying about it... but I wonder if he knows... stop—just stop!

Bud Battle started toward the cash registers at checkout. Although prior to this August day Kristi Lou hadn't seen him in the store since July, she chose to not approach him, satisfied with their brief greeting awhile earlier. She turned and walked away to find her mother.

She impulsively changed her mind. Walking fast with her strides that still doubled those of Mr. Battle, she stopped about 12 feet away and called out to him.

"Hey, Mr. Battle."

Bud turned around, recognizing the voice before seeing its face.

"Hey there, Kristi Lou. How are you, young lady?"

"I'm fine. How are you?"

"Oh, I'm all right. Thanks for asking."

"Sure. Well, I say I'm fine, but, uh ... I ... I still miss Guinevere and Marsha. They both moved away. I don't know if you knew."

"Yes. I already knew that. But you know what?"

"What?"

"Sometimes life goes in circles and, presto, sprinkles some sugar on you. You never know what good things might be about to blossom like early-spring daffodils. That's a lesson I've been trying to get myself to accept."

"Yes, I know you're right."

"Yeah, well ..."

"Oh, Mr. Battle. I, well, I just wanted to say, uh ..."

Kristi Lou, for a moment, wanted to tell him something encouraging about his height, but in an instant knew she couldn't find the perfect words for such a profoundly sensitive subject, so she redirected her remarks.

"… I just wanted to say that I think you're a really good teacher and a nice man. I'm glad I was in your class."

"Well, thank you so much, Kristi Lou. Thank you. That means a lot to me to hear you say that. I feel the same way toward you; you're a very smart student, smarter than you think, and you're a very nice girl."

"Oh, thank you, sir. Thanks."

"You're welcome. Your friends Marsha and Guinevere helped me learn how to properly say 'you're welcome,' as I'm sure you'll recall."

"Ha-ha. I do. I do; that was earlier this year in class. OMG, it's funny to look back at it now, but you were so stressed. OMG. And poor little Marsha. But you tried so hard and you wound up handling it so well."

"Thanks, but Guinevere is the one who really handled the situation well."

"Yes, she did, but so did you."

"Well, thanks. Thank you. Well, I, uh, I better get home and feed my puppy and take her outside for her walk. It was nice seeing you again. We seem to run into each other now and then in this store, don't we?"

"Yes, we do. Anyway, it was so nice seeing you again, too."

"All right, bye now."

"Bye, Mr. Battle."

****

As she and her mom rode home, Kristi Lou thought how she had already come to accept Mr. Battle as a goodhearted gentleman, even before overhearing the discussion in the woods between their respective therapists, but that her congenial feeling toward him had elevated and become cemented afterward. She remembered how, for the remainder of the school year, she had reserved an understanding and a sentiment of kindness toward the teacher who feared that he was a micro man.

Kristi Lou then realized that she was, yet again, spending a quasi-eternity of time thinking about her former teacher. Although she'd just enjoyed a pleasant conversation with him in the grocery store, she still saw herself as astonishingly strange to be her age and having all these many thoughts about Mr. Battle rather than preoccupying herself with thoughts about boy bands or what's cool on the Internet or getting her hair just right or having or trying to have a crush on some guy from one of her classes.

"Mom, I'm still not normal."

"I'll second that."

"Gee whillikers! Thanks a lot, Mom."

"Don't mention it."

"So, how many kids my age do you think say gee whillikers these days?"

"You're probably the only one in the known universe."

"So, I'm just weird."

"You're unique, my dear."

"You're taking lemons and making lemonade."

"Well, you are my daughter, sweetheart."

"I love you, Mom."

"I love you, Kristi Lou."

While riding peaceably in her mom's car, Kristi Lou recalled how she had shared her knowledge of overhearing this would-be private conversation, which had not been intended for her ears even though it was about her, with no people other than her mom, her therapist, and Guinevere. Kristi Lou thought she might tell Marsha someday. With the exception of a couple of grownups who, for these purposes, didn't count, this knowledge had been viewed by Kristi Lou and Guinevere as essentially their secret. Kristi Lou had enjoyed knowing that only they knew—until less than an hour before when the specter of Mr. Battle's possible knowledge of the event had bushwhacked her brain.

I'll deal with it.

****

Following Marsha's move to Fayetteville in June and Guinevere's move to Toledo in July, a communication pattern developed. Over the next two years, till just before all three girls entered the tenth grade, they kept in touch regularly via telephone, texting, and email, usually making contact at least once weekly. Eventually, they went to occasional texts and emails, only. Finally, during the last two months of that period, their comradely communiqués had diminished to infrequent emails. Soon thereafter they became engrossed in new friends and activities as sophomores in their respective schools, and the girls eventually just faded out of contact, obliging Kristi Lou to concede that what she, back in the seventh grade, had feared might happen to them had indeed happened: they were, after all of their our-relationship-won't-atrophy protestations, merely another group of school-days friends whose vow to maintain their friendship forever was conquered by time, distance, and the entrance of other people into their lives.

Spanning the following five years after Kristi Lou and Guinevere walked away from Marsha while waving goodbye the night before Marsha moved to Fayetteville, Kristi Lou never saw Marsha again. Before Kristi Lou could drive, she rode with her parents to Fayetteville, as she had done since she was a toddler, to visit Aunt Charlene. But those trips from Little Rock to Fayetteville had always been scarce. On average, they made the journey once, maybe twice, per year. Whenever Kristi Lou called Marsha to arrange a get-together based on her and her parents trekking to Fayetteville, Marsha's family, it just so happened, was always going out of town to visit relatives, going on vacation, or going somewhere.

After Kristi Lou obtained her driver's license and drove herself to Fayetteville, the same thing repeated; Marsha, for whatever reasons, wasn't home when Kristi Lou was in town. Plus, Marsha's house was on the opposite side of the city from Aunt Charlene's house. The best Kristi Lou could manage was to drive over to Marsha's house even though she knew there wasn't going to be anyone home, just for the satisfaction of being near where Marsha lived. Kristi Lou visited Marsha's Marsha-less house in Fayetteville thrice before graduating from high school and going off to college in Detroit.

Once, on her final stopover at Marsha's empty house, Kristi Lou pulled into the front yard, got out and left Marsha a handwritten note, taping it to the front door, stating she had grown even taller since the last texted photo of herself sent several years earlier, and that she still missed her, and was saddened and a bit freaked out that they lived somewhat close but couldn't seem to be in Fayetteville at the same time.

Kristi Lou knew that she and Marsha, as well as Guinevere, had, because of the ever-present absence of their former around-the-corner propinquity, entered the fade-away zone of youthful relationships, just as Kristi Lou had dreaded.

****

Despite the fading, the three girl-amigos believed that they maintained an unwavering, albeit muted, shared affection which, while forced into hibernation, retained a pulse. They would often think of one another, sometimes in the midst of joking around and laughing with whoever was their present company.

18

AS KRISTI LOU STOOD ON MIRACLE BOULEVARD REMINISCING about how she transitioned from very tall seventh-grade middle school student at Mary Our Lady of Mercy to high school as an angst-ridden freshman on her first day in grade nine, she was juddered back to her hic et nunc, August 2, 2018, by the sound of skidding tires.

"Whoa!" she exclaimed as her inerrable body shook from a shot of fear; she was ready to leap aside, if necessary.

She looked up and immediately realized what had happened, as the driver of an upscale roadster carrying two other men had to slam on his brakes to avoid crashing into a nearby light pole. Upon ascertaining that no wreck had befallen them, the two passengers gathered themselves in less than two seconds to turn their heads in unison and resume their Cro-Magnon staring at Kristi Lou's enticing curves. She saw the driver, now driving away slowly, also look back at her over his shoulder while his car swerved for another 15 feet.

She watched the car turn the corner and go out of sight. She then spoke inwardly to herself.

I think they're all OK. Thanks for the kudos.

Kristi Lou continued standing on the street corner outside Downtown Secrets for another few minutes, and soon returned to dreaming about her tribulations with Mr. Battle and all that happened during that year of discovery. A pensive but warm smile subtly creased her face. It hadn't been all that bad—and some of it had been quite good. Standing there, in the dusty, humid breeze on the hard city street eight years later, she greeted the recurrent remembrance of how Mr. Battle, despite his tormenting humiliation, had indeed given her that munificent B+ in general science, at the conclusion of the first semester—before they had come to convivial terms.

Kristi Lou had long felt that she really had deserved no higher than a C+ for that class.

She hoped to hear scuttlebutt someday from a reliable ex-classmate to the effect that ole Bud Battle was doing all right these days, maybe still teaching at Mary Our Lady, and that he had perhaps finally found someone to marry—if she treated him right and brought him happiness. She envisioned that he might've even firmed up his tummy.

While wondering why she cared so much, Kristi Lou felt a sense of gladness upon imagining that her ex-teacher may've gotten his life ably underway, and she felt an appreciation for Mr. Battle having bumbled into a key developmental year in her life. He now seemed bigger and taller in her recollections, the recollected image of his stature having been nourished by the reflective yearnings for her yesteryear—of which she knew that no small part was her warmly inextricable nexus with him and her two lost-in-time girlfriends.

The three of them ... just one year ... but a triad of profoundness for me and my adolescent development ... for sure, they were ...

As she found herself in yet another instance of recalling that conversation in the woods she wasn't supposed to overhear, Kristi Lou realized she was once again catching herself in another state of flagrant abnormality.

How many twenty-one-year-olds stand on street corners making speeches about men being sexually discriminated against and also fondly think about their seventh-grade teachers? Then again, he and I did go through a strange, well, relationship, I guess… strange episodes… strange times … strange personalities … strange brains. Holy moly, I am strange.

She was aware of the fervor of her self-awareness.

Shooting a casual impromptu glance downward at the soaring hemline of her crimson miniskirt, Kristi Lou wistfully pined for those old days of drama which had been laced with innocence.

But, wait a moment, here. Over the years, yeah sure, I've thought back to Mr. Battle and the girls, but just lately it's… I don't know… it seems like it's sorta increased. Something's maybe triggering me to think about those middle school days more than I usually do, but… I don't know what that would be.

As Kristi Lou continued to stand still on the sidewalk, she looked around at the ramshackle buildings and again listened to her thoughts.

Yeah, as I was just saying, I don't think most people my age are so nostalgic and daydream so much about the past. But that's OK; I don't care that I'm odd like that. But, on the other hand, I do care. But anyhow, I'm not going to only look ahead; I'm going to continue to look back to bygone times, too. The past is where I've learned lessons and from where I owe debts of gratitude for those who've helped me along my pathways. I'll do breaststrokes in my mind's Lake Anamnesis. I will be both futuristic and pastistic. Pastistic? Did I just say 'pastistic'? Yes. English language, with thee I taketh liberty. Anyhow, there's no contradiction 'cause I've got room for both polarities. That's me. That's how I roll. How I roll? Did I just say 'how I roll'? Yes. Nobody says that anymore. Oh well, it seems that you do. And, so do I. Yes, we do. Good grief. Did I just say 'good grief'? Yes. Nobody who's twenty-one says that. Well, it seems that you … Stop. Now. OK.

****

Her whimsical self-analysis was suddenly blotted by the sight of that bizarre car, rolling slowly but gracefully—almost floating—down the dimly lit street. "There it is again," she uttered. "It moves sorta like a gazelle on wheels."

Kristi Lou thought she had seen it on Miracle Boulevard about 12 to 15 times recently, and there was always something odd about it. The windows were tinted to near opaqueness, which would seem to offer a logical reason as to why she never saw a person behind the steering wheel. But she noted to herself that these windows were not just tinted; these windows were very, very, very darkly tinted—darker than she'd ever seen windows on an automobile. She wondered how the driver could see to drive.

Beyond the black-dark tinted windows, there's some overall weird thing about that car. I just can't put my finger on it.

The car, hazel in color, wearing a glossy yellowish-brown coat, appeared to Kristi Lou to be domestic or Asian—maybe a Ford or Chevrolet or Toyota—but any raised metallic letters around the car's trunk to identify the make or model or any other brand markings were not evident. Kristi Lou could not tell whether it was an older or late-model car. But it was always eerily quiet; it would glide so smoothly and silently it almost seemed to have no engine under the hood.

19

WHILE KRISTI LOU OBSERVED THE VELVETY AUTOMOBILE slithering down Miracle Boulevard, about three-quarters of a mile away an animated account of events was underway at police headquarters in the Drollman precinct.

****

"He came runnin' and bleedin' up the street lookin' scared as hell and yellin' 'that got-damn car got me, man! Shit! It just reached out and got me and slammed me around! That got-damn car grabbed my ass and started doin' shit to me, man—shit! I'm hurt bad. I gotta get help, man!' And then Willie, man, he just like kept tryin' to get away from whoever was after him, you know? He had like this terror shit in his eyes, man, and he started staggerin' round and he fell off the overpass there, man. You-know-what-I'm-sayin'? And that's where he landed. Right there on the freeway and got run the fuck over by that 18-wheeler, man. It was a got-damn mess. You-know-what-I'm-sayin'? That shit brutal, man."

The agitated eyewitness stroked his goatee, looked down at the two recorders—one digital and the other microcassette—lying on the table recording his testimony. He looked quickly at and away from the two officers who were interviewing him, and then restarted his theatrical description of events.

"Hey, like, I mean I known Willie since school, man, like for 20 years or more, and I ain't never seen him terrified like that of nothin'. He musta lost his mind when whoever they was got hold of him, 'cause he was screamin' that fucked-in-the-head bullshit, man, about some car gettin' him. I mean, not sayin' that some dudes got out of the car and got him, but, like that, some car got him, you know, man? Like, everybody in the 'hood here know Willie be stealin' and breakin' into cars since forever, man, but ain't no piece of metal car goan put a payback on him. You-know-what-I'm-sayin'?"

"So, he said a car got him?"

"Yeah, you cops, I know—you think I'm just some fucked up dope-head. Well, whether I is or whether I ain't, it went down just like I done said, man. I saw it all and I'm truthin' on ya. You-know-what-I'm-sayin'? Believe it or leave it, man."

The policemen gave each other a rather knowing look, which Franklin recognized and was puzzled by but did not ask about. Franklin sensed that the officers seemed to believe him more than he expected and were not all that surprised at hearing the details of his story. The officers released him from custody.

One officer spoke to Franklin as he walked out of the interrogation room.

"We know where to find you if we have any more questions."

"Yeah, I know that."

"Watch out for cars with bad attitudes that don't belong to you. It seems that some of them might defend themselves very aggressively. Believable or not, Willie could've truthed on you, you know?"

"Huh? Oh yeah, man. I know that, too."

****

Kristi Lou, after feeling calmly mesmerized by the bizarre car in a way she did not understand, followed her feet more than her brain as she wandered back into Downtown Secrets where she spent the remainder of her work shift not working. Exceptionally slow for a Thursday night, Secrets did not draw any of Kristi Lou's regulars. Rochelle, by contrast, was beyond busy with two of her most devoted consumers. All the other girls with whom Kristi Lou felt camaraderie were similarly occupied and thus unavailable for protracted conversation or as an audience for obsession-fueled discourses. She mostly sat alone at *my main table*, near the rear of the club, which for tonight, was fine with her. Kristi Lou felt not motivated by money this evening; she simply wanted to *chill and think*.

20

WHAT FRANKLIN WOULD NOT ALLUDE TO, REGARDLESS OF being preoccupied with Willie's melodrama, was his own preoccupation with stealing cars. He knew the cops knew, but they had never caught him in the act. He stole cars with thin gloves, like the other thieves trained in the art of auto-thievery around town, leaving no fingerprints, and made his deliveries quickly to various chop shops, not all of which had yet been found in Detroit. The shop operators were proficient about packing up and moving when the heat was on.

Franklin Loper, dark black, 5'9", slightly overweight, heavily bejeweled with multiple gold chains and an earring in his left ear, was always adorned in the brightest bling. Franklin, the personification of a prancing popinjay, had turned 26 in December. He had spent his entire life in Drollman, which, for decades, had continuously defined the stereotype of a simmering, crime-plagued, working-class community surviving deep in the bowels of Detroit.

Some of the citizens of Drollman managed to muster varying degrees of happiness. Most led grim lives, as they battled rampant unemployment and broken dreams. There were Drollmanians who were honest, caring, family people; Franklin was not one of them.

Halfway through his junior year, Franklin had chosen the route of high school dropout, surmising that education was for weak, dumb punks who didn't have the sense or guts he had to get The Mean Green fast by selling The White Girl.

He continued to employ such outmoded terminology into his 20s. He knew it was no longer considered cool among young people near his age to refer to heroin as The White Girl, but he knew to still say it to some of his older clientele. When dealing with most of his younger purchasers, his preferred jargon for heroin included Hot Dope, Antifreeze, Aunt Hazel, and Dog Food. Franklin wore with pride his street job designation as a professional supplier of heroin; he was proud to be a Balloon.

Although heroin, crack, and marijuana were his specialties, Franklin's business with no storefront could supply, sometimes via special order, just about any intoxicant desired.

Smooth Frank, an alias he had assigned to himself when he was eighteen and by which he had encouraged others to call him, had few ambitions besides daily drug sales, using his own products, and getting laid. He enjoyed boasting about multitudinous amorous conquests, regardless of whether they happened. And, when he did manage to implement *my ramrod*, such exercise was usually by way of a handy self-application or a $35 hooker—inconvenient details he omitted from his steamily embellished accounts of seductive studism.

Franklin envisioned himself as one day becoming an X-rated movie star—*I just need to grow my thing a bit longer and I can do that whenever I want to get in the porn industry*—or a skin-flick producer or director.

Franklin's real-life treatment of women included his penchant for intimidation mixed with crudeness, such as routinely addressing many of the women he encountered with "Hey, slut," or "Yo, hoe," not as retaliation against particular women having been abusive toward him or somehow deserving of such invective, but rather as his boilerplate salutation to them.

He occasionally remembered his former counselor, a vivacious LSW by the name of Victoria Beam. After a conviction for shoplifting three years before, he was required by the magistrate judge to see her for general counseling twice per week for eight months.

Yeah, that LSW bitch—she was a licensed social worker—Ms. Beam—with the name that fit her happy ass 'cause she was a sunbeam bitch, always actin' chirpy and cheerful. But, I don't know ... she was kinda nice and she did help me, so yeah, she was all right for a white bitch.

Ms. Beam told Franklin that the primary problem with his crude wordage was less about the words themselves and more about the attitude behind them, in that he seemed to truly think that sluts, whores, and bitches were all that any women amounted to, as in their *total essence.*

He recalled the sprightly Ms. Beam's phrase, "total essence," more than anything else she had said.

Ms. Beam actually was a nice lady, with all her total essence shit. Yeah, she was cool. She was nice. And she had a nice rack.

When in one of his more reflective moods, and especially when he thought of his departed mother, who had been instantly killed by a stray bullet from a drive-by shooting when he was fifteen after having sacrificed greatly to raise him the best she could as a single parent with limited income, Franklin would conclude that maybe there was some substance to Ms. Beam's total essence theory.

There are times when I get on down deep into my thoughts, when I meditate, yeah—deep ... I get deep, man.

He would think that maybe—in addition to viewing attractive females as, yes, objects of sexual desire, which he knew was dictated by nature, and that *girls do the same thing every got-damn day when they're turned on to men they're gazin' at and fantasizin' about*—he should concede that chicadees have the potential to be more than just fuck dolls.

Franklin was nevertheless proud of his raw approach to women, and decreed his own brand of "street decency." He had often boasted over the years to his contemporaries that "I treat my bitches right."

****

Franklin threw a post-obit party for "lewd dudes and their hoochies" at his '80s-style, stroboscope-lit, three-bedroom apartment Friday, August 3, in belated honor, ostensibly, of Willie Morgan's twenty-fifth and final birthday, which had come nine months earlier, way back in early November of 2017. Veracity was neither Franklin's, nor the late Willie's, chief virtue. In truth, Smooth Frank's little shebang, which merged retro disco with modern hip-hop, was a calculated business investment designed to attract potential new as well as repeat customers. The partygoers were expected to purchase his "mind-elevating commodities," as Franklin called his sundry array of illicit pharmaceuticals. Many purchases were made this Friday night.

There were copious displays of carnality going on at the party, in various rooms. Franklin stood in several doorways, enjoying the role of voyeur as he took in the orgy of sex and drugs he had assembled.

Finally, after englutting a bottle of high-alcohol wine, Franklin had enough of touring other people's sexual activities. *I'm gonna get some.* And he got some from two girls, both 19, drunk, high from smoking weed, and who had already had sex with other men during the festivities. He told them to "come into my office and I will cum in your orifice."

The three of them indulged in bacchanalia in Franklin's walk-in closet.

Aside from the focus on business and sales, Franklin felt his party was rather cool, packaged as it was to posthumously celebrate Willie having made it halfway through the turbulent 20s. And Willie's mysterious but dramatic death carried a macho component, and thus an element of coolness. Franklin felt he was cool to associate himself with such melodrama.

Franklin had all revelers bring their own food and beverage. "Simple cost control, man, in an *unstable economic climate*." Smooth Frank emphasized these words when enunciating them to sound intellectually impressive to his patrons.

As the night of old-school discoing and new-school hip-hop and rap moved past midnight, Franklin gathered some of his clientele, "my people," as he referred importantly to his acquaintances who also purchased his contraband. He wanted to assure them of the low-level of risk involved with doing business with him.

"You don't gotta worry 'bout shit. They know what I got on 'em," reassured the illimitably gasconading Franklin.

He went on to explain that most of the officers on the scene above the interstate working the aftermath of Willie's demise knew Franklin was a dealer. "They know what I do. You-know-what-I'm-sayin'? They know I'm a hemp consultant."

Franklin further explained to his guests that although he had been caught peddling his wares red-handed on several occasions, that "nobody goan do nothin'."

After the busts, charges were always dropped. Prosecution was seen as a procedure which they knew just might impel Franklin to be less than esoteric regarding the names of policemen who enjoyed his hedonistic products. That was not a revelation any of them wanted to surface.

Franklin concluded his speech. "Cops on ganja and scag ain't what they wanna get known for."

****

Franklin closed down his party about 4:45 a.m. and got everyone through the door. "How many y'all used condoms?" laughed

Franklin as the last of the merrymakers departed down the breeze-way stairs.

"I don't do no condoms. They kill the feel," replied one man over his shoulder. "Ask my female, here. She don't like 'em none, neither."

"He don't do condoms. But I do IUDs. And I do the pill," said the woman, smiling, as she playfully pushed her man-friend while they descended the outside stairway.

****

Franklin, without undressing, went to bed a little after five o'clock this Friday night, which he realized was technically Saturday morning, and fell asleep instantly, his slothfulness facilitated with help from some of his merchandise. He drugged himself whenever he wanted to sleep—and whenever he wanted to stay awake—and did not place himself onto the bed in the normal way for most people who sit butt or legs-first, but rather collapsed onto the bed in a free-falling blob.

Prior to dropping himself on his bed, he had swallowed, as usual, one of the brightly colored capsules from his collection of barbiturates—*my sleeping pills*. Franklin knew, of course, all the drug culture nicknames for any of his barbital-like capsules; he and his customers knew they were color-coded for those with streetwise lingo. Offerings included yellow jackets, blue birds, red devils, pink ladies, green Christmas trees, and his favorite, blue clouds. For this night/day of somnolence, he chose a blue cloud.

21

FRANKLIN AROSE SATURDAY, AUGUST 4, JUST AFTER 1:30 P.M. He pulled himself off his maroon-colored waterbed, on which he never placed sheets, preferring only ornate bedspreads and quilts. Smooth Frank staggered to his top-of-the-line, CD-changer stereo system. He put on some society-coarsening 2 Live Crew hip-hop, to be followed directly by loud-rapping British grime—a word that both named his preferred style of music and described the squalor of his bathroom, into which he entered, sat down inattentively, and then worried that he might not have enough toilet tissue, but finished with a paper towel dropped on the floor by a party-pooper. Without washing his hands, he exited to the sound of flushing water and navigated his way over and through bountiful debris to the refrigerator where he found a can of beer that had been remarkably left. He dropped himself onto his living room floor, leaning against the back of a dark-purple chair coated with several streaks of formerly-yellow-but-now-brown, partially dried mustard.

He spotted three leftover hamburgers from the party still in their wrappers but spilled out of the bag. He ate them. He spoke to himself as he wiped his mouth with someone else's napkin which he tossed back onto the carpet where he had found it.

"Man, this shit ain't been in the refrigerator; I hope it don't get me sick."

He watched TV, popped in some porn, and then climbed onto his couch and dozed off in the middle of the afternoon. He got up just after four o'clock and transferred himself to the bed.

Franklin awoke at 8:25. He thought about cleaning himself of the various odors from his party, now a day old, but eschewed a quick shower.

I gotta get me some action right now. They expectin' me to deliver over at the shop. I owe 'em some shit. Goan get me some car tonight.

Smooth Frank voided his bladder into his filthy toilet which was caked over with yellowish urine crust, then did not, as usual, bother to flush. As he sometimes reminded himself: *All I done is peed. Piss don't need to be flushed.*

He grabbed his stolen Smith & Wesson 9mm handgun, stuffed some car-stealing tools into his backpack and deep pants pockets, pulled his chocolate-colored hoodie over his head and stepped outside afoot, on the prowl.

Franklin was quite proud of boasting to his comrades that he had flipped—as they say in the car-theft industry for stealing cars—"'bout as many cars as General Motors ever made in this town."

I be fixin' to be flippin'. Yeah, it be time to flip some mo of dem mofos.

****

After about 45 minutes of peripatetic hunting, he found what he thought he was searching for.

Having walked six blocks from his apartment building and then turning right onto dimly lit Tracer Avenue, Franklin spotted what appeared to be a dark-red Toyota Camry. The car was locked and parked alone at the curb.

He looked around and no one was in sight.

I bet some dude done parked here and walked a few blocks to Downtown

Secrets to get some. Didn't wanna pay in them pay lots by the club. He goan pay now.

Franklin felt he had hit the jackpot with this serendipitous find.

A Camry—number 1 with a bullet—right in front of me. Perfect. I must be livin' right.

Smooth Frank, being a pro, knew that stealing cars was greatly a crime of opportunity. And he knew that few cars were currently more in demand at chop shops than Camrys, whose parts sold like the emblematic hotcakes on the automobile black market.

This shit is mine.

Franklin removed his backpack and reached into it, grabbing his slide hammer puller to bust by the car's door locks. While he had his hands inside his backpack, he shuffled his spare wires—tools of the trade typically used to connect a vehicle's battery to its ignition after breaking inside the cabin—to the top of the backpack, readying himself for a quick crank and a masterfully fast getaway.

He changed his mind about which device to use for entry. He returned the slide hammer puller into his backpack and replaced it with his rod and hook combo.

I got my Slim Jim. We ready.

Franklin made his move.

He started to position his rod between the driver-side window and the car frame to snap open the lock just beyond the glass.

He felt a sudden pain.

Something had him by his ill-fated balls.

Upon detecting Franklin's raised hammer coming toward the window, three of the cars pliant iron tentacles with finger-style appendages at their ends instantly commoved forth from behind the front wheels like steel eels, snatching and lifting him by his crotch 11 feet above the pavement. While he was being car-handled in midair, he wasn't sure if his yelping was due more to agony, fear, or humiliation.

Franklin's S&W 9mm was immediately impounded. One tentacle extracted the gun from his raggedy trousers and secured it inside the vehicle.

Franklin was held in place for about 12 seconds above the grille of the car so he could see its appearance transform from what had at first seemed to be a burgundy-colored Camry, complete with the standard chrome lettering on the rear that spelled out the name, to a gray, generic automobile. He then saw the color go quickly from gray to purple to blue and then back to gray.

After revealing itself to not be a Camry, the counterattacking car commenced playing with Smooth Frank.

The tentacles suspended Franklin upside down for about one second, and then flipped him upright for a moment, then turned him topsy-turvy again, shaking him as if he were a fear-stricken rag doll.

Franklin squealed in horror. Cigarettes, cash, coins, keys, toothpicks, syringes, lottery tickets, crumpled nude centerfolds, and extra-large condoms—which didn't fit him though the package labeling looked impressive—fell from his pockets in a bizarre shower of incongruous objects. One tentacle coiled pythonishly around his waist and held him airborne, while another unsheathed its claws to expertly shred and then remove his loose-fitting baggy pants. The third tentacle rudely maintained its clench upon his disgruntled testicles for about 20 seconds, before rising to play with Franklin's face by thumping him on his forehead, and sticking its fingertips in and out of his ears and up his nostrils, tweaking his nose and pulling olfactory hairs.

Then one tentacle raised him five yards into the air and forced him into a bent-over posture. A different tentacle pulled down his fluorescent red underpants. While held thusly in place, another tentacle brandished a device that resembled an old-fashioned wooden paddle and administered a harsh spanking to Franklin's exposed buttocks.

The car's loudspeakers blared:

"Here he is—another urban nasty boy gone amok! He enjoys vandalizing and stealing things, but he doesn't want to be vandalized or stolen from. He likes theft by taking, but dislikes the thief who takes from him, including any speck of dignity that he might somehow possess. His machismo is less impressive when he is dangled and spanked. He disapproves of being forced to swallow a dose of his own medicine. The flavor is foul."

A Polaroid-type camera arose from underneath an aperture in the hood to snap incriminating pictures of his dishonorable behavior and emasculating plight. The car, equipped with its own internal photocopier, mass-reproduced the libelous snapshots, preparing to cruise a few of the local streets and fling them around the 'hood. This was humiliation by litter.

But Franklin had more immediate and literal concerns, wondering whether he would suffer castration by car. Would he be merely squeezed into soprano inflections for several days of what would have been his usual boasts, or would he be slashed into a eunuch?'

The car disposed of Smooth Frank by depositing him in a narrow, unlit alleyway.

22

FRANKLIN SURVIVED HIS EMASCULATION WITH NO MORE than several bruises and whelps. He was arrested very early the next day, Sunday, August 5, by the Michigan Criminal Justice Bureau, which had been quickly informed of Franklin's caper by Drollman cops.

Sergeant Sean Nelson took the account of what happened from two beat patrolmen, officers Markus and Donnelly, who had espied Franklin at 12:14 a.m. Sunday, interrogated him on the spot, kept him there, and then notified the CJB, per their instructions should they encounter any suspect indicating he'd been assailed by an automobile.

Markus and Donnelly found Franklin curled in a fetus-like ball blubbering about being attacked by some "motherfucking goddamn car. Willie weren't telling no lie, man."

CJB agents arrived in a matter of minutes to make the arrest.

After interrogating Franklin and researching his criminal history, the CJB charged him with felony auto theft, carjacking, and transporting stolen materials across state lines.

The CJB, citing overcrowding at other facilities, decided to warehouse Franklin in the Drollman jailhouse, with no objections emanating from Drollman authorities. Franklin knew that some local cops would be nervous as to whether he would reveal their indiscretions as purchasers of his black-market substances. But he was unsure as to how he could use such knowledge to leverage any breaks from the CJB, as its people were with the state law enforcement division and he had nothing on them to damn them if they pushed for prosecution.

Most potential legal witnesses in Drollman did not like cops. They liked Franklin's hallucinogenic products, though, so there was reluctance to rat Franklin out.

Loyalty and getting high were not the only things preventing local denizens from talking; they were just as scared of the castigatory car as were the thieves.

****

"So, Franklin finally got his," said Sergeant Nelson.

"Yeah, we knew we'd get him someday," agreed Donnelly.

"We didn't get him; that mercenary car got him," corrected Markus.

"Yeah, that's true. Of course, some among us—present company excluded, I'm sure—don't necessarily want Franklin to go down. Anyhow, I just checked on him. He's huddled back there in his cell shaking like a pompom, staring at the floor," said Donnelly.

Nelson sat at his desk and looked around at some working girls that had just been brought in for their customary one-nighter in the slammer before being bailed out and back on the street again the next night.

"Damn. There's Nellie Jean again. When's she gonna quit the whore life? And there's Wilhelmina. They used to be over at Downtown Secrets till a few months ago. We didn't mess with 'em when they stayed indoors at Secrets."

"They'll quit when men quit liking sex," said Donnelly. "I'm not sure that'll happen anytime soon."

"Yeah," replied Nelson, "I think you might be right with that prediction. Anyways, I gotta tell the captain tomorrow about another one of these car assaults," said Nelson. "I'll tell him first thing when he comes in in the morning. I really don't know if he wants to do anything to stop it, seeing as how auto-theft and carjacks are down to about nothing 'round here. But I know he wants to know what the hell is going on. What is this car?"

****

The local police as well as the Criminal Justice Bureau were, as August progressed, learning more about the car. For every episode of the car fighting back against its attackers, they were finding copies of the perpetrator in action as he was first getting ready to strike the vehicle; the authorities then knew he was guilty—a vandal or bandit. The authorities also knew the macho street cred of thieves and jackers always took a hit to the scrotum. They knew that when accosting this car, the intrepid car snatcher, whoever he was, became swallowed by instant ignominy. The effect was, as Marcus once put it, "Reputation annihilation."

The cops on the local beats, as well as the station commanders, knew of this recently manifested cryptic phenomenon. But, the decision had been made to not go public via the media.

Some of the political powers that be, including city council members, were still in denial that such an aggressively retaliatory vehicle could exist. None of them had actually seen it, and, for them, believing would require seeing. Even when they entertained the possibility that such a car existed, these people were unsure what to make of it and, of greater import, what to do about it.

The top politico, however, knew about the car. Detroit Mayor Anthony Okoye had been briefed by law enforcement. His position was: monitor but don't interfere. "Crime is down in the streets in Drollman. Considering that fact, we shouldn't allow our egos to feel so threatened about someone else doing our job maybe better than we've been doing it that we let it cause us to try to stop something that's obviously working. Let's see how it plays out the next few days."

Then there was the worry living within some cops as to whether Franklin would retaliate against his arrest and incarceration by spilling the figurative beans about his supplier/customer relationship with those certain venal officers, who were bribed not by money but by the ongoing purchasability of Franklin's pleasure-drugs. The local cops who had been Franklin's clients hoped that he would emphasize that A, he was nabbed not by them but rather by the CJB, and B, they had always protected him from arrest and prosecution. They also knew that, should Franklin levy their worst case scenario and blow the whistle on them, their collective response would be to evoke the uncomplicated and time-tested L&D stratagem: lie and deny.

23

SUNDAY BECAME MONDAY WITH NO REPORTED ATTACKS ON—
or by—cars in Drollman.

District Attorney Susanna Willis wanted to quiz Franklin about the car. She called the jail Monday morning and spoke with Lieutenant Alfonso Ferguson.

"I want to stop in and interview this guy, Franklin Loper. Today is Monday, the 6th. How about if I come by tomorrow afternoon?"

"That'll work," replied Ferguson. "He'll be here. I'll be here. I'll put it on the docket."

"Good. I'll see you then."

She had seen the pictures and the defaming documents the car had produced and spewed, which the cops had become accustomed to gathering after each episode of an attempted car-grab gone bad.

****

Franklin festered in his cell. Four of his chums came by to visit, more as something to do, an event about which to yak amongst themselves later, than from genuine concern about Franklin; he had no real friends with whom he shared mutual trust. They spoke with Franklin in the visitation room. All five of them sat on black-plastic chairs around a small-circumference, two-foot-high, metal table with an ersatz-wood top. Smooth Frank viewed incarceration as a stopover with some decent free meals and a cot that was just slightly uncomfortable on which to sleep.

Ever rep-conscious, the best thing about being arrested, thought Franklin, was that his street cred was raised a notch—though he also dreaded the offsetting effect of his credibility being tarnished because of the humiliating defeat inflicted by an automotive punisher.

He knew the public defender would liberate him; the system had worse criminals than him to prosecute and deliver to the penitentiary. Notwithstanding the fact that although stealing cars was indeed a felony punishable by a trip to the big house, such lawbreakers were often not thus imprisoned; he felt such reprimand would never be imposed upon him.

But Monday night was different. He still shook with trepidation and anger about what that car had done to him. He recognized some of his convoluted emotions and became angrier each moment he let himself realize his fear, which he attempted to suppress when talking with his crew. Franklin abominated smelling terror within himself, even more than he resented its revelation to his minions. He told his homeslices about his episode.

"Yo—that car, man—I told you what it done to me, man. I'm goan holla at you what I'm goan do to that car, man. I'm goan fuck that car up, man."

"Yeah, man, we been hearin' some shit 'bout some badass car and all that shit, but, I don't know, dawg. But, yeah, man, you probably right 'bout that shit."

****

His bros left, not sure whether to believe him. "Franklin's fucked up,

253

man," said one of them, echoing the stated sentiments of the others. "Anybody be talkin' bout some car fuckin''im up and how he goan fuck it up back is fucked up."

But inwardly they couldn't deny that his story just might not be a prevarication; despite not yet seeing any of the humiliating pictures flung onto the streets by the vengeful vehicle, they were quite famil- iar with the mounting urban legend about a hardcore car plundering thieves in the neighborhood.

****

Monday night and then Tuesday morning rolled by, with Franklin still festering in his cell, sometimes pacing, often sitting and staring at the floor, always obsessing about the car. He told himself he was *goan get that car.*

But he also feared he might be scared away from the car-stealing business forever, though he loathed admitting any such fear, even in- wardly to himself.

Damn, I might have to get a job.

****

D.A. Willis arrived at the jail Tuesday afternoon, August 7, at two o'clock. Everyone recognized her. She started to quick-step by the desk sergeant, Fred Mackey, as she had phoned about 10:30 a.m. and said she was coming to speak with Franklin, saying that Lieutenant Ferguson was expecting her to come in. Sergeant Mackey called out to her.

"He's in unit 11, by himself. He was so spooked last night he was scaring the other guys. I don't think he's had hardly any sleep."

"Oh really? Interesting. Thanks, Fred. I'll catch you on my way out."

****

Susanna Willis, thirty-one years old, was 5'8", 121 pounds, with brown eyes, shoulder-length, brownish-auburn hair and slightly above non-descript facial features—somewhat pretty but not with the symmetry that unleashes blatant beauty, though she was certainly not a *butterface*, as Franklin and those of his ilk who espoused such street lingo would describe a woman who showcased a curvy anatomy but was facially repellant:

"She's got the body—*but her face!*"

Ms. Willis had given birth 10 weeks earlier to her and her husband's second child, but, unlike with her first-born, she hardly ever showed a pregnancy bulge. As of this day in early August, her figure was once again streamlined and comely.

While not solicitous of affirmation, she was neither hostile nor indifferent to reasonable, respectful male attention.

Besides, being a looker helped her get elected, and she knew it.

"Of course, I was also the most qualified candidate," she would non-boastingly tell others, and her self-assessment was accurate.

Ms. Willis had never met Franklin, but knew his type. She knew he'd see her as an educated piece of white ass. She always dressed with appropriate professional modesty, but, when dealing with suspects like Franklin, made sure the hemlines of her dresses fell about an inch over her knees so as not to create any distractions for them or for her.

As she strode toward cell number 11, while deliberately exhibiting the gait and deportment of overstated confidence with which many professional women comport themselves while working in a tradition-ally male-dominated environment, she heard five, maybe six catcalls and/or sexual innuendo remarks, though all utterances were subdued and barely discernible. She was unflustered.

She wanted to offer Franklin a quotidian plea bargain. If he would simply confess to his latest felonious indiscretion and pledge to no further lapses into recidivous recklessness, she would seek a significantly reduced sentence—with the standard-stock caveat that he blow the allegorical whistle on as many of his fellow car thieves transacting in his sphere of operations as possible. She knew he might invoke a strain of "honor among thieves" philosophy. She also knew he might dread merciless retaliation if he ratted on any other community outlaws.

Susanna Willis stopped in front of cell 11. She peered in at Franklin and noticed that he looked rougher than he did in his mug shot. She also saw that he was sound asleep.

She started to awaken him, uttering a partial syllable that went unheard. She cut herself off.

For some reason, I don't feel like talking to this guy now. Later. Let him sleep.

Willis spun around and walked the gantlet back the way she came in. She didn't stop at Sergeant Mackey's desk, but calmly glanced at him as she continued toward the station's exit door.

"As you said, he didn't sleep last night. He's doing that now."

"Well, wake his ass up," exclaimed Mackey.

"No, I'll catch him another time; I know where to find him."

"You can count on that. He's not goin' nowhere."

"Really? I'd say that's exactly where he's going."

Willis exited the building.

<h1 style="text-align:center">24</h1>

AFTER AN ANOMALOUSLY SWELTERING WEDNESDAY AND AN even fierier Thursday, Detroiters yearned for a break from an oppressive heatwave incompatible with a locality so close to Canada. They didn't get it. Friday came with one of the hottest August 10 nights in Detroit in several generations, so said the local weather reporters on TV and radio about this particular calendar date. By mid-evening, thermometer readings neared their prognosticated ascent to 101° Fahrenheit. The air was muggy and viscid, feeling as sticky as a partially melted cough drop that someone had spat into his hand to set aside for later, as if Michigan had somehow slipped southward into deep Dixie.

About eight blocks from the precinct station where Franklin was being warehoused, Bosco was looking for a car to steal.

****

Bosco Mason was never abused by relatives or anyone. But he bullied other kids as a toddler, as a first-grader, and uninterruptedly afterward. He was once classified by a well-educated, longtime-next-door neighbor who had often stopped Bosco from brutalizing smaller childern: "I hate to say it, but Bosco is a bad-seed child; he is congenitally diabolical."

Now twenty-three years old, 5'11", 125 pounds, with chest-length blond hair and small, beady, gray eyeballs, Bosco had dropped out of Michigan State University in East Lansing at age nineteen after his freshman year, sacrificing his studies for the pleasures of inordinate usage of alcohol and other recreational drugs. He broke off all ties with family and bummed around East Lansing till he was almost twenty-one, working as a hireling in short-duration, low-paying jobs with janitorial staffing services. Then he discovered the joy of stealing cars.

Bosco hitchhiked his way from East Lansing to Detroit around eight months earlier. He soon thereafter met Franklin through Willie, and had been one of Willie's "operatives," as Willie used to call his assistant car-thief malfeasants.

He knew Franklin had been apprehended, but didn't care.

He shouldn't of let himself get caught … dumbass.

Bosco loved to play video games, especially Grand Theft Wheels, often nattering to himself that *GTW inspires me to work harder at what I do.*

As an artificer of solipsism, ultra-hyper Bosco Mason unapologetically prided himself on living his life within his me-not-you ideation as an arrogant, peevish, one-dimensional go-getter, revolving around only himself. He hardly ever slept in his low-rent, efficiency apartment. He was a classic case of a high-strung super-fidgeter with shifty eyes always darting side to side, up and down, matching his bodily mannerisms—choppy and spastic.

Can't sit still. Gotta go. Outta my way. Life's short and it's all about me.

When he did have to put his gluteus in a chair, his hyperkinesia would not authorize him to stop fidgeting. His metabolism was so fast he *couldn't add no body fat if I ate 20 super-size-me burgers a day till Satan's ass got frostbite.*

"Besides," Bosco often said, "eating is like love—overrated."

Compounding his inability to gain weight was his cacoëthes for tobacco and coffee, of which he drank gallons per week.

Caffeine keeps me lean, mean, and obscene.

Almost never without a cigarette between his slit-thin lips, Bosco was a pack-a-day chain smoker, looking like an anachronism who fell off the screen of a 1940s film noir where seemingly everyone smoked in every scene. He often secreted so many pallid swirls from his nose and mouth that he resembled a robotic ventilation shaft.

"I can't live without my cancer sticks," he was fond of saying to his cohorts, seeking to be clever through irony but entirely missing the grim actuality inherent in his aphorism.

Bosco felt a fondness for hitting cars parked at apartment complexes. Lately, however, his top targets included parking lots outside of gyms anywhere on this side of Detroit.

****

This Friday evening Bosco was trolling the avenues for a grab. He would walk till he found something he liked.

A few minutes before nine o'clock, he set his sights on Lost Angels Fitness, located at Fifth and Geronimo St. on the outskirts of the Drollman borough. This was the lone gym in Drollman.

I been meanin' to do this place. I been passin' it to do gyms elsewhere in Detroit. Maybe that don't make much sense but it does 'cause those other gyms got lots of fine-ass automobiles.

Lost Angels Fitness's corporate management accepted the calculated hazard of opening shop in Drollman. But, at least their gym was in one of the lower-crime areas of a high-crime district, situated in the far corner of a not-too-run-down strip mall. The only roof-covered section of the parking lot was adjacent to LAF, which attracted a goodly number of non-locals to the Drollman gym via discreetly advertised discounts.

Bosco stepped under the roof and approached a quartz-gray minivan.

A Dodge Caravan callin' to me.

Irreverent-and-proud-of-it Bosco read the bumper sticker averring that "My child is an honor student at Chapel Valley Middle School."

So some rug rat fell outta your fuck-hole and you gotta tell everybody about his report card. Fuck you.

Wearing dark sunshades and a blackish-brown hoodie over his head, Bosco felt adequately anonymous. Hence, he audaciously ignored the multiple surveillance cameras peering down upon his worksite.

He got within five feet of the driver's side of the minivan when a custom-installed alarm system activated in the well-preserved, 1976 green Oldsmobile Cutlass Supreme parked in the slot next to the van, bellowing obnoxiously, with the outside lights flashing like fireworks.

As a crackerjack carjacker and thief, Bosco felt alarm systems were either an amusing joke or an irritation, depending on his mood. He knew that car alarms had long ago become very commonplace and were widely known as devices that were sometimes set off at the slightest provocation—such as a pop of lightning or another car's door slamming shut. He believed that alarms were so boringly ubiquitous that most people in public locations generally ignored them.

Despite his brazenness, he felt some concern during his advance. He saw most of the spaces filled with vehicles, and he realized someone could be seated inside one of them.

But he would not be deterred by such potential pitfalls. Unfazed by the alarm, he peered through the front driver-side window of the Caravan. He then walked around and looked across the van's interior through the front passenger-side window. As the Cutlass's alarm continued squawking, he observed an unusually large mischief of gym rats at Lost Angels for a Friday evening, including about a dozen willowy femmes pedaling maniacally on stationary bikes while several other women ran like lab mice on treadmills.

The dumbass moron bitches ain't goin' nowhere. They're so fucking feeble-minded. They look like a bunch of gerbils in a laboratory.

Bosco Mason zeroed in on one voluptuous, dark-eyed brunette whose rubber-banded, ponytailed coiffure wampished bewitchingly with each stride, exquisitely moving to and fro in unisonous accordance with her derrière and her breasts. He froze still in a lustful gaze as her curves in motion summoned his instincts.

Bosco wasn't alone in his primeval obedience to nature. He was surprised by two men who had just left the gym. Equally oblivious to the theatrics of yet another mundane car alarm, they seemed not to see the lurking larcener, as their attention was focused on the same feminine form that had mesmerized Bosco.

"Damn—I'd tread her mill," said one man as he and the other guy walked slowly to their cars.

"Yeah, you and I, both. She's a really nice girl; her name's Celeste," said his friend.

"Hell, I don't deny that she's nice; I'm just saying I'd like to get into her pants."

"Yeah, like about 99.9 percent of all straight guys anywhere between age thirteen and one-hundred-thirteen."

"Actually, being nice makes her even sexier."

"Yeah, I agree with that. Yeah, it does, yeah."

Bosco, having moved to behind the Caravan, looked at the men as they passed by, observing that they did not observe him, and then realized he couldn't stop himself from looking back one more time at the entrancing body on the treadmill.

As the two men drove from the parking garage, Bosco peeled himself away from the Dodge van next to the still braying Cutlass. *Damn things usually don't stay on this long. Somebody just might notice the son-of-a-bitch. Too close to the van. Fuck it.*

He stepped about 20 feet, and then stopped. He had an impulse. *Fuck that dumbass alarm.*

Just for *good measure*, he decided, in defiance of the uncomfortably nearby alarm, to go ahead and take the Caravan, of which he had stolen so many in recent years, Caravans being among the most in-demand vehicles at chop shops.

Moreover, he surmised, *it probably belongs to one of those dumbass ignoramus suburban sluts in there who thinks she's too good for me. A dumbass husband, two dumbass kids, a dumbass cat, a dumbass dog, and some dumbass fish in a dumbass bowl of water. All them slut-holes cheat on their loser-ass men, anyway. Fuck 'em.*

Bosco defiantly re-approached the Caravan. He intended to disarm the Cutlass's alarm, which he knew how to do with deftness.

He halted in his tracks in reaction to the Cutlass seeming to quiver. He thought he may've seen something go from the Caravan to the Cutlass. The alarm fell silent.

Why'd it quit? What—the van turned off the car's alarm? Screw it.

Bosco stopped next to the Caravan's driver-side door. He glanced quickly left and right. Seeing no one, the left-handed Bosco dexterously removed his pry tool from his front pants pocket and made his move.

He thought to himself, *I gotta upgrade to one of those things the cops use to pop open locks—you know, for those dumb-fuck assholes who lock themselves out of their own cars. Yeah.*

The Caravan's door slid open in a flash. Two tentacles with blunt-tipped claws grabbed Bosco on either side of his buttocks, squeezed his loose butt skin through his pants into fleshy handlebars and pulled him airborne inside the van, holding him over the bench seat behind the front section.

Bosco squalled and cursed.

'Fuck you, you fuckin' fucker! No, you goddamn fuck!"

A tentacle instantly took from Bosco's front left pants pocket the Ruger LCP 380 pistol he had purloined from the glove box of one of his recent car victims.

With a singular motion, Bosco's britches were stripped off over his misappropriated $300 running shoes, revealing sequin-covered fuchsia boxer shorts. In a millisecond, Bosco was thrust up through the moon-roof, then back in, then up again, repeating up and down like a pop-goes-the-weasel, which was the song played by the van's sound system.

At the apex of each rise through the roof, his long mane was forced downward and tight around his face while each violent descent back into the Caravan caused his hair to fly up and bear a resemblance to flapping jellyfish arms.

The up-and-down action stopped.

"Shiiiiiiitttt!"

One tentacle held Bosco several feet above the roof while another tentacle released a lavender plastic hand which repeatedly slapped his face on both sides and made his head turn back and forth as if he were a villain being pummeled in Saturday morning cartoons.

A third tentacle grabbed Bosco's balls and squeezed.

"Owwww! Fuuuuucccckkkk!"

While that tentacle provided his testicles with an unloving embrace, a fourth tentacle imposed itself near Bosco's throat and, with perfect execution, touched his skin with a tickly small brush while applying a fast-drying liquid that immediately gave Bosco a scaly red rash surrounding his Adam's apple, causing an itch so gruesome that he was maddened by it even though his scrotum was being compressed.

Frantically scratching his throat with his left hand while trying to free his jewels with his right hand, Bosco looked as if he were choking himself while trying to get himself off in midair.

"Shit! What the fuck? Help! Let go of my gonads, you fucker! You goddamn fuckin' fuck fucker! Fuck you, fucker! Fuuuuuuuccccckkkkk!"

The tentacles then jerked Bosco and his bleeding throat back down through the roof into the interior, cut open the bottom of his sparkling pink briefs and pushed his boney buns onto the console. After a tentacle removed the round handle from over the silver shaft gear shift, up and down Bosco went as he endured six seconds of two-inch anal insertions of metal.

Being ass-raped by a joystick was not what Bosco had anticipated; he just wanted to steal a van. It was not supposed to fight back, especially with such disturbing tactics.

Bosco screamed and then whimpered like a terrified schoolgirl as he saw the flash of a dozen pictures taken of him from numerous angles.

"No! Help! Shit! No! Fuck! No! Fuck fucker! No!"

Bosco momentarily lost the ability to form intelligible words, as he was reduced to incoherent and shrill ululations.

He felt confident that he was going to die.

The Caravan's tentacles jerked Bosco across the bench seat toward the rear doors which flew open with poor Bosco hollering as he was plunged down to the exhaust pipe. He was greeted by a spray of motor oil which one tentacle neatly smeared everywhere on his face. Bug-eyed Bosco resembled a 1920s blackface vaudeville actor with bulbous white sclera trying to jump out of his forehead.

The Caravan left with Bosco instead of vice versa. As the van screeched and sped out of the gym parking garage, Bosco, now entirely naked, itching, and hemorrhaging from his own fingernail-inflicted wounds, was relocated to the front exterior of the rapidly moving vehicle.

Two tentacles with large grippers repeatedly tossed him precisely five feet into the air—upward and forward—above the slope of the windshield, catching him on his descent just enough ahead of the shield to prevent him from becoming splatter. His nose and mouth were recurrently pressed hard onto the glass, granting his bloody face the appearance of mashed potatoes with seasoning sauce. With each toss, Bosco was spun around as if he were a gaggle of laundry in a wash cycle. Whenever motorists or pedestrians came into view, the van would hide Bosco by pulling him in through the roof, then flinging him again when the coast was clear.

Bosco's break-in slide hammer, screwdriver, and two packs of cigarettes went flying like aimless satellites into the night.

In the midst of such a violent crisis, choosing an imploration for rescue put neither coolness nor originality at a premium. Bosco, at this juncture, could think of only one thing to exclaim.

"Help!"

He yelled his invocation more than a dozen times, his pleas no longer laced with obscenities, looking shamelessly around for anyone to save him from calamity.

The retaliatory van moved onto the backstreet where Bosco always delivered his ill-gotten gains for profit. The Caravan took photos of Bosco's indignity and scattered about a hundred of them outside the chop shop.

The van pulled Bosco back into the interior and held him flush against the stereo loudspeakers, which yelled to him in disconcerting monotone.

"You steal but don't wish to be stolen from. You are a level-one hypocrite. You lose. You lose. You lose. You lose. If you pilfer again, I will find you. More unpleasant things will be done to you. You are advised to adjust your lifestyle. I am the van of your dreams."

As Bosco's ears throbbed from the up-close decibels at 120dB, he was rudely deposited with no clothes. One huge tentacle dangled him by his left ankle for about five seconds before dropping him head-first into a large waste barrel.

"Fuuuuuucccckkkk," whined Bosco in a feeble voice, with one last reversion to his preferred profanity. Exhausted and shaking, he removed pieces of moist garbage from his knotted yellow hair while sitting up inside the barrel amidst a pile of wet filth.

After rocking berserkly and overturning the barrel, Bosco extricated himself from the damp rubbish and turtle-crawled out. He tottered to the chop shop's front door, pounding upon it while shouting for someone to let him in.

"Open the goddamn door!"

His petition was heeded by Red Roofus. Known by the red bandana he always, as in his every waking moment, wore wrapped around the entirety of his head-crown, Red Roofus was one of the chop shop's chief enforcers and watchdogs. Red, one of Smooth Frank's occasional customers, was almost always at the shop, even sleeping there, as guarding the headquarters was his occupation.

He opened the door and Bosco stumbled in, bloodstained and terrified.

"What happened to your ugly flat ass?"

"This van…like I've been hearin' about these cars with these arm-type things that grab you when you're goin' for it…this van it…it…I was about to get it and…"

"Fuck. Another one of 'em? Got-damn things. Yeah, I know 'bout that. We all been knowin' 'bout that. One of 'em got Franklin. Is it gone?"

Red stepped over to a window and peered onto the street.

"Uh-huh, I think it is," said Bosco. "It told me with some voice in the radio, I guess, some bullshit sayin' 'you lose, you lose, you lose' and sayin' I ought not to be stealin' no more cars."

"Yeah," said Red Roofus, as he snatched some old mechanics overalls from a nearby locker and flung them at Bosco.

"You can wear this. Get in the bathroom and get cleaned up. I would say you look like shit but you don't look that good."

****

After about 20 minutes, Red dozed off in his recliner. He snapped awake upon hearing the bathroom door hinges squeak as Bosco exited the bathroom, wiping water and blood off his washed face with a ragged, not entirely clean towel.

At the same instant, they both saw flashing blue lights just outside the shop. About one second later they heard what they didn't want to hear.

"Police! Open the door. The building is surrounded!"

They both started to run toward the back exit by the alley but stopped themselves upon the word "surrounded" fully registering. They also saw that their presence was brightly irradiated via multiple flashlights intermittently shining toward them through the window glass along with surging streaks of illumination emanating from the searchlights mounted on the police cruisers. They scampered into an unilluminated locus.

Bosco, roiling within a full-blown panic—but opportunistically conjuring a quick and sociopathic, self-serving strategy—grabbed a nearby tire iron and savagely struck Red over the back of his head. Red crumpled into a heap against the side of a chair. Bosco, hearing the police about to finish breaking down the front and back metal-plated heavy doors, hurriedly reached into Red's hip pocket and seized his wallet, which he tossed aside after extracting three $100 bills, a 50 and several smaller denominations. *These ducats are mine now.* Bosco then lowered the attic staircase. He snapped off and pocketed the pull-chord, and then clambered up the ladder, turning around and raising the ladder at the rivet hinges one section at a time.

He hid from the raid.

Bosco overheard the commentary below, including confirmation that Red Roofus had been discovered.

"Here's somebody. His head's been busted open. Get an ambulance for this guy."

Bosco huddled with intense but quiet anxiety till the cops had finished their sweep of the premises. After about three hours of waiting, at about 12:30 a.m., Bosco pushed the stairway back down and then descended from his hiding place.

Bosco had been mauled, bloodied, and denigrated by a paranormal minivan while working his craft, as well as permanently ruining a working relationship with a colleague who would now surely want to kill him. He had narrowly averted apprehension by the gendarmes. He was thinking even less lucidly than usual, and the myopic Bosco was never a very lucid thinker.

There was a stash of opiates and stimulants, not found by the police, hidden under pull-up floorboards beneath the hollowed-out, bathroom-sink cabinet bottoms, where also lay a decades-old, rusty switchblade that had lain fallow for about 11 years. After pocketing the rust-coated, handmade-of-cheap-materials-in-prison, snap-open shiv, he smoked hashish—Acapulco Gold. He did some crack. He drank a half-pint of liquor.

He nudged the need to evade law enforcement to the back of his mind. He wanted relief from his turmoil. He felt deserving of something blithesome, a diversion from the unfairness he believed the unfair world imposed upon his assiduously effort-loaded life … *I work hard. I pay retail-store taxes. I ain't on no welfare. I deserve to have what I want.*

Bosco, perspiring profusely, slithered past the yellow police-crime-scene tape at the rear exit and absconded into the alley, blending into the sultry August night.

****

Bosco's tumultuous evening, which began before midnight as Friday, August 10, had morphed into a humidity-drenched Saturday morning. Bosco—notwithstanding sliced skin, whelps, and a predictably dismal near future—staggered along the streets seeking an oasis, anything that might grant him an assuaging distraction that would allay his reality.

25

MEANWHILE, JUST UNDER A MILE AWAY, ANOTHER BUSINESS night of blues music and carnality was underway at Downtown Secrets.

Kristi Lou had moved through an unremarkable eight days since Thursday of the previous week, including her monthly trip to the grocery store. She arrived at Secrets about 25 minutes early, coming in around 7:05. Upon learning that Rochelle had called in sick and was thus absent from the club, Kristi Lou chose to just hang out awhile, leaning against the bar and chitchatting with coworkers, primarily a 5'9" green-eyed redhead from Bloomfield Hills named Satine, with whom she got along famously.

Satine's real name was Bonnie Bell. She chose Satine as her stage name upon seeing a movie with a Parisian setting and whose heroine was a courtesan named Satine.

Kristi Lou liked Satine's choice for her stage name. Satine, despite the privacy concerns that prompt most sex-industry workers to opt for anonymity, was impressed by the fact that her beautiful coworker eschewed a stage name. Satine once told Rochelle that "most of us go by our stage names. Kristi Lou goes by Kristi Lou."

****

The night wore tranquilly on for Kristi Lou, composed of routine dances with calm customers to blues songs and nothing more. Kristi Lou glimpsed the gigantic cuckoo clock mounted and centered above the main bar. The hour and minute hands, illuminated in amber, were at 1:41 a.m.

As Kristi Lou, standing in the center of a human quincunx, chatted with another dance instructor, Hannah Savannah, who had walked into a congenial chitchat between Kristi Lou, Satine, and two other dancers, Satine gazed across the chockablock room crowded with sex-seekers. Someone caught her eye. She looked back at Kristi Lou, waiting several seconds for her to finish delivering her sentence to Hannah, and then issued an advisory.

"Someone's here waiting for you," said Satine, with a mordant frown.

Kristi Lou knew instantly who she meant. He was standing about 30 feet away, partially hidden by a support beam, intently watching the leggy belle.

"Yes, I know. I saw him out of the corner of my eye when he came in. I looked away before he saw me. I wish Hoke wouldn't let him in. He should be officially persona non grata here," said Kristi Lou, as both women refrained from glancing again in Bosco's direction.

Bosco had come into Downtown Secrets on several occasions during the summer, hungering for backroom gratification with Kristi Lou, who always assertively but politely rejected him. Per her immutable personal protocol, she was charily discriminating in her selection process as to with whom she would, as she put it, "do the thing."

"Bosco sorta creeps me out, not because he wants sex—which, as you know, I think is normative and fine—but because he talks so big and acts mean and steals other people's property, their cars. At least that's what they say about him. He just makes me have the creeps because of all that," Kristi Lou said to Satine.

"He gives you the creeps because he *is* a creep," replied Satine.

"Yeah, but it's because of what I said, not because of wanting…"

Almost on cue, Bosco approached Kristi Lou, walking at her—more than toward her—with his herky-jerky strides.

He was high, which all five girls sensed immediately. They were taken aback by the sight of his blood-stained face and arms. Bosco was a natural bleeder, and although the wounds inflicted by the retaliatory Caravan had clotted after his shower at the chop shop, some had reopened with his intense thrashing around, specifically when he ambushed Red and then rubbed and bumped against the floor and walls of the attic while hiding. His disturbing appearance was worsened by his badly tousled hippie-long hair, as well as the ill-fitting mechanics overalls, which were two sizes too large for his gaunt physique. Bosco's combustible personality was on hyperdrive.

"I want a dance in the back and I want it now. I'm tired of you turnin' me down. I got the money," insisted the irascible and importuning Bosco.

"No, I don't want to. I'm sorry. I'm flattered that you find me attractive. Thank you. But, I've told you before that I just don't feel right about it. It's like there are girls you wouldn't feel right with and you wouldn't want to be with them that way, so it's really …"

"Then go fuck *yourself,* bitch!"

Bosco, detonating into a paroxysmal fever, whipped out his squalid switchblade-shank from the overall's left-side pocket and swung at Kristi Lou. As the other women disbanded frightfully, she ducked backward and spun around. Before her spin, Bosco's knife cut through her pleat-style skirt above her underwear and sliced the lower-right flank of her abdomen. The lancination was just deep enough to elicit a three-inch crimson stria that immediately soaked into the fabric fractionally below the waistband of her light-teal plissé. The abrupt blood-streak coloration that marred Kristi Lou's clothing was accompanied by an incursion of stinging pain, which, for a lurid half-moment, metastasized to the farthest reaches of her body. The onset of agony, combined with a rush of visceral fear, caused her to scream.

"Oh-God-No!"

Kristi Lou retreated, turning sideways against Bosco's advance while instinctively raising her arms to cover her face. While still left-handedly gripping his knife, he seized her ferally, with his right hand snagging her throat and his forearm under her shoulder.

Growling like a rabid lupine, Bosco jerked her and lifted her an inch off the floor, then heaved her onto a table. But he did not stab her.

Summoning her natural athleticism, she quickly rolled off the table onto her feet and readied herself for self-defense. Bosco came at her. Kristi Lou tactically dipped herself and smartly shoulder-feinted a leftward escape run but then gyrated abruptly toward her right side and instantly—in one fluid, seamless motion—cocked her long left leg and unleashed a ferocious kick. Fortunately for Bosco, the heel tip of her four-inch pump missed his temple and thus he was not killed. The upper sole of Kristi Lou's shoe caught Bosco under his chin and launched him airborne over the same table onto which he had thrown her.

The explosion of her powerful gam sent hapless Bosco ricocheting off the wall into a spindly heap. As he staggered to maintain his equilibrium, he looked not unlike an inflatable air dancer wobbling spastically in a used car lot.

The collision jarred Bosco's knife loose from his clutch. It dropped to the floor. He inadvertently kicked it under a nearby table without knowing.

Bosco took a second to gather his senses. He searched in vain for his switchblade, and then went after Kristi Lou again. He landed a punch to her chest, making her reel backward against a chair. She fired her right hand with fingers bent and fingernails wielded like a cat's claw, scraping him downward along his ear, cheek, and throat, leaving four red streaks.

"I'll hunt you down, cunt!"

Bosco spat on Kristi Lou, with his spit landing in her eyes. As she wiped her face with the back of her hand, Bosco rediscovered his switchblade lying on the floor. As he squatted down to retrieve the knife, Satine grabbed a chair and smashed it across Bosco's negligible neck, sending him tumbling downward. But he put his hand on the floor and regained his balance, snapping back upright like a coil spring. After standing again, though, he stumbled forward, dizzy and confused, drifting sideward, left then right, and almost fell down.

Satine, still holding the same chair, whacked him with it again, this time banging the chair on Bosco's head. He collapsed to the floor. His efforts to stand and assail interdicted, Bosco commenced crawling on his hands and knees, with no idea where he was going.

Rushing from a dark corner came Soul Sister Raven, who had chosen a stage name from the 1970s and with whom Kristi Lou had nothing in common as far as attitudes toward men. Raven was the embodiment of a sex-industry worker who hates the very people she lures for money by exploiting their natural cravings. She grew up in a middle-class, mostly black neighborhood in Ann Arbor densely inhabited by embittered anti-male—more so if white—radical feminists, whose proponents comprised many of Raven's high school teachers and then professors at the University of Michigan's Women's and Gender Studies program.

Raven squirted lighter fluid at Bosco, but missed high, dousing the left side of Kristi Lou's face, with some getting in her nose. Raven quickly threw a three-candle table candelabrum at Bosco, intending to set him on fire, but misfired again, as the candles flew loose and then deflected off the back of Doris, the nearest server, who began whacking Bosco with her phosphorescent-green, glow-in-the-dark serving tray, launching shot glasses and splattering vodka over an 8-foot radius.

"Fucking goddamnit!" screamed Raven, venting her disappointment from missing her target and then dashing the squeeze-can of lighter fluid onto the floor, where it happened to land beside the only still-lit candle. As Raven stormed away toward another room, two drops of fluid were jarred out of the can, igniting a narrow, seven-inch stream of flames, which Hannah Savannah blasted with a nearby fire extinguisher.

"Hokey! Help!" screamed Satine.

Hoke, just arriving after being summoned to the scene by Dopey, heard Satine's scream. He dragged the thoroughly disoriented Bosco outside and beat him to the pavement.

****

Kristi Lou's raw wound was not deep enough to be dangerous, but stung viciously.

"It feels like a hundred hornets got me," she told Satine, who had put her arm around Kristi Lou's waist and was helping her stagger away from the main dance area of the club.

"You wanna call 9-1-1, don't you?" asked Satine as they walked.

"No, I don't. I don't," said Kristi Lou, wincing and holding her hand over her stomach as she steadied herself within Satine's gentle embrace.

"Why?" asked Satine, as she used two water-wetted cloths handed to her by another dancer to clean Kristi Lou's face—one to wipe lighter fluid off her left cheek, nostrils, and chin, and the other to dab out tobacco-mucus sputum from around her eyes.

"I just don't. I don't want to get involved in any legal situations if I can help it. And police coming here is not good for Secrets."

"I know, but…all right," replied Satine.

The gaggle of customers, having been treated to dazzling bar-fight entertainment, began to talk about the raucous affray they had just witnessed, with some laughing. The blues music, which had never been halted by DJ YoCrunk, became louder. DJ YoCrunk knew he needed to get the crowd refocused on dancing and sex.

****

Bosco, battered and bleeding anew on his face from Hokey's fists and Kristi Lou's claws, was released by Hokey, in keeping with Big Sam's policy of no killing, if avoidable, and no police, unless absolutely necessary.

"Our boss-man, Big Sam, ain't here tonight, but you best be glad for 'is policy—he say 'police and killin' be bad for business'—'cause if it wuz up ta me, I'd kill yo ass right here!" yelled Hokey.

"I'm gonna kill you to death someday, bitch boy!" hollered Bosco as he temporarily ignored Hokey, looking beyond him and glaring toward the front of Downtown Secrets, not knowing whether Kristi Lou, who was still inside and softly crying, could hear him.

"I'll take you out! You're gonna be a dead bitch!"

"If'n you come back here or mess wit' Kristi you da one goan get killed and I'll do da killin', you scrawny little car-stealin' punk!" thundered Hokey.

Bosco staggered down the street, not knowing where he was going.

"You're already a dead nigger! I just ain't wasted you yet! I'm gonna fuck you up! I'm gonna slice your throat one day, homie!" bayed Bosco, spiraling himself circularly while still moving away from Secrets.

"Uh-huh. I hear dat punk-boy talk. You best be keepin' yo ass away from here, you punk-ass sorry sack of shit."

"I'll kill you!" screamed Bosco, with spit droplets aerosolizing from his mouth. "I'll take you out! I'll take your ass out! I'll take you out like the garbage!"

Bosco regurgitated his thersitical threats in his hyper, shrieking way. Having been pounded and stomped so many times during his life by different angry people, he no longer cared about pride or any shame associated with losing a skirmish.

26

AFTER THE COMMOTION HAD SETTLED, KRISTI LOU, WHO HAD been seated by Satine in the first-floor, assistant-manager's office, received first aid attention from sixty-nine-year-old Doris Danielson. Doris, the club's eximious, would-shut-down-without-her factotum, pulled quad duty, serving nightly as waitress, supervisor, and house mother for the young women as well as on-staff nurse. She was an accredited LPN.

Doris, who viewed herself as among the mesdames who take their responsibilities very seriously, had fulfilled these roles at Downtown Secrets for 32 years, longer than most of the working girls had been alive. She seldom took a night off work.

"You'll be fine," reassured Doris as she tenderly lifted Kristi Lou's coal-black, sequined tank top while slightly lowering her teal plissé miniskirt. Doris then applied a topical antiseptic cream and adjoined a germicide-coated bandage. "It's mostly, as they say, just a flesh wound."

"But it sure makes my flesh hurt bad," moaned Kristi Lou, but with a forced faint smile as she sank herself more deeply into the large, spongy chair in which Satine had reposed her.

"I know. Have you had a tetanus shot in recent years?"

"No—not since I was about six or so."

"Well, you should go to the doctor and tell him that and let him take a look at it. It probably won't get infected, but it's better to be on the safe side."

"OK."

As Doris returned to her desk, in walked Raven, confrontational to the hilt.

"Hey, Kristi Lou, you know I tried to kill that motherfucking bastard. I wanted to light him up—make him a shish kebab, an asshole kebab. I guess I missed but I wound up saving your ass. Whaddaya think about that, miss goodie-goodie?"

"Thank you, but I don't want Bosco to die. I don't like him. He should be punished. Hoke did punish him. But I know he's got some good qualities somewhere in him and he doesn't need to get killed, especially not burned to death."

"What? He was about to fuck you up with a knife."

"Before you ask—yes, if I just had to do it I would've killed him or incapacitated him, if I had the power to do it, if—and only if—I felt like he was about to kill me, such as if I thought he was close to delivering a death blow.

"So, yeah, if I had a gun, I would've shot him as a last resort. But I ... I would've tried—if I were a trained marksman and I felt I had enough time to aim—I would've tried to shoot him in the leg or shoulder or whatever so he'd live on. But I would appreciate another person killing him or somehow controlling him if it really looked like he was about to kill me or maybe severely hurt me or someone else. OK?"

"Bullshit!" raved Raven, unharnessing the me-only, single-layered selfhood that calcified her as a practitioner of anti-multidimensionality as well as hyper-shrewish termagancy.

"But Bosco—when you tried to set him on fire—Bosco couldn't, he couldn't ... he couldn't do anything more. He was down. He was on the floor 'cause Satine had busted him at least twice with that chair."

"Yeah? So what the fuck?"

"He was under control when you were going to burn him alive. It wasn't necessary to do anything else to him to keep him from hurting me. If you'd done what you were trying to do, he could've survived and been mutilated with third-degree burns."

"Why the fuck should you care? He's not only a man—he's a straight white man, a white-boy pig. I'm working in this male-pit shithole as part of my future Ph.D—gathering information for my dissertation. I know what's real about these people. He's a man, so he deserves hell."

"Look, Raven, we've had this argument before. I do not consider men to be pigs, and definitely not in the pejorative sense that you intend."

"The what sense? Oh, yeah, I know that word; that's a white-girl word. You're very…you're very…professorial. How about that one? You like my white-girl word?"

"I'm ignoring your racially bigoted remarks. Most men are good."

"Bullshit! That's smiley-face, have-a-nice-day, white-society bullshit! They're all scum, especially white ones—patriarchal oppressors within the oligarchy. That slave-driver asshole just tried to kill you. Do you not get that? What is it about that that you don't get, you dumb-blonde hoe?"

"I don't believe he wanted to kill me. He went low with the knife. And a moment later, he didn't try to cut my throat when he had the chance."

"Holy shit, bitch! Have you ever heard of toxic masculinity? What *are* you?—the goddamn heart-of-gold hooker around here?"

"Well, thanks, Raven. But no, I don't try to portray myself as that."

"You may as fucking well. I saved you. I saved your lily-white ass. You owe me. You need to pay me at least two of those C-notes you fucked out of some sleazebag. Pay up, bitch. Pay up. I saved your girl-next-door ass back there. Pay up!"

"Actually, that would be Satine and Hokey who saved me. And if Rochelle were working tonight, I know she would've been in there fighting to help me, too. As for you and what you did, we both know your purpose in intervening was not to rescue me from Bosco but rather to inflict harm upon a heterosexual male—particularly if he's white. Right? Bosco and his toxicity represent the exception, not the rule. You never look at each guy individually. And when you paint them with a wide brush, it's always calumnious. You refuse to consider any general positive traits of men."

"What, bitch? What? Fuck you!"

"You came at Bosco only because what he did to me was an excuse to attack a man—any man."

"You goody-two-shoes, ivory-ass sluthole. You deserved to be cut."

Before Kristi Lou could retort, she was defended by another workmate, who stepped between the two adversaries.

"Shut up, Raven, you foul-mouthed little black-bitch bigot!"

Doris, after medically treating Kristi Lou's injury, had been standing silently and observing the escalating tension. Doris would brook no more abuse of Kristi Lou.

All dancers, including Raven, knew that Doris, despite her nearing septuagenarian status, was no one to cross.

"Kristi Lou didn't deserve anything of the kind. She's a good girl, an honorable person. I can't believe you actually want her to pay you. Then again, considering it's you, I guess I can.

"And she's right about everything she says about men. There are plenty of good men throughout the planet, including most of the men who come in here; the majority of them are just looking for some warm caress or yes, sex, but how's that so bad? She's right; Kristi Lou is right with what she thinks and what she says about that—about men, about men and wanting sex. You're just a bigot against them."

"Bigot? I can't be a bigot—I'm black. So, I can say it like it is. I can be blunt. You're just as fucked up in the head as…"

"Be silent, blunt cunt!" commanded Doris. "Did you hear me grant your uncouth ass permission to speak? I swear to God you're a bellicose bitch! Bosco called Kristi a cunt. She's not. You are."

After Raven clammed up, with a stunned expression on her face, Doris continued.

"Trying to confer upon yourself false immunity from bigotry just because you're a member of a certain race or whatever group is one of the worst forms of bigotry. If you're a bigot, then you're a bigot. And you're a bigot. And you know what, cunt? You're more of a creep than Bosco. You're a creep because you're so hateful against a whole world of people—men—especially the ones you tempt in here and make money off of like a damn hypocrite—just like Kristi Lou says in her wild-ass lectures—because of what they can't help wanting and what you make 'em want even more and then you wanna piss in their faces."

"Or find an excuse to kill them," interjected Satine.

"Yes, Doris is right," said Kristi Lou, vocally agreeing in order to express appreciation for Doris's support but also because she agreed with Doris's points. "You usually hear the word creep used against men, but women can be creeps, too."

"You cream-colored bitches are fucked up. Go fuck yourselves."

"Stay away from me, Raven," warned Kristi Lou, invoking an incongruously masculine, deep-toned voice no one had heard from her before, while wearing a severely serious expression on her now-rigid face.

Having stomached enough of Raven's contumelious derision, Kristi Lou, still resting in the soothing comfort of the foam-cushioned chair in which Satine had gently placed her, temporarily forgot about the throbbing pain smoldering upon her slashed stomach and rose to her feet.

"You don't want me to lose my temper with you. That would bode unwell for you. And I know you know that."

Raven did indeed know that.

"Fuck off and die, hoe—and that also goes for Miss Rochelle, that Aunt Thomasina of yours," said the perpetually petulant Raven, as she whirled around to return to the dance floor to earn a living with artificial affability and the tempting of the same people she bigotedly despised.

"Rochelle is benevolent-hearted whereas you are irredeemably odious!"

Kristi Lou watched Raven strut through the door. She then looked away blankly, toward the wall, somewhat shaken by the exchange—and stupefied by Raven's clamorous insistence on fiscal remuneration for trying to slay someone while prevaricating that the unsolicited attempted homicide was on Kristi Lou's behalf.

Six seconds later, she walked to the doorway. Herself incapable of equivocation, Kristi Lou saw Raven already tilting herself enticingly toward and smiling in the face of a timorous, lonely-looking, sandy-haired, white man, inveigling him remorselessly. Kristi Lou was shocked by how suddenly Raven, inured to volatile tempests, had gotten over their clash and how she could instantly return to her fabricated persona to drain more money from the same people she would be glad to murder.

Kristi Lou, extemporarily sensing that her differences with the misandry-suffused Raven were irreconcilable, stared at Doris and then at Satine for two seconds apiece. She realized she'd forgotten something.

"I've somehow not yet thanked you. Thank you, so much, for what you did for me—both of you and Hokey. Nevermore shall I forget."

"You're welcome," replied Doris and Satine simultaneously, as Kristi Lou was startled at how their tonalities seemed to merge so harmoniously, almost with a musical harmony.

She walked several feet away from her two allies, and then looked upward toward the corner of the ceiling. She melted into the moment, and then summoned her Singing Seraphs, who had faithfully stayed with her into adulthood. They remained her supportive friends, still wearing the same colors: one in red, one in orange, one in green, and one in blue. Unchanging through the years, they sang privately and with soothing tranquility to Kristi Lou, melodizing some of the same unadorned lyrics as they had always sung before: "It's immortally true; God is with Kristi Lou," and "Warm is the blessing of time; You're going to be God-blessedly fine."

27

KRISTI LOU INSISTED UPON STAYING AND WORKING. SHE KNEW Big Sam, were he present, would send her home. *But he's not here so I'm gonna stay. The cut's not all that bad. But I know I'm being prideful and obstinate. But I'm not gonna let either Bosco or Raven run me off.*

Avoiding any eye contact with Raven, she did indeed refrain from leaving immediately after Doris had patched her wound. But, the combination of steadily increasing pain from the laceration and worsening nerves compelled Kristi Lou to finish her work night about two hours earlier than usual, at about 2:30, around 50 minutes after Bosco knifed her.

She went outside to wait for a cab.

After lingering for a couple of minutes, she was relieved to see Dan Cobain, her favorite cabbie, pulling alongside her. Kristi Lou knew Dan would not only take her home to Moonbeam Landing, but would make her enjoy the short trip. After being attacked twice, one attack physical and the other psychological, she felt especially grateful that she could count on Dan to provide her with not just safe transportation but also reassuring affirmation that chivalrous people can be found anywhere.

Oh, thank you, God—I don't have to peregrinate home on a night like this; I've got somebody nice to drive me.

Dan pulled his yellow cab to the curb. Kristi Lou got in.

"Hey, sweetie pie. Let's get you back to the Beam. Whoa—are you OK? You seem extra tired or something."

"Yeah, I'm all right. I'm OK. I'm, uh, I'm kinda OK. Yeah, you're right. I'm really tired. I had a long night, tonight."

"I understand."

Feeling a sharp sting from her Bosco-carved lesion as she fastened her seatbelt across the bandage that Doris had affixed, she started to tell Dan all about her near-fiasco with Bosco, but halted herself.

I'll tell Dan about it some other time. I've had enough melodrama. And I don't want to get into a protracted conversation now, not even with Dan; I just want to go home and rub and love on Mr. Dooflotcher and go to bed.

"You seem a bit off the mark," observed Dan, after they had traveled about a half-mile.

"When am I not off the mark?"

"Never. You're always *on* the mark."

"Oh, well…thanks. That's sweet of you to say."

They both fell silent, and, as Dan drove another 60 yards down Miracle Boulevard, he slowed at the sight of a convergence of blue lights. There were four squad cars.

"Look at that; they got that guy," said Dan. "I've seen that guy around before. He always strikes me as a bad guy. As a matter of fact, I saw him at about that same spot, right there where they've got him handcuffed— about a half-hour ago when I went by. He was kinda staggering and walking in circles, looking all hyper and amped-up-like. I wonder what he's getting arrested for."

"Yeah," said Kristi Lou, as they rolled past the arrest scene. "That's Bosco. He was in the club tonight—just a little while ago—and he caused plenty of trouble. I guess somebody at Secrets decided to call the police on him after all. Well, obviously they did, unless they're nabbing him for something else. You saw him moiling about and acting disoriented a half-hour ago, huh? That probably explains it; he was crazy when he left the club. He just erratically walked a ways and freaked out in one spot, it seems, and that made it easy for the police to find him."

"What did he do at Secrets?" asked Dan.

"He, well, he started a big fight. I'll tell you the details later. Please don't make me tell you now; I'm just…I'm so fatigued."

"Oh, I know you are. That's OK, baby. As long as you're all right, it's OK. So, yeah, you can tell me more about it another time. It's OK."

"Thanks, Dan."

Kristi Lou got out of Dan's cab after leaving him with a much larger-than-normal tip—a $50 bill.

"Hey, what's this for? You can't be tipping me this much."

"Yes I can. You deserve it."

"I do? Really? Well, you might get me spoiled to expecting this type of tip every time, you know?"

"Ha-ha-ha. I'm not worried about that. It's just that you're always nice to me and sometimes I feel like rewarding people who've been nice and kind to me; I feel that way right now—and you happen to be the nice guy who's around to benefit from it!"

"Well, in that case, I hope you have some more of these long and nasty nights—just joking."

"I know. I know you are. I'll see you tomorrow, all right? Nite, Dan."

"Nitey-nite, Kristi Lou. Sleep tight. Don't bite the bedbugs."

"Ha-ha. I won't."

Kristi Lou dislodged herself slowly from Dan's cab, moving gingerly to diminish the on/off pulsating pain from her wound. She and Dan exchanged "bye-byes," spoken synchronously. As Dan drove away while she stepped slowly toward her door, she looked introspectively at her pained midsection. *Bosco almost kerfed my umbilicus. I really like my innie. But I hope I don't develop omphaloskepsis. I needeth not another obsession.*

28

SHE BARELY SLEPT; THREE SLEEPING PILLS AND THREE acetaminophen capsules, rather than the standard dosage of two of each, helped her fetch three hours of poor-quality, doze off/snap awake sleep rather than none. The burning cut kept her wakeful, as did flash recollections of Bosco's rage. But neither of those distresses weighed on her more than the emotional aftermath of the imbroglio with Raven.

However, what disturbed her this night more than Bosco, Raven, or pain were doubts and fears about the direction of her life, the resurfacing of this anxiety having been triggered by the intense clash.

****

She was awakened at about seven o'clock Saturday morning by a strange sensation. She looked toward her torso and saw Mr. Dooflotcher licking her wound. Either Doris's bandage had come off on its own or Kristi Lou's wily cat had removed it with his claws and/or teeth.

"Oh my goodness, that feels good. Thank you, sweet boy."

Giving up on the notion of sleeping anymore, Kristi Lou pulled herself off her bed, but went no further than her rocking chair across the bedroom before she slumped down again.

Kristi Lou had one of her conversations with herself.

I hope I don't get an infection. I'm still not going to the doctor unless I have to, though. I know I had a tetanus shot a few years ago back home; it should still be good. I told Doris I hadn't had one since I was a kid but I forgot about that last one. I believe I'll be OK. I'll keep an eye on it, won't I? Yes, you will. Thank me. We're welcome.

Kristi Lou stayed in her apartment the entire day, Saturday, August 11, spending many hours at her computer, surfing the Internet without specific topics in mind, till that thought she had been avoiding broke through and exploded into her awareness. She didn't want to think about it anymore. Using several different search engines, she surfed some more, but now semi-maniacally, deliberately seeking subjects that would serve to distract her from the decisions she knew she would soon have to make—about going back to college, and what she felt she should be doing with herself.

I'll cross the Rubicon regarding those issues before too long, but not today. My cut hurts, but it's OK. I don't guess Bosco will come back. I won't worry about that. At least, I don't think I will, will I?

After applying medicated salve to her cut and affixing a new bandage, she walked out her door at 6:27 p.m., intending to meander rather slowly as she trekked to work.

****

Kristi Lou reported early, as always, to Downtown Secrets, arriving Saturday evening about 15 minutes before her regular Saturday start time of 7:30. As she approached the entrance to the club, she quizzed herself.

It's 7:30 for Saturdays, right? Yes, it is. Why am I having to check with myself about that? Am I starting to have short-term memory deficiencies? No, I don't think so; I'm just . . . I've just had . . . I've had a lot going on and . . . but, anyway, even if I were a bit late, it wouldn't matter 'cause they enforce the promptness rule only on habitual laters . . . wait . . . what? Did you say 'laters'? Yes, I said laters—you know, people who are habitually late could be called laters . . . couldn't they? Yeah, they could—laters.

Uncharacteristically, Big Sam was positioned at the front entrance. No one else was around, due to orders from Big Sam for all staff to be inside till he said otherwise. Upon seeing Kristi Lou, he hustled her upstairs to his office. The stairs were just six feet past the doorway, and she was whisked away before any of her coworkers could spot her.

Big Sam felt his girls earned some leeway in their work schedules now and then. And, that status certainly applied, in spades, he surmised, to his tallest dancer, who impressed him immensely by coming back—as he anticipated she would—to her job less than 24 hours after being attacked with Bosco's five-inch, razor-sharp dagger.

"You just survived a knife attack," said Big Sam to Kristi Lou immediately after closing the door behind her back, as he rifled off his amalgamated points in his no-frills, staccato style.

"You always treat everybody right and nice—too nice, maybe, but you're always nice. Besides, I don't want you here tonight when Raven comes in; I'll be dealing with her. Take some time off, with pay. Of course, you make most of your money from client interaction but I'll let you have your base salary. Doris called me after what the bastard Bosco did and I called 9-1-1 and told them to look for Bosco on foot down the street from here. I didn't want him free to come hunting for you. I learned later they were already after him anyway because he'd tried to do a car before he came to the club. You should go to the doctor. I'll see you in a few days, on, let's say, Tuesday. I know you're off every other Wednesday. Next Wednesday is your night off. Keep it. Work on Tuesday; off Wednesday; back on Thursday. Got it? Get out of here."

"Oh, thank you so much. But there is one thing, though. Last Wednesday was my off Wednesday, so …"

"Oh," said Big Sam, while checking the employee-shift calendar on his online business ledger. "My mistake. Take off next Wednesday, anyway. Then off again the following Wednesday, the 22nd, to get you back on track."

"I really do appreciate it, Big Sam. I do. I truly do."

"Yeah, OK," grumbled her gruff but surprisingly sensitive boss.

Kristi Lou turned around, quick-stepped down the stairs and out through Secret's entrance door without being seen by anyone. A quick glance back into the club allowed her to see Rochelle sitting at a table playing a game on her phone. Kristi Lou began to stroll toward home, the daylight of early evening still lingering and providing a degree of cover against the jeopardy of an ambuscade, such as for robbery or rape.

****

Within a half-minute after arriving, Kristi Lou gave Mr. Dooflotcher a few crunchy cat treats. Next, she disrobed, used the toilet, and then entertained an impulse. Preparing to fulfill her whim, she removed the bandages on her sliced stomach. Kristi Lou had decided to do something she'd thought about doing since she moved to Detroit but had not actualized. She loaded her always clean bathtub with very warm water, close to scalding hot, drawing the water level almost too close to full. She then slid herself slowly into the wet warmth, wishing she had a bottle of bubble-bath. Her wound stung for about a minute, but then the stinging vanished. Feeling luxurious and carefree, she fell asleep and slept for nearly two hours, awaking just before ten o'clock, with the water no longer warm but still pleasant to her touch.

Oh wow! I did it; I eschewed another modern-day shower and took an old-timey bath. A bath! A real bath! I'd better check myself for wrinkles. I may look like the shriveled prune that you're supposed to look like when you stay in the water too long. Oh good; I don't look ninety-five after all. Of course, there's nothing wrong with being or looking ninety-five and having those nature-dictated wrinkles and if I keep living long enough I will be that age and so I'll have the associated infirmities, and, in the meantime, I should always be respectful to my elders, but… well, that's a long ways off now and my mind appears to be trying to whisk the rest of me away on another tangent. OK, stop that.

Kristi Lou dried off, donned her fire-engine red bathrobe, fed Mr. Dooflotcher and herself a light meal, and retired for the evening with her pussycat.

She pulled back and then neatly folded her seashell-patterned bedspread, placing it on the recently vacuumed floor at the foot-end of the bed. She lay face up under her chartreuse top sheet as Mr. Dooflotcher quickly completed his burrowing down to and then beside her right foot.

Hoped-for torpor, blocked by the intermittent stinging that was discourtesy of Bosco's blade-work on her stomach, did not set in immediately. She already knew she'd have to wait awhile before feeling dozy. She let her thoughts rove.

While Mr. Dooflotcher took turns grooming both himself and Kristi Lou's toes, something compelled her to think of an anecdote relayed by her Aunt Charlene several years earlier. One of Charlene's Fayetteville neighbors, a retired nurse in her nineties, once told Charlene about a wicked prank she and other nurses would pull on unsuspecting neophytic switchboard operators in their 1950s hospital. A rascally nurse, feigning exigency, would ask an unwary tyronic operator to announce over the hospital-wide loudspeakers, "Paging Dr. Rubin, Dr. Billy Rubin" and "Paging Dr. Bumin, Dr. Al Bumin."

Ha-ha-ha. Poor rookies. Faked-out novitiates. Maybe you need to know your pigments and proteins if you're going to work in a hospital and not get punked. But, I imagine those beguiled novice operators could take a joke.

29

Lounging through a mundane, homebound Sunday and
Monday, Kristi Lou spent her unplanned mini-vacation peacefully re-
posing, briefly venturing outside just thrice and only during the daylight hours. She went beyond the walls of her interior apartment for
no longer than five minutes on each occasion, twice Sunday morning
and once Sunday evening, each time stepping through the door of her
screened-in, second-floor porch and onto the cement square comprising her back-of-the-apartment patio that was surrounded by wooden
guardrails she always pushed and pulled to ensure their stability.

Kristi Lou thought, as she often had before, about how architectur-
ally unusual it was for a porch and patio to extend out from a bedroom
rather than from a living room.

*Well, this is The Moonbeam. Maybe that was an aspect of hippie-style
architecture in the '60s.*

She wanted to scan the cityscape, breathe some outdoor oxygen,
pollution notwithstanding, as well as observe any animal activity, such
as capering squirrels or nesting birds, which might be happening to
her left on the patio of the unoccupied, next-door apartment.

Before going to bed Monday night, August 13, Kristi Lou thought about the fact that she had not exchanged phone numbers with any of her Secrets coworkers. None had asked. She hadn't offered.

I believe … I sorta sense … that it's some kind of understood thing at Secrets. But I don't know if that's an industry-wide thing, a sex worker thing. I should know that, though. I'll find out. I think Rochelle would give me her number. Maybe I'd be less lonely if … but, I'm not all that overly lonely … not extremely lonely or anything, but … no … maybe it's better to just leave well enough alone, as they say.

****

Soon after arising Tuesday, August 14, at midmorning, Kristi Lou felt compelled to look back on her miniature personal holiday. She sat in her roller chair at her computer desk, which she kept in the bedroom, turned on her desktop and 24-inch LED monitor, opened her media player, and selected her downloaded copy of Rachmaninoff's classics. She chose Piano Concerto No. 2: Adagio. She climbed onto her bike and leaned against the wall with the kickstand up while thinking about what she had done or not done the previous few days.

I really didn't do much but that's OK sometimes, as I was telling myself yesterday.

She recalled that on Sunday morning, during one of her brief observational ventures onto the patio, she had become aware that she often, while scanning the sky and the buildings in the Detroit skyline, craned her neck and held her head tilted way back, with her eyes rolled down.

While perched upon her bicycle, she anticipated returning to the patio and repeating her head-slanting scan later this day, Tuesday, and knew that while doing it, she'd be thinking about having done it Sunday, but this time with a sharpened awareness of the extreme arc of her oblique tilt.

I actually think I do this a lot. I'm like a dog sniffing the air. Right now, I think I'm thinking too much about the fact that I think about it.

She remembered that her Sunday was followed by a Monday during which she was even more reclusive, never leaving her apartment to even step onto the porch or patio, preferring to spend the day exploring the Web, watching reality TV reruns, and petting Mr. Dooflotcher.

Continuing to straddle her bike, Kristi Lou recalled that at bedtime Monday night she had sat on her bed and looked through her window at some gathering cirrus clouds, viewable via the luminous moonlight and resembling swirling argent puffs, and how innocent and carefree they appeared as they floated gracefully across the sky. She spoke to herself out loud.

"Those clouds last night were so pretty. Man, I've been a totally totalized lazybones with several consecutive days of my life. And I'm going to do it again today before I go back to work. But that's cool. I enjoyed resting. I think it's salubrious and revivifying to now and then just rest and relax and do a load of nothing—analeptic idleness."

Still straddling her bicycle as her Tuesday morning progressed, Kristi Lou wheeled herself around gracefully on the bike seat, facing away from the wall, and stretched both her long, toned arms straight up and then outward at 45-degree angles for seven seconds and then released them in a blissful collapse. She then exhaled audibly while pushing her butt into the wall and pinning her arms behind her back, with her fingers intertwined and pressing down hard for deeper stretching. She heard most of her knuckles pop, which she liked.

Oh my goodness. Aunt Charlene hates it when I pop my knuckles. She says "don't pop 'em!" And why have I not fallen off this bike? I must be unintentionally applying some law of physics just the right way.

Kristi Lou dismounted from her bike lest her luck end. After switching off Rachmaninoff, she drifted downstairs and into the kitchen. As she stepped to the refrigerator for a gulp of limeade, Kristi Lou felt pleased, mostly, with her restorative hiatus from the wild-side life. But she realized a tinge of disappointment upon recognizing that, as usual, there was some strain of cautionary qualification blocking her from completely unfettered satisfaction.

She walked into the living room and dropped herself onto her couch.

I can't just totally enjoy anything, big or small. There's always at least one hitch. Yeah, I kinda recharged my battery. But I need to watch it, though; I could get too used to this laziness. But, it's great that nobody stopped by or called. Of course, as I was noticing earlier, no one I work with at the club has my number, well, other than Big Sam and Doris. Mom called Sunday, as she always does, without fail. But that doesn't count because she's my mother—but, of course, that's a good-type version of not counting. But, otherwise ... no interruptions to my blissful vegetating. Hunkering down alone can be really good for that— for not being interrupted by any darn thing. So, aloneness is sometimes a fine thing, a sanatory thing ... as long as it doesn't turn into loneliness.

Kristi Lou stood up and looked at her feet.

Sometimes it's good, really, it is, I guess, except when it's not. That is, when it's too much. But I don't have that going on, that is, being too lonely ... well, not too much, I don't suppose, do I? I do seem to talk to myself, though. I guess a potentially scary aspect of that is that I answer myself, don't I? Yes, you do.

Kristi Lou persuaded herself to march back upstairs and into the bedroom, followed dutifully by Mr. Dooflotcher. She grabbed her two 10-pound dumbbells, which she called smartbells. While standing erect, she completed one set of eight military presses per arm and then dropped the weights from about two inches off the floor onto her posh, purple bedside rug. She paused for 18 seconds. She did a second set. She sighed. She did a third set, with tedium overtaking her.

OK. You're stretching your Bosco wound and it's stinging. Enough. I'm not into this now. More later.

Kristi Lou checked the time on her cellphone and was mildly surprised that her day had moved to just past noon. Feeling drowsy all at once, she succumbed to the temptation of an afternoon nap. Pushing through her semi-guilt, she allowed her bed to draw her to it. She threw back the seashell-themed bedspread and started to slide onto her queen-size, sleep-numbered mattress, intending to do her napping atop the chartreuse top sheet. But, four pieces of paper she had laid on her dresser one night the week before caught her eye. She walked across the bedroom, grabbed the papers, and then returned to the bedside.

What are these papers? Oh yeah; someone's been leaving me notes in the mailbox at Secrets. I brought 'em home the other day. Same handwriting. They all say about the same thing. Nothing threatening, at least not overtly. They've all got 'Hello leggy, longgy girl' or something like that.

As she stood and sifted through the notes with her slender fingers, she noticed she couldn't discern with any confidence whether the cursive strokes were likely written by a male or a female; there was no distinct masculine or feminine gender.

Oh well, I guess maybe I have a classic secret admirer. These notes aren't billets-doux. But I'm not gonna delve into the ever-popular and ever-over-used stalking concept. Then again, maybe I will. The person leaving me notes is not necessarily some guy who's stalking me. I won't jump to that conclusion. Stalking, stalking, stalking. No, I won't. Yes, I realize it does happen, and sometimes the stalking culminates in violence. But I believe those outcomes are comparatively rare. The large majority of followers or stalkers just follow; they don't attack anybody. I know that many up-to-date modernists like to jump on the stalking bandwagon because it's very popular nowadays to talk about stalking this and stalking that every time we turn around. It's wise to be aware of these things. But it's overdone. It's now sewn into the public psyche. It's so Zeitgeisty. Zeitgeisty? Did I just say Zeitgeisty? Yes, you did.

Kristi Lou plopped onto the side of her bed and then slid slowly onto the floor, placing the paper notes, which she had neatly stacked, under the edge of the bedframe. She pushed a cluster of hair off her face and rubbed a scarcely perceptible but still irritating itch inside her right eyebrow. She glanced at Mr. Dooflotcher, who was blissfully asleep under a small end table, snoozing in his circular poly-cotton kitty nest with its leopard-spots pattern.

Or every time a guy just follows a woman a little bit, even if there's really no indication he means any harm, as in he might just be shy but wants to meet her or talk to her more than he already has—it's a stalking thing. Our current culture trains us to think it's fashionable to portray a male-someone as being a stalker. It's cooler than ice to view some guy as stalking. And the stalkee gets to feel complimented for being so desirable while she's frightened and say things like, "I don't need those types of compliments." I know there's such a thing as aggressive stalking, which can be scary. And there can be a serious crime when the so-called stalker becomes violent. But it's still an over-the-top thing these days. Jeezamanelly! There are misinformed YouTubers who've posted in the Comment Section under the heartwarming old '60s song by The Vogues called "Turn Around Look At Me" that it's a creepy stalker song. Unadulterated falderal! It's one of the loveliest love songs of all time, about this guy yearning to fulfill unrequited loving feelings for a lady he thus far can't win over; he yearningly watches her footsteps and figuratively, or perhaps literally, follows her—innocently. He's following—not stalking, as does a hunter who stalks his ravin to commit an act of violence—with hopes of someday winning her heart, romantically. And while he's nearby, if somebody were to indeed attack her, he would surely rush in to rescue her. It's an example of modernized, frosty-cold cynicism. Here's what's creepy: the feeling itself that such a song is creepy. Now, that's reallllllllly creepy. It's a love song, for Pete's sake—a tender-sweet love song! Oh, and let us revel in anti-penis apoplexy over songs like "Standing on the Corner" and "Girl Watcher." Anyway, as far as my unsigned notes, it's kinda cool 'cause it's kinda fun 'cause it's kinda mysterious. Should I feel threatened? No. Am I glad I don't? Yes.

Kristi Lou extemporaneously tapped all of her fingertips together several times, and then descried a few minor cracks in her ceiling.

Do these internal analytical dialogues between me, myself and I indicate that I'm terribly lonely? I'm supposedly so sexy and attractive. Thus, I'm not supposed to be lonely. How lonely am I? I wonder whether… never mind.

She got up off the floor, fell face first onto the bed, and then decided to wriggle underneath the effulgent chartreuse top sheet. After about 12 seconds, she turned over. Kristi Lou always slept on her back, as lying on her stomach—even without the discomfort provided by a knife wound—for much more than half a minute put too much pressure on her trachea and made her unable to breathe with normal air flow. She slept well for a couple of hours of guiltlessly self-indulgent naptime.

Kristi Lou was roused from her slumber by the musical alarm on her smartphone at 2:30, finding Mr. Dooflotcher curled into a feline sleepy semicircle on her chest, nestled between her breasts. After using the bathroom, she brushed her teeth, scrubbed the toilet with bleach, and then shaved her longer-than-long legs.

She spent the remainder of Tuesday midafternoon reading news articles on the Internet, watching TV, and laundering a mixture of bed linen and undergarments, briefly dozing off in her laundry-room chair.

****

At about 4:15, she gratified an impulsive urge to browse the shops in the mall several miles away from her apartment.

Kristi Lou took a taxi, as usual, to go to the mall. Sometimes she would recognize a cabbie as someone who had driven her before. She compared all other cabbies to Dan, and they never quite measured up.

She did not recall having seen this driver before. His probable nationality was a mystery to her; he looked as if he could be Indian or Latino or Greek or some ethnic conglomeration. He spoke very limited English, but he understood that her destination was the mall.

"Mall, yes, you want mall. I take you go to mall."

"That's right. Thank you."

He never spoke again for the duration of the trip and avoided eye contact with her altogether. Kristi Lou observed that, unlike almost all taxi drivers who drove her, he seemed to carefully avoid looking at her reflection in the rearview mirror. Most cabbies, she knew, would try to stare into the backseat at her body, often discreetly inclining the mirror downward, especially if she was wearing a dress or a skirt, for as long as they felt they could get away with it without receiving scorn from her—a censure which, unbeknownst to them, she would not administer. But she knew they did not know.

Upon arrival at the mall, she added a generous tip, as was her custom, to the fare, to which the quiet cabbie responded with a nearly inaudible "thank you."

****

As Kristi Lou sauntered through this local apotheosis of American retail, she noted that malls seemed like small towns whose citizens and businesses were crammed closely under a communal ceiling.

She drifted for 18 minutes, bought nothing, and spoke to no one.

I guess I'm a mallrat loner today. Actually, I hardly ever go anywhere with friends anymore. Oh well, such as it is…

While perusing merchandise in an avant-garde gift shop, Kristi Lou sensed the attraction of a male shopper and the likely chronic resentment of a young, nondescript, and apparently jealous female employee. Neither reaction surprised her, as the attraction/resentment causality was standard fare when Kristi Lou moved among other people.

I just got here. But I want to go home.

She left the store and roamed to the center-court fountain. She stared almost nonstop for about six minutes at the water, into which she then tossed three coins. She removed her phone from her pocket and called the same taxi company in whose cab she had ridden to the mall.

After hanging up, she sat on the mint-green circular brick wall surrounding the fount, looked back at the water and impulsively hummed and then whisperingly sang "Three Coins in the Fountain" audibly enough to draw the attention of three little girls, all blue-eyed blondes about seven years old, passing by in the tow of a young woman who appeared to be their mother. Rosy-cheeked and adorned in matching powder-blue cotton dresses, the children smiled warmly at Kristi Lou. She smiled back.

Oh my goodness. They all look alike. They're all wearing the same type of dress. They all smiled at me at the same time. I wonder if they're triplets. Oh my goodness. Wow. They all look the way I used to look. Cool.

As she slowly arose to walk outside to await the taxi, she obeyed an impulse to reach into her change purse and toss a fourth coin, a penny, into the fountain.

Kristi Lou then sang softly again:

"Four coins in the fountain..."

She looked at her watery likeness for a few seconds, noticing her well-formed figure was distorted by the ripples caused by her coin.

*Oh my goodness. Who are **you**? My body is shapely, all right. But look at the shape. I'm freaky—a butt-ugly freak-uh-muh-thing. Only space aliens would find this sexy. I'm yucky-looking in this reflection pool. Ewwww...*

Kristi Lou stuck her tongue out at herself as she turned away. She walked briskly along the aisle to and through the automatic doors and out onto the sidewalk.

****

Given to observing her own mood swings, Kristi Lou realized she had, just a few moments earlier, felt amused and thus energized by her jovial self-effacement back at the fountain.

While waiting for her cab, she assuaged the intermittent burning sensation that emanated from her abdominal laceration by using her smartphone to read websites carrying local and national news reports. Her next diversion was to count green cars in the parking lot.

I counted red cars last time. Green this time. Next time I'll count blue cars. RGB—red, green, blue. As long and winding as I am, maybe I was a component cable in another life. OK. That was a dumb thing to say. Oh well.

The same driver returned to take her home. She tipped him generously again. He gave her the slightest of smiles at receiving the money, with Kristi Lou easily sensing his shyness. She smiled back and spoke to him cordially as she got out of the taxi.

"Thanks for the ride. Have a really nice evening. Bye."

He surprised her. While responding in his still-fragmented English, he intoned an inflection that was sonorously louder and more animated than before.

"OK. You also too have nice evening, really, too. OK. Bye you."

"Oh, OK. I will. You have a nice evening, yourself. Bye you, too. I mean, uh, bye. Goodbye. Bye, now."

As she was closing the taxi's door, she already felt guilty about the content of the farewell she had given to the foreign cabbie. She looked through the cab's rear window at the back of his head for a moment as he drove off, and then gazed down at her shoes.

Gosh darn it. I was trying to be cute, I think, but also to copy him to relate to him when I said his 'bye you' back to him. I hope he didn't think I was mocking him, making fun of him. And I wasn't necessarily doing him any favors by reinforcing his not-so-perfect English. He'll probably do better here in America by speaking the language properly. But, I don't imagine I hurt him too much, though. Besides, right after I said 'bye you' to him I caught myself kinda mistreating him even though I was trying to be nice and I corrected myself to a normal 'bye,' so it's OK…I guess. And I wonder if he knows Dan Cobain. Then again, just because Dan is a cabbie doesn't mean he knows all the other cabbies in town. And Dan works at night. Oh well.

****

After expunging her guilt, at least most of it, Kristi Lou felt unexpectedly buoyed by the pleasant exchange with the bashful expatriate. She quick-stepped into her home, grabbed a handful of cat toys, and then tossed them for Mr. Dooflotcher to chase. She played with him joyfully for about five minutes.

Kristi Lou observed that she felt tired, unaccountably, within a matter of seconds.

All right, my whole mall expedition lasted around an hour-and-a-half or … I think less than that, actually. That's not such a long time. But I feel tired. I am tired. Why am I tired?

A moment later, Kristi Lou felt a resurgence of energy. Shrugging off any remnants of her brief but inscrutable lethargy, she loped into the living room, thoroughly idealess as to what she was going to do there. She glimpsed at a stack of magazines on the coffee table and then spontaneously lobbed herself onto the sofa to take a late-afternoon nap. Mr. Dooflotcher immediately leapt onto her stomach, without hurting her wound, preparing to snooze on his human eiderdown.

Wow. I'm taking my second nap of the day. Why? I don't feel sleepy. Within one minute, I've felt tired, then energized, and then ready to take a nap. I feel so very nonplussed. What's going on here? I just want to take another nap. Maybe it's Bosco's knife cut kinda sapping me or whatever. But, as I just said, I don't feel tired anymore. If I'm no longer tired, why do I crave a nap? Maybe I'm tired in a different way that I don't quite recognize. But, then again … oh stop quizzing yourself and take a nap. But … I don't know … but you don't always have to know … yes, I do … no, you don't … it's 5:47 … just take a nap, for goodness' sake … yes, I will, but … no!—no more buts!—but … shut up!

30

AFTER HER SUNDRY NAPS AND RECUPERATIVE NIGHTS OFF,
Kristi Lou and her wounded abdomen returned to work at the blues
brothel on Miracle.

Seven members of the day-shift crew, who had been there since soon
before the club's daily opening at 11:30 a.m. and were just leaving, had
heard about the vicious assault Bosco had perpetrated against Kristi
Lou four nights before. They saw her sitting at a table beside the bar
and swarmed around her, inquiring about her well-being.

Some of the girls wanted to see her gash, the way orthodox women
want to look at baby pictures.

"It's not really that deep," reassured Kristi Lou, who was genuinely
surprised and heart-warmed by the attention and concern.

*Well, I hope they're more concerned about me than they are just curious
about what my cut looks like. I'm gonna go ahead and believe they sincerely care.*

Rochelle arrived at work late, as usual, but she was not as late as
she usually was. She rushed to Kristi Lou and gave her a gripping hug.

"Oh Kristi Lou! Oh sweetie! Oh my god-a-mighty! I heard what
dat dude did ta you. Oh, man, he needs ta die. Is you OK? Why ain't
you in da hospital?" asked Rochelle as she swiftly sat next to Kristi Lou.

"Hey, Rochelle. It's really not that bad, really it's not. It could've been much worse. Thankfully, I got rescued."

"Yeah, I heard all about it. Hoke and Satine—dey had yo back. But I heard dat nasty-ass bitch Raven tried ta shake you down for money, right there wit' you juzz been almost gutted, by sayin' she saved you and you owe 'er and all dat shit. She didn't save nothin'. It was Hoke and Satine. Dat ole hoe-hole Raven always be like 'All y'all keep watchin' at me 'cause I'm Miss Thang.' Anyways, you don'ts gotta worry no mo 'bout dat hoe."

"Why so?"

"Dat hoe be out da doe. Big Sam fired 'er sorry ass."

"He did? Big Sam fired Raven?"

"Hell fuckin' yeah. He knew he had to. What else could he *do*? He had'ta ditch dat bitch. Doris told 'im what happened and he fired dat attention hoe, dat athoe. He fired da athoe bitch over da phone. I heard him firin' 'er athoe ass an' tellin' 'er 'Don't come back here. After how you treated Kristi Lou last night plus da fact you coulda burned down da buildin', you aren't workin' here anymore.' Dat's what he said."

"Oh my goodness. Well, he told me to take some time off and one reason was he didn't want me here when Raven came back in. I guess he changed his mind about firing her in person."

"He did. He decided he didn't want 'er ass back here no mo, period."

"Oh."

"And then I heard 'im tell 'er he'd already busted open 'er locker and she didn't have nothin' in it so dere ain't nothin' for 'er ta come back here ta get. Nothin'. So, she gone. Gone, gone, gone. And I say damn good riddance. Me and 'er was goan throw down one of deez nights. Now she takin' 'er athoe, nigga-bitch act somewhere else."

"Well, I don't know how I entirely feel about this. I hope she'll be all right and be able to get work and that she'll…"

"'Get work'? Whatch you talkin' on 'bout 'get work'? Of course she'll get work. She'll be workin'—on 'er back, like da rest of us. Unless all dem straight dudes you so crazy 'bout defendin' turn homo, she *goan* get work."

"Well, I guess you're right. I know, but, it's just that … well. You know, Raven is just 22, right? And she does have a college education from U-M. I think she graduated last year. So, I suppose that's in her favor. She was yelling about working here to help her toward a Ph.D, presumably in a women-centric discipline. For now, she's got a Bachelor of Arts in something. I don't know exactly what her B.A. degree is in, but…"

"She gotta degree in hoe-bitch-ology. She be a bachelor of bitch."

"Well, that's a bit harsh, Rochelle. Anyhow, I hope she'll get herself on the right track and not be so violent and so hateful toward men and maybe she'll find some happiness and…"

"Oh, Kristi Lou, you juzz so concerned 'bout everybody else, even some lowlife athoe like Raven who don't care 'bout nobody or nothin' but 'erself. You too sweet ta be workin' here."

"Thank you, Rochelle."

"But I dread when you leave."

"Thank you, again. I don't want to go, but…"

"But you gotta go. Dis is my kinda life; it ain't yozs."

"After I do leave, I'll come back to visit you and Hoke and Satine and Doris and everyone. I'll miss some of my regulars, and … I don't know."

"I know you'll come back. I know when you say you'll come back dat you really mean you'll come back. You goan be fine, sweetie. You goan be fine, juzz fine. Ooh, look at dat. Dere's Mr. McNamara, speakin' of regulars. I gotta go see what me and 'im goan do wit' 'is money. Dat man likes ta spend 'is cash on me, and I like for it ta get spent on me."

"Oh, Rochelle, before you go over to Mr. McNamara, there's this one thing I've been meaning to say. I've been thinking—obsessing—about it a lot."

"Whaz dat?"

"It's about … to say it directly, it's about prostitution. Should it be legalized everywhere, especially in designated red-light communities, not just in certain parts of the Las Vegas, Nevada area? I say yes, absolutely."

"Oh lordy, here we go. All right, does I need ta get me some snacks anna Co-Cola for dis?"

"No, this one won't be that long…well, not by my standards. Anyhow, I just wanna say that without sex-industry workers—like you…and me, too—that there would probably be a lot more rapes around the world. A guy's horny and he's got some dollars and he buys it from us. He doesn't steal it. I know they say that rape is about violence and dominating and punishing, and I believe those elements are often there and the main reason some rapists commit rape. But sex is still a component of rape. A guy could dominate and punish by just beating someone up. But when you add sex to the domination mix, then you've got the recipe for rape.

"There are many guys, I'm sure, who feel they're about to explode from unsatisfied desires and who can't get it the normal way for whatever reason. Maybe they're physically unattractive or socially clumsy. So, these men purchase it from us—as in prostitution—rather than stealing it from other women—as in rape. I believe the number of rapes would go way up, and maybe skyrocket, were we not available. So, well, if I'm right, then, despite all the hostile revulsion and condemnation from standard society about our supposed turpitude, ladies of the evening such as you and me, encased in our beckoning habiliments, are quietly doing mainstream women and girls a huge favor. Yes, we are. We can't actually know, but many of those ladies may've been ravaged over the years without us sex mavens shielding them from being raped."

"Wow," replied Rochelle, eyeing Mr. McNamara with a quick glimpse to confirm he was still waiting on her. "Wow? What? I said 'wow'? Now I sound like you. Fuck. Now I sound like me. Anyways, I ain't even goan ask nothin' 'bout no mavens or billy-mints or turditudes."

"That's turpitude, and it means shameful depravity."

"Oh yeah, dat's right—good ole turpitude—one of my favorite words; I juzz forgot it, yeah."

"And that's habiliments, and it means clothes. And mavens—that means connoisseurs. Wait, before you ask, connoisseurs means experts, as in we have expertise in the sex-for-pay industry."

"Maybe if you wrote all dat shit down for me, I'd study it."

"Sure you would. Also, you and I are both part of the regal demimonde."

"Oh, we is? Well, of course we is. I always did think I was part of dat. OK, what da fuck is it? If I'z part of it, I may as well know what it is."

"We are both demimondaines."

"I'm pleased as shit ta know dat. So, what we is?"

"Ladies—and I'm using the word ladies with defiance here—ladies back in the 1800s who were seen by polite society as having sacrificed their moral honor because of sexually promiscuous behavior were known as comprising a certain disdained class of people called the demimonde. Such improper ladies of ill repute were, and still are, correctly described as demimondaines."

"Yeah, well we definitely be some of dem demi-whatevers."

"You don't hear those words too often, anymore, though."

"I don't hear 'em none. But I don't hear 'bout half da words you say. At least I ain't heard 'em from nobody else but you."

"You are a succubus," said Kristi Lou, with a mildly wicked smile.

"Oh, is dat so? Well, you suck juzz as much as I do. Well, all right, probably not as *much* as I do, but you still suck…don't you? I mean, I think we all do, don't we? I'm thinkin' every one of us workin' girls 'round here do some serious suckin'; it kinda goes wit' da job, don't it? So, whaz dis succubus shit? I can tell you right now I ain't wrappin' my funky-chunky lips 'round the tailpipe of no bus."

"Being a succubus doesn't involve sucking busses. And, uh, I'm not really much for, ahem, sucking, but yes, I'm also a succubus. You are a succubus and I am a succubus … that is, as far as one particular connotation goes. Together, we are succubi—plural."

"Well, if we ain't suckin' buses, then we supposta be suckin' somethin' else. So, what we suckin'? What kinda suckin' does us suck-u-byes do?"

"Interestingly, the words succubus and succubi don't refer literally to the action of sucking, although I readily concede that that activity does, uh … well … sorta tie into the overall theme of what we, or some of us … well … OK, a succubus, according to old-time folklore, is a devil's disciple who manifests as a sneaky female demon and has sexual intercourse with men in their sleep. It's a form of rape; since the guys are asleep, their consenting to sex is impossible. But I don't quite believe that we are that type of succubi. Another more generalized, demon-less definition of a succubus is simply a strumpet—in other words, a harlot … like you and me."

"Kaint I juzz be a hooker wit'-out bein' a fuckin', suckin' succubus?"

"Well, I suppose you can, but … of course you can. You can call yourself whatever you wish. The main point I wanted to make is that we—ladies of the evening—perform a valuable service to society. Even though we are immoral in the classic religious and conservative sense, we provide something that helps satisfy the needs of many men who might otherwise be out of control in light-of-day society."

"All right. Good. Damn, Bosco didn't cut out yo personality; you still you. You still be droppin' word-bombs in my ears. You still do dem all-a-sudden lectures. And you be right wit' what you was juzz lecturin' 'bout, definitely. Whaz dat word dey like ta say nowadays on TV talk shows? 'Empowered'—dat's it—empowered. You juzz done made my self-esteem feel empowered. Nobody'll ever know how many regular females woulda been raped in da past or would be raped in da future wit'-out us workin' girls satisfyin' dem dudes who need ta get some but don't got no normal 'bility to get it. Dem bitches owes us some gratitude. Anyways, Mr. McNamara should thank you, too, babydoll."

"Oh, should he? Why's that?"

"Well, 'cause you juzz stopped me 'fore I could get over to 'im and then you got me so pumped up 'bout what I does dat I'm goan give 'is ass a discount. And dat's in addition to 'im usin' 'is Secrets coupons. He fixin' to get a real fine fuck for his buck."

"Oh my goodness; I bet he is. That's a rather crafty way of wording it. Mr. McNamara doesn't have to thank me, but I'm glad he'll enjoy some savings. And I'm really pleased that I could help you feel better about yourself—empowered, that is; you deserve it."

"You such a sweetie. All right, I'll be back wit'-chu after while," said Rochelle, as she got up from the table and started to step toward the eagerly waiting Mr. McNamara.

"All right, see you later. Oh—one more thing. There's an old song from the '60s you should listen to; it pertains precisely to what we've been talking about and how we're important. It's called 'Sweet Cream Ladies, Forward March,' and it's from a great band called The Box Tops."

"Oh yeah, babydoll. I be listenin' da dat shit real soon."

"Well, you should."

"OK. I'll get right on it."

"Please do. And you just memorized the song title so you can find it, right, Rochelle?"

"Oh yeah. I sure did—'Creamy Ladies' by Da Marchin' Sweet Pops."

"'Sweet Cream Ladies, Forward March,' by The Box Tops."

"Oh yeah, dat's it. I'll be a music critic and write a review for you."

"Yes, I'm so sure you will."

"Yeah, baby—I will!" Rochelle said over her shoulder as she began walking to her john. "I'd best be steppin' toward Mr. McNamara while 'is money and 'is britches is still burnin'."

Rochelle disappeared across the room from Kristi Lou's view, making her way through the crowd to learn what Mr. McNamara wanted to do about his wallet fattened with C-notes.

31

AFTER ABOUT FIVE HOURS OF WHAT HAD BEEN A ROUTINE work night, with numerous dances, some actual dance instruction, and one event of coital union in the back room with a semi-regular gentleman, Arnold Anderson, who owned a vacuum cleaner repair business and whom Kristi Lou liked and trusted—*he's so quiet and clean and always smells really good*—she strolled outside into the steamy August heat.

She spotted Rochelle talking with Hokey, who was on sentry duty at the front door.

"Hey, Rochelle. Hey, Hoke. Wow, it's torridly hot out here tonight. This feels almost like Arkansas."

"It ain't *dat* hot, Kristi Lou," argued Hokey.

"I know. I said 'almost.'"

"Dat's right. You sure did," agreed Rochelle, turning to face Hokey. "She said 'almost.'"

"Oh, so you gettin' all literal on me here, huh?" said Hoke as he looked down at Rochelle.

"Damn straight. And dat's OK 'cause ..."

Their conversation was interrupted by the sound of door hinges and a familiar abrasive voice.

Dopey McGillicuddy—the semi-albino, blueish-green-eyed, cantankerous, eighty-three-year-old bartender/curmudgeon who took pride in still having all of his natural teeth—stuck his narrow, hairless head past the front door of the club and hollered at Hokey.

"Hey Hoke. You know that little European customer, you know, the scrawny bald guy who always wears a suit that's a hunnert times too big for 'im?"

"Yeah, I seen 'im go in."

"He done went 'n' poked his French face from behind da door of da shitroom 'n' said he needs some tee-*shew* of toy-*let*."

"He wants toilet tissue?" asked Hokey.

"*Hell* no. His ass gotta have some tee-*shew* of toy-*let*. I tried to tell 'im we say 'toilet tissue' in these here United American USA States of America, but he don't get it. Them Frenchies is always hittin' that last syllable."

"Got-damn. When dat Euro dude goan be learnin' himself how ta be talkin' proper-ass English? Sheeeet."

Kristi Lou giggled.

"Whatch you say? Who you be talkin' shit 'bout somebody else not usin' no proper English?" said Rochelle. "You wide-ass hypocrite!"

"Oh, Hoke, he always says things like tee-*shew* of toy-*let*," confirmed Kristi Lou. "I think the way he talks is enjoyably cute."

"You would, baby. OK, Dope, tell 'im I'll get Chris ta bring 'im some, uh, tissue of toilet. I ain't *even* goan *pro*nounce it da way he do. Sheeeet."

"By the way, Hokey," said Kristi Lou, "his name is Francois. He's 51. He's French. He's kinda sad, actually, but he's very romantic."

"Oh, dat's right; I yous-ta knew dat was 'is name. I just forgot. But anyways, it ain't just any ole body who can think a dude sounds romantic while talkin' 'bout toilet tissue in a hoe-house."

"Well," said Kristi Lou, "he's still rhythmically romantic, regardless of topic or location."

"Oh yeah, Miss Kristi, Downtown Secrets definitely be da right place for romance," continued Hokey.

"Shut up, Hokey. Whatch you know 'bout romance?" said Rochelle in defense, as usual, of Kristi Lou. "You probably think dogs fuckin' in da park is romantic."

Kristi Lou patiently, but intensely, challenged Hokey's premise.

"Hokey, come on. Please dispense with the cynicism about romance."

"Dispense? Yes, ma'am, Kristi Lou, my darlin', I'll see if I can dispense," replied Hokey with a slight bow. "And, in honor of you, I'm goan try ta get 'Enchant You Some Evenin' put on da music list. You know DJ YoCrunk sho'nuff goan love ta play dat."

"Oh wow, Hoke, that would be delightful. Oh my goodness. I guess DJ YoCrunk would have to make an announcement or something, you know, saying that that song is just a temporary departure from our blues music. But, anyway, the actual name of that wonderful old song is 'Some Enchanted Evening,' composed by Rodgers and Hammerstein. And it's from their Broadway production of *South Pacific* and later the classic 1958 movie by the same name."

"Well, excuuuusssseeee me for not knowin' dat high-culture shit. What-the-fuck-ever. Dis night's some kinda enchanted evenin', ain't it?"

As if on cue, Kristi Lou, ignoring the stinging from her stomach wound, began to sing "Some Enchanted Evening." Hokey stared with mock disgust. Rochelle looked on with admiration, swaying her head in unison with Kristi Lou's impromptu musical outburst.

Crafting an exaggerated sourpuss, Hokey tilted his chin upward and commenced howling like a wolf.

Kristi Lou, wearing a wide grin, paused her impromptu performance to listen to Hokey's zinging of her singing.

"Lordy-mercy, I gotta getta away from dis shit! Sheeeet. Speakin' of shit, dat reminds me—I gotta go be seein' 'bout dat tissue of toilet for France Shaw."

Hokey trotted toward the front door, sporting a wide grin while cupping his hands over his ears and looking back with convivial sarcasm at Kristi Lou.

"Man, Kristi be singin' what France Shaw be needin' tissue for—shit," Hokey hollered, then laughed. "And I got 'er started on it. Sheeeet."

"Shut da fuck up, Hoke—you big, dumb, thug-ass gorilla," commanded Rochelle as Hoke departed into Secrets to seek Chris, the young janitor/maintenance attendant. "You don't know nothin'!"

Kristi Lou resumed crooning and smiling while sashaying and pirouetting over the curb and onto the street, gazing gaily into the stars beyond the Detroit skyscrapers.

"You sing on, girlfriend," encouraged Rochelle. "Dat's some lovely shit."

Jubilantly traversing all the nearby lampposts while moving with grace-laced élan from one to another, Kristi Lou grabbed the posts and spun around them as she sang, imagining herself as performing in a '50s musical.

She finished singing "Some Enchanted Evening," sighed a gushing sigh, and then smiled broadly at Rochelle and six passersby on the sidewalk—four men and two women—who stopped walking and gave her a rousing ovation.

"Oh my goodness, thank you so much," replied a truly grateful and blushing Kristi Lou, as she curtsied.

"You should be on Broadway," shouted one of the guys as they resumed their stroll.

"Well, I don't know about that. I don't think I'm a very good singer. But thank you. Thank you. Thank you very much."

"Now you sound like Elvis," said one of the friends of the shouting man as they continued to amble along.

"Oh my goodness; I guess you're right."

"But you don't sing with a deep voice like Elvis. And you sure as hell don't look like Elvis."

"Oh, thank you again," yelled Kristi Lou as the men and women disappeared down the side street next to Spinoza Tires. "But I'm certainly no chanteuse."

"You ain't no what?" inquired Rochelle.

"Chanteuse—a professional female singer."

"Yeah—deez days you another type of *pro*fessional."

"I know."

"But hey—dat's all right. You juzz a songbird, babydoll," said Rochelle. "Dat was *dee*-vine."

"Well, golly. Thanks."

Rochelle looked up at Kristi Lou and freeze-framed herself.

"'Golly'? Nah. Really? Golly? For real—really? *Really*? Golly? It juzz keep-own comin', don't it? You don't know how outta place you is."

"Yes I do. In addition to being rather socially unorthodox in these whereabouts, I'm also decidedly anachronistic."

"No. No. No. No, I ain't," said Rochelle while wittingly turning the corners of her large lips down and shaking her artificial-afro-crowned head as she began to walk back toward Secrets. "Dis time, I ain't even goan say da word you juzz said, much less axe what it…no, I ain't even *sayin'* it."

"OK," said Kristi Lou, as she smiled, then laughed warmly.

****

The remainder of the night for Kristi Lou was mostly unnoteworthy. She danced with several patrons on the main floor as well as dancing for a few others in the private area, but did not entertain another of her few "coitus customers," as she sometimes called them.

I think Arnie Anderson will be it for tonight. It didn't hurt my wound too much. Francois hasn't asked. He might've had a stomachache.

Alhough they didn't have sex, Kristi Lou danced and conversed cordially with Francois, whom she considered an ensorcelling *interlocutor*, the word she and Francois mutually used to describe their shared conversational prowess. She recognized that she was attracted to Francois beyond enjoyment of ordinary conversation and moderate animality.

After parting with Francois at the completion of their last dance, Kristi Lou called out to him as he walked toward the exit door.

"Oh, Francois, I almost forgot to ask: Did you get what you wanted? You know—the tee-*shew* of toy-*let*? I hope everything came out well for you." She smiled coquettishly and then giggled.

"Oui, Kristi Lou, it came out wondrously well. Merci. You are such a wise-crac*ker*. I say again—wise-crac*ker*. My observay-she-*own* can have a double enten*dre*, as you are indeed a Southern American white girl. I am so clay-*ver*, myself, no?"

"Yes, I mean Oui. I got it—cracker. And I know you don't mean that in a regionally and racially bigoted, anti-Southern-white way. And yes, you certainly are clever, or clay-*ver*. And, uh, although I didn't mention it while we were dancing, I've been meaning to tell you that—though we only danced tonight—I'm most grateful whenever you, umm, help me deliver myself into the quaverous jubilance of *jouissance*—my new French word I found on an online dictionary that I, well, relate to you."

"Jouissance! Oui, I am honored whenever I guide your entrée into the orgasmic tremors of jouissance. You, my lovely Kristi Lou, my mistress of the spasms of orgasms, have such *joie de vivre*. I love this about you. This, my leggy-sexy wench, is French. And its meaning is …"

"I know what it means, Francois—joy of living!"

"Oui! Absolute-*lee*! You have the zeal. You have the zest. Even more than the soap. Good night, my dear Kristi Lou, my kittenish coquette, and safe har*bor* for you."

"Soap? Oh, I get it—that brand of soap. Ha-ha. Thank you, Francois. You're quite zesty, yourself. And you're so piquant! That's also French, right? Anyway, you go to a safe har*bor*, too. I'll see you later. Bye."

Well, I haven't really felt too zestful about my life, lately. But I don't show it so Francois doesn't know it.

****

Near the end of the work night, Kristi Lou and Rochelle chatted at the bar before they both departed a bit early.

"I'm off tomorrow, too," said Kristi Lou.

"You is? Oh yeah, tomorrow's Wednesday. You ain't workin' much lately, girl. But dat's all right, considerin' whatch you been through."

"I know. Big Sam said to keep to my schedule. So yeah, I'm off every other Wednesday but tomorrow is supposed to be a work Wednesday but he said to go ahead and take it off anyway, despite all those other nights in a row I had off—you know, last Saturday, Sunday, Monday— so I'm gonna do that. I'll be back Thursday."

"OK. See ya Thursday. Good to have ya back, sweetie."

"Thanks, Rochelle. It's good to be back here. Secrets can be, perhaps quite surprisingly, a rather nice place to work, especially for a bagnio."

"What?" queried Rochelle. "Another one of yo scholar words. So, dis place be a banjo? But I know what a bango is and Secrets ain't no unfancy fiddle."

"Bagnio. It does sound similar to banjo, though. But it means, well, it means the type of place where we work, here. That is, it means where sweet-cream ladies like us can be found plying our trade."

"Huh? Oh…dat song."

"Some sweet-cream ladies work in bagnios."

"So, it's a *poe*-lite way of sayin' hoe-house."

"Well, as you so bluntly put it, sure, yes. Bagnio can be considered a euphemism for…for that, for what you just said."

"Euphemism. You know what, girl," observed Rochelle, "you juzz kaint help yo-self wit' usin' mo big words. You use big words ta 'splain da big words you juzz finished usin' in da first place. Dem big words juzz keep on movin' outta yo mouth."

"I know. That's just how I talk."

"I know it is. Dat's all right, though. You juzz keep bein' who you is."

"I will. Thanks."

"OK. I be gone," said Rochelle as she turned away from Kristi Lou and left the club.

"Bye-bye, Rochelle."

****

Kristi Lou went to the locker room, changed into her plain-Jane baggy blue jeans that she sometimes wore to maximize comfort, and walked out of Secrets. She decided to eschew a taxi ride with Dan, this being sometimes her preference when in the mood for light exercise upon leaving work. She wanted to stroll the several blocks to her apartment on this night. She saw Dan's parked cab, as he was waiting for her at curbside. She walked over to him and explained her decision, rather than just giving him a simple, "I don't need a ride tonight," as she usually called out to him without stopping on nights she chose to walk home. She remembered her covenant with Dan from Friday night to particularize what had happened with Bosco.

"Hi, Dan. I know I told you last Friday night—well, it was literally early Saturday morning and I know you know how technical I can be but I still like to call any night, meaning while it's still dark, by the name of the day that was going on before midnight—that, er…where was I before I interrupted myself?"

"Uh, you were…" answered Dan, attempting to keep pace.

"Oh yeah, I told you I'd tell you more about Bosco's behavior and all that. I didn't feel like talking much that night. But tonight, I feel much better, so much so better that I just want to hoof it home. But since I am feeling better, I'll go ahead and tell you what Bosco did."

"All right. What did he do?"

"He attacked me."

"He what?"

"He got mad. He got really angry because I wouldn't go into the back room and be intimate with him. I told him as nicely as I could that he just wasn't my type for such interplay, but he was drunk and high and he didn't want to take no for an answer so he came at me with a knife. He cut my tummy, and it still hurts some, but it wasn't too deep so it's not all that awful. Hokey and some of the girls rescued me. I'm OK. I'm convalescing quite well."

"What an asshole. Oh God, if I'd been there I woulda protected you."

"I know you would have. Thanks."

"So that's what those cops were arresting him for, then?"

"As it turned out, yes—that was one of the things for which he got arrested. Big Sam told me that Doris called him about Bosco jumping me in the club and that he called 9-1-1 and told them about it. The people at Secrets, including me, weren't going to call 9-1-1, what with me hurt but not all that terribly. Everyone there knows that Big Sam doesn't like emergency vehicles around his building. But he made the decision. Flashing lights aren't too terrific for business reputations."

"Yeah, I guess not."

"Anyway, I'm going to be fine."

"Really? Then you went to the doctor, right?"

"No. No, I didn't."

"What? Why not? Why didn't you go to the doctor? You got cut by a knife, didn't you? Tetanus and whatnot, you know?"

"I know. You sound like Big Sam and Doris and some of the girls. And they were right and so are you, but I just didn't go. I don't like to go to the doctor if I can help it. I've been monitoring my wound. It hasn't become infected or anything. It's OK, really. As for tetanus, I had a tetanus shot recently enough, in Arkansas."

"Well, if you say so. I hope that SOB doesn't come looking for you after he gets out."

"Yes, I'm hoping not…obviously. I, I, I don't think he will. But…"

Kristi Lou looked down and away from Dan.

Dan was on the brink of asking Kristi Lou multiple questions but chose to not protract the conversation any further. He sensed that Kristi Lou would benefit more by simply being allowed to begin her stroll and getting some mild exercise while relaxing quietly as she walked.

"All right then, baby. You better get to walking so you can get home and get some more rest. You take it easy, girl."

"I'll be riding home with you again soon, though."

"Hey, that's fine," replied the almost always agreeable Dan. "I'll miss taking you home but the main thing is that you're OK."

"Yes—much better. I got to sing tonight. I wish you could've been there."

"Oh, I bet you were great! You, uh, you can sing for me sometime. I'd be honored."

"OK. I will. At least, I hope we both remember that I'm supposed to sing for you."

"Yeah, I'll hold you to that; you're going to sing for me."

"I promise I will. OK, I'll see you later."

"All right. You be safe walking home. Bye."

"I will. Thanks, Dan. Bye."

Kristi Lou walked about 25 yards. A thunderclap rumbled overhead.

"Hey," shouted Dan, sticking his head out the taxi window and looking back over his left shoulder. "You hear that? There's a storm coming to town. You sure you wanna walk?"

"Yeah, I heard it, and I saw a lightning bolt flash up there, too," she replied as she stopped walking and turned to look at Dan. "But, if I don't dawdle, I think I can outpace the rain, or at least get caught in only a dinky sprinkle-dinkle. And if there's any skywater, I've got my super-duper tote bumbershoot," which she waved at Dan and then returned to her purse.

"Yeah, OK."

"Also, I can stretch out these long legs and cover a bunch of ground fast, you know?" Kristi Lou smiled at Dan as she spoke.

"Yeah, baby—those legs were made for getting you where you want to go—in more ways than one—no doubt about that. OK, OK, well … OK. We're having trouble getting you going. I keep sayin' something to you to hold you up, so, if you're gonna beat the rain …"

"Oh no, that's all right. You're just trying to look out for me."

"Yeah, well, get on goin' then, Kristi Lou. I'll be seein' ya."

"OK. Thank you, Dan. Bye—again."

****

Kristi Lou began trekking in earnest toward her apartment, glancing back to her left at Downtown Secret's tenuously hung sign, then at Dan's still-parked cab, and finally at the pluvious sky.

As she speed-walked homeward, she was ever ready to reach into her purse for her pepper spray or her umbrella, if needed. They weren't.

Despite what smelled like the earthy, musky scent of petrichor—though there was precious-little soil nearby—no rain fell on her.

She arrived home without incident and went to her door.

I'm back home again at good ole A-207, my one-bedroom domicile in my rough, but not unlivable, neighborhood. Yeah, I'm home again. Home again, Finnegan; that's what Aunt Charlene used to say a lot when she got home. I imagine she still says that. I'll have to ask her if she does.

As Kristi Lou inserted the key into the keyhole, she heard car tires wheeling on wet pavement and an engine's acceleration. Letting the

318

key-chain dangle from the door, she turned around and saw Dan's cab turning and heading toward Miracle Boulevard, into the procellous night.

Dan and the rain followed me home. But neither one caught up with me. He probably trailed me and gave me an escort the whole way to ensure I'd get back safely. Oh my goodness. That's incredibly sweet. There are some nice people in this world. And I know some of them and they treat me so well. I'll miss them when they're no longer in my life. I won't forget them, though.

She unlocked the deadbolt. Stepping into her living room and then on into the kitchen, she dropped her purse onto the countertop, fed Mr. Dooflotcher, and drank a half-glass of limeade. She then used the bathroom, brushed her teeth, and readied herself for bed.

It's not so horrific here, thought Kristi Lou in her upstairs bedroom as she undressed while standing beside the bed, as her kitty sat on a pillow next to the headboard and post-meal groomed himself.

As Kristi Lou dropped her jeans to the floor around her ankles, she happened to look down at her body. Her eyes' focus traveled slowly upward with a side-to-side sweep from her feet to the top of her breasts, her chin pressed against her collarbone. She next scrutinized her dorsal anatomical assets. Completing her extemporaneous self-scanning, she felt almost detached from herself while issuing her assessment amid hearing raindrops pattering upon the roofing shingles above her head.

So, this is what men find so appealing. They like it. As I say, that's what they're supposed to feel, if they find a woman attractive. But, for me, well, it's just me. Funny, I see these curves whenever I get out of the tub, so it's no big deal to me. I take it for granted. I guess if I were a man I'd be turned on by myself. But if I were a man I wouldn't be me, so . . . oh shut up and go to bed.

She glanced at the amethyst-colored wall clock her mom had given her, and observed that the time was about what it normally was at this juncture when she chose to walk home from Secrets—almost five o'clock.

I don't think I feel like reading tonight. I'm weary. I'm just going to crash.

32

SHE SLEPT LIKE A MONTH-OLD BABY, AND THEN GREETED August 15, a sunny Wednesday morning—what was left of it at 11:15—with the alarm on her smartphone playing "Chopsticks."

She pressed "Snooze" on the touchscreen and rolled over, clutching her pillow and dozing for another seven minutes till the music repeated.

Kristi Lou looked at her old turquoise-colored, soundless, alarm clock on the bedside table while deftly touching the "Stop" button on her phone.

She got up, went to the bathroom and then to the kitchen for two brunches—one for her and the other for her best friend, who meowed unremittingly till his bowl was lowered under his whiskers.

On the menu for Kristi Lou were food and beverage items of questionable congruence: grapefruit juice, pickles, jalapeño biscuits, So Delicious bananas foster frozen dessert, grits, hazelnuts, and green grapes.

What a wacky smorgasbord. Am I pregnant? No, you do weird food combos.

Kristi Lou emoted to Mr. Dooflotcher, who sat and listened, head cocked while staring, as if performing his perfunctory duty, while she gestured intensely with open arms and pretended to be seriously perturbed about an issue that was, indeed, mildly aggravating to her.

"I'm kinda being a fusspot here, but I find it somewhat annoying when the grocers place signs calling green grapes white. I know they're technically supposed to be known as Thompson Seedless White Grapes. I care-eth not. They're not white. They're green. Reality says hi. I'm being literal on purpose. The correct color identity of grapes is a subject that should be treated with literalness. White grapes would be white. Green grapes are green. That color is the one-and-only color that makes sense to assign to these grapes. Why? Because green is what color they are.

"And, expanding on vendor-inflicted irritants, I find myself abominating those ubiquitously everywhere-you-turn retail prices ending in 90-something, especially the star-of-obnoxiousness price of decimal 99 cents. Jeez. It's psychologically lying to shoppers' faces while making them like the lie. Generations of people have been conditioned to accept this left-digit-sleaze, psychological deception tactic as if they're herded sheeple: 'Oh, preeminently trustable retailers, please train my brain!' We're supposed to focus semi-subconsciously on the digits toward the left end of the price, with the brain-training guiding us to be more concerned about leftward digits since they represent the bigger sum of money to be spent. $19.99? You wanna sell an item for $20.00, then sell it for $20.00. Why quibble against adding one more cent? Because, with impulse buying, that 19 on the left looks psychically juicier than 20. That 1 is smaller than a 2. They get you feeling 19 but take 20. Minus a penny. But—*more* than 20 with tax. Merchants believe they'd sell less merchandise or fewer services if shoppers could use rounded numbers and easily summate their totals as they shop. Hey! Howz aboutcha including sales tax in your listed prices, wouldya? Sellers connive at making it non-easy for shoppers to keep track of their money. But, they rebut, isn't that 99¢ front and center? Sometimes, except when those tricky cents integers appear in wee-bitty typeface. However, being honest about being dishonest doesn't eliminate dishonesty. Plus, if you protest, both retailers and, sadly, some brain-trained customers, who wish to defend their compliance, are liable to accuse you of being priggishly petty. Is honesty in business dealings petty? Is it petty to oppose trying to greedily trick people into spending money that they maybe can't afford to spend? If emphasizing a few pennies is so petty, then why do retail marketers themselves place that emphasis? Because *their* penny-pettiness might mean more dollars in corporate coffers. But, small retailers are often guilty of doing it, too. By psych-lying, marketing staffers can get paid more in pay raises and/or bonuses. Because to sellers, maximizing profits, even at the expense of selling to gullible customers more things that are both unneeded and unaffordable, is very *non*-petty. All that said, consumers, unless they're mentally challenged—and some are—bear responsibility for their spending. But, from my perspective, in addition to the actual-life, practicality issue of using advertising sophistry to slyly take too much of other folks' money that they could otherwise save and thus enhance their financial security, it's also a matter of, as they say, 'the principle of the thing.' Why? Because these legerdemain specialists are deliberately attempting to deceive. Retailer skullduggery! Am I right, Dooflotch?"

Mr. Dooflotcher continued to stare.

"Thank you. I was hoping you'd agree with my memorized rant-burst."

You talk with your cat. Well, many people talk with their cats or dogs or whatever pets, so … No, many people talk **to** *their cats and dogs. You talk* **with** *your cat … as if you expect him to comprehend every detail and then reply. Yes, sometimes I do. But … so what? As long as you're OK with it … Yes, I am. Well, all righty then.*

****

Kristi Lou spent much of the day captivated by her magazines and English literature textbooks, which she declined to sell back to the campus bookstore. She wanted to read every story and passage, beyond the material she had needed to learn for her Wayne State lit classes, of which she had taken three—one course being an elective and two being mandatory for her degree in education. She had no subscription to any magazines, preferring to purchase her magazines at the store, based on what appeared on the front cover plus a quick perusal of the content.

By late afternoon, she was ready to jog. She donned her running shoes and ran her four-mile route, pepper spray in her sweatpants pocket, trotting through the local blocks amidst their run-down buildings.

She came home, having spoken with no one all day, showered, took a nap from five to six o'clock, and microwaved herself a frozen vegetarian meal for dinner, consisting of broccoli, cauliflower, and squash.

Kristi Lou watched television in her living room during the early evening for a couple of hours, switching arbitrarily among movies, local and national news, and her favorite reality-TV programs.

Football being her favorite sport, she also surfed the sports-themed networks, listening to commentators discuss the upcoming gridiron season. The NFL preseason had already begun, the first exhibition games having been played the weekend before. Kristi Lou, however, being from the South, strongly preferred college football. She was eager for the season-opening ballgames to be played during the first week of September. Her favorite team was the Arkansas Razorbacks, though there were about a half-dozen teams for which she rooted.

After swallowing a combination of one sleeping pill and one-half teaspoon of cough syrup—for the codeine-induced drowsiness effect, as she was not coughing—she and Mr. Dooflotcher went to bed at just after 10:15.

As Kristi Lou began feeling slumberous at about 10:20, she stared at what looked like a mini-mountain of fabric created by her toes' elevation of the bedspread. Mr. Dooflotcher, purring rapturously, was nestled against her right ankle. A philosophical concept, emanating from sources unknown, inserted itself into her mind. *I believe human character is muchly grounded in what we do when we believe no one is watching and what we permit ourselves to continue thinking when we believe no one is reading our thoughts. Muchly? Yes, muchly.*

33

KRISTI LOU, WITH MR. DOOFLOTCHER NOW DECUMBENT ON her bosom under the top sheet and bedspread, awoke, with no musical alarm set on her cellphone, close to 9:45 Thursday morning.

"Is this August 16? Is this Thursday? Did I just hibernate for almost 12 hours?" she asked herself aloud as she engaged herself in whole-body pandiculation, stretching and yawning satisfyingly. She then rolled over with Mr. Dooflotcher pouring off her chest onto the bottom sheet in a gracefully flowing lump of fur. She rubbed her eyes, blinked to clear her focus, and checked her *Horses of the World* calendar to confirm the date. "Get up and get to percolating."

Kristi Lou spent the entire day at her apartment, venturing onto the patio deck once in midafternoon to soak up some sunshine for about 45 minutes. After slathering on tanning oil containing 30 SPF, she stretched out on her chaise longue while wearing what she termed "my Confederate-gray bikini."

She heard a catcall from one neighboring apartment building and a whistle from another. Whenever she sunned herself, Kristi Lou would, without exception, spot some blind slats cracked open. She knew peering eyes were behind them. She knew at least two sets of those eyes belonged to women neighbors, one of whom she knew was a lesbian and the other she suspected was at least bisexual. Kristi Lou took the attention in harmonious stride, well-pleased, but not egotistically pleased, to receive the flattery.

Eschewing her standardized food routine but keeping the grapefruit juice, Kristi Lou acquiesced to her cravings, and she craved a mostly empty digestive track. Her daytime nourishment, for this particular Thursday, consisted of three glasses of grapefruit juice.

I hope all this grapefruit juice I like to drink doesn't give me kidney stones. OMG. Uncle Harvey got stones and his doctor told him to stop drinking grapefruit juice 'cause that can cause their formation, although some case studies dispute those findings. Uncle Harvey said he hurt so bad he just wanted to be put out of his misery. He said he wouldn't have minded if someone had grabbed a gun and shot him. According to what I've read, men get kidney stones more often than women. But we can still get them. Maybe I'd better switch from grapefruit juice to grape juice. OK. I can do that. But I don't think I will. And I wonder how many demented feminists have wondered whether male hetero-beasts secretly drop the g prefix so they can enjoy mind-raping women while eating rapefruit and drinking rape juice.

At just past 4:30, Kristi Lou, sitting on her living room sofa voraciously reading about word etymologies and geographical hotspots in her unabridged, twelve-inch-high, nine-inch-wide, five-inch-thick, illustration-packed hardcover dictionary/gazetteer amalgam, slammed the eleven-pound tome shut and chunked it off her lap onto the sofa cushion next to her. Her mind had been invaded by an urgent thought.

This ongoing hashtag Me Too movement thing that I've been hearing and reading about… that I've been researching on the Internet… it's gotten… it's become… it's now extreme extremism… extreme extremism? Did I say ex… never mind. But you've gotta excogitate a speech and memorize it… about this Me Too, uh… extreme extremism. OK, let's do it.

With Mr. Dooflotcher snoozing at her feet, Kristi Lou firmly pressed both hands flat upon the sofa on either side of her traffic-stopping thighs, leaned forward, and closed her eyes. She plugged herself frenetically into a highly ordered, obsession-filled memorization of facts and counterpoints that she'd already gleaned from her Web searches. She immobilized herself, almost freezing her body into a forward-leaning statue, and obsessed for about an hour's worth of motionless speech-memorizing. She abruptly stopped. She raised her eyelids. Mentally drained by her intensity and with a slightly sore spine, she lay back on her sofa and let her limbs go limp. Feeling luxuriously lassitudinous, Kristi Lou felt she had earned a period of intensive relaxation; she wanted to relax on her sofa and then lounge lazily, lollygagging anywhere in her apartment.

After lounging around, Kristi Lou noted the time as 6:11. She adjusted her thermostat's AC setting from 78 to 75, took a shower, brushed her teeth, relieved herself, and got ready for another night of work.

****

Walking at a brisker-than-usual pace, she arrived at Downtown Secrets more than promptly, at 7:13.

Kristi Lou's night was going along uneventfully. She danced with several regulars as well as a few first-timers. Then, sitting alone at a table after defending her decision to Rochelle and Satine to not seek medical treatment from a physician for the handiwork Bosco had done on her stomach, she overheard a nearby conversation between Hokey and Dopey, who was away from his bartending duties on a 10-minute break.

"Yeah, there he is, Hoke. That's Skinny Denny sittin' in the corner, yonder. See 'im?"

"Oh, is dat Denny? Yeah, now dat I look closer, I can see dat is Denny. I must notta been at da door when he walked in."

"Hell, you mightta not even *seen* 'im walk in, the skinny-bones rascal."

"I know dat's right. Sometimes you gotta look real close to be *able* to see 'im, specially if he be sideways whenya lookin' at 'im."

"Uh-huh. He's over there right now sorta twistin' around. I think he may gotta go here at Secrets," said Dopey, with a spasmodic head-shake as if to say, "Oh no."

"Damn dat shit," said Hoke. "Speakin' of shit, I hope he goan go outta here for dat. On da other hand, it's kinda funny to see him go through his worryin' 'n' frettn' so maybe we oughta hope he stays here for it. I know we laughin' at somebody else's trouble, but I kaint stop. You-know-what-I-mean?"

"Hell, yeah. Poor thing, though. He kaint help it."

"Yeah, no, he sho kaint," agreed Hoke, shaking his head. "Between him 'n' our French dude, France Shaw, 'n' his tissue of toilet…I just don't know."

Dopey looked at Hokey and colorfully described Denny's disorder. "Poor Denny. He's a shit-a-phobe."

Dopey elaborated, although he knew Hoke, as well as most of the dancers and staff, already knew of Denny's plight.

"He got shit-a-phobia—fear of shit. That's why Denny's so skinny; he's so scared of shit, he don't eat. Not much, anyway. He wants to hold down his shittin' to a bare minimum."

"I know dat's right," bellowed Hoke, as they both looked across the room to the emaciated Denny Thomas, looking hapless and forlorn, as he squirmed in his chair.

"Watch at 'im fidget. He might gotta go. He might be over there in a state of terror," theorized Hoke, hoping for more levity at Denny's expense. Hoke's schadenfreude-ish feeling was more of a selfish desire to enjoy opportunistic humor than a cruel hankering to see another in pain; he felt that *if it's goan happen anyway, I may as well get some fun out of it.*

"I bet he don't swallow no fiber!" said old Dopey.

"No, I bet he don't!" concurred Hoke, while laughing heartily. "I bet he be terrified of a can of beans!"

Dopey mustered no compunctions about further mockery of Denny.

"I wonder if he's ever been scared shitless."

"Oh no, Dopey, you didn't just say dat!" bantered Hokey.

"I reckon the answer is yes. He's so scared of shittin' he don't do no eatin'. So, he's scared into shitlessness."

"Yeah. I know dat's right," sniggered Hokey.

"But what little he gots gets backed up bad!" yawped Dopey.

"I don't wanna be 'round *dat*!"

Both men laughed so loud they were worried that Denny might realize they were laughing at him, as he glanced their way through the haze of cigarette smoke and dim lighting. Dopey and Hokey quickly looked away, their countenances reeking with we-may've-been-caught culpability, with Hokey turning completely around in his chair.

****

Kristi Lou knew about Denny's fear factor and felt sympathetic toward him. But that didn't stop her from giggling. She was still sitting by herself, next to Hokey and Dopey's table. She began counting her dollars. Easily in earshot of her two coworkers' conversation, she did feel a smattering of guilt about her amusement, though her glee at another's troubles was without harshness, as Kristi Lou's unimpeachable moral compass rendered her incapable of true schadenfreude.

He's a shit-a-phobe. Kristi Lou felt her face grinning. *Of course, the proper medical terminology for Denny's condition is coprophobia—extreme fear of feces.*

Kristi Lou felt a pinch of puzzlement. She opened a selfie picture on her smartphone and looked at herself. *Coprophobia? Why do we know that word? I know we know lots of words, but why do we know that one? Where did we learn it? Why do we know about being petrified by poop?*

She closed her gallery folder and put the phone on the table.

Oh well, I must've read it or heard it somewhere.

She then returned to thinking about Denny's travails.

But, like Dopey just said, he can't help it. Poor Denny—he's really a nice guy. I hope Denny takes good-quality multiple vitamins, though. I'll have to ask him sometime, but I'll do it very discreetly; I don't want to embarrass him. How did we'all here at Secrets come to know about Denny's issue, anyway? He must've told someone and it got out and word spread around or whatever. Of course, there are worse things than having shit-a-phobia, I suppose—not many, though.

Kristi Lou giggled to herself, again. Her brain suppressed her lips' urge to grin.

****

Meanwhile, there was action across the room near the other end of the bar.

Davey Burton, a twenty-four-year-old drywall hanger with a GED diploma and a Secrets regular, had fallen into a heated foofaraw with an inebriated anonymous patron of about the same age who was sitting at the next table. The matter of contention, which carried great gravitas for both debaters, was establishing the identity of what is the world's best whiskey.

Dopey, having seen the wino's inebriation worsen to the level of Downtown Secrets no longer being able to legally serve him, had, about 15 minutes earlier, cut off all drinks for the first-time, tope-happy customer, who exited the bar and lurched onto the street. He was trailed by Davey as they tenaciously continued their verbal combat.

Davey was the customer who cursed backward.

Kristi Lou, upon hearing the commotion while sitting alone at her table and amusing herself over Denny's shit-a-phobia, had looked up to observe the ensuing squabble. The upheaval caused her to recall a conversation with one of her former dorm-mates back in late March when she still lived in an on-campus dormitory but occasionally visited Secrets after becoming fascinated with the club's hustle and bustle. She remembered explaining Davey to her girlfriend:

"Davey's a crazy guy. He gets so batty sometimes, especially when he's been drinking. He's a … well, he's a dyslexic curser. Davey doesn't have sequencing issues with other words—just profanity and related phrases. He gets 'em mixed up."

The two drunken debaters, having carried their pettifoggery onto Miracle Boulevard, continued blasting each other with unshackled billingsgate. Kristi Lou, Hokey, and Dopey went outdoors to continue watching the ongoing rumpus between the two tacky tongue-lashers. Rochelle and a few other dancers were already on the sidewalk. All onlookers nourished the hope that this blossoming enmity, filled with incendiary insolence and the promise of more richly tasteless jollity, would escalate.

"Whaddaya know 'bout what's good swishkey, you stupid-butt, slun-a-bitch. Yours juss shum fuck-head who wears ugly clothes," inveighed the drunkard, oblivious to his slurred syllables.

"I've already forgotten more about whiskey than you'll ever know," protested Davey Burton. "I bet you don't know the difference between whiskey and beer."

"Yeah, and I bet you think bourbon whissey is made outta blar-ley."

"Shit-bull, you ass-dumb sucker-cock. I know well damn that bourbon is made with corn and it's malt whiskey that's gots barley in it—you disrespectful pig!"

"No—you so stupid 'bout whissey you thinks it's got rubbin' alcohol in it, you shithead moron!"

"Off fuck! Out the fuck get of here! Off fuck and die, head-shit!"

"What?"

"You heard me, you idiot. Off fuck! Hell to go!"

"You sound like a retard. And flurthermore, I bet you gotta really schmal gherkin-pickle pecker."

Davey, indifferent to the vituperation directed at his penis, was offended solely because his knowledge of libations was being doubted. His anger rose.

"You fuck! I know my whiskey, you ass-dumb shit of piece! You fuck!"

"Whad the hell you shayin, you dumbass fucker? You stupid arse. You don't even makes no shense when youse cussin', you fluckin' fluck!"

Davey, becoming more antagonized, retaliated.

"You fuck! You fuck!"

"What?"

"You fuck!"

"Youse sayin' I fuck? Yeah, I fuck. I fuck your sister whenever I feels like it. I don't need no $10 bill—just a little sack of quarters. She's cheap but she's gots lots of 'sperience."

As the two adversaries walked obstreperously along about 12 feet from each other, Davey leaned toward his opponent and screamed.

"Yeah? I don't got no sister, but if I did she'd rather do it with a possum than with you, you bitch-of-a-son, you shit of sack! I know my whiskey! Dick my suck, sucker-cock! You disgusting degenerator!"

"What'd youse say? That's 'degenerate,' you mow-ron. You idiot-ass. You dunno whisk-ley and you can't even cuss right, you retarded butt-flucker!" retorted the cantankerous man, as he turned and stumbled away.

"No that's you, fucker-butt. I know my whiskey! You fuck! Hell in rot, you tard-bas hole-ass!"

"Listen at 'im. Davey goan holler some mo mess at dat dude," exclaimed Hokey, wild-eyed and grinning as he spoke. "He fixin' to be fussin' 'n' cussin' back-ards again. Here he go. Here he go. He goan cuss bass-ackards some mo. Here he go."

"Oh shit," said Rochelle. "Davey goan go off bad on dat dude. Davey ain't done fuckin' with his cussin'."

As the drunken antagonist staggered down Miracle Boulevard toward another tavern, he turned and gave Davey the middle-finger salute.

"You a looooooooosssseeeeerrrrrrrrr!" bellowed the polluted interloper, baying with laughter and sounding like a disorderly mule.

Davey fired back.

"Ass my kiss!"

The drunk, after stepping backward and almost falling down, stopped to grab his crotch and obscenely thrust his pelvis in and out at Davey. He then waved his left forefinger in a circular motion while pointing at the confused curser for what he now knew with certainty was—for Davey—a cataclysmic slander.

"And youse never will know shit 'bout whiskey!"

Over the course of about four seconds, and upon fully grasping the level of impudence inherent in this final and insufferable affront, Davey felt a gush of primitive indignation surge through his ribcage. He trembled with rage.

His fury detonated.

"Shit eat, fuckermother!"

Rochelle, dancing and cheering, screamed her support of the red-faced Davey.

"You tell 'im Davey! Woooo, yeah! Dat drunk-ass dude ain't dealin' wit' it! He kaint deal wit' it! I know dat's right! He don't know what it is! He kaint handle no ass-backards cussin'!"

Returning to the classic middle-finger gesture bomb, the drunken enemy forged his concluding retaliation, which was nearly reminiscent of a choreographed Olympic routine designed to close with dynamism in front of the judges. He opted for a double-handed flip-off, alternatingly pumping both hands up and down into the night air, and closed his masterwork with two full body spins like a human top. After almost flopping on his face, he then disappeared behind a building.

****

Hokey rubbed his scalp and looked down while walking back into the club.

"Does we gots any normal-ass people dat comes in here? Sheeeet."

"Oh my god—Davey," sighed Kristi Lou, turning away with her hand to her mouth and a coyly bemused smile.

"You know somethin', girl?" asked Rochelle, walking up to Kristi Lou on the sidewalk as Davey reentered Secrets.

"I know a few things."

"We got us a weird-ass bunch of fucked-up customers in dis place."

"Yes, you're right; that's surely for sure," agreed Kristi Lou, laughing. "We indeed do attract some rather unconventional people. It's commonly called 'an assortment of characters.' And we've definitely got 'em."

"You got dat right," affirmed Dark Rochelle. "Dey be *real* assorted."

"I know, right?"

Rochelle saw a figure emerging from the shadows across the street.

"Oh, here come dat funky-talkin' black dude who likes you. He likes Satine, too. He likes a white girl who's gots a mighty-fine bee-hind. He goan extra-like you tonight wearin' dat long peach-yellow dress huggin' dat booty tight and wit' dat slit so yo legs be flashin' in and out when you steppin'. I bet he got pockets stuffed wit' Secrets coupons."

Kristi Lou thought about, but did not speak about, the raw street-word that Rochelle, in a reversal of roles, had recently donated to Kristi Lou's ever-expanding vocabulary. Kristi Lou felt that, although both she and Satine were God-blessed with prominent, underbutt-crease-gifted, bounce-a-quarter-off-of, Grade-A nates, most competent ass assessors would conclude that neither of their rear-ends were of a sufficiently wide dimension as to warrant either curvy woman being accurately pegged as a "PAWG," an acronym that Kristi Lou learned abbreviates "phat-ass-white-girl," and, non-coincidentally, rhymes with "HAWG." Rochelle, however, during that earlier conversation, had purposively accentuated, in her flamboyantly idiomatic way, that such a crafted Caucasian keister "didn't hafta be no fat-ass vanilla ass, just a big'un."

"Yeah. He's OK. He keeps trying to get me to do the thing with him, but I don't feel comfortable with him that way. He's just not my cup of tea to do the thing with. Anyway, you can use only one coupon per night, so why does he carry those extra coupons with him?"

"Maybe 'cause—I dunno—'cause he might wanna try to get away with usin' more than one, or, maybe give 'em to other customers or somethin', you know, to try to get in good with somebody. He might even try to sell 'em. Who knows?" speculated Rochelle.

Rochelle and Kristi Lou strolled together back into Secrets and sat at a table near the front door, adjacent to the bar. Kristi Lou did not opt to hide from the customer whose backroom advances she knew she'd have to spurn again, preferring to do what she normally did and just politely deal with the quandary upfront. Unlike Bosco Mason, he always accepted no for an answer, on a per night basis, and thus she didn't have to fret over dealing with him throughout the remainder of his visit to the club.

The man spotted Satine first and went straight to her, sparing Kristi Lou any discomfort. About an hour later, after enjoying his time with Satine, he left, nodding and waving at Kristi Lou from about 25 feet away as he exited. Kristi Lou smiled and waved back.

Kristi Lou didn't have much to do from midnight till about one o'clock, having danced with just two men, neither of whom she knew. She danced with one man for three dances and danced with the other man for five dances. They both tipped her generously. Soon thereafter, Kristi Lou struck up a conversation with a well-groomed, articulate man wearing a tannish-gold suit sans a tie, and they spoke amicably for about 15 or 20 minutes, laughing often about Davey's unique style of swearing.

34

After spending about an hour chatting with Rochelle and Satine, Kristi Lou had been sitting by herself at the bar for around 12 minutes, playing games on her cellphone, when, just after 2:00, she spotted a familiar figure seated alone in the back of the main room. Bent over with his forearms on his lap and his chin tucked between the open collar of his crumpled dark-gray dress shirt, he sat—as motionless as a tombstone—staring at his mug of beer. He had removed all the ashtrays from his table. Although his face was obscured by darkness, Kristi Lou knew instantly who he was.

She put her phone in her purse and galvanized herself for another tête-à-tête with this unique man, knowing she was a lifeline for him and he for her. Of all the bizarre folks who ventured into Secrets and of all the people she had ever known anywhere, there was no one reminiscent of Mr. Winston Wilmont III.

Mr. Wilmont impressed everyone who worked at Downtown Secrets as a pleasant, courteous, and quite sophisticated gentleman.

His early life, however, was fraught with cataclysm. During a family vacation in 1930 when he was almost one year old, his parents perished together in a predawn motel immolation ignited by an arsonist who had doused the flammable carpeting and walls of several first-floor rooms below

335

with gasoline and tossed a lighted match into his igneous, death-dealing pyromaniacal stunt. Awakened and then weakened by the fire's baneful fumes that had rapidly seeped upward in the poorly insulated economy motel, Winston Wilmont II, after opening the door and learning that the entire second-floor hallway was glutted with flames and lung-singeing smoke, as his final act before succumbing to asphyxiation, managed to use his elbow to smash a good-sized hole in the cheap-glass window of the hostelry's bathroom and drop baby-Winston III, who had been quickly wrapped in a bright-blue bath towel by his mother, into the un-mowed, ultra-thick and cushiony Kentucky Bluegrass abutting the rear of the motel. Winston, with pudgy arms and legs threshing turbulently out of the slapdash fardel, was sighted by a firefighter a split-moment before he would have otherwise aimed his pressurized water-cannon hose—discharging water with enough velocity to easily kill an infant—at the bottom of the motel a half-yard beyond where Winston lay.

Orphaned and left with no close relatives, Winston was an oft-de-pressed ward of the state in a Michigan multi-child foster home until he joined the armed forces at eighteen. Within a month of completing his 12-year military stint in 1959, the then-30 and recently married Mr. Wilmont, utilizing G.I. Bill benefits, enrolled at Central Michigan University where he earned a four-year statistics degree that propelled him to a lucrative career as a federal-government statistician.

Now at the age of eighty-nine, the uncommonly unsenile Winston Wilmont, of German/Polish heritage, was the establishment's oldest known consistent customer. As Dopey once said, "You know he's got some mileage on his tires; he's six years older than I am."

No one knew of any other octogenarians who regularly ventured into the club. Mr. Wilmont, as Kristi Lou always respectfully called him, was a quiet man, dutifully polite toward all dancers, and often saturated with palpable loneliness. His was the isolation often endured by many elderly people who still live self-sufficiently alone.

Although he was old enough to vividly recall the Great Depression and 10-cent fudge sundaes, his reproductive instincts, while attenuated by the biology of aging, remained intact and therefore he was attracted to the sensual young women who graced Secrets. But there was another more personal and stronger reason he felt compelled to maintain his status as a regular patron in this decadent venue where he seemed to most onlookers so strikingly incongruous with the habitat.

Kristi Lou, from their many conversations over the previous three-and-a-half months, knew his story. His wife of 59 years had worked as a burlesque-style ecdysiast in New Orleans. The night they met, in 1958, she was stripping at a dive in the French Quarter. He was a U.S. Marine, stationed aboard a destroyer-class naval ship, on shore leave. He was five years her senior. Their wedding was seven months later.

As Mr. Wilmont once told Kristi Lou, "My wife married one of her customers! That's considered a taboo boo-boo for gals working in the sex industry. But it happens. And it can be fruitful. Maybe it's rare, but it worked for us. And besides, Mary and I were both odd as hell, anyway."

Mary Wilmont died of lymphoma in March. Winston Wilmont began frequenting Secrets in May.

Mr. and Mrs. Wilmont never had children. He had told Kristi Lou one night in June that, "We didn't want to have kids but we wanted to have kids. Over the years, while we were trying to make up our minds about having kids, her biological clock ticked out."

Winston Wilmont lived in an upscale five-bedroom house in Lake Orion, but only one bedroom was ever used, as he had no family or anyone else to come and stay with him. He employed a young Frenchwoman as an au pair girl. She came by once every two weeks to vacuum, mop, and do whatever else needed to be done, and, other than when he visited Secrets, she was usually his sole company—though she spoke limited English.

Embodying old-age cognitive acuity, Mr. Wilmont commuted safely to Downtown Secrets in his plum-burgundy, late-model, full-size Cadillac.

Kristi Lou realized that not only did Mr. Wilmont—despite always keeping himself clean-shaven and immaculately groomed—usually look like a sad, lost pup looking for Mary, he was also truly suffering. Physically, Mr. Wilmont was remarkably healthy. Emotionally, he was lugubrious beyond disconsolation, his unyielding grief having carried him into the clutches of clinical depression, for which, despite his diminishing appetite and increasingly insufficient sleep, he obstinately refused to seek psychiatric help.

Remembering her own obstinacy in initially rejecting admonitions for her to go for counseling during her trauma-laden schooldays, Kristi Lou feared for him, that he might permit himself to be claimed by suicide's cold but effective pathway of escape from unrelenting anguish. He merely alluded to taking his life, never saying directly that he would. But he and Kristi Lou both harbored religious concerns regarding his fate should he choose to travel on that path, fearful for his soul if the rumors were true that God just might punish those who reject the gift of mortal living, despite its agony, by condemning such escapers to eternal damnation—although neither believed God would be so unkind.

Uniquely concerned—ad infinitum—with the well-being of others for whom she cared, Kristi Lou could not permit such anathema to be the destiny that would befall her aged friend.

****

"Hey, Mr. Wilmont," said Kristi Lou as she arrived at his table. "I haven't seen you in a couple of weeks. I've missed you. May I sit down, please?"

"No, get the hell out of here."

Kristi Lou giggled and asked again.

"Will you please let me sit down?"

"Oh, OK then, if you insist, go ahead and have a seat. I suppose I can tolerate your presence awhile."

Although rather saturnine toward most people, Mr. Wilmont gladly opened up conversationally to Kristi Lou, and here he grinned widely, revealing a Hollywood-worthy, bright-white smile festooned with the best dentures dentistry had to offer.

Kristi Lou bent forward and gave him a tight, firm hug for about three seconds, followed by a quick peck-kiss on his right cheek. She then sat in the chair across the table from Mr. Wilmont.

"You know, about the only time I smile is when I come into this place and talk to you," he said, intending to compliment Kristi Lou, which was achieved, but also serving to deepen her sincere concern, little of which would be felt, she immediately sensed, by most twenty-one-year-old women, much less shady ladies of the nighttime.

"Well, we've just got to fix that. I love seeing you in here. I really do. But—and I hope you won't get mad at me for saying this again—but I still think you should look into going to one of the senior centers in Lake Orion, or somewhere. Why not?"

"I know your advice is well-intended, and it's also very sound, but…I don't think, I just don't think that, that I'd find too many ex-strippers in there and this joint here…it looks a helluva lot like where I came across my Mary back in '58. I know I'm supposed to let it go, as they say, but I…I just can't. I'm sorry, but I just…"

"It's OK. I know. It's OK, sir. You cannot—and furthermore, you should not—just let Mary go. It would be good if you could let go of most—but not all—of the yearning, the grief. But, I'll never tell you to just let the whole thing go. That's not reasonable and it's not right. You can't do that—and you shouldn't. You should keep Mary with you and you should miss her—but to a less painful degree than now. We need to get you there. It's degrees. It's degrees; it's not a total cutoff.

Anyhow, it's going to be OK. I promise you. God knows, I haven't endured what you have. But I know you know I often feel lonely, too."

"I know, I know," said Mr. Wilmont, "and we've got to bust you loose from that snare."

"Yeah, loneliness," said Kristi Lou, sighing.

"There is no bloodshed," stated the taciturn Mr. Wilmont in a breathy voice while peering raptly at Kristi Lou. "There are no damaged organs. There are no severed limbs, nor are there any broken bones. But you can be certain that loneliness, when it becomes overwhelming, is quietly violent. The subtle violence of loneliness, if it wins, can rip away your spirit and crush your soul … a dull ripping, a slow crushing … and your pride makes you deny to everyone that you care whether anyone likes you or wants to be with you, but … there are few forces more devastating than deep loneliness … Did you know you can be surrounded by people and loud sounds and still be drowning in loneliness?"

"Yes, I know that fact quite well."

"On any given day or night, anywhere around the world, you can step into a bar and find a sampling of the most godforsaken people you could ever meet; some of the loneliest people on Earth come into bars. I don't blame them a'tall, though, 'cause they're trying. Look at me; I'm here in this bar."

Mr. Wilmont started to drink a swig of beer but then put the mug back on the table.

"Too much loneliness creeps up on you like a treacherous shadow and when you realize it's got ahold of you it can seem like it's too late to get away; it's … uh, it's both depressing and softly terrifying. It's like being in a building and seeing the walls slowly closing in on you but somehow you can't make yourself run out the door."

"Yes," assented Kristi Lou, "with loneliness and depression it's sometimes as if we're immobilized and we can't persuade ourselves to try to move anymore, and I …"

"But, Kristi Lou, despite what I just said, don't let it defeat you without a fight. It's worth it to fight it, to fight it hard and bravely."

"Yes, we'll fight back against it," vowed Kristi Lou. "As I said, I struggle with loneliness daily, myself, and…I often try to deny that I do but when I'm honest with myself I know that…well…I know that when I cry myself to sleep, as I sometimes do, that my denials are lies."

"You've never told me that sometimes you cry yourself to sleep. But, I knew you did."

"I know you knew. Yes, loneliness is an acquaintance of mine."

"Yeah, I know you're lonely, and I'm sensitive to your loneliness, but…"

"I know you are, Mr. Wilmont, and I thank you for that."

"…but, unlike me, you're young and vital and have all those years ahead of you. You're going to be happy; I damn well guarantee it. I promise you; you will be happy. You'll be a happy girl. You'll meet new friends—people you can relate to better than you can with the folks you work with in here, or that you see in here as customers, including me. Or, you'll get back together with old friends, maybe down there in Arkansas. And you're going to find a goodhearted young man to marry. You mark my word. You're going to make it; you're going to have a good life."

"You know something, Mr. Wilmont, if I were a bit older, you'd have to beat me off you with a stick."

"Yeah…'a bit,' huh? If I were 400 years younger, you'd be running from me because I would be after you."

"I would not run from you. I'd run to you."

Mr. Wilmont, a classic crusty codger and still ever the Marine, tried to react curmudgeonly, mustering a contrived hardboiled face while also feeling an upsurge of fidelity toward Mary. But a spontaneous smile and extra moisture in his eyes manifested against his will and belied his unsentimental fascia. Kristi Lou, whose perspicacity matched her height, easily intuited his discomfort with the sweetness she had elicited from him. Recovering masterfully, she gave them both a verbal out.

"Of course, you might throw me over your shoulder like a Neanderthal caveman and make me do housework all day."

"Oh, I would not."

They both laughed, averting a continuance of the tenderness—at least in its overt form—with which he was uncomfortable but in which they mutually reveled. Kristi Lou knew, regardless of outer protestations to the contrary, that Mr. Wilmont cherished such moments of shared warmth.

"Look, Kristi Lou," said Mr. Wilmont, "there's this thing, this … well, this … uh, this awful thing that's been upsetting me for, for, well, for decades. I never told anyone a'tall about it but Mary. I still talk to Mary about it, and about other things, too, as you know, with her up in heaven and all. But, it's—this thing—it's, uh, it's been happening more just in recent weeks, and, well, I was just wondering if I could … I don't know … if I could, uh …"

"Talk to me about it? Are you kidding, Mr. Wilmont? You can talk to me about anything."

"Well, all right. Thank you, Kristi Lou. Uh, well, I mean, uh … yeah, thank you. Anyway, this may sound technical, but I want to talk *with* you more than talk *to* you."

"Oh yes, I like that much better; I'll have to remember that. It's better to talk with than to talk to. I agree."

"OK, then. Well, what it is, is that … well, it's that … oh, hell! I probably should be living in a nuthouse and taking loony-bin medication."

"Yeah, you might be right. Just joking … sorta. Anyway, let's have at it. I wanna know. What is it? Tell me. Go ahead. Tell me about it."

"Well, all right. You see, after I left the Marine Corps, I uh, I … I don't know if I should … I …"

"You what? Come on—out with it. You can't get me interested like this and just leave me in limbo; that would be rude and I know you're not that way. I've gotta hear it. After you left the Marine Corps, you did what?"

"I…I don't know if I should really divulge…"

"Mr. Wilmont! You did what? Tell me now!"

"I dropped acid."

'You did?"

"Yeah, I did. I took LSD. Mary didn't. I did. She was always smarter than I was."

"Oh, I've heard and read about the effects of LSD, but I don't know a bunch about it. I know it was popular in the 1960s. But, is that the one with…the drug with…the wild dreaming—the trips? Isn't it good trips and bad trips?"

"Yes, that's it. That's LSD."

"Well," said Kristi Lou, "there was this old band from the '60s, from back in that decade. It was called The Doors, whose lead singer and his bandmates were thought to be rather LSD-centric. So, I'm guessing you know of the Doors."

"The Doors? Are you serious? One of my all-time favorite bands."

"Well, I'm somewhat of a freak in that I like to listen to a lot of vintage music and one of their songs kinda sorta helped inspire—if that's the right word—me to venture into this life I'm now living, working in Secrets and so forth. It's called 'Break on Through to the Other Side.'"

"Damn, you like that song? I've got that song on about four or five different records or tapes or CDs. How about that?"

"Yeah. So, your sitting here telling me, coincidentally—I guess—about dropping LSD acid back then, in the '60s, brought to mind how that song was part of my decision to do this…what I'm doing in here in this place and all. But, so, so…OK…what's going on? What's been happening for 'decades,' as you put it?"

"Well, you kinda just hit on it. You sure did. You just…I…I, uh…"

"What?"

"I keep having the same bad trip, the same very, very, very bad trip."

"Oh. Well, so it's a bad trip thing, then. All right, I'm sorry that's been happening to you, hanging over you for all these years."

"Yeah."

"OK, tell me about it. I won't let anyone interrupt us for more time than it takes for me to politely say 'I'm busy now.' OK, I'm listening; get it out."

Mr. Wilmont looked at the fingers of his right hand as he slowly tapped his fingertips on the table for about five seconds.

"OK. Here goes. I used to take acid in the mid-'60s. I took it on and off for a couple of years. As they used to say, I 'experimented with it.' You know, if I'd taken it to open my mind to be more receptive of spiritual enlightenment, then it could've been viewed as an entheogen—and thus maybe I wouldn't have pissed off God. Hell, I don't know."

"Yeah—entheogen. I read that word in my dictionary one day. As you said, it's using a mind-altering drug to enhance spirituality."

"Yes. Literally translated, entheogen means 'generating the divine within.'"

"I didn't know that. Thanks for enriching my vocab knowledge."

"You're welcome. But, the thing is, I just took LSD recreationally."

"Oh."

"So, one day—it was on a Saturday afternoon in October—I had to survive one intensely bad trip. Let's just say it was *very* intense; it jacked the bejesus out of me. Mary had to drive me to the VA Hospital. They had me strapped down on a gurney in the psych ward. I was a certifiable lunatic there for 13 days till I was kinda detoxed and then the lead shrink released me. I think they needed to free up the bed for some other vet. Anyway, ever since that day I've eschewed LSD."

"I'm glad you quit."

"But—there's been no eschewal of me by LSD. Those nightmarish visions remain embedded in my brain and still surface now and then, and in vivid lucidity. And I'm talking really lucid, like I'm still tripping. When I get hit with one of these flashbacks, I, I don't, uh, I don't actually know whether I'm having another occurrence of the same actual acid trip I had 50-plus years ago or if I'm just having terrifying memories of those trips. But, I do know that when it happens I'm scared shitless."

"I don't want anything scaring you," reassured Kristi Lou, as she couldn't stop herself from being reminded of Denny.

"Thanks. I so much appreciate your caring. So, well…uh…so far, it happens only when I'm home. I dread it happening when I'm out somewhere, like here at Secrets or wherever. But, I just have to bury my face in my hands till it passes, and that usually takes two or three minutes, though it always seems almost unending. I'm not sure what triggers it, but since it happens exclusively in the damn house, so far, I'm thinking there may be something in that environment that sets me off.

"It used to happen once or twice monthly. But lately, for what-the-hell-ever reason, it's been happening every other day or so—been going on like that for about a month, sometimes more often, I think. And damn if I'm not wide awake when it happens. I'll be watching television or reading a book and it comes and gets me."

Kristi Lou reached over to Mr. Wilmont and stroked his hair twice.

"It's always the same thing that happens? The same visions? It's a reoccurring dream, or trip?"

"Yes, basically it's almost always identical, though there are occasionally some slight variations. But it's easily recognizable to me as the same damn thing.

"I've read up on it online. The APA—that's the American Psychiatric Association—has a guidebook called the Diagnostic and Statistical Manual of Mental Disorders. So, what I've got is a rare thing, but it has a name. Technically, I've got HPPD—Hallucinogen Persisting Perception Disorder. I think it's also called Flashback Hallucinosis. I call it a '60s flower-child-style LSD trip gone hell's-bells haywire."

"OK, I'm sure it's awful, but…"

"The dealer sold me what they now call Jesus Christ acid."

"Why do they call it…?"

"They call it that because it's super goddamn, uh…I'm sorry…super…it's super potent. It's so potent…so potent it might let you see Jesus."

"Oh, it is that, that potent? I see. All right, I can tell it's terrible and it's terribly hard to talk about. But give me the details, please. I won't think less of you, if you're possibly worried about that. I absolutely won't. As you know, I've uh, well, I've had some shuddersome trauma in my lifetime, too. Anyhow, I'm on your side. I'm going to help you."

"I know you won't be judgmental against me. I'm very grateful for that."

Mr. Wilmont began sweating at the top of his forehead, and Kristi Lou saw a bead of perspiration roll down and into his bushy left eyebrow. Kristi Lou took a tissue from her mini bag and wiped his face.

"Thank you," said Mr. Wilmont, peering through the thick lenses of his bifocals and locking his gaze on his mug of beer, the object at which he had chosen to stare after commencing to tell his tale.

"All right, here is my trip."

"I'm nothing but ears. Tell me everything."

"I'm engulfed in an iridescent milieu of phantasmagoria within a kaleidoscope of harshly bright, multi-colored strobe lights, mostly orange, red, and purple—all glaringly prismatic. Everything is 1960s psychedelic. I turn into a donkey."

Mr. Wilmont, knowing that donkeys are animals that humans often reference in their comicality, looked up at Kristi Lou to check her facial expression. He saw that her face was imbued with not only fascination but also deep sincerity, and sans even a trace of cynicism or budding amusement. He expected no less from her, but he needed assurance, and was thus encouraged to continue his humiliating revelation.

"You, you turn into a donk…OK, I got it. Go ahead."

"Yes. I do. After I become a donkey, I'm forced to coil into a fetal contortion with all four hirsute legs in an equine ball next to a heating vent on the floor of a bedroom—I think it's my own bedroom—and then I have to unfold just enough to eat parts of myself to avoid starvation because my digestive system won't accept any other food. The heat blazing up from the furnace in the basement and through the floor vent is so hot that it cooks me, with bubbling skin like bacon in a skillet, to make me taste more succulent for myself; in a gruesome way, it's a highly personalized meal.

"I vibrantly see blood spurting when I bite into my body with enlarged wolf-like fangs that are affixed inside my otherwise donkey's mouth. I hear one sound—my screams resulting from the pain I inflict upon myself, but my screams are blood-curdling—literally—because my blood is in my mouth, and it's gurgling and then it curdles as I scream; it's like I'm gargling. I'm forced to gargle with my own body fluids, and since I'm screaming I'm vigorously exhaling and so there's a grotesque red mess with grossly oversized blood droplets spraying into the air like a wild crimson cloudburst and then splashing with heavy thuds that vibrate the floor and walls.

"And I…I, I normally consume my upper arms that look like donkey legs first and then bend forward to start eating my donkey-looking shins and then my ankles.

"But, now and then, it makes me devour my testicles.

"I become a carnivorous donkey. I have to swallow myself. I'm a cannibal. But I'm my own victim. You know the old saying that 'you are what you eat'?"

Mr. Wilmont did not smile, nor did Kristi Lou, who knew the moment held no humor.

"But there is a treacherous trap that catches me.

"I have a ghastly Catch-22. The damn thing…it torments me psychologically with the realization—and I constantly realize it—that always hammers home to my mind that I'm devouring my only source of nourishment. Ultimately, I'll run out of meat. I'll eventually eat myself up and then I'll starve. But, if I've devoured all of myself, then there's not only nothing left to eat, there's nothing left to feed. So, I should be dead; even if I didn't kill myself from self-inflicted trauma wounds, I would cause myself to cease to exist because I'd have eaten all of me which would make me vanish.

"But, I, uh, I … it gets so confusing. During the trip, I'm compelled to view an image of myself trying to eat my mouth but … but, you can't eat the very thing you use to do your eating, so I, I … I'm trapped in a double-bind deadlock I can't get out of, and …"

Mr. Wilmont quickly peeked up from his glass of beer at Kristi Lou. Seeing that she was mesmerized with her gaze locked in on his face and her lips open, and the environs of Downtown Secrets utterly obstructed from her awareness, he instantly reaffixed his eyes back upon the mug. He felt that the golden hue living in the beer, bathed in candlelight, somehow afforded a soothing ambience against his desperate revelation to his young, beautiful, full-of-life-and-potential friend from the other end of the age spectrum.

" … and, during a period of only several minutes of actual, real-time dreaming, my virtual world—I guess you can call it that—that I'm caught in will span weeks of self-consumption. That's right—weeks; the whole ordeal, in my mind, goes on for weeks. I don't know whether I'll eventually die from eating myself to death because of devastating my flesh and organs, or from starvation when, after consuming so much of myself, there would remain only a few morsels of myself left to eat. Like I was saying, by eating all of myself, I would extinguish my sole supply of sustenance, but … but I'd also disappear so there'd be nothing left to feed, anyway.

"But when I have to eat my stomach, that's, uh … that's when it gets unbearable. I can look down and see there is nowhere for my food that is my own flesh to go to. So, I can't digest. And then I would truly famish. My mind, during the trips, conjures the image of my donkey canine incisors biting off a large chunk of my stomach and then swallowing and seeing that piece of my stomach drop to the floor after passing through the hole in my stomach that I had just bitten open. I have to pick it up and eat it again but it keeps dropping out because the part of me that's supposed to hold the food was just eaten *as* food. And I'm in this cycle of eating my stomach till the damn trip lets me go."

"Oh God," said Kristi Lou. "I'm so sorry…"

"Another be-damned thing is that my trip doesn't explain why I'm a donkey, or how a donkey could require meat, because donkeys are vegetarians; they're supposed to be cud-chewing herbivores, not flesh-eating carnivores. I remember once when I was a little kid of about six or so that I was at a petting farm and I petted a donkey and I felt he looked sort of sad.

"So, anyhow, this … uh … this, this recurring nightmare of mine, this trip, often, but not always, ends with the same brutal termination. Sometimes, after I've cannibalized my anatomy down to a small, bloody remnant of myself and I'm mostly just a huge mouth with teeth that won't quit their chomping motions, the furnace in the basement changes from an oven that is cooking me through the floor vent to a suction device sucking my scanty remains into the wall and then what's left of me is eaten by the donkey-eating anthropophagus monster who, himself, is a giant donkey—but as huge as a Tyrannosaurus—living and lurking in the soggy ground below the house's ventilation ducts.

"My screaming when I eat myself is the only sound that happens, because there is no other sound allowed. Other than my screams, there's no sound a'tall. It's soundless. It's, it's, it's perfectly sterile silence, so cold, so hopeless, and so filled with Lordless despair. I know no one can hear me and nothing can save me—unless I wake up.

"But the worst horror is that some entity, some evil element of the trip that I can't see or explain but that can communicate more directly with me, keeps telling me—the real, semi-conscious me—that one day I won't wake up. It says to me 'You won't wake up—but you won't die.' Oh dear God…It's telling me that I can't be freed a'tall, even by death. It's telling me that someday I'll be locked into this sequence forever. I'm pretty damn sure that's biologically impossible—that it could keep on keeping me alive and making me continue devouring my cannibal donkey self into perpetuity. I mean, I have to be awake to swallow some real food and use the toilet and, uh, other real-life necessities, but…I don't know. It scares the hell out of me.

"I'm a man, a grown man, an old man; I shouldn't let this be happening to me, but, I can't…I can't seem to make it stop. I, uh, I just can't. It seems ineluctable. Is there no escape?

"Acid doesn't hit everyone like this. Why me? I want to live. I so very much want to live. With the time I have left, Kristi Lou, I want to live."

Mr. Wilmont was softly crying. He wiped his nose on his sleeve as would a child.

Kristi Lou, transcendentally sympathetic as her modus operandi, wanted to deliver Mr. Wilmont into rescue with immediacy; she needed to birth his deliverance with one all-embracing induction of instantaneous salvation.

But her mind had trouble picturing this highly intelligent, educated, tough ancient mariner, who was also most convivial and suitably mature, as trapped inside such an isochronal cauldron of unimaginable excruciation. She felt ambuscaded. And, to her surprise, she felt badly shaken. This data did not compute. Kristi Lou, before Mr. Wilmont presented the details of his inconceivable predicament, did not anticipate that what he was going to tell her would be so disturbingly bizarre. She struggled to process what he had told her and how she should go about helping him.

Unaccustomed to feeling so perplexed over anyone's problems besides her own, Kristi Lou looked away, looking through lit candles and billows of cigar smoke over at Hokey laughing with a customer, and then looked back at Mr. Wilmont. She then looked down at the table and then at her hands. She observed what her brain had not previously detected, that she was nervously twisting her fingers into pretzel-like deformities.

Kristi Lou then received an intrusive insight. She realized that not only did she seek to aid Mr. Wilmont for his sake, but that she also felt motivated by a surge of vanity. She felt a serious challenge to her ability to understand and to say the right things to be empathic toward another person in need of compassion. She took pride in being a capable confidante, and now she felt somewhat lost.

Inwardly, she quickly chided herself.

Oh, don't be vain about yourself. This is about Mr. Wilmont, not you.

"OK. Give me just a few moments, please, Mr. Wilmont, OK? I'm digesting, uh … no … I'm sor … I mean I'm thinking about what you've said. I want to give you a really good response. So just hold on, OK?"

"Sure, that's fine," replied Mr. Wilmont, with a trembling voice and a face that appeared to Kristi Lou to say: *You're my final hope … please.*

Mr. Wilmont had perspired throughout his confession. His tears had stopped falling within a few seconds. He took the pink tissue that Kristi Lou had used on him earlier and wiped his face. She reached into her small pocket purse and gave him two more tissues, one of which he immediately used, causing her to be taken aback by the sight of a rugged old Marine shamelessly wiping his hard face with a soft, pink tissue.

"I knew you wouldn't gloss over it, that you'd take me seriously. That's why I chose you to talk with about it."

"Thank you for trusting me. I'm touched by your trust in me. I really am. Let me contemplate. I'll be right with you."

"OK."

It's dawning on me amid all this LSD tumult that Mr. Wilmont hasn't heard about Bosco knifing me ... he would've been upset and asked me how I'm doing. Don't tell him. Focus on him. OK, OK, OK ... Mr. Wilmont is probably the last person I know who I'd think would see himself as a donkey eating himself. So shockingly unfathomable. But this is a terrible, ungodly thing for him. He's such a good man. I, I want to, I want to say the best things I can say. Think before you speak. Think carefully. Be calculating as well as spontaneous. Just get it down pat before you talk to him, OK? Oh my goodness ... he's counting on you. Just don't, don't ... Right now, he's as fragile as thin glass. Don't shatter him.

Kristi Lou gazed at her thumbnails in her lap while cogitating intensively, poring through her ruminations for 14 seconds.

"All right. There are three main words I want to say right away."

"OK," said Mr. Wilmont, looking up from his beer with a child-like yearning to be protected.

"The first word is 'listened' and the second word is 'therapy' and the third word is 'concrete.'"

"OK, good. That's good. Those are good words."

"I listened to every syllable you said."

"I know you did."

"And just to zoom in very directly, I believe what you really need to swallow here is your you-know-what that starts with a P and go to a top-notch therapist, a psychologist or psychiatrist. But make sure you feel comfortable with him or her before you get hooked into going back for multiple sessions. You need, need, need therapy."

"OK, my pride can be swallowed."

"And I want to say in a very concrete way that, regardless of what your vicious LSD trip keeps screaming at you, I know that you will never morph into a donkey and you will never cannibalize yourself. Those things will never, never, never happen. I say that expressly. I say that concretely. And I know that, intellectually and logically, you actually know that, too. We both know that. You know you literally can't make such an unnatural transformation. You cannot morph into a donkey; that evolution is not possible.

"But, it's the trip—the reoccurring gory trip—that is so horrible to visualize, especially during those moments while you're locked into it. And that part, that is, being captured and held like a prisoner, is what you identified as almost the worst thing. Your trip has some type of voice and it torments you by threatening you with one day getting stuck forever in the nightmare because you can't wake up, and that you won't be able to get out of it even by dying. And that scenario … that's truly the worst thing, the ultimate worst thing. Well, I'm here to tell you unequivocally, to tell you concretely, that you will never, ever, be unable to wake up. I know for a fact that you will *always* be able to wake up."

"Thank you so much. I hope you're right."

"I'm always right about such things. Your trip voice is a bully. Personally, I loathe bullying. He or she or it is lying to you because it takes pleasure in tormenting you. It's a bully and it can't win—not in the long run. Yes, I know, in a way it's been winning as far as scaring you for all this long time and haunting you so you're more tired than you should be, and all that is certainly not good because it detracts awfully from the quality of your life and adversely impacts your health. But, don't forget the truth that all bullies, at their core, are cowardly invertebrates and that they operate from an underpinning of weakness.

"Listen to me when I say this, Mr. Wilmont. The next time your hateful LSD trip bully starts telling you that someday you won't wake up, just remember what I'm telling you now—it's a liar; it's a lying bully and bullies will eventually always lose, and because you are good you will win. You are a good-hearted man and you will be the winner because that's what's right. I am Kristi Lou Jones from Little Rock, Arkansas and I'm your true friend and I promise you that you will always wake up and that you will be happy to live your life."

Mr. Wilmont's rutted brow, gnarled with agedness, relaxed just perceptibly enough so Kristi Lou could see some of the skin folds in his forehead smooth out. As she saw the wetness gather unavoidably in his weary eyes, tears welled up under her own eyelids. As if scripted, all four eyes released the same-sized tear in each of their corners, yielding four streaks of commensurate moisture that halted their cascades at the same moment upon reaching their respective mandibles.

There in a tenebrous corner of a house of ill repute, two disparate faces intersected, one face with supple, delicate, healthy skin and the passion of youth juxtaposed in unlikely unison with a face enclosed in wrinkles that revealed the brave endurance of countless tribulations that must accompany the bearer of nine decades of living. Two people, both intellectually capable of grasping paradox, sensed unisonously, without wordage, how they were so far away and different and how they were so intimately close and exactly the same.

Like Kristi Lou's other speeches, this one was laced with her impassioned sincerity. Unlike her other speeches, this one seemed to save an isolated near-nonagenarian from desolation and death.

Mr. Wilmont thought he would have to force a smile. The ends of his mouth moved upward with natural ease.

"Thank you, young lady. I think that your resounding reassurance, stated so firmly and, yes, concretely, is precisely what I wanted you to give to me. You gave me a gift. I know you're not a shrink. But you're right, as you usually are about most things, when you say I should go and talk with one. I knew you'd really listen and, well, that you'd just…I don't know…that you'd care about me, an old man still on an old LSD trip from half a century ago.

"You know," continued Mr. Wilmont, "I'm remembering a wise thing my foster-home granddaddy told me one day while I sat on his lap: 'People who talk but don't listen don't know what they're talking about.'

You're perfectly the opposite of that. You listen earnestly. And, I can't thank you too much. No, I can't thank you enough."

"Oh, well, you're welcome. I know I didn't say anything earthshaking, but I …"

"Yes, you did."

Kristi Lou recognized that her own vanity—her pride in being an effectual helper—was being tended to by Mr. Wilmont. She felt a wave of warmth and reassurance, but primarily gratitude, because she knew that, although his appreciation for her kindness was rampant with candor, he was also bolstering her ego—and doing so quite purposely. But she wanted to keep any focus on herself in check.

"I did? Well, OK, that makes me feel good that you say I helped. But the main thing is that you, that you … the main thing is your well-being," she replied as she reached across the table and refastened a button that was hanging loose on Mr. Wilmont's shirt.

"Yeah, that one keeps coming unbuttoned. Thanks. You know, Kristi Lou, you're such a winsome distaff."

"I'm a what?"

"Well now, did I use a word that you don't know, Miss Vocabulary?"

"You used two of them—in a row."

"I better go get Rochelle and tell her about this."

"No! Please don't! You'll ruin my rep and devastate my pride!" said Kristi Lou, feigning peril by pushing the top of her right hand onto her forehead. "I'm prideful about my wordsmithery, or, in my case, my wordjonesery, as I goofily say."

"OK, I won't, then. All right. Winsome means charming and innocent and sweet. And distaff means a girl—though that definition of distaff might be considered archaic today. But I'm not what you'd call non-archaic, myself, so that makes it OK."

"I love to learn new words and this time, with you, I didn't even have to read my favorite book that I love—the almighty dictionary. Cool."

I love it when he talks vocabulary to me ... much more titillating than dirty talking from whomever ... but he's almost 90, so we can't ... uh ... bummer! Ha-ha!

They both looked around for a moment at dancers and patrons interacting in Secrets. Mr. Wilmont took Kristi Lou by her shoulders and gently turned her toward him.

"Kristi Lou, I want to tell you ... well, I just want to say, uh, don't ... don't keep working here too much longer. I don't think you'd ever let yourself get crustal—there's another word for you—that is, hardened with a roughened crust, but ... look—there are some good people that toil in these places, like my Mary, and some good people who come in as customers ... good people. But, just don't stay too long. Do you understand what I'm telling you?"

"Oh, do I ever—yes, I ... yes ... I most certainly do. I think about that subject a lot—daily, the truth be known. You know we've talked about it a few times before."

"Yes, we have."

"You know what?" asked Kristi Lou, preparing to share with Mr. Wilmont the resurfaced thought of commonality that had occurred to her while he was describing his bad trip but that she had since temporarily forgotten.

"What?"

"You kinda remind me of—I mean with your repugnant LSD trip that's not really real but seems like it—you remind me of one of my teachers from a long time ago back in Little Rock. He didn't have any LSD trips, I don't think, but he had these bizarro-world, dire dreams."

"Really?"

"Yeah."

"Your teacher told you about his dreams?"

"Oh, no—he didn't tell me. But I knew about them 'cause there was this one day that Mom let me wander off after my counseling session with my therapist and I wound up walking in the woods behind the store down the street from the therapist's office and I overheard my therapist talking to Mr. Bat…I heard mine talking to his—my therapist talking to his therapist—and his told mine all about the dreams that my teacher had. And I, well, I, I was very prominently in his dreams—me. And I happened to come along there to overhear it."

"Well, was it a case of, you know, a pedophile-type attraction he felt toward you—that sort of thing that goes on sometimes?"

"No. Absolutely not. It wasn't that whatsoever. That actually would've been closer to normal, as odd as that might sound. In ye olde nutshell, he was extremely insecure about being so short and I was extremely insecure about being so tall. And we were in the same classroom; he was my general science teacher and I also had him for homeroom, wouldn't you know it? We both hated it … well, for a while, we did. Then we started sorta liking each other, after we, you know, kinda gained a better understanding.

"Anyway, there I was having wandered into the woods with no idea I'd have a chance to eavesdrop on a conversation between my shrink and his shrink and hear myself being talked about as a giant 50-foot beastess attacking him in a selcouth, freak-out dream he had one night. It was weirder than weirdness."

Mr. Wilmont, now glad the conversational focus had shifted away from him and onto Kristi Lou, paused for a few moments to think about what she had said and then nodded his head up and down.

"Yes, not only selcouth-ish and weird as far as his weird dream, but also weird that there was such a weird coincidence that you had actually wandered into the perfect position to overhear that conversation. I mean, you had to wind up in just about the perfect place to be close enough to hear them talking—and without being seen because that would've shut them up and you wouldn't have learned about his dream—and you also had to be there when—that is, at just the right time—when they actually talked about the subject of this dream in which you were, I guess from what you just said, stalking him as a King-Kong-ish symbol signifying the futility of his shortness. You were there during the period of just a few minutes when they talked about you. That is, you could've overheard them talking about the weather on the moon or one of them having a car in the repair shop or whatever random topic. The odds would've been pretty high against you coming along at just the perfecto time to overhear them talking about the strange situation between you and your teacher."

"Exactly! I'm utterly fascinated by coincidences. I don't know, but I believe maybe I have more of them than most people have."

"Yeah, you probably do. But that's fine. There's nothing wrong with that."

Mr. Wilmont tilted his left wrist inward and glanced at the mid-1990s wristwatch Mary had given him shortly before her death. She had bought the watch for him as a gift in 1995 but had misplaced it soon after the purchase, only to find it back in January a few days before hospice arrived to provide in-home care for her final days. Mary found the watch buried at the bottom of a ceramic cookie jar that she used for stashing store-bought, pre-tied ribbon bows that are glued onto gift-wrapping paper. When Mary was seven, her mother baked the cookie jar in a kiln for her. Neither Winston nor Mary knew how the watch got into the cookie jar.

"I call this my Mary Watch, with a capital W. Mary got this watch for me back in '95 for my birthday but she lost it and didn't turn it up till earlier this year. So, she gave it to me a bit later than she expected to."

"Well, never better than late. I just convoluted a cliché."

"Yeah, you sounded like nutty Davey with his cockeyed cussing."

"Oh my. I kinda did, didn't I? Look—there's Davey sitting over there right now. You know, he had an episode just about an hour or so ago. He had this verbal fight with this drunken guy I'd never seen in here before. They went out onto the street blabbering to each other but they started yelling in here and Davey…"

"Oh yeah—I know. I heard 'em. I was so depressed I couldn't enjoy it too much. If it happened now, since you've cheered me up, I'd get a fine laugh out of it."

He pressed the button on his Mary Watch to illuminate the blue Indiglo backlight.

"It's way past my bedtime. I'm going home. If the donkey trip comes after me tonight and tells me I won't wake up, I'll be coming back at it strong with what you reassured me is true—I damn well will always wake up."

"You're darn right you will."

"I'll be back in here before too long."

"I hope so."

"Remember what I told you: Know when to go."

"I will."

"Thanks again, Kristi Lou. See you later."

Mr. Wilmont arose from the table. At 6'5", his height matched that of Kristi Lou when wearing her four-inch high heels. He pushed back his white hair with both hands and started to slowly walk toward the door. Kristi Lou pounced at him like a congenial cat, throwing her arms around his neck and giving him a quick, affectionate kiss between his eyes, which were perfectly level with her own.

"Well, I won't wash my face for a long time."

"Oh no. I don't want you to stop practicing good hygiene."

"That's funny. Don't worry; I won't do that. All right, you have a safe trip home tonight."

"You have a safe trip home as well, Mr. Wilmont. I'll be seeing you. Oh, there's another thing. You said something when we first started talking tonight about how I'll meet people I can relate to better than anyone I come across in here, including you."

"Yes."

"I'll never meet anyone I can relate to better than you."

"Well, OK. I mean, that's nice of you to say, but…"

"*But?* But … it's the truth. Really, it is."

"Thank you, my dear Kristi Lou."

"You're welcome. And thank you for being who you are—loving Mary forever and always. Thank you for being my true-life friend. I better let you go home now, right? Otherwise, you're going to get fussy 'cause I made you feel mushy!"

"Yeah, I think you're maybe right about that. Well, no, not really, but…anyhow…OK, bye now, Kristi Lou."

Winston Wilmont III turned and began moving once again toward the door. He looked back at Kristi Lou and waved, and was pleased to see her reciprocate.

"Bye-bye, Mr. Wilmont. See you later," she called out after he was almost 20 feet away from her.

Kristi Lou stood still and watched Mr. Wilmont, her bosom-buddy helpmate in a symbiotic consanguinity, use his slow, deliberate gait to gradually trudge through the cloudlike nicotine smaze and cola-in-a-glass, dark-red lighting as he negotiated his way across the old, wooden floor of Downtown Secrets. She kept watching him till he had vanished from her sight by stepping through the exit door. She saw Hokey pat him gently on his shoulder as he took himself into the summer night.

I believe maybe I should be friends with Mr. Wilmont because I…I feel—even though I'm a young woman, I feel—I feel like an old soul. I can't explain that.

The story of a grossly bad LSD trip, though not needed to maintain her abstinence, did nothing to diminish her commitment to avert usage of any nonmedicinal drugs stronger than the caffeine in soda. She reaffirmed within herself that the only Coke consumed by Kristi Lou would be the liquid version.

35

FINISHING A SEXUALLY UNADVENTUROUS EVENING OF WORK, Kristi Lou spent her final hour at Secrets this Thursday night dancing with customers to antique blues tunes from the 1940s and '50s, receiving generous tips for swaying closely and sensually, but, as usual, with no backroom goings-on.

Kristi Lou felt notably wearier than usual, walking out the front door within one minute of the club's closing at 4:30 without stopping to change from her peachy, slit-sided dress or chat with anyone, even though such end-of-work brief socializing was her custom. As she had observed the past several days, these bouts of tiredness had recently begun to sweep over her rather quickly; she would feel alert, and then in a matter of seconds she would notice she felt weary.

Now and then, it just catches up with me all of a sudden.

She stopped walking.

I think I'm having an epiphany.

She accepted an undeniable recognition that a significant source of her malaise was her recently intensified angst over when to stop doing what she was doing—when to go back to school, graduate with her bachelor's degree, and pursue normality.

Mr. Wilmont was right. I helped him believe, and he helped me see.

Come on now; get yourself back to a beautifully boring normal life. Get your college degree. You've got to get it soon; you've just got to.

Kristi Lou had been repeating this mantra with similar or identical wording quite often over the preceding week, but after the profound interaction with her near-century-old friend, the urgency began pounding her like a padded hammer.

****

As she stepped onto the sidewalk in front of Secrets, Kristi Lou saw that Dan, as usual, had parked his taxi at the curb to wait for her so he could drive her safely back to Moonbeam Landing. She stepped slowly toward the cab's passenger side and stopped. She dropped her shoulders in a droopy dangle while smiling softly at Dan without speaking.

"Get in, girl. You look worn-out, like you're about to capsize. You need to go home and go to bed."

"Hey, Dan," said Kristi Lou as she pushed through her weariness to give Dan a warm greeting. "You're right on both counts. I look obviously worn-out, huh? So, it shows that much?"

"Yeah, it shows. You really do look worn-out. What's wrong? And don't bother saying 'oh nothing' because I can tell something's gotten ahold of you and, like I said, you're worn-out-looking."

Kristi Lou slid the strap of her pleather duffel bag, which contained her purse as well as some work clothing, off her shoulder and down her left arm into her hand. Dan—as he sometimes did for Kristi Lou but not for anyone else except handicapped or very elderly passengers—got out of the cab and held open the car door. She entered the backseat and plopped down in a heap, immediately flinging her head backward and pressing firmly against the top of the headrest. As usual, she had to bend her knees to one side to fit her ropelike pins into the limited seating space afforded by the aft of Dan's cab.

Dan reentered his cab but did not start driving. Sometimes he and Kristi Lou would sit and talk before he drove her to her apartment.

"I mean, you're still very good-looking, of course, but you're just tired-looking, in a way you don't usually look."

"I know. Thanks for the complimentary comment and thanks for noticing that I look tired. Well, all right. What it is, is that I had an emotionally and physically draining conversation with Mr. Wilmont earlier tonight. He told me his problem. I told him to tell me the details and he did and it was profoundly disturbing. He's getting more fragile. And I…well, I believe I helped him. But giving him an outlet and listening to his situation made me feel more tired, but not as tired as he's been. His felicity for daily living has been almost totally depleted and he's eighty-nine years old, so what the heck am I fussing about? I don't know. It's just that I've been thinking—I don't always excel at thinking—and I think my thinking has taken its toll."

"I'm glad you tried to help Mr. Wilmont; I'm sure you did. You're very talented when it comes to helping someone else. As far as your thinking adventures—you aren't paid to think," quipped Dan with a quick grin, knowing Kristi Lou would not take offense at his sexual innuendo riposte.

"Ha-ha-ha."

"In reality, you're quite a gifted thinker; you're a very smart girl."

"Oh, thank you, Dan. But, anyway, it's just that I've been, well, telling myself it's probably time for me, myself, and I to get out of this lifestyle and get back to classes. I've just got one more year—a couple of semesters—and I'll be done. Rising senior, that's me. I've actually liked working at Secrets, for the most part, and I've made a bunch of money. But, I don't know, I just, I just think it's time to stop."

Kristi Lou abruptly leaned forward and pushed the right side of her face into the thick wire mesh between the front and back seats of Dan's taxi.

"You know, Dan, I don't think I ever would do this—that is, what

I'm about to say, but … I mean, I just don't, I don't want to ever become hardcore and, as they say, 'rough around the edges' with my personality. Mr. Wilmont was just cautioning me about that and getting onto me about it. I know you know what I'm talking about, about becoming hardened and all that, because I've told you that before."

"Yeah, you have. And don't worry, sweetie. You'll never become hard and rough like that; you're too damn sweet. But, yeah, it's time for you to get out. You've been doing this for about a year. That's long enough."

"Well, actually, it's been only around four months—April till now in August, so …"

"Oh, well then, that's even better. You've got less of, uh, an attachment, timewise, you know? So, this is your life—and it's your time to go."

"Yeah, Dan, I think that's true. Thank you. Oh, man, I feel *so* drained …"

Kristi Lou, in her elegant, slit-style, peach-colored dress, crash-landed herself rearward onto the seat, leaning back and letting herself relax in toto, spreading her supermodel-quality legs and her arms and her fingers and permitting her fatigue to overtake her, allowing her worries to stream from her like grimy water swooshing through a drainage hole, as she felt uncompromisingly safe in Dan's taxicab; she trusted him without the slightest misgiving.

"But, anyway, yeah, I know, Dan. That's what, uh, what I've been … what I've been, uh, telling myself … I've been, uh, saying that to myself when I, uh, when I have these talks with myself, but I … ohhhh …"

"It's all right," assured Dan, who saw Kristi Lou was near exhaustion.

Within a few moments, Kristi Lou fell into ocean-deep sleep.

While letting his taxi idle for about 40 minutes, with the air conditioning set on low, the setting he knew Kristi Lou preferred at this hour of these August nights, Dan seized the opportunity for the ultimate in guiltless voyeurism. At first, he utilized the rearview mirror. Later, he progressed to turning his head around and staring down at Kristi Lou's perfect body.

He knew the sleeping beauty whose dress he intermittently looked up while she slept would not even remotely object to this eyeful indulgence of his heterosexual carnality. Knowing that Kristi Lou was quite at ease with men staring lustfully at her body, he speculated—without specifically wording his thoughts—that, in addition to sprawling loosely because of lassitude, she might've been sweetly gifting him with private visual nirvana by granting him unfettered optical access to God's layout for female calves and thighs. After all, he knew that she knew he was demonstrably a "leg man."

He also knew that she knew he would look but never touch without her permission, and that no such consent could be granted while she was asleep.

But he also thought that, based on some of Kristi Lou's comments about sex, that even if he did unhook and slide open his slidable wire mesh security screen, then reach back and touch her gently but sensually while she slept, she wouldn't mind at all if she learned about it later. She would likely say something akin to, "It didn't harm me, physically, did it? If the average man discovered that a woman touched him sexually a bit while he was not awake, would he get upset about being somehow harmed or his dignity being assaulted? A woman should react the same way."

Nonetheless, I will not.

After having several erections, then going flaccid, and then becoming erect again, but never ejaculating, Dan drove her quietly home.

He kept the meter turned off.

Dan realized that he felt peculiarly but pleasurably tired as a result of guiltlessly gawking at a body and pair of legs worthy of goddess-level stardom in the reverie of a crurophile.

"Wake up, sleepyhead."

"Oh, I think I was sleeping."

"You snore real loud."

"What? Snore? I do not. I do not snore," said Kristi Lou, rubbing her face.

"Just joking."

"Oh, you're so hilarious."

"I'll miss you when you're gone."

"I'll miss you back, Dan. Maybe I'll call you sometimes to drive me to class. Oh wait, you don't work in the mornings—well, at least not in the daylight hours of mornings."

"Yeah, but I'll still see you around."

"Here." Kristi Lou extended a $20 bill to Dan, not knowing that she had been asleep in Dan's taxi for nearly three-quarters of an hour, which, applying the normal fare rates, would yield a charge well above 20 dollars.

"Nah, you ain't payin' me tonight. Get your sexy ass in there and get some sleep."

"But Dan, that's not right; that's not fair to you. I have to pay you, so …"

"No, you don't. This one's on the house. Or on the cab. Or on the whatever. Besides, you've already paid me …uh, visually, I must confess …you know?"

"Oh, you were looking up my dress?"

Kristi Lou giggled loudly.

"Well, I, uh …yeah, I kinda did, uh, but, uh …maybe you maybe thought I maybe would, so, you know …"

"Of course—I *knew* you would. I didn't exactly keep my legs together when I knew I was about to doze off, now did I?"

Kristi Lou gave Dan a wink and a smile.

"Uh, no."

"So, yeah. As I just said, I knew you would. And that's fine 'cause I wanted you to, for your pleasure. And I know you're beyond trustworthy."

"You're actually amazing with that …that is, instead of getting all irate and calling me a pervert, you laugh and tell me you wanted me to. That niceness instead of nastiness makes you even sexier and, uh, really and truly down-to-earth sweet."

"Thanks. You're sweeter than I am. Oops…you're a guy, so you don't want to be too sweet…sorry," said Kristi Lou, laughing again.

"Yeah, well…OK, then. When you quittin'?"

"I think probably within a few weeks, or days. Well, I suppose I should say nights."

"I want to take you home on your last night, please."

"You will."

"All right. Good night. Sleep tight."

"You always say that; you tell me to sleep tight. That's what my dad used to say."

"Father knows best."

"Right."

"Your dad and I—we both want you to be OK."

"Right."

"Your dad and I—we're the same type of guy."

"Well…"

"That was another joke, maybe not a very good one, but…"

"No, it was good—good'n silly."

"Yeah, all right. You better go hit the sack."

"Yeah, I know. OK."

"One more thing."

"What's that?"

"Sleep tight."

Kristi Lou grinned through her weariness.

"Thanks. You sleep tight, too. Nighty-nighty, Dan—or should I say naughty-naughty Dan?"

Kristi Lou inconspicuously slipped the repudiated $20 bill, which she had furled into a tube shape, through a hole in the lattice security screen directly behind Dan's head, knowing he wouldn't feel it touching his neck till she was gone. She exited the cab and walked to her front door as Dan drove away.

****

She towed herself into her apartment. She petted and fed Mr. Dooflotcher. She used the toilet. She brushed her teeth briefly, with 13 strokes of her bright-fuchsia toothbrush, and then rinsed the sink.

I hope Mr. Wilmont is sawing logs now, with no fiendish LSD demons rampaging in his handsome head. I've gotta deposit myself onto my bed and do my own log-sawing. I'm totally bleary. I'm a total wipeout. But, I'm awake enough at this moment to understand this: I am blessed. I often don't appreciate as much as I should my too-many-to-count blessings. I mustn't misunderstand how morally wrong that is. I must do better. And I will.

As Kristi Lou approached her bed, she saw out of the corner of her eye an article she had printed from the Web and tossed on her dresser about two weeks earlier, with the intention of putting it in her news-items scrapbook. Though its headline intrigued her, she had not gotten around to reading the article. She whimsically snatched it, then climbed into bed with it and Mr. Dooflotcher. Compulsively defying her fatigue and her body's demand for sleep ASAP, she read a few paragraphs in which a female psychoanalyst discussed a type of bitterness-driven older woman who in her youth had been both very attractive and sexually freewheeling but had not aged as well as she would have liked, and who tended to artfully renounce her younger-days venereal feistiness with renunciations such as, "My sexual imprudence was one of my worst-ever youthful mistakes." The therapist averred that such a woman's misleading renouncements are, in reality, based on her resentment that she is no longer as alluring as she once was and thus resents younger women whom she observes flaunting their looks as she used to flaunt hers while resenting men who reveal an attraction to them.

Noting that her mouth was open and her eyelids felt like flickering barbells, she dropped the article onto her chest.

Within 30 seconds, she was sleeping soundly.

36

KRISTI LOU SLEPT TILL JUST AFTER 10:30 THE NEXT MORN-
ing, Friday, August 17.

After spending most of Friday afternoon with earbuds appended
to the sides of her head and listening to contemporary rock music,
she watched TV from four till six o'clock, but barely paid attention to
reruns of her favorite reality shows.

****

Arriving at work around 7:15, Kristi Lou spent most of the first hour
dancing with a few customers, none of whom she recognized as previous patrons. She knew Mr. Wilmont would not come back till another
few days had passed, and she hoped for a glowing report from him
about how he had dispatched his LSD demon.

Despite not recognizing any individuals, a quick scan of the terrain
permitted her to easily ascertain the distinctiveness of her environment.
There was nothing distinctive. She beheld what appeared to be a typical
assemblage of sex-seeking men on an average night at Downtown Secrets.

She was graphically aware that this night marked the one-week anniversary of Bosco and his cutlery carving an incision into her mid-section.

All right, Bosco cut me after midnight last Friday night/Saturday morning so, to be technical, it won't be a week, officially, till after midnight tonight. But that's very technical. I shouldn't be so technical. But I am. But not always. But now I am, so ... Oh, stop being such a dipwad and just shut up, will you? OK.

As she looked down at the section of her dress that covered her ruptured flesh, Kristi Lou felt a resurgence of the wound's sting, just a tiny bit, even though it had almost entirely quit hurting two days earlier.

It's psychosomatic ... that's why it's stinging again. I think of it; it hurts. I don't think of it; it doesn't hu ... it doesn't hurt as much.

At about 8:15, Kristi Lou had Dopey serve her a straight ginger ale. She drank alone at the end of the bar, enjoying a few minutes of silent, unobtrusive people-watching.

I don't know any of these people—no regulars, yet—but they sorta look like a run-of-the-mill Secrets group. Umm ... for a week or two, after I started working here back in April, I fretted betimes over the possibility that I might see some guys from Wayne State venturing into Secrets or—more worrisome—that they might see me. Andrew, whom I was dating till I broke it off, could come in. But, thus far, I don't recall seeing anyone in the club I recognize from WSU. Interesting. Of course, the minimum age for admittance is 21, so, you know, that'd disqualify the eligibility of most students—but not Andrew, who's 23. But, uh, with my strident pro-sex ideology, I shouldn't care that much. And I don't. Do I? But, it's understandable that I'd feel some discomfort. But, I'd get over it quickly, but ... oh well. I'm glad I'm no longer worrying about such eventualities. Am I? Not a lot ... I guess ...

She noted the crowd had grown over the past 45 minutes and that the current populace now included an eclectic mix of what looked to be several young urbanite males, both black and white; a few lesbian females and/or bisexual females, some of whom, she thought, were likely strippers across town; and numerous middle-age and senior-male suburbanites and even exurbanites visiting from metro Detroit's calmer, more refined outliers, such as Auburn Hills, Ann Arbor, Warren, Lapeer, Port Huron, and Flint.

Yes, I still always wonder, every night, how many of these men are married or have girlfriends. Of course, most all of them who are attached remove their rings before they come in here, but … I don't know. I won't be with them if I know they are un-single, but I feel guilty about having anything to do with that situation, even without knowing, but …

She reconnoitered the front room again. She spotted someone she knew.

There in the far left corner of the lounge area sat Skinny Denny.

Oh my goodness. There he is. I wonder if he's used the bathroom this week. Hmm, I don't think I've ever wondered about that about anybody before. OK, I'm going to talk with Denny. But I'm not gonna tell him that some of us were laughing at his shit-a-phobia last night. But I, yeah, I wanna ask him whether he takes some really good-quality vitamins. I mean, yeah, he really should … yeah, he really oughta be augmenting his nutritional ingestion with supplements.

Unnoticed by Denny, she walked to his table and crouched behind his chair. She knew that when he turned around in response to her imminent greeting, that her face would greet his up close.

"Hey, Denny."

Kristi Lou welcomed Denny's awareness of her by smiling warmly as she stood up and then sidling next to him, her hip playfully bumping his shoulder, before she sat in the chair beside his chair.

"Hey there, skip to my Lou, my darlin'," undertoned Denny, sotto voce, disclosing his small smile formed by his minikin mouth as he set down his glass of wine without sipping the first drop. "I know that's corny. And you may not even know what I'm talking about, 'cause even though we're about the same age, that's from a really old song, but …"

"Oh, I do, too, know that song. I love old songs. I love lots of old things. I'm kinda odd in that regard. Anyhow, it goes 'Skip to my Lou, my darlin',' I think."

"Yeah, that's it."

"As a matter of fact," said Kristi Lou, glancing askance to summon a more precise recollection, "I did that song—I and the other kids in my kindergarten class did that song. It was one of our nursery rhymes. Now, the tune, the melody, and uh, yeah—some of the lyrics are coming back to me: 'a fly in my buttermilk, shoo fly shoo' or something like that, isn't it? The teacher had us do a dance. We were dancing when we did it. It was cool…and so innocent."

"Yes," agreed Denny, smiling shyly but enthusiastically. "That's it. We did it in my kindergarten, too."

"Oh, good; maybe it'll live on forever in kindergartens."

Kristi Lou glanced quickly down at the table and then at Denny.

"Well, so, I…I, uh, just wanted to come over and say hi and see how you're doing and all."

"Oh, cool. I'm glad you did. I'm all right, sorta, I suppose."

"Oh, I'm glad. Well, uh, anyway, I also wanted to…I hope this isn't too personal, but I kinda wanted to talk with you about a thing that's not so cool … your, uh, well, uh…I mean, uh, condition."

"Yeah, it's a real shitty problem."

"Oh my goodness," said Kristi Lou, cringing. "OK. Yes, I think you're right about that. But, well, uh, I just wanted to know whether you take some top-quality vitamins, what with your tendency to not eat much at all. So, I was just, you know, wondering…"

"Yes, I do. I pay $27 per bottle with 120 easy-to-swallow capsules."

"Oh, that's great; I'm so heartened to hear that."

"Yeah, well, thanks for being concerned, but…"

"Sure. I want you to be all right—really. But I really wish you'd get yourself refocused so you can eat more real food, with lots of nutrition in the food. I know you'll have to get over your fear of uh, that stuff and all, but…"

"Thanks. But that'd be really hard for me because…"

"Would it really be all that difficult, really, if you really tried?"

"Yeah."

"You could put your mind to it. You could resolve to get in the habit of eating healthy foods more regularly and then you could be more regular."

"Maybe, but I doubt it."

"Why?"

"I hate shit."

Kristi Lou looked silently at Denny for a couple of seconds, trying to maintain a stoic expression.

"You make that bowel, uh, I mean that avowal, you know, sound so deeply profound."

"In my life, shit is deep."

"I hardly know what to say in response to that statement."

"I understand. But, it's like this: I don't want to see it, smell it, touch it—it's so disgusting. But an equal source of disgust is contemplating that I might have some in me at any given moment. I know I have a contradiction because since I abhor having it in me I should be glad to get it out of me by going to the bathroom, which I detest but that's because then I have to look at it and deal with it directly so I'm in conflict and trapped up shit creek. Shit awareness is my revolting and constant nemesis."

"Shit awareness? OK. But really, that's kinda what bowels are sorta for—temporary housing, you might say, you know, so bowels are …"

"I know. I don't care. My Uncle Doug's toilet overflowed with his grody diarrhea when I was five and I ran into the bathroom playing and I slipped and fell in it and it all happened 'cause he stuffed the damn thing with too much paper. Ever since then I've had it in for shit. It was traumatic and I screamed in terror. It took my mom two weeks to get me clean. OK, maybe two weeks is an exaggeration. I'm a bigot against shit. It's Uncle Doug's fault. I got older and started calling him Uncle Dung. But anyway, I've got no use for shit. It terrifies me. I despise it. Enemas are my enemies. Shit is evil. Down with shit! It's so grooooosssss! So I just try to avoid it altogether. Shit avoidance requires avoiding food."

"Well, uh, I mean, it is *waste* material, Denny, so I guess it's destined to be like garbage in us that we're going to be dumping … uh, well, uh … rejecting. So, you know, I think perhaps it's bound to be unpleasant and all, but nature dictates, er … anyhow, medically speaking, it's called …"

"Coprophobia. When I'm not eating, I read a lot. And that means I'm underfed but well-read. Constipation and literacy are not mutually exclusive."

"Well, I guess they aren't. But, despite taking your vitamins—which is healthful—your nourishment from real food is, uh …"

"… lacking."

"Yes, that would seem to be a highly probable probability. Wait—did I just say 'probable proba'…"

"Yeah, but that is quite all right. I'm backed up. You're redundant. Your occasionally occurring polarity-of-pithiness flaw is a better defect."

"I suppose maybe it is, but …"

"Oh, speaking of kindergarten, it was about that time I started liking girls. Then, I learned they also had to use the bathroom. I was so dismayed."

"Sorry about that! Despite sugar and spice, we gotta go, too, ha-ha!"

"Perhaps, one day, you won't. Look, Kristi Lou, you came over here to talk to me, right? I wanna take advantage of this opportunity. I've gotta really tell you something that's grandly unshitty."

"Ooh, that sounds exciting and sanitized. All right. I'm ready."

"I haven't told anyone under the stars about my secret project."

"You have a project? A secret project?"

"I do. I'll tell you my secret in Secrets. I know that was corny as hell, but I just said it, anyhow."

"Oh, that's OK. Anyway, I'll be glad to hear about it—your secret project. Someone told me his secret last night here in Secrets and now you're going to tell me your secret tonight here in Secrets. If this keeps up, I'll start to see a pattern. Oh well, lemme have it—this highly guarded clandestine secret."

"All secrets are clandestine," said Denny. "More redundancy."

"I know. I was being verbose—again," said Kristi Lou, laughing.

"But, anyway, yeah, I saw you at the table last night for a long time with old Mr. Wilmont. You both looked intense. I bet he was the secret-teller."

"Yes, he was. And yes, there was much intensity—for both of us."

"Yeah, I could tell."

"So anyhow, Denny, you've got this super-secret thing of your own to let me in on?"

"I do. OK, listen up. I'm working on creating an anti-shit pill. My specialized pill will alter our innards. After people ingest my no-poop pill they won't have to egest any more shit."

"Oh, really?" said Kristi Lou, stoically. "A panacean remedy for fecal accumulation? An undoing of doo-doo?"

"Yes! I won't be able to actually make the pills, myself; some drug-con-cocter scientists or alchemists in a laboratory somewhere will have to handle that part. Pharmaceutically, I envision that my shit-deleter pill will function via facilitating the extraction of nutrients from our food and then somehow dissolving the would-be caca before it can form by causing the aspiring shit to dissolve into liquid when it's processed in the bowels—said liquification being their new bowellian duty—and then get rerouted from there to the bladder and exit our bodies as a urinary-type discharge that will have just finished blending with traditional urine. And, there you have it! Regardless, I'm the creator of the concept. I'll get it patented. I've got to sell it…make it believable in my proposal so rich sponsors will pay for its being made. It's called R&D and it means…"

"…research and development," said Kristi Lou.

"Right. But, anyhow, the toilet tissue companies won't like it; they'll try to block my invention, my pill, from reaching materialization."

"Oh, I'm convinced they will."

"They'll be afraid I'll wipe them out."

Kristi Lou caught on immediately and giggled while tipping her head sideways.

"They'll lose a shitload of money," said Denny.

"Oh Denny, you're too witty."

"But I'm sure not shitty."

"Oh no, I saw that one coming after I said 'witty.'"

"That's right. I hardly ever eat. I can be full of wit but not full of shit."

"Yes, well, I doubt I've ever wished for someone to be full of that before, but in your case, it might be a good thing for you to be full of, well …"

"I'll call my product something suitable. I'm thinking maybe I'll call it Shit-Be-Gone," boasted Denny.

"Oh, that sounds appropriate."

"Or maybe PO, S! for Piss Off, Shit! … to, you know, tell it to go away."

"That's quite apropos, too."

"I've also got Farewell Feces and Arrivederci Anus."

"Those have catchy little alliterations going for them."

"Yes, they do—and the first one has two straight F-words."

"Yeah, F-words!" said Kristi Lou, with a quick laugh.

"I considered FO, F for Fuck Off, Feces but, no—too graphic. I could go with a straight-forward strategy, like So Happy It's Terminated, with the first letters in caps—trying to be candid and sly simultaneously."

"That has a rather blunt acronym in it."

"Or also, for my religious customers, maybe I'll offer a special God-themed formula called Excrement, I Smite Thee!"

"That sounds righteous," said Kristi Lou.

"Exactly! My TV marketing will include angels humming and harpsichords playing and the tag-line admonition that the Lord would likely say, 'Thou shalt flusheth not that which I have created.' Hence, in order to avoid rejecting God's creation, they'd buy my pills so they wouldn't manufacture any holy shit."

"Holy shit!" exclaimed Kristi Lou, as she spontaneously covered her mouth with both hands. "Oh my goodness! I can't believe I said that!" exclaimed Kristi Lou through parted fingers.

"No, that's—I like that. I'll put that in my infomercial. Of course, I'll have to censor it for television."

"You know, Denny," said Kristi Lou, "if your product is successful, then Francois—I've seen you talking to Francois, including just a few nights ago—he wouldn't need any more tee-*shew* of toy-*let*."

"Indeed, he would not. And I guess that'd be a shame 'cause not just anybody can talk about toilet tissue and make it sound charming."

"I know, right?" agreed Kristi Lou.

Denny's excitement was intensifying, as he edged nearer the front end of his chair.

"I'm thinking maybe that, to be able to sell it on the mainstream market, like in stores and all, that, uh, that I'll have to nuance those names somewhat to maybe something like Stuff-Be-Gone or No More Crap or something people can relate to, you know? Well, whaddaya think?"

"Well, Denny, I think you've got some really solid ideas. If your product is as effective as you envision, just think of all the inconvenience of going to the bathroom that could be eliminated, plus all the personal monetary savings from not only less toilet tissue being bought but also from less water usage and hence lower monthly bills due to fewer flushes—flushing used only for peeing, I presume, since you indicated that your pill not only won't extirpate urine but will create more—and from having to purchase commode-related replacement parts less frequently—you know, such as valves and flappers, etcetera—'cause they'd wear out at a slower rate, and, well, all the energy conservation and whatnot. So, it sounds like a plan to me. Good luck with that."

"Thanks. I knew I could count on you for serious support—that you wouldn't make fun of me. I knew you wouldn't mock me by telling me that I'm so full of shit that I need an enema."

"Absolutely," said Kristi Lou. "I think you're about the least likely person anywhere who would be full of…that…because you almost don't eat. Anyway, when your pills are available, I'll sure-as-shootin' be among the early-bird triers. I promise."

"Par excellence, as Francois would sprucely say," said Denny. "After talking with you, Kristi Lou, I can now go take a dump."

"Oh. OK."

"Your fellowship has had that cathartic effect on me. Since I have not yet invented my pills, I still have to occasionally defecate. This is a defecation occasion. Thanks to you, I now feel a rare I-want-to-shit feeling churning within me. You've inspired me to actually want to go. Thank you for stimulating my bowels."

Kristi Lou paused for a moment.

"Oh sure, Denny. You're most welcome. I don't think anyone's ever rewarded me with that compliment before. And I'm fairly confident that it will never come again. So, thank you."

"You got it. I'm going to the restroom now, all right?"

"Please do."

"I'll be thinking of you while I'm in there," assured Denny, with sincerity.

"That's wonderful. Thank you for sharing that thought."

"You're most defecatingly welcome."

Denny strode confidently to the men's room.

After almost a minute had passed, Kristi Lou looked at her deformed reflection in Denny's candlelit, still-full wine glass and then conversed inwardly with herself.

Did I just have that cringeworthy conversation? Yes, I think you did. Oh well, if it helps Denny…Has he begun to think of me while he's…? No, don't even go there. Think of something else—golf leaderboards or what-

the-heck-ever. Oh, good grief. You're so preternatural. I know I am and so are you. Yes, we are.

Though Kristi Lou was quite accustomed to her practice of answering herself extensively, she sometimes felt worrisomely dumfounded by her intrapersonal interlocutions. She caught herself reminding herself of herself plus someone she used to know, and her mind, without alerting her in advance, launched into a pleonastic avalanche of full-bore, obsession overdrive writ large.

OMG. I know I do this too much; I'm doing it right now. As a direct result of thinking about doing less of it—I'm doing more of it. I can't think about doing it less without doing it more, because the act of using thoughts as the means to convince myself to talk less to myself requires that I think thoughts to myself which leads to me talking to myself about how I shouldn't be talking to myself. In other words, the very action I'm taking to get myself to stop doing something is, itself, the precise thing I'm trying to stop doing. While in the process of trying to quit doing it, I'm doing it with that very process. When I'm talking to myself about how I shouldn't talk to myself, I'm talking to myself. It's like a catch-22. It's self-defecating. No. That's Denny's dilemma worming shitily through my encephalon. Shitily? Yes, shitily. Be gone, Denny doo-doo. I hereby douche thee outta my cerebrum. I meant to say that my anti-talking-to-myself efforts are self-defeating; I'm defeating myself. My method of trying to get rid of something is the very same thing I'm trying to get rid of. The only way I can get rid of it is to do it. It's like I wind up doing more of a thing to try to eliminate that same thing. The very thing I'm using to get rid of something is the same thing I'm trying to get rid of. I can't think about it without doing the very thing I'm trying to diminish. I mean, I'm talking to myself about how I go too far with talking to myself. That is, in the very course of telling myself I shouldn't do this so much, I'm once again doing more of the very same thing that I'm telling myself to do less of. Aren't you? Yes, you are. And in this inverse-of-concision outburst right here, do you know what you're doing? You're manically using somewhat different words to pleonastically repeat the same points—over and over and over and over. It's an inescapable impasse. It's like a junkyard crane discarded a car I'm driving into a no-outlet cul-de-sac. Round and round and round and round I go. Make yourself stop! But wait; it doesn't have to be a go-in-circles contradiction. OK? Rather, it can be an irony. That is, I can ideally talk to myself just enough to persuade me to do less of the very thing I'm using as a tool to do less of the original behavior, which is the same as the tool. That is, I can reasonably use a thing against itself: use thinking to convince me to do less thinking and use self-talking to convince me to do less self-talking. Also, just because I think to myself does not automatically mean that I have to talk to myself. They're not mutually inclusive entities; yes—they can be separate. Yeah—the talking to myself part occurs when I, when I, uh ... when I answer myself. That's it! I think I can just maybe think without envisioning, the way I tend to do, specific questions and specific answers. Yes—I will be thinking but not really conversing with myself. OK. Try that approach. That's what I should've figured out long ago. You can still talk to yourself some, just not as much. All right. But, you know, this is how Mr. Battle used to talk to himself—in such detail, back and forth and actually answering himself multiple times. I know about that from that day I overheard our shrinks talking about it in the woods—that afternoon back when I was in seventh grade. And Mr. Battle had that time like the time I just had with trying to get Denny Thomas to go to the bathroom when Mr. Battle was trying to get Marsha Mellow to go to the bathroom. All these coincidental things ... Coincidence overload ... Life has its ebbs and flows, doesn't it? Yes, it does, but ... Oh, stop it, stop it, stop it—just stop it and hush!

Kristi Lou, during the entirety of her internal eruption, had sat perfectly motionless while fixating her eyes on the home screen of her phone. Now bewildered, mentally sapped, and internally embarrassed, she needed a break from the self-assailment exacted by her maniacal minutiae.

I didn't see that coming—that crazed self-talk about not talking to myself. Where did it come from? It just leaped into me. I know I need help. Mr. Wilmont and I, in our own ways…

Fortuitously, no one was approaching her. She chose to leave the table where she and Denny had been sitting. She required about 90 seconds to regather herself after her unexpected and draining inner flare-up. And she also caught herself dreading a detailed report from Denny as to just how the inspiration she had imparted to him had manifested itself in the latrine.

She escaped a potential contretemps with Denny by quick-stepping outside and onto the sidewalk.

****

Kristi Lou glimpsed at her watch and saw the time was almost nine o'clock. A sliver of dusk remained, with full darkness setting in imminently. A gentle-but-strong summer breeze gusted toward her, as if greeting her arrival, and blew a large leaf onto her right cheek, where the piece of stray vegetation seemed to have enough moisture to stick.

How did this leaf get here? There aren't any trees, just concrete.

As she brushed the frond into the air with her long fingers, something entered the peripheral vision of her left eye. The object looked familiar but somehow odd.

It's just a car.

Another abrupt zephyr prehended the leaf that Kristi Lou had expelled from her face, causing the roaming flora to swirl around and float onto the driver's side of the approaching automobile's seemingly opaque windshield.

37

Kristi Lou did a double-take. She saw *THAT* car again.
This was the peculiar hazel-colored car she had seen several times over the past week; this car fascinated her without her knowing definitively why.

Maybe it's the car's uncanny quietness and smoothness. It's extremely quiet.

This time, though, the car rolled up to the curbside, stopping almost two yards afore the stretch of curb behind which Kristi Lou stood about four feet from the edge of the sidewalk. The car remained there idling, silently, for almost one minute. The leaf blew off the windshield.

Kristi Lou felt compelled for some reason unknown to her to not leave but to remain positioned next to this odd car that had blatantly encroached upon her personal space.

After another 15 seconds, the car slowly pulled directly alongside her, and then stopped.

She sensed no threat. But, she looked away so as not to stare too long at whoever was seated behind the dark windshield. Following a few moments of fixated curiosity, she blocked her focus on the car, opting to return to pondering her various issues.

After about a half-minute of thinking again about her life's challenges, she began to pay overt attention to the car, staring at it without interruption for seven or eight seconds. She wondered why she felt that this car and its unknown occupants were so non-threatening to her.

Why am I not threatened, at least a tad, by this car that has come right up on me and keeps staying next to me?

Realizing that, for whatever reason, she continued to be strangely unintimidated, she turned away and quickly returned to willful oblivion, lost in her thoughts about her future and her past.

Another 60 or 70 seconds passed in silence. The quietude was shattered by the famous pounding riff in Beethoven's Symphony No. 5: "da da da DUM, da da da DUM." The powerful music emanated from the automotive visitant lingering just over a yard from where Kristi Lou was still standing. Startled by the musical explosion, she looked down at the car and saw the front right-side window slowly descending, revealing a cherubic countenance in the hazy light.

Kristi Lou, having been jolted out of her trance, bent over and looked beyond the passenger seat to the person behind the steering wheel. She watched as a pair of hands removed a hat from a head. Long, elegantly coiffed, chestnut-colored hair suddenly flowed downward over the shoulders of the driver, whose face did not immediately look up. Kristi Lou could see only a few facial features, but there was an instantaneous familiarity, which grew over the next two seconds. The driver's head turned toward the beautiful girl. Kristi Lou, still bending, broke the conversational ice.

"Do I know you?"

"Hi, Kristi Lou." As the driver shifted her head rightward, a pleasingly toothy smile slowly unfolded.

"Oh my god—Guinevere? Is that you? Guinevere? Guin...are you my old friend, Guinevere Lindsay? Yes, it is you! You're all grown up. Oh my god! I haven't seen you in forever and...but...but, I mean...I haven't seen you since the seventh grade. And…I don't know where to start. But…"

"It's OK," reassured Guinevere.

Kristi Lou instantly recognized her erstwhile friend's characteristic calm demeanor, almost as if eight years had not passed.

"Guinevere, you still have your face!"

"Well, I find that observation to be reassuring."

"I mean, I know that's your face, albeit it's now a young adult face."

"'Albeit'—good word choice, Kristi Lou. And I knew what you meant."

"Of course you did; you always did know things about things, all sorts of things. Anyway, I can't believe you're sitting there in that crazy car. It's a nice car, I'm sure, since you're driving it, but it seems, I don't know…"

Kristi Lou, her mind racing and her words gushing, made no effort to bridle her elation.

"Do you think it's safe for me to get out in this neighborhood?" asked Guinevere with a suspicious tone that Kristi Lou sensed as perhaps intending feigned concern.

"Oh, yeah. Yeah, it is. It's OK right around this part of the block. Hokey—my, uh, coworker—he's right over there and he won't let anything get us."

Guinevere exited the uber-sophisticated automobile and stood two feet in front of Kristi Lou.

"Well, I'm glad he's around to protect you, though I'd bet you'd be pretty tough in protecting yourself. As for my own safety, I wasn't really worried," said Guinevere, who glanced down at the sleek car with its inerrant aerodynamics and glistening metallic exterior.

"Let's just say that this car has been knocking over criminals around here like dominoes for about a week now."

"Huh? Oh, you mean the car? The car will…it will defend you? It, the car…"

"Yes, you could say that," said Guinevere.

"Oh, wait. Oh, oh my god. You're the one behind the car? The car that gets the car thieves? This is that car? It's the car I've been hearing about, that people have been talking about? The car that … uh, I mean, that's you doing that, those things to the car thieves—grabbing them and hurting them and putting them in women's clothing and shooting out embarrassing photos and so on? You? How … how do you do it?"

"I'll answer all—well, many—of your questions about the car in due time. But first let's talk about other things, about us then and now."

They stood and looked at each other for about three seconds, 6'1" Kristi Lou gazing straight down and Guinevere, now 5'3", gazing straight up.

"Oh my goodness," said Kristi Lou. "We're still Mutt and Jeff."

"Yes, we certainly still are," agreed Guinevere with a quick laugh. "Anyway, I guess we've got a lot to talk about, catching up, as they say. You haven't shrunk a bit; in fact, you're even taller. Remember I told you back in the seventh grade that you'd grow to like all your growing? That you'd come to embrace your skyscraper-ness? How do you feel about it now?"

"I love it. You were right, as usual."

Kristi Lou and Guinevere looked at each other, smiling. In sudden unison, they bounded into one another's arms, melding their mismatched bodies into a mutual hug, Kristi Lou hugging downhill and Guinevere hugging heavenward.

"I can't believe you're here!" exclaimed Kristi Lou.

"I know. I've never forgotten you," averred Guinevere.

"Nor I, you," reassured Kristi Lou, as they disengaged from their embrace.

"Of course," said Guinevere, "it's not as if we haven't talked over the phone now and then through the years."

"That's true, but, but—not since the tenth grade! So the last time we talked on the phone was about five whopping years ago. And we haven't exchanged texts or email or anything in almost forever. Anyhow, it's better face to face; it's more real."

"I know. Get in, Kristi Lou. Let's go for a ride. It's all right; your safety is assured in here."

"OK. But, I've got to…well, I actually work over in that building…and I…well, I need to tell someone—I'll tell Hokey—that I'm going off for a little while. They won't mind if I'm not gone too long, but I've got to tell them. I know you must be thinking I'm bad for…well, for being dressed like this and out here in the middle of the night, but, I'll explain, but, I hope you don't…"

"No, Kristi Lou, I don't. I don't hold where you work against you. I kinda figured it out—not that too much figuring is required. That comment was intended to be zingy but amiable."

"I know it was. Well, I'll tell you more. Let me go check out with Hokey," said Kristi Lou over her shoulder after she had already begun stepping in Hokey's direction.

"All right."

"I'll be right back."

Kristi Lou sprinted to Hokey like an eager puppy-dog running to her master.

Guinevere observed Hokey nodding in approval, and then moved the passenger seat next to her as far back as it would go.

Kristi Lou galloped like a deer in high heels as she returned to the car, which was idling with its silent power.

"Hop in, Kristi Lou."

As the girls rode slowly down the road, Kristi Lou noted the windshield did not seem ultra-dark from the inside; she didn't ask why. There was silence for about 45 seconds. Finally, Guinevere tilted her head toward Kristi Lou.

"You're my long, lost friend, Kristi Lou—long, as in really long."

"Long—ha-ha-ha. Yes, I'm less lost and more long … though, actually, sometimes I'm not so sure about the first part of that formulary."

Kristi Lou felt both fascination and panic rush into her. Her thoughts and her speech became pressured.

"And you know what? It's just now occurring to me that, believe it or not, I swear I was—a mere half-handful of minutes before you pulled up beside me in this car—I was thinking about Mr. Battle, from the seventh grade, in Little Rock—and you were one of the stars of my life during that period. But anyway, so, I was sitting at a table in Secrets here in Detroit—nowhere near Little Rock—and I was talking to myself and after I caught myself answering myself it hit me that that's how Mr. Battle used to converse with himself, back in seventh grade, when you and I became hip-joined. And the whole time I was having those thoughts, you—the very person who helped me the most, by far, in dealing with my pain back then over being so tall while Mr. Battle was so short—and a person I haven't seen since summertime of that very year, eight years ago, you—that very person—you were somewhere so physically very nearby, in this Batmobile, in this neighborhood in Detroit, more than 850 miles from Little Rock, at those very moments I was recalling an aspect—Mr. Battle and his neurotic self-conversing—from that stretch of my life."

"Coincidences can be fascinating," said Guinevere.

"Yeah, they totally can. I mean, about the only way it could've been more unbelievable would've been if—while I was sitting at the table—if, if I had thought *directly about you* while you were, unbeknownst to me, so close by rather than thinking of someone else—Mr. Battle—who we both knew from back then. Nonetheless, Mr. Battle has a direct nexus to you because he was such a prominent figure during that same period when you and I … when we, when we, uh, came to be … when we developed such closeness. So, while I was mulling at the table and thinking about that period that starred you, you were quite literally just down the street, even though as far as I knew, when I was at the table, you were about a decade and a thousand miles removed from me, and…darn it to heck. I'm getting exhausted from suddenly obsessing about this. My confused brain is so tired. But, still, what are the odds of all those things defying time and distance and…I…Did you…Could you, uh, sift through my babbling ramble and understand what I think I was trying to say?"

"Yes, Kristi Lou, of course I understood," said Guinevere. "Sometimes the combination of timing and coincidence is remarkable."

"Yeah, truly, it is. I'm just flabbergasted by it all."

"I know. But you did a much better job of analyzing the details of all those tie-ins than you realize. Don't let these against-all-odds events frustrate or frighten you so much; rather, let these seeming coincidences fascinate you and reveal to you once again how life can be rich and filled with bright surprises. We don't really know what things are around the next corner, and when those twists of fate are strange but benevolent, as is true of this impromptu rendezvous, then don't be disturbed—be charmed."

"My goodness, that's precisely how I should filter my coincidences. Your advice, your interpretation, is so much like you that you could be you! Oh…why do I say things like that? I can't keep up with myself when I get giddy. But, yeah, Guinevere, you are still you, aren't you?"

"As far as I know, I am."

"Thankfully, you are."

"Look, we've got so much to catch up on," said Guinevere.

"I know we do. We really do."

"I just changed my mind," said Guinevere. "A few moments ago, I said I wanted to reminisce and talk about us first, and then talk about the car later. I'm reversing that order. I do want to get into all the nostalgia with you, but for now, I'm going to tell you about my mission."

"Your mission? I've heard two secrets the past two nights and now

I'm going to hear about a secret mission. So you have a mission? That sounds so James Bondishly cool."

"Yes, I have a mission. You asked how I do it. How do I punish the thieves that steal cars? I know you won't reveal anything, Kristi Lou."

"Never."

"It's me and my dad. We're like a wrestling tag team. You may recall we moved after the seventh grade, and …"

"Like it was yesterday," interrupted Kristi Lou. "I watched your car roll out of sight and I cried on and off all day … and for days and days and days."

"You weren't the only one crying," said Guinevere as she turned onto a long, dark avenue lined with more streetlamps that were burned out or smashed in than lamps that glowed. "Even though it was ages ago, I remember missing you for days before we even left town. We moved to Toledo. Anyway, we're back in Little Rock now. But, after we left Toledo, we lived in Atlanta awhile. Dad had wanted to go back there for a long time. He was born and reared in a small town about 25 miles outside of Atlanta, in Conyers, Georgia."

"Oh, your dad's from Georgia? I think I thought he was from Arkansas. I guess I sorta assumed."

"That's all right. Anyway, he has his degrees in M.E., mechanical engineering—a bachelor's and a master's and a Ph.D.—all from Georgia Tech. As far as his B.S. degree, he graduated from Tech at the usual age, when he was 22. So, next, he got the master's degree and then went on to get the Ph.D., which he got when he was 28. And then Dad, he just sifted through his employment offers after sending out his résumé and took the job in Little Rock. And that's where he met Mom who was in college at the University of Central Arkansas—you know, out a ways from Little Rock, over in Conway. I may've told you all or most of this when we were at Our Lady—that seventh-grade year when we were friends. It seems as if I did, but I don't know."

"You maybe did, but we talked about so many things that year. I guess we might've even talked about where our parents went to college. But I can't honestly say I remember you telling me that—that is, about your dad's education and all."

"Anyway, what I might not have told you when we were kids is that he's very … well, how can I put it? Dad is very, very eccentric. He's also brilliant. He's a genius. Really. He is, in the literal sense of the word."

"No, wait," exclaimed Kristi Lou. "You just called your dad a genius. Now I remember. You did tell me that. When you said 'genius,' that blew away the clouds that were fogging up my memory. I'm sure you told me about him being a genius when you told me you were moving. That's right. You told me you were moving to Toledo, Ohio 'cause your dad got a job there too good to turn down, and … Actually, no, I think you said he was transferred by his company. Right?"

"Right."

"And you explained to me that he was a genius. Yeah, you said something about him being one of the smartest people in Mensa. Right?"

"Yes," confirmed Guinevere. "You're absolutely correct. Now I remember, too. I did tell you all that about Dad."

"Yeah. Anyhow, as far as your dad being a true genius, I believe you. As smart as you are, I have no trouble believing that one of your parents is a real, live genius."

"Well, thank you, darling," said Guinevere in an improvised impersonation of a haughty European sophisticate, nose aimed sharply upward.

"So, yeah, he's an actual certified genius, but he's also somewhat crazy—good crazy, but still crazy; sometimes he's about five sandwiches shy of a picnic."

"Oh. Well, I guess that's better than missing six sandwiches," replied the quite-nervous Kristi Lou, with a giggly chirp. "Umm, I know that was a pathetic and lunkheaded attempt at humor."

"No, not at all. But anyway, yeah, you see, after we moved to Toledo, two of our cars were stolen. We never saw them again and we still don't know where they went; they were probably chopped up into parts that went who-knows-where? And my uncle Ralph—my mom's brother—had his car vandalized three different times. They keyed his old Oldsmobile—a car he dearly loves—in the parking lot of his condominium complex, here in the Detroit area, over in Ann Arbor where he and Mom grew up and where he still lives. Not once, not twice, but thrice."

"I'm sorry they got your cars and your uncle's car. But wait…your mom…uh, your mom is originally from around here? In Detroit? Wait, no, you said Ann Arbor, which is very close. I don't recall ever knowing that. And your uncle still lives in Ann Arbor?"

"Yes."

"What a coincidence."

"Yeah, how about that?"

"That's just, well, it's just too coincidental. But, so, these car-crime committers did those things to the family cars, as you were saying?"

"Yeah. All that was bad enough, but one day about three years ago, about two months after we moved back to Little Rock, they went after my grandmother—my dad's mother, in Conyers. That was the drop of water that burst the dam. My grandmother's car was hijacked with her in it. A little old lady was carjacked. She told us and the authorities all about it. And…"

"Oh my goodness."

"Those guys were sliders."

"They were what-ers?"

"Sliders. Those are carjackers who capitalize on an opportunity to slide fast onto the seat of an unlocked car that is stopped and make off with it. They often strike at places like gas stations. That's where Grandma was. She'd just finished filling her tank. The punks were lurking over to the side and when she got back in her car, they hopped in and knocked her aside and drove away."

"Oh, no, that's …"

"They took her to an isolated area. At first, they threatened to kill her. She was terrified. They stole all her money. And, for good measure, they took their knives—the two guys did—and ripped her seats to shreds, then pushed her out onto the side of the road. They drove away about 20 yards, but then they came back. One guy got out and kicked my grandmother several times in the face till she was almost, but not quite, unconscious. They evidently were trying to make good on that threat so she wouldn't I.D. them or testify against them in court. Lying there in a beaten pulp and looking lifeless, she heard one of them say: 'She's too old to be here. At her age, she done lived long enough. She'd be dead soon, anyway, even if we didn't gank her wrinkled ass. She ain't nothin' but an old hag; she don't matter none. She's just takin' up space.'"

"Oh dear God. That's unforgivable. I'm so sorry, Guinevere."

"They left her, thinking she was dead. That was the tropological final straw for my dad—and me."

Guinevere stopped at a red light, as two cars going in opposite directions crossed in front of her and Kristi Lou, with passengers in both vehicles shouting and gesturing at one another through rolled-down windows.

"They were wrong. She didn't die. They were right. She testified. My grandmother is, as the ancient axiom goes, a tough old cuss. The gas station's security cameras got 'em on video. Those assholes were apprehended, tried, convicted, and put away for what's supposed to be most of the rest of their lives. You should've seen their rap sheet; their names should be in the lawyer's lexicon as part of the definition of recidivism. And, as the years go by, Dad and/or I will appear before the parole board in Georgia whenever they're eligible to be paroled and argue passionately against it—long after Grandma has moved on to heaven.

"Regarding forgiveness from Grandma, and Dad and I moving on—people love to talk about how they want to move on—from wanting them to be punished more, Grandma has basically already forgiven them. But we—Dad and I—we'd have to see their records that, according to prison officials, document perfect behavior for, let's say, several decades. And, we'd have to see them consistently humble themselves with groveling apologies over many years, and then, maybe…"

"Oh no," interjected Kristi Lou. "I'm so sorry all that happened. But, so, now you're…you're on a vendetta against any and all car criminals?"

"Yes," said Guinevere with her same old calm and confident smile, accelerating slowly off the green light. "And when I say yes I say that as an emphatic yes. Perhaps one day my and Dad's name will be in the dictionary as part of the definition of vigilante."

"You're starting to remind me of Charles Bronson in *Death Wish*."

"One of my all-time favorites. I have it on a DVD."

"That's a must-have movie for you."

"Anyhow, Dad and I simmered with anger in Little Rock over what happened to his mother and my grandmother in Conyers. Dad finally decided on his plan of action to go after car criminals—more on the specifics later. Our first operation was back home, in Little Rock.

"As for our present purposes, we have only one operation scheduled for this month, August, and that's here in Detroit. As you may know, car crimes around here have dwindled eminently. Dad and I will reevaluate Detroit later as to whether we'll come back here, but in the meantime, we'll take our show on the road."

"On the road, huh?"

"Sorry. I couldn't resist. Well, maybe I could've but I didn't."

"So, you started in Little Rock, huh? And you've lowered car crimes here in Detroit and you're going to go to other places to nail car criminals? But, uh …what are you …how do you …I mean, how are you and your dad somehow making these cars do these things to these bad guys? How? Your cars—I guess including this car I'm in now and ..."

"Our arsenal-on-wheels contains one car and one minivan. We have the car you're in now—which is a shape-shifting automobile—and one Dodge Caravan. Those are our two vehicles."

"Oh, uh …shape shifting? Uh, what? So, two vehicles—this car and a van?"

"Yes—both reconfigured to be AEVs, i.e., all-electric vehicles."

"OK, then. Well, uh, so they, uh …they reach out and grab the criminals and do hardcore things to them. How do your cars do all that?"

"All right, Kristi Lou, I'll begin with…"

"And some more thoughts just stumbled into my head. What about the police? How do you resolve what you're doing—terrorizing these car criminal people—with the police? I mean, aren't you kind of doing their job? Do they feel territorially threatened? Do you get along with them—the cops—as well as politicians and other local government officials? Do they know? Did I ask enough questions? Would you like more?"

Guinevere responded with an almost noiseless utterance, opening her mouth and laughing with the only audible sound being the end of her exhalation.

"OK. Those are all fair and understandable questions—and a ton of them bunched together."

"I know. That's just me, again. Sorry," said Kristi Lou with a slight blush and a quick laugh.

"No, that's fine. And yes, that is you. You get all your questions out in one big burst and then you sit back and listen. I like it—at least I like it when *you* do it."

"Thanks."

"To answer your questions in reverse order, yes, here in Detroit, the police and the mayor and some government officials do indeed know.

Yes, the police, at first, felt their territory was threatened, and our methodologies took some getting used to. So, yes, the police and politicos here in Detroit felt threatened by us. And before that, the police and politicos in Little Rock felt threatened by us. But, at some point, after a few days of our activities, when they see what a genius Dad is, most of them seem to accept that he and his creations brilliantly combat crime and they get over it."

"I'm glad they come around to accepting it."

"Yeah, most of them seem to. So, my dad sought out the Detroit authorities. They had a backdoor meeting—like in a movie—at the city hall building about two weeks back. Yeah, several of them, as would be expected, did not approve—some still don't—but the decision was made to not interfere. Since then, they've seen what we've been able to get done, which validates that non-interference. Dad lets them know we are friends, not foes. We are bizarre friends, from their perspective, but friends, nonetheless. They know we're doing what used to be called God's work."

"But, OK, so how do you prevent these melodramatic attacks on these car criminals from getting all over television and the Internet?"

Guinevere accelerated from 20 to 45 mph in about one second as she took a right turn at a green light. Kristi Lou felt the burst of power course through the vehicle and her body, but noticed there was almost no noise from the engine.

"Law enforcement is handling the news media by spinning the reports and rumors a bit, saying that, yes, there have been claims by some of the suspects and other people—witnesses—on the streets of some wild cars fighting back against car thieves and carjackers but that it's all just exaggerated talk. And that's basically the storyline given to any news people who get wind of our operations. We do want the news media to occasionally offer a little limited reporting about tales of a car that fights back, but we want the stories on television, radio, newspapers, online, etcetera to be reported with a skeptical tone and a heavy touch of 'it's likely just another urban legend.' So, we want some exposure, but we're not ready to go exoteric. It's a managed balancing act."

"Yeah, I can see that you want to balance it."

"Yes. Some publicity is part of creating and sustaining a fear factor so we can intimidate—that is, of course, intimidating the perps so we can deter them from doing more car crimes. But, we don't want everyone and his cousin believing we're for real because we don't want investigative reporters or paparazzi or groups of regular citizens to try to come after us and publicize us every-which-a-where. As I said earlier, we don't want the government to make us quit. We want to maintain a good deal of anonymity so we can operate without interference."

"Oh, all right."

"And consider, if you will, the humiliating fliers with the pictures we take on the scene and then unload onto the street that show the car punks bloody, beaten, and kissing or in other forced homoerotic poses, as well as all the verbal accounts from the car punks themselves or the occasional eyewitness. Most of those humiliation-drenched photos get grabbed up and destroyed or kept hidden away—just as we anticipated—by those who have an interest in keeping too much publicity from happening, especially the photographs. That's the police and sometimes the criminal car punks themselves, if they can get ahold of the pictures. Sometimes other car punks, who know their coworkers have been photographed, will clean up any remaining pictures or fliers the authorities don't gather."

"Yeah, I can get how both of those disparate groups would not want too much of it getting around."

"That's right," said Guinevere. "OK, the TV news and newspapers have covered us *some*—a smidgen. Have you not seen anything about us?"

"No, not really," said Kristi Lou. "But I confess I haven't kept up with local news as much as I should have, as of recently."

"That's all right. Well, anyway, the thing is that a couple of our embarrassing pictures of car punks have indeed made it onto local TV and one appeared next to a small write-up in the paper. But, rather luckily to this point, not too many news reporters and not a bunch of the Detroit, city-wide general public seem to believe there's too much to it; it's just, from their perspective, it's just some trumped-up stuff, perhaps doctored photos and claims from hysterical criminals who lack credibility to begin with."

"Oh," said Kristi Lou, who was enthralled by the experience of listening to Guinevere talk more than she was by what Guinevere was talking about. For Kristi Lou, the sound of Guinevere's long-missing voice was nirvanic.

"But the car punks know," continued Guinevere. "And lots of local Drollman street people know. They get to know fast. Anyway, Dad and I are hoping that the media in whatever other cities we visit won't start putting two and two together too well when and if they obtain all the detailed stats—that is, the statistics showing dramatic drops in car break-ins and carjackings and car vandalism."

"OK," said Kristi Lou, "so far, then, it seems that you and Mr. Lindsay have had the perfect balance of some publicity but not too much—just enough to help discourage the car criminal types, which is obviously your target audience for any publicity, anyway. And law enforcement has cooperated, after you've won them over by gaining their trust."

"Yeah, that pretty much summarizes the situation."

"It's still hard to comprehend, though."

"I know it is."

Kristi Lou wanted Guinevere to continue talking, continuously, but sensed the topic that motivated her to speak with atypical loquaciousness was nearing its completion.

"So," said Kristi Lou as she shoved her naturally blond hair back from her forehead, "part of it is kinda like a disinformation approach, an orchestrated denial, right?"

"Yes, that's mostly correct, though, as I've tried to say, we want there to be a tinge of believability. The official disavowal is reminiscent of the Air Force's attempts at dismissing valid UFO sightings as weather balloons, swamp gas, atmospheric phenomena, or other curveballs."

"Oh, right. I believe there may indeed be visitors, you know, space aliens, among us here on Earth. I'm pretty open-minded about that possibility."

"Good. I would anticipate your open-mindedness about that and anything else. I think extraterrestrials have probably been here on and off for centuries.

"Anyhow, regarding your query as to how we do it, I will expound upon that topic for you, my trusted friend from yesteryear, because I know you haven't changed as far as your integrity."

"Thank you. But how do you know—about my integrity, that is? Do you know what I do? For money?"

"Yes, I believe I do. I know that you've not exactly become a prude. You work in the, uh, erotic entertainment industry. As I said earlier, I figured it out. But, even if you were the Whore of Babylon incarnate, that wouldn't make you a treacherous wretch."

"Ha—just a regular wretch, huh?"

"Yes, but a nice, trustworthy, regular wretch, though. Those are the best kinds of wretches."

"Gee, thanks."

Kristi Lou smiled and leaned back in the seat.

"If I'm going to be a wretch, I'd prefer to be a nice and trustworthy one."

"Of course. Maybe an amazing grace will save you."

"Yeah—save a wretch like me, as the old spiritual hymn goes. I really like that song."

"Yeah—so do I," agreed Guinevere.

"You want me to sing it for you?" asked Kristi Lou.

"Sure. But, maybe you could wait for, say, 50 years or so—maybe 500; that'll give me something to which I can look forward."

"Yeah, right. OK, I'll give you a raincheck on my singing," replied Kristi Lou, as she and Guinevere simultaneously smiled.

Silence, pleasantly felt by both friends, swept over them for about 12 seconds. Kristi Lou temporarily forgot about learning more from Guinevere about how she and Mr. Lindsay used their supercar to fight car crime.

"You know all those tall-girl notes that kept showing up in Downtown Secrets?" inquired Guinevere.

"Yes. Oh wow. They were from you, weren't they?"

"No, they were from Bud Battle."

"What? Mr. Battle? My—our—seventh-grade teacher? Mr. Battle? I was just talking about Mr. Battle a few minutes ago—saying to you that I was sitting at the table in Secrets thinking of him while I had no idea that during those same moments you were in town here and actually in or near the neighborhood and, uh … are you kidding?"

"No."

"No?" queried Kristi Lou, having twisted sideways in her seat and staring wide-eyed at Guinevere.

"OK, yes, I am," Guinevere replied with a muted laugh. "You're incredibly naïve … OK, you're very trusting and ingenuous. Yeah, the notes were from me. I drove by the club several times and put them in the big brown Secrets mailbox."

"Oh."

"So, when Dad and I got here about three weeks ago and scouted about the community to arrange our maneuvers, I saw you on the sidewalk. You were wearing a dark-red miniskirt—and heels you definitely don't need—speaking of Mr. Battle, if you know what I mean."

Guinevere grinned, then laughed out loud, as both girls remembered Kristi Lou's middle school trauma over her dreaded height.

"Yes, I definitely know what you mean," said Kristi Lou while smiling broadly. "As I was talking about earlier, it was so hard, emotionally. Oh, man, do I ever remember me towering over Mr. Battle. He hated it and I hated it. And there was that dreadful day when I poked him in the eye with my boob. It's funny now, but back then I wanted to curl up and die."

"Yes, you were miserable until toward the end of that year, when you began to feel better. You were a kid. I also remember that you and I got to be friends with Marsha Mellow."

"Oh, yeah, little Marsha. She was so sweet with her obsessions and rituals—though I know she suffered with it; I'm not making light of it."

"Well, I should hope not."

"I'm *not*."

"I know you're not; I'm teasing. Anyhow, I told you you'd eventually come to accept and enjoy your height. And, well …"

"And you were so right, as always."

"No, I'm not always right, but thanks."

Kristi Lou looked out the window as the graceful car glided along. She then turned back toward Guinevere.

"But anyways, nowadays … did I just say 'anyways, nowadays'?"

"Yes, you did," answered Guinevere.

"OK, well—as I said a little while ago—now I really like my tallness. And, as for the pumps, the other ladies wear pumps and I don't want to be too different so I wear pumps, too. And men expect pumps. Besides, my heels aren't too high."

"I know they're not. Anyhow, I told Dad about you. He remembered you from school days back at Our Lady. He knew you came over to the house a few times. He said 'Was she the tall, gangly girl who was scared of her own height?' And I said 'yeah, that's her.'"

"Funny," said Kristi Lou.

"So, he went to Downtown Secrets on two or three nights to confirm what we thought you were doing. And, well, he also went there because he's single and he's a man and he's a heterosexual and you know how that goes. At any rate, he could tell—we could tell—that the club was more than a place to dance."

"Is it that obvious?"

"To someone who's observant, it kinda is."

"Oh."

"I kinda remember your dad. But I don't recall seeing him in Secrets."

"You probably didn't pay much attention to him back when we were twelve and thirteen, during those few times you came over to visit with me. Also, since then Dad has gotten a lot of gray hairs, and he's bigger. Well, he's bigger, but it's good bigger because since he and Mom got divorced he's been dedicated to going to the gym."

"Oh. I wonder if I saw him."

"You approached Dad to talk with him. You had a really good conversation."

Kristi Lou glanced at Guinevere and turned away in the same moment, fixating for about two seconds upon a freckle on her left knee.

"Oh, Guinevere I didn't, did I? Not your dad."

"No," replied Guinevere, smiling. "You just talked. Besides, Dad and Mom split six years ago—over his personality, his eccentricity, you might say—so he's non-committed. It wouldn't have bothered me if he and you did do it. I'm not hung up against sex as are so many people, even though I've rarely had it—sex, that is. But, the point is, coitus and other forms of sexual pleasure are natural and I don't believe God is opposed to it, despite what certain passages in the Bible seem to declare. For example, consider the verse in Matthew, chapter 5, that says 'If a man lusts after a woman he has committed adultery in his heart.' I think that's how it goes. Well, all people, including women, feel lust when they see someone who inspires lusty feelings. I guess the idea is that we're supposed to extinguish the urge really soon after it comes upon us. But I just don't buy it—not literally; it needs context."

"Guinevere, I'm simply…I, uh, I, I'm listening to you talk about how sex is really an OK thing and uh…you're saying the same things I say and believe. It's just…I was just saying almost those same things the other night, just over from where we're riding right now—at the club, with me making a speech outside. And now you're sounding like me so much that…"

"Twisted minds think alike."

"Oh, right."

"So, anyhow, with my dad, you doing it with him would not have rattled me at all."

"Well, uh, I don't know," said Kristi Lou, embarrassed and now looking at the dashboard while nervously fingering the glove compartment lock hole for a tactile release of stress. "Does a super-teched-to-the-max car like this actually have to have a key in a keyhole to unlock it? I'd think you'd just use some—I don't know—some type of laser beam aimed at it or cryptic number code or…I don't know, but…"

"It's just for looks. No, actually, a key, while unnecessary, can indeed unlock it; that feature makes the car appear more normalized to anyone Dad and I might want to, uh, well, deceive, if there was such a need. But, we both know you just abruptly changed the subject. Get back on it, please. It's OK, Kristi Lou; you don't have to be uncomfortable about it."

"Well, OK. It appears my diversionary tactic was less than a booming success. So, anyway, I, uh, anyway, I'm glad—I'm really glad to learn that you've grown up to not be hung up against men wanting sex; as I just said, that's one of my big things, philosophically. As I just got through saying, what you just said sounds amazingly just like me during one of my pro-sex soapbox rants. In fact, you'd be amazed at how much you just sounded like me, really. It's a purebred coincidental happening that you said all that since I say the same sorta…but—your dad—I don't know. It might've seemed weirder than I could handle. It might've gotten to me, I mean, after I'd found out, that is, that he was your dad. But, I don't know. Maybe it shouldn't, but, anyway, I don't know, I …"

"Now, you're sounding hung up a bit over sex, yourself. Yes, you are."

"I know, but despite me agreeing with everything you said and me saying about the exact same type of things, I was still raised in this society and, well, I don't know, I'm sure I would've been OK with it after you told me it was OK," said Kristi Lou.

"It's OK."

"OK."

After another pause of silence that lasted about 15 seconds, Kristi Lou thought of something about which she felt she should have already asked.

"Did you just happen to land in Detroit for your project, with me living here by freak coincidence? I mean, I guess I should just realize that your mom and your uncle are from near here and his car was attacked and, uh, and those connections were what drew you here. But, anyway, did you just come here to get car criminals and you happened to, as you said, see me on the street? Of all places, of all cities, you could've chosen, did you just happen to choose one with someone—me—in it with whom you used to be close friends and just happen to be in a part of town here where I was and just happen to look over at the perfect moment so you could spot me outside? That just seems like too much to be entirely coincidental."

"All right. I'll explain things. There is some coincidence, but not as much as you were getting at. Detroit is our second target. We came here because Mom is from here, as you were just saying, and also because of Uncle Ralph living in the area and because they got his car.

"That's it; that's the main connection. Mom is from here. She and

Dad are divorced, but they still love each other. Yes, it's one of *those* divorces. So, Dad wants to do something good in Detroit because it's her original hometown. And they got my uncle, Dad's ex-brother-in-law."

"I understand," said Kristi Lou. "So, it really wasn't me, because, I mean ... not that I'm that important, but I was just wonder ..."

"But, also," continued Guinevere, "the other hugely important reason I wanted to come here was because I heard you were here, going to college. So, yes, to a strong degree, you are one of the reasons I'm here—absolutely. And don't go thinking you aren't."

"Thanks. That makes me feel kinda warm and reassured."

"But, I didn't know you'd temporarily dropped out of classes and were a working girl, as they say."

"Who told you I was in Detroit?"

"Do you remember David Darnell?"

"Yeah, I remember David. He called me a giraffe in the seventh grade. He wasn't being derisive, though. He was nice. I always liked David."

"I'm glad. He remembers you fondly, too."

"Really? How do you know? Did he tell you that? So, how did David know I was here? I haven't seen him since high school."

"His mom talked to your mom one day in the grocery store in Little Rock, and your mom told Mrs. Darnell you were in Detroit. David's mom told him. And I saw David at the movies—at the multiplex in the mall—and he told me."

"Oh. How is David doing?"

"He seems to be doing fine. He's a senior at U of A, where, parenthetically, I'll be a junior majoring in geophysics upon resumption of my education there—whenever that will be. Anyhow, David's an equipment manager for the Razorbacks football team. And yes, he did indeed tell me he always liked you, too. He used to feel sorry for you because he knew you were virtually deranged over being so much taller than the other kids."

"Yeah, I was."

"Oh, by the way, that night at the movies, he also told me that back then in the seventh grade that he put the word on Nate Perkins to leave you be or else."

"Oh my goodness. He did? He defended me? I never knew that. David always was kinda quiet. Anyway, that's really, uh …touching."

"Yes, I concur. Noteworthily, David's grown into a good-looking, nice guy, and, quirkily, a cat-daddy who's somewhat of a harborer of ailurophilia."

"Oh. Has he?"

"He has."

"Good-looking, nice, and ailurophile-ish is a great combo."

"It is."

"Is he still tall?"

"He's 6'3"."

"Oh. Is he?"

"He is."

"Oh. David kept growing?"

"He did."

"So, he's taller…"

" …than you."

"Oh."

Guinevere turned onto the same side street she and Kristi Lou had already ridden along three times during their joyride. Kristi Lou felt a wave of pensive sadness drift into her head, and she felt this despondency settle literally into her abdomen. She whispered in a sad tone loudly enough for Guinevere to hear.

"I guess David's opinion of me would take a substantial nosedive if he knew what …what I'm doing with my life now. I know he's been reared in the same culture as the rest of us. Maybe, Guinevere, when-ever you see him again when you're back in Little Rock, perhaps you won't have to, you know, tell him about, uh …"

"Please," assured Guinevere. "I wouldn't say a thing about that. If you were to ever get with David, then you could determine whether you wanted to tell him. You'll have to make such decisions, anyway, with your Valentine's Day pash, your true-heart beau, your soulmate into whose arms you'll melt—that is, whoever becomes the indescribably lucky man you marry. And I know that one day you will get married."

"You do? You know that—that someday I'll find me a fella? I hope so. I hope you're right. I hope I haven't blown it forever."

"You haven't. You indisputably have not."

"I hope you're prescient. OK, I just used a medium-size big word that I knew you'd know."

"Yes, I can be quite vatic; I just used a small-size big word that most people don't know. But anyhow, whoever he might prove to be, if I knew you had already informed him of your descent into brazen dissoluteness, and I knew he was worthy of you but he was understandably struggling with your past life activities, then, well, I would indeed talk to him about it. I'd try to inspire him to see how wonderful you are and to accept you and your previous undertakings. I'd let him know you were more than worth his commitment."

"Thank you so very much for saying those things."

"You're welcome, Kristi Lou."

"Vatic?"

"Look it up."

"I will. I can hardly wait."

"I'm thrilled that you're excited."

"Oh," said Kristi Lou, "going back to what we were saying about David and, you know, whether he and other men can love a woman who's been, uh, sexually unconservative, I want to say some things I've been thinking about in recent weeks. People naturally want to know they're special to those they love. For those romantically in love, there are various specials—plural with an s. Here are two premier specials for a man in love with a woman. If a female mate has led a prior life of chastity or close to it and now loves one man, that fellow who loves her gets two specials. If a female mate has had many casual-sex partners, that fellow who loves her gets only one of those specials—but it's the paramount special: she did not love them but she does love him. If he finds himself feeling heavy-hearted because she qualifies as being or having been a so-called *thot*—that hoe over there—and comfort is needed by him to be taken, he can take it in knowing that."

"Agreed, from A to Z."

The car glided with eerie smoothness across the fractured asphalt at 30 mph, still no traffic in sight. Kristi Lou was aware, without thinking about it, of an unusually steady, barely hearable humming as well as a slight vibration, which she found oddly pleasing, even comforting. She felt a resurgence of confidence regarding her ideology and occupational choices concerning human sexuality.

She looked through the window, then at Guinevere.

"What does your dad look like?"

"He's 6'1"—about the same height as some skyscraper you know."

"Ha. Funny."

"But he doesn't wear high-heel pumps."

"He doesn't? That's admirable."

"He's very distinguished-looking and speaks eloquently."

"Like father, like daughter."

"I think so. One night—wait, it was just last night—he wore a camel-colored suit but with no tie. He said he saw and heard one of the most bizarre conversations he'd ever witnessed. There was this 20-something man who had a verbal altercation with another customer and he, uh, he seemed to reverse the order of his curse-words. Dad thought it was hilarious and …"

"Oh my god! I remember him, your dad. OMG! OMG! He was cracking up at Davey, our backward cusser. He's dyslexic only when he curses. But your dad—he was so nice—so very nice. The guy I'm remembering fits the height and clothing description you just gave: a little over six-foot tall and in a suit with no tie and all that. That had to be him. Actually, there was something kinda familiar about him. Now I know why. I might've remembered him subconsciously from our seventh-grade days when I was over at your house.

"Anyway, we talked for almost half an hour. He was so intelligent and nice—I guess that's where you got your intelligence and niceness from. Well, maybe from your mom, too. And he smelled really nice with his cologne. I still remember his aroma. So many guys come into Secrets wearing cologne because, I think, they want to smell good for the girls because they think it'll help their chances of getting, well, you know, laid. And that makes sense, even though, you know, if they have the money, then…but, anyway, your dad—he wore cologne I didn't recognize at all. But, more importantly, I didn't recognize him from being in your home those four or five times eight years ago. But maybe I did sense something familiar about him when he was in Secrets; I can't remember whether I felt that way or not."

"But you just said less than a minute ago that quote there was something kinda familiar about him unquote. Right?"

"Oh my goodness, I did just say that, didn't I? Is my short-term memory going kaput?"

"Probably. Too much sex. Kidding. No, I doubt it; we all sometimes forget things we did or said very recently. But, yeah, Dad didn't absolute-ly recognize you either from eight years back when we were in middle school, but he knew who you were because I'd told him you were working in there and that I'd driven by and seen you on the sidewalk. I told him that, just for fun, I'd put enigmatic notes to you in the club's mailbox. I described you as, well, a very tall and very curvy and very bomb-shelly blonde. Besides, he told me you introduced yourself to him as 'Kristi Lou.' So, you use your real name while agitating male instincts? Interesting.

"And, by the way, Dad wears old-fashioned British Sterling."

"Oh, then he had the advantage of knowing I was me but I didn't know he was him. Oh my goodness; did I just sound as convoluted as I think I sounded? Anyhow, British Sterling?"

"Yes, you did sound like you thought you sounded, but I could figure it out. Just funning, ha-ha. Yes, it's—the British Sterling—from the '60s. Back then, Dad says, it was all the rage with teenagers in high school throughout America. His dad, my granddad, used to use it and used to give it to him as Christmas and birthday presents. It's not easy to find in stores anymore. But he orders it over the Internet."

"He smelled so good I could've … never mind …"

Giggling ensued from both friends, followed by a half-minute of silence as the car continued to roll across the dimly illumined causeways with what seemed to Kristi Lou to be unreal smoothness, as if underneath her seat were the finest shock absorbers ever attached to any vehicle.

"You know, Kristi Lou, when you get excited you still do what you used to do when we were kids—you talk nineteen to the dozen."

"Oh my gah … I just learned that phrase the other day, when I was reading this magazine and I came across it. And now you've just said it: nineteen to the dozen. Coincidences really get me. I mean, they're fascinating, but sometimes they bother me a bit if they pile up because I don't understand how or why they're happening, but, anyway …"

"Yeah, but as I said earlier, don't be bothered by coincidences; be charmed by them."

"Right."

Kristi Lou looked at the only green illumination amongst the futuristic cluster of gauges, all brightly lit by light-emitting diode technology. She spotted the car clock.

"Oh my goodness, Guinevere. I've got to get back. We've been riding around for a long while. Hokey is cutting me some slack, and I don't know if he told Doris, our kinda-like den mother. But, anyway, I don't want to stay gone too long 'cause I'm supposed to be at Secrets."

"I understand. Actually, I was about to say the same thing; you need to go back to work."

Guinevere reset the navigation system to return through the side streets to Downtown Secrets.

"How about tomorrow, in the daytime—if you're active during the daylight hours?" asked Guinevere.

"Oh my. That's a zapper. Yes, as a matter of fact, I am out and about even when the sun is shining. I make it a point to get outside during the day."

"I know. I was just joshing."

"I know you were."

"Dad and I have some potential targets tomorrow, but we're not certain as to whether any of the local car punks will do anything. But we'll be on patrol, as they say. You can ride with me."

"I can?"

"Yes, it'll be fine."

"OK. Why don't you come over to my place, my apartment—we almost rode by it a little while ago—tomorrow around…well, what time is convenient for you and your dad?"

"Let's say I pick you up at 1:00, if that's compatible with your plans."

"I am positively planless. So, yeah, 1:00 is swell."

"Swell? Really? Swell? All right. And, just to clarify—that's 1:00 p.m., not a.m. I was thinking you might become a bit unsure because you're often a mite more vigorous in the post-vespertine hours," said Guinevere, mischievously winking.

"Vespertine! Hardy-har-har," replied Kristi Lou. "Yes, I knew you meant p.m.; we were remarking about me being active during the day. And, inasmuch as I'm crepuscular, I know what vespertine means. And yes—swell. And you were teasing me again. I love it! My address is …"

"I know where you live."

"You do?"

"Yes."

"How do you even know that?"

"We can get data on anyone or anything super-fast using Dad's 22nd-century software. His seek-and-collate programs can dig up information better than the NSA."

"Do you have my phone number?" queried Kristi Lou. "If you do, that would be most impressive since it's unlisted."

Guinevere immediately recited Kristi Lou's phone number.

"Gollll-**lee**," said Kristi Lou, channeling her inner Gomer Pyle from late-night TV reruns she'd seen of *Gomer Pyle, U.S.M.C.* "You probably expect me to say that that's somewhat frightening. That's somewhat frightening. But it's really not frightening when I consider the source—you—and your dad, of course. But I still feel doxed, ha-ha!"

"Never worry. The privacy of any info we have about you is more than 100 percent secure."

"How can you have more than 100 percent? Is that actually possible? Because 100 percent is, of course, the pinnacle of percentages, so you can't really..."

"You haven't become a literal-o-phile have you?"

"A what? Oh. No. I have not. Of course not. It's just that you must know that 100 is literally the zenith, so it's ... oops."

****

Several more minutes of remember-when chattering ensued, and then Guinevere returned Kristi Lou to Downtown Secrets.

38

KRISTI LOU SPENT A HUMDRUM FINAL SIX HOURS ON THE dance floor and then rode home in Dan's cab. Too wired from her unanticipated reunion with Guinevere to fall asleep easily, she eventually did doze off, but not until about 30 minutes after sunrise. She slept for a few hours, awakening with her alarm at 11:30, Saturday, August 18.

After quickly showering at 11:55, Kristi Lou spent most of the early afternoon's first hour deciding what clothes to wear for her get-together with Guinevere at 1:00, as well as writing a list of topics to discuss, including reminiscences, though she knew that memory lane would deliver them both to recollections about which she had not written in her notes.

****

By 12:50, Kristi Lou, having aerosol-bombed every room in her apartment with Citrus Meadows air freshener while almost emptying the previously half-full can, was primed, at least as far as physical preparation, for Guinevere's arrival. Wearing a pair of threadbare, faded, gray-denim jeans and a lemon-yellow T-shirt, she sat still in her living room with Mr. Dooflotcher snoozing in her lap. Recognizing that she

412

was unreservedly agog over Guinevere's pending visit, she analyzed herself while waiting.

Ohhhhhh, I've got the collywobbles, the jumpy jimjams. I am so big-time nervous. Why am I nervous? I think I'm nervous 'cause I'm worried I'll forget to talk about some things. But I've got my notes—but don't take them with you. I won't. No notes. I can't be talking to Guinevere and suddenly whip reference notes out of my pocket—too unnatural. And what we don't talk about today we can talk about another time. People often say the word anxious to mean they're hepped up and excited in a happy way about something good they anticipate when they should say they're eager. But I feel both anxious and eager. Please, oh God, let it go well. I hope she won't be too late. I can't believe she's here in town. I'm so aflutter. I'm so jittery. I'm so neurotic. Oh, maaannnnn …

Guinevere pulled the marauding supercar along the curbside in front of Kristi Lou's apartment building at precisely one o'clock.

Having transferred herself, Mr. Dooflotcher and the chair directly next to the living room window out of which she had been staring for the previous seven minutes, Kristi Lou marveled at the exactitude of Guinevere's punctuality.

Not late and not early. Arriving too early can be just as inconvenient to whoever is receiving the visit as arriving too late. Guinevere got it just right; from remembering her as a kid, I should've known she would grow up to be considerate and dependable. Yeah, I should've expected that. Actually, I did expect that.

Kristi Lou arose, lifted Mr. Dooflotcher from her/their lap and carefully placed him onto the chair.

"This chair is all yours, Dooflotch."

Mr. Dooflotcher looked up at his human. One second later, he jumped down, bolted across the living room and hopped onto the glider recliner, decisively his favorite chair. At the moment Mr. Dooflotcher bolted, Kristi Lou bolted in the opposite direction. She raced across the living room, positioning herself behind her doorbell-less and knocker-less front door. She bent forward to peer through the peephole.

She watched her friend approach. Timing her move and feeling clever, Kristi Lou swung open the door just before Guinevere could knock, leaving Guinevere's fisted hand suspended in midair.

"Hey," said Kristi Lou, "you look like a mime."

"Great. I used to want to be a mime," japed Guinevere without pause. "There's nothing like living in a world made of air."

"Come on in. It's no majestic castle; it's just my humble, haimish abode."

Guinevere strode six feet inside, stopped, and then looked around.

"Oh, it's comfily nice in here, very attractively arranged with pleasing colors. And it smells like an orange grove. Hmm … did you clean up because I was coming over?"

"No. I always keep things cle…yes."

"I thought so. But that's OK," said Guinevere with a warm smile.

"There are several tons of dust and garbage piled up in another room."

"Yeah, I see a giant germ right over there," said Guinevere, frowning as if repulsed.

"No you don't!"

"I can't believe you live in a place called Moonbeam Landing, partially patterned after a '60s hippie commune."

"Far out, man!"

Kristi Lou looked across the room.

"Oh, here's someone I want you to meet. This is Mr. Dooflotcher, AKA Dooflotch. I almost told you about him last night when you told me about David Darnell's affinity for felines."

"Hi, handsome baby!" exclaimed Guinevere, as Mr. Dooflotcher, as if he had anticipated Guinevere's geniality, had already trekked over to her and commenced dipping his head and rubbing his vibrissae against her ankles.

"I'm the same as David—I love cats," she added as she crouched and used her fingertips to stroke Mr. Dooflotcher underneath the tip end of his chin. "Wow, he purrs so loudly," said Guinevere, as Mr. Dooflotcher stepped forward and began convivially head-butting her knee.

"Now, he's gracing you with happy-head-butts, known as bunting. Did you know those friendly head-butts are also called head-bonks?"

"No, I did not. Head-bonks, huh? Well, if I must be head-butted, from now on I'll want them to be head-bonks."

"You didn't use to have a cat back when I was coming over to see you, did you? I don't remember a cat in your house or in your yard."

"No. Although I'm a cat fancier, I didn't have one growing up. Mom is allergic to cat dander; she gets hives and sternutations her head off."

"Super-dandy word! She gets the sneezies! But, that's too bad, that she can't be around kitties. I've become a certifiably cat-crazy ailurophile—like David, it would seem … hmm. Well, OK, anyway, allergies aside, I hope I don't seem like a lousy hostess, but could I give you the grand tour of my lovely apartment some other time? I just feel … I don't know … I feel like I want to get on the road in that splendiferous car of yours and literally roll down memory lane. I just feel like talking in your car, for whatever reason. So …"

"Let's go. Nice meeting you, Sir Dooflotch."

Kristi Lou peered down at the usually skittish Mr. Dooflotcher, who continued to rub against Guinevere and clamor for her attention.

"You like Guinevere better than me? You just met her. You're ordinarily a single-human kitty, standoffish toward maintenance men and such. Anyhow, I've gotta go. I'll be back before too long, though. As I always tell you, I'll always come home. I always do. I always will. I promise," said Kristi Lou as her kitty came to her. "Play with your catnip toys and eat some treats. You know I'll never not come home to you," assured Kristi Lou, squatting and using both hands to gently rub Mr. Dooflotcher behind his ears.

"Give me a sniff-finger kiss."

Kristi Lou and Mr. Dooflotcher, as was their custom, exchanged a sniff-finger kiss, whereby she extended her forefinger to an inch from his face and he moved his nose softly onto her fingertip.

Kristi Lou stood up, as did Guinevere. As they walked toward the doorway, Kristi Lou switched her floor lamp onto the 15-watt setting.

"I always leave a little dim light in here so I can see Dooflotch from the street at night or so someone who would hopefully rescue him if something went wrong—a fire or whatnot—could see him. You can often see him through the window when I'm not here 'cause he enjoys perching on the back of the sofa and gazing outside waiting for the first sight of me."

"That's so sweet. Your give-and-take affection is very sweet. You need to get a guy who's man enough to appreciate that sweetness as a form of strength. And you will."

"Thanks. That's what you said last night—that I will meet someone like that. Thanks, again."

The two reunited girlfriends stepped outside and onto the concrete walkway. Kristi Lou, with the bottom of her avocado-colored, mini crossbody-bag purse resting on her left palm, turned and looked back through the doorway into the living room.

"Bye, Dooflotch. Don't worry; I shall return."

Kristi Lou closed and locked the door. She took two steps and halted.

"Guinevere?"

"Yes?"

"I'm sorry; I uh, I feel the need to … I have to … I have to go back in and change clothes. I want to wear a dress."

"Change clothes? Well, Okayyyy. But you look fine now. You're wearing jeans. I'm wearing jeans. I'd think you'd like to wear jeans as a switch from wearing short, tight skirts, etcetera—for the sake of comfort."

"I know. I like jeans. I wanted to relax in jeans while going out with you; that's why I put them on. But, I don't know … but, it's just that, I think that … that this new cotton-ish type dress I bought the other day but haven't worn yet—that it kinda reminds me a bit of the dresses I used to wear back home when we'd go somewhere, you know? It's really peculiar, I know, but…"

"Go change. It's fine. I'll wait outside the door here."

"All right. Thanks. I'm sorry."

"No need to be sorry. It's OK."

"All righty. I'll be back before you know it. I can get in and out of clothes really fast."

"Yes, I'm sure you can."

"Oh my goodness, I think I detect a zinger."

"No, I would never…"

"Ha-ha—right," said Kristi Lou with a laugh as she dropped her purse onto the pavement beside Guinevere's feet and reentered her apartment. She peeped down at Mr. Dooflotcher as she raced past him toward the stairs leading to the upstairs bedroom. "I told you I'd return. I'm back. And it took me only 45 seconds to come back. But I'll be going right back out, though."

Kristi Lou, after titivating her sleekly molded lower arms by clamping two lightweight, green-and-gold grass bangle bracelets onto each wrist, disrobed rapidly and then slipped into her new pastel-green summer dress, almost in one motion. Hurrying, she felt part of herself wanting to leave her T-shirt and jeans crumpled on the floor where she had tossed them. But she could not resist the compulsion to fold and neatly place her clothing into their proper dresser drawers.

"As usual, the neat-freak in me prevails," she said outwardly to herself as she descended the stairway.

She reached down and petted Mr. Dooflotcher without breaking her stride across the living room.

"Bye again, Dooflotch. See you before too long. My green dress and my matching bangles look nice, don't they? Thanks. I knew you'd like them," said Kristi Lou as she was closing the door, after which she deadbolted the lock, snatched up her purse, and then looked, with an exaggerated wide-eyed expression, at Guinevere.

"I'm here again. Remember me from a few moments ago?"

"Yes, I haven't forgotten you. You look good in that dress; it becomes you nicely."

"Thanks. OK, we can go now."

"Are you sure?"

"Yes, I … well … as far as I can tell I am. Let's get going before I have another impulse."

She and Guinevere walked toward the vehicle now dreaded by local car malefactors.

As Kristi Lou approached Guinevere's space-age automobile and reached to open the door, it opened automatically, producing a muffled, pleasant swooshing sound as it swung outward gracefully and moved past her.

"Oh. Well, okey-dokey, Mr. Car. Thank you, thank you."

Kristi Lou sat down, placing her purse on the floorboard under her knees. The door closed automatically, emitting a pleasantly dull, puissant *thunk*.

Guinevere's driver-side door also opened itself, and, upon her seating herself, thunked itself shut.

"This car is a gentleman," remarked Guinevere,

"Yes, it sure is. It opened and closed the door for me. I'm impressed. Maybe I'll ask this car for a date."

"He would consider you a hot date, especially when you sit on him— as you are now."

"Yes, I'm so sure, ha-ha. Anyway, I've been dreaming about this— about us, you know, but I … I'm so glad you found my place, here."

"No problem. With space-age navigation, it was as easy as ye olde pie. And, by the way, as an etymological sidebar, there is debate as to whether 'ye' in the French-influenced old-English phrase 'ye olde' should be pronounced 'yee' or 'thee.' But even though centuries ago 'ye' was used on printing presses as a shortcut for the word 'the' I'm going with 'yee' because some things evolve, and, over much time, countless instances of extensive usage have morphed the popularly preferred pronunciation away from the original 'thee' and to the altered version of 'yee.'"

"You just did me with that tangent; after you interrupted yourself and took off about…it was as if you were channeling me."

"I did that as a tribute to you," confirmed Guinevere. "Did you like it?"

"Uhhhhh—it was just wonderful. But…do I really sound like that? I mean, it was quite interesting to learn those things about the historical origins of how 'ye olde' can be pronounced properly. As a matter of fact, I said 'ye olde' just the other night—I said 'ye olde nutshell'—to Mr. Wilmont, one of my friends who comes into Secrets. But, do I…uh, do I actually…never mind."

"I could never match your matchless talent for tangential ramblings; you're simply the best," said Guinevere. "And, yes, I've been looking forward to our continued visiting, too. It's so unbelievably good to be back with you; really, it is."

"Same here," proclaimed Kristi Lou.

"Anyway, I want to pick back up where we basically left off last night."

"OK," replied Kristi Lou.

"Oh, would you be interested in storing your little crossbody bag in our slide-out, mini-storehouse," an inexplicably deep box which Guinevere caused to slide forward from a smooth-surface, borderless section of the center dashboard area. "As you can see, I have my small purse in there."

"Wow, that's uh … that thing fits in the dash? How does …? It must somehow undergo compaction, but I don't understa … oh my. Anyway, thanks but no thanks; I'll just keep mine here with me for now."

"All righty," said Guinevere, smiling.

They rolled quietly and slowly away from Moonbeam Landing.

39

"TO ANSWER YOUR QUESTIONS—AS I'VE SAID BEFORE, MY dad's a genius. And he's not, well, he's also not all that mentally normal, which I've also pointed out. He's not a psycho, but he's psychologically aberrant. He almost redefines eccentric. Put those two elements together and then couple them with an obsessive revenge motive and a deep understanding of automobiles and mechanics and you've got trouble for car thieves and carjackers."

"So, as you told me last night, you've got two vehicles that you and your dad sic on them—our car, here, plus the menacing meanie-van?"

"Yes—very good—the van can be marvelously mean, when needed. This car, as you can readily see, is now in regular-car, sedan-ish, structural form. But, you'll recollect from yesterday that I told you it's a shape shifter. It can change shapes and colors, making it very hard to detect or trace. Let's become SUV riders."

Guinevere typed in commands on the dashboard touchscreen. The vehicle's interior, particularly the seating, underwent limited but noticeable changes, but the exterior of the car metamorphosed into what appeared to be a well-known SUV.

"Oh my goodness!" said Kristi Lou. "I just went higher and the seats and the dash—that's not possible to do what we just did. How…"

"OK, let's go back to riding in a sedan. Incidentally, no one saw our transformation; I would know."

"But…what? We just changed cars while we were riding? How can that…"

"Remember, I told you before about how this is a shape-shifting car."

"Yeah, you did say that, but how can that hap…"

"There actually are shape-shifting vehicles. That technology is cutting-edge, but the technology is there. You can see shape-shifting cars on YouTube.

"Think along the lines of the metal retractable roofs found on some upscale convertibles, except brilliantly applied to essentially the entire vehicle. The technology that Dad invented is a groundbreaking, brilliant expansion of the already-existing shape-shifting technology.

"Anyhow, we sometimes call this car the 'Bad Car,' with a capital B and C. We also call it the 'attack car,' but we're not capping the first letters of those words yet. That inconsistency somewhat troubles me. Anyway, you could say it shouldn't matter as to the grammar because it's not as if there are any official documents bearing the titles we've chosen. The car names are not being printed in any publication such as a newspaper and they aren't appearing on TV or on the Internet and so on. As I told you, we're holding down the pub. But, still, the grammatical discordance nags me somewhat—that is, when notes are hand-written by Dad to me or occasionally to the authorities. But it's his call."

"Oh. So, I'm riding in the Bad Car?" asked Kristi Lou, still bedazzled and breathing harder than usual.

"Yes, you are thus privileged."

"I am, indeed," agreed Kristi Lou. "All right then, you told me yesterday the van is really a Dodge Caravan. So what is this car? It's really, uh…it's really a what? It has roots, too, right?…a base car underneath all this, this…rocket-ship stuff, right?"

"Honda Accord. The Accord is consistently near or at the top of the list of sedans popular with car thieves."

"Umm…I'm almost scared to ask, but my parents' Nissan Sentra has 130 horsepower. I'm going to venture a guess that this car has more. So, what's the supersonic horsepower in here?"

"2,070. Zero to 60 in 1.9."

"Can we fly?"

"Not yet. But we're working on it."

"This car with that horsepower is not street legal, is it?"

"Nope."

On a straight path of road, Guinevere gunned the engine, which elicited only the slightest sound, almost instantly jolting from 25 to 77 mph. Kristi Lou felt the silent power surge through her buttocks and then flow into her torso and legs. Then Guinevere slowed herself and Kristi Lou to a meek speed as quickly as they had accelerated a moment before. For Kristi Lou, the suddenness of the transition was surreal; there seemed to be virtually no elapse of time between warp acceleration and docile slowness—almost as if it hadn't happened, though she knew it had.

They continued to cruise calmly, as the car trundled along at about 30 mph. Kristi Lou could not tell she was moving without looking out the window.

Guinevere continued her revelations.

"Also notable is that when our uber-tech exterior lights are on, the taillights on our attack car here as well as the taillights on our van of violence are green, except when the brake pedal is pressed, which rubifies them in red—the way it should be for taillights on all vehicles everywhere. The smaragdine color illuming the rear lights clarifies more clearly to onlooking motorists or pedestrians as to whether the vehicle is rolling sans braking versus halting or already halted. Onlookers receive a color-bomb alert. The taillights gleam emerald-green—then quickly fire-red. Contrasting colors render a vehicle's movements more distinguishable than causing one color—red—to merely become brighter when braking. How is it commonsensical to have same-color lights for both stopping and going? As we know, it's red for stop and green for go.

"In any case, Dad invented a system that he'll probably make a fortune selling someday. He'll probably sell it to the U.S. government, probably to the military, for some type of weaponization. He uses a technology involving, well … I can't quite explain it. The Caravan is used because it's still one of the most-often stolen vehicles in America because its parts are so valuable to these people and their criminal customers. A minute ago, we spent several seconds in what appeared to be a Cadillac Escalade. Why? Because the Escalade is the current sports utility vehicle champ. It's a rather dubious championship. The Escalade has been numero uno for many years; it's the top-of-the-list fave SUV for car gangsters to steal."

"Oh. The Cadillac Escalade is? I didn't know that at all. Then again, I don't know most things that there are to know. So, going back to the van, does the van change colors, too?"

"No. Actually, no, it doesn't. But, you've gotta wonder how the car's color changes when I push some buttons. One day, Dad will explain it to me exhaustively, but it's truly vanguard technology, pioneering technology that he's originated. It has to do with taking leading-edge MicroLED technology that's commercially designed for ultra-modern TVs and miraculously applying it to the, well, to the dermis of our car, with zillions of unfragile, protected pixels inlaid barely beneath the car's clear-glass-like but ultra-hard, quasi-metal surface. MicroLED expands on what's called emissive technology. Then, Dad somehow applies that to the car. So, anyhow, the literal paint on the car, of course, stays the same—a yellowy off-white—but a color-illusion is created for any onlookers. But, anyway … no. As for now, the Caravan will stay gray."

"'Stay gray.' I like little rhymes that are inadvertent that don't seem too earthshaking," Kristi Lou said with a placid smile as she looked at Guinevere while leaning completely forward and tilting her head against the dashboard above the glove compartment.

"Yes, I know. I remember. You like rhymes. And you like words such as inadvertent. By the way, if you lean too hard where your right ear is now you will inadvertently activate a set of tentacles that could snatch up that man walking with the grocery bags on the sidewalk we're approaching."

"Oh no! I don't want to do that. He hasn't done anything wrong that I know of," said Kristi Lou while raising up with a grin.

"I don't see a button that I was pushing with my head or anything."

"A type of button is there. There's a pressure point where your head was. It serves as a button. You have to know where it is."

The girls cruised by the unsuspecting man who would never know that a beautiful prostitute's resting head had brought him razor-close to being shanghaied as if plucked off the pavement by a Mesozoic raptor.

Guinevere explained the system further.

"You've probably heard or read about the recent surge in cars manufactured with rear-view cameras."

"Yes, I have heard of them. But I don't know much about them."

"Well," said Guinevere, "rear-view cameras, at this point, are found mostly in luxury cars. But, anyhow, those are cameras that are mounted inside cars' rear bumpers that alert drivers that they're about to back into an object. They hear a warning beep or a buzz. Our cameras go way beyond simply ensuring against a back-up collision. Our rear-view, side-view, and front-view cameras record what's going on, including criminal activity, and that includes break-ins."

"So there's always a record of what happened?"

"Yes, right; everything is recorded. Our cameras, if used on commercial vehicles, could also come in handy in helping to help prosecute tailgaters. Personally, I absolutely detest being tailgated. Of course, if someone tailgates us we can just, well, take the law into our own tentacles. We can discourage further tailgating with our own personalized methods of dissuasion."

"Oh," replied Kristi Lou. "I don't doubt that."

"We haven't imposed anti-tailgate reprisals very often—yet. Let's suffice to say that our discouragement methodology involves the thickest, strongest tentacles lifting and then shaking cars in midair while being carried for a little jaunt behind us, with the tailgating driver still inside. Until we set his or her car down off the side of the road, that individual is usually screaming—and likely hesitant to tailgate again as much."

"Oh my goodness, so you're … uh, you're saying that, that some of these tentacles are actually strong enough to lift and shake an entire car? But how can … how can that be?"

"Yes, they can and do pick up other cars—easily. The tentacles have the power to do it. Plus, this car and the van somehow have their bases maintained perfectly while dangling other vehicles, so we don't overturn. I don't know all the tech details and physics and counterpoise stases and weight-distribution aspects—but Dad does."

"Oh, well. OK, then."

"But, back to the cameras. So, both the Caravan and the Bad Car have multiple hidden cameras. We utilize both video cameras and standard still-photography cameras."

"I guess that's how you generate all those humiliating pictures that the van and the car fling about. Those pictures get scattered around the neighborhood. I know you said yesterday that the pics get gathered up rather quickly, but, nonetheless, a few guys have come into the club and talked about how they grabbed a copy of some of those pictures. I even saw one with these terrified-looking men being dangled in the air and all. I just thought like many people that they were just some fake pictures from some screwy Internet website and that they were just part of a hoax—you know, an urban legend. I thought they were just uh, regular pictures, and printed out and Photoshopped or something. But now I know the pictures were real, and I know who took them."

"Yes," said Guinevere, as she drove through an intersection that carried them beyond the Drollman district. "And, as I was indicating to you yesterday, that's the basic spiel the authorities give to any news-hounds who want to maybe believe eyewitness claims and want to think the pictures are valid. We want criminals to know, but Dad and I are dubious about the general public believing too much. Deciding how much information about what we do that we want disseminated publicly remains a work in progress. And how many websites do you know of that aren't on the Internet?"

"Huh? Oh, did I say…oh my…I did say those words consecutively, didn't I? I should've chosen just one. I ditzy-ed out—never happened before," said Kristi Lou, as Guinevere looked at her and grinned.

"So, for our license plates, we create counterfeit plates that correspond to the state in which we're operating—now Michigan, as you may've noticed—with bogus plate numbers that don't exist in the state's DMV database. If necessary, we can push a couple of buttons and quickly change to another plate with a different number, or just retract the plate.

"And another thing—when the van or this car makes a counterat-tack on a criminal, we're not normally in the vehicle. That being said, there are many retaliatory things we can do while driving or sitting inside. Dad usually manages everything, every action, from what is essentially a remote-control panel—maybe sitting in the other vehicle parked someplace or maybe from a hotel room. Our command centers are quite mobile. Let's just suffice to say that he's somewhere in town; he sees us right now."

"Where is he? Is he in the van? Or…"

"Well, as I was saying, he can be in the van or in this car. Or he—or I—can be in our hotel room with our system tools, which involves ba-sically a laptop and our very, very, very, proprietary software. We use wired, Wi-Fi and satellite connections. We can control the car or van from any isolated location."

"OK, so how did your dad get all these parts and computers and gadgets and everything? How did he get all these adjustments made to the van and the car? I mean, does he have some secretive place in a building where he has tools and big machines to put in all this stuff? Did he do it by himself? He couldn't…he couldn't have done all this alone."

"Those are very good questions. If you sequester anyone in an unoccupied champaign somewhere and say 'build a car' or 'build a house' or 'build a refrigerator' or whatever, constructing those things would be nigh impossible. You have to gather all these parts and then make them interact functionally with one another—the large metal and iron pieces, the wiring, the electronics, the lights, the computer chips, the plastic, the buttons, the turn knobs, the rubber, and the cutting and shaping of every little and big thing, and the nuts, bolts, screws, paint, and on and on and on. And machines are used to make molds that assist in making many of these parts on assembly lines, but other machines are needed to make the machines that make the molds, etcetera. Just a comparative very few people in the world possess the recondite knowledge of how to make these individual things, and they know how to make only their things, not the other things. Thus, you must combine the work of diverse experts.

"So, to make the long story shorter—and I know I've been sounding like you again—Dad drove the Caravan and the Accord into the shop he had built with a massive bank loan of more than $3 million. The shop is in a very obscure neck of the woods in Arkansas. Parts are ordered and delivered sagely. Dad hired a crew of seven professionals—five ingenious mechanical engineers who are Mensa members plus two auto assembly line staff—and swore them to secrecy and brought them into the shop. And, of course, in exchange for their discretion, they have been promised an immense share of the inevitable profits that will eventually come to Dad when he goes commercial or goes military—as long as they keep quiet. So, we have co-conspirators. And they are available, PRN, to do any further work, redesigns, or repairs.

"And we—Dad and I—aren't employed while we're crusading against car criminals. But, Dad is so valuable to his company that he can go back to work there anytime he pleases, although he may never work for anyone else again. We're using part of that three million to pay for our operational expenses—EV charging stations, food, hotels, and so on. Plus, Dad has always been a prolific saver of money—and so am I.

"And I've just imparted to you, my friend whom I haven't seen in eons, all of this level-10 confidential information. And I didn't know I was going to tell you. And I hope Dad won't send me to Siberia in the wintertime. Please keep it to yourself—the details, primarily."

"Oh, oh my god. That's uh, completely fascinating and impressive. It actually frightens me. And no, of course, I won't reveal any of this. I...I, uh, well..."

"Don't be scared. It'll be fine."

Guinevere turned left onto a narrow street that put them back into the Drollman community.

"All right. But, well, what happens to the car criminals after you and your dad and the cars finish with them? Do you, uh, keep them tied up in ligatures or trapped or something so they can't get away? Do they just kinda lie around manacled till they're caught and taken to jail?"

"Yes. Actually, yeah—with an occasional exception—they do. They essentially do find themselves lying around, just feebly waiting for incarceration. Sometimes they're hanging around, though, if we leave them tied up and dangling. That's never any fun. The local police in whatever city we're operating in are summoned after the perpetrators are secured. Sometimes they're conscious; other times they're not. Often, when the authorities find them, they are bound and gagged. Sometimes there's no gagging, and they are moaning or cursing or crying when the cops arrive. They are often found twisted in knots, having undergone human pretzelization. Sometimes, as you've indicated that you already know, they're found wearing women's underwear, such as braziers or girdles or panties—not respectable attire for crime-committing macho men."

"I know. Yeah, that's what we've been hearing at the club for a couple of weeks as to how they're found. It sounds kinda cruel, though."

"Yes, it is."

"Well…"

"By design."

"But…"

"They deserve it."

Guinevere looked over at her school-days friend with whom she had warmly reunited.

"Kristi Lou, with some age on you, you've really brought out more of your soft-hearted side. In middle school back in Little Rock you were, it seems, more aggressive. I had to almost stop you from pulverizing some of the kids that razzed you about your height. But, even then, you were still basically a sweet girl; you were just going through the adolescent angst thing, but intensified, because of your uh, fear of heights. Sorry, I felt compelled to say that. In fact, I'll tell you now that, in the privacy of my own mind, I used to affectionately call you Acrophobe Girl."

Kristi Lou smiled a closed-mouth smile.

"That was clever. And, ironically, you did indeed calm me and I definitely recall you telling me I shouldn't be physically violent—and now look at what you're doing to these car thieves and vandals. Not that I'm criticizing you for it, though. I'm not. It's just, I don't know, it's…it's just a somewhat strange reversal for the two of us."

"So, you're not calling me a hypocrite?"

"Oh, no, definitely not. It's just the irony. I would say the word is not 'hypocritical' but rather it's 'ironic.' I'm sorry. I…"

"I know. I was just joking," assured Guinevere.

"I knew you were, or, well, I thought you were…hopefully," replied

Kristi Lou, who paused a moment before turning toward Guinevere and grinning.

"'Acrophobe Girl,' huh?"

"Yes…sorry. But I never said it out loud. And I always thought it with affection."

"I know you did. But I'm still glad you didn't say it to me back then. I was so raw and hypersensitive that that name coming from you, even though you were only kidding, might've crushed me."

"Of course I knew that."

"I know you knew that."

"Well, I knew that you'd know that I knew that."

"Oh my goodness, Guinevere, my brain is telling me to not even try to keep up. You win."

"I like winning."

"Doubtlessly, you do, ha-ha. OK, now I'm flashbacking to last night's brief chat about sex and scripture. I thought about your remarks in bed when I was trying to fall asleep. We agreed. Properly understanding the meaning of some verses may need proper contextualization, right?"

"Posilutely. Interpreting accurately requires contextualizing correctly. Regarding Matthew, chapter 5, sex isn't adulterous unless there's marital infidelity. But, Matthew likely used the word adultery to refer to any sexual intimacy outside marriage. I'm still not buying it, just as I reject a literal interpretation of the *shut-up-bitch* admonishments found in Corinthians, chapter 15, ordaining that women must remain silent in church because we're apparently unworthy of being permitted to speak there. Likewise, in Timothy, chapter 2, we learn that a woman, while learning, shall be docilely quiet and in full submission."

"Oh my!" said Kristi Lou, laughing. "God says 'Hush, ladies!'"

40

As the reconvened femme-buddies were riding along the avenue parallel to Miracle Boulevard, Guinevere received a call on the phone built into the dash.

"Guinevere?"

"Hey, Dad. Guess whom I have here with me."

"You've got someone with you? What? What are you thinking?"

"It's all right. You actually know her. You both had a big laugh listening to Davey with his inverted profanity."

"Oh. Your friend? The girl who's as tall as me and then taller with the high heels? Kristi Lynn?"

Kristi Lou giggled.

"Her name is Kristi Lou, Dad."

"Oh, it's OK; I don't mind," said Kristi Lou while right-handedly waving off any notion of being bothered.

"Oh right, sorry. Hi, Misty Lou."

"Dad."

"I enjoyed talking with you Thursday night. That guy who curses backward is hilarious. I was there another night, too. I even corrected you on the last name of the scientist—Dawkins, not Hawkins."

"Hi, Mr. Lindsay. Oh my goodness, that was you in the crowd that set me right on the scientist's last name. I'm sure I was confusing Richard Dawkins with Stephen Hawking, who sadly passed away earlier this year. Anyway, I was just telling Guinevere how much I liked talking with you. And I remember talking with you when I was a kid when I was over at your house a few times with Guinevere, when I was in the seventh grade back in Little Rock."

"I'm glad I made a good impression—or re-impression. I do remember you from back then as the tall girl who hated being tall."

"Yes, that terribly insecure girl was me. But I eventually learned to love it, and Guinevere, here, was a big part of that."

"My daughter has always been very supportive of people she cares about, even as a child."

"Yes, she certainly was—and is. Anyway, so I guess that was also you that same night a week or so ago who agreed with me after I finished my ranting speech against atheism? There was some man who spoke up whose voice sounded like the correcter man—correcter man?—that is, the man who was the correcter when I, uh … the same man who had corrected me earlier over getting the scientist's name wrong, so …"

"Yeah, that was me, too. I walked up and filtered into the group on the sidewalk as you were getting started with your artful oratory and I just stayed outside and listened to the entire thing. That was some speech. Do you make these speeches often at the nightclub? Do you employ a speechwriter for your curb-side speeches?"

"Ha-ha. No, I sorta write them myself and then memorize them. Really, though, believe it or not, my speeches on the sidewalk are almost always spontaneous. And yes, although I don't spruik—oh, I ought to say that's s-p-r-u-i-k, which is a verb and, for my purposes, means to make a public speech brimming with advocacy. So, anyhow, despite not spruiking like every other day at Secrets, it's far from rare for me to burst into such spieling."

"Interesting. So you don't plan ahead to make these impassioned street speeches. You just delve into them when the spirit moves you?"

"Yeah, that's pretty much it. But, as I said, I do have major parts already committed to memory, usually from a theme paper I've composed."

"That explains, at least partly, why your sentence syntax was so well structured while you were speaking. Though, with your anti-atheism speech, you were reading from papers. You dropped them dramatically on the sidewalk when you finished. But still, you sounded like a young, polished orator."

"Yes, that's a legit explanation. And yes, for that treatise about atheism I did have those papers I had written, but I didn't know—honestly—that I was going to use them that night. But, anyhow, thanks for … for complimenting my oratorical skills. That was nice of you to say. I know, though, that I'm not exactly the reincarnation of Socrates."

"Maybe Plato, though; you know he was Socrates's number-one aficionado. If you can't be Socrates Junior you can be Plato Junior," joked Pete, followed by mild laughter from all three conversationalists.

As Guinevere turned onto an obscure side street and then onto Miracle Boulevard, there were a few moments of silence.

"Oh, Mr. Lindsay, I was wondering about something. You knew who I was when we were talking Thursday night in Secrets, and you could tell that I didn't recognize you from eight years ago. But, you didn't tell me you were Guinevere's dad. Was that omission of information because I … because, well … because of where we were and, uh … because of my, you know, activities … and because of what I, uh … what I …"

"It had nothing to do with you being in Secrets or what you do. I didn't want to spoil the surprise of Guinevere showing up one day in front of you. I thought that—who knows?—if I told you I was me, then the conversation might lead to you catching on that Guinevere was in town. I left that moment for her and for you."

"Oh. That was, that was actually very sweet. Thanks, Mr. Lindsay."

"You're welcome. And you're old enough now to call me Pete."

Guinevere chimed in.

"Call him Pete. You should be on a first-name basis. After all, you almost screwed him."

Kristi Lou, instantly embarrassed to think that Pete heard his daughter's brash remark, blushed and then gushed her defensive reply.

"Guinevere! I did not! Well…"

"I know; his British Sterling was so alluring, right?"

"What was that? You faded out," said Pete.

"Oh, sorry about that, Dad. I must've accidentally hit the mute button."

Kristi Lou sighed loudly.

"OK. Listen, Kristi Jean…"

"Dad, please, it's Kristi Lou."

"Right, I'm sorry, again. Kristal Lou, you, er, well, you know to not talk about what Guinevere has been, I presume, telling you and showing you—don't you…please?"

"Oh my goodness, no, certainly not; I won't say anything. I love Guinevere. I think she saved my life, or at least my adolescent sanity, back in the seventh grade, when I was so tall and my teacher was so short. And, well, I suspect he still is short because he was about 40 or whatever already and he was probably finished growing and well, I just threw that comment in there and I'm rambling. But, anyway, no, I won't tell anybody anything. I won't talk about your car thing. I wouldn't do anything to upset Guinevere, or you. I'll never forget all that she did for me when I was suffering. That is, what I went through and how Guinevere stood beside me."

"I mostly stood beneath you."

"Oh, that's ha-ha hilarious. That comment would've wrecked me back then. But now I know that you know that we both know that I'm over it."

"Yes, I know that you know that I know that," assured Guinevere, with a light chuckle.

"Besides, Mr. Lindsay, I mean, Pete, I approve of what you're doing, as long as you don't kill anybody or hurt them too much. Well, there was that one guy—Willie was his name, and he died.

"But, anyhow, the police and the mayor know what you're doing, according to Guinevere. And, I think it's justified as condign punishment as well as to deter other car crimes—and I was so awfully sorry to hear about what happened to your mom."

"Kristi Lou changes subjects very quickly—in the same paragraph," explained Guinevere.

"I know; I still do that. Being digressive is something I'm really good at," concurred Kristi Lou, with a brief laugh.

"Yes, well, I do thank you for your concern and sympathy; I can tell you're sincere, just as Guinevere said."

"You're welcome."

"Regarding Willie, well, that wasn't planned and I'm—well, I'm sorry, really sorry, about his death. That was our first retaliation in this town, and I activated an action I shouldn't have at the moment I did it, and after I saw that he was wounded too severely, I just released him. But, mainly, Willie just still had enough get-up-and-go left in him to bust out running and he ran himself over the overpass in front of that truck. Of course, if he hadn't been stealing cars, we wouldn't have gone after him and he wouldn't have suffered such a fate. But, still, I'm sorry it happened."

Kristi Lou, having listened attentively, responded without hesitation.

"I believe you when you say that, that is, that you're sorry about Willie dying. And yes, I hope these other guys who are stealing cars will learn from what happened to Willie and also from what's happening to the rest of them that you and Guinevere are doing these rough and embarrassing things to, and ..."

As Kristi Lou was speaking, Pete interrupted her.

"Pardon me for interrupting, Krissy Sue, but we now have a situation that's …"

"Again, Dad, she's Kristi Lou."

"Oh, that's all right, Guinevere; it's no big deal," said Kristi Lou as she shook her head and smiled.

"Yes, I know her name. I was just checking to see if you were paying attention."

"Umm, as they say, Dad, 'yeah, right.' Your attempt at funniness is acknowledged."

"Thank you for that acknowledgement, dear."

"Uh-huh. You're quite welcome."

41

"OK, GUINEVERE, WE HAVE A TARGET. IT JUST CAME UP, BY COIN-cidence, about 10 seconds ago, while we were in this conversation. You never know when something will happen. Activity is on 41st Street. I see you're on Miracle. You're much closer than I am. You can take a live action with the Bad Car. Can you drop off Christmas Lou at a safe place? The GPS says you're so far down Miracle away from the Secrets club that if you took the time to deliver her there you wouldn't be able to get to these people on 41st Street before they stripped the cars and left—even though now they're just milling about, getting ready to strip them.

"I want to get these A-holes. There are four of them, two black, one white, and one kind of a south-of-the-border-looking type. They're probably the ones we heard about the other day. They're going after those six cars we saw them loitering around yesterday from one of our temp-mounted surveillance cameras I planted near the garbage dumpster at those apartments. Remember, we were watching them at the hotel? They didn't do anything then but now they're about to. These are those cars belonging to those elderly ladies and one of their husbands."

"Yes, I remember seeing them on-screen. You mounted those cameras in just the right spot."

437

"Yeah. I'm looking at them as we speak."

"All right, I'll take it. I can't put Kristi Lou out in this neighborhood by herself—not with her wearing her pretty, green dress. She might get raped or killed."

"It's OK," said Kristi Lou. "I'll be all right. I actually know some of these people who live around here, though I don't feel all that safe around them, at least not all of them. My regular walking route from home to Secrets is a bit safer than this area, but I've got my pepper spray and ..."

"No. Forget it. I'm not releasing you onto any of these streets."

Guinevere redirected her remarks to her dad.

"No. I'm taking her with me, Dad."

"All right, but be careful with her."

Guinevere, as she began driving toward 41st Street, turned to Kristi Lou.

"You're safer in here than out there. In fact, this car will protect you; it can take down almost anything. Do you want to see one of our battles from the frontlines?"

"Uh, frontlines? That sounds very military-ish. Well, I'd ... I'd say I probably perhaps do. I guess so, but I don't know ... OK, sure, I think. But, maybe I shouldn't, though. But, well ... no ... I mean—yes!"

"Way to be decisive, Kristi Lou."

"Oh, thank you, Guinevere."

"All right, here we go, and we will festinate. Look it up later. We've got to get there. Hold on tight."

Guinevere's right foot mashed the accelerator almost to the floor, after which she immediately withdrew, no longer touching the pedal at all. The sleek car did not burn rubber onto the blacktop but rather hastened its celerity, as if it were floating along the traffic-less street, with a disturbing but incongruously soothing quietude. It moved from about 35 to 65 mph in 1.2 seconds, but could've easily gone faster.

Kristi Lou sensed that she should've heard at least a modicum of noise, and its absence was eerie.

Guinevere shot a quick glance over at Kristi Lou, whose face revealed her disquiet.

"Keep your pants on. Well, for you, that may be a tall order."

"Oh no-no! A double-edged zinger—risqué *and* heightism-istic … heightism-istic? I'm word-mangling, but … Whoa! We have liftoff!"

Guinevere and the attack car had just bolted amain to 73 mph on an urban street. Still, there were no other vehicles moving, just a few parked against the curbsides.

****

As they scurried toward the targeted crime scene, the speeding car came upon a sharp curve and thus had to slow down. At that point, Kristi Lou spotted commotion down a narrow side alley.

"Oh my god, Guinevere! That's Davey they've got! They've got Davey! We were just talking about him. They're mugging Davey—those two guys are. He was trying to walk to Secrets. They might kill him! Please stop—we've gotta get him outta there!"

"I know. I see it. The car saw it before we did; it's programmed to detect any aggressive behavior anywhere near. OK, get ready."

The voice of Mr. Lindsay, who was monitoring Guinevere's functions from his remote location, vaulted from the sound system.

"Guinevere, what are you …"

"I've got a slight diversion, Dad. We were on the way to the target and we spotted one of Kristi Lou's friends being attacked by two thugs. In fact, he's the backward curser you found so entertaining. I've got to get him out of there."

"OK, but …"

"I've got this, Dad. Over."

Guinevere had already slammed on the brakes. The car glided to a sudden and silent stop on Miracle, without any whiplash effect whatsoever, a phenomenon which startled Kristi Lou even while she was focused on rescuing Davey. Guinevere pulled over near the curb, about 15 yards away from the brouhaha raging between Davey and his two young assailants, twenty-something black males covered with tattoos. All three combatants were so immersed in their skirmish they did not notice the presence of the car on the main street.

Davey, while being dragged toward a nearby ashcan for indecorous disposal, was being pummeled intermittently with ring-covered fists and stomped with stolen $200 sneakers. Having already taken Davey's wallet, the muggers were working on stripping him of all valuables, visible and hidden.

They stopped dragging him. One man began to undo the strap on Davey's watch while the other attempted to wrench all five of Davey's various rings from his bleeding fingers.

Davey, stricken with fear, screamed his disapproval of the proceedings.

"Let go of me you tard-bas hole-ass! Help! Damn god it hell to! Off the get fuck me!"

Kristi Lou started to exit the car to rush to Davey's aid.

"No, Kristi Lou, no!" blurted Guinevere, who agilely tapped a tiny auto-lock dot on the dash, trapping Kristi Lou safely inside. "Don't worry. I've got it covered."

Guinevere pushed a button and out came a control panel with an LED touchscreen. Exerting placid and guiltless truculence, she deftly actuated the attack car's retaliatory brutality.

Kristi Lou's eyes bulged wide as she took it all in.

Guinevere spoke expeditiously.

"OK. These guys are gun-less. Even though this car is about 85 percent bullet-proof, it's equipped with a firearm detection sensor. Guns are the first things detected and confiscated."

Six tentacles rose to greet Davey's attackers, who had progressively hauled the floundering and blood-spattered Davey nearer to the dumpster. The tentacles, sporting small and prickly spikes, soared upward from a quickly opened aperture—where a moment earlier there had been smooth paint and metal—located behind the passenger-side headlight. They bolted forward.

The first tentacle wrapped around the waist of thug number one, planting him forcefully face down flat upon the pavement next to a drainage gutter, then turning him over. The second tentacle used its claw-like tip end to harshly grip his misfortunate groin, exerting force sufficient to inflict pain and bleeding but sans castration. The third tentacle sheared thug number one's head and collected the hair, which was shoved into his mouth, causing his screams to mingle with his spitting of hair-nuggets.

As thug number one screamed and spat, he looked up and observed the ill-favored fate of his thug-mate. The fourth tentacle, which had instantly encircled both feet of thug number two to hold him in place, pulled him high into the air and dangled him there, as he squirmed upside down about 20 yards above the pavement.

Sensing that any punches would prove feckless in combating this overpowering adversary, the punks did not even try to form fists to fight. Their hands impotently gripped the tentacles in hapless efforts to push them away.

Four more tentacles appeared and, within 25 seconds, unceremoniously stripped both thugs of their clothing, re-garmented them with pink panties, and then disappeared back into the attack car, leaving the original six tentacles to carry on. Thug number two underwent his wardrobe change while airborne.

Thug number one watched the third tentacle slap him under his chin repeatedly, as audio emanated from the Bad Car, proclaiming "You are being bitch-slapped, bitch," which was repeated loudly 17 times for anyone around to hear.

Thug number two, still 20 yards up in the air, was uprighted by the fourth tentacle and forced to accommodate the unfriendly presence of the fifth tentacle that hovered about an inch from his face, repeatedly opening and slamming shut what appeared to be a tiger-like mouth filled with saber-toothed steel incisors, all the while unleashing a vocal fusion of deafening snarls and roars that perfectly emulated the battle declarations of an unrestrained Felidae apex predator. The tentacle intermittently pulled back a foot then charged in, while thug number two hollered shamelessly as he foresaw what seemed the realistic possibility that his head would be bitten away from his neck.

The sixth tentacle, from the vantage point of both thugs, was the most disturbing of all, as it carried in its end segment a simple, round, 3-feet-in-circumference mirror, which was moved back and forth between the thug criminals and always positioned in front of their fear-filled eyes.

Davey lay still and watched.

The slapping and chomping proceeded for about a half-minute, as the arms and legs of both thugs flailed spastically.

The tiger-istic fifth tentacle withdrew back into the attack car as the fourth tentacle lowered thug number two and placed him alongside thug number one beside the drainage gutter.

Then, the tentacles hoisted both thugs eight feet above the ground for five seconds, as the shame-filled visual account of their futile kicking and squirming continued to be mirrored back to them.

Both thugs were spun upside down, then right-side up again.

Nearing the coup d'etat, the tentacles next punitive measure took the two perpetrators and adhered them to the same lamppost, which they were made to straddle while facing one another, causing their legs to interlock in a rather intimate arrangement. Then they, two machismo marauders, were forced into a lip-locked kiss while being tethered to the post wearing their new garb of pink-lace panties, which was all they were left to wear as their apparel, including the stolen shoes, was shredded into ribbons.

As the forcible kissing persisted, the unenthusiastic kissers, faces pressed inescapably one upon the other, realized that the only verbal protests they could emit were unintelligible muffled groans that carried a frantic buzzing sound as little pockets of breath leaked occasionally through small openings in their otherwise hermetically sealed lips.

Steely-eyed while summoning her usual visions of her grandmother being abused and horrified, Guinevere received a sudden idea. *Let's have these guys put their fuck-you fingers to constructive use. Yeah, they can substantiate their bond as hardass criminals via sharing the penetrative intimacy found within these two femininely attired recta.* She compelled two tentacles to assail one assailant apiece by grabbing the left digitus medius of each thug and inserting it beyond the pink panties and into the unwilling anus of his fellow hooligan.

Guinevere turned to a stunned and mesmerized Kristi Lou, saying, "I realize these guys aren't known car criminals, but they're cut from the same loathsome cloth."

Kristi Lou could not register an answer.

Another tentacle quickly applied the standard nylon strapping to the thugs to hold them in place in their humiliating and painful positions till the police arrived. Guinevere directed the tentacle that was forcing the thugs into a protracted French kiss to release their entwined lips, allowing five inches of space between each nose.

As the forced finger fornication continued unabated, the defeated thugs screamed in horror and repugnance. Madly spitting away invasive spit, they expectorated one another's slaver, which their mouths had exchanged via violent kissing, back onto the original owner's face.

Rapt in the full, guilt-free vengeance mode she always manifested during what were normally counterattacks against car criminals, Guinevere withdrew all tentacles. She had enjoyed defending Davey against these common street muggers.

Guinevere's mouth unveiled a barely discernible but slightly macabre Mona Lisa-ish smile that alarmed Kristi Lou, who happened to glance over at her friend at just the precise moment to see Guinevere's unsettling simper.

Always piercingly alert, Guinevere perceived Kristi Lou's concern.

"I loathe bullies," justified Guinevere as she confirmed all tentacles were re-embedded inside the fierce vehicle.

Davey, though terrified as he witnessed the ferocity that was defending him, could still easily sense that the dumbfounded thugs felt an un-macho abasement that penetrated straight through their terror. As he watched the thugs flailing their forearms pathetically while trying in vain to unfasten themselves from their disinclined intimacy, Davey lodged a hodgepodge of emotions that were dominated by a fusion of fear and shame, fury and satisfaction, and what he recognized as a strange feeling of being entertained.

After the assailants were dispatched and hogtied, there was the need to bring in Davey, who had crawled away from the severely admonished thugs and was huddled under a No Parking sign. A tentacle snatched Davey off the sidewalk and lifted him about 30 feet toward the Detroit skyline before reeling him in toward the Bad Car.

"Shit holy!"

The rear window flashed open and just as quickly closed behind Davey, who was safely deposited onto the backseat. Arising from his prostrate placement, during which he had buried his head by enveloping it inside his arms, Davey attempted to gather his wits.

"Fuck the what? Kristi Lou? Why are you here? What is this? Fuck the what's going on here?"

Kristi Lou leaned back reassuringly between the front bucket seats toward the naturally nervous Davey, who blubbered again.

"Fuck the what? Those punks—those things grabbed 'em—and then me. I'm cut! What…? Bitch of a son! Bastard of a daughter! Fuck the what!"

"Davey, it's OK. You're OK. Everything's OK. Davey, meet my old friend, Guinevere. She just saved you and your whole body."

"I know. I know. Oh my god! I know. Thanks for my ass. I mean, thanks for ass my savin'. But, this car…those things got ahold of them and then me and …I mean…fuck the what?"

"Hi, Davey. You're a stellar curser. I so admire your cursing style," deadpanned Guinevere in her usual understated manner. In spite of his distress, Davey detected her peculiar calm amidst intense turmoil.

"Oh, well, thank you, thank you very much."

"You sound like Elvis," remarked Guinevere.

Davey, arranging himself in a crumpled lump, mustered an attempt at levity to express convivial gratitude as well as to ease his nerves.

"Well, thank you, thank-you-very-much," replied Davey in a rather high-pitched tone.

"Wow, coincidentally, I was told just the other night by some people strolling by outside Secrets that I sounded like Elvis. As you both know, I'm truly fascinated by coincidences," interjected Kristi Lou.

"You sounded like Elvis?" asked Guinevere.

"Yeah, I was singing and…I'll tell you later."

"OK. Speaking of 'later,' I'll explain things to you later, Davey, but we're in a huge hurry now—not much time—gotta move lickety-split. You're going to see more of what you just saw, so just brace yourself, OK?"

"Uh, OK, but…"

The car sped away, accelerating like a terrestrial F-22, pinning Kristi Lou and Davey against their back-rests with G-force domination.

"Shiiiiiiiiitttt holy!" exclaimed Davey. "Did you ge, ge, ge, get my wallet? My wallet …" Davey forced the words out of his mouth against the pressure caused by the extreme speed, which seemed to almost shove each syllable back into his knotted face.

Guinevere slowed the car to 15 mph going forward, and then, without the car seeming to stop, she sent the car into reverse at 50 mph, backing up about 85 yards on the street in a flawless straight line and coming to a halt around 60 feet from the side-street assault site. With hand speed that astonished Kristi Lou and unnerved the already discombobulated Davey, she began nimbly pushing buttons and twisting dials.

A camera view of the ambush locale from which they had just departed a few seconds earlier was displayed on the dashboard screen. Turning a selection knob with impeccable deftness, Guinevere homed in with a super-magnified close-up on the location of Davey's mugging, where the two attackers remained attached to the lamppost wearing their pink lace panties, still locked into pederast-style penetrations.

"What are you do … are you gonna get my wallet back?"

Spotting the wallet on-screen, she unleashed a string-thin tentacle that shot backward and retrieved Davey's trifold by snatching it with surgical precision from the back pocket of one of the mugger's decimated cargo pants. Most of the tentacle then recoiled back into the underbelly of the automobile, except the tail end, which entered the car through the snapped-open-then-shut-rear-right-side window to gently drop Davey's wallet onto his lap.

"Oh, thank you, thank-you-very-much," gasped Davey.

"You're welcome, Delvis. I combined Davey and Elvis. That's corny; I know. Anyway, GPS, that is, global positioning satellite, which is provided by the U.S. Space Force, is amazing technology," offered Guinevere, as she reestablished warp speed on Miracle Boulevard.

Driving the speeding attack car with her left hand, Guinevere, with animal-like dexterity, reached between her knees and pulled open a cubbyhole at the front-center of the driver's seat and extracted a kit containing a sanitary cloth towel, a small bottle of liquid antiseptic, a tube of rub-on, pain-obtunding gel, and a box of Band-Aids. She tossed the plastic box over her right shoulder to Davey while instructing him to "Undertake doctoring yourself, Mr. Reverser Curser."

Guinevere then whooshed down a privacy partition that attached flawlessly to the floorboard in front of Davey, who could no longer hear the slightest sound originating from the front, shielded-off section.

She slowed down as she approached a somewhat more peopled area, populated with a few curious pedestrians, vagrants, and shop employees and their customers on or near the roadway. Kristi Lou knew they were approaching Downtown Secrets. She managed to speak for the first time in almost two minutes.

"Pardon me for daring to question your doing anything with this car, but aren't we going the wrong way? I mean, we were headed away from Secrets and now we're headed toward it. And I thought your dad said on the CB radio you shouldn't go this route because of not enough time. Plus, we've also obviously had this unanticipated delay with salvaging Davey."

"Yes, all of that is true, but his calculations were inaccurate. We were going out of our way and would've had to circle back to 41st Street. He must've realized he screwed up 'cause he's not calling in correcting me. I checked the navigation options and we're rerouting to go slightly past Secrets and then a couple of turns and we'll be on 41st. A miscalculation from Dad is profoundly rare because he's usually right about everything."

"As I've already said, like father, like daughter, huh?"

"Truthfully true."

Downtown Secrets came into view.

Guinevere abruptly withdrew the privacy partition.

"As you know, that's where I work," said Kristi Lou, pointing at the club.

"Well, I suppose it's reasonably considered a form of working," said Guinevere.

Kristi Lou giggled while facepalming into her right hand.

"She's a doozy of a floozy. She's really good fucking at what she does," offered Davey unaffectedly, his recovery from pain having quickened and his heebie-jeebies having swiftly ameliorated after patching his gashes.

"I believe you mean she's really good at fucking—which is what she does," clarified Guinevere.

"That's what I sorta said, except what I meant was…"

Kristi Lou grinned sheepishly while applying another facepalm.

"Thanks to both of you…sorta."

42

AFTER BLOWING BY DOWNTOWN SECRETS, GUINEVERE, KRISTI Lou, and the still-stunned Davey rolled on just under a half-mile when Kristi Lou saw a familiar countenance loping slowly along the sidewalk. "There's Smilin' Al going back to work at Spinoza Tire Factory after lunch at that little tumbledown Chinese restaurant where he eats every single day—The Crouching Dragon."

Kristi Lou waved quickly, skimming her hand over the surface of the ultra-advanced, bullet-resistant, laminated safety glass of the closed window as they passed.

"Hey, Smilin' Al," she called out, knowing the old gentleman would neither see nor hear her.

Guinevere hightailed on Miracle for about a mile, then turned right onto Nikki Avenue, drove about 250 feet and made a left onto 41st Street, bolted ahead a half-mile and saw her quarry.

She spotted four hoodlums, two black males, one white male, and one brown Latino male, all in their late 20s to early 30s, about 70 yards ahead, inflicting havoc on two parked automobiles. Brazenly operating in lambent sunlight, their effrontery was lessened by the absence of any people or traffic within their sight range. And they knew they worked fast.

"They're banging those two cars right now—to strip them or steal them, but they'll go after those other cars, maybe another three or four, if they get the chance to flip them. They won't."

"Of course they won't. 'Cause you're gonna stop them," said Kristi Lou.

"'Cause we are gonna stop them."

"'We'? What do you mean 'we'?"

Guinevere, ignoring Kristi Lou's query, stared unflinchingly at the criminals for about three seconds.

"Those are surely the guys the cops told Dad about—a little ring with a couple of black guys and one white guy and one guy from Colombia. They didn't have any hard evidence and of course these guys—when they were questioned—denied everything witnesses said about them, naturally. See their hands? Like some of them do, they wear micro-thin gloves so they don't leave fingerprints. We'll amass plenty of evidence here. Our video devices are already merrily recording."

She stopped the car.

"Brace yourself, Kristi Lou."

"OK, I'm braced. Unless there's excessive harshness, this is going to be so cool."

"Brace yourself, Davey."

"Shit oh. This is going to be a shit of bunch. Me fuck."

"It'll be fine, Davey," reassured Kristi Lou. "Don't be such a nervous Nellie. Relax."

"Relax? You want me to relax? She just said 'Brace yourself.'"

Davey leaned forward toward Guinevere.

"Why should I brace myself?"

"Because we're about to swing into action that you may regard as rather intense."

"Shit oh. Hell it to damn. Shit oh. Damn god it, this is shit bull," stammered the frightened Davey while ducking his head behind his raised elbows.

"Well said, Davey." Guinevere, as when she was a child, was almost never incapable of droll offerings, regardless of circumstances, and made no exception in this instance.

"I'm enamored with your elocution, as you are quite the interlocutor."

"Huh? I'm an inter-what-er?"

"Interlocutor. I'm saying that you're a skillful conversationalist. And, by the way, I'm sure you're a genuine expert on the subject of alcoholic beverages—and your knowledge should be respected."

"Oh, well, thank you. Thank you…"

"…very much," said Guinevere. "I rarely finish people when they're talking, but I made an exception for you."

"Are you ready, Kristi Lou?"

"Yes."

"Are you ready, Davey?"

"No."

"Perfection. Here we go."

Davey reassumed the face-under-arms prostration into which he had flattened himself upon being placed in the backseat. But then his curiosity supplanted his trepidation, and he chose to emerge and observe, albeit with lip-furled consternation and a fixed frown of fear.

Guinevere, accelerating slowly at 16, then 17, then 18 mph, shot the car forward to 55 mph in about one second and then suddenly slowed to a snail's pace, with the car's abrupt acceleration yielding no sound beyond a whoosh. Guinevere, with feline stealth, moved the stalking car toward the thieves, one car rolling into action to rescue other cars. She stopped the Bad Car precisely 15 yards out from the miscreants; she pulled to a halt alongside the curb and nestled behind a parked, full-size tan van.

"What—why aren't they reacting? Couldn't they see us coming st them?" inquired Kristi Lou.

Guinevere, talking faster than Kristi Lou had ever heard her talk, proffered a quick elucidation.

"I didn't tell you a few moments ago, but I adjusted the exterior color of our car. I can't perfectly explain Dad's technology, but there's a modified-MicroLED color scheme available that I activated that takes advantage of any current environment and causes the color of the car to appear to absorb the environmental colors that are prevailing—in this case, bright sunshine. Think of a chameleon lizard that's permitted by nature to alter his body color so as not to be seen by predators. We're kinda like that, except we are the predators. They could see us if they looked and concentrated on us; we're not totally invisible, just camouflaged. Their concentration is on harvesting those cars."

"Oh sure," said Kristi Lou.

"Shit oh," said Davey.

Kristi Lou thought that these bandits seemed to have somehow not heard the scuttlebutt around the community about a retaliatory car that fought back against those who transgress against cars.

Did they not get that memo?

Guinevere turned her head toward Kristi Lou, who sat wide-eyed with arms crossed while gripping her triceps with anticipation.

"Do you see the depraved ruffian with the striped pants?"

"Yeah. He's stripping off the tires."

"Ill-mannered things are about to happen to him."

"Oh, Guinevere, please don't be too harsh."

"Don't worry. He won't get more than he deserves—for raiding old folks' property. Dad and I consider such deviant behavior a form of elder abuse."

"Oh. Well now, I can certainly understand and appreciate that reasoning."

"You know what they did to my grandmother—assholes just like these goons."

"Your grandmother—yes, I know. That linkage will always be there."

"Can we just do this and leave?" asked Davey.

"Sure," responded Guinevere.

Calmly enraged, Guinevere took her left ring finger and tapped the 2" x 2" touchscreen in the middle of the steering wheel. With quiet suddenness, three-quarters of the dashboard seamlessly flipped over, displaying an even more electronically futuristic set of apparatuses than those on the default dash, different and larger than the panel from which Guinevere worked to dispatch Davey's assailants.

Guinevere, with hand speed that once again astounded Kristi Lou, adroitly programmed and synchronized her predacious system, manipulating three illuminated knobs with flashing blue, green, and white lights as preparation for unchaining her coup de main tailored to rout these specific archenemies.

The high-tech dashboard looked to Kristi Lou, herself a dedicated Trekkie from late-night TV reruns of Star Trek, like the instrument panel on the starship USS Enterprise.

Guinevere summoned to her screen a live camera view with target scope markers.

"All right, Kristi Lou, push that red button, if you will, please."

"Who? Me?"

"Yes. You. I don't see another Kristi Lou. I have all vomitous scofflaws registered on my screen. I've chosen a retaliation program. Let's expedite our sweet-violence proceedings."

"But, that button is so bright red. Will the car really, I mean, uh, hurt those guys?"

"Yes, with gusto."

"But…"

"Come on, Kristi Lou. Push the button. They'll live. You know what happens by now. They're going to get cut and bruised. But, as I just said, they'll live—they'll be allowed to continue living. Primarily, they're going to be untenderly intercepted and then humiliated, with copious scattered photos—you know, the usual delicious degradation."

"But…"

"Kristi Lou, those guys are full-grown Nate Perkinses. Yes, I said Perkinses. I know you remember Nate from the seventh grade; his name came up last night when we were talking about David Darnell and how David told him to stop hassling you. There was that day at school in the hall when you were going into the bathroom and I alleviated your anger and humiliation when Nate was trashing you, right? These guys humiliate old people like my grandma and make them feel even more vulnerable. And they don't care. But I care. And you care. Look, I want to say this quickly. The lividity Dad and I feel toward these people doesn't mean we don't want them to get straightened out and maybe have a good life later. We do have a philosophy of wanting them to be rehabilitated. But first, we want to stop them. And we want to punish them. I'll say it again—they'll live."

Kristi Lou replied rhetorically. She sought moral justification for possibly making herself an active part of Guinevere's grand mission of vehicular justice. She needed to saturate her qualms with permission-granting rationalization, and she needed to think fast.

"OK. So, these are the type of people who hurt your granny? And they're like Nate used to be? And, despite your retribution tactics being so Draconian, you do truly want them to get better after getting punished?"

"Yes, to everything."

Kristi Lou pushed the button.

She felt a surging vibration, strangely arousing, that lasted just over a second.

Davey felt the same sexual frisson. His eyes widened. He grabbed his crotch.

"Woo-hoo!"

Four tentacles rocketed from the underside of the attack car, three from the chassis under the driver's side and the other from the chassis under Kristi Lou on the passenger side.

The three tentacles that shot forward from beneath Guinevere grabbed one hoodlum apiece, selecting the two black guys and the white guy.

The tentacle that fired out from beneath Kristi Lou snatched the remaining criminal, a short, wiry Colombian, who commenced screeching and cursing in Spanish as he was held 21 feet above the ground and upside down by his ankles after the posterior part of his jeans had been surgically removed, allowing the Bad Car's metal paddle, favored by Guinevere, with the small prickly spikes similar to a carrot shredding board, to have access to the thief's buttocks for a pitiless spanking.

The same punitive paddling technique was applied to the other three wrongdoers who were also held seven yards into the air.

A smaller sub-tentacle, as always, held the punitory paddle. The four airborne automobile abusers were spanked hard, with enough force to cause a loud slapping sound upon the paddle's repeated contact with their uncovered fannies, as their skin was stabbed and thus besieged by minor puncture wounds that weren't deep but were quite bloody and painful, feeling at once like multiple paper cuts.

The paddle spanked the men violently 12 times within four seconds, paused for two seconds, and then resumed paddling the upturned lawbreakers, repeating this punishment for exactly one minute, per the prerecorded instructions Guinevere had entered into the Bad Car's computerized assault system.

Finally, the car culprits were completely undressed by another full-size tentacle that charged out from the chassis underneath the trunk. They were then redressed in ladies' hot-pink, lacey undies, with a fuchsia-colored child's bonnet and a hyper-adhesive pacifier rammed into their mouths. Guinevere lowered them to 15 feet from the pavement and within two feet of one another. Sub-tentacles forced both hands belonging to each man to twist their crime partners' nipples.

One of the bestial car's movable cameras, held firmly by yet another tentacle, flashed brightly in front of the criminals' faces, purposely conveying to them, in certain terms, that their shameful condition was being photographed. They were made to see a sudden scattering of multiple copies of said photos fly through the air like elementary school paper airplanes carrying a bomb payload of infamy.

Hailing from a macho culture, the Columbian was almost hurt worse by the psychological castration than by the corporal pain.

All four men were bleeding. Although they bled not profusely to the point of danger, the visualization was sufficiently gory so as to disturb Kristi Lou.

"Oh God, Guinevere, please don't kill these guys!"

"They won't die," replied Guinevere, who continued to adjust a few manual levers at the bottom of the control panel that she had slid out from under the dashboard.

Davey sat huddled in the backseat, watching through the windshield but not moving or uttering a syllable.

Finally, following nearly three minutes of levying vigilante-justice agony and humiliation, Guinevere's preprogrammed procedure administered the grand coup d'état of dishonor. The primary tentacles lassoed around the four criminals, quickly jettisoned the pacifiers, and then pressed their bodies together while powerful sub-tentacles opened their mouths, abrading patches of surface skin on their lips and forcing them to take turns French-kissing one another, with tongues rolling spastically and cameras flashing brightly.

Davey erupted from his silence.

"Hey, yeah baby, that's what this thing made those guys back there who jumped me do. This car makes 'em kiss. That's really a gross-out. They gotta be shit this hatin'."

"That's the whole idea, Davey," affirmed Guinevere, in a staid tone.

"Yeah," said Davey. "Them fuck! You team up with some other guys to mess with a car around this thing and you're gonna be homo-kissin' on your teammates."

Guinevere wore a thoroughly serious expression on her face; Kristi Lou observed that, unlike Guinevere's uncharacteristic smirk of a few minutes earlier while counterattacking Davey's attackers, there was nary a trace of smirking satisfaction or cruel enjoyment. Guinevere liked what she was doing, thought Kristi Lou, but was doing it as somber punishment, not as entertainment.

"OK, we're almost done with these scumbags."

After continuously holding the car muggers 15 feet above the pavement, the tentacles applied unyielding ropes made from the strongest of fibrous materials, along with the regular nylon straps, thereby enveloping the degenerates and leaving them bundled together cozily in an up-in-the-air intimate package. Their wrists and ankles were bound by stock-issue handcuffs stowed neatly in the Bad Car's equipment storage chamber, which had been flawlessly designed by Pete for maximization of space.

****

Kristi Lou, sitting transfixed in a space-age warrior automobile, found herself, to her mild disappointment, somewhat afraid of Guinevere. She felt not a wrenching, deep fear, but she did feel a flicker of fear, nonetheless. She thought to herself that the passive, nonviolent aggression Guinevere manifested as a twelve-year-old, while still there, was now mingled with the same capacity for physical aggression that Guinevere had stymied in Kristi Lou during that childhood year.

Kristi Lou's unexpected feeling of fear toward her friend, however tepid, troubled her; she did not want to feel any trepidation toward Guinevere, not even a smidgen.

Kristi Lou noted that Guinevere's extreme equanimity in the midst of duress, however, had not contracted by the littlest whit. While exacting her automotive rabidity against dangerous criminals, Guinevere exhibited, in her mannerisms and intonations, a steely sang-froid. While engulfing herself in her own intrepidity, Guinevere was so self-possessed she seemed almost robotically phlegmatic.

Kristi Lou could not prevent herself from feeling that perhaps Guinevere was almost too composed.

****

The car criminals were lowered to the pavement and deposited in a heap of feminine underwear and blood-streaked flesh, bound and gagged with one another's mouths strapped together to achieve continued forced kissing. As the four captives squirmed, they grunted gutturally through their coworkers' lips, sounding like excitable pigs.

"Oh my god, Guinevere, those people are bleeding, just like Davey's assailants were bleeding. They're all bleeding. You said earlier they weren't going to die—like that guy Willie who did die. They're not going to die, are they? They'll be all right, right?" implored Kristi Lou.

"Yes. And they're going to bleed some more before they clot up. Don't worry; they will recover. There really isn't that much blood oozing out of them. Their rubricated skin just has lots of painful slices."

"Slices?"

"Yeah, slices."

Guinevere looked at Kristi Lou and then at the car criminals. She made a spontaneous decision. The felons' mouths were allowed to disengage from kissing and then covered with ordinary duct tape, stuck on with split-second speed by one of the sub-tentacles.

"Sometimes I just feel compelled to tape their mouths shut rather than leave them in homoerotic kisses," explained Guinevere. "Either way, they'll never forget the experience."

"I'm sure they won't."

Guinevere turned and glanced back at Davey. "They'll be here waiting conveniently for the police, just like those punks that were mugging you a little while ago."

"Cool. They're all head-shits."

"OK, Kristi Lou, it's over. We can go now."

"All right," replied the nearly verklempt Kristi Lou, who, uncharacteristically, could think of nothing else to say.

Guinevere drove the Bad Car slowly and quietly away from the scene of hard justice, another mission of vehicular vigilantism having been completed.

43

AFTER ABOUT 50 YARDS OF VERBAL SILENCE, KRISTI LOU PUT her right hand gently on her abdomen and looked at Guinevere.

"Those guys you just dispatched have something in common with me."

"Oh, what's that?"

"Slices. They've been cut and so have I."

"Really? How were you cut?"

"Bosco Mason—this guy who used to come into the club—he assaulted me the other night with a knife. He was angry because I kept saying no to him for the backroom because I just don't feel…wait! He steals cars. You might know him or know about him. Have you heard of Bosco?"

"So, the little punk attacked you with a knife? Not surprising. Bastard. You seem OK. Are you?"

"Yeah, I'm OK. But, so, you do know—you know him? You know who Bosco is? Well, I suppose that makes sense, what with him being a car thief and so forth and that's what you're after, what you and your dad are fighting to…"

"We got Bosco. We got him Friday, August 10—it was late that Friday night; actually, it was early Saturday morning, still dark, when

460

he was picked up by the cops. We nailed him and the whole damn chop shop he worked out of."

"Oh, you did?"

"Yeah, we did. The van got him and busted him up some, with Dad working the controls from the hotel. We dumped Bosco in front of the chop shop. Dad alerted the police and they executed a raid of said chop shop. They got this guy who calls himself Red Roofus. Neat name. Ass-trash person. Everybody else associated with that place was nailed within a few hours. Warrants were issued by a judge. Clean sweep."

"But Bosco…"

"But you know what? Bosco got away from the chop shop. His apprehension was delayed, at least for a few hours. The cops were looking everywhere for him. They had an APB out on him. That's an all-points bulletin, in case you didn't know. Bosco's in jail. We basically nailed the entire outfit with which he was in cahoots. They're in jail. They're all in jail."

"Oh, I knew Bosco was arrested. I saw it. Dan was driving me home from Sec…oh my. I'm just now figuring some things out. It just dawned on me—about the timing. It's another coincidence, yet another one. The coincidences just keep coming into my life. Oh my goodness. I was just telling you about Bosco knifing me and then you told me that he was nabbed early Saturday a.m. So, it was your car—your van, I should say— that Bosco tried to steal. So, anyhow, when I looked from Dan's cab at Bosco being arrested, I thought maybe someone from the club broke down and called the cops, anyway, on Bosco because he'd mugged me. You see, Big Sam doesn't like to get cops coming around Secrets 'cause it looks bad and could discourage people from coming to the club and all that. But Bosco was just down the street, so I thought maybe they'd changed their minds about calling 9-1-1—and I was right. Big Sam told me later—the day he gave me time off to recover—that he called the cops after Bosco had walked a ways from Secrets hoping they'd find him and pick him up 'cause he—Big Sam—he didn't want Bosco on the loose where he could hunt me down.

"But…so, uh, it seems Bosco was arrested for two crimes at once: because he'd tried to steal your van and because he knifed me. The police were already looking for him from your having told them he was at that chop shop, earlier, you know, when he got away. And then they were looking for him because of, I guess, assault with a deadly weapon or whatnot. His behaviors were contiguous, time-wise—you know, time-adjacent.

"OK, what I'm saying, Guinevere, is that when the police arrested him I was riding home in pain from a cut stomach that Bosco gave me. He had just finished cutting me a few minutes earlier, evidently just a little while after your van got him and after he got away from the chop shop. My mind is trying to comprehend. By the way, I already knew what APB stands for, but thanks anyway for telling me."

"Wow," replied Guinevere, as she turned onto Miracle Boulevard, directing the Bad Car to mosey along at 37 mph. "Yes, it appears that's how it happened. If he hadn't gotten away from the chop shop, he wouldn't have had the chance to assault you. He could've killed you. Now, knowing this, that he did that to you, I wish we'd just left his low-class ass tied up for the cops to arrest him. I offer my heart-rendered apologies. I feel bad about…"

"No, it's all right. Don't feel guilty about that. You couldn't have known that he would escape the chop shop and you couldn't have known he would show up at Secrets and you couldn't have known what he was going to do to me when he got there. So Bosco's still in jail?"

"Yes, he is," said Guinevere.

Kristi Lou leaned to one side and raised her summer dress above her legs and waist, high enough to display her bandage-covered injury.

"I apologize for my immodesty without forewarning. I hope I don't offend you…but this is what Bosco did to me."

"Oh God, I'm glad you're not dead. I'm so sorry that happened to you, Kristi Lou."

"Yeah, me too, Kristi Lou," Davey chimed in. "I heard about it. I'm glad you're all right. That Bosco is an ing-fuck tard-bas."

"Thanks. I'll be fine," said Kristi Lou, as she lowered her dress back to her knees.

Kristi Lou's memory perked again, and she felt a compulsion to rehash, in summary form, what she and Guinevere had just discussed.

"Yeah—that was Friday night when Bosco hurt me. I was riding home in my taxi, with my friend, Dan, the night Bosco knifed me and I saw all these cop cars on Miracle. That was Bosco getting arrested. And it happened Friday night or you could say—as you did say a few moments ago—very early Saturday morning."

"Just say 'Friday night,'" petitioned Davey.

"OK. Friday night."

"Yes, that was it," concurred Guinevere.

"But," said Kristi Lou with a look of ambiguity, "I still don't know, for sure, why he would be so brazen as to come into Secrets right after that raid at the chop shop that your dad called for—that he barely escaped from. Had I been him, I would've tried to think of, uh, you know…"

"He wasn't thinking. He was seeking. He was just a gallivanting prowler with a to-hell-with-it mindset," explicated Guinevere. "Look, Bosco seems entirely unacquainted with scruples. He doesn't burden himself with inconveniences such as restraints based on morals or ethics. If he wants it, he believes he should be entitled to take it."

A voice spat out of the Citizens Band radio.

"Good work, Guinevere," said Pete, who had been monitoring the action from his location via the camera system on the attack car that relayed all events back to him. "I know we can trust Krissy Coo. What about the gentleman in the car, there? The guy you rescued?"

"Oh, I believe Davey will prove most trustworthy. I'll talk to him about it, though."

"Yes, Mr. Lindsay, uh, Pete, Davey here won't say anything. He's a good fellow."

"It's all right, sir. I ain't goan shit say."

"Oh, you're the backward cuss man, right?"

"Yeah, I reckon that'd likely be me."

"Yes, Dad, this is Davey. He's exceptionally entertaining."

"All right, Davey. Please keep these matters to yourself, for the most part. Use your judgment. Guinevere will give you some guidelines that we'll request that you follow."

"OK. But, like I said, you don't gotta worry 'bout me. I'm tight."

"All right. Good. OK, Guinevere. I'll see you girls later."

"Yeah, thanks, Dad. We're outta here. See you later."

"All right, then. Be seeing ya," replied Pete Lindsay to his daughter, of whom he was very proud.

"Bye, Mr. Lind…uh, Pete."

"See you later, Missy…"

Guinevere cut the call.

"Oh, I seem to have hit that button a bit prematurely. We've been deprived of another mispronunciation—at least a complete one—of your name. Darn."

"I know. That's kinda disappointing. I was starting to like it—seeing what he could come up with."

"Well, Kristi Lou, what do you think about what we do?"

"I don't know yet. I, uh, well, I may have to get back to you on that. I'll need to have more time for some umm, well, psychological digestion."

Then she quickly added her follow-up discernment.

"But I do believe those guys might be discouraged from messing with cars again."

"Oh, I think so," said Guinevere. "I'm quite glad that the old folks who own those cars or any of their friends or neighbors didn't come outside. And no one else saw any of this."

"Really? How can you be so sure that nobody sees what you do when you do these vengeful things, especially in broad daylight like now?" inquired Kristi Lou as they continued to drive slowly away from the carnage. "They could've been peeking through curtains or blinds in their apartments or whatever."

"This car is equipped with sensors worthy of a NASA spacecraft. If anyone else is even so much as looking out a window in a nearby building, Dad and I will know."

"Wow. I don't really know how your equipment could … well, anyway. But then what? What if someone is watching? Do you go through with the attack on the car criminals, anyway?"

"Well, sometimes we do and sometimes we don't. We get close-ups of the people who see this car or the Caravan and have our computer do a blazing fast analysis of who they are. In seconds, we have an idea of whether they would or would not likely blow our cover to the news media by presenting a story that was too credible to be dismissed as a loony hoax. If they were about to switch on a video camera, like in a smartphone or any type of camcorder, we would know instantly. As I've been harping on, we do want the news media to report our work—to a degree—because, as I've repeatedly emphasized, that's part of deterring car crime; we also want the news media to have some healthy doubt as to our existence—kind of a happy medium—because we want government agencies to not feel forced to shut us down due to us being vigilantes, which we are. Since we're running a quasi-covert operation, a goodly level of skepticism is our ally."

"Got it. Thanks for explaining that so it makes more sense to me. Wow. This is really … I don't know. It's really something else; what you and your dad do is … my goodness."

"I know," said Guinevere in her understanding way.

44

GUINEVERE DROVE DAVEY TO DOWNTOWN SECRETS. AS THEY approached, they saw a few dancers and patrons outside milling about on the sidewalk. They all noticed one rollicking discussion about 12 yards to the left of the entrance, with waving arms and pointing fingers.

"Oh look. There's Miranda refereeing Rochelle and Hoke while they argue about who-knows-what? Those two arguing—that's never happened before," scoffed Kristi Lou.

"Only all the time," said Davey.

"Yes, like Guinevere, sometimes I'm facetious."

"There's probably some medicine you can take for that," said Davey.

"No, facetious is a dreaded disease and we cannot be cured," replied Guinevere with mock graveness.

The two girls giggled, somewhat at Davey's expense, as Guinevere pulled alongside the curb and stopped about 25 feet to the right of Secrets's front door.

"Facetious kinda means sarcastic, in a silly way, like being flippant," explained Kristi Lou, with feigned condescension.

"Well, why didn't you just say sarcastic?"

"Uh, 'cause I wanted to get a rise out of you."

"You get a rise outta lotsa guys," poetically rejoined grinning Davey, with a snuffle.

"Oh, he zinged you into never-never land with that one, Kristi Lou," said Guinevere. "He blistered you big-time."

"He definitely did zing me," conceded Kristi Lou, turning to face Davey. "You got me. You zapped me, Davey, you witty zapmaster, you. You are a ripsnorting and scintillating voon-duhr-kint. Or—to English-i-fy it for you from German, including pronunciation—you are a wunderkind."

"Yessiree, that's me—wonderful and kind. That's what you just said, right?"

"It may as well be, yes."

"Yeah, I'm all that and more."

"Now, you're being sardonic toward yourself."

"Huh? Here you go again, with sayin' them ole ass-fat, forty-dollar college words."

"Yes, I know," said Kristi Lou with a smile. "I just can't help myself."

Davey then leaned up from the backseat and spoke to Kristi Lou.

"Are you workin' tonight? It's a Saturday night, you know? Of course, just about everybody else besides you comes in early on Saturdays, about the middle of the afternoon—Satine and Rochelle and all them—to get a head start on makin' that Saturday money. You don't get in till 7:30 or 8. So anyhow, you comin' in or not?"

"I haven't decided yet. I might. I don't know. I think I want to spend some more time with Guinevere, since I haven't seen her in ages. And there is all this wildness that I just saw. You saw it. I might need time to just wind down."

"Yeah, you should do that," replied Davey. "I might oughta do that same wind-down thing, myself."

"No, you go on in and have a nice time. Order your usual beverages," encouraged Kristi Lou.

Davey did an eye roll.

"You're such an oddball, sayin' beverages. Just about everybody else on Earth would say drinks, but you let loose with beverages, like your fah-cee-tus and your sar-donkle-ik."

"Well, thank you, Davey, for calling me an oddball. And those words that you so creatively enunciated are facetious and sardonic. But you know that we both know that I know that you know that I talk like that."

"And so does your friend, here," added Davey, glimpsing at Guinevere. "You're two peas in a puddle."

"Pod."

"Huh?"

"Two peas in a pod, not pud…"

"Oh, OK. Yeah. That's what I meant. But like I just said, both you girls are so high and fine—almost hoity-toity."

"No, Davey, Guinevere and I are not hoity-toity, which means putting on airs and being pretentious, essentially meaning stuck up. We use some so-called big words, but they just flow out from us, especially from Guinevere. We're not trying to act hoity-toity or better than anyone; that's just the way we've learned to talk over the years. Yes, Davey, some people do say obscure words to try to make themselves seem so superior to everyone else. We do not. Admittedly, we do indeed sometimes tend toward sesquipedalian dialogue, but at other times our conversational style is quite demotic. Speaking of big words, such uppityness would make us guilty of pedantry. Guinevere would never be that way; she's a down-to-earth lady."

"Kristi Lou has defended me," said Guinevere, upturning her lips' corners. "Drums are drumming and trumpets are trumpeting. "Thank you, Kristi Lou."

"Why, you're most welcome, I'm sure, dahhhling," replied Kristi Lou, with feigned snobbery, implemented for Davey's consumption.

"You can nutsac my polish! Says-Quaalude-aliens and demon-tick—you big-word-usin', college-edumacated girls," rebutted a grinning Davey. "Kristi Lou works in a cathouse and talks like a professor."

"And I live in a cathouse 'cause there's a cat in my house. Well, OK, I live in a cat-apartment."

"Well," interjected Guinevere, cordially smirking," at least she curses with her words in the right order."

"No, she don't," snorted Davey. "She don't curse in *no* order. She don't curse none. Kristi Lou don't curse no which-a-ways. The girl don't curse."

"Doesn't," corrected Kristi Lou.

"What?"

"Doesn't."

"Huh?"

"Doesn't curse."

"OK, then. You doesn't curse."

"Davey!"

Kristi Lou started to genially admonish Davey again regarding his linguistic indiscretions, but decided to refrain, thinking to herself: *What's the use?*

She smiled back at Davey.

"Never mind."

"What? Never mind what?"

"Just, well, never mind," said Kristi Lou, still smiling pleasantly.

"Whatever. I'm goin' in," said Davey.

After unlocking the back door for him, Guinevere sought reassurance from Davey.

"Regarding your observations of the past half hour, Davey, you can be surreptitious about it, can't you?"

Guinevere rolled her eyeballs at herself in a full circle and then reprimanded herself under her breath.

"I can't believe I just said 'surreptitious' to this individual."

Overhearing Guinevere's self-scolding soliloquy and anticipating Davey's indignant reaction, Kristi Lou snickered audibly.

"Huh? Can I what? I'll damn be. Before I can even get outta the car, you done it again. What was I just sayin'? I was just sayin' you talk like Kristi Lou. Speak English and I'll know hell the what you're talkin' about."

"Ok. Let's try it one more time, and I'll recast my query," offered Guinevere. "You, Davey, can keep your experience with our car and what you discovered about its abilities to yourself, right? Please?"

"I dunno what you mean 'bout queers and I ain't gonna ask, but, yeah hell, I can stay hush-hush about what I saw with your ass-wild car and all. Besides, no one would believe…well, maybe they would with all the rumor-mill talk around the neighborhood about these cars attacking people who mess with 'em and like shit that. But, no, I won't spoil them top-secret beans."

"Spill," said Kristi Lou. "You won't idiomatically spill, not spoil, the beans."

"You screw, Kristi Lou; you're an idiot, too," said Davey, grinning.

Guinevere looked intensely at Davey.

"You promise? Even when you're less than sober?"

"Yeah, I promise—even when my drunk is ass."

Guinevere became pensive for a moment before replying to Davey.

"Good. Thank you. Look, along the lines of what I was telling Kristi Lou a few minutes ago, we would actually like for you and anyone else to spread the word about how it's not safe for criminals to abuse cars around here anymore. That's the deterrent we seek. But, we just don't want you to tell them all the details you learned about me and Dad, and the technical aspects of how our vehicles operate. And we definitely don't want you to let it be known that we've left the area."

"OK," agreed Davey. "But remember you had that thing, that wall, up when you and Kristi Lou were talkin', so I didn't hear all that much."

Kristi Lou echoed that point.

"Yes, I guess he couldn't hear too much because of that partition that came down when you flipped some switch. I still don't understand where it goes when it's not down because—how does it not go through the roof? But, oh well."

"Almost correct. He couldn't hear anything back there when the partition was down. The partition and overall insulation of this car Dad and his crew built does indeed perfectly mute any sound emanating from the front seat. But, as you will recall, the partition was in place for only a very brief time. So, he's heard me tell you some things. And, before I lowered the partition, he'd already observed that I was controlling the car's penal actions. I decided to withdraw it after thinking that he'd already seen and heard so much that hiding anything else from him wouldn't matter. Dad and I want to maintain anonymity. We won't mind if some of the punks believe it is supernatural—anything to frighten them into compliance, to scare them away from other people's cars."

"All right," said Kristi Lou. "Yeah, that makes sense."

"And, regarding where the sound shield partition goes when it's not visible, it has panel hinges that unfold the shield when it goes down but refold the shield, flat-ways, when it goes up to flatten it so it slides horizontally and fits underneath the metal roof of the car but above the leatherette lining, snugged compactly in its own integument."

"Leatherette?" asked Kristi Lou. "Oh—I'm so glad you use imitation leather."

"Right. We like animals, including cows. Thankfully, Dad used only pseudo leather—leatherette."

"Oh, man, I've gotta say that the whole thing about the car and the van and what you and Pete do is truly amazing."

"Thank you."

"Davey," said Kristi Lou, "I know you've already said you can, but once more, can you—will you—keep quiet about what happened?"

"My lips are peeled."

"Sealed."

"I know, Kristi Lou. That was a joke. I was making a joke—you know, one of them joke-type things that people say when they're tryin' to be funny? I guess I was being fa-seed-us."

"Facetious—all right, I'm sorry."

"That's OK. You can correct me alls you wants."

"All you want."

"Grammar Nazi! Hi Hitler!"

"That's 'Heil Hitler.'"

"That's what I said—Hi Hitler!"

"No, Davey. The Nazi's weren't telling Hitler hi; they were saying h-e-i-l for 'Heil Hitler,' which, in German, means 'Hail Hitler,' so they really weren't … oh, never mind."

"Oh, good grief. On that note, I'm ass my takin' into Secrets."

"Well all righty then, you better go on in. And please note that I never correct your cursing reversals and your dropped g's at the end of your gerunds. For example, what you just said should be 'taking my ass' but I realize you can't stop your backward cursing and you often just don't do word-ending g's so I stetted it, uh … I let it stand."

"Yes, you do *refrain* from correcting my cussin'—I mean cussing, and that's very *tolerant* of you. You like my words 'refrain' and 'tolerant'? And I ain't *even* 'bout to ask what 'gerunds' is."

"Are—gerunds are. And, I do like your words—very impressive. Gerunds are words with i-n-g suffixes."

Guinevere nodded and interjected her input.

"Well, actually, a word with an i-n-g ending is a gerund only when it's a verb that is functioning as a noun. Consequently, Davey's use of 'taking'—with the g elided, of course, in his case—is not really a gerund because 'taking' in his phrase is a verb used as a verb. He's taking his ass into Secrets. Contrariwise, if Davey were unreversing his cursing and saying 'My ass is here for the taking,' then we would have a gerund."

"You're right, Guinevere. Thanks for setting me straight on that," said Kristi Lou with a mild blush.

"Woo-hoo—somebody done corrected Kristi Lou! I love it! Your girlfriend just caught you makin' a mistake. The tables are turned."

"I make lots of mistakes, Davey. Come on."

"No, ya don't. I tease you but I know you're almost always right 'bout most things. Anyway, I'm tired of tryin' to go but not goin' so now I'm really gonna go. Here I go. Watch at me go. See ya, Kristi Lou."

"I'll see you sometime soon, Davey—maybe tonight, maybe tomorrow night. And thanks for complimenting me."

"OK. Bye."

Davey exited the car but then stuck his head back inside the open door, looking beyond Kristi Lou at Guinevere.

"I 'preciate your ass my savin' back there. Those guys mighta killed me for a few dollars and my watch. And thanks for that mind-blowin' ride in your flyin' saucer car," said Davey, with his hand on the outside door handle. "You know, I've been jokin' about it, but, uh, when I think about it—about what you and that car did and all that, it hell the scares out of me. It's, uh, it's . . . I don't know what it is but it's too hard to believe, but . . . OK. Anyhow, it was really real and somehow I did not pants in my piss."

"You're welcome," replied Guinevere. "And thank you so much for appreciating my ass. I'm also thankful for your having decorously refrained from incontinence."

"For what from what?"

Kristi Lou laughed and interceded as would an interpreter.

"She's thanking you for kindly not urinating in her car."

"Lord amighty—you brainiac girls and your ass-big words." Davey chuckled and closed the door.

Guinevere lowered the front passenger-side window next to Kristi Lou.

"And thank you for cursing backward in my presence. That was a blast," said Guinevere.

"It was my damn god pleasure. I hope to see you again sometime. I guess I might if you hang out with Kristi Lou and come into the club. Anyway, bye."

Kristi Lou scolded Davey, calmly but with earnest intent.

"Davey, you really shouldn't take the Lord's name in vain like that, even in reverse."

"I know; you're right. I'm sorry, Kristi Lou."

"I'm not the one to whom you should apologize."

"All right. Please accept my apology up there, Big G," exclaimed Davey, while gazing skyward and waving apologetically toward God.

"That's better," said Kristi Lou with a sincere smile.

"Your approval of me just cocks my warm," said Davey.

"What? Oh. No. No, Davey, no. It's not, it's not … that. It's cockles, not … what you said. Cockles are actually mollusks in the water or weeds on the ground. The colloquialism you're reversing, in your own special way, is 'warms my cockles,' which is an amended version of the retro-saying 'warms the chambers of my heart,' which etymologically derives from the Latin term for the human heart's chambers, which is 'cochleae cordis,' which led to the vernacularism 'cockles,' which eventually became a key part of the adage 'warms my cockles,' so, so—oh, golly, I'm jibber-jabbering—so, it doesn't have a dagnab thing to do with heating up your … uh, it's not about warming your … never mind."

"I like it when mine gets warm."

"Yes, of course you do."

"OK it-damn, keep watchin' me. Watch what I'm fixin' to do here. I'm actually gonna go now. Bye. Bye. Bye. Good freakin' bye."

Davey exchanged final waves with both Kristi Lou and Guinevere, and then walked up to Hokey, Rochelle, and Miranda to join in their still-ebullient repartee.

Guinevere then drove Kristi Lou home.

45

THEY SAT IN THE CAR IN THE PARKING LOT OF MOONBEAM Landing, near Kristi Lou's apartment, with the engine running and the AC on near-medium setting.

"Look," said Kristi Lou, "there's Dooflotch sprawled on the back of the sofa, looking out the window for me and waiting faithfully."

"Yeah, he hasn't seen us yet; we're parked at an angle and off to the side."

Kristi Lou looked pensively at the palms of her hands, observing the creases, as she examined her thoughts. She rubbed her hands together. She glanced up at Guinevere, then back at her hands, then back at Guinevere.

"So, you'll soon be off to the next town to do more of this—to go after car criminals. Where? Where are you going?"

"Atlanta."

"Oh. Why are you going to Atlanta? Because your dad's from around there?"

"I'll elaborate later."

"All right."

Guinevere gazed at the dashboard for about three seconds while tapping her fingers on the steering wheel, and then, smiling, turned toward Kristi Lou.

"I thought about, well, trying to recruit you as a partner, but I don't know that you're harsh enough for it. Besides, Dad wouldn't allow it. He wants to keep this strictly a father/daughter project for now—maybe till some government somewhere makes us stop and commandeers our technology."

"No, I, I uh, I wouldn't work out too well as a partner doing this, though it does appeal to me on some levels—stopping the car criminals and all. But, I've been thinking—something I do too much of, it seems, and not always very effectively—that, uh, after my walk-on-the-wild-side life of the past several months, and after being reunited with you, I'm going to reunite myself with school. I'm going back to college. It's time. But I don't regret my adventure. Maybe one day I will. But right now, I don't. Anyway, in about two weeks, I'm going to reenroll for my senior year. I'm going to graduate next spring."

Kristi Lou looked at Guinevere for approval.

"I was always going to go back."

"Of course, you were; I knew that," agreed Guinevere as she turned on classical music, in a low volume, from a disc that was already loaded in the CD player, which her dad chose to install despite the trend toward phasing out CD players from automobiles. The 10-speaker, state-of-the-art stereo system, with its Wi-Fi functionality and surround sound stereophonic reverberations, combined with an airtight cabin that canceled all outside noise, occasioned Kristi Lou to feel as if she had been transported into a concert chamber.

"Oh, that's one of my all-time favorites—Pachelbel's Canon in D Major—so strong but so soothing, and the spire of Pachelbel's oeuvre," said Kristi Lou, as she blithely sunk herself deeper into the soft leatherette-covered seat and realized she was experiencing some of her rarest moments, those when she felt perfectly safe and void of any anxiety.

The girls sat nonverbally still for almost four-and-a-half minutes, watching birds and squirrels playing in the trees while listening to the serenely inspiriting violins in Johann Pachelbel's musical masterpiece from the 17th century. Guinevere added more bass, and then slightly increased the treble. As the next track, Tchaikovsky's Swan Lake Waltz, began to play, Guinevere decreased the volume and looked at Kristi Lou, who was already looking at Guinevere. Kristi Lou spoke instantly.

"Thanks for playing Canon; you seemed to know that I would love to hear it. Anyhow, as I was saying, I'm going to go back to school and finish what I started. I just needed, or maybe I just wanted, to try this other stuff. It's hard to explain, but I have these non-mainstream thoughts and feelings about men being just as sexually exploited as women and maybe more—in a different way—because of being vilified every day for being attracted to nice-looking women who try to make themselves attractive and I know I've got this face and these long legs which, the last time you saw me, I hated, but not anymore and guys really like them and…well, I think I'm starting to ramble. Actually, I know I am. But, nonetheless, perhaps you can follow and grasp the gist of what I'm trying to say."

Guinevere tilted herself sideways, leaning against the driver's door, and nodded in agreement as she laughed for about one second, and then peered up at Kristi Lou.

"I have no trouble grasping your gist. I'm a good gist-grasper. I can be very prehensile—look it up. And I think you're right."

"Oh, good—and I believe you when you say that; I know you're sincere. And I care what you think. Many people love to say 'I don't care what anybody thinks.' And sometimes that attitude is appropriate. But I do care what some people think about me, and you're one of those people. I'll tell you more later because I plan on us getting together again—and often. That's what I want. That's what I've always wanted. I remember we talked about this back in the seventh grade when you told me your dad was moving you away. That is, about how most people our age say they'll always be friends, always, always, but then they just fade away. But you said that wouldn't happen with us. I think it kinda did happen for the past several years but the fading is not permanent, 'cause here we are back together again. So, but I … I want us to stay friends and see each other and for you to be in my life and … and all that. And yes, I'll look up 'prehensile.'"

Kristi Lou looked upon her old friend and eagerly awaited what she hoped would be a reassuring reply.

"Yes, I do, too—that's what I want," said Guinevere. "Very much so. I can come back here and see you. Dad's got plenty of money—and frankly, so do I because he pays me quite well for my services. You probably have made quite a bit of money yourself, considering, well, the lucrative nature of the world's most time-honored—or dishonored— profession. And I would bet that you've saved most of it."

Guinevere smiled and winked.

"Yes. Please come back. Yes. I've made a bunch of money. Yes. I've saved most of it. I really don't know what to do with all of it. I'm going to have to decide whether or not to accept Mom and Dad's check they'll mail to me for tuition after I tell them I'm going back to classes. I'd told them I wasn't going back till next January. They think I don't make much as a part-time dance instructor. If I take their money, I could feel guilty. But, I can honestly say, without rationalizing, that taking their money I don't need is worth it to help prevent them from knowing what their daughter has been doing. I'll still be their little girl 50 years from now. They would ask, 'Where did you get all that money so you can afford to pay for college, yourself?'"

"You can tell them someday, if you wish, when you believe you and they are ready."

"Yeah. I might. I might tell them when … that is, I might tell them, well, someday. Then again, I might not. But, maybe I might. I don't know. I might not, but I might, possibly."

"There you go being decisive again."

"I know. I think I really shine at that, but, then again …"

Kristi Lou and Guinevere fell silent for about a half-minute.

"Anyway, I'm glad I reached that decision."

"What's that? You reached a decision?"

"What I just told you a few moments ago—when I was in ramble mode. I'm going back to school starting next semester. I'm going to tender my resignation from Secrets and provide them with a two-weeks notice."

"'Tender my resignation'? You're going to tender your resignation?"

Both girls laughed for a couple of seconds.

"OK. I'm glad you're going to, ahem, tender your resignation—from a whorehouse."

"I know; it's funny. Well, all righty then. I'm going to discontinue my vocational association with my current place of endeavor. Hmm. That doesn't sound too normal, either. Pompous? Maybe. Normal? No."

"Actually, I like 'tender my resignation' better," replied Guinevere. "And you're definitely not normal—like me."

"Yeah, right. You're so normal, you car assassin, you."

"I said 'like me,' though, yeah, that was ambiguous. I didn't mean 'normal just as I am normal.' Rather, I meant 'not normal just as I am not normal.' I meant that you're like me in that I also am *not* normal. That is, to correctly interpret my meaning when I said that phrase a moment ago, you would've had to, in effect, mentally merge the 'not' and the 'normal' so that it'd be: How are you like me? You're not-normal. But, I made that denotation abundantly unclear. I'm flawed, so I screw up."

"You don't screw up often. And, back in school at Our Lady, I used to consider you to be the most admirably normal person who had ever lived—a paragon of well-adjusted-ness."

"Right. And now you've learned the truth about me. Anyway, however you say it, it's the right thing to do. Get yourself back into a healthier lifestyle with no social-disease worries looming over your head, or between your legs, and go ahead and complete your coursework and get your degree. And, I must reiterate, I've never thought of someone in your occupational field tendering a resignation and submitting a two-weeks notice. I think hookers banging in a brothel generally just up and quit, don't they? I realize we just covered that subject."

"Yeah, we did, but people talk in circles," said Kristi Lou. "Everyone does, to varying extents. We circle back to main points and repeat some things, and that's usually for the sake of emphasis. Many people who like to ridicule others for talking in circles usually talk in circles as much as or more than the people they're ridiculing because the ridiculers want to deflect attention away from their own circular talking 'cause they're not comfortable with it. I read—it was in one of my psych textbooks—that many people do that with other issues as well and do it often. That is, they hypocritically criticize other folks harshly for doing what they do, hoping to get away with it, to lessen the focus on their own tendency to do that same thing, that behavior—whatever it might be. The psychology term for it is 'projection.' We project onto others what we perceive as our own flaws that we're insecure about. No, make that: about which we're insecure. Anyhow, I try not to do that, but as flaw-filled as I am, I reckon I do do it, some, now and then."

"All right." Guinevere's succinct response was escorted by a soft grin.

"Did I just ramble again?" Kristi Lou queried with an impish grin.

"Yes, I believe you did. But, it just seems natural for you, and you're so good at it that I admire you for it. You actually turn rambling into a skillset."

"Gee thanks, I guess."

Both friends looked at each other and guffawed.

"Oh, Kristi Lou, I'm curious about something, if you don't object to me asking."

"I'll let you know after you ask—kidding."

"All right. To cut to the chase—how many men have you, uh, done it with? I'm referring only to your occupational undertaking at Downtown

Secrets. Whatever you say, I won't condemn you for it; I know you know I won't. But I was wondering about that. Realizing that in your line of work you can't exactly be abstemious, you don't seem like you've turned into someone who would, despite your job, sleep around indiscriminately—at least not too much."

"Thank you. And you're right; although I'm, uh, well, something other than sexually austere, and I'm clearly not a sexual ascetic, I don't do it too much, at least not considering what I do, that is, work-wise."

"OK. I didn't think so."

"I started at Secrets in mid-April. This is mid-August. I've done the thing with 11 guys. Of course, I've done it with some of those guys more than once, but I've been with only 11 different guys, all total. I'm very, very, very, very discriminating. Big Sam has no problem with my pickiness."

"Condoms always?"

"Yes, without concessions. I'm a no-glove, no-love girl."

"Davey?"

"Yes, Davey—four times."

"Oh my god. Does he curse backward when he gets, uh, excited?"

"Yes. It's really hilarious. But I don't laugh out loud, of course. Anyway, his backward cursing doesn't last long, because he doesn't."

"He doesn't?"

"No."

"Davey doesn't last long?"

"No, not really," replied Kristi Lou with a quick giggle.

"I can visualize Davey not lasting long, especially with you. That is, what with all those muscular curves wrapped around his bony anatomy. 'Kristi Lou! Me fuck! Me fuck! Me fuck! Oh, oh, oh—fuck the what! You cum me made too soon!'"

"Oh my goodness! He's not that bad. Well…"

"How old is Davey?"

"Twenty-four."

"You do like Davey, don't you?"

"Yes, I do."

"Anyone else, in particular, who's maybe a favorite regular customer?"

"Francois."

"Francois? Is he French?"

"Yeah. He is. Very. He's, uh … well, you know what they say about the French usually being good lovers. Let's just say he does his part to fulfill that stereotype."

"He's better than Davey?"

"Ha-ha. Yes, but I don't want to pick on Davey. He tries and I try to help him, but, umm, oh well. But yes, Francois is quite accomplished and he makes me feel, uh, well, you know. He sets my amative sectors atingle. He helps me reach jouissance."

"Jouissance! Oui, feminine-centric orgasm. So, How old is Francois?"

"Fifty-one."

"Is he married?"

"No, he's not. But he does have a girlfriend. But I don't feel too guilty about doing the thing with him because his girlfriend is unfaithful to him—and has been in the past with at least one other guy. That's what he says and I believe him."

"Why do they stay together?"

"I don't know, but I think they're just so attracted to each other, physically and personality-wise, that, for now, they don't wish to split. But they won't get married. Eventually, they'll go their separate ways."

"OK, so Francois rather excels at Don Juan sensualism?"

"You could definitely say that. He's thin, bald—and very handsome. But also his voice with his French intonations—you know that French is a romance language—is disarmingly charming, so mellifluous. But beyond those attributes, he's really a nice man. He is not mean; he has a good-hearted spirit."

"He sounds like quite the silky-smooth charmer."

"Yeah, he sure is. Hokey—he's our bouncer, as you know—calls him France Shaw."

"And that mocking mispronunciation, I presume, has to do with Hokey making fun of Francois's rather sophisticated-sounding French accent, including the proper pronunciation of his name."

"Yep. You got it. But Hokey likes him, though."

"I'm glad."

"Francois has heard me sing—I don't believe I'm very good—and said he'd like to be the manager of a band of Secrets girls led by me. He said we should call ourselves Kristi Lou and the Clitoridean Climaxers."

"That's a very snatchy-sounding name," said Guinevere.

"I think so. He also suggested that it might be catchier—or snatchier, to use your iteration—if we pared it to Kristi and the Klits—with a K."

"I like both versions. I'm not sure that many mainstreamers would feel entirely comfortable with it or the music I presume would follow. So, your on-air radio time could be limited."

"Yeah, I think we'd try to target a uniquely underground audience."

"Yes, looney-eyed, cliquish fans thinking their musical partialities are oh-so superiorly uncommercialized, so abstruse, so rarefied—all of them shrouded and self-quarantined in a buried 1950s railway station underneath a hidey-hole city street and head-banging to your ribald, clit-centric music. OK—kidding, kidding, kidding."

"Wow! That was a super-weird effusion! Ha-ha! How'd you conjure that up so unrehearsedly? What? Unrehearsedly? Oh—speaking of music—that music that's just starting in here … that's Concerto No. 2 by my pal, Rachmaninoff. I play it often on my 'puter at home," said Kristi Lou, as Guinevere simply smiled. "Unrehearsedly? Yes, I said that."

Following about 25 seconds of wordless serenity, and Rachmaninoff's lengthy Piano Concerto No. 2 having begun, Kristi Lou's facial expression assumed a more serious form, and she spoke with earnest gravitas.

46

"GUINEVERE, MAY I DISCHARGE SOME VENTING YOUR WAY, IF that's OK? It's about a subject I referred to a little while ago. Sometimes, I have these obsessive urges to proclaim what I think is right or wrong. I can squelch myself so I don't impose on people who don't want to hear it—at least when it comes to up-close conversations as opposed to speeches to an audience of bystanders who are maybe several feet away from me. I do that all the time—stifle myself from saying a word or at least saying only an abridged version. Other times, such as when I cut loose outside Secrets, I detonate and bloviate. I cannonball myself into pure prolix orating. But, whether I uncage my garrulous ramblings or I block myself, I feel this compulsion to express my intense tidings."

"Tidings? It's OK. Sure, I'm up for some high-intensity ramblings and tidings. What are you going to ramble about?"

"Uh, well, I was recently rambling to Rochelle and some of the other girls at Secrets about this subject—just the other night I was. It's, well, it's the unfair treatment of straight men when they are vilified for their sexuality. You know, what I've been commenting to you on and off about? They're always being made out to be villains just because they're sexually attracted to females they believe are sexy-looking and want to have sex with them. Well, I ask, what's wrong with that?"

"OK. I find that to be an interesting topic. And, I think you can probably count on me to agree with you a bunch, and maybe entirely."

"I know," said Kristi Lou with a wide-eyed nod of gladness. "I recall a while ago, when you were talking about me and your dad and how he came into Secrets and you thought that maybe he and I—well, you know. And, you made a joke about it instead of getting all huffy and puffy and hostile or offended."

"Yep, I did. In fact, you're the one—not I—who became a bit flustered at that suggestion."

"Yes, I know; that's true. And speaking of you agreeing with me, another thing that's occurred to me is that most of the people with whom I've shared my views about wrongminded discrimination against straight-male sexuality have indeed agreed with me. From the folks at Secrets to you here, I haven't been challenged that much, which is surprising 'cause my raison d'être is quite outré. Well, there was Raven at Secrets. I had a big-time blowout with her. She's a dedicated man-hater."

"'Outré,' huh," said Guinevere. "Nifty word, outré."

"It means…"

"…beyond the boundaries of normalcy or what society considers as proper or conventional."

"Yeah. It's nice talking with someone who knows so-called big words. But, on the other hand, it deprives me of that feeling of superiority I relish so much. No—just joking."

"Are you sure that's a joke, Miss Egotist?"

"Well, I hope I'm not actually that way. Do you, uh, do you think that, that, that I'm really…"

"No, of course not. I was just joking."

"Oh, OK. I knew you were just joking, but…"

"You wanted to be sure."

"Yes. I did. OK, well anyway, I'll start by saying that the anti-sex elements of our society make males exist in a perpetual state of apology for feeling—and certainly for revealing—sexual attraction to females. But, women can show it and it's oh-so copacetic. Women can show all the physical attraction to guys they find to be good-looking that they want to show without being condemned with words such as pervert, lecher, lech, sleaze, creep, yada-yada-yada. When a male expresses sexual attraction toward a sex-sensitive female—unless she's given explicit permission or unless he's paying for it such as at a sex club or marriage—then she, and plenty of onlookers, will view his being attracted to her as something that's dark, dark, dark. Why is it dark?

"But, if she expresses her feeling that he's hot, then it's more or less 'You go, girl! You're uninhibited!'

"Oh, and ruminate, if you will, on what I saw on reality TV recently with this not-a-stitch-of-fabric-on-her woman standing in a nudist camp ordering this man who stood in front of her while they conversed to keep his "eyes up!" She even gesticulated with her hands, lowering her forefingers and pointing down toward her au naturel body and then raising them to point at her own eyes as sort of mapped-out directions by which he should reroute his. It's the same, standard-society thing—looking at eyes doesn't inspire sexual feelings in the looker. Looking at ordinarily-covered body parts often does. 'Don't let me catch you looking at any of my erogenous zones 'cause you might get inwardly stimulated and your stimulation would assail my dignity.' Oh my! Risible ridiculousness! She's in a nudist camp. Hello!?! They're just as naked there as are nude dancers in a nightclub. Also, the guy wasn't exactly gawking while drooling with an 'I'm-gonna-rape-you-at-any-moment' expression, either; he was just glancing now and then at her exposed-to-the-maximum attributes. There she was wearing her Eve-tempting-Adam accoutrement—by her own unforced choosing—and she self-righteously commands him to not, I suppose, eye-assault her. Of course, despite her protestations, you can be certain she was gladdened by her ego having been stroked via his wickedly impertinent eyeball naughtiness. To me, her response to his wanderlusting eyes was simultaneously perturbing and hilarious. Wanderlusting? Yes, wanderlusting. Rather than positioning men to be rejected by inviting them to give her the attention she supposedly sought to avoid, shouldn't she have been wearing clothes to lessen the likelihood of receiving what she had preprogrammed herself to reject? Otherwise, she's encouraging men to do the very thing she is allegedly opposed to being done. I felt like jumping through the television and asking her, 'If you're so sensitive about your body being looked at while nude, why are you in a nudist camp?'

"And when I model, which often includes modeling swimsuits as well as lingerie such as negligees and camisoles, we have assistants called 'changers' backstage to help us change from one outfit to another quickly. Many are males and they see us mostly unclothed for a few moments per scene. But they have to be gay. Why? Because if they're straight, they might get aroused. What difference should it…does it…could it…make if one guy who sees our bodies remains flaccid but the other guy who sees our bodies gets a hard-on? The idea is that the girls would be uptight—since this is how we're brought up—'cause they're somehow being harmed by a guy just gazing some at them and feeling sexual arousal. But there are no busted bones, there is no cutting of skin, there is no physical damage whatsoever any more so when the straight-guy gazer has a woody than when the gay-guy gazer has a floppy.

"So, the key thing there is, once again, the male feeling of stimulation—the sex, itself. 'That gay guy is unaroused and that's good. That straight guy is aroused and that's bad.' It's so absurd. It's remindful of the perennial and societally reinforced, tier-one absurdity that men can be totally topless in public places—such as the beach—but women's boobs can't be completely exteriorized. It's a puerile double standard that routinely goes mindlessly unchallenged. Why? Female-nipple-o-phobia! Some male onlookers might become sexually stoked! As a society, we cannot tolerate such heterosexual wickedness germinating within penis people!

"To broaden that theme with some more memorized obsessiveness, when we react with that reaction, we're predicating our mindset not on her being corporeally injured, but rather on what we suspect is happening mentally within him. You're a guy and you feel that the other fellow is offensive if you believe he's sexually stimulated, even slightly, by looking at, or especially touching, your wife or sister or daughter or girlfriend, etcetera. But—magically—as long as he's not stimulated, it's OK. For instance, consider this classic disclaimer: 'It's all right; I'm a doctor.' The doc is merely examining her, professionally, and he's supposedly not stimulated, right? But sometimes he doubtless is.

"But what about this scenario? You're a boyfriend or a husband or a dad or whatever relative, including a female relation, and you get angry and defensive because a male is looking your lady's way. FODs—Fathers of Daughters—are particularly prone to these reactionaryisms. The more attractive she is, in your mind—and probably hers—the more offended you—and she—will become. Your level of being offended correlates unambiguously with what you presume is her level of attractiveness to him plus his consequent perceived level of stimulation. The stronger the turn-on you believe he feels, the more upset you are. But … you then learn that he's a homosexual. Or, you learn that he's blind. Or, you learn that he's a eunuch. Or, you learn that he wasn't really looking at her, but at something else. In other words, he wasn't sexually stimulated by her whatsoever. 'Whew. I was upset, but now I'm not upset at all.' Yeah, since there was apparently no sex sloshing around in his mind and he therefore likely didn't get a hard-on or hopefully not even a teensy tingle, then, you know, it's hunky-dory.

"Translation: We're not responding to any impact on her body. We're responding to what we perceive is going on inside his mind.

"But, if he is straight and he is looking at her and his urges cause him to have a body-change moment, i.e., an erection, well, that's troublesome. Because, you know, that boner confirms that he feels sexual feelings toward your female, and the sex part is what's wrong, because the sensual feeling he harbors—despite existing entirely within his own interiors—is somehow harmful because it's, well, it's offensive.

"'It's, it's, it's … it just is. It's a sex-type thing when he's eyeballing her, and hence since it's sex that's involved, I need to be offended by it.'

"Yeah. Beware of that looker-man. His sexual feelings took off flying through the air and invaded her underwear.

"Anyway, touching is definitely a stronger action than looking; I agree with that viewpoint. If someone, male or female, without me signaling a go-ahead, taps my forearm with his/her fingertip to get my attention, I don't feel uncomfortable. But, if he or she were to tap my breast with his/her fingertip to get my attention, I'm societally habituated so that I do feel uncomfortable. But, just as my forearm is unharmed by that unforceful touch, so is my breast equally unharmed by that unforceful touch. Nonetheless, the forearm is not a known erogenous zone; the breast is. We, including me—oops, grammatically, I should say I—are reacting straight-out exclusively to one thing: what we perceive as a sexual feeling living inside of someone else. That is, we're concerned that the looker or toucher is somehow harming the lookee or touchee, because while he's looking or touching, he feels sexual feelings within his own personhood, which is supposed to somehow deprecate her dignity. But, as I said a minute or two ago while I was talking about models' changer assistants, there's no bone-busting or whatnot. When I stop and think about that, it seems to be somewhat baffling. I'm thinking it's perhaps a natural-selection, competition-based possessiveness buried in our genetics—'that person is mine and if you aim sexual vibes at her or him you might wanna take her or him away from me and that's a threat, so get lost'—combined with cultural reinforcement.

"However, when I get touched sexually without green-lighting it,

I don't—and I emphasize this—unless the touching is abusively aggressive, I don't fly off the handle. Unless it continues on too much, I often won't do or say anything or act irate. If I do have to say *no*, I typically will, at first, say something such as 'Hey, I'd rather you not do that; I don't feel comfortable with it,' and say it assertively but calmly. It almost always works. And I certainly don't let an unwanted sexual touch diminish my self-esteem. Contrarily, regardless of how it was presented, it's usually still at least measurably laudatory.

"Also, we're taught, as kids, to feel icky when an older person touches us beyond normal contact. While we should learn to oppose being molested by anyone, regardless of age, it's sensible to discourage adults from unsuitably touching us while we're young children. Otherwise, *mores-spurred* psychological issues might supervene. But, I say that, unless there's extreme sexual assault such as coercive, penetrative rape, that this discouragement can usually be achieved without all the typical hysterical rage and draconic punishment. The grownup, despite him or her—and yes, there are women molesters—sometimes being sad and sick but nevertheless non-violent and non-crude, is often publicly excoriated and imprisoned for a lengthy sentence in a penitentiary. That's where he could be murdered by some pseudo-heroical fellow prisoner trying to put a feather in his own machismo cap and impress other inmates as a hardcore justice-imposer via personally fulfilling the faux-hero prison tradition of murdering child molesters, as in the poetic injustice of 'Make your life worthwhile; Waste a pedophile,' while he's probably using this savage custom as an excuse to pursue the joy of inflicting violence and scoring macho points.

"Harkening back to women molesters, there's all too frequently an asymmetrically applied lax attitude toward them as contrasted with the auto-severity with which heterosexual men molesters are treated. Female molesters, both hetero and homo, are far more likely to be viewed pitiably as being mentally ill. Male molesters are ordinarily granted no such psychogenic leniency. 'She's disturbed, poor thing. Take it easy on her.' But: 'He's a pervert-sleazer. Kill him.' Once again, we encounter the infantilization of females. 'That instable, sad-sack woman must've been abused or whatnot when she was young, so she's not significantly accountable for her molesting miscues.' But, for the selfsame type of molestation wreaked by a male: 'It don't matter none what's happened to him. He's a perv-scummer.' This mentality is contrastively condescending toward women and signally inequitable toward men, often leading to astringent punition of male pedophiles while their female pedophilic counterparts receive comparative kid-glove penalties. *Possibly* consequential *might be* an infliction of a marginally worsened, societally-fueled dosage of sex-shame on kids molested by males than on kids molested by females. We might've heard of studies purporting that hetero-molested girls normally suffer worse psychical detriment than do hetero-molested boys. *If* true, why? Because that's the drumbeat, societal messaging drilled into girls from tyke-hood on. This tendentious, detrimental-to-men-and-girls discrepancy could be annulled. How? Grownups in kids' daily lives plus society's authoritative spokespersons need to effing stop in essence telling underage girls molested by men that they're *damaged goods* while concurrently telling underage boys molested by women that they *got lucky.*

"For the perversion-afflicted molester, he or she—ordinarily he—is melodramatically diabolized by local and maybe national society as well as, of course, the judicial system and is portrayed as having done something horrible. The child sees that portrayal. Something horrible was done, thinks the child. Who was this horrible thing done to? 'It was done to me. So, I must be horrible, too. I must be shameful. I must be damaged. I must be trash.' Although I realize there are other confusing complications, developmentally, if incest is involved, why not train kids to refrain from automatically viewing non-violent adult sexual touchers as totally vile predators, but rather as psychologically maladapted persons whose advances should be rejected in a firm but calm manner? Many of these adults are otherwise kind-natured, such as the agonizingly chary individuals whose suppressive shyness forces them to be frightened by adult relationships and who non-violently stroke, fondle, or pet kids for sexual gratification but also sometimes for a yearned-for exchange of affection. How about some solace rather than odium for them? Care about the best interest of the child *and* the adult, in that order. Wouldn't a non-histrionic approach more likely result in a child experiencing less or no sexual confusion, internalized shame, and fear of unworthiness as well as better long-term mental health? I recommend a black-and-white, non-sensationalistic movie from the '60s I saw on late-night TV several years ago—*The Mark*.

"Amplifying on the subject of feeling creeped-out or grossed-out or whatevered-out, I say this: There are hostile and rude expressions of feeling someone is creepy and there are non-hostile and non-rude expressions of feeling someone is creepy. I can feel creepily repulsed by a person because he has a particularly off-putting facial or bodily appearance, or he's too sweaty, or he's mephitic and smelling repelling…smelling repelling? Anyhow, unless he deserves to be rejected harshly due to abusiveness or crudity or meanness, I don't need to reject him with hostility and rudeness if he asks me to dance with him—or to have sex with him. Uh, I even rejected Bosco Mason un-harshly. And, this includes when I'm away from Secrets, that is, when I'm in most regular-society places. I can't necessarily prevent myself from feeling that so-and-such person seems creepy. He could be the grossest guy I've ever seen; maybe he's old, obese, wrinkled, hairless, malodorous, scarred and looks like a leper-colony castoff. But, in response to his expressing a flattering attraction to *me*, I don't have to be hardhearted to *him*—either there on the spot, or later on if I talk to somebody else about him. I don't have to insult him or put him in a fix by getting him in trouble.

"Finally, I do wish to say emphatically that I apply these questioningsof-the-norm to my own reactions as well as to those of other people. OK … I know, I know, I know … I went from venting about what irks me backstage when modeling to expounding upon those other tied-in things. My brain just goes off. You realize, Guinevere, that you don't have to reply to my entire vent-burst heresy, so …"

"So, you did indeed become a model, as I predicted you would that day back in seventh grade when I was consoling you about how it's a plus not a negative to be a tall girl and how models are pretty and tall, and that you had both of those qualities. You'd just finished barely stopping yourself from annihilating Nate Perkins. Remember that?"

"Oh yeah, I do recall that incident. You referred to it earlier today when you were persuading me to push the red butt-kicker button. You told me back then that I should be a model," said Kristi Lou, smiling.

Guinevere adjusted the left-center AC vent so it would blow a cold gust directly onto the side of her head, which made her hair fly up in the air, and then leaned back in her seat as she nodded her agreement with Kristi Lou's fundamental premise. Piano Concerto No. 2: Adagio Sostenuto continued to waft unobtrusively, blending into the artificially cooled summer air that was chilled by Freon MO99, an innovatory and cost-effective refrigerant that does not deplete the ozone.

"Yes, of course you're right with your fervidly heretical, sussed-out scrutinies," said Guinevere. "But, according to society's rubrics, it's not something that people—especially women—are supposed to challenge. Your peccancy makes you a disloyal dissident, an iconoclast. We girls, most of us, anyway, whether we admit it or not—or even consciously know it's going on—like the power. We're conditioned to feel disrespected if males optically express sexual attraction and we revere the power to make them feel ashamed for supposedly shaming us and then some-times we'll escalate to trying to get them in trouble for said expression."

"Yes!" said Kristi Lou. "Power. It's the power. The anti-straight-male-sex-uality bigotry is greatly about power. It's about other things, too, but, to a great degree, that's it. It's about the power to control men by making them feel like creeps or bad guys when they look at us sexually or whistle or make some non-crude catcall or stare at our body parts. We debase them for allegedly debasing us and we secretly keep the compliment."

"Yes, that's right," agreed Guinevere.

"Power," said Kristi Lou. "Feminists fear and resent what they perceive, even if they deny the perceiving, as the power of the penis. They idolize power; they just want to take it all away from men and somehow give it to women—a logicless nonstarter. Hysterical hostility toward straight-male sexuality seems boundless, has existed for centuries, and continues on unabated—grossly worsened by modern rad-fems and socially ingrained within us. Truth-filled propaganda can spread propitious ideas. But—here we have the deceivingly propagandistic penises-are-putrid-anti-female-weaponry trope, which is deeply connected to penis envy and penis enmity. The penis goes in, in a power action. Our genitalia receive, in a passive non-action. The penis acts; the vagina is acted upon.

"Halt your thoughts and focus on the meaning of such biologism. Many overwrought religionists and their uneasy allies in penis opposition—extremist-feminists—are focusing, often subconsciously, quite deeply on what the male does with his genitals. What does he do? He thrusts. He penetrates. He ejaculates. He does those acts inside of the female. What does he thrust with? He thrusts with his *junk*, an instrument seen by overwrought religionists and extremist-feminists as an attacking rod of dominance and danger: a supremacist intruder and inflictor of possible pregnancy, which can be a struggle, even when desired.

"The female body gets thrust into, in a sort of invasion—natural for creating life but still viewed as a threatening act of violent entry interlaced with sin by carried-away members of the former population and as a resented act of unequal power by the latter. Thrusting is what the man is supposed to do. But, many mean-ass rad-fems want sexual intercourse, the bodily boulevard on which we travel for the continuation of our species, to be done only with the man reduced to an inert receiver lying decumbently motionless on his back and the woman on top powerfully thrusting down on him with her ass. She gets to be the thruster, and that arrangement grants rad-fems the illusion that they are somehow negating the unalterable fact that, regardless of what position is chosen, the penis remains the organ that goes in and the vagina remains the organ that gets gone into. Men have a plug. We have a receptacle. Men have a jackhammer. We have a manhole, sans the cover plate.

"And, so say some rad-fems, due to the violative violence of male penetration—during which he repeatedly stabs her—there must be a rule for all coitus, including within marriage: the man stays on the bottom and the woman must initiate to forestall a case of stabbing rape.

"Those conflictions are going on psychologically in our subconsciouses, exacerbated by ossified, anti-straight-male-sexuality cultural conditioning. We must inflict punishment. Penis punishment is a perdurable societal norm. Punishment of the penis is encouraged and expected. For an un-biting attestation of said expectation, check out *vagina dentata*, which, BTW, is a toothless, feminist fantasy—both physically and figuratively—as penises after entry and departure are neither chomped nor diminished.

"Some women, notably feverish feminists, are often significantly more approving of men performing cunnilingus than they are of men drilling for coochie oil. With cunnilingual licking, we avoid the inequality of copula-tive dicking. We're on equal tonguing-footing—tonguing-footing?—yes, tonguing-footing—with men because we've got tongues in our mouths, too. So, body-parts-wise, we gots what they gots. Thusfore—yes, Guinevere, that's a word—when it comes to administration of penetration, there's no jealously/resentment factor based on males being biologically equipped for shoving something into a human body that we can't shove in, albeit a tongue, gallingly to such feminists, can't go diving to the depth that a man's penile penetrator can. 'Aw shucks! I wish I had a short-for-Rich-ard!' However, God does not affix to our anatomies a short-for-Richard.

Our singular recourse is simulation. If we want to enjoy the pounding power of a short-for-Richard, we have to use, ahem, a strap-on, which is both artificial and a de facto admission that we marvel at the thruster men naturally have while resenting them for having it 'cause we don'ts gots what they doeses gots. Doeses? Yes, doeses.

"Not only must a man who gets himself into a position of power in the workplace, e.g., an office manager, not be rewarded with gratification of sexual attraction to a female who just happens to hold a subordinate rank, he must be punished for such pursuits—even if she has been pursuing him. Any attempt to obtain sex from her is auto-deemed to be an abuse of said power, including when all he wanted was sex, with zero I-will-do-bad-things-to-you-if-you-refuse qualifications. According to feminist dogma, the higher up the success/power ladder a man climbs, the less he should be carnally rewarded and the more he should be punished. Jealously-based resentment of traditional male power in the workplace abounds with many feminists, and sex—especially since radical feminists hate straight-male sexuality—is a convenient on-the-surface excuse for punishing him for having any kind of power at all. Men could rightfully say about some of these extremist-feminists that 'you despise us 'cause you ain't us.'

"And, while we're on this subject, guess what, Guinevere! I have some more committed-to-memory, ranter-raver remarks."

"Shocking," replied Guinevere.

"I know. Anyway, we now have the 'Me Too' movement, based on anecdotes of episodes whereby men supposedly inflicted sexual mistreatment upon women. From what I've read and heard, some of the grievances stated by Me Too complainants seem quite believable and are highly justifiable. Some of the grievances are iffy. Some of the grievances, even if about true events, are preposterous mole-hill-meet-mountain grumbles and reek of standardized anti-straight-male sexism. Here's a litmus test for the Me Too-ers: When women in the workplace do the same things to men—and yes, they sometimes do—do you consider those leering, touching, sexual-innuendo-commenting, have-sex-with-me come-on behaviors to be equally wrong?

"Men could form their own movement—the 'I Also' crusade:

"'I Also have been falsely accused of sexual harassment;

"'I Also have been reprimanded or even terminated from my company because I, as a supervisor or manager, tried—non-crudely—to get sex from a flirtatious job applicant or subordinate employee, but, upon being rejected did not use that rejection as a reason to refuse to hire the former or to demote the latter, to deny her a promotion, to refuse to award her with any merit-based salary raise, or to fire her, and I did not marginalize or attack her in any way;

"'I Also have sought sex from women, or merely engaged in sexual conversational banter and, when I was told to stop, I…stopped…but still was portrayed as predatory—despite stopping;

"'I Also have been approached by manipulative Jezebels who came on to me seductively, weaponizing their feminine wiles to get ahead or *sleep to the top*. After they extorted from me a Pavlovian response and I was intimate with them—even if the intimacy was limited to a few lewd jokes—they pulled a 180° bait-and-switch and went from turning me on to turning on me. They made that U-turn because they didn't get the advancement or perks they demanded. Or, they were cunningly contriving a conniving setup game from the outset with initial charming/cordial come-ons and I took the honey-trap bait. I showed the sexuality they were duplicitously trying to elicit within their entrapment inveiglements. They then became strategically angry or tearful or accusatory, followed by the corporate and/or judicial system punishing me while excusing and rewarding the gyneco-saboteurs with payoff money;

"'I Also have been cast as a demon in the workplace for mild peccadilloes for which women, when they do the same things, are rarely, if ever, chastised. And I have been demonized just for calling a woman "sexy" or the equivalent thereof, as if such a verbalization somehow constitutes an awful affront rather than what it is, which is a harmless compliment;

"'I Also—without treating any of them as my rightful appanage due to outranking them—have engaged in behavior such as libidinous remarks and/or sexual touching with adjunct women who, at the time, *liked it and did it back*, but later complained about what they had previously enjoyed. Or, some other subaltern females, who may've been jealous because it was another woman to whom I was exhibiting attraction and who were uninvolved themselves in the sexual conduct but were present in the environment and were offended, chose to protest *my* conduct but wholly refrained from protesting the conduct of the flirty woman who the complainers could see was mutually flirting with me as much as I was with her;

"'I Also have been embarrassingly vilified, or sued, or have lost employment or have been accused of and/or arrested for nonexistent assault or otherwise suffered colluded sabotage and punishment because of mere flirtatious interactions with a female, even if *she initiated* said flirtations—with a copious coating of cherry-red lipstick on her facial lips that has forever beckoned men by conveying to them the subliminal message of an enraptured and joyful vagina imaginarily relocated to between her nose and her chin; and with her short and/or tight skirts; and with her rubbing against me sensually; and with her grabbing my haunches; and with various other aggressively provocative behaviors and purposeful allurements—while she went utterly unpunished.'

"And then there's this. According to the predilections of the I-might-have-rabies genus of Me Too-ers, any and all females who claim they've been raped or sexually abused should be automatically seen as *survivors*. One of their fave mottos is 'I believe survivors!' This motto appears on signs some of them wave riotously at public protests where many of them can be found yelling it and chanting it like bug-eyed, brainwashed cultists.

"They play word chicanery right in front of everyone—blatantly. Automatically believing either the accused or the accusers—unless you personally know them very well and trust them—is egregiously inappropriate. But, instead of their rallying-cry motto being the slightly less dumb and discriminatory 'I believe accusers!' they arrogantly replace what should be—by all rational and fair applications of logic—the word accusers with the word survivors, thereby skipping a critical step in the process of assigning guilt within the framework of fairness and justice. They skip the inconvenient stage of equitably examining pertinent empirical evidence, applying reason, and weighing facts. Those things should be done in order to dispassionately determine whether or not any atrocious behavior, against which the alleged victim would've needed to *survive*, actually happened. Rather, the accusers are automatically hailed as survivors. Accusing is magically conflated with surviving. And, the word survivors is drenched with drama, which is, of course, by design: what befell them was so awful that they've had to survive it."

Kristi Lou paused and, seeking reassurance, looked at Guinevere.

"Keep going," said Guinevere, with a knowing smile.

"OK. I will. So, in the never-ending saga of sex-based he said/she said, only the people on one side are supposed to be believed, primarily because, it seems, credence is auto-granted to their claims based on, on, on—their genitalia, which make them virtuosos of veracity, whereas members of the enemy class have genitalia that make them merchants of mendacity. This ukase is delightfully uncomplicated: Females must be automatically believed. Males must be automatically disbelieved. Translation: We people who wear a vagina are never liars about being sexually assaulted—or, if we females are lying, it's irrelevant. Those people who wear a penis are always guilty when a vagina-wearer accuses them of sexual assault—or, if those males aren't lying, it's irrelevant. Ergo, we have our verdict: Vagina? Innocent. Penis? Guilty. Eureka!

"Speaking of vaginas and wearing things, Guinevere, do you have a, ahem, pussycat hat—meow-meow, hiss-hiss—in your wardrobe?"

"No. And I grant to God the grandest gratitude that I don't."

"Neither do I. I'll keep my pink thing where it belongs; I don't wish to wear it on my head. Anyway, another current who-you-should-instantly-believe slogan is 'Believe women!' Really? Again—automatically? Why not 'Believe men!'—and do so automatically? Oh no, we can't have that, because men who are accused are always guilty, right? No, they're not.

"How about letting ourselves be guided by this concept: Believe who's believable, on a per-case basis, while overlooking or deemphasizing gender.

"Regarding Me Too, there is already an ever-growing backlash, and it's going to strengthen. Some men—and males own and control most businesses in America and worldwide—have already for years now been reluctant to hire females, especially young and attractive ladies, because of fears of losing money through sexual-harassment-type lawsuit awards or settlements. I believe that trend started within the past couple of decades or so as a direct result of steadily worsening anti-male-sexuality-in-the-workplace hysteria perpetrated by femicommies. These business owners are willing to take a calculated risk and hope they're not sued by the woman who's applying or by the federal government for directly defying the Civil Rights Act of 1964 whose legislation bans employment discrimination based on multiple elements, including the sex of a job applicant.

"Look, I am categorically *not* referring to valid concerns and justifiable reprisals based on truly egregious sexual misbehavior by men; those men are wrong—just as those same behaviors by women in the workplace are wrongful. I am, however, talking about rampant female overreactions to relatively mild expressions of sexuality that used to be mutually liked or, if disliked, handled without melodrama and without the consequent money snatching from the company and sometimes loss of profits from public boycotts or whatnot, not to mention lost daily productivity due to internal dissension. They understandably think it's not worth it. What businessman—or businesswoman—wants an atmosphere riddled with constant fretting about whether some gal is going to raise a ruckus over 'that guy in that cubicle stared at my body for three seconds' and then possibly escalate her victimhood from there?

"And, some women are undoubtedly secretly resenting Me Too for one aspect of this backlash reaction phenomenon. Their feelings, put into words, could go something like this: 'Hey—what about *my* pay-day? Some of you in Me Too have already got yours but now you're going to block me from getting mine! I know it feels fulfilling to be part of a social movement, but you're making it so that, even if I can get hired—which you've helped ensure is now less likely—the guys in the office will subdue their natural libido urges and won't pursue me even mildly, including if I try to manipulate them and tempt them as I was planning to do and thus I won't have grounds for setting up a money-grubbing sexual harassment claim. Thanks a freakin' lot!'

"How many millions of dollars over the past say, 25 years, have gone from companies to women who've claimed sexual mistreatment? Yes, some of the claims have been valid. But, many of them have not.

"Also, you might notice that, with some exceptions, these guys who are publicly accused of sexual misbehavior are not overly handsome. How many good-looking male coworkers, including bosses, go unreported?

"For the women who've received a sexual mistreatment payload and were not plotting a sexcapade money-heist from the outset of their employment, I have this question: How many of you, if you could put yourselves on a tape deck and rewind your lives, would trade in that life-enriching sum of money your hot-in-the-eyes-of-some-guys body earned you in exchange for never having been sexually pursued in the office? Call it 'moot' all you want. Say 'it doesn't matter,' and other dismissive comments. Nevertheless, the query remains. If you could, would you? Would you? Well—how 'bout it?—would you? How many of you who are now rich to the extent you likely never would've been had your curves not elicited some office-space male sexuality can look back—if you dare do so, even within your private thoughts—and honestly say that those male sexual expressions were *not* worthwhile? 'If I could time-travel back…I'd gladly return all this money if I could just undo what my ex-boss did with his asking me out and trying to get in my pants!' You'd kiss off that settlement that has given you thousands, sometimes millions, of dollars that you otherwise would've seen only in a dream? Really? How many of you who haven't yet obtained office sex-scandal money, if you knew you could hit the monetary motherlode, would be more than happy to endure an oh-so-degrading boob-touch or a butt-grab or some prolonged leering in order to have your pocketbooks and your bank accounts bursting at the seams, drive a BMW, live wherever you wish and have no financial worries?"

"Well," said Guinevere, "it's obvious that—while evincing stupefying tenacity—you do, indeed, have all of those intensity-packed statements thoroughly memorized, which suggests considerable effort devoted to memorization that is so intense that it is, uh, obsessive."

"Mistaken, you're not," replied Kristi Lou. "My paramour is Mr. Talking Points."

"Any more grand visions?" asked Guinevere.

"Yeah, envision this: What would be wrong with having a culture in which people could simply ask, non-aggressively, for possible sexual pleasure from either acquaintances or strangers, almost like asking for directions—and then receive a calm, mature reply? I'm referring to calmly approaching someone we think is not in a relationship and who, at the time of the approach, is usually sitting or standing alone. Widespread acceptance of this sex-is-no-longer-the-elephant-in-the-room etiquette would necessitate a culture-wide de-hysteria-a-tizing. What? De-hysteria-a-tizing? OK, I'm coining a word. There would need to be a de-hysteria-a-tizing of human sexuality in general and an elimination of anti-hetero-male bigotry in particular.

"'Hi. I find you to be attractive. I'm interested in possibly having sex with you. If the attraction is mutual, can we talk and see if it might work out?'

"Presently, if a woman approached a man with such a proposition—not usually much of a problem. If a man approached a woman with such a proposition—hysterics.

"Furthermore, when the average man nowadays *does* receive pellucid sexual interest from a woman in whom he's not sexually interested, he acts like a gentleman and rejects her with a smile and sensitivity so as not to hurt her feelings, while showing that he's flattered. Unless bluntness is necessary, he often lies, with kindhearted dishonest excuses, by saying something like 'I'm not feeling too well' or 'I have a girlfriend,' and then thanks her for her interest.

"By contrast, the average woman rejects a sex-seeking man to whom she's sexually unattracted with insensitivity and often with nasty nastiness. Nasty nastiness? Anyhow, we women blow right on by being concerned about making him feel inadequate. In fact, we pour it on. From us, there is no apology or humbleness. There is no explanation, such as commiserative fibbing. There is no expression of feeling complimented by him for being carnally attracted to us. Do we let him down easy? Are you kidding me? Unless he engages in the mandatory denial game by choosing words that indicate he's hiding his real intention—even though both sides know what he *really* wants—we typically go directly to the opposite extreme with societally required—and glorified—hostility: Pervert! Lecher! Creep! Sleaze! Pig! Loser!

"Regarding revulsionary reactions, it seems to me that many straight females are programmed to confine their revulsion to being triggered only by sexual attention from straight males to whom they're unattracted the way many straight males confine their revulsion to being triggered only by sexual attention from gay males. That said, I know of straight females who are comfortable with non-crass sexual attention from men but are uncomfortable with sexual attention from lesbians and bisexual women.

However, for the former group of straight females, their programming is somewhat heteroclite, nature-wise, in part because—and I'm not trying to dis Sapphic females or any homosexual persons—because, well, it's not natural in the sense that interweaving members of the same gender cannot continue our species. Females being sexual with females can't reproduce. But, Guinevere, as I've told other people, men who copulate with hetero women and keep the human race going, do so by pushing these women into the unpleasantness of pregnancy. So, that undercurrent psychological concern, combined with the corrupting cultural influence of flaming feminism's bigotry and misandry, contributes to many females being resentful and intolerant of straight males—especially the guys to whom the females might want to say 'I find you to be unfetching so don't aim your deoxyribonucleic acid at my vagina'—when those men compliment them with expressions of sexual attraction.

"I'm not contradictorily making excuses for enmity toward males who show physical attraction to females' bodies—au contraire, I continue to denounce it. However, it's somewhat understandable that females—and males, too—have adverse reactions to males expressing attraction to females 'cause that propensity is so deeply ingrained in us via cultural conditioning. A female knows that the guy knows that he's *supposed* to hide it, and, when he doesn't, his non-hiding can seem disrespectful to her 'cause even if the societal rule is unfair—it is—and doesn't make sense—it doesn't—he still knows that said societal rule is there. Thus, he's not culturally permitted to openly show attraction because to do so, according to society's edict, means he is disrespecting the incumbent rule, and, by extension, he is *supposedly* disrespecting her. That's one of the major things I'm complaining about and want to drastically change.

"Also, due to the long-entrenched societal warping of women's minds that pre-prejudices us against men's sexual feelings, it's unsurprising that a man might overreact to a woman reacting positively to his expression of attraction to her body by jumping to the conclusion that she is definitely reciprocating sexual interest in him when, in reality, she may or may not be. His experiences could be that those positive reactions from us females to ooh-la-la come-ons from males seem so seldom-occurring that he may misinterpret her smile or whatever expression of acceptance of his flattery as a signal that she's blatantly declaring that she's panty-less and lascivious, and that she wants him to come and get it. In fact, merely a neutral reaction by her to a cat-call or whatnot could result in a guy misreading her response. That is, because of society's bigotry against straight-male sexuality, he may respond inaccurately not only to the presence of her friendliness but also to the absence of her unfriendliness. We need to move away from that pervasive standard. In the meantime, we girls still don't, in most instances, have to huff and puff about it.

"There's also this. When people communicate with other persons, the form of the communication's delivery matters as to the way the receiver receives it. A female is more likely to accept a carnal comment and/or a lusty gaze from a male if his tone of voice does not seem cold and churlish but rather seems warm and breezy, and if his face does not seem seamy, surly, scowling but rather seems complaisant, good-humor-ed, smiley. 'Hey, great ass' delivered with churlishness can seem creepy and deservedly flops, whereas such a gluteal assessment given buoyantly ordinarily deserves to be accepted as a well-received plaudit. So, it's not just what we say, but how we say it; it's not just that we look, but how we look when we look.

"I, as a female type of person—female type of person?—I neither enforce nor obey that ridiculous rule in that if a guy shows attraction to me, as long as he's not extremely crude without permission, I'm not offended at all—either personally or as a woman. Rather, I'm flattered. And—unless it's a 2 a.m.-and-alone-in-a-parking-garage type of situ-ation—I'll display to him and any onlookers a friendly response to his expression of being attracted to me.

"A big ongoing problem is that most females, and many male observers, go way too far in applying this cultural regulation of taking offense and then wanting to punish a male who non-grossly but overtly manifests sexual attraction. If you're a girl or woman, your sense of dignity does *not* have to be so lame that you feel required to apply this idiotic, bigotry-based, double-standard rule!

"OK, Guinevere. I'm all wound up in ranting mode sitting here in your ass-kicker car. I've got one more memorized rant and I'll be done."

"Are you sure?"

"No. But here I go. So, societally ingrained in our collective subconscious is the irrational and sexist notion that straight-male sexuality is essentially misogyny incarnate and that heterosexual sex is somehow basically something that males inflict and against which females must be protected. That misandrous sensibility is on full display and deeply entrenched within the mainstream media's rarely challenged and time-dishonored discriminatory practice of refusing to name female accusers who don't clearly reveal themselves when accusing men of sexual misconduct, while such news editors evidently have no compunctions about printing or broadcasting the names of males who've been accused. Operating under a flaming double standard, she conveniently gets to accuse him of shameful behavior and remain publicly anonymous while he gets accused by her of said shameful behavior and is publicly identified. This policy says: 'to hell with the accused man's anonymity. He's another cisgender male who's been accused of aiming some sort of non-romantic—i.e., unethically and/or illegally prurient—sex toward a female. And, if she says he went overboard, he's probably guilty.'

"Wait for a conviction or, at the very least, formal charges to be filed? Nah, not necessary. And, we should, as the feminists tell us, just automatically believe the accuser, as long as—of course—the accuser is female and the accused is male. After all, women deserve to be believed, without question. That's because we women never lie about being sexually mistreated by men … right? We shouldn't be bothered by such chauvinistic things as corroboration of any witness testimony or pursuing in-depth investigations. So, don't you dare go questioning the veracity of our allegations, 'cause, with us, accusations equal facts. And if you dispute the factuality of our accusations, then you're hatefully insensitive and you're disrespecting women.

"And frequently, maybe usually, after the female's accusations of sexual impropriety have been exposed as fallacy, the media will still refuse to reveal her name. Oh my, if our names were revealed, we women could be embarrassed or ashamed. And many women would be scared to come forward, they say, because of all the hassle of people questioning our accusations and digging into our sex lives and maybe saying that we might be a bit promiscuous. The fallback refrain is that of 'blaming the victim and punishing her twice.' Hence, we girls can't be IDed in the newspaper or in magazines or on TV or on radio or on the Internet. I say 'get over it.' What have we ladies got to be ashamed of? If our accusations are true, then we haven't done anything wrong—the man is the bad guy … right? He's the one who should be ashamed, which is a huge part of the whole idea. But, we're not named 'cause we're supposedly on the receiving end of … of … of … of … what? Sex—that's what.

"So, females often won't come forward to report sex abuse? And that reluctance is because of shame? As I said, what do we women have to be ashamed of? She's the victim; he's the perpetrator—of a societally shameful behavior. Thus, he's the person who, logically, should be ashamed. But, yeah, there can be shame for the female, because she received sex— never mind that it was unjustly forced upon her. Therefore, some females won't report the offense and the male abuser goes unpunished. Most females are indoctrinated at an early age with a strong strain of what I call sex-shame. I remarked on sex-shame when I was talking about molesters. Anyway, that sex-shame flows directly from subtle-but-powerful bigotry against straight-male sexuality. I don't want to be insensitive; I really don't, but these women need to do what those other women do: overcome it—the sex-shame factor—and report the abuser, anyway, so such men can hopefully be stopped from hurting anyone else.

"But, I didn't report Bosco for his knife attack on me," said Kristi Lou, glancing at her now knocking knees. "Management at Secrets did, but I didn't. It wasn't sex, though; it was violence. He didn't get sex, so he became non-sexually violent. Still, I didn't report him, so maybe I'm being hypocritical. Sex-shame, however, wasn't the reason I didn't report him; I was protecting the reputation of my employer's business.

"Anyhow, if she does report an event, it should be reported only if he's truly guilty of doing a truly bad thing that she made clear she truly didn't want done. Otherwise, if it was mutually consensual, she could be outed as the wrongdoer. She *should* be afraid of that outcome. But, she frequently isn't because she's confident she can get away with it. Sadly, she often does—because of societal bias in her favor, especially in the workplace or on college campuses, a prejudice which the Me Too zealots want to intensify even more.

"So, we have some women who were, in fact, abused but are unfortunately afraid to file a report, while we have some women who were, in fact, not abused but are unfortunately unafraid to file a report.

"But, returning to the shame factor, if a wrongdoing indeed occurred, and he did it, why does she feel ashamed? It's greatly, as I've been saying, because Western societies' influentially dominant forces in the media and popular culture, as well as in feminism and other matriarchates, ceaselessly reinforce general anti-straight-male-sexuality hysteria. She received some degree of forcible sex? Well then, by God, she's been shamed—shamed by sex. She's been conditioned to feel and then claim sex-shame, as an aspect of her victimhood and justification for not reporting the abuse, even if the male would be viewed as the offender.

"By contrast, if he punches her senseless or he robs her at knifepoint or he guns a bullet into her or he burns her house down or he forges checks in her name or he, he…he steals her car—Guinevere, that one was for you—or if he does whatever sexless bad thing to her, then she's unashamed, or at least not nearly *as* ashamed. But, civilization norms demand that she can't be entirely shame-free if non-love, hetero sex is involved because straight-male sexuality, outside of romance, is wicked. Hence, she's saddled with sex-shame, and he and his abuse goes unreported.

"Yes, gynocentric fem-activists need for females who've been groped, stroked, molested, or whatnot—even if those touching misbehaviors were quite mild and the man stopped when he was told to stop—to educe as much sex-shame sensationalism as possible. Their contradictory signal to women is: 'We're on your side and we really want you to be mentally and emotionally well. Buuuutttt…we sorta don't because we also require that you be damaged goods. Because, if you're not damaged goods—you know, miserable with low self-esteem caused by unwanted male sexual conduct—then we've got nothing to beat men over the head with, which, uh, we really enjoy doing. So, yeah…please be those sex-damaged goods we keep telling you from the time you're a young kid that you should be, with a full package of psychological misery, which, of course, can be sensationally confirmed by academic studies, so we can get 'em punished. We just love self-fulfilling prophecies. But, don't worry, 'cause after you've been damaged goods for months or years' worth of that depression and rotted self-concept that we sorta-kinda want you to have, which you'll help us blame entirely on male sex perps, then you can recover…but don't go recovering too much, please, since we need to be able to point to the long-term, damaging effects of straight-male bad behavior on innocent female victims.'

"We even have what is known as a 'sex offender registry' in jurisdictions throughout the U.S. And the federal government operates its National Sex Offender Public Website. I know these registries are advertised as serving to warn neighbors of an offender's nearby presence, which, while understandable as a means of fostering protection, is somewhat of a ruse. The flagship function of these registries is for the purpose of inflicting sex-shame. You can see names, pictures, and addresses of these offenders. And these people have indeed been convicted of committing crimes. But where are the *murder-offender registries?* The *vicious-beating-offender registries?* The *home-invasion-offender registries?* The *recidivistic robbery, stealing, and larceny-offender registries?* The *auto-theft-and-carjacking-offender registries?* Right now, in 2018, only five states have what's called 'violent offender registries,' those being Illinois, Indiana, Kansas, Montana, and Oklahoma. That's it. Why? Because there's no sex involved. Shouldn't society say someone should be more ashamed of committing homicide than committing rape, sexual assault, voyeurism, or inappropriate touching? To achieve the infliction of shame, how about going with the traditional shaming of a writeup in the newspaper and maybe a report on TV, radio, and the Internet? Does perpetual, you're-a-pariah-forever denigration really help, overall, more than harm? He could think, 'I can't get employment. I can't get a relationship. I'm publicly broadcast as a scum-of-the-earth thing unendingly. It's hopeless. So, back to crime I go.'

"What about women not ashamed to be publicly pregnant? That's because she realizes that, as far as the general public knows, that child she's carrying who's causing her bulging midsection was conceived in love, whether true or not.

"I know you radical feminists want to turn into victims any women who've received even the slightest male sexual advancements in order to set them—and by vicarious extension—yourselves—up to be heroic fighter-backers. And you seek to make these women out to be double victims because they're ashamed to, as you say, come forward. Then, you believe you accomplish a likewise doubling of male villainy—one, he threw some type of straight-male sex at her, and two, he made her feel so ashamed she can't report it. Well, shouldn't they be I-am-woman-hear-me-roar enough to honestly tell their stories? If they aren't, maybe it's because they sense they'd look foolish by reporting some male sexual behavior that was so non-terrible that it didn't warrant reporting. When you feminists mollycoddle them over their shame, you can't so victimize them and not infantilize them.

"Some girls, especially in my situation and at my age—college, where I'm about to go back to—have consensual sex after downing a few drinks—but are still completely capable of consenting to an activity, sex or anything else. They're feeling frisky or hormonal or wild and carefree. But, with the arrival of the next morning, they feel—ofttimes because of sex-shame—disheartened about what they've done. So, they, maybe with the encouragement of a feminist friend or acquaintance, manage to defeat any ashamed-to-report-it-feeling, which they replace with one or more of the following statuses: one, glorious power to—speaking of shame—punish and thus shame some guy for inflicting sex upon her; two, a feeling of 'I'm so sexy he couldn't resist me'; and three, 'I feel slut-shame 'cause I didn't really know him too well or at all and he's not that attractive to me anymore and he took advantage of me just because I wasn't keeping my legs together. Although I won't say this out loud—couldn't he realize that I'm just another strengthless and gullible girl? How dare he not make the effort to convince me to keep my own thighs closed!'

"She's regretful about her own-volition choice of participatory sex. But, if she can get him in deep trouble, she can assuage her sex-shame by psychologically exonerating herself from what she or other people might conclude: she fain engaged in whorey/slutty behavior. She uses the existing anti-straight-male-sexuality system on campus to clear her conscience while he—and likely his family—is unfairly punished, sometimes including suspension, lowered grades, delays in graduation and career pursuits, physical violence, and long-lasting repercussions such as a dark mark on his various permanent records as well as ongoing, unwarrantable, shame-based infamy.

"The poor guy was thinking that it was consensual sex and it was last night and it's all over. But, no …

"She effectively transfers her irrational shame onto him. Unless contrition seeps in later, she feels no guilt in saddling him with her self-loathing."

I feel ashamed in the bright light of day. But soon everything will be A-OK. An assault allegation will make it all go away.

"She should not be allowed to successfully weaponize her sex-shame regret by hypermagically retracting consent later—after the fact of what he had unambiguous reason to believe was a mutually consensual sexual encounter. I say no to such justiceless retroactivity. No to regret rape. No to reconstructive rape. No to recant rape. No to retroactive rape.

"Patronizing university administrators are her cheerleading coconspirators, whether it's helping her attack a male student or, especially, a professor with whom she voluntarily consented, knowing exactly what she was doing, to 100-percent consensual sex, including an ongoing affair. The prof's in a position of authority. He's older. Hence, he's been, uh, unethical. The age-gap thing is mainly another demonizer-bomb dropped on straight-male sexuality. Gradational developmental advantage? So what? How's any younger person *not* auto-harmed physically or mentally by sexual contact with someone, say, two or five years older but somehow *is* auto-harmed by someone, say, 32 or 105 years older? Never mind the female student's level of ethics within her totally willing participation—including if she was the real so-called predator because of actively pursuing him. As they say without saying it: 'She's such a feeble, helpless little girl…wait! No! She's still a hear-me-roar powerhouse! However, for our current purposes, we administrative warriors need to temporarily deemphasize her powerhouse-ness and portray her as a taken-advantage-of flimsy female, while simultaneously hiding our emphasis on her flimsiness. Then, after she's been suitably cast as the helpless, ineffectual, not-responsible-for-controlling-her-own-self victim, we proprietors can help her rise up and resurge her feminist powerhouse-ism via riding the power comet to damage or destroy his teaching career!'

"She should say to herself what, thankfully, many women in college or elsewhere do indeed essentially tell themselves after they've willfully participated in sex—with anyone—that they later regretted:"

*No, I will not make to any authorities those false accusations of sexual assault I was contemplating. For starters, I might get exposed and justifiably punished for lying about a serious offense. Then again, I might not, because I hear and read about many other girls triumphantly gaming the system, which is a deck of cards that is already pre-stacked against males, who are often judged as guilty of sexual misconduct merely because they're accused by a female, as if the accusation is a conviction. Yeah, I drank some alcohol and smoked some weed, but not to the point of out-of-it intoxication. I knew perspicuously what was going on when he was sexual toward me—and when I was sexual toward him. Besides, we both had a few drinks. If I'm to be treated by the powers-that-be like a big baby and not held responsible for my conduct when I've had a few drinks, then why shouldn't he likewise not be held responsible for his behavior when he's had a few drinks? Am I stupid? No. Am I a complete weakling? No. Do I have the self-control and the maturity of an infant? No. Do I relish infantilizing myself to serve the grandiose cause of anti-male feminism? No. Was I totally able to **say** "No"? Yes. But I didn't. I consented. I need to put on my big-girl panties and accept that my regret does not equal his rape.*

"Affirmative consent is now quite the craze in some localities. Affirmative consent? Really? How often? Must he rely on her to repeatedly re-grant affirmative consent at regular intervals during their sexual transaction? Should he be required to check with her every, say, 15 seconds—glancing at a nearby clock or watch—at each step of the way to secure from her permission to proceed? If feminists succeed in entrenching this movement into society, perhaps men will someday hear women say, for example, 'Yes, you may unfasten that button but then halt till I see how I feel about unfastening the next one' or 'Yes, you are permitted to move your hand in a caressing motion four but currently not five inches above my knee but then pause to await further instructions and possible authorization to reactivate.'

"Would such supervisory regimentation just maybe, uh, cause a ruination of the natural spontaneity that normally accompanies the enjoyment of sex? Umm … yeah.

"Non-verbal cues—that's what he's expected to read nowadays as if he's a mind-reading psychic. Non-verbal cues? Really? OK—feminists and Me Too-ers carry within themselves an overmastering zealotry for female control before and during intimacy. However, what if the woman initiates sex—female initiation of sexual interactions being something that feminists also covet—and he naturally responds to her touching him sexually by touching her sexually, and they get hot and bothered, but then—whamo!—she has a female-freeze moment? If she doesn't tell him to stop by speaking or at least gesticulating saliently or frowning noticeably—and she allegedly can't verbalize or use her hands or frown because of sudden-onset trauma, maybe traceable to, as she may thereafter claim, having been molested earlier in her life—and he keeps going, then she can later cry 'So what if I came on to him and touched him first? I didn't consent to him continuing. I froze. I couldn't move my hands to push him away or gesture "No!" He ignored my non-verbals. He should've been reading my non-verbals, my expressionless facial expression, and the fact that I was unresponsive. He disrespected my non-verbals. He raped me.'

"The reality is that many girls are, well, not too responsive during the early—or latter—stages of sex, because they're shy, or not enjoying it—or simply take a while to get warmed up. The guy, again not being proficient in reading minds, could think, especially if they don't know each other well, that she just needs more, you know, warming.

"A woman who knows she's prone to paralysis during sexual episodes, should, in my view, consider herself responsible for somehow alerting her potential partner to the possibility that if he commences sexually touching her that she might become congealed into a state of catatonia that renders her incapable of saying no to any further sexual proceedings. And, if she, at any juncture, becomes very still and quiet, she may be traumatized and he should stop seeking carnal pleasure from her posthaste.

"She could tell him, orally. Or, she could perhaps keep handy in her purse an oversized, explanatory plastic badge attached to a necklace chain that she could quickly sling onto her neck if sex seems likely. Or maybe she could stick upon her blouse a large sticker, such as an enlarged paper nametag with glue on the back. Both communiqués would display text explaining that 'If I'm sexually touched, I might become catatonic. Hence, being disabled, I will be unable to verbally speak a no, gesture a no, or produce a frowny-face no. Therefore, if you observe that I'm not writhing and moaning, you shall check me for total motionlessness. Upon noting that I've become catatonically paralyzed, your sexual pursuits must cease and desist immediately.'

"Otherwise, if she decides later that she doesn't like him—'cause maybe he didn't give her a follow-up phone call or email her or text her or ask her on a date, or he somehow elsewise offended her, or, very typically, she no longer finds him all that attractive, looks-wise or money-wise or status-wise—she can retroactively proclaim that 'I was frozen. But he failed to obey my non-verbals. He assaulted me. I'm devastated. He's going down.'

"Therefore, the man, after screwing her consensually—so he thought—is screwed by her accusatorially. She is immorally assaulting him, via her mind-flip caprice in choosing to fallaciously cry 'assault!'

"Also, I would advise guys that, unless they know her profoundly well, the days of trying to read a woman's reactions as to whether she wants to be seduced—despite the fact that she just said no—are over. Those women who want their beguiling resistance to be erotically broken down by, as they say, the art of seduction, will just have to be disappointed. For the men, the reward is not worth the risk. So, even if he senses she's giving him one of those ' no, no, no—yes!' invitations or slyly saying 'stop, stop, stop—I'll give you 35 minutes to stop!' he should, nowadays, upon hearing even the slightest utterances from her of anything that remotely resembles a 'no,' slam on the sex brakes and altogether quit touching her, lest she cry rape. For him, it's self-preservation.

"It's getting extreme," said Kristi Lou. "A man, prior to contact, might require a contract. She'll have to sign on the dotted line. He should get it notarized. I can foresee a new type of pre-sex business arising: Notary Public For Understood Consent—NPFUC—with some offices staying open 24 hours for those late-night assignations."

"Would you like some water…or a cup of Coke?" asked Guinevere. "You're a virtual typhoon of vivacity that may need a rest-break. We've got a soda dispenser in here that'll slide forth from inside the dashboard."

"No, thank you. I'm not thirsty. I just need to…uh, I need to…"

"You need to quench your obsession by upchucking the remainder of your diatribe."

"Yes."

"I remain stunned that not only are you ineffably indefatigable but that you've committed to memory all of these detail-drenched perspectives."

"I know. I stun myself. For my various issues about which I obsess, I sit at home and freeze myself motionless on the couch and I shut everything off and I just delve into memorization of my speeches, not knowing if I'll ever say them to anyone. Mr. Dooflotcher knows not to interrupt me. This speech is so very not abridged. I apologize."

"Don't. Go for it."

"Thank you, Guinevere. So, OK, I was going to say…er…oh—yeah,

I was going to say that some anti-malers…what? Uh, malers? Yes. Some anti-malers are stridently oppositional to any and every acquittal of men in sexual misconduct cases 'cause they claim that acquitting men serves to discourage women from—here it comes, again—coming forward with sex-crime victim reports. Is that true? Well, aside from, once again, a thorough ignoring of the plight of the wrongfully accused guy, there's a two-fold answer to that question: no and yes.

"No—public not-guilty verdicts should not—and, among non-childish individuals, do not—dissuade women who are true victims of sexual abuse, whether perpetrated by a straight man or a lesbian woman—which happens more than many people might realize but I guess that's another storyline—from reporting an assault.

"Yes—public not-guilty verdicts should—and hopefully will—dissuade false accusers from alleging potentially life-wrecking, fictitious assaults.

"Also, note that these feminist complainers are concerned about the chilling effect of merely acquitting the falsely accused man. Therefore, by logical extension, these feminists must be wildly adamant against lying females having the tables turned on them by being charged themselves with commission of a crime—specifically, making false statements to detectives—because, you know, actual punishment of women for wrongly accusing males of sexual misbehavior could, you know, chill women even more than mere acquittal of males and therefore cause them to not report male sex abusers.

"Hence—because some women, who already are reeling with sex-shame even though they are presumably the people who were victimized and thus did nothing wrong, might be discouraged from reporting authentic abuse—not only should an innocent male not be acquitted, but a guilty female should most definitely not be punished, despite her lies and/or exaggerations resulting in a waste of school-faculty and/or government resources, taxpayer money, and officials' time, and perhaps permanently slandering and defaming the falsely accused man who is the real victim. However, unless truly victimized females are utterly moronic, they can read and hear the publicity in media sources that inform them that there was overwhelming evidence that the male who was acquitted was innocent and that the female who was punished was guilty. Consequently, these honest, non-infantilized women would surmise that, 'I've got nothing to be ashamed about or to worry about because my report is based on the truth.'

"As an apt addendum, if our culture dropped its vitriolic and illogical anti-straight-guy bias, the opprobrium that begets the unholy trilogy of slut/whore/tramp that's sometimes attached like a deer tick to girls and women who are known to or believed to engage in even moderate promiscuity would, over time, greatly diminish or disappear altogether, with those slurs evaporating into verificatory misnomers. Along with that diminishment or disappearance would come, for us females, less shamefulness and less spiritless self-esteem and less depression and less of a feeling of sex-based worthlessness. Therefore, a conclusion that should be reached is that the blindly accepted and rarely questioned phenomenon of anti-straight-male-sexuality madness, in addition to hurting men, hurts the very people it's ostensibly designed to protect."

Kristi Lou unlocked her entangled fingers and threw her hands over both sides of her forehead, pressing her palms forcefully against her temples, and then stared at her shoes, which she noticed were frantically tapping the floorboard.

"Oh my god, Guinevere, I'm going kablooey into one of those rants when my ranting is like a locomotive! It's as if I'm a senator doing a filibuster, though, of course, I'm not that important. I love that fili-bustering scene with Jimmy Stewart in *Mr. Smith Goes to Washington*. Anyway, sometimes I write parts of my speeches on a notepad; some-times I don't. Anyhow, I'm sorry. It's all memorized—but, it's all deeply sincere. I'm … I'm very earnest with everything I'm saying. But when am I going to stop? I realize that I could be seen as intolerable when I do this, but, as usual, I have a compulsion that I .... I can't seem to get myself to just ..."

"It's OK, Kristi Lou. I know you've got to get through. So, go ahead."

"Thanks," said Kristi Lou, inhaling and exhaling audibly, then resuming her car-seat disquisition.

"Sex was imposed upon us in some unwanted way and, as everyone should know by now, sex from a male, outside of narrowly defined parameters such as romantic relationship commitments, is a thing from which we must be defended. So, she makes an accusation against him and to avoid discomforting her she gets to remain anonymous. He gets accused by her and he gets named and—since he's the villain—he suffers more than discomfort. He is often disgraced, with his family perhaps humiliated and then shunning him or never accepting him the same way again, with his ability to earn a living damaged. Yes, he's greatly responsible for bringing those consequences upon himself and his loved ones—if he's guilty. But, what if he's innocent? Does that even matter?

"Does *due process* ring a bell?"

Kristi Lou, after looking at and then quickly away from Guinevere, sat comfortably upright, placed her hands upon her knees, fixed her gaze on the dashboard, and then spiritedly—but equably—re-detonated.

"OK, revisiting the motif of surviving, how many men have been forced to survive—while enduring extreme hardship—the sometimes brutal aftermath of being falsely accused of sexually mistreating a female?"

"Yes," said Guinevere, "as you were just saying, men can suffer horrendous consequences as a result of sexual abuse allegations."

"Yes, they certainly can—and do. Yeah ... so ... if the lynch-mob feminists discover later that the targeted man was one of many countless victims who, through the years, have been falsely accused of sexual misconduct, then, well, from where they sit, that's just tough toenails.

These feminazis won't feel guilty or offer a sincere apology for torpe-doing his life. They'll be content to dismiss him as necessary collateral damage. He needed to 'take one for our team.' After all, 'he probably deserved it, anyhow, for something else he did but has heretofore gotten away with.' Yeah, maybe he was observed ogling a girl's backside for five seconds or some other shocking eye-rape objectification. So, it's time for snide sarcasm designed to be dismissive, such as 'cry me a river' or 'oh, you poor men' because, 'you know, we might need to sacrifice some innocent guys like him along the road to achieving our goal of inflicting indiscriminate punishment upon hetero males…uh, that is…er, protecting women from being afraid to report rapists. So, you know, he's a breeder-type man whose pants hide a power tool aimed at women he finds appealing. Therefore, even though he may not have committed this particular crime of which he's been accused, he's still packing guilty genitals. So, screw him; let's convict him, anyway.'

"Don't forget that 'innocent until proven guilty' has forever been the sine qua non of our entire American judiciary. The burden of proof is always supposed to be on the accuser/plaintiff. And you can bet your butt that feminist/extremist Me Too-er types are supporters of applying that injunction—as long as the accused are women. Indeed, when females are accused of an infraction, feminists will insist on its application. However, when the accuser is a female, especially if the alleged crime/misbehavior that supposedly victimized her involves sexual behavior from a straight male, then 'innocent until proven guilty' is defenestrated through the nearest window.

"All right, I think, based on long-sustained and documented evidence plus common sense, that most females through the centuries around the world who've reported being sexually assaulted have been veracious. But, that being said, there have been—and continue to be—bushels of false allegations of sexual assault perpetrated against males by vin-dictive females who have misused the age-old-but-now-on-steroids tendency of civilized cultures to be prejudicially sympathetic toward females—especially in matters of sexual assault claims—as a weapon to get back at men over things like relationship breakups, or refusal of a boss to promote her or raise her pay, or for being ignored, or for whatever reason. Fallacious sexual assault allegations against men made by unstable or unethical women are nowhere near rare. On the contrary, I believe they're much more abundant than is widely known.

"Hey ladies!" said Kristi Lou, after glancing at Guinevere and then looking down at her folded hands in her lap. "Do you have fathers, husbands, brothers, sons, grandfathers, uncles, male cousins, or boyfriends or guy friends whom you love? The fanaticized, overly emotional, to-hell-with-reason-and-fairness Me Too-ers may be coming after them—even if they're guiltless. These fanatics, some of whom may be temptingly attractive femmes fatales, and their comrades will be armed with their girl-power theme of 'Believe women because they're women!' They not only won't feel remorse if they unjustly cause at least a partial but hopefully complete demise of your beloved menfolk, but will derive intense delight in inflicting whatever ruthless harm they can inflict.

"And, if you're a woman who's fair-minded toward men, you know what these femifascists will do to you? They'll try to shame you, as a female, for not sweepingly supporting their eyes-wide-shut, auto-guilt agenda. 'Women must band together as women! Tragically, some women are not supporting women!' You must be obsequious and bow to their radicalism—or else! If you don't sycophantically hurl yourself into their boiling cauldron of She-Said-It-So-He-Did-It lunacy, you will be summarily branded as a traitor to vaginas everywhere. Such apostasy!

"But—men should not—natch—think even the remotest half-thought about closing ranks as men and supporting one another when they are mistreated in these matters. That would elicit cries of 'sexist!' In other words—and here's a genuine tragedy regarding this issue—radical Me Too-ers' ideology is not focused on supporting who's in the right, per-incident, but rather on supporting other people because they share the same type of between-the-legs body part—as long as it's the one that resembles a taco shell.

"Perhaps they could amend their outlook and proclaim that women should support other women who are truly victims of abuse while agreeing with men supporting other men who, likewise, are truly victims of abuse, including A—being abused, sometimes with tragic results, by fallacious or inflated accusations of sexual misconduct and B—who, as men, are themselves victims of unwanted female sexual aggression. And yes, while less commonplace, that aggressive conduct coming from women, as I said in my 'I Also' comments, does indeed happen.

"The goal of many members of the extremist faction within feminism and the Me Too social club seems to me to be less about protecting women and more about attacking men. It's to the point that a lot of these Me Too-ers and their kowtowing, ingratiating male enablers—when an accuser admits she lied or exculpatory evidence, such as a previously unknown video or whatever, surfaces and exonerates the man—are disappointed that no woman was actually hurt. Then they fail to be particularly angry toward the female who made a phony or inflated accusation, even though she publicly weakened the integrity of their mission. Rather than genuinely saying 'Well, I'm glad that, in this case, a woman wasn't really assaulted. But, she damaged us. And, she lied and harmed that un-guilty guy,' their attitude is more like 'Damn! We wanted to nail that penile bastard!'

"Don't automatically dismiss the female accuser's story because of no witness testimony? Agreed. Often, there are no other people, i.e., witnesses, around when and where the alleged maltreatment occurred. But," said Kristi Lou, with the intensity in her voice rising, "are you willing to reverse that formula and agree we should not automatically dismiss the accused male's story because of no witness testimony? If not, why not? Regarding witnesses who were present, yeah, I know—witnesses could testify falsely in support of the male. But, witnesses could also testify falsely in support of the female. Both males and females sometimes lie in these matters. This population of liars can include the accused, the accuser, and any witnesses. Thus, it's critical for anyone judging, particularly law enforcement and judicial officials, to perform due diligence and make informed judgments regarding the probable probity—probable probity?—of all parties who are involved in each episode, and to judge these participants primarily as people, regardless of to which sex slash gender they belong. Probable probity?

"You feminists portray sexual abuse as profoundly serious misconduct, right? Therefore, there should be profoundly serious punishment for whoever is guilty—if he's male—right? Consequently, it's a profoundly serious allegation, right? His life could be profoundly wrecked, right? But, when he complains that he's being treated unjustly, you still sarcastically say things like those I mentioned a few minutes ago—'cry me a river' and 'oh, you poor men'? Where is your magnanimity?

"And, off-topic somewhat—and yes, Guinevere, I have this harangue memorized, too—I want to say that men and women, while the same in many aspects such as both having the desire to obtain sexual fulfillment, are designed, genetically, to be significantly different in other ways, not only physically—which should be obvious—but also psychologically, emotionally, and mentally. Nature dictates that males and females of any species—especially we Homo sapiens—are, ideally, supposed to pair-bond and complement one another with their differences, filling in the other's blanks. Modern matriarchal feminism, frothing with misandry, seems to not get that—or gets it but resents it.

"We women garner more sympathy because we are the weaker sex. Radicalized, foaming-at-the-mouth feminists, envious of naturally superior male strength, are offended by that old idea. But, it's logically irrefutable. Regarding their condemnation of old-fashioned masculinity, foaminists—foaminists?—yes, foaminists—hypocritically condemn in men what they really want to reassign into women. But foaminists are rankled to the core by the fact that manliness seems much more natural residing in a man. The traditional rule that proclaims 'guys shouldn't hit girls'—without an exceptionally good reason—is predicated completely upon that concept—of we being the weaker sex.

"And, now we've got gender-jumbling in athletic competitions. Female-i-tized males, some of whom no longer need jock straps but, despite gender-bender hormone swap-outs, remain biologically male-endowed after their sex-change alterations, are competing in female sports—which they inequitably dominate by benefitting from their retained manpower.

"Oh…I realize that, regarding foaming at the mouth, that I can seem that way myself, what with all my spumescent semi-rabid ranting. So, is all mouth foam the same as far as justification and logic? No. I believe my foaming is rational because it's a response to foaminists' unjust and irrational foaming. But, yes, I'm prejudiced in favor of myself. But, anyway, so…continuing…what was I about to talk about? Oh—I know…

"Unbelievably—and pathetically—some Western militaries have timorously raised the white flag of surrender and shamefully yielded to feminist we're-just-as-powerful-as-men egoism and have agreed—policy-wise—to send women into combat on offensive missions. That's what they say. Perhaps it's just a paper-only policy. I don't know if it's actually happened, yet; maybe it has not and will not. As far as the policy goes, some congressmen and generals may've seen too many Hollywood productions. Should they let foaminist-type feminists enjoin them to become progressive sociologists? Is the primary purpose of a military to defend its homeland, including, as necessary, levying lethality pursuant to subjugating an enemy? Or, is it to turn battlefields into social-experiment laboratories in pursuit of feministic egalitarianism?

"Women soldiers should be trained to fight—defensively—meaning that they will do battle if they're attacked, cornered, and have no choice.

But, they should never, never, never be sent into the field—offensively—seeking to engage the enemy. There are bad double standards and there are good double standards. Approval of females expressing sexuality toward males while condemning as predatory those same expressions of sexuality by males toward females falls squarely into the former category. Approval of sending men but not women to the frontlines falls squarely into the latter category. They can be as butch as they want, but women, with very few exceptions, aren't nearly as physically strong or as mentally tough as men, can't handle the heavy equipment over protracted periods nearly as well as men, and simply can't fight—against an enemy's male forces—nearly as well as men. There are all sorts of other problematic matters that can arise—modesty issues in base-camp and bivouac encampments, menstrual cycles, and sex and pregnancy and romance conflicts. Primarily, though, there is the unavoidable, overall comparative weakness factor: women simply aren't capable, strength-wise, of pulling their own weight on a battlefield nearly as well as men can pull theirs—not even close—and in the process of getting themselves killed will probably get men killed as well.

"Bear in mind that, if your workplace is a battlefield, you're working not with a keyboard but with an M4 carbine. And a typical day at the office involves going out to try to kill somebody who's going to try to kill your body. Each breath could be your last. You're living within the quintessence of kill or be killed. Are women pragmatically on par with men here?

"Plus, women have often been—since the B.C. era—the spoils of war. And, speaking of sex, I think you know what that means. Not all nations produce armies infested with a surfeit of rapist soldiers, but some do. What a pitiful antilogy for feminists who want to prematurely brand a man as guilty and then demolish him because he, in a nightclub or in an office or on a campus, might've flirtatiously touched some woman's hiney-tail—which is portrayed as having inflicted severe sexual degradation upon her—but then turn around and essentially advocate handing a woman over to a foreign male army to be brutally used as a run-a-train-on-her rape toy. Why? More equality, right? I suspect that most of these foaministic feminists—both female feminists and male feminists—who advocate the deadly nonsense of dumping women into combat know that they will not be dumping themselves into combat. Yeah—in the name of equal rights, while getting men killed in battle, give women the equal right to die an equally gruesome death and the unequal right to be gang-raped in a ditch.

"Anyhow, I did some research, and it seems that, since about the 1970s, feminism has sent painfully mixed messages to men on the subject of aggression toward the other sex. Consequently, many men are, without their awareness, reared from youth with related psychological confusion. Men are ordered to slam on the brakes—note the feminist-inspired U.S. legislation titled the Violence Against Women Act—while women are encouraged, in popular culture such as movies and television and books, to step on the accelerator, with not only glorified physical fury toward men, but as having the power to routinely prevail in inter-sex fighting.

"Well, Guinevere, you know, personally, I guess I did perform kinda well against Bosco when he assaulted me, but I'm actually taller than him and I think I weigh more than him, too, and I'm—not to boast— quite an exceptional athlete. But, I don't know if I would've prevailed without Satine and Hokey helping me."

Kristi Lou, having barely altered her posture since sitting up straight several minutes earlier, shifted herself in the car seat, turning slightly to her left and then glancing at Guinevere, hoping her friend did not appear to be bored, confused, or turned off by the volcano erupting beside her. Upon seeing that Guinevere was smiling while wearing an amused but warm, understanding expression, Kristi Lou quickly commenced gazing at the dashboard and resumed her maniacally memorized oratory.

"Anyhow, consider all these tough-gal toughies in movies such as *Wonder Woman* and *Lara Croft: Tomb Raider* and *Atomic Blonde* and *La Femme Nikita*, et al., who thrash bad-guy villains in women-coopting-testosterone fantasies. Guys don't hit girls? Or, guys do hit girls? If we women are as badass as they are, why should they take it easy on us? Well, feminists, which is it? Make up your minds. Nonetheless, we females, overall, clearly are, in real-life reality…real-life reality?…we indeed are the physically weaker sex.

"But, over the course of multiple millennia and uncountable male inventions, we've proved that we're also the weaker sex in the intellectual arena of creating things of immense value and making them function, such as, to name a few things that we have not brought into creation but that men have: summit-level artistic creativity, as in the greatest works of music, painting, and literature; science; technological advancements; mathematics; physics; mechanical engineering; industrial designs; space travel—let's walk on the moon!; electricity; electrical wiring and interior lighting with lightbulbs—let's flip a switch and see the lights come on!; electronics; televisions—let's watch a ballgame on the other side of the country!; meteorological weather forecasting and tracking; radios; stereos; computers; construction of edifices from housing to skyscrapers to bridges over water; telephones—let's speak with someone who's hundreds of miles away!; air-conditioning and furnaces—let's be cool in the summer and warm in the winter!; indoor plumbing—let's flush the toilet and pee-pee goes bye-bye!; planes; trains; automobiles; paved roads; appliances such as refrigerators and stoves—let's cook a meal while in the house!; washing machines and dryers; escalators, elevators, and vertical architecture—let's stand still while we're carried up and down from one floor to the next in a building that saves ground space by rising upward into the sky!; life-extending and lifesaving medicine; mass manufacturing and distribution of clothing and food—in many non-Western countries women stand in line outside in inclement weather waiting for food…our women stroll into climate-controlled, *man*made grocery stores where food is waiting for them; highly functional and mostly ethical judicial, business, and educational systems; soundly organized monetary cash and banking structures that prevent financial- and property-ownership chaos; and countless innovations through the years and the maintenance and improvements of such things that make our daily living easier, safer, and more enjoyable.

"How many of us ladies often offer only a scantiness of gratitude—or none at all—to men for these life-enhancing things with which creative and hardworking gentlemen have benefited us? I know I'm guilty.

"OK, feminists, I'll say it outright—women are genetically predisposed to be the familial nurturing gender more so than men, as in our nature-based…here it comes…*roles*. There you go—I said it. So shoot me.

"Feminists persist in claiming that modern feminism's mission is a noble pursuit of equality for women. That claim, with its pretty-on-the-surface arguments, is specious. Women in first-world Western nations such as the United States face inequality, all right—in favor of women. Pursuing equality sounds too honorable to criticize, so they duck behind it as an unassailable lifework. But that's a smokescreen for feminist fakery whose partisans' real impetus seems to be the enjoyment of a feeling of belonging to a dramatic avocation combined with the fulfillment of releasing their jealousy-based hatred of men for being better at being men. The extremist-feminists who hate masculine and successful men wish they could be masculine and successful men. They are resentful that they can't successfully take for themselves the very traits they berate in those who harbor them naturally. Rad-fems condemn in men the same characteristics—aggression, power, dominance, achievement, confidence, leadership—they covet the most but functionalize the least.

"Sadly, the lioness's share of modern extremist feminism seems to be jam-packed with vicious women who marinate themselves in Victim Mentality Disorder. You can find many of them woofing on YouTube. And, this unrecognized or denied VMD pathology, when combined with envy-based vitriol toward men as a class, leads these women into a state of seething misandry and often, I believe, self-inflicted personal misery. Nobody does VMD better than an extremist-feminist.

"Femi-fascism is singularly the most destructive phenomenon ever unleashed upon female/male relationships. Maybe I'm a conspiracy theorist. So? Are there conspiracies? Yes. Gabillions of theories about conspiratorial machinations—about all sorts of disparate subjects—have been proved valid. Consider the trajectory of radical feminism, which has moved steadily toward blatant anti-maleism. Perhaps around a century ago there were plotters foisting a covert subversion into our societies by machinating to sow seeds of distrust and animus between the two sexes to pit us, men versus women, against each other to destabilize and weaken our societal stability from within ... a type of Marxist cabal, a communist plot designed to stir nocuous strife and unreel over the course of generations. Boom! I'm a nutcase. Ooh, I just *must* adjust my tinfoil hat.

"We 21st-century women residing in places such as America, Australia, Canada, New Zealand and the countries of Europe—Western countries within the East-West dichotomy of cultural hemispheres—are privileged to be able to live our lives in societies that offer us the highest levels of respect, protection, outright legislated favoritism, and opportunities for female happiness found anytime or anywhere in Earth's history. No, we don't reside in Utopia-ville, but, if Ms. Extremist-Feminist has her way, we may wind up living under a gynarchy and wallowing in Dystopia-ville within a half-century or so. Why do the masses of female immigrants entering our Western countries dwarf the trickle of female emigrants leaving our Western countries? Most cultural and law-enforced discrimination is not against us; it is for us. Try a scrumptious slice of the 97-percent-of-alimony American pie! Overall, we women in the West are not victims of our mostly benevolent patriarchy; we are protected, coddled, and often coshered by it. Without it, we'd probably be awakening every morning in lean-to hovels and peeing in outhouses.

"As a group of people, we pampered ladies, comparatively and historically speaking, have very little to rationally carp, niggle, and bitch about. So, some among us should stop carping, niggling, and bitching.

"There are two opposing fems, with different ends. The fem-inine is not anti-men, but the fem-inist wants to do them in. Feminist is antithetical to feminine. Feminism is the enemy of femininity.

"OK, Guinevere, after that off-the-rails digression, I'm about to redirect my lunatic self back to my rant about my original topic—accusations by females of male sexual impropriety and the, uh, the importance of responding reasonably. OK … OK, just a moment, please … OK."

Kristi Lou inhaled and exhaled deeply. She cleared her throat. She glanced at her living room window. Observing that Mr. Dooflotcher had departed from the back of the sofa to sploot somewhere else, she looked at the calmly attentive Guinevere and resumed her tirade.

"What if, A—he didn't do it? Or, B—he did it but it's not—or shouldn't be—a big deal, as defined by her not being hurt in any serious way plus, when comparable conduct is directed toward virtually any male, he doesn't protest, doesn't become hysterical, or doesn't claim victim status at all? In these cases, the male is the victim—of a false or grossly unfair and potentially damning allegation—and the female is the perp. Can you put the toothpaste back into the tube? His name is out there in public perpetuity as associated with this slanderous assertion—a damnable ipse dixit—and the impugning of his reputation is amplified since the type of bad behavior of which he is accused is lascivious and thus shame-worthy. That's because it's drenched with none other than you-know-what: sex.

"And, even if he's exonerated from all formal charges or accusations, there may always be people, of whom some could affect his life, who will doubt his inculpability. Of course, there's one primary reason that name-dropping by the media is so lopsided in favor of accusers of sex misdoings as opposed to those who are accused, and it has a little something to do with gender favoritism—the cultural mantra that, typically, all female participants in non-romantic heterosexual sexual episodes are, on some level, always victims of male sex. And that attitudinal inclination is combined with the reality that close to 100 percent of alleged and/or actual sex misbehavior is reported by females casting themselves as the victims and males as the perpetrators. If those roles were reversed, even for a short period, I think the feminism-centric media would want to stop IDing people who are accused until substantial evidence was accrued, but would feel inclined to ID the accuser right away. After all, the media would aver, the accused, if she's guilty, is the person who misbehaved and should be ashamed and therefore stands to suffer possible loss of employment opportunities, ridicule and shame, and thus she has the most to lose and be embarrassed about. Concomitantly, if these accusers are lying, then she's the real victim … right?

"In regard to benefitting from power in locations such as the workplace or on a college campus, feminists want to emphasize power in different ways, with the male cast as the heavy—invariably. The man, as in a boss or professor, is in charge so, yeah, feminists have to concede that he has bossman power. But, they emphasize, he abuses that power when he exhibits any kind of sexuality at all toward a less powerful female so his power is corrupt and must be weakened or— even better—eliminated. In the subtly disguised power-versus-power game that some feminist types like to trickily play, the subordinate female, by exercising her own power—her sensuality power—and deceptively luring him into some type of sexual display and then later revealing his provoked-by-her indiscretion to his politically correct, anti-straight-male-sex superiors while knowing her culpability will go un-reprimanded, scores a game-ending touchdown and a grand triumph: he's fired, jailed, humiliated, loses his pension and/or his family or he suffers other such really wonderful he-must-pay-for-having-a-stim-ulated-sex-stick retribution.

"The girl or woman, being younger and/or subordinate in the pecking order hierarchy at school and/or work, is in a position of comparative weakness, but feminists will deemphasize that weakness—as I was saying a few minutes ago about recrimination against professors—because feminists don't ever wish to show females as weak, even though that's exactly what they're strategically doing and promoting to create his image as a power abuser; they instead recast her weakness as 'vulnerability' as they mask her weakness and accentuate his power, but portray his power as tainted and thus his power is of a vile quality and it—and he himself—must be punished and sterilized. When he is brought down, even if—sometimes especially if—she manipulated the situation and him via her Eve-in-the-Garden-of-Eden enticements, they cruelly celebrate her victory and his demise. They want money as well as punishment. 'Pay me!' However, if they can't finagle any subtle sex-payoff, they'll settle for his head but hopefully his penis on a pole. You can almost hear them cheering 'Another dick bites the dust! Hooray!'

"So, you see, feminist selectively condemn one power but laud the other. When a male manager seems to use his power of higher rank to try to get sex from a subordinate female employee, his power is villainous. But, when a sexy subordinate female employee seems to use her power of curves and feminine wiles to try to flirt, entice, or seduce her way to job advancement—or to get him to try to get sex from her so she can scream 'Sexual harassment! Pay me!'—her power is valiant. She's a power user. He's a power abuser. These feminists and their cronies might describe her sly, scheming utilization of her own power with adjectives such as shrewd or crafty or resourceful or gutsy.

"Furthermore, when it comes to office hanky-panky in the form of subordinate-rank women getting bawdy with bosses, many women, since time immemorial, have felt—especially if the man is at least fairly good-looking—that power held by a male is aphrodisiacal. So, sometimes a woman uses her seductive powers to cajole her boss because she's attracted to him. She's not trying to catch him in a web to harm him and benefit herself; she just likes him. And then some type of sex transpires. It's almost like hypergamy minus the marriage. In my opinion, regardless of any age difference or who gets it going by initiating the fling—unless the woman is willfully deceived or she's obviously mentally handicapped—this truthful truism is truly true: It ain't sexual mistreatment if you like it, too!

"Actually, I think that, were I working in an office, I might erect one of those deliciously anti-PC signs at my workstation announcing that: 'Sexual harassment will not be tolerated. Rather, it will be graded!'

"Also, consider the woman who files a sexual harassment claim even though she's worked for that employer for about a full year—or even longer—*after* she began receiving sex-themed behavior that she now declares has been intolerable. But she stayed in the exact place where she had to continue tolerating it. If she starts seeing sexual conduct of which she strongly disapproves and it's so rampant in the environment, why not—since she presumably hasn't been kidnapped and enslaved and forced into indentured thralldom—just quit and go work somewhere else? Frequently, the answer is, of course, that she's foxily building a case for having interminably endured enough severe penis-inspired abuse to the point whereby she finally feels her cry-foul portfolio is fattened with ample grab-ass anecdotes and he-called-me-sexy episodes sufficient to strike hammer-hard with a complaint or lawsuit that will maximize her payoff. 'I put up with this dehumanizing debasement for soooo long! I've been objectified! I've been thought-raped! Pay me!'

"The longer she stays the more harassment she has a chance to receive and report to HR or to a judge in a courtroom. Thus, ideally, the worse is the man's punishment and the greater is the woman's reward. On the other hand, thinking logically, the longer she willingly remains in an atmosphere that is supposedly so bad, so oppressive, and so debasing against her humanity, the question arises: How bad can it be? Evidently, it's not so bad as to impede her drawn-out case building. Cha-ching.

"Finally, although I'm critical of modern male-hating feminists because of their mistreatment of men, I acknowledge these feminists can have good qualities as people. And, when I'm around them, I'm usually not directly confrontational toward them in conversation. I make my speeches to a general audience in which they may or may not be present, but I don't normally say rough, anti-feminists things directly to them, as a matter of courtesy and civility. Unless incensed by them to *my* face, I don't say my anti-feminist rants in *their* faces. It's just that, with feminists, I much prefer what I consider to be the ones who are more temperate and reasonable.

"All right, Guinevere, please summarize me."

"So," summarized Guinevere, "my compendium of you and your dissenting outlook is that, apart from being quasi-insane, one of the major themes during the waking moments of your current lifecycle combines the view that males should not be vilified, directly or indirectly, for being physically attracted to females, with the precept that sex, overall, should not be viewed hysterically and as a bad thing, and that we should stop—other than outright sexual abuse—seeing sex as something of which females are victims and of which males are perpetrators," surmised Guinevere.

"Yes, that's an accurate recapitulation."

"Thank you," said Guinevere. "I realize, as do you, that it's beneficial to our beliefs to have them intelligently contravened sometimes so we can defend them successfully or we can see them defeated and then improve our intellect by dropping or adjusting our beliefs. Right? Or…but, if we prevail in the argument, then we protect our currently held concepts by preserving the beliefs we already have because we've seen that our status quo beliefs about whatever subject are superior to the challenging beliefs. And we see that changing would be a negative change. But, well, I can't offer any challenge to your beliefs about sex because, in truth, I basically believe the same things you believe."

"Well, I'm relieved that you agree with me, Guinevere. Being agreed with by someone like you makes me feel as if I just might be right. Or, at the very least, it makes me feel that I maybe make some sense."

"You make plenty of sense. You always have."

"Thanks. I do believe sex is one of the leading causes of life," averred Kristi Lou with devout unpretentiousness.

"That premise seems plausible," agreed Guinevere, with an elvish smile.

"Oh, thanks."

"That reminds me," added Guinevere, "of what this guy I was dating a couple of years ago said when we were talking about legalizing marijuana, which we both favored. He was being totally serious for a few seconds while he thought about the widespread availability of cannabis. And then, speaking rather profoundly, he said: 'It's common where it grows.'

"We looked at each other. I laughed at him. Then, he laughed at himself."

"That has some deepness to it," said Kristi Lou, sans any sarcasm. "Sometimes we think too much about something and then what should've been clear all along sneaks up on us and just for a moment it seems like a stunning unraveling of a mystery."

"I know," said Guinevere. "That's a remarkable phenomenon. There are times when it's useful to state the obvious or hear it stated to us; it reels us back in from fool-yourself thinking. We're over-analyzing water and then surprise ourselves when we realize that we just said, sincerely, that 'water is wet.' And then it hits us that we dug so deep beyond our ability to comprehend that we got lost and had to be jolted back to the basics. Sometimes we need to declutter our brains."

"Yeah," said Kristi Lou. "I know my brain could use some decluttering. Or defragmenting. I confuse myself when my obsessive thinking causes me to have too many thoughts too fast and too close together and I wind up sounding like a dolt by fervently proclaiming some conclusion—as if I've brilliantly cracked the code to some stringently guarded omertà—such as one day a few years ago when I earnestly blubbered to someone, 'you'll be less heavy if you lose more weight.'

"And there was this time when I was a senior in high school in Little Rock and I saw a distant uncle I hadn't seen since I was nine years old and he had become partially bald and gotten chubby and I said to Mom that 'Uncle Chuck has gotten older with age.'"

"Or when you commented a couple of minutes ago about sex contributing to causing life."

"Yeah, that one, too. Thanks."

"My pleasure."

"Guinevere, a puzzling thought just catapulted into my cranium. Although, I'm well-acclimated to my own obsessive ranting, how did I manage to concentrate on delivering to you my memorized pro-male-sexuality rant so soon after witnessing firsthand your, uh, your shock-the-senses, car-combat bedlam? It was pure pandemonium like I'd never seen or even imagined. How could I…how… how did I, you know, how did I concentrate enough to, well, block out all of that craziness and talk as if it hadn't happened? I mean, shouldn't I have been—and Davey, too, have been—in a state of shock so that…so that I couldn't just, just carry on normally like I…"

"The word for that phenomenon is compartmentalize. That's what you did. Also, your obsessions are so force-of-nature impregnable that totally quashing them for too long is nigh on impossible."

"Oh. Yeah. Compartmentalization. OK."

47

"**hey, kristi lou …**"

"Hey, Guinevere."

"OK, well, I wasn't quite finished with what I was going to say after 'Hey, Kristi Lou,' but hey…"

"Hey, I know. I'm just feeling sorta carefree right now and when that happens I sometimes get silly…or sillier … and talk sillily … which BTW, is a real adverb."

"Your silliness is perfectly perfected perfection," assured Guinevere. "Anyhow, instead of sitting here in the car in front of your apartment, may we ride around some more? That is, if you don't need to go and do something, we can just, well, have a change of scenery."

"Sure, that'll be fine. Mr. Dooflotcher got up a few minutes ago while we were yakking and left his observational tower on the sofa, so he's not obsessing at the window anymore about watching for me to step inside; he's obsessing somewhere else. But, he'll be all right while he's obsessing 'cause he knows I will always come back to him."

"OK, then let's just go…wherever. It's your town; maybe we can hang out awhile in some abandoned area."

"Abandoned? Why abandoned?"

"Well," replied Guinevere, "Abandoned just feels right to me, for now, but not in a woeful way."

"OK, then. We won't have trouble finding abandoned places in Detroit, especially around here in the Drollman community."

Guinevere, with classical music still oozing pleasantly from the indefectible speaker system, drove the Bad Car about two miles from Kristi Lou's apartment complex. She parked on a hard-dirt lot coated unevenly with scattered gravel and nestled within a cluster of three- and four-story deserted edifices.

"My goodness," said Kristi Lou, "I thought I knew my way completely around here, but I don't know that I know this place. It sure looks abandoned, though."

The girls communed lightheartedly, zigzagging amongst a potpourri of disparate topics, such as philosophical perspectives regarding politics, social issues, what matters in life, and then on to opining about lighter-but-still-important matters such as TV programs they liked and disliked and about fashion and celebrities and music and lipstick colors and flavors of soda and chewing gum.

Guinevere and Kristi Lou easily reached a concurrence that scenes in movies and TV sitcoms typically presented inaccurate—so they hoped—and gross-looking portrayals of people who've just finished brushing their teeth by showing the actors expectorating a mucky mix of spittle and toothpaste without rinsing the yuckiness down the drain with faucet water. "Who leaves all that gunk and mire to dry in the sink?" asked an incredulous Kristi Lou.

After confirming they both unashamedly enjoyed reality shows and laughing about the travails of one particular contestant whom they agreed was arrogant and obnoxious, they simultaneously sighed with a gush of satisfaction from deep in their paunches. They became aware at the same instant that they both appreciated their mutually shared laughter; they felt good about the realization of the appreciation.

With their minds refreshingly empty, they stared straight ahead through the windshield for about five seconds.

Guinevere checked the dashboard clock.

"Hey, it's 4:30. Do you want to get something to eat?"

"No. I'm not hungry. But, if I was, since it's late for lunch but early for dinner, we could scoot over to a local hashery I know for a low-cost quickie lundinn**cher**. As you just heard, that's pronounced with the last syllable punched, sorta in honor of Francois, though I haven't used my syllable-salad word on him, yet. So, you know, if we can have brunch, when it's late for breakfast but early for lunch, I figure we can have lundinn**cher**. OK? Well, anyhoo, I'd rather just keep talking with you, that is, till your dad calls for you or whatever. But, even though I'm not hungry, if you're hungry, we can …

"Lundinn**cher**, huh? I'm quite sure Francois will be rose chatouillé, ha-ha. But I think **lun**dinncher or just **lun**dinnch are OK, too. Anyhow, no, I'm not hungry, either. So, have you decided whether you're going to work tonight?"

"Well, la-dee-da, Guinevere, you're still fluently trilingual with English, French, and Spanish, aren't you?" asked Kristi Lou, with cordial sarcasm.

"Yes. Oui. Si."

"You are just too polyglottally cool. Polyglottally? Yes, polyglottally. But, yes, when I tell Francois about my French-ish, portman**teau**-word tribute to him, he'll likely be tickled pink. But, no, I have not yet made my decision as to going in or not going in to Secrets. I just don't know, but … anyway, I was thinking …"

"Was that painful?"

"Was what painful? Oh—thinking. No, it wasn't too painful, but it's sometimes an exercise in futility."

"No it isn't. As you know, I was kidding. So, what was your painless thinking about?"

"Well, it's just that … uh, it's that … I know you want to be very aggressive toward these guys, and I know there are all sorts of veritable vindications, uh, but…doesn't what you're doing have a level of, well, ruthlessness to it? I mean, uh, it's…it seems so…"

Kristi Lou's voice trailed off into silence. She looked down at her green summer dress as she fearfully sought to acquire any truth-based, allaying reasons that would enable her to conscientiously avert seeing Guinevere and Pete as sadists.

Guinevere, as she prepared to answer Kristi Lou's inquiry, grabbed a pendant from a compartment in the center of the dash and pinned her shoulder-length brown hair into a ponytail.

"Yes, Kristi Lou, we are indeed rather ruthless. I said earlier that we're sorta doing God's work. So far, it's working quite ruthlessly well. We're on a dedicated mission—maybe not directly from God but perhaps from the deity of deterrence and unapologetic revenge."

"Well, uh, all this extreme harshness coming from an otherwise very nice you is just—it just seems incongruous, but I know why you're doing it and there's justification for it. It's just kinda hard for me to…I don't know, but it's OK, though, 'cause I can get used to it…somewhat."

Guinevere switched off the classical music and then twisted a knob that turned her driver's seat to the right while folding and then submerging the entire center console, enabling her to sit directly facing Kristi Lou.

"I want you to realize, Kristi Lou, that I care deeply what you think of me. Please try to direct your focus less on the harshness part and more on the justification part."

"I will. I absolutely will," said Kristi Lou as she bumped her knee on the door handle.

"Ouch."

"Long legs—still causing botheration," cordially chided Guinevere, smiling daintily.

"But, as you know, I like them, now."

"Yes, you overcame the lengthy-legs phobia that had infixed hellish adolescent self-rejection in your blonde head. I wish I had such a long-leggy problem. So do most other girls throughout Earth. As I've been saying, I recall assuring you of that reality back in the seventh grade."

"Yes, and I remember everything."

"Anyway, Dad will submit a report of this activity to the police and the D.A."

"The D.A.?"

"Yeah, the district attorney here is …"

"… Susanna Willis," said Kristi Lou.

"Right. You know her? Or you know of her? Oh, were you, uh, picked up for your work activities and perhaps she prosecuted you? No, I don't think so. D.A.s typically don't get into prosecution of prosti …"

"… unless it's time for reelection or some other political motivation," chimed in Pete.

"Dad? Have you been listening in the whole time?"

"Define 'whole time.'"

"Dad …"

"No, I've heard merely a brief snippet of your conversation—maybe about 40 or 50 seconds' worth."

"That's too much."

"Get over it. You left your send feature on, on the CB."

"Oh, so I did," admitted Guinevere as she turned her seat back around so it was toward the windshield and directed the center console to reemerge.

"All right, Dad, I see you're in the Caravan at the hotel. So, what's going on?"

"I'm just hanging out right now. Is that OK with you?"

"I suppose so."

"Thanks, my dear. So, Christine Jean, you were saying you know the local D.A.?"

"Dad, you're teasing, again, I know. But, for the umpteenth time and the unofficial record, her name remains Kristi Lou."

"Sorry. I may've simply forgotten it. As you know, I have no sense of humor and I never tease."

"It's OK," said Kristi Lou, giggling. She then looked toward the dashboard, looking for the embedded microphone to ensure she was audibly directing her reply to Pete, but she couldn't find it and realized she'd never seen it. She then recalled that there had been no problems heretofore with Pete hearing her or Guinevere, so she just spoke.

"But, about Susanna Willis, yes, I know her, or, I should say I know about her. But, no, it's not from being prosecuted for my illegal work activities. This man from her D.A.'s office called me with a bunch of questions, so I was involved in providing testimony against Bosco Mason. He didn't have me come in; he just questioned me over the phone. Anyhow, Guinevere and I were talking about Bosco earlier. So, you must know about Bosco, obviously. One of your cars—the van, actually—got him."

"Sure, I remember Bosco—from about a week or so ago, or whenever it was," replied Pete. "Yeah, the Caravan got him, outside the gym. We dumped him off at what we knew was the chop shop he worked out of—just to screw with them at first, but to also send them a message that they were going to get shut down, which they were. Everybody there was arrested. They're all still in jail. As I said before, car crimes in this part of Detroit have dropped off the charts. We like that—a lot."

"I know about all that," replied Kristi Lou. "Guinevere told me."

"Yeah, but you have to be careful about believing anything that that Guinevere girl says. She's a bit shady; she might've had a shaky upbringing with, you know, poor parental influence."

"I'll second that motion," agreed Guinevere.

"That's funny," said Kristi Lou. "Her parents must've done something right 'cause Guinevere has more integrity than just about anybody I've ever known."

"Yeah, I suppose Guinevere's kinda all right."

"Thanks, Dad."

"Sure. I thought I'd toss you a breadcrumb of praise. Anyway, I need to cut out and check on a few things. Back at you later."

"OK, Dad."

"That was great—you and your dad jabbing at each other, but good-naturedly."

"Yeah, he expects me to retaliate. We have fun."

"So," said Kristi Lou as she looked through the side window and then turned toward Guinevere, "I have a few additional questions. I wanna hear you talk about these things some more. All right? How many more places are you going to go to, to get car criminals? I mean, is this what you're going to keep doing with your life for the foreseeable future? And what about your mom? How is she? What does she think of all this? Will I see you again?"

"Do you think you could cram some more questions together? Those weren't quite enough."

"I know. As we've noted, I'm rather capable of asking multiple questions when they flood my mind. Sorry."

"That's OK. And you know I was just joking. Joking before. Joking now."

"Yes, I know. You keep reminding me about that—about how you're 'just joking.'" Kristi Lou smiled and then tittered a quick laugh.

The third voice rejoined the mix.

"All right, I'm just checking in again," said Mr. Lindsay. "I'll leave it with you two; I'm sure you've got some more catching up to do now that we can relax a bit. Guinevere, I'm going into my hotel room."

The CB spat a little static which surprised Kristi Lou, as all other audio in the grandiloquent car was crème de la crème.

"OK, Dad, I'll see you there in a little while."

"Bye. It was nice meeting you—or re-meeting you," said Kristi Lou as she rushed in her farewell before Pete could disconnect.

"Same here, Krystal Lou."

"Dad…"

"Krystal Who?"

"Dad…"

"OK. Kristi Lou."

"I kinda think you've known my name all along."

"Maybe. Bye-bye Misty Goo. See you later."

"Ha-ha. I hope so. Bye."

"Oh wait—hold on, Dad. I just had a thought."

"That's impressive, sweetheart."

"Yes, I know. Thank you. I think I think maybe this is a good time for that uh, that reunion thing we talked about. Can you, you know, get that going?"

"You think you think?"

"OK, Mr. Smarty-Pants," rejoined Guinevere with a snarky but convivial smile, noted by Kristi Lou. "I stumbled with the delivery of my words. Forgive me."

"I'll consider it. But, can I get that going? Sure, I can get that going. I can take care of that fast. I took our subject to the coffee shop a few minutes before I contacted you about that assignment you just finished, protecting those old folks' cars. It's just down the road a short ways. We'll be there soon. Keep Krystal Blue company."

"OK Dad. See you soon."

Guinevere and Pete disconnected.

"Parents," said Guinevere as she laughed a little and looked at Kristi Lou.

"I think it's funny—all your frantic questions that spilled from your face just before Dad interceded with his name-butchering gobbledygook. All right, in no particular order, I'll answer your questions. If I forget any of them, remind me."

"OK. I will. But, what was that about a reunion? What reunion?"

"Let me answer your previous questions first. Anyhow, I told you about how I learned you were here from the happenchance conversation with David Darnell's mom and your mom and then David told me when I bumped into him at the movie theater."

"Yeah."

"So, my grandmother—my dad's mother—as I told you, was attacked in Conyers. After Dad got his revenge thing going full force in his mind, we decided to start, as I told you, at home, in Little Rock."

"Yeah, you told me."

"So, we did Little Rock. Now, we're doing Detroit. After we leave here, we'll do Atlanta—as I told you a little while ago outside your apartment when you asked about our next destination. Atlanta starts in September."

"Yeah, but you told me you'd elaborate later as to why. So elaborate. Why Atlanta?"

"Because, when Dad was a Ramblin' Wreck from Georgia Tech—actually, he still is and says he always will be—he saw or heard about car thieves and vandals on campus and around Atlanta. And, well, because he went so long to college there, it's like one of his homes, no matter how far away he might live. And we'all lived in Atlanta for about two years before moving back to Little Rock. And, of course, an obvious aspect is that Atlanta is close to Conyers, where his mother was almost killed by carjackers. So, he wants to fight the bad guys in and around his college town as well as in his hometown, Conyers."

"Oh, I see. Well, sure, that makes sense."

"After Atlanta, we'll be heading out west, where there are cities that are hotbeds for automobile thievery. In fact, every jurisdiction in the current top ten for per capita car theft is located in a Western state, with California, by far, the overall leader for this dubious distinction.

"But we're going to Albuquerque, New Mexico first. Albuquerque just recently skyrocketed to number 1 in America for car thefts as a per capita percentage of the city's population. In 2016, Los Angeles saw about 61,000 car grabs, way more than Albuquerque's 10,000. But, to accurately assess the problem, you have to look at the stats on a per capita basis. Greater L.A. metro has about 13,000 million residents compared to about 900,000 folks living in the Albuquerque area. So, per-capita-wise and compared to the national average, the subpopulation of car-theft douchebags residing in Albuquerque is off the reservation.

"After Albuquerque, we're going to Bakersfield to start a California carnage tour against car criminals. We'll be out there—New Mexico and particularly California—awhile, that is, if law enforcement doesn't make us stop. But, before we go westward, we'll be home in Arkansas for a breather—maybe several weeks—after we do Atlanta."

"Well, busy you'll be 'cause that's quite an itinerary you have there. It's all extremely mind-boggling."

"Yes, I know it is. Anyway, you asked about my mother. Yes, she's OK with what her ex-husband and her daughter are doing; she's very supportive—conditional upon Dad not overexposing me to danger, plus we have to take extended and fairly frequent time-off periods. We'll be checking back in with her on the phone in a little while."

"I'm glad she's onboard with what you're doing."

"Yeah, her endorsement is imperative. OK, it's almost 5:00. Have you still not decided whether you're going to work tonight? Do you know, yet, what you're going to do?"

Kristi Lou's brain had to check in with itself.

"OK, lemme contemplate. It's August 18, Saturday. Big Sam, for his own personal, unstated-to-me reasons, is quite lenient about girls working or not on Saturdays. But, I always work on Saturdays. But, am I going to work this particular Saturday, this evening? Hmm…yes. I mean no. Uh, that's yes, that I still haven't decided, and so it's no, that I don't know. What did I just say? Golly, that was even confusing to me and I'm the one who said it. Translation: I haven't quite made up my mind, but I'm sorta leaning against it. So, I probably won't work tonight, but I might. I don't know. Wow … I'm mixed up."

"Did you just say 'golly'?"

"Well, I … yes, I did. Sometimes, I'll say good golly, too. Rochelle at Secrets nails me when I say golly—like I'm a Buffy-style white girl … which I suppose I am."

"That's fine; it sounds natural coming from you."

"Of course it does."

Guinevere touched a touchscreen embedded in the windshield point-blank in front of her, and her seat and Kristi Lou's passenger seat reclined back seven inches while a completely disguised sunroof simultaneously opened above. "Whoa," Kristi Lou calmly exclaimed. "This is nice; it's kinda like I've been beam-me-up-Scotty-ied to the beach."

"Like you've been what-ed to the beach?" queried Guinevere.

"It's a Star Trek reference. You know—haven't you ever seen Star Trek? Scotty beams crew members down from the Enterprise to some other place such as another planet that maybe they're hovering nearby to, and then he beams them back up and onto the spaceship when they're done with their exploration or whatever. I like to watch Star Trek reruns."

"Well, of course you do. You would."

"Yes, I would. And I do."

"Let's look at clouds, Kristi Lou."

"OK. I love looking at floating clouds. I like to see faces and different things in them. These ones look like giant cotton-candy balls at the county fair in Arkansas."

Guinevere tilted her and Kristi Lou's seats back another two inches.

Both friends gazed serenely at several thick, low-hanging cumulus clouds scudding gracefully under the vast sapphire expanse above their eyes, staring silently for about seven minutes.

48

GUINEVERE LOOKED OVER AT KRISTI LOU AND SPOKE SO SOFT-
ly that her voice seemed to extend the pleasant silence while ending it.

"There is one more person of interest to you, though, about whom
you did not ask in your flurry of questions a little while ago—though the
name did come up in one of our earlier conversations," said Guinevere,
as she sat up and brushed her fingertip across the windshield to raise
her and Kristi Lou's seatbacks to their standard positions.

"Oh, really? Who's that?"

"I said I knew you were in Detroit, right? Well, since Dad and I
were coming here anyway to throttle car punks, I thought I might try
to arrange something—kind of a way for you to tie up some loose ends
from your yesteryear, though you obviously have gotten way over the
hump—well, in a manner of speaking."

"Huh? Oh—I see what you mean—humping. Ha-ha! Chortle chortle
and yet another chortle. That's funny—you're wickedly clever."

"Yes, thank you. I'm just teasing, affably, of course."

"Of course. And you keep reassuring me of the good-naturedness
of your zappers, implying that I need that reassurance."

"For now, you do."

"Yeah, I suppose I kinda do."

"Anyhow, there's someone here to whom you shall be reintroduced. You won't believe it. But I think it'll work out just fine for you two to talk."

"What? What are you talking about? Are you saying you actually brought someone I used to know here, to Detroit, to see me?"

"Yep."

"You're kidding."

"Nope."

"Oh my goodness. But, all right. Wow. That's cool. Now you've got me really wondering. Umm, OK, who is it? Where? Where is she or he? When is this happening? Or…I don't know, but are you…what or who?"

"Knowledge of those things is about to penetrate your awareness. Well, I could've refrained from making any reference to penetration, but…"

"Chortle again! You just can't resist these crafty little quips. OK, where is…all right, I'm ready, maybe."

"You didn't notice, but when you were chirping about Star Trek, I contacted Dad and quickly whispered to him to bring our guest on over here. Then, I neutralized your side-view mirror with an inconspicuous cloudy-ish cover—this car can do almost anything—so you couldn't see what was behind you without knowing you couldn't see what was behind you. The mirror took on barely discernible little wavy images that distorted your view just enough so you couldn't see any reflections very discernably although you didn't realize any interference was happening. And we chilled out for some cloud gazing."

"Oh yeah?"

"Check what is now your clear-view mirror."

"Oh, there's Pete in the vendetta van."

"Right."

"So, you mean, uh, when he and you were talking a few minutes ago about how 'now would be a good time for the reunion' and how he would 'take care of that fast' and he was maybe going 'down the road a short ways' to get this, uh, subject from some coffee shop to bring here and all that stuff that, uh, that he really went and did that, and came here with this individual—and I didn't see your super-van pull up behind us?"

"Uh-huh. The little out-of-way coffee shop is indeed nearby; you might not have seen it before, though, since you were surprised that you weren't familiar with this abandoned area."

"You're kinda like a spy in a movie with these super-tech cars, these spy-mobiles, of yours."

"I know," agreed Guinevere. "We're the coolest people you know."

"Nonpareil."

"Yes, we're peerless."

"But, I don't see anyone else in the van with your dad. Of course, he or she could be ducking down on the seat or in the back of the van or …"

Guinevere snapped down Kristi Lou's window, an action that took less than a second and yielded a whooshing sound.

"Oh my," said a startled Kristi Lou.

Pete moved the Caravan alongside the passenger side of the attack car, next to and about three yards away from Kristi Lou. He pushed a button to trigger the action he had preprogrammed into the van's system.

Kristi Lou gazed at a grinning Mr. Lindsay. Then, she saw two large tentacles, emanating from the minivan's undercarriage, slowly enter through an open window into the van's rear seating area. She strained her eyes and saw through the glaring sunshine that the tentacles appeared to be wrapping some object, elevated about two feet above the seat, in white rags. Next, she saw one tentacle gently lift up and out of the van a bundle of something that resembled a human shape and that was about five or so feet long, enclosed in wrap-around swaths of cloth-like material. She spotted four holes near one end, which she quickly ascertained were intended to accommodate facial orifices.

Kristi Lou watched as the parcel was raised and left dangling next to a fourth-story window in an adjacent abandoned building.

"Oh my goodness. What is that?"

The thing dangled there for about a quarter of a minute.

Kristi Lou's first impulse was that this apparition looked somewhat like a burqa.

She spoke to herself with a quick thought.

I don't think I know any Muslims, do I?

She glanced over at Guinevere, who had broken out her makeup compact case and was nonchalantly powdering her nose and checking her hair.

"Oh, I see what you're doing—acting so blasé and all. This is a game, huh?" inquired Kristi Lou.

The tentacle, with a movement so sudden that Kristi Lou was startled into a state of motionlessness with her eyelids opened wide, swept the thing down from the building within four seconds and held it aloft directly beside Kristi Lou's open window.

A muffled voice, greatly altered by fabric surrounding the thing's lowest aperture, spoke through partially separated strands of cloth. Kristi Lou immediately realized that she was unable to determine the gender of the speaker.

"Hi, Kristi Lou. Long time, no see. Of course, right now I can see you but you can't see me. So, it's still a long time for you. But I think they'll unwrap me soon and you can see me, too. You're really pretty, even prettier than back then—and I will take the liberty of saying you look very sexy, which is not a sin," said the thing, which stopped wiggling.

"Oh, well thank you," replied Kristi Lou who turned and looked at Guinevere.

"So this is someone from back, uh, when … the last time we—you and I—were together?"

"Yes. One number to think of is seven. Think seven."

"Seven? OK. Think seven what? Oh, as in seventh grade?"

"Yes."

"Well, this person is uh, not too big."

"Penetrating observation," agreed Guinevere. "Well, perhaps I should have chosen another adjective to describe your observational acumen."

"Oh, please—more penetrate-themed innuendo. If you'd thought of it, you woulda said penis-trating observation. You can't stop zinging me, even in the midst of this weirdness."

The thing wiggled again.

Kristi Lou grinned and blushed.

"Oh Guinevere, that's—in there in that bundle—that's not Mr...."

"Hello. Please excuse me. If you please, may I please be unwrapped, please?" pleaded the grumbling thing, with distorted inflections.

"Oh my goodness," exclaimed an amused but concerned Kristi Lou. "You look like a mummy on a string. Oh, I didn't mean that as an unflattering remark. I'm sorry."

She looked at Guinevere. "May we unwrap him now? He might get circulation problems or something."

Guinevere ignored Kristi Lou's request and spoke to the thing.

"I bet you know how many times you said 'please,' don't you?"

"Yes, I do. I do. I do. I do," said the thing.

"You'll be unwrapped—in four seconds."

"Oh, that's perfection," said the thing. "Four, three, two, one—I'm really ready to be undone. Other than mild claustrophobia and a bit of trouble breathing, this is really so much fun. So, may I be unraveled now, please?"

Kristi Lou looked at Guinevere and then back at her visitor, still being softly gripped by the tentacle and suspended about a foot off the ground.

"Why four seconds? Is that some kind of hint? A clue or something? Oh! OMG! Oh my god! I know who it is! At least I think I know."

The tentacle placed its package onto a dirt patch next to the car and then sucked in the calico-ish cloth, one bandage-looking sliver at a time, unfurling its detainee from the bottom up and revealing a smiling, bespectacled, freckle-laden Marsha Mellow, who, at 5'1", had lengthened by three inches since the seventh grade.

Marsha, clutching her purse against her midsection with both hands, was wearing medium-gray, high-waist, relaxed-fit, holes-above-the-knees jeans and a cornflower-blue T-shirt that matched her blue socks and blue tennis shoes. Pete had the tentacle place Marsha upright next to Kristi Lou, who, with her mouth gaping, was gazing wide-eyed through the open passenger window as her latest unforeseen reunion unfolded.

"It's me, Kristi Lou; it's Marsha Mellow. Marsha, Marsha, Marsha. Yes, I like *The Brady Bunch*. Hey, long-tall-old friend!"

Kristi Lou, before she could speak her reply, recognized her sense that Marsha's aura seemed to convey instantly that she remained as much the ingénue as she ever was, compelling Kristi Lou to contrast such apparent unworldliness with her own antithesis-of-ingénue lifestyle.

"Marsha! I see it's you! Oh my goodness! Wow, you are so very lovely! Look how good-looking you've grown up to be," gushed Kristi Lou with sincerity, cupping both hands aside her mouth as the tentacle gracefully slid back into the Caravan.

"Well, you may be exaggerating, but it's still nice to hear," said Marsha, grinning though gasping after enduring her over-the-top entrance.

"No, I'm not—there's no exaggeration at all. I mean it."

Kristi Lou and Marsha spontaneously lunged at each other through the still-open window, embracing for four seconds.

"Anyhow, how are you? It's, it's so great to see you again," said Kristi Lou, rewinding her upper body back into the car.

"Yeah, I know. It is great. Well, actually, I don't mean it's great for you to be able to see me again because that would be quite egotistical; I mean it's so great for me to be able to see you."

"Oh, that's OK. But—are you still doing 4s? Well, that is, I hope you don't mind me saying that, you know, about how you used to, well…"

Guinevere interrupted.

"She was doing 4s during our theatrical intro routine. You just caught on to that tipoff a moment ago, remember?"

"Oh, so I did."

"And she also did a *Brady Bunch* reference that enabled her to say her name four times."

"Oh, so she did."

"Yes, I'm still an OCD-4 girl. But, it's not as bad as it was," explained a giddy Marsha, continuing to catch her breath after the drama of her planned but unrehearsed aerial delivery into Kristi Lou's presence, as she stood and swayed shyly outside the passenger door.

Marsha, smiling and blushing, dipped and then lifted her eyes to look directly at Kristi Lou.

"When we were in seventh grade at Our Lady I was almost completely dominated by my OCD. But now I've got it under better control—somewhat. I still need to go to counseling. I go to my psychiatrist, but I go only once a month, now. Except, that is, when I go twice a month. Or when I go thrice a month. Or when I go four times a…OK, I go PRN—as needed."

****

Pete moved the van to the other side of the attack car, about 15 feet to the left of Guinevere, and shut off the engine.

"I'm going to take a snooze right here, with the windows up and the AC on. It's a little after 5:20. There's a decent bit of daylight left. You girls reminisce to your hearts' content. Guinevere, wake me up after an hour or thereabouts goes by."

"OK, Dad. I will. Enjoy your catnap."

****

Kristi Lou looked at Guinevere with the sincerest of expressions.

"Guinevere, may Marsha get in and sit in the backseat?"

"No. We're going to make her stand outside in the summer heat and then leave her stranded in downtown Detroit," scoffed Guinevere playfully as she unlocked the passenger-side back door. "Get in Marsha."

"Okey-doke," replied Marsha, as she entered the attack car and plopped giddily onto the same seat where Davey had cowered in dread just a little while earlier.

Kristi Lou remembered her manners. "Marsha, you can have the front seat. I should've offered it a moment ago. I'm sor…"

"No. Your legs won't fit back here nearly as well as mine. But thanks, anyhow."

"OK," said Kristi Lou as she used her left fingertips to flip hair away from over her right eyebrow and off her forehead, though a large blond tuft instantly fell back where it had been, prompting her to blow upward past her nose toward the recalcitrant plumage.

"Well," said Guinevere, who felt compelled to defend the capabilities of her dad's creation, "I could easily expand the legroom of the backseat, but the most important thing is your intended courtesy."

While Marsha arranged herself to get comfortable in the seat, Kristi Lou turned around and stared tenderly at her for several moments. Kristi Lou noticed that she billeted a mollifying feeling of being relocated into her past, which now seemed warm and soothing, including the recollections of her torturous adolescent angst.

A realization swept through her that, although she was only twenty-one, she felt displaced in the present, longing for those days when she had friends such as Guinevere and Marsha, people who housed different but still significantly similar personalities, and with whom—despite their physical shortness—she effortlessly felt a kinship, even during a period when being too tall was her worst trepidation. She commented to herself before speaking to Marsha.

I don't live in the past, but I do feel happier when I visit there often.

Kristi Lou burbled the next thoughts that surfaced in her mind, the words spilling out of her face like vetoed English peas escaping from the mouth of a highchair-bound child.

"I can't believe you're here. And Guinevere's here. And I'm here. We're all here—at the same time. How did we all get here? That is, I mean, how did we all get here together?"

Marsha waved her left forefinger at Guinevere four times and asserted an explanation.

"Guinevere made it happen. She's smart. She and her dad arranged it. Anyway, they—Guinevere and her dad—mostly Guinevere, told me about your life."

"Oh, that. My life. Well, yeah, I've got one of those … to an extent, it seems. I assume—no, make that presume—that she told you what I do and all. But, I'm about to go back to school, to college," said Kristi Lou.

"Oh, that's good. But, I'm not putting down the other things you've been doing—as long as you're happy and healthy."

Kristi Lou looked down at her fingernails, and then at Marsha.

"Oh my goodness. Thanks for that. Thank you. That, uh, that means a lot to me, really it does. That makes two old friends I've gotten back together with that don't condemn … that don't … that do accept me without holding that, you know, that … what I do … those work-activity things that I do, uh, against me, and …"

"Of course we don't hold it against you," asseverated Guinevere.

"No, we certainly don't," agreed Marsha.

"That's so meaningful to me that I just can't say how much. I … thank you."

Kristi Lou glanced over at Pete, now sleeping, and then looked back at Marsha in the backseat.

"All right. Well, I'm OK. Anyway, I'm sitting here looking at you and remembering all those times we had together back in the last part of the—the final few months of the seventh grade at Our Lady of Mercy in Little Rock. Oh my goodness, I used to worry about you and your OCD and whether you were going to—I don't know—blow up in a gooey explosion or something."

"Gross!" said Marsha.

"There was that day with you and Mr. Battle when it really got weird. You know, when you had to pee really bad and poor Mr. Battle couldn't say the right type of 'you're welcome' that you needed to hear him say. And you and Guinevere and I had such good times when we went out to the movies or to the mall or to your house or to Guinevere's house or to my house. Your parents were so nice."

"Yes. I remember all that. Of course, as you know, I learned later that some of the kids in class had made bets about whether I was going to tinkle on the floor in Mr. Battle's classroom."

"I know. I hope you knew I didn't place any bet on that," said Kristi Lou.

"I knew you didn't."

"Of course, I didn't."

"Thank you for not betting on my peeing."

Kristi Lou was about to roll off onto another desultory tangent. But, in one of those moments of quick and fortuitous perspicacity, combined with swift clarity regarding what they were in the midst of discussing about Marsha's yesteryear, Kristi Lou observed a serious expression on Marsha's face. Kristi Lou saw that Marsha tried to smile but looked scared and disappointed at the same instant. She correctly sensed that Marsha wanted to continue her lightheartedness but needed her, Kristi Lou, to erect a crossable bridge, the same passageway for which she thirsted all those years ago.

Kristi Lou and Marsha had just finished speaking about fondly remembering Marsha's trying times and about her disorder. And here it was again—Marsha's OCD requirement for the proper "you're wel-come"—but, in this instance, there was no colloquial reference to it as had been the case only seconds earlier. Rather, it was now actually manifesting, seriously, in the present, mere moments after referring to it, humorously, as having manifested eight years in the past.

Kristi Lou, wearing a calm and sensitive smile, looked down at the headrest and then at Marsha.

"You're welcome."

Marsha released an audible gush of air she had held in her diaphragm.

"Oh, that was so good. You didn't forget—after all these years, you remembered" said Marsha as she breathed another sigh of relief.

"Was that a coincidence?" Kristi Lou asked. "I mean, 'thank you' and 'you're welcome' do come up a lot between people all the time. So maybe it was only slightly coincidental. But we were just talking about it—the exact same thing, that is, that particular OCD hang-up of yours as opposed to your other specific OCD hang-ups, meaning specifically your OCD 'you're welcome' hang-up—from when it happened in seventh grade and then lo and behold it popped up in front of us right here today. In fact, what you had thanked me for that you needed me to properly say 'you're welcome' for here in this car was me saying how I didn't do something—place a bet on you—that happened as a direct result of you not getting one of those 'you're welcomes' from Mr. Battle back then. So, in other words, the exact thing we were talking about that happened eight-and-a-half years ago re-happened in the here-and-now—and it happened precisely when we were talking about that very thing that had happened in the past. And right now I'm yammering obsessively, myself, and I don't know if I'm making sense but I know what I'm trying to say. Anyway, I counted to four before I said 'You're welcome,'" said Kristi Lou, who had actually done just that.

"I know you did; I counted with you. And you made sense 'cause, as you said, it happened again here while we were talking about it happening before."

"Yeah," Kristi Lou sighed, "I still obsess, too. Yes, I do. My own mind is bewildering to me. Anyway, you said a few moments ago your OCD is not as bad, right? But…"

"Well, yeah, I still have OCD, and sometimes it's still bad, but, overall, it's less bad. But sometimes I still have these irrational fears, though, that something bad will happen to me or someone I love if I don't complete my rituals the right way. It can be such a strong compulsion, sometimes overwhelming. Sometimes I can deny the ritual and feel like not doing it won't cause any disasters but other times I'm still not sure so I give in."

"It's OK," assured Kristi Lou.

"Well, Kristi Lou," interjected Guinevere, "speaking of OCD, your analysis of your conversation with Marsha and how the same thing happened here in the present that had happened in the past right while you were talking about the past incident was very detailed and precise—in the extreme."

"I know," concurred Kristi Lou. "I've got it, too—as I was just talking about. I've got a degree of OCD. I always have. I know you obviously know that—like the tall girl thing back in the day and so on. And these days, I obsess about other things. I don't do cool rituals like Marsha, but I've still got it, some of it, definitely."

"But your OCD is way cooler than mine," reassured Marsha.

"No, it's not, Marsha. It's just the opposite. Your OCD is sorta funny. Your OCD is superior, and vastly so. My obsessiveness is just…obsessive."

"I still like your obsessions better than my obsessions," said Marsha with a defiant but cordial grin. "Do you wanna swap obsessions?"

"We better not," said Kristi Lou. "I'm not sure I could do justice to your OCD. The number 4 might get really mad at me and start screaming 'Bring back Marsha!'"

"Yeah, right," replied Marsha with a gushy smile. "But, in any event, this is really wonderful. I've been here with you only a few minutes and our conversation and our reminiscing is just rolling along—like we didn't skip a beat, as if it hasn't been eight years since we last saw each other. And there's a wee tad of difference between thirteen and twenty-one. Of course, it helps that we've exchanged those greeting cards and emails once or twice every two years or so. And we talked on the phone—what?—maybe three or four times before you left Little Rock to come up here for college."

"Yeah, that's about right," replied Kristi Lou. "But we haven't talked on the phone in about four years. How many years did I just say?"

"Four," said Marsha.

"Yeah, four. I think it's been about that long since we swapped emails, too. I'll have to check my Inbox and my Sent Items folder. I save all my old email."

"So do I," said Marsha.

"Of course," chimed in Guinevere. "You both save all your old email— no shocker there."

Kristi Lou grinned as she concurred.

"Yes, Marsha and I both have obsessions, plus I kinda like partially residing in the past—taking vacations there. We're kinda like the old two peas in a pod."

"Or in a pud—channeling Davey here," said Guinevere.

"Oh yeah, right," said Kristi Lou.

"Who's Davey," asked Marsha.

"He's this nuthead guy who comes into the nightclub where I work. Guinevere met him, and he said 'two peas in a puddle,' about me and Guinevere, when he was being zany."

"Oh. And, in addition to both of us being obsessive, we sure do look alike, too, especially our body types," offered Marsha as she reached forward with her right forefinger and gently tapped four different freckles exposed between long strands of golden hair on Kristi Lou's neck.

"Oh my goodness. You poked me four times! You're doing your rituals on me; that's pure awesomeness. I'm so honored," said Kristi Lou with a burst of laughter.

"Sorry. You have four freckles and I had a compulsory need to touch them so things would be all right for you. I wouldn't have done it, though, if I thought you'd mind."

"No, it's OK. I liked it. It felt sorta soothing, like we kinda bonded even more with an actually literal OCD exchange."

Kristi Lou leaned to her left and glimpsed at herself in the rear-view mirror.

"Did I just say 'actually literal'?"

"You sure did," answered Marsha Mellow.

"Sometimes, the things that spill off my tongue … derp-derp," said Kristi Lou. "So … but, anyway, you've obviously remained loyal to your grand ole number, 'quatro' in Spanish—the magnifical 4."

"Whether it's good or whether it's bad, I belong to the mighty tetrad."

"You belong to the what?" queried Kristi Lou. "What was that word?"

"Tetrad? I don't know that word, either," confessed Guinevere.

"Yes. It's tetrad: t-e-t-r-a-d, of Greek etymology. It's an obscure fancy-butt word for the number 4. I don't know when I started knowing it. But I *gotta* know it. Also, I like driving through intersections 'cause they're quadrivial. And, my main metal is beryllium because its atomic number is … yeah."

Guinevere, laughing lightly, looked back over her right shoulder.

"I can't recall if you told me—I think you did, though, when we were kids. But, is it God you think might cause some bad things to happen or either let them happen? Or, is there some other entity or force you feel just might exist that would cause or let these bad things happen?" inquired Guinevere.

"I believe I remember you asking me that, yeah. So, well, for some OCDers, it is indeed God; I know that from what I've heard them say in group therapy sessions for OCD people, and from what I've read.

But for me, no, it's not God. I never blame God. He's not doing it to me; it's the second thing you said."

"OK then, what other force? What kinds of bad things?" asked Kristi Lou.

"I've never been able in my whole life to identify the OCD force. I mean, I can't, I can't pinpoint who or what…I don't know. I don't. As far as the bad things that could happen, it's various possible bad things. They just jump into my mind suddenly. I rarely tell anybody the specifics, except for telling my shrink."

"Really?" said Kristi Lou. "Well, do you feel like sharing some of those specifics with Guinevere and me? Of course, you don't have to, but…"

"OK. Well, for instance, if I see someone—or just think of him, even if he's imaginary—who looks or seems threatening, I feel compelled to do, to perform, one of my protection procedures to stop something from happening like him, or maybe her, hauling off and shooting me or my loved ones or doing some horrible thing such as bombing us or running our car off the road—or causing us to feel ashamed or defeated or disgraced."

"Oh," said Kristi Lou, fascinated again. "Protection procedures? Is that what you call them, your rituals?"

"Often I do call them that, yeah."

"You could also call them ritualistic safeguards," said Guinevere.

"Yes, yeah I could. Ritualistic safeguards. I like that one. I might use it sometimes. Thanks."

"You're welcome."

Marsha resumed her self-disclosure.

"Another goblin that chases me in my mind is that sometimes I get scared of something strangling me, or, even worse, someone I love, if I don't perform my protection procedures, or my, uh, my ritualistic safeguards. Trepidation will just sweep over me. It can be terrifying. So, I have to do my protection procedures. I have to do a thing like move my shoe four times just perfectly on a line on the floor or maybe tap my teeth four times or grind them four times or whatnot, because, if I don't, I'm afraid that this image that flashes into my brain such as some person or thing choking someone in my family might come to fruition.

"Sometimes I can make myself not do it. But, when I don't, although intellectually I know that no one will get choked just because I didn't do a four-based protection procedure, I just, well … there's still that nagging—no—that burning doubt. There's that doubt. There's the doubt—the doubt that if I don't obey the compulsion then someone could get choked. Or something else awful could happen, like being humiliated or, uh—I got degraded a lot in school, called packrat and all that—those type of petrifying potentialities.

"A byname for OCD is 'the doubting disease.' And my doubts make me … I just have this feeling that I'm protecting myself or them from such terrible events. And I love them so I do the protection procedures because I couldn't bear to let them down, to allow them to be hurt."

"So," surmised Kristi Lou, "you just can't help it. You realize, from a perspective of logic, that these bad things are probably never going to happen. And, if they did happen, it wouldn't really be because you didn't properly perform your protection procedures. That is, you logically know that you can't actually control whether they do happen or they don't happen by activating your rituals. But, well, you want to cover all the bases and be on the safe side—just in case that OCD nemesis is actually, really there."

"Yes. Right. Yeah, that's right."

"I think I understand," said Kristi Lou.

"I know you do. And I want to be understood; I'm not one of those people who relish being supposedly so mysterious and who gets off on dramatically complaining that 'Oh, no one understands me!' and then secretly enjoys the idea of not being understandable."

"You're too genuine and unpretentious to be that way," said Guinevere.

"Thanks. But, there is one more important thing, an aspect of my OCD. You both know—well, if you remember from school, you know—about how I sometimes have to finish some of my routines, and ..."

"Your rituals," said Kristi Lou.

"Yes, my rituals—in a set period of time, like within four-point-whatever seconds. Well, other times—lots of times, actually, I have a similar but different type of challenge. My OCD will tell me that I have to complete one thing—a thing that suddenly turns into a ritual—before this other thing happens—or else. In other words, I don't have to finish it perfectly before a certain time expires; rather, I have to finish it perfectly before another particular thing occurs. It's sorta hard to explain, but ... well, like I might be walking or typing, and then the message flashes into my mind that I have to walk this or that many steps or to the edge of a marking or a crack on the floor or sidewalk, or I have to type this or that many letters—with no mistakes—before that person over there who's about to sit in a chair finishes seating himself—or before that approaching car out on the road gets by an imaginary line I see extending out from the window I'm looking through, or ..."

"It's like a roundabout trap that encircles you, and you want to find the egress," said Kristi Lou.

"Yes. Some of my rituals, just like back in school, are not so distressing and some are even amusing to me. But others ... others are disturbing—and they hurt me so very much. It's like what you just said—I feel trapped. I want to say 'No!' and quit the rituals that are hurtful. And sometimes I can. But ... OK ... wait. Here's another one. Often—no, make that almost every time—when I brush my teeth, which I do four times per day, of course, I uh, I have to spit just the correct way or just the correct number of times—usually a variation on four times—into the area of the sink to the right of the metal stopper to protect my loved ones—such as parents, grandparents, aunts, uncles, cousins, or friends—who have conservative and Republican-type political leanings, and then I have to spit just the correct way or correct number of times to the left of the stopper to protect my more liberal and Democrat-type loved ones. So, my right-wingers are associated with the right area of the sink and my left-wingers are associated with the left area of the sink.

"Often I have to make my accurate spits before I hear an extraneous sound from outside the bathroom. Like, uh, if I have guests at my apartment—I don't have any roommates—and I overhear someone speak on the other side of the door or whatever sound, then I have to start over.

"I know it's absurd; technically, I know that. And it sounds just goofy when I describe it to myself, and even more so when I tell someone else—which means my shrink and the two of you. I haven't told Mom—even though she's also, as you know, an OCDer—about my mandatory spits.

"So…but…so, I have to do my proper spits. I *have* to do them, and, well, it's…it's not so funny for me 'cause sometimes this is, well, it's actually debilitating. It's painful when I have those times when I just can't break away from the sink 'cause I'm scared that since I haven't spat with adequately accurate aim or exactly the required number of times, then these harmful things—sometimes horrible things—that flash through my mind that my OCD master says might happen to my loved ones if I don't spit properly…that they might, might, you know, just really might come true.

"I can't let anything hurt my loved ones 'cause I love them. So, I'm stuck leaning over the sink. And I can't…I can't get away. Sometimes I'm at the sink so long that, uh, that what started as a near-full hot water tank when I began brushing drains out, and the sink water goes cold. And why don't I just run only cold water? Because my OCD master tells me I have to mix in hot water or my protection procedures will be neutered or spayed and won't produce any protection. And yes, my protection procedures are male or female.

"And sometimes when I lean forward too long my back or my neck or both hurt so awfully that I cry. And when I look up at myself in the big bathroom mirror, which I try to not do, I see myself enslaved for 15 minutes, 30 minutes, 60 minutes hysterically spitting. And, I just start crying 'cause I look like such a pitiful loser.

"So, it's freak-out tasks like that that I have to complete," said Marsha, now breathing laboredly. "I have to do them. And, despite what I just said about how some of my protection procedures, whether it's the teeth-brushing spits or some other requirement, aren't timed, sometimes they are timed. Or, if they're not timed, it's still like I have to do them—for instance, my accurate spits—before, as I was saying, some particular thing happens such as someone knocking to get in the bathroom or before a man working in a nearby yard revs his lawn mower. I have to do them just right and do them fast before the buzzer. I'm under the gun. I have the compulsion to get these unplanned-for OCD necessities done before those all-of-a-sudden deadlines expire or someone I love may be hurt or…I…I sometimes panic really bad and I get so tense and terrified.

"I don't believe, though, that I have *harm OCD*—people irrationally fearing that they themselves might inflict harm. My fear is of failure to stop harm from being inflicted by another entity.

"And, if I fail, I often feel that I've failed my loved ones by endangering them and then I get enraged with myself, and I cry and curse myself inside my head with words you might not think I even know. And, sometimes I get so spellbound repeating an OCD rite over and over and over and over and I just can't stop and by the time I do get myself stopped I'm exhausted. And, sometimes it's so painful, that I just…"

"But, you said a few minutes ago your OCD isn't as severe as it used to be when we were kids. But, going by these things you've just finished saying, it's still there—sometimes like an evil demon from hell," said Kristi Lou, now virtually swimming in earnest sympathy for Marsha.

"I'm so sorry it's there, especially when it gets ugly like that. Sometimes your OCD is, well, it seems kinda funny and cute—but, not when you seriously suffer. I'll do anything I can to help. I want you to be happy."

"I know you do. Thank you so much. All that—that you just said—is right. I'm better but I'm not totally well. I know it's not logical; I've always known that, even when I was a little girl. Sometimes I just can't stop; my thoughts race like NASCAR. But, as I said, I'm better now—despite what I just finished describing—at stopping myself and not believing I've left the door open for a pending catastrophe. I wish I could just bring it to a halt. But there's still that lingering doubt.

"Thankfully, one obsession thing I don't have is orthorexia."

"Is that related to anorexia?" asked Kristi Lou. "That's the only rexia of which I know."

"In a sense it is—in that both are eating disorders. With anorexia, you're scared to eat; with orthorexia, you're morbidly obsessed with consuming nothing but flawless food. It's like a health-food diet on steroids"

"I can't have that obsession. I'm not that finicky. Nope. I would feel too gustatorily deprived. I have too many sweet toothes in my mouth to swear off molecular formula $C_{12}H_{22}O_{11}$. By the way, Guinevere—lest you correct me—'sweet teeth' doesn't work with my colloquialism."

"Correcting you is something I would never do, Kristi Lou."

"No, of course not."

"Anyway," said Marsha, "I've obviously still got OCD issues, but I'm going to keep fighting…at least I think I will. Since I, for now, continue to decline drug treatment, which would be with SSRIs—selective serotonin reuptake inhibitors—my therapist treats me with ERP, which abbreviates Exposure and Response Prevention. It's been helping. I'd be much worse without it. With ERP, I have to deliberately expose myself to thoughts or things or whatever stimuli that trigger my irrational anxieties, and then I have to be mentally tough enough to prevent myself from responding with the rituals I usually use to protect myself or anyone else I'm protecting. So, after I compel myself to eschew my protection procedures, I'm supposed to see that nothing bad happens. And, ideally, I will learn to trust that my, uh, my ritualistic safeguards have no impact whatsoever and are hence unnecessary and that, you know, that I'll eventually eradicate them altogether. But, even with the ERP, I still get vexed and I get entrapped, and I, I, I just…"

"You'll conquer it someday; I know you will," averred Kristi Lou. "And I know that, personally, I've also got work of my own to do. But, this isn't about me; the focus is on you."

"You'll both get there," avowed Guinevere, who, having sat quietly during most of Marsha and Kristi Lou's discussion of Marsha's OCD, felt that one of her supportive interventions was now urgently needed. Guinevere submerged the console and then turned her pseudo-leather bucket seat 135° to her right to face Marsha, who was now huddling in the center of the backseat looking at the floorboard with her chin buried between her upraised knees, with her forearms wrapped around her shins. Guinevere leaned back between the bucket seats toward Marsha.

"Marsha, lift your head and look at me."

"OK," said Marsha, as she complied with Guinevere's diktat.

Guinevere put both of her hands firmly on Marsha's slender shoulders.

"Marsha, regardless of whether or not you complete the oppressive requirements of those popup rituals that suddenly invade your head, you will never, never, never, and I mean never—and I know you counted my nevers—cause even the slightest, tiniest tinge of harm to befall anyone you love; it's not going to happen—ever. Kristi Lou and I will always help you—always, always. OK, one more—always."

"Thanks. Thank you. I love you both," said Marsha, whose eyes moistened but did not drop tears.

"Well," said Marsha, "there is this professional organization that's really top-flight that's set up to help people with OCD that's called the International OCD Foundation. It's at www.IOCDF.org. It's for people like me snared in the clutches of OCD. It's for their families. It's for therapists and so on. I keep going to their website. I've been going to it for…I don't know…for a long while. I go there obsessively. Yes, that's how I go there, which I suppose is fitting.

"But I, well…one of these days I'm going to take the plunge and sign up for a membership. That is, I think maybe I might. It costs a measly $50 per year and, if you're a member, you get helpful stuff like the OCD Newsletter and emails with OCD news and a discount on the price of attending their big get-together—their annual OCD conference. I know I'd meet some good people who also have OCD and we would commiserate and support one another and I'd feel a kinship and all. But, anyway, so far, I just haven't because…I…I'm…OK, I'm scared to do it because…'cause I'm afraid it won't work for me.

"So, you know, since I haven't tried it yet it, it…it gives me something practicable to hold out in front of myself and say to myself, 'If I get unbearably miserable and I can't take it anymore then I can get with the OCD Foundation and that'll fix me.' But if I try it and it doesn't help me then I won't be able to look forward to it as, uh, you know, as an ace in the hole that will do the trick. I will have, in effect, killed something I can now comfort myself with 'cause I can still say 'it might work' but if I actually try it and it doesn't work—it's gone.

"So, keeping it in my back pocket as something that *might* help blocks me from literally trying it to see if it *will* help. If I don't try it, then it won't fail me and I can keep it as a source of hope. That way, even though I'll never find out if it will work, at least I'll never find out that it won't.

"And I won't have that despair. I dread exhausting all my options. So I keep on not utilizing this potential source of alleviating my problem 'cause I don't want to lose the potentiality. I'm obsessed with not using up my ways to end my obsessing. In short, I'm screwed to the max. Most people would say, 'You got that right.' I'm just so ridiculous that I …"

"Marsha," said Guinevere, re-grabbing Marsha's shoulders and applying an even firmer grip, "what did I just tell you? Kristi Lou and I will stand by you, and so will your family. And the therapy has helped you and will continue helping you. And that International OCD Foundation—that sounds like an excellent source of guidance and empathy to add on to your current help. The risk of disappointment is defeated by the possible—and probable—reward. Sign up for it, Marsha Mellow. Sign up for it after you get back to Arkansas."

Guinevere reset her seat to its standard position facing the steering wheel and reestablished the console.

"Yes," said Kristi Lou. "Go directly to that site and join. Guinevere is right, as usual. That program, in all probability, will work, with time and effort on your part. And you can't just keep going on wasting that opportunity because of fears that it might not benefit you, which it probably will."

"I know I should."

"I hope," said Kristi Lou, "that you don't believe Guinevere and I are kibitzers."

"Kib-what-zers?"

"Kibitzers," repeated Kristi Lou. "Sorry—one of my words I learned, by coincidence, a few days ago when I was reading one of my dictionaries. A kibitzer is someone who gives unwanted advice."

"Oh. No, you're not—both of you are not kibitzers, then. I wanted you to give me sympathy—and, OK, empathy—and to advise me."

"All right," said Kristi Lou. "Jump in, Marsha. Give that foundation a whirl."

"OK. When I get home, I'll do it."

"Excellent," said Guinevere.

"Excellent, excellent, excellent," added Kristi Lou.

****

Marsha then looked at her lap and began blushing in anticipation of the OCD confession she felt she was about to offer. She hesitated, but then forged ahead by informing Guinevere and Kristi Lou of an OCD demand about which she had never shared the slightest information with anyone else.

"Well, while we're talking about, uh, OCD rituals, there is, well, there is one more I sorta think I'm about to tell you about. Even my shrink doesn't know about it. It doesn't cause depression. But it's somewhat uncool."

"Oh, come on," said Kristi Lou. "Go for it. We want to hear it. I bet it's just too cool."

"Uh, I don't know about that. But, well, you see, it's uh … well, whenever I see somebody wearing a purple shirt that touches orange pants or an orange skirt or orange shorts or orange whatever-kind-of-bottom clothing, well, there's something I have to do to prevent the total devastation of all living organisms."

"Well, that's a prohibitively garish combination of colors," said Guinevere. "Most people will not make that sartorial choice, so I would expect that whatever ritual you're about to tell us that you're compelled to perform does not happen frequently."

"No, fortunately, it does not."

"So, what is it?" asked Kristi Lou, peering intently into the backseat at Marsha.

"So, well, OK … it's that … it's this, well … I dunno … OK …" said Marsha, hemming and hawing with hesitation lasting about eight seconds.

"Okaaaay," said Kristi Lou.

"When I see a person who's wearing a purple top that's touching an orange bottom I feel that I have to grab a penis."

"You have to grab a what?" asked Kristi Lou.

"I have to grab … I have to grab what I said I have to grab."

"And then I have to squeeze it 4.1 times within 1.4 seconds."

"You've never told me about that one," said Guinevere, calmly. "I would surmise that such behavior could create some socially awkward moments."

"You're not wrong."

"So," inquired Kristi Lou, "if you see a purple clothing top touching an orange clothing bottom, you have this powerful urge to uh, grab, some man's thingy? I mean, does it have to be the thing, the penis, of the guy wearing the purple and orange clothes? Or, could the person whose thing you want to grab be just a male bystander nearby or … well, you know …"

"It could be any guy within grabbing range who has a penis. Most of them do. I think."

"That equipment comes standard on most male models," confirmed Guinevere.

"Oh my goodness," replied Kristi Lou.

"But, if it's in reverse I don't have to do it. That is, if the top I spot is orange and it touches a purple bottom, it's OK. If I see that clothing arrangement, nothing bad will come true if I don't squeeze a penis."

"Well, that's good that you and the penises catch a bit of a break, there," said Kristi Lou. "Penises in your immediate area are safe, you know, from a surprise squeeze."

"Yes, and penis safety is important to many guys," averred Marsha. "Well, I'll amend that remark to say most guys. OK—all guys. But also, even if the top is purple and the bottom is orange, it doesn't count if the top doesn't literally touch the bottom. So, if some girl wears a midriff purple top/orange bottom combination and I can see whether she has an innie or an outie, then my OCD will not object and I won't feel that I have to squeeze a ding-dong four times."

"Have you ever in real life manifested this compulsion upon an unsuspecting penis?" queried Guinevere.

"Yeah—have you? Have you ever actually, uh, done that?" asked Kristi Lou.

"You must know," cautioned Guinevere, "that your grabbing conduct—though you might get away with it because of approbative discrimination since you're a girl—could be considered sexual assault or illegal groping."

"Yes. I'm well aware of that possible debacle. I believe that grabbing random penises would be generally frowned upon by the American judiciary."

"I agree with that assessment," harmonized Kristi Lou, with a serious face sans a trace of facetiousness.

"I'm glad that you grasp the inappropriateness of such behavior," said Guinevere.

"I see what you did there," said Marsha.

"You could have a hairy situation," added Guinevere.

"Yes, depending on shaving choices, I could."

"So," surmised Kristi Lou, "you mean you've never literally satisfied this OCD urge, ever? How do you not pop? You have to satisfy the OCD demands at least part of the time to not go brainsick bonkers because of fearing that some devastating thing will happen if you don't, right? That's what you said. And we discussed your agonizing rituals a few minutes earlier. Now, this potentially embarrassing and even dangerous sexual-assault-style bizarreness, so …"

"But I do satisfy that OCD demand … sort of. In my purse, here, I always have a big Cuban cigar."

"Oh my goodness," said Kristi Lou.

"I use that. Whenever I see that rare clothing combo of purple over orange I just reach into my purse and inconspicuously grab and squeeze. See," said Marsha as she put her hand into her purse and removed a partially mutilated cigar. "Here's the cigar I'm carrying now, in case I need to perform a proxy penis squeeze."

"Well, it's a bit mangled," observed Guinevere. "But it does somewhat resemble the appendage coveted by your OCD."

"Yes. I've used this one only twice in several weeks. It's about time to replace it so my purse won't smell stinky."

"Good idea," said Guinevere.

"I used to use a dildo whenever this compulsion first came into my head, which was almost two years ago when it started. But, I kept my dildo for just four days, and then I sneaked off with it to a dumpster in Little Rock and threw it away and replaced it with the cigar I'd already bought. I got scared that if I were in an accident that someone might go through my purse and discover my dildo. I wouldn't want anyone to find my dildo. I would be too embarrassed. Even if I were dead. I could become temporarily reanimated and see someone reach into my purse and it would be 'Oh no, they found my dildo!' So, I ditched my dildo."

"So, you no longer do dildos," said Kristi Lou.

"No, I don't do dildos. Not anymore. And you may wonder how, if I find a dildo so potentially embarrassing, I ever got ahold of one to begin with. Well, I wore a disguise and went incognito and I slipped into The Sex Shoppe in the red-light part of Little Rock and bought one.

"Anyhow, both of the last two times I've seen purple tops touching orange bottoms were on TV—one time on one of those reality modeling fashion shows and the other time it was a sanitation gentleman dumping garbage into the big trash truck.

"But, anyway, I fix up the cigars by picking at the bottom of them so some tobacco is kinda hanging out 'cause that sorta resembles pubic hair and that makes the cigar seem more like an authentic penis."

"Authenticity is always important for penis replicas," opined Guinevere.

"Oh my goodness," said Kristi Lou. "It really does kind of resemble a penis with hairs."

"So you would know what they look like?" asked Guinevere.

"I think you know that I would."

"But, anyhow, I usually feel reasonably confident that my OCD accepts grabbing the cigar in my purse and squeezing it 4.1 times as a viable substitute for sticking my hand down some guy's britches and running the risk of getting punched out—maybe by a girlfriend or a wife, if not the man."

"My goodness, Marsha, I'm a little flabbergasted by this particular obsessive-compulsive requirement of yours," said Kristi Lou, "but, OCD is, by definition, rather abnormal, isn't it?"

"Yes, it is."

"So, you don't ever want to get caught seeing a purple shirt touching orange pants without your purse. Because, in that case, you might actually try to—no, you wouldn't—not really…would you?"

"If I don't have my purse with me I make sure to stuff a cigar in a pocket."

"Oh. That's a wise precaution," concurred Kristi Lou. "So, yeah, it seems that you must be ever-vigilant about avoiding purple-on-orange sightings."

"Yes. I've already thought ahead that if I'm ever in South Carolina, unless I know the choice of uniforms in advance for that day, I'll not be attending a Clemson ballgame. And I avoid TV channels carrying Clemson games if I don't know the color combos first. It's a shame, too, 'cause, even though I don't have any tie-ins with Clemson people, I otherwise like Clemson. But, I can't let them compel me to want to be a pecker-snatcher. Also, as a postscript, there is Clemson's number one rival. I can't be watching Clemson wearing purple jerseys and orange pants and playing the Gamecocks."

****

Guinevere, turning to Kristi Lou, decided to change the subject.

"Hey, Kristi Lou, just out of curiosity, considering the vocation in which you've been working, do you watch porn?"

"No, I don't. OK, well…OK. Every now and then on the computer—I don't own any videos—but not very often. It's OK, though, as long as all the participants are of adult age. Of course, I'm against the child pornography industry.

"And I don't like the X-rated movies that depict rape, including involuntary irrumation, as a sexy thing. I know it's all acted out by willing and paid models, but I don't care for it, anyway. Some of the rape movies, just like some of the other porn movies, are only about 15 or so minutes long. But that's more than enough. I figured out that some of the sites use the uppercase letter D or past-tense D'ed as self-censoring code for the word rape. They might have the caption saying something like 'so and such D'ed in the alley.' I've actually watched just two of these D'ed movies and they were vicious and disturbing. But, however, distasteful or brutal, it's still freedom of speech."

"Interesting," replied Guinevere.

"I didn't know they made movies like that," said Marsha.

"I didn't, either, till someone at Secrets told me about them. I'd never even heard of anything like that. You know the maxim: 'It takes all types to make up the world.' But, yeah, there are such movies, whether we like it or not. That's because there's a market for it.

"If you've got enough money and you know where to look, you can get just about whatever you want," said Kristi Lou. "Somebody somewhere will sell it to you. Money has always meant power and always will. Money, in sufficient sums, can cause just about anything you can imagine to happen. I don't want to seem too cynical. But, if you can pay for it, there are very few things you can't buy some place in the darker corners of the planet."

"I won't win any originality contests for saying this. But, well, you can't buy love," Marsha softly avowed. "That relic band from way-back-when that Mom likes—you know, The Beatles—sang about that."

"Yes, you are absolutely right. And, so are The Beatles when they sing 'Can't Buy Me Love,'" agreed Kristi Lou. "Love is not—and cannot be—purchasable; it's never for sale."

"Marsha is almost always right about everything," said Guinevere, with genuineness.

"Oh, I am not."

"Oh, yes you are. You're wrong when you say you're not right," said Guinevere.

"I love irony," quipped Kristi Lou. "Well, sometimes I do, but other times I don't, so, but…"

"I know men go for you in Secrets—and everywhere else," said Marsha. "You're a *picolit* girl; you can have your pick of the litter. You're God-gifted, naturally blonde with sky-blue eyes, a curvy bod, and ropey legs up to your ears. They've gotta like you. You're not lanky-gangly; you're—what's the word?—svelte, with natural sexiness. You smell good. You're sweet. I'm sure you do well with the guys, financially and popularity-wise."

"Picolit? OK, picolit, ha-ha. Thanks for saying those nice things. Yeah, I guess they like me pretty much, and I am sorta lucky, soma-wise."

"But, coincidentally, you mentioned blond hair," continued Kristi Lou. "Just the other day I was watching this TV talk show and they had this psychologist on and she had the theory that one reason a lot of men supposedly like blondes, or 'gentlemen prefer blondes,' as the old proverb goes, is that blondes have light-colored hair and lighter colors are insentiently associated with a form of innocence. She basically said men are generally kinda turned on, whether or not they consciously realize it, by thinking they're conquering a woman's so-called sexual innocence. So, you know, darker colors, as in brunettes, when it comes to hair, are supposed to subliminally convey being more openly non-innocent, while blondes with their blond hair are supposed to subliminally convey being more openly innocent."

"How many blondes do you know who don't have blond hair?" inquired Guinevere.

"Huh? Not a whole lot. Why do you …oh wait …I'm retracing what I said …oh my goodness."

"Guinevere, don't pick on Kristi Lou!" pleaded Marsha, grinning.

"It's OK; I enjoy it. I'm masochistic when Guinevere does it."

"Ha-ha-ha-ha!" said Marsha.

"Anyway," resumed Kristi Lou, "she wasn't saying that most men are desirous of being brutal, as in forcible rapists—like we were just talking about with some dirty movies—when they're cutting into this so-called innocence—though rape could amount to this theory in fantasticated form. She was referring to the idea that many men just like the idea of seducing blondes more because of the basic notion of light hair is somehow tied into a form of purity and it's a conquest and thus more sexy if they, the men, get there. It's something like being the guy who ends a girl's virginity, regardless of her hair color; it's an achievement and thus a turn-on."

"Believe it or not," said Guinevere, "I have actually thought the same or similar thing once or twice. I don't recall hearing or reading it anywhere: the notion of men being enticed by blondes because blondes may seem fairer, and therefore having—or at least projecting—a type of innocence which men are maybe extra attracted to conquering. It's perhaps somewhat related, to a degree, to the concept of 'forbidden fruit is more tempting.'"

"Yes," said Kristi Lou, "but it's also a manifestation of the ludicrous, in my opinion, nexus that is typically drawn by many people in our culture between female activeness in sex and the loss of innocence and between female abstinence from sex and the presence of innocence. The theory goes that if you have sex and you are a female—especially if you are young—you are no longer innocent. If you have sex and you are a male you are beyond non-innocent—you are guilty. Of what? Of inflicting sex on the female, hence depriving her of the continuance of her alleged innocence. According to this mindset, sex not enclosed within love is so intrinsically wretched that once a female does it, she is no longer innocent. And what could be worse than taking away—stealing, as they dramatically proclaim—a female's innocence? Therefore, more vilification of oh-so-sordid, heterosexual-male sexuality is accomplished.

"And yes, I know that if a female is sexually active outside of a devoted relationship, especially if she's, well, let's say, generous with her number of sex partners, she can be condemned as a slut, whore, tramp, or hussy, while a male is often described flatteringly by some onlookers as a stud, Romeo, or Casanova. That sex-name bias is a function of the fact that most women are highly guarded about giving their sex. But, that guardedness is not there only because of pregnancy concerns. No, it's also there because of culture-imposed, don't-let-'em-get-it requirements with which she's obligated to define her dignity. It's easier for women to get sex from men than vice versa, and conclusively so if she's attractive, because men are more unconstrained about giving their sex and therefore seducing them is frequently—though not always—a breeze. However, many males are much pickier than some observers realize. Men reject women's come-ons daily. Still, men—if a coming-on female is attractive to them—typically accede to unbridling their sex less guardedly than do women pursued by an attractive male.

"So, should a female choose to engage with numerous male sex partners, then A/, the relative ease with which she can obtain sex, combined with B/, her failure to not severely restrict and/or punish men who want it, results in her getting ladened with sullying labels such as unchaste or loose or promiscuous, and particularly the classic SWT invectives of slut, whore, tramp. Contrastingly, it's harder for men to get sex from numerous female partners, and thus men score a type of accomplishment when they succeed, hence the SRC credits of stud, Romeo, Casanova.

"But, that said, many current-day critics—who are usually religionists and/or feminists—will, without hesitation, condemn a lots-of-women man with slams such as selfish, irresponsible, Lothario, horndog, cad, or womanizer—while ridiculously and hypocritically demanding that no lots-of-men woman ever deserves to be condemned with slams such as selfish, irresponsible, slut, whore, tramp, or hussy. One thing I call a hyper-sleeper-arounder, including myself because of my current occupation, is a *many-sex-partners person*, which I'm terming an MSPer and pronouncing, as you can hear, Guinevere, as M-S-Per. But you can pronounce it however you wish. It's spelled with one P, which pulls double duty. So, an MSPer comes in both male and female flavors. Whether or not an MSPer is deserving of being fired at with sex-shame word-bullets should be significantly predicated, among other predications, upon how he or she treats those partners beyond just having sex with them. And, if the MSPer meets the family or friends of his/her many lovers, is he/she reasonably respectful to them?

"Another test of justification for fairly applying sex-based slurs—if we feel we must apply them—is whether or not the promiscuity practitioner—female MSPer or male MSPer—is or isn't serially unfaithful to a presumably faithful significant other whom she or he might have. Unless both parties agree to participate in the swinger lifestyle, the presumption is that serial betrayal is there. Men who are serially unfaithful to a girlfriend, a fiancée, or—especially—a wife have a derogatory word hung on them: *philanderer*. What is the equivalent incriminating word for women who are serially unfaithful to a boyfriend, a fiancé, or—especially—a husband? Shouldn't she be called something like a philanderer-ette or a philanderer-ina or a philanderer-tress? As for SWT defamations—slut, whore, tramp—those denigrating labels refer to a female who is generally very promiscuous; it doesn't address the specific behavior of infidelity.

"Double standards? While we're examining cultural double standards regarding sex-slur usage, let's look at these contrastable examples.

"Here is a double standard based on a popularized fictional character that favors men. Casanova is a centuries-old, fictional male super-seducer whose name has entered Western culture as a term with primarily positive connotations for a modern man whom it describes. A Casanova is very successful with obtaining sex from numerous women. He is generally not viewed as a jerk and an immoral reprobate, but rather as a sexually appealing stud, whereas a woman who is very successful with obtaining sex from numerous men is generally viewed as a jerk as well as an immoral reprobate and a slut. Some feminists will complain that there's no label equivalency in the form of a favorable name for females who are Casanova-ish with their MSPer behavior. That inequity probably goes to the fact that most females are known for being considerably more inhibited with uncaging their sex than are most males with theirs.

"Here is a double standard based on a popularized fictional character that favors women. Lothario is a centuries-old, fictional male super-seducer whose name has entered Western culture as a term with primarily negative connotations for a modern man whom it describes. A Lothario is very successful with obtaining sex from numerous women. He is generally viewed as a jerk and an immoral reprobate who is deceptive, hubristic, cold-hearted, and apathetic toward the fate of the women he seduces. Feminist are predictively either silent or they are rationalizers about the absence of label equivalency in the form of an unfavorable name for females who are Lothario-ish with their MSPer behavior.

"So, we have Lothario—the name of the selfish, unfeeling, treacherous MSPer cad in the 1702 stage play *The Fair Penitent*. What about a proper debasing term for female Lotharios, of which there is no dearth, who don't just, as they say, 'get around town' by bedding copious men—that falls into SWT territory—but who unscrupulously seduce and then do life-damaging harm to men? How about a Lothario-ette or a Lothario-ina or a Lothario-tress? I suppose those terms, with feminine suffixes, would be constructed along the lines of temptress and seductress and so forth. But just because some women tempt and seduce—and they do—doesn't automatically mean they're indifferently or calculatingly poisonous. Should there be a Lothario-equivalent, sex-shame nickname for those who are?

"Anyway, on a per sexual episode basis, males, despite some people hailing them as SRCs, are still vilified by other people for participating in sex with multiple females. Womanizer? OK. However, are those women who are seduced responsible for their acquiescence? Do feminists excuse seduced men from their responsibility when they acquiesce? And, how many times have you heard or read that a woman is a manizer? Loads of lady-Lotharios callously take sexual advantage of men. Why aren't they izers?

"And, although I don't recommend typically doing this, if someone is confronted with an unjustly abusive, mean-natured, truculent individual, you know, an outright bully—particularly an MSPer—use of those horrid sex-shame words might be warranted. If a bullying person has recently behaved very abusively, whether or not the abusiveness involves sex, then use of some of these degradations can be justifiable simply because of the targeted abuser's meanness. You know, he or she, as they say, 'had it coming.' And, although I ordinarily dislike calling people nasty names, these denigrations can be effective retaliatory verbal weapons because of the top-level insult value they carry.

"A male who has many sex partners has to have something exceptionally seductive going on for him, such as mucho money, uncommon charm, status power and/or handsomeness. And, speaking of a guy being handsome, women, as I've often said, are overall just as *visual* as men or very close to it—oh yes they are! 'Look at that guy! He's hot!'

"Anyhow, the primary point I'm trying to make is that—along the lines of the shame factor that I talked to you about earlier today, Guinevere, before Marsha joined us—is that … that if society were to eliminate or demonstrably lessen its systemic bigotry against straight-male sexuality, unattached girls and women who have slept around would, ultimately—though it might take a long while—probably come to be generally viewed not so much as shamefully dissolute, unchaste, loose, or promiscuous, or as SWTs. Rather, they would be calmly accepted as non-monogamous, sexually active females who simply choose to have more sex partners. This ongoing acceptance would, blessedly, co-incide with a scarcity of the hysterical slut/whore/tramp degradations as well as those besmirching susurrations murmuring that she's '*that* type of girl.' I suspect that the SWT debasement would then be more appropriately relegated to describing women who unjustly stray pro-miscuously while in love-filled, commitment relationships, especially marriage, with a good and faithful man."

Guinevere nodded in agreement while Kristi Lou continued her circuitous and hyper-rambling observations.

"But, cirlcing back to the issue of innocence, it's more hysteria against sex, straight-male sex in particular. If she is virginal, either literally or in her attitude—as in very limited, non-intercourse sexual experience with maybe only one, perhaps two, partners—she is innocent. By contrast, should she undergo deflowerment—I think I just created a word—via non-marital or non-romantic sex with a straight male, innocence is ter-minated. She is not viewed—by the people to whom I'm referring—as guilty. She is always condescendingly given a pass by them, as if she's too dumb or weak to be responsible for her intimacy choices. 'Oh, did he seduce you? Then he's evil.'

"Rather, she can no longer be characterized as innocent, because her innocence has been taken—ripped away—from her. There needs to be a noxious villain who does the taking and ripping, and guess who that always is. Thus, so they surmise, for the female of the human species, the absence of sex equals the presence of innocence; the presence of sex equals the absence of innocence. And, by syllogistic extension, the presence of that sex must equal the guilt of the taker—the nefarious straight male, he who has disgracefully rendered her unclean by depriving her of her maidenhood and hence terminating her immaculacy.

"Societally reinforced sex-shame is calibrated to include the hiding of human sexuality—penis goes into vagina, etcetera—from early-age children, supposedly to protect them because they're allegedly not ready to be educated about the humiliation and disgustingness associated with that shameful thing called sex because such education would cause kids' innocence to somehow be robbed away from them. So, not only is actual sex itself guilty of being an innocence-killer, but even knowledge of sex means a child can no longer be innocent. How in tarnation does being knowledgeable about sex make anyone, including a little kid, non-innocent? Once again, possession of sex is ridiculously aligned with obliteration of innocence. 'You're guilty of depriving that child of the innocence of ignorance!'

"Of course, all that sex-is-dirty-even-though-we-adults-crave-it habituation will itself cause pain and thus backfire when puberty and its attendant natural sexual desires arise, as many of the kids—prevalently girls—who've been trained to connect sex with guilt will vacillate neurotically between feeling stimulated and feeling guilty—a youthful mindset that could potentially augur a lifetime of sexual neurosis.

"Via andragogy, we adults should unlearn the sex-shame we've learned. Because, if we're sex-negative alarmists, we're the plunderers robbing kids of their innocence. We're stealing their internal perception of their innocence by claiming they don't have innocence anymore because they had some form of deemed-inappropriate sexual encounter, thus burdening them with guilt. Those kids are still innocent—external perception be damned. They just engaged in voluntary sexual conduct—that's all. Or, they merely acquired more information about it at school in sex-education class or wherever, for goodness' sake.

"The perception of guilt that we culturally force upon them does not make them non-innocent people; they can be kind-spirited, magnanimous, respectful, law-abiding, non-me-first, non-selfish, non-mean, non-thieving, non-abusive when no one is looking, and non-malevolent in most of their private thoughts about which nobody will ever know. However, our anti-sexuality indoctrination of their minds compels them to believe that society's perception of their supposed non-innocence equals the guilt of their essential, head-to-toe selves. We ransack their feeling of innocence: 'You participated in sex? Or you've been informed about sex? I'm sorry, but your innocence is dead. You'rrrrreeeee guilty!'

"Rather than having achieved protection of kids, we've mind-screwed another generation of conflicted, guilt-ridden-while-naturally-pining-for-pleasure individuals who will one day repeat and pass on to their kids the same inadvertent stealing of childhood innocence while Orwellianly claiming that the hiding of sexual realities from children is to prevent their innocence from being stolen. The backwash here is etiological inversion; this prevention causes causation.

"Hence, by not edifying kids about sex before they develop their foreordained nature-gifted appetence because we are supposedly safeguarding and extending their innocence, we are ironically guilty of pickpocketing an aspect of their innocence by infructuously setting them up to feel neurotically non-innocent for carrying within them or for trying to satisfy and especially for actually satisfying the inevitable and entirely normal feelings they will soon receive that direct them to engage in conduct—non-forced sexual behavior—that is non-abusive and thoroughly natural. And our training instructs them to be derogatorily judgmental against others who engage in non-commitment sexuality: 'She's a slut tramp! He's a horndog perv!'

"Such adults are guilty of the potential infliction of future self-esteem-assaulting confusion plus emotional and sometimes physical agony. When they're still quite young and finally learn about the birds and the bees and sexual desire, but realize that grownups have been actively engaged in hiding this phenomenon from them, they easily and logically ascertain that since it was bad enough to warrant being hidden from them for all the prior years of their lives, it—human sexuality—must be God-awfully bad. And when their puberty hormones charge to the foreground, here they go with a strong urge to engage in something that was so wretchedly bad that its reality had to be masked by the big folks as if it were a dungeon-dark conundrum. Or, if unhidden, sex is explained to kids in overwhelmingly negative and critical terms. Many lawmakers legislate with various legislation against kids being exposed to or connected with sex, sometimes including just being non-hysterically edified about it. And once something becomes unlawful, then, over time, as the years go along, the shame factor—if they participate in whatever illegal acttiviy, which, in this case, is sex-related conduct, even if they're not the ones who are legally liable—seeps deeper into their psyche and then continues to increase. 'It's so terribly bad that it's against the law!' These combined elements may, sadly, portend that girls and then women will be even more slutified and that boys and then men will be even more horndogified. Sex-negative ideology annunciates that 'If you are even partially libertine, you are totally debauched.'

"And, I wish to now interrupt myself to say that, yes, Marsha and Guinevere, I've memorized almost all of this current didacticism, including specific sentences, of course, and I … uh … but … I, well, so I just wanted to insert an apology for being so obsessively didactic. So …

"Umm, OK … what was I going on about? Oh, yeah. So, another overriding reason for the coverup seems to be parents' and other grownups' own classically indurated sex-shame that imposes upon them intense discomfort when faced with the idea of being forthcoming about sex with elementary-school-age kids. That's why scenes in motion pictures and on television—and in real life—in which a young kid surprises her or his parents by popping unexpectantly into their bedroom while they're enfolded in intimacy reveal a super-embarrassed and suddenly panicked Mom and Dad duo dramatically disengaging their bodies and scrambling frantically to pull the covers over themselves while sometimes lying via nosexplaining to their child that they were just play-wrestling or whatnot. Parents are desperate to stop their kids from knowing about the very phenomenon they utilized to make their kids happen. They're ashamed for their kids to know about the thing that enables their kids know anything. 'Hey! There's this thing we did to get you into the world. But it's so gross we don't want you to know about it! We'll tell you about it one day, though, maybe after you've already learned about it from older kids and the Internet. But, for now, stork-story evasions are so much less unnerving.'

"OK, in case you're wondering, I doubt I'll let my future very-young kids watch me do the thing—and definitely not after they enter pre-pubescence; that might be too much—for them and for me, as I was reared in this society whose concepts I'm questioning but by which I'm affected. However, I will uninhibitedly tell them things such as 'Your dad and I are now going to go make love in the bedroom. Check the doorknob and you'll see the Do Not Disturb card we borrowed from that hotel during our vacation.' Ha-ha.

"But, anyhow, consider the discourse in the movie *The Silence of the Lambs* during which FBI-agent-in-training Clarice Starling is asked by caged-cannibal Hannibal Lecter to describe what happened on a Montana sheep-slaughter-for-profit ranch where she as an orphan child was sent to live with distant relatives.

"Clarice recalled how the screams of the titular lambs were silenced by their deaths. She recounted the fateful night when she grabbed one of the young sheep and ran away with him to try to save his life. She and the lamb were caught and brought back to the ranch. The rancher killed that lamb, too. Rather than sparing the little woolly as special because Clarice, powered by compassion, had tried to rescue him, the rancher conferred no mercy—upon the lamb or the girl.

"In an earlier scene, Lecter had inquired as to whether the rancher had sexually molested her. She said 'No,' and then added, unprompted, that 'He was a very decent man.' The scriptwriter didn't have her say 'decent in that regard' or 'decent in that sense' or 'decent in that way.' And, I underline that some persons who do abhorrent things such as wreaking cruelty on animals are what I call 'otherwise decent people.' Nonetheless, despite her clear-cut recollection of what she revealed to Lecter later in the story—that the rancher had dealt in brutality for money—Starling semi-knights him with a title of decency. Why? Because, while subjecting helpless animals to screaming demises, he refrained from any sexual delinquency toward her.

"Yes, it's decent to not molest children—no quarrel there. But what did it take to get this woman to typecast as decent, as an implied overall characterization, someone who had horrified her by ruthlessly butchering animals to fatten his bank account, including a lone lamb, just one lamb, a lamb the rancher knew that Clarice, as a gentle girl, had held tenderly and protectively in her arms and whom she zealously wanted to receive merciful clemency that was coldly denied—a scarring horror still afflicting her into adulthood? All it took was a recollection of the absence of sex, while disregarding the presence of barbarity. Starling, on cultural-conditioning auto-drive, obliviously vomited more societal, feminist-fabling, indoctrination against the nefariousness of straight-male sexuality, which, of course, must be correlated with indecency. Even viewed through the lenses of a sensitive, kindness-to-animals devotee, lack of outside-the-lines, potentially harmful male sex qualifies somebody for a decency rating despite his infliction of ghoulish, horror-story killings on picture-of-innocence animals. Sex is once again the enemy.

"Onward goes the deception. Teach children about sexuality when they're very young, but in mostly positive terms. Put a sensible emphasis on sensible caution and sensible modesty. Wouldn't such augmented sophistication promote real innocence—non-abusive sex ≠ guilt—while enhancing psychological well-being? Indoctrinating kids to feel that unsanitized sex is dirty is itself deleterious—and ironically unwholesome.

"Actually, this monologue I just frothed at you referencing the savagely slaughtered sheep in *The Silence of the Lambs* and the ugliness of animal abuse segues my current thoughts into one thing about which I was speaking outside at Secrets 10 or 20 or so days ago. I was once again serving as Miss Speechmaker. And, while I was pontificating to Rochelle and an audience of sidewalk listeners about the societal fragility of human sexuality, I addressed the following topic, which I've since expanded upon by adding more memorized slants.

"OK, so, we've all heard those standardized, animal-oriented critiques applied to instances of people engaging in unusually immodest or not-so-restrained sexual conduct. Here are two ever-popular such condemnations: 'They're acting like animals!' and 'He's disgustingly dehumanizing her by objectifying her body!'

"The standard insistence on separating us from non-human animals probably comes from centuries-old religious values that have been revised and hyper-ized in modern times by radical feminism with an anti-sex-object, feminist flair.

"Well, we are, in fact—when you get right down to it—animals. We are not plants. We are not inanimate, lifeless things. We are, in actuality, the same as the beings we hubristically disregard as mere animals when we're sending sexual signals and when we're feeling carnal attraction and when we're manifesting those desires with corporeal contact. We physically touch as do animals. We make a male reproductive organ go into a female reproductive organ as do animals. We feel lust—whether or not our lustiness is mingled with human love—as do animals.

"Societies, because of entrenched discomfort, embarrassment, and shame felt by their citizens toward their own human sexuality, insist on modesty regarding sex, such as wearing clothes on our bodies. And that clothing isn't supposed to be too revealing and sexy except in exceptional locations, such as swimsuits at the beach, lingerie in the bedroom, and in places like Secrets. And, as we're all aware, we're restricted to doing just about any and all sex-type things only in private. Hence, we are required to refrain from so-called public displays of affection.

"But, regardless of where we are when we do the deed or who does or doesn't see us doing the deeding, when we're rutting rawly and getting our estrus on, especially when we're enjoying our sex, we are absolutely doing what all other animals do—literally wriggling and banging. Nobody seeing us do it doesn't undo what we're doing.

"Anyway, as far as when human sexuality is animalistic, I believe it comes down discernibly to where we draw the ASS line—the Animalism-Sex-Shame line—above which we are not behaving sexually like animals and below which we are. As I often say, I think the latter, undesirable phenomenon occurs when we see another person in a thoroughly crude way and not just as an object of sexual desire—which, whether or not we realize it, is morally and humanly healthy during moments of arousal—but rather as *nothing else but* an object of sexual desire, as defined by holding no regard for or recognition of the attractive individual's status as a human with a distinct personality, beliefs, emotions, attitudes, wants, and needs.

"We don't dismiss another person's potential spirituality and uniquely human qualities and animalize her or him simply because we're turned on—during the moments we're experiencing the turn-on—by her or his body. That dismissal occurs whenever we take an overarching, 1-to-100 view of a sexually appealing person as *exclusively* a sex-object thing, even when we're not feeling heated up thinking about, looking at, touching, or being touched by that person. The ASS line is not crossed with me just because some man finds my body parts to be appealing and sees me as a sex object while still seeing me as a human with thoughts and feelings. Not at all. I feel quite complimented, just as do most men when they are seen as sex objects by women.

"The ASS line is crossed if he so views me wholly and solely, to the exclusion of my inner self. He doesn't have to love me, like me, or even know me from Adam and Eve, as in seeing me for the first time; he merely has to view me, in an overall way, as a sex object who is also a human being.

"Finally, as I have said before, if a guy is not bestially stimulated by sheep or horses or kangaroos or carburetors or whatnot, the fact that he sees me—a female human—as an object of sexual desire does not deny but rather confirms my humanness in his eyes.

"OK, do you two think some of these cultural concepts are worth thinking about and perhaps challenging?"

"ASS line, huh. That's a mind-sticker acronym. But, yes," concurred Guinevere, "those associations have been entrenched in civilized society for eons. However, upon close examination, those connections don't hold up. You, Kristi Lou, have become someone who excels at marshaling the moxie to expose illogic and unfairness in anti-male-sexuality social systems. Most people simply don't challenge these concepts. And they're bound to be uncomfortable with your heterodoxy when you do. But I know you'll forge ahead."

"Thank you. And yes, I'll continue to be a forger. Forger? Did I say 'forger'?—not to be confused with a forger who falsely signs somebody else's name such as a crook who tries to peddle a counterfeit check and I may be interrupting myself and rambling discursively again—though anyway, yeah, I'll try to be courteous while forging and ruffling feathers with my sexuality ideology."

"I know you will," said Guinevere.

"And, by the way," said Kristi Lou, "when's the last time you heard anyone expressing remorse over a male having sex because that resulted in him 'losing his innocence'?

"You know, since there's such abundant bigotry and/or hysteria against straight-male sexuality, sometimes I look around and wonder to myself: How did all these people get here? It's because we do the sex thing, anyway.

"Oh, BTW, I propagandize. But all outspread advocacy is propaganda, whether true or false or we agree or disagree. Often, it's 'I Agree? Truth! I Disagree? Propaganda!' Nope. OK, Marsha, what thinketh you?"

"I think all that you've said here seems to make rational sense," concurred Marsha. "But I'll have to have time to compute those things. I'll get back to you on that."

"OK. You don't have to concur. But it'll be splendidly cool if you do."

"Speaking of cool—I know this is a cheap segue—it has become rather chilly in here," said Guinevere, as she adjusted the air conditioner to a lower air speed. "So, Kristi Lou, tell us something about the misery factor of the women who work in the sex industry, based on your personal experiences this year. I can tell you're ready to break away, but you don't seem truly miserable—isolated, self-doubting, sad, but not actually miserable. But, the misery thing—that's what we hear and read—that most of the girls, whether they're strippers or ..."

"Nude dancers," interjected Kristi Lou. "Generally, they prefer to be called nude dancers or just dancers; it sounds more respectful, and besides, most of them don't really do the old-time burlesque routine whereby they make a big to-do out of slowly removing clothing, like a long, frilly glove or whatnot. They just quickly shed a top or a bottom or whatever betwixt sets and dance rock 'n' roll style. But, well ..." concluded Kristi Lou, as her voice trailed off.

"OK then," said Guinevere. "So, sex girls are supposed to be miserable, so say society's denouncers, whether they're nude dancers or porn actresses or courtesans like you. What do you say, from an insider's perspective?"

"I say that I've had only about four months of it, but, nonetheless, I've met a lot of girls, including nude dancers who visit Secrets from strip clubs. Oh wow, I just realized … despite what I just said about how they want to be known as dancers and not strippers that, really, the places they work at are called strip clubs, not nude-dancer clubs. So, go figure. But, anyhow, as I was saying before interrupting myself, I've gotten to know a number of them and they sometimes tell me— very candidly—about what's going on with other dancers as well as what's going on with them themselves. I just used an intensive pronoun.

"But, anyway, I've gotten acquainted with a goodly many of my fellow women at Secrets—some, of course, better than others. There are about 40 of us at Secrets, but I haven't had many dealings with some of them 'cause they work the day shift; I see them when I'm coming and they're going. But sometimes we'll have good conversations, though. And, of course, some girls don't stay in the job very long; they come and go kinda quickly but most of 'em I know about, believe it or not, stay for a least maybe half a year or … did I say 'fellow women'?"

"Yes," said Guinevere. "So, how many of them do you think are miserable?"

"OK, the feeling I get is that most of the girls, who are usually millennial-age women but some are older in their 40s or even a few in their 50s, are not miserable at all. But, that said, some are. I believe the ones who leave and then look at it as a dark, shame-pit episode in their lives probably make it more Stygian than it has to be. You know—slut, whore, tramp, 'cause as we were just discussing, sex is something men are guilty about and if women just let them do it without inflicting the society-required dutiful punishment upon them, then they have to be condemned along with the men.

"Or, if the experience really was such an abomination, they did a lot to make it that way when they didn't have to. Some girls get too much into the drug scene, and, if they do, that's ordinarily on them."

Kristi Lou, who had been staring at her hands as she twisted her fingers while discoursing, decided to look directly at Guinevere next to her in the driver's seat, and then turn around to check on Marsha's level of attention. Seeing that both friends wore faces that conveyed to her that they were listening intently, Kristi Lou drew a deep breath and resumed her protracted answer.

"But, unfortunately, some sex women work in a club with mean owners or mean bouncers or mean other girls or for a ruthless-type pimp who abuses them. So, yeah, those girls are likely either miserable or their senses have become so dulled and their self-concept so low that misery and depression aren't felt 'cause they don't feel much anymore. With them, the light in their eyes grows dull.

"Some of the girls who are truly miserable have let the societal shame factor get to them too much—you know, as I was saying a moment ago, you're a whore and/or a slut and therefore you're riffraff and all that. But I think many girls don't work in such terrible places or with such awful coworkers and don't let the shame factor affect them so deeply.

"And not all of us become man-haters. That is, not all of us become misandrists. And while there may be a higher percentage of us in the sex industry who were sexually molested as little kids—I don't know about any scientific research data on this subject—most of the girls I've met and heard about were not. Most of us do it for the money. I chose to do it for the money, too. Yes, for the money, but, with me, I, I, well, I also did it for ... because I wanted to do it just to do it.

"Of course, anyone—female or male—who chooses to do porn has made a lifetime commitment to the sex industry, whether or not she or he has thought that aspect through beforehand. Because, unless someone can gather up and destroy all the DVDs, VHSs, and archived website videos, one or more of those movies will be out there somewhere, potentially forever, and could be seen by somebody you'd rather not see it, such as a potential employer or your parents or your kids. If other kids see it, your kids could be ridiculed at school. That's just the way it is. But, I'd think that X-movie actors could cope with the situation proactively, if they wish, by preparing family and friends in advance so they, you know, hopefully won't be too shocked if they see one of the movies or are confronted by someone else who's seen them. X actors could ask relatives or whoever to not watch the movies, or explain things the best they can to their kids before they maybe come across those movies in the future. Or, if the wrong person has already seen such cinematic sinfulness and finds it alarming, the X actor might have to talk it through with him or her to try to get things emotionally settled.

"As a side-note thought, I'll say that, oddly enough, despite—or maybe *because* of—the ongoing tidal-wave proliferation of pornography over the past 25 or so years, there seems to me, based on my anecdotal observations plus my wide-ranging research, to be just as much hysteria and cultural tabooing—perhaps externalizing as an overcorrection to porn—within the vox populi against non-romantic human sexuality as there ever was. Sex is often a wide-open, dirty big secret hidden in everyday, plain view.

"Anyhow, we know that many regular people in society want us to be miserable. So, I think that since we were raised with such a mindset, that this expectancy can seep in perniciously and contribute greatly to the misery of those of us who actually are miserable.

"But, in conclusion—and I know this has been a stream-of-consciousness outpouring—I'm not, and many sex-industry women are not—miserable. I'm lonely. I'm self-doubting. I'm obsessive. I'm … I'm not happy—but I'm not miserable.

"Girls like me, of course, are young and have some collegiate education—many are working their way through college and earning money to pay for tuition, books, room-and-board, and so forth—and know they're going other places. For the less-educated women who don't want to stay in but don't have any other marketable skill, yeah, some of them are sad or angry or frightened because they fear they lack the ability to earn a living doing anything else. So, they wonder if they'll be stuck in the industry forever. But, retraining should result in them procuring new job knacks, which thankfully often capacitates their extrication.

"Some girls, I know, harbor hopes that they'll meet a nice man with enough money to take them away from the sex-industry life—especially if they have, as a fair many of them do have, a kid they're trying to support—but they may feel that no decent man will want to marry them or have a deep-rooted relationship with them because of so many other stranger-type men having seen them denuded or having been intimate with them, and so on. Uh, as a matter of fact, I personally kinda have that worry myself, as you know, Guinevere."

"Yes, I know."

"However, it doesn't have to be that way. I believe there've been countless reputedly promiscuous women who've found happy relationships, including matrimony, even during the Victorian Era in Europe, with men of decency. The selection pool may downsize somewhat, making their search harder, but it can be and is done. I've seen it happen.

"But, anyway, some women, particularly those with the aforesaid skillset deficiency, are just looking to use their sex in the old gold-digging way to get into a fake romance with the plan all along to take as much of the guy's money as possible and then make off with it.

"So, well…OK…I'll say that some of us are miserable, or, if not miserable, then quite unhappy with our lot in life. But many of us are quite surprisingly—and, I suspect, in the minds of many mainstreamers, quite disappointingly—not miserable at all. And some of us are happy—as long as we don't let the whole thing get to us too much or don't fail to move on when it's time to go.

"The idea, as I see it, is to do it long enough to make some serious money, save a bunch of it, then recognize when it's your time to get out of the industry and then persuade yourself to actually leave—even if you're tempted to remain 'cause the lucre continues to flow gushingly like a dead-presidents waterfall—while you're still not hardened toward life in general and men in particular and while you still have other dreams to fulfill in front of you.

"Then go, but keep the memories as good-spirited as you can. Don't hide from all the recollections by burying every one of them in your mind's bitterness basement. Don't remember everyone and everything in the industry with nothing but bitterness; remember bitterly only the people who, as individuals, because of their meanness, deserve to be remembered that way—that is, use selective bitterness. So, instead of being nothing but bitter, embrace the remembrances of those good times and those good people you met and knew while you were in it. That's what I'm going to do, and that mindset is going to work just fine for me.

"All right, I guess I've streamed enough with my rambling remarks. I, uh, I didn't know you were going to ask me about that. But, it's something I've thought about a lot, as, well, you can tell. So, any-ole-hoo, I hope I've at least sorta answered your question."

"Yes, and then some," said Guinevere. "You know, Kristi Lou, sometimes you lob yourself into cavalry-charge vehemency, a firebrand who's so bombastic and loquacious. Yet, at other times you're calmly quite brief or you display normal-person brevity when conversing. And, you're an exceptionally considerate conversationalist, when, that is, you're in a normal speak-and-listen conversation. You're truly a very attentive listener. It's almost hard to know what to make of you. That said, I get you. I do."

"I get you, too," said Marsha.

"Thanks. I know you both get me. And I'm so glad to be gotten. I'm beyond grateful for the godsent blessing of getting getted. Huh? Getting what-ed? Getted? Getting getted? Yes, getting getted."

The three young women sat in the attack car for another quarter hour, further reminiscing and informing one another as to the ebb and flow of their present-day lives.

49

"LET'S STEP OUTSIDE AND MOVE ABOUT SOME," SAID GUINEVERE. "Sitting for too long is not healthy."

"Yes, let's do that," said Kristi Lou. "I wanna do that."

"I wanna do that, too," said Marsha, as the trifecta of friends stepped into the late-day August sunshine.

The girls, arranged in ascending order of height, walked in tandem around the car four times, led by Marsha, followed by Guinevere and then Kristi Lou.

Kristi Lou spontaneously flung her fanny onto the hood of the automotive avenger above the grille and slightly to the inside of the left headlight, with the remaining regions of her sinuous body seeming to follow. She then looked over at Guinevere.

"Oh, can I sit here? This car won't eat me or anything, will it?"

"It's not hungry. As you know, it's munched recently on car hooligans. Its appetite was whetted but then satiated. Thus, you shan't be consumed."

"That's reassuring."

"I'm glad," said Guinevere, as she also climbed onto the car, sitting next to Kristi Lou. "As soon as I saw you mount the car, I knew you'd express such a concern. Umm, well, I suppose I could've said 'get on' rather than 'mount,' but, c'est la vie."

"Again!" exclaimed Kristi Lou.

"Of course," said Guinevere, smiling.

"Hey, Marsha," said Kristi Lou, "Guinevere keeps getting me. She gets me every chance she gets about my sex-job activities and all that. She won't let up."

"I know; she gets you good, too."

Marsha, last to get onto the car, positioned herself directly above the right headlamp. As Marsha was raising and lowering her posterior four times before settling into her makeshift metal seat, Kristi Lou turned rightward and began querying Marsha about the soothing subject of life in their mutual Arkansas hometown.

"So, Marsh, can you tell me about your job back home?"

"Marsh? No one's ever called me that."

"Oh. I'm sorry. I didn't even know I was going to say it before I said it."

"No. It's fine. Anyway, about my job, yeah, in the summer between semesters at U of A, I work at JCPenney in Little Rock—you know, the one near Walmart Supercenter. I took time off to come up here. I'm in the shoe department. I sell shoes. Maybe that clarification was unnecessary. What else would I do in the shoe department?"

"Well," answered Kristi Lou, "you could be plain-clothes security, guarding against shoe heists."

"Oh yeah, right—the perfect job for a powerhouse like me. I'd really excel in that role. I'm superformidable! All five feet plus maybe an inch of me and weighing in at a fearsome 81 pounds! Nobody messes with me. I'm Mighty Marsha Mellow, the Intimidator!"

"You sure are," agreed Kristi Lou, immensely enjoying the frivolous but fulfilling banter. "And, at 5'13", I'm exactly one foot taller than you."

"I know. One whole foot. Anyway, sometimes when they page me over the store intercom for this or that—'Marsha Mellow, please dial extension 3-1-4'—some of the customers will pause and then yuck it up, because of my name and all."

"But they're not really ridiculing you, Marsha, as I'm sure you know," said Guinevere.

"Oh yes, I know."

"I think that's cool and so is your name. I'd love to hear your name called out in a store," said Kristi Lou with genuine earnestness.

Guinevere chimed in.

"You make it sound as if hearing Marsha's name called out in a store would be breathtaking. Would that be a highlight of your life?"

"Oh my goodness—you're talking about *my* life—yes it would!

"Oh, Marsha, when you get back on campus in Fayetteville, you could, if you feel like it, drop in on my Aunt Charlene. She doesn't live all that far from U of A. She'd be thrilled to see someone who's seen me recently. And, you could, you know, just tell her that I'm healthy and OK and, well, kinda, uh, refrain from telling her other things, and, well, all that. You know, if you want to, you could. I just think that'd be a nice thing for both of you. And, oh yeah, she's the lady that if you ever get in trouble or need anything, she'll be there with Johnny-on-the-spot help. So, you know ..."

"Yeah, yes, I'd love to do that. Give me her phone number, please."

As Kristi Lou recited her Aunt Charlene's number, Marsha employed her left-hand thumb and forefinger to spread strands of frayed denim in the factory-serrated, precut hole of her gray distressed jeans four inches north of her right knee and then wrote the number on her skin in lime-green ink with a pen she'd withdrawn from the far side of her spacious, on-the-butt, flap pocket.

"I'll put her number in my phone later."

"OK. Cool," said Kristi Lou. "Thanks."

"You're welcome," said Marsha.

No one spoke for eight seconds as Marsha playfully kick-swung her feet in and out, followed immediately by Guinevere's and then Kristi

Lou's copycat kick-swinging, accompanied by everyone grinning and giggling with a merry enjoyment of being carefreely silly.

"Hey, Kristi Lou," said Marsha. "What's your sign? No, I'm not hitting on you. But I guess I do sound like some guy trying to pick you up in a nightclub—maybe Downtown Secrets. Anyway, what is it?"

"Oh, OK, now we're talking astrology, which I find fascinating. Don't know for sure if there's anything to it—don't know, don't know. But there might be, somehow. It fascinates me 'cause sometimes it seems so accurate about some people and it involves abstract thinking; I believe it's metaphysical. Anyhow, my birthday is April 1. I'm an Aries and a fool."

"That's right, yeah," replied Marsha, nodding her head. "I knew you were an Aries and that your birthday is April 1. I knew that back in school; I just forgot. But, yes, you seem like an Aries—a rambunctious ram who is fiery and determined. But you're still so nice and sweet. And you're also much more enamored with the past than most Aries. So you must have some strong influence from other planetary constellations."

"Oh, well, thanks for describing me with those good traits, but I don't know about other planets and influences or whatever. So what are you?"

"My birthday is May 25, so I'm a loopy Gemini. I'm the one with the mixed-up twins trying to go in different directions at once. I think that helps me produce some high-quality OCD weirdness. If I'm gonna do OCD, I may as well excel at it."

"I know a girl who works with me at Secrets who's a Gemini; she's a chatterbox and a mite flighty—a flibbertigibbet. And she's very sweet and highly intelligent, just like you," said Kristi Lou, who then was visited by a surge of introspection. "I think I may have just described my-sometimes-scatterbrained self; who's more flibbertigibbet-ish than I?"

"Nobody! Anyway, does that other girl at Secrets often confuse herself when she talks? And does she have an obsession with the number 4? Does she insist on getting things just right?" inquired Marsha in a chirpy tone while grinning broadly.

"Well, now that I think of it, yes, sometimes she does want everything just right—but not quite on your level. She's not as adept at OCD as you. You're the best!"

"You make me feel kinda proud to be an OCDer. I never woulda thought that could be possible."

"I'm glad I could be of assistance."

"Hmm, maybe I shouldn't tell you this, but you know one way to oppress an OCDer and cause her some at-home aggrievement? Pelt her bathroom mirror with drip-down water droplets and make those gunky white streaks."

"OK. Thanks for telling us how to getcha, ha-ha!" said Kristi Lou, as everyone laughed.

Kristi Lou then shifted her focus onto Guinevere.

"OK. It's your turn, Guinevere. I'm on the verge of remembering when your birthday is—when is it?—but I don't know your sign. What is it?"

"I don't have one."

"Oh, phooey!" said Marsha. "You have to have one, whether you want one or not. I think I know what it is. I think I knew your birthday from back in seventh grade, like I knew Kristi Lou's birthday, but I'd forgotten. Anyway, I think I know what your sign is, but come on. You gotta tell us."

"Yeah," agreed Kristi Lou. "What is it?"

"I don't have a sign—or a birthday. I was created over a period of several weeks in a laboratory."

"That's what I thought all along," said Marsha.

"So," said Kristi Lou, "that means that Pete and your mom maybe purchased you from a lab, perhaps soon after some bioscientists completed most of the assembly?"

"You finally figured me out."

"Oh good. I feel smart."

"OK," said Marsha. "Really—what is it? Come on. Don't be an uncooperative fussbudget."

"Fussbudget? I'm not sure if I've ever been called a fussbudget before."

"Do you like being called that? If you do, I can keep on calling you a fussbudget—fussbudget, fussbudget, fussbudget."

"Excellent. I'll look forward to that. All right," said Guinevere, smiling while capitulating. "My birthday is March 3."

"Oh, that's it. I do remember, now," said Marsha. "You told me a long time ago. You're a Pisces. You're kind, supportive, compassionate, and stronger than many people would think because your strength is expressed quite quietly. But, though, you've got an edge to you, an ability and willingness to retaliate—as you did against those mean kids back in school and against these car stealers nowadays. So, just like with Kristi Lou, you've got some other..."

"... planetary influences," interposed Guinevere.

"Exactly," concurred Marsha. "As a matter of fact, I think I'll go and get that indispensable information right now," as she accessed the Internet with her smartphone. "Stand by, please."

"Oh, all right," said Kristi Lou. "So you're going to find an astrology website and explain our personalities to us?"

"No, the stars will."

"Of course, that's what I meant. This might be fun...possibly, maybe," said Kristi Lou.

No one spoke for about 45 seconds while Marsha surfed the Web.

"All right. I found one here. I'm at 'Astrological Mandates—Heavenly Bodies and you.'"

"There are just so many ways to apply that theme to Kristi Lou and her work skills that I don't know where to begin so I won't," said Guinevere.

"Oh, please," replied Kristi Lou.

"It's not those kinds of heavenly bodies, Guinevere, as I'm quite sure you know," said Marsha.

"Yes, I do actually know that."

"OK. I've got our day-and-month birthdays and I know the year the stork delivered us was 1997 'cause it's 2018 and I know we're all twenty-one. But, I've gotta get the exact minute of birth for the Starometer."

"The what-uh-ter?" asked Kristi Lou.

"The Starometer. At least I think that's how you'd pronounce it: star-ahm-uh-ter. Or, I suppose you could say it as star-o-meet-er. See, it says it right here—Starometer. It'll pull up a chart that shows the alignment of all your planets when you hatched and then you can learn more about your traits and so forth."

"That's fascinating stuff," said Kristi Lou.

"That's hard science," said Guinevere.

"OK," said Kristi Lou, "I know Mom told me a long time ago that I was born at 2:40 a.m. on April 1. I was a jerk; I kept her awake all night."

Guinevere winked at Kristi Lou. "If only she knew how her daughter keeps her*self* awake all night now."

"Oh my goodness. Guinevere won't give me a break."

"OK, Guinevere," said Marsha. "You popped out when on March 3? Do you know?"

"Yes. I made my grand entrance—officially, and it's on my birth certificate—at 6 p.m. on the dot, just in time for the evening news."

"And you *are* newsworthy," said Marsha, who was using a pen with bright-pink ink to write birth times on the top of her left wrist.

"Right. Thanks. And your arrival time, my dear?" asked Guinevere. "Let me hazard a wild guess: 4:44—right?"

"No," replied Marsha Mellow, glancing down, as she finished writing, with a somewhat serious expression that did not escape the notice of both Guinevere and Kristi Lou. "I came out at 3:59 a.m. That means that I, uh, that…that I didn't quite make it."

"Oh yes you did," said Kristi Lou. "That's close enough."

"Yeah," said Guinevere. "Kristi Lou's right. You were a paltry one minute away from your celestial four. So, you should look at it as an auspicious omen—you were predestined to be number 1!"

"No, I'm not number 1 at anything."

"Yes you are," said Kristi Lou. "You're a number-1 good person."

"Oh, well, thanks, but . . ."

"You're welcome," injected Guinevere. "I said 'you're welcome' on behalf of Kristi Lou. But there are no buts about what she said—you are indeed a tip-top good person. OK?"

"OK," said Marsha, unenthusiastically. "One way I try to reassure myself of the possible, minuscule OK-ness of my 3:59 origin is this arithmetical formula: 3+5=8; 8x9=72; 7x2=14; 1x4=4."

"Bingo!" said Guinevere. "There you go, good-person girl. That formulation is logical and gets your consecrated 4 into you. You're sheltered—by being fortified—from what you view as an inauspicious origination."

"Yeah, I guess it does fortify me. Of course, that word needs a u. But thanks, Guinevere."

"You're welcome. Anyway, back to astrology and the Starometer. I see you keying in those times. So, what are we? Explain us to ourselves."

"Give me a few more seconds."

The girls were quiet for about half a minute.

"OK, this is really interesting," said Marsha.

"Uh-oh," said Kristi Lou. "Watch Guinevere say something like 'It says that Kristi Lou was preordained to be a streetwalker.'"

"I hate it when someone steals my lines," retorted Guinevere.

"Ha-ha-ha. You're becoming predictable with your zingers against me."

"All right," said Marsha. "Here it is. Oh wow! Your moon sign is reflective of your inner self and provides insight into how you filter and manage your emotions. And it says here that your rising sign is also known as your ascendant and that your rising sign greatly determines how other people view you. And then there's your Mars planet and your Mars thing governs your anger and aggression and willingness to fight. And there are Earth signs and Sun signs and Air signs and Water signs and—this is so cool, really enthralling."

Marsha read her smartphone screen silently for another 35 seconds.

"Uh…" said Kristi Lou.

"Are we still sharing?" inquired Guinevere.

"Oh, sorry. So, OK, check this out. Kristi Lou's sun sign is Aries—fire type—but her moon sign and her rising sign and her Mars sign are all Pisces—water type. Guinevere's sun sign is Pisces but her moon sign and her rising sign and her Mars sign are all Aries. How about that?"

"So," said Kristi Lou, "there is a real nexus, astrologically, between Guinevere and me? Is this another one of my coincidences?"

"I'm not certain about the validity of the astrology," said Guinevere. "But I could've told you there is some type of connection between us, coincidental or not."

"Yeah, we are connected," replied Kristi Lou, as she looked at Guinevere.

"All right, Marsha—what about you?" asked Guinevere, gazing at Marsha with a warmer-than-usual smile. "I suspect that whatever your, uh, combination is that you're going to put some semi-paranoid, obsessive spin on it and make it more negative than it needs to be."

Guinevere and Kristi Lou saw that Marsha, while continuing to read, had progressively slipped into her frowny face.

"Well, I think it says here that…I'm effed up."

"That's basically true," offered Guinevere with her standard sardonic reassurance.

"Gee thanks, Guinevere. I knew I could count—one, two, three, four— on you."

"Oh, you're welcome. But, you know what? We're all effed up. But you're effed up in an especially charming way."

"I think maybe I should thank you for saying that. But…I…I've known for years that I'm a Gemini sun sign, which is an air type, but it's saying here that…oh my god…OMG…that my sun sign is Gemini, my moon sign is Gemini, my rising sign is Gemini, and that my Mars is in—what else?—Gemini. I'm overloaded with Gemini. I guess that explains why I'm a total airhead."

"Oh, you are not," said Kristi Lou, reassuringly. "I'm certain that Gemini is one of the grander signs 'cause you have so much of it. All that extra air is needed to let your brilliant brain breathe."

"Well, ha-ha-ha. Thanks. Ha. That's very supportive, and nicely alliterative—three straight b-words. But I've got the sign of the twin-type doppelgänger clones and they're thought to be highly contradictory or tugging each other to go toward different destinations or what-not-ever. I had heard or read that before. And I'm seeing here about flightiness and I'm thinking my obsessiveness might be tied into my Gemini excesses and I'm getting tired of reading this so I just might stop."

"I think you can safely not worry too much about what that website is telling you," said Guinevere. "It's probably right on some things but not on all things. Besides, you're an inimitably special person who's more deserving of high self-esteem than most people who go through life loaded with confidence and no OCD."

"Thanks," said Marsha. "You—both of you—help me feel better about myself."

Guinevere and Kristi Lou looked at each other, then at Marsha, and delivered to her a simultaneous "You're welcome."

"Changing the subject, I noticed something a while ago, before we got off onto the astrology tangent," said Kristi Lou. "You called Guinevere a fussbudget four times in a row."

"Of course. That made the name safer for Guinevere. Saying it four times diluted any bad karma that otherwise might accompany being called a fussbudget."

"So, that's a laudable aspect of your OCD," concluded Kristi Lou.

"I suppose you could say that," said Marsha. "OCD, OCD, OCD, OCD. There. That's better."

"OK, then," said Kristi Lou, gigglingly, with a quick-giggle laugh.

"However," said Marsha while gently poking the back of Guinevere's head four times, "I plan on making a change next May 29, four days after my birthday. On that day, I'll stop always calling it OCD and begin to sometimes call it CDO for 'compulsive disorder obsession.'"

"Why?" asked Kristi Lou.

"Because then the letters will be abecedarian, prudently arranged in alphabetical order—the way they ought to be."

"But," offered Guinevere, "it really should have four words, shouldn't it? May I suggest 'compulsive disorder obsession psychoquadnutsis'?"

"Yeah," said Marsha. "I like it. It comes out C-D-O-P. That's perfect for me; I'll pronounce it 'see-dope,' as in, 'See the dope who turns everything into a four-fest.'"

****

As the girls chuckled in unison, they heard someone yawn loudly.

Pete Lindsay had awakened from his catnap and had rolled down the Caravan's window. His yawning was sufficiently loud so as to sound as if it emanated from inside the attack car rather than several yards away. Stretching with both arms sprawled at 45-degree angles, he hailed Guinevere.

"Hey girls, get back in the car, please; we've got to get going. I've got to go to the police station and submit a full report on our activities for today and the past couple of days. Then, I need to discuss some things with you, Guinevere, back at the hotel."

"OK, Dad. I know," replied Guinevere. "Oh, Dad, by the way, at what precise hour and minute were you born?"

"Huh?"

"When, in terms of the exact hour and minute, were you born?"

"Hell, I don't know when I was born—that precisely. The day was March 4, but the rest of it—I don't know. Why?"

"We're doing star-studded research over here, astrologically speaking."

"Oh, that. Well, I don't know."

"OK. I'll ask Grandmother about the time of your hatching."

"I'm sure she was glad to get rid of me."

"Probably," said Guinevere, who turned to Marsha. "I'll get back to you with that info."

"OK. Cool," said Marsha.

"Oh wait," said Pete. "I recall now that this woman at the office where I used to work a few years ago—she was really into astrology— went around getting her coworkers' birthdays and doing one of those astro-chart things, or whatnot. She told me that I was sun Pisces with a moon Taurus and a Mars Scorpio and I had a Virgo this or that."

"Oh, Virgo," said Marsha. "With your Virgo, you're the only one of us who has any earth-type influence, that I know of."

"Oh, is that a good thing?"

"Why, sure it is," said Marsha. "As for me, I'm just full of air."

"A lot of people are full of something else. Anyway, Marsha, you're a smart, good-character girl."

"Thank you, Mr. Lindsay."

"You got it. OK, Guinevere, y'all wrap it up in a few minutes, OK? You and Marsha and Christine LouAnn get ready to roll."

"Dad, please," said Guinevere, continuing to feign aggravation at her father's purposeful mispronunciation of her friend's name.

****

Believing they were about to crank up and go, Kristi Lou had some quick and urgent questions. She felt her eyes move toward looking at

609

Marsha without her brain following them. Hence, for a half-second, she didn't know what she was looking at.

"Well, when are you leaving town? And where are you staying, Marsha—in the same hotel as them? Do you have your own room?"

"Tomorrow, I think. Yes, I am. No, I don't."

"Yeah, she's my roommate on this trip," said Guinevere. "Whenever she goes to the bathroom, the toilet flushes four times."

"Sorry."

"Not a problem; the toilet-flushing obsession is kinda funny, as long as it's not disturbing you. But, wait. I'm just now remembering that day back in seventh grade. You were about to tinkle on the floor because Mr. Battle couldn't say the right type of 'you're welcome,' and he had me intervene. And I escorted you to the restroom. And you had some elaborate flushing system, profoundly obsessive, that required some precise point-something-or-other number of flushes—I think it was .4 flushes. So now it's just four regular flushes?"

"Oh my! I do remember that day. Poor Bud…I mean, Mr. Battle. But, yes, my OCD flushing regimen required more fractional precision back in the day. I had to do three-and-one-quarter flushes—which are actually .25 flushes rather than .4 flushes, Guinevere, but, oh well. So, yes, now I just have to perform four normal full flushes—no partial flushes."

"Oh, that's right. It used to be three-and-one-quarter flushes," said Guinevere.

"Correct."

"I'm guessing your OCD has an impact on water bills."

"Yes. My water bills at my apartment back in Little Rock are always about $45 per month, when they probably should be only about $20 per month. I didn't mention this, but every time I go to the bathroom I let the water run in the sink for four minutes and then before I leave the bathroom I have to let it run for another four minutes. I have a clock with second hands on the wall.

"But I don't get stuck there when I just have to use the bathroom. As I explained earlier, it's when I brush my teeth that my OCD sometimes gets serious and hurtful in that room—when I get trapped in spitting fits to take care of my Republicans and my Democrats. Since I brush four times per day, I know that's the main thing that causes my water bill to inflate like a blimp.

"And my next-door neighbors are this family of—yes, I know you're both guessing what I'm about to say—this family of four—the perfect size for a family. They have two kids and the mom washes lots more loads of clothes than I do and she told me their water bill is usually about $25 per month. And I know I'm not doing the environment any favors by wasting water. I'm sorry."

"Don't worry about it, Marsha," comforted Kristi Lou. "You're not going to desiccate the rivers, the lakes, the watercourses, and the rivulets. Ain'ta gonna happena. And it's not a total waste 'cause—other than your teeth-brushing trap, which is seriously painful—you're getting something—your comfort—in exchange for the flowing and flushing water. And one of these days you'll kiss your OCD goodbye."

Kristi Lou turned to Guinevere and unleashed another flurry of queries.

"So, you're leaving tomorrow? What about your next stop to go after car criminals? You said that's Atlanta, right? Are you taking Marsha to Atlanta with you?" inquired Kristi Lou.

"No, we're flying Marsha back to Little Rock," said Guinevere.

"Yeah, I'm going home. This was all Guinevere's idea and Mr. Lindsay said yes and he paid for my plane ticket and everything."

"That was very generous of him," said Kristi Lou. "This has been so cool. Thanks again, Guinevere. And Marsh …Marsha, when I get back home to Little Rock I'm going to call you and you and I are going to hang out. I can tell from our get-together here today that we've grown up in a way that we can still be friends."

"I know. I agree. We're on the same wavelength. I feel as comfortable with you now as I did when we were kids," concurred Marsha Mellow, as she leaned behind Guinevere on the hood of the car and used her left forefinger to gently touch one of Kristi Lou's face freckles four times.

"Oh, good," said Kristi Lou, blinking rapidly upon the approach of Marsha's finger. "That's how I feel, too. And I'm very sincere when I say I will call you and that I want to get together; I will call you and we *will* get together, as in incessantly. I hope to be back for the Christmas holidays. You know, weirdly, I haven't been back home since I came up here three years ago. I'm quitting Secrets, as I told you a while ago, and I'm going back to classes fulltime, and the fall semester starts in a couple of weeks, in late August. That reminds me; I've got to go to the registrar's office and register."

"Registering is a judicious thing to do at the registrar's office," said Guinevere.

"Smart butt," said Kristi Lou. "But, no wait—my brain fizzled. I'll register at the WSU website, as I've been doing. I won't go to the registrar's office unless I have to."

Kristi Lou fumbled through an unnoticeable side pocket on her green summer dress and brandished a pen and piece of scratch paper. "Give me your phone number, Marsh, and I'll give you mine. All of our mobile numbers may or may not have changed since a few years ago."

"We can just swap phone numbers the modern way—into our phones."

"Oh yeah, right," agreed Kristi Lou. "Why didn't I think of that?"

"What about my phone number? Are you interested in my number, too? Or am I just not important?" asked Guinevere with mock sadness.

"Oh my; you're so sensitive all of a sudden, like I and Marsha. I suppose I might sorta want your phone number, maybe. I don't know, though. Of course I want your number."

"Well," said Marsha, "Guinevere is probably more sensitive, overall, than us 'cause she's a Pisces."

"Yes, I'm a sensitive Pisces. Dad is also a Pisces. He says that since I'm his daughter that I get to be a Pisces but he's a piss-eeze. Then he'll say that 'it's better than being a feces.'"

Grinning, all three friends exchanged updated phone numbers, inputting them into their cellphones.

"Mr. Lindsay already asked us to get back in the car and get ready to go," said Marsha. "And it's gotten a bit toasty out here. So, can we get back in and have the air conditioner on, please?" requested Marsha, who ordinarily would not speak up and ask for a change of pace involving other people. But she felt comfortable asserting herself in her present company.

"Kristi Lou and I will get back inside where it's cool but you have to stay out here and simmer," said Guinevere.

"Gee, thanks," said Marsha.

"You're welcome."

The girls reentered the car. Guinevere made the AC unload a blast of icy air that cooled everyone almost instantly.

****

"About ready over there, seriously now?" asked Pete. "You need to take Krystal Lynn back…"

"Kristi Lou, Dad," said Guinevere as she lowered her window to better hear Pete.

"…Kristi Louie back to, well, wherever she wants to go."

"I want to go home, please. And it really was nice meeting you, Mr. Lindsay, I mean Pete, at the club and out here with Guinevere. Well, I suppose I should once again say what I said to you an hour or two ago—that it was nice to re-meet you, since, you know, I met you before when I was little…uh…not so lit…when I was a kid."

"It was nice to re-meet you, too, Kristi Lou. I'm sure I'll see you again someday. When you're back in town, I know Guinevere would like to bring you over to the house. And Margie Ann lives just two blocks away. I know Margie Ann would enjoy talking with you."

"Margie Ann is Mom, in case you don't remember," explained Guinevere.

"Oh, as soon as he said 'Margie Ann' I remembered."

"Yeah, my dad's ex-wife—my current and forever mom—lives only a couple of streets away from him. And, if you're wondering, when I'm not sleeping in my apartment, I'll split time between their houses; I sleep over now and then. It all works out rather harmoniously."

"Oh, good. I'm so glad it does," said Kristi Lou.

Pete cranked the violent van; the startup sound was barely audible, just as faint as that of the attack car. The van's engine purred like a contented cat.

"OK, Guinevere. I'm out. See you back at the hotel, Marsha."

"OK. Drive carefully, Mr. Lindsay."

"I might," said Pete.

"Later, Dad."

Kristi Lou waved goodbye. Pete returned the wave and drove on.

50

AS PETE DROVE QUIETLY AWAY IN THE GRAY CARAVAN, HEAD-
ed toward the police station, he spotted a small, rumpled paper wedged between the storage console and the passenger bucket seat. He picked it up and saw it was a coupon for Downtown Secrets, with the name scribbled in the "For" box reading "Bosco Mason." Pete smiled as he thought about how he was driving the Caravan that Bosco had tried to steal.

Bosco dropped his sex discount. On the video review, I thought I saw something like this fall out of his pocket while he was being thrashed about. Oh well, he won't need it. He doesn't see too many women in his current neighborhood; he may have to adjust his sexual preferences.

51

AFTER 17 SECONDS OF NO TALKING, GUINEVERE SPOKE UP.

"Hey Marsha, don't you have some information about your family that you want to share with Kristi Lou?"

"Oh, that—yeah."

Marsha tapped her left nostril four times with her right pinky finger, tapped her knees together four times, tapped her upper and lower right molars against each other four times, and took exactly four seconds to finish all these movements combined.

Kristi Lou, ever observant, needed to inquire.

"Did you just do a ritual in your mouth?"

"Uh-huh. I did my quadruple teeth tap; it's one of my best protection procedures."

"Oh, all right. That's cool. I just wanted to confirm. So, what's up with your family? I hope everyone's OK."

"My daddy died," said Marsha with a serene but somber countenance.

Kristi Lou at first did not know what to say, and her mind urgently rummaged for the most appropriate reply, sifting hurriedly through sundry phrasal candidates. After about three seconds, she just sputtered.

"Oh no. I'm sorry. I'm so sorry. When did he go? What happened? I'm sorry, Marsha," stammered Kristi Lou.

"Thank you; you're very sweet. The last time we exchanged one of our occasional letters was before he left, so I know I never told you before. He passed away about two and a half years ago—on April 4. He had fast-growing cancer. He deteriorated so fast. The doctors discovered it and he was gone in five months."

Marsha gently tapped her chest over her heart four times with her right thumb.

"He'd been feeling really tired and bad before the diagnosis, but he just didn't go for medical help soon enough. He, I don't know, he just procrastinated, I guess. It's almost as if he … I don't know. He suffered but the morphine held down his suffering. We became even closer during that time. He told me that someday I'll beat my OCD and that I'm already much better with holding it down and that he knows I'm angelic and without guile and that he'd be with me—always. He told me he'd always be with me no matter what. We had hospice care in the house. He passed with Mom and me sitting on his bed. And we were holding his hands; Mom held his right hand and I held his left hand. And we were stroking his head. And we were telling him we will love him forever and always. He went quietly. He just seemed to stop breathing … and the last word Daddy said to me was 'always.'

"And, he didn't tell us, Mom and me, he didn't, didn't let us know till four days before he went to his heavenly home that he had done something quite sub rosa. He told us from his bed in a soft-but-audible voice that he'd kept a secret from us, that he had long ago, without telling even Mom, that, uh, that because he knew how we were and all with, you know, our OCD and its incapacitating effect and how, for Mom, a job is hard to get and harder to keep, that he had, uh, that years and years and years and years ago—long before the cancer—that he had purchased a super-value life insurance policy to cover our future living needs in case he were to pass away early. He'd been paying these stratospheric monthly premiums from a non-joint bank account about which he'd never told Mom. And the insurer insured him because back then he was a low-risker because he was healthy and fairly young—and he was willing to pay all that money 12 times per year for the premiums. And my father was such a reliably great provider for his wife and daughter because of his hard-work dedication to his high-paying-with-bonuses position of national distribution manager for his company that he could afford those premiums. And now we're financially secure. And you know what that means? Daddy is *still* providing for us—taking care of us from beyond the grave—from heaven."

"Oh, oh, that's so, oh, that's so tender and strong. I'm sorry. I'm so sorry," sympathized Kristi Lou, with tears beginning to roll over her arched cheekbones as she empathically felt Marsha's dolorous feelings.

"It's OK, but thank you."

"Oh … You're, you're welcome."

"I was a freshman at Arkansas, at U of A," continued Marsha.

"I'm glad he didn't suffer too much—well, I mean," Kristi Lou spluttered helplessly. "I, I know he, I mean, he had pain, and, but, I mean …"

"I know what you mean. And that's very kind of you, as usual—no, as always," assured Marsha.

"Oh, OK … sure. But, it's hard to know what to say," said Kristi Lou, stopping herself from further crying but still speaking with a crackled voice.

"I know. It's OK, though, really. It's OK," assured Marsha.

Guinevere smiled knowingly and with warmhearted sympathy. She handed Kristi Lou a tissue. "This Kleenex is just slightly used. I blew my nose on it a couple of days ago, but not too much."

"Oh, right. Ha-ha. I really wouldn't care right now if you actually had. Thanks," replied Kristi Lou while wiping her face.

The girls sat silently and somberly for about a half-minute, all peering straight down at their laps.

52

"NOW TELL HER ABOUT YOUR MOM'S CURRENT HOUSEHOLD arrangement," prodded Guinevere, breaking the somber silence as she moved her head past the inside end of the headrest to peek back at Marsha.

"Well, all righty then," agreed Marsha while leaning forward in the backseat, elbows on knees and chin placed in open palms which were touching each other 44 millimeters above her wrists. Marsha then began smiling directly at Kristi Lou, albeit with a tired smile that revealed her emotional weariness, as she was depleted from having just described the demise of her father.

"Well, we moved back to Little Rock. You might recall that we moved to Fayetteville after seventh grade. But after Dad passed away, Mom decided we should move back to Little Rock. So we did. We even got our old therapist back for our OCD."

"Oh, good," said Kristi Lou. "That's so cool that you're back home in Little Rock. As I was saying, when I get back there, I can see you without any problem."

"Yeah, I know. That'll be really great."

"Yeah, it will. But, anyhow, I definitely recall that you moved to

Fayetteville after seventh grade. For years, I'd go up there to visit you but you'd never be home."

"We just kept missing each other," replied Marsha. "But I got that note you left taped to the house that day—and I still have it somewhere!"

"Oh, that's so tender-sweet that you've kept it."

"There's another thing, though."

"What?"

"Mom remarried."

"Oh, I'm glad for her. Does he treat her well? Is he a good guy? Do you like him? Is he nice to you?"

"Yes, yes, yes, and yes. He was nice to you, too. Well, maybe not at first, but you grew on him, although maybe too much."

"What does what you just said actually mean?"

"He never looked down on you, though. That was impossible."

"Oh, we're playing games again. So, I know the fellow who married your mom?"

Guinevere, her perspicacity in perfect form, looked at Kristi Lou at the precise moment of comprehension. Kristi Lou raised the eyelids atop her large blue eyes. Her mouth opened wide before she spoke.

"You're kidding. Oh my god! Your mom married—no, she didn't. Yes, she did? She married Mr. Battle? Bud Battle is your stepfather? Is he still short?"

"Yes, yes, yes, and yes."

"Oh my goodness!" said Kristi Lou as she grinned and looked out the window, envisioning a remembered image of this one teacher with whom she shared a peculiar past and a bond of deep, two-way insecurity melded with mutual forgiveness.

"OMG, Oh my god."

Kristi Lou began to laugh robustly, but with no impertinence, as she bent forward and covered her face with her hands, and then turned back to face Marsha.

"A few moments ago I was crying about your dad and now I'm laughing about your stepdad. It's Mr. Battle! Oh my god. I'm sorry I keep saying oh my god, but—oh my god!"

Marsha tugged her left ear four times, preparing to amplify further.

"You don't think it's bad, do you?"

"No, no, definitely no. I don't. No. It's just that…I…I have to get used to the idea. Mr. Battle—your mom lives with Mr. Battle! All these memories come flooding back, and, I don't know. But, no—it's wonderful, it's superb. If you and your mom are happy, and if Mr. Battle is happy, then it's super-superb. I'm really happy for all of you."

"Oh, good. I'm glad you approve—really, no sarcasm."

"Oh, I do. Not that you need my approval, but you have it."

"Well, regarding his height, he was in his late 40s when we were in the seventh grade and he was our teacher," said Marsha. "So, he wouldn't have exactly grown too much—at least not vertically. Width-wise, well, that could be a different story. But, really, he hasn't developed much more of a paunch than he used to have back in the day."

"Oh my goodness. My mind is working overtime to try to appraise this. OK—this is magnifique! It's great! It's frankly kinda weird to me but, well, it's still great; it's really great."

Guinevere broached her perspective.

"We knew you'd find this marital development to be, at a bare minimum, interesting. I assured Marsha that you would probably respond positively. Hmm … I suppose I could've omitted the adjective 'bare' to qualify 'minimum,' but, oh well."

"What? Oh, 'bare'—ha-ha. I get it. You still just can't, you just, you simply just can't refrain from these little equivoque-ish digs."

"Evidently, I can't. Equivoques are so jocose."

"Yes, they are, aren't they? Particularly when you're dishin''em and I'm takin''em, ha-ha. But, anyway, yes, I'm positive about it, about Marsha's mom being married to Mr. Battle. It's cool. I was just thinking about

Mr. Battle a few days ago outside Secrets. I don't know why. Freakishly coincidental. I can't overstate how fascinated I am by coincidences. Anyway, I'd already begun seeing your car—this car I'm sitting in right now, I guess, except it's currently a different color—and I thought back to my seventh-grade year and about Mr. Battle and how he was so little and I was so big and we both hated each other for that, that is, until the second part of the school year when we started kinda liking each other."

"Yeah," said Guinevere, "we all remember those issues."

"And, as I told Mr. Lindsay…"

"Pete," corrected Guinevere. "As he said, he wants you to call him Pete."

"Oh, that's right. As I told Pete, you pulled me through that trauma."

"And both of you helped pull me through my trauma with the school bullies and my OCD," proclaimed Marsha.

"We really had some times that year," said Kristi Lou.

"We sure did," concurred Marsha.

"So, about Mr. Battle—he, I mean, he, he's your stepdad. How's that going? And, well, how is he? How is he doing? How is life with Mr. Bud Battle in the family?"

Marsha inconspicuously tapped her nose tip four times.

"Zowie—you sure can ask mega-multiple questions, can't you?"

"She's the undisputed champion of the world at that," said Guinevere.

"I know. I'm sorry."

"Oh, it's fine. I like it, sorta. No, it's fine. And fine. And fine. OK, well, here goes. Mom and Bud kept running into each other in the grocery store—coincidence, Kristi Lou?—where they would talk happily and they eventually started dating and romance blossomed and then down the church aisle they walked. After their wedding, Bud moved into Mom and Dad's house and then sold his house. Bud and Mom love each other. He'd never been married before. He's not the handsomest man on the planet, but he's so intelligent and he's very thoughtful. He's kind to Mom and he's kind to me; he's kind to us about our OCD. He's too sensitive sometimes and he can overact to things but the kindness is there; he's a good-hearted man. He was kind to me in school; he was very understanding and concerned about my OCD and all. Remember?"

"Yes," said Guinevere and Kristi Lou at the same moment.

"They've got a dog and two cats—all quadrupeds! Bud—he wants me to call him Bud but that took some getting used to since he was my teacher and I always called him Mr. Battle and now he's my stepfather—well, Bud still doesn't like being short, but he's not as perpetually upset about it as he used to be. He's less insecure about it; he's still insecure about it, mind you, but not *as* insecure about it as he used to be."

Marsha abruptly opened and closed her mouth four times, making four popping sounds.

"He and Mom and I have something in common; his preoccupation with his shortness is an obsession, in and of itself, and Mom, like me, has OCD. So, we're all sensitive about our own personal issues. But, since we all know we're all screwed up, we all show sensitivity to each other's screwy-ness. And, our mutual screwed-up-ness actually benefits us, in a way, by making us stronger together because we all understand our need to be understood. Does that make sense? And so, we're not as dysfunctional of a family as some people might speculate us to be. Not that we're not dysfunctional. We are dysfunctional. But we're only somewhat dysfunctional; it's functional dysfunctional-ness. And also, Bud says that we should be grateful that, unlike many families, our family is, as he says, 'financially solvent.' He's fond of quipping that 'We've got gas in the tank and money in the bank.' He gets that from this song he likes to walk around the house singing called 'The Man,' which is from this band with the macho name of The Killers. Did I just say 'screwed-up-ness' and 'functional dysfunctional-ness'?"

"Yes, you did," confirmed Guinevere, "but that's OK."

"Oh dear," said Marsha. "My grandmother says that: 'oh dear.'"

Kristi Lou blurted her thoughts.

"I'm really so glad to hear about all this, to know you and your mom and Mr. Battle are happy together. Does he have any hair left?"

"What?" asked Marsha.

"Oh, I hope that question wasn't too blunt. I didn't mean to be rude. I think I blather more than I should. I was blathering without my filter on because I believe you know I wouldn't say anything that was meant to be hurtful. But, as you were just saying, you are sensitive and, well, anyway, I was just wondering about his alopecia because…"

"No, it's all right; it's funny you should ask about his alopecia—good word, by the way. So, but, anyway, just four months ago, in April, he was down to—believe it or not—14 hairs. I know; I might sound like I'm making it up about how long ago it was and how many hairs he had—14. But I'm not. One day when I was visiting at Mom's house, I stood over him while he sat sprawling on the living room recliner and I counted 'em. Of course, he had already done a hair count and he'd found 15 hairs but I told him one hair didn't count because it belonged to Muffin, who is one of their kitties, and it had floated onto his head and stuck in his mousse."

"Oh, so," asked Kristi Lou, "he still plasters his hairs in place?"

"Yes, actually-factually—like cement. Every now and then they'll stand up straight and he looks like a cockatoo. Anyhow, he finally started using this hair-growth product they advertise on television and it's sorta working. He's up to 31 whole hairs!"

"That's wonderful!" exclaimed Kristi Lou, with undiluted sincerity.

"Wasn't your mom's OCD rather pernicious? Is she doing any better? Does she manage her compulsions more effectively, as you do with yours?"

"Yes, yes, and yes. She still goes to therapy once a month with me, though. She still has to flex her butt cheeks at mile markers."

"Oh, she does?" asked Kristi Lou. "Oh my goodness; I remember that."

"Yes, but now she flexes her butt only at certain mile markers, but not all of them. They are designated butt-flex markers. It's a form of selective butt-cheek flexing."

"Yeah, that's probably the best kind of butt-cheek flexing," agreed the very earnest Kristi Lou.

"Yes, it is. It's really a good thing that with some mile markers, she's butt-flex free."

Kristi Lou nodded while responding with more genuine enthusiasm. "That's splendid."

"Yeah, she's much better about it."

"I'm so glad she's rebutting her butt-cheek flexing," said Kristi Lou.

"I also applaud her rebuttal," said Guinevere.

"You're both funny-bunnies. Anyway, Bud's very cool about it, too; he's really come to accept that his wife is a butt-cheek flexer," said Marsha in a solemn tone, demonstrating pride in Bud's tolerance.

"Well," said Kristi Lou, "I must say that I've never talked so much about butt-cheek flexing in my entire life as I have this past minute. I'm not complaining, though. It's really a unique and intriguing topic. But—oops, I said 'but,' but I meant the regular 'but' even though we're talking about somebody's buttocks butt. But, I'm well-pleased that he's flexible about her butt. Uh, he's flexible about her butt-cheek flexing. OK, but … I'm confusing myself."

"Well said," said Guinevere.

"So," said Kristi Lou as she formed her next battery of questions, "I have to ask: Did Mr. Battle know you were coming up here and that you'd try to see me? Did he ask you to tell me hi or anything? Does he know what I've been doing for work while I've taken time off from college?"

"Yes, yes and … no. How could he know? I didn't know, myself—that is, what you do for, uh, work. I didn't know when I got here to Detroit. Guinevere told me in the hotel room. She had gone for a spin soon after we checked in at the hotel, and she saw you in front of your nightclub."

"Well, maybe you could not tell him, if you don't mind, about my work goings-on. But, on the other hand, since I'm committed to my philosophy that non-violent sex is mostly a good thing and something many people should stop being hysterical against, I suppose I shouldn't care if he knows. But, I don't know, but, I mean, he's your stepdad so you can tell him anything you darn well please, of course, but, I guess I …"

"Don't worry. We don't have to be absolutely perfectly in line all the time with our convictions. You're mostly consistent, I'm sure, but I think some inconsistencies are normal. And no, I won't tell Bud about your, uh, occupational field. So, it's OK. But he wouldn't hold it against you even if he did know … well, maybe a tad … but not too much."

"Thanks," said Kristi Lou.

"You're welcome."

"Please tell him I said hi back at him. Tell him I'm glad to learn that he's happily married. Tell him that I think he was one of my better teachers."

"I will."

"And please tell him that I'm very sorry if I ever hurt his feelings by being taller than him. I didn't do it on purpose. Genetics did it. My body had a mind of its own."

"OK, I'll tell him," said Marsha as she laughed mildly, "but he bears no grudge against you whatsoever. He actually has a fond memory of you. He said you were one of his super-smart students—as he says about Guinevere. And, of course, he says that about me, too."

"Oh, that's so good to hear. I'm very flattered. I was just so tall and he was just so, uh, un-tall. Man, how we wanted to swap. But it seems it worked out for both of us."

"Yes, and as Marsha was saying, he's as vertically challenged as he ever was," said Guinevere. "I've seen him around town a few times in recent years, and he was home when we stopped by to pick up Marsha. He's really a nice guy. He always was, deep down; he was just so insecure back when we were in school because of his exiguous stature that he sometimes let that insecurity make him a bit ornery. He was the same as you on that note but in reverse. And fate threw you in together. Life is sometimes strange."

"Exiguous," said Kristi Lou. "Darn it to heck. I know—or at least I knew—that word, but I can't think of what it means now, dang it."

"Please curb the obscene language," said Guinevere.

"Oh, gee whiz—sorry"

"Exiguous means meager, scanty, exceptionally small."

"Oh yeah, that's it. Also, I should've known that by the context in which you used it in your sentence—to describe Mr. Battle's insecurity. Anyway, if you see Davey again, please don't tell him I didn't know that word."

"You can count on me. Or can you? Kidding."

"But," said Kristi Lou as she looked back at Marsha, "he doesn't … that is, Mr. Battle doesn't … you know, regarding being littlish, he doesn't worry about it so much anymore, right? That's what you were saying earlier, wasn't it? Weren't you saying … ?"

"No, not a lot—just a little bit, now and then. He's mostly accepted his littleness. And being married to Mom has helped him a lot because he knows a woman found him masculine enough to marry him. Plus, she's only two inches taller than he is, which means she's two inches taller than I am because Bud and I are both 5'1", which means that since you're 5'13", you're 12 inches taller than your ex-teacher, which means you're even more taller than Bud than you used to be. Ha-ha-ha … wait for it … ha. But, anyway, Mom and Bud give each other companionship and that makes him feel a heapin' helpin' of happiness."

"So, I have come to like my height while Mr. Battle has come to tolerate his."

"I'd say that's an accurate assessment," agreed Marsha Mellow.

53

GUINEVERE LIGHTLY TAPPED A TOUCHSCREEN BUTTON AND revved the Bad Car's engine, which emitted the usual almost inaudible murmur, joined by a pulsing, sensual vibration felt throughout the vehicle's cabin.

"Why did you do that?" inquired Kristi Lou. "The car was already on. Are we getting ready for takeoff or something? As in flying through the air? Oh wait. You said earlier that this car can't fly—yet"

"I was just juicing the car a bit because it's been idling with the AC on while we've been gabbing. I also turned down the air conditioning so we won't freeze."

"Oh, all right. Not freezing us is commendable."

Marsha reached into her pocket and pulled out a small bottle of alcohol-based liquid hand sanitizer. She squirted some onto her hands and rubbed them together aggressively. She looked at Kristi Lou and then at Guinevere.

"Want some?"

"Oh, no thank you," replied Kristi Lou, who glanced down at her hands. "On second thought, yes, I'll have some, please."

"As will I. Thanks, Marsha," said Guinevere. "But, are you insinuating that my car is germy?"

"Oh no. It seems quite pristine, compared to most cars. But germs are everywhere, and they're always a menace. I'm already mentally sick. So I try to avoid being physically sick. Being sick is bad."

"That statement is profound," said Guinevere.

"Thank you," said Marsha.

"You're welcome," said Guinevere and Kristi Lou in unison.

"Now, both of you stick your hands back here."

Guinevere and Kristi Lou complied with Marsha's instructions and received four button-pushes apiece worth of hand sanitizer.

"That fourth squirt yielded the best sanitizer," assured Kristi Lou as she and Guinevere rubbed the clear, lemon-scented product all over their hands, getting it between their fingers and beneath their fingernails, just as they'd observed Marsha do a few moments earlier.

"I know," agreed Marsha. "The fourth squirt was definitely the most bestest and goodest."

"Marsha's vocabulary is expansive," said Guinevere.

"Thank you."

"You're welcome," replied Guinevere, with perfect timing.

"I was glad to see both of you push some sanitizer underneath your fingernails," said Marsha. "Germs have parties under fingernails."

"So, Marsha," asked Kristi Lou, "are you a full-fledged germaphobe, AKA mysophobe?"

"Yes. My fledge is phobically full. I'm fully mysophobic. You might say I'm kind of obsessed with fighting off germs. Me obsessed? Who woulda ever thunked it?"

"Not I," said Kristi Lou with a giggle. "I know someone else who's a germaphobe."

"You!" said Marsha.

"Yes, me—what a shocker, huh?"

"Not really," said Guinevere.

Marsha twined her arms behind her head, bumping her frail biceps against her ears four times, and then prepared to describe one of her colorful fantasies.

"I've read and heard, as I know both of you have, also, that after we pick up germs from strangers in public places, the primary way those germs enter our bodies is through our fingers touching our faces."

"Yeah, that's what they say," concurred Guinevere. "There was a man on our hotel-room TV last night saying precisely that same thing."

"There was?" asked Marsha.

"Yes, but you were conked out in dreamland. He talked about germs for about half a minute or less."

"Wow. What a coincidence," said Kristi Lou. "I mean, that Marsha is now talking about that and just last night you happened to be watching a certain channel out of gazillions of channels at just the right time to hear this man talking about the same topic. And Marsha isn't now simply recalling what he said; she couldn't 'cause she was sleeping and presumably never heard him say a word. I'm just…"

"…fascinated by coincidences," said Guinevere, interrupting with a smile.

"You finished me!" exclaimed Kristi Lou, also smiling.

"Yes, I did. I'm sorry about that."

"No, that's OK with me."

"But you're right; it is a coinkydink," reassured Marsha. "Or is it? But anyway, as I was saying, that's mainly how germs get into us—through us touching our faces and transmitting germs into our insides."

"Yeah," said Kristi Lou.

"So, sometimes I sorta, well…I see germs."

"You see germs?" inquired Kristi Lou.

"I see germs."

"What do they look like?"

"They look like germs. They always look the same. They're purple and brown and ugly and mean-looking little rectangles with nasty hairs that prickle me when they crawl across my face. I look in the mirror and watch them trying to sneak into my nose or into my ears, or sometimes they try to raid my skin pores on my cheeks and my chin, trying to scale my epidermis's ramparts."

"Yuck," said Kristi Lou.

"But, thankfully, I always also see my face-friends, as I call them. They—my face-friends—they, they are little Army men or little Marine men—little military men, and they come charging out from behind my skin's parapets and repel the germ invaders. My face-friends have little bayonets and they impale some of the germs and other germs turn and flee and I see germs falling off my face and they always decompose while they fall and they vanish into the air before they can hit the floor. Then my face-friends turn and salute me and I counter-salute them and they go back inside my face to lie in wait to retaliate against more germ attackers. So, my face-friends plus my washing my hands prolifically and my using hand sanitizer helps me almost never get sick…well, at least not in a physical sense."

"Well, Marsha," said Guinevere, "that part of your inner world is truly, uh—Kristi Lou—fascinating. Thank you for sharing that account with us."

"Oh my god. OMG, Marsha!" exclaimed Kristi Lou. "That was amazing. And, well, I, I've got to tell you that…that…I see germs, too!"

"Yes, of course you see germs," said Guinevere. "Another nottashocka."

"I do. My germs don't get run off by any face-friend soldiers or anything that cool. My germs that I see are small and kinda translucent—I can see through them—and they just are there and then I stop thinking about them after a few seconds and they just go away. But anyhow, the thing is that…what a…well, it is. It is. It really is another you-know-what that starts with a C. It's just fascinating. OK, I know I said my F-word again while talking about my C-word again."

Kristi Lou looked at Guinevere and then back at Marsha and then at her shoes now pressed very hard against the car's floorboard.

"I'm just besieged by coincidences."

"I believe you," said Guinevere with a warm smile.

"Anyhow," said Kristi Lou, "this is so much fun—what we're doing—just sitting and talking. I could do this everlastingly."

54

THE REUNITED FRIENDS YAKKED FOR ANOTHER FEW MINUTES.
Guinevere checked her watch.

"We better go. We've stayed here jabbering way too long after Dad
asked us to go. He'll be done at the police station soon and we need to
get back to the hotel room. I'm not sure about everyone else's bladder
but I need to tinkle."

"Do you already have everything packed?" asked Kristi Lou, who was
not concerned about suitcases but wanted to delay her friends' departure, though without being inconsiderate to their and Pete's time needs.
Upon realizing the core of her own question—everything packed—she
felt a sudden sadness sweep into her body, even glancing down at her
stomach to where the melancholic feeling had plummeted. Her mouth
opened and her face sunk.

Kristi Lou realized in a millisecond that she'd never felt so lonely
so fast.

Oh God, I feel empty.

The onset of emptiness frightened her, imposing a terror that had
arisen in a heartbeat and for which she was wholly unprepared.

"Yes. Our packing is done," answered the perspicacious Guinevere,
who immediately read the woebegone expression on her friend's face.

633

"Marsha is flying home to Little Rock and Dad and I are on our way to Atlanta for more work. We'll be driving—of course."

"Of course," said Kristi Lou, as she looked up at Guinevere and displayed a forced smile that fused incongruously with the gloom in her eyes. "Your vehicles are the tools of the trade."

Guinevere and Marsha, who also sensed Kristi Lou's dejection, looked at each other, knowing what they had to do.

"Hey, Kristi Lou," said Guinevere, "do you have any friends here in Detroit—any close friends, real friends. I'm talking about friends you can talk with—on your level, people to whom you can intellectually and culturally relate?"

Kristi Lou, not expecting such a stark inquiry to be asked at this moment, glimpsed at her shoes and then looked outside the car while rubbing her neck.

"No."

"That's what I thought," said Guinevere.

Marsha silently tapped her knees together four times.

"Well, there's Rochelle at Secrets. I love Rochelle. There are a few other girls there. There's Hokey, our bouncer. He protects me. I love him, too. Then there's Satine; she's actually quite bright and fairly well-educated, as is my coprophobic friend, Denny. But, well, I really enjoy talking to them, but, I guess, as far as what you said about culturally relating and the intellect angle and so forth, well, I … well … no.

"Wait. Yes, there is one true friend to whom I can relate very well-ly, despite one obvious difference between us. Well-ly? I think I just took a word that's already an adverb and added an extra l and a y. Oh, well."

"Who's that to whom you relate so, uh, well-ly," asked Marsha, smiling.

"His name is Mr. Wilmont."

"You mentioned him earlier today," said Guinevere. "You said you'd said 'ye olde' to him recently. Considering that you refer to him as mister, I gather that he's an older gentleman."

"You might say that. He's in his late 80s—eighty-nine, to be exact."

"Yeah, that's a sizable age gap," said Marsha. "But, if you can relate well—and you just said you do relate 'very well-ly' to him—despite being from such different backgrounds, age-wise, then the age doesn't matter as far as having fulfilling conversations and feeling a warm kinship."

"We have wonderful conversations, though our conversations are sometimes emotionally taxing. He helps me with my deepest doubts about my life choices while I'm young, and I help him grapple with, well…with his drug-based demons from when he was young. He, uh, he used to take LSD, and he's still coping with what has been for him this inexorable, implacable nightmare—a bad trip from hell. And he practically doesn't go anywhere or socialize with anybody—and he profoundly misses his beloved wife, Mary, whom he lost to cancer in March."

Guinevere knew what to say.

"You and Mr. Wilmont share a deep commonality. You're both exemplary people. And you're both two of the loneliest people in the world."

"Do you think I'm *that* lonely?"

"Yes."

"Uh, 'in the world,' you say? Not just regular lonely, but *that* lonely? You could, of course, be maybe-possibly-sorta right. Actually, Mr. Wilmont and I have talked about that issue, uh, quite candidly. All right, I'll tell you that, mostly, I work and go to my apartment. There's a goofball modern meme making the rounds about how a woman who lives with a cat but no humans is likely lonely. Yeah, well, that's quite overblown, but regardless, that's me. But, if I had an orphanage full of two-legged kids, Mr. Dooflotcher would still be my fur-kid. Anyway, the loneliness thing is…yeah, it's true. But, 'in-the-world' lonely? OK, well, I don't have anyone over to visit. It's rare that I go out to eat or go to a movie, and when I do go, I go by myself. I go to the grocery store, but I, uh, I typically go only once per month to stock up because some studies have been said to show that most shoppers save money with getting more groceries on fewer trips than with getting fewer groceries on more trips because of, they say, fewer opportunities for, you know, impulse buying and all that. But, that's also fewer opportunities to happenchancily meet people while shopping, and … happenchancily? But, uh, I occasionally go to the mall, but rather infrequently and … well … that's about it. So, umm … super-extreme loneliness? I suppose you could make a case that I may be trending toward 'in-the-world'-level loneliness, a little. But, I don't know that it's that awf … that extre … that I'm really *that* lon … OK. I disclosed to Mr. Wilmont that sometimes I'm so lonely I cry myself to sleep. So … yeah."

Kristi Lou, after conceding, nose-dived her eyes, then her head, with her chin looking as if it sought to meld into her sternum.

"But Marsha and I are going to help you fix that."

"You are?"

"We are," concurred Marsha.

"Oh, I'm more than ready for that," said Kristi Lou, hoisting her melancholy face and looking at Marsha, then Guinevere.

"I know you are," said Guinevere, now presenting herself as the same soothing rescuer for Kristi Lou as she was in the seventh grade at Mary Our Lady of Mercy Catholic School for Gifted Pupils in Little Rock eight-and-a-half years earlier.

"But," said Kristi Lou, "after you've fixed me and my loneliness, I'll still have to be available for my old—my much older—friend, Mr. Wilmont. Sometimes, he's like the archetypal lost puppy. And he's helped me so much. I can't just abandon him. If I leave Detroit, I'll have to stay in touch with him—for real, really."

"You can do that," assured Guinevere. "But, you know what? You just might break through to him so he's … well, number one, so he's not having his bad trips anymore and, number two, so he's somehow getting around other people—of whatever age—he can relate to warmly and intelligently and therefore he wouldn't miss you quite as much. Some, but not as much."

"Yes. I've been trying to convince him to do essentially just that—to get involved in some of the local group programs for seniors and so forth. And, by the way, I'll miss him, too."

"I know you will," said Guinevere. "You're too sentimental and too deep to not miss someone for whom you care after you've parted, and you will never coldly dismiss anyone because they're quote in the past unquote. You have the depth to keep them near when they're afar. You keep the memories. You keep a yearning for them.

"However, we need to get you somewhat more normalized, for lack of a better word, in an overall sense. Of course, you, just as Marsha and I are not, will never be completely normal. But, I'm talking about whether there are currently any potential friends around here in your own age bracket and on your intellectual level with whom you can go dancing—not work-dancing at Secrets but regular dancing—or that you can go out with to wherever, or hang out with them at your home or theirs, or maybe…"

"No."

"No?"

"No. There aren't any, unless you maybe count Satine, as I said, but…"

"How about when you're on campus? It's Wayne State, right? You're about to go back to classes. Any true friends there? You must've made some friends during your freshman, sophomore, and junior years."

"I used to have several friends at WSU, but they're gone. Two of them graduated. Another two or three left school. And then I myself left school to earn more money and also to, well, to…to just experience what it'd be like to step over into an X-rated version of Neverland—that is, to learn for myself what goes on over on the so-called wild side, the outcast side, the other side. Yes, I wanted the money, but I actually…I just…I really wanted the adventure as well as the money.

"I think I've already basically told you much of this stuff already, and I know I'm rambling. But anyway, I had intended to stay with Secrets till at least next January but I thought that if I took classes and worked at Secrets at the same time it would be so draining that I'd always be exhausted because of the overload. And I did confirm that concern by doing just that—school daytime and nightclub nighttime—for a brief while in the spring. I was so tuckered out. So, I was gonna skip the fall semester—remove my life from ordinary mode and live on the shadowy side of the tracks. And I suspect that right about now I'm sounding like the plot to a late-night movie. Anyhow, maybe I'll make some new friends in a couple of weeks when I reenroll."

"Yes, you definitely will," said Marsha. "That's exactly what you'll do."

"Yeah, I probably will. Thanks for encouraging me. Oh—and after resigning, uh, quitting at Secrets, I'm gonna go back to church, perhaps maybe possibly in September. I've just had to stay away from church while I've been … well … you know, but—I'm fixin' to go back."

"Yes," said Marsha. "You definitely should, speaking of an ideal place to meet new friends—and hopefully reconnect with old ones."

"That's a marvelous decision, Kristi Lou," said Guinevere.

"Gee, thanks. Occasionally, I can be intelligently decisive. By the way, speaking of relating to other living beings, I wish to say that ships are bigger, stronger, and go farther than boats, though both can be good."

"Uh-oh," said Guinevere, as Marsha grinned widely. "You're about to unfurl some of your word-spinning, gymnastical morphology, aren't you?"

"No, not I, ha-ha. OK, what I'm about to say already has some attention on the Internet. Here's my take: I believe that with a deep-feeling, trust-packed bond, you can have a *relationship*. Whereas with a nice-but-casual-acquaintance involvement, you can have a *relationboat*."

As Marsha commenced tittering, Guinevere offered her reply. "Your brain should be studied intensely by a team of A-list scientists using the Hubble Telescope."

"Ooh, that might be fun, albeit necessitating a ratherish size-of-device overreach. I'm up for having my head examined, but I'm afraid they wouldn't find anything."

"They'd unearth a thing or two—or four," said Marsha, grinning. "Oh, I've been meaning to ask you: Where do you put all that money?"

"Hoarded and squirreled away in a guhnormous, treasure-trove cardboard box under my bed."

"Yeah, right," said Marsha.

Guinevere interceded.

"So, you hide money under a bed after making money on a bed. And sometimes you even sleep on a bed, too, right? Beds can have multiple uses."

"No, I do not … make money on a bed. We, uh … we don't have beds at Secrets. They're sorta sofa … ish. But, anyhow, at present, I choose to not have a checking account, but I do have one bank card—a MasterCard—for occasional purchases and to build credit. And I can buy a money order when I need to, which is what I use for paying my rent. And when I go shopping for groceries or whatnot, I usually pay for my stuff with old-fashioned cash. And I have a Bank of America savings account for a secure place to keep my money and for convenient, quick-access withdrawal from an ATM. And I have my savings account linked to my online money market account into which I electronically transfer a lot of money 'cause it provides much better APY interest. And so I deposit almost all of my money into the bank so there's no bed involved so—so there!"

Kristi Lou stuck her tongue out at Guinevere.

"Kidding," said Guinevere, with a teeth-flashing grin.

"I know, Miss Wiseacre. Anyway, nobody's been on my bed besides Mr. Dooflotcher. And we don't have that type of relationship."

"You're not into bestiality, AKA zoophilia?"

"So far, no. But I may be zo-curious."

"Oh stop, you two," said Marsha, giggling.

55

"ATTENTION! HERE IS A MAJOR ANNOUNCEMENT CONCERNING you," Guinevere forthrightly proclaimed while looking at Kristi Lou.

"OK."

Guinevere continued to look directly at Kristi Lou, while pausing her words for effect, waiting three seconds before speaking again.

"I have decided to map out and revamp part of your life."

"Really? Oh my goodness. OK. Gee, thanks, I think."

"Ready?"

"Go for it."

"Next year," said Guinevere, "after you've graduated, you are required to move back to Little Rock. I'm propounding this relocation as a friendship requirement—but in a friendly fashion, of course. So, I'm not really making any demands. Well, OK, I'm not making any demanding-type demands, and I know you know what I mean."

"Yes, I know."

"We'd love to have you back home. Dad and I may or may not be finished with our attacks on car punks in California by then. After we do Bakersfield, we will, as I was saying earlier, aggressively keep going in that state, if allowed. We'll at least take some periodic breaks for long periods—like a sabbatical. Mom made it clear that she requires such respites if she's not going to interfere with Dad taking their daughter on these potentially dangerous sorties, and he knows she's serious. Regardless, you're moving back to Arkansas for refurbishment."

"Oh, good, good; that's very good. You're such a good mapper-outer and a good revamper and a good life planner and a good refurbisher. Yes, as I sit here right now, that's what I want to do in my future. I'll have to see how I feel about it next year. But, as of now, I want to move back. That axiom that 'you can't go home again' is wrong; you can indeed go home—both literally and allegorically. Yes, you can. Your old home may not be exactly the same as it was when you departed but it can still be almost the same or at least plenty close enough to being the same."

"Absolutely," agreed Guinevere. "I assure you that you'll quite easily recognize Little Rock as home."

"Yes, I know I will. It'll be life in Little Rock redux. I want to see Mom and Dad again. I want to be in their lives again. I want to continue being independent but I still want to be with them again, and often. I want to try to work in Little Rock. But not, of course, in the world's oldest profession—of prostitution; I'm calling it what it is, and that's all right. That is, I want to work in Little Rock with a career in my degree field—a major in Education with a minor in English. And that obviously aims me toward a work-life in the classroom. I'll have to get certified to teach in Arkansas. I can do that. And, no one's mentioned it, but yeah, I know I could transfer my credits to a university in Arkansas and move home in just a few weeks. But no, I won't, because, among other reasons, psychologically, for me, that'd be too timewise close to what I'm, uh, what I'm about to stop doing. I need more distance, so … Oh my god! I just thought—what if I wind up teaching at the same school as Mr. Battle? That would be majorly weird. What school does he teach at, Marsha? He's not still at Our Lady, is he?"

Marsha smiled her toothiest smile and folded her arms. She then rocked to and fro on her backseat perch.

"Yes, he is. He sure is still there. Actually, he left and taught high school over in Mabelvale for four—yes, four, my precious number four—for four years. But, I guess he's somewhat of a glutton for punishment, as they say, so he went back to teaching middle school kids at his old stomping grounds—and ours—at Our Lady."

"Oh my goodness," said Kristi Lou.

"They say," offered Guinevere, "that life is often circular, even when we don't see the circles."

"Yeah, I agree with that," said Kristi Lou, who had joined fellow interlocutors Guinevere and Marsha in sharing that feeling that sometimes rises between trusting friends when they feel a soothing satisfaction—almost tantamount to a psychotropic high—upon comfortably losing themselves in their conversation. They all sensed it, though none directly spoke of it.

Kristi Lou's saudade of moments earlier had not vanished but had diminished; she had come to feel certain that she would return to her hometown after graduating, and that Guinevere and Marsha would be there waiting for her.

She felt her mind hurtling ahead to envision meeting a man for romance. And the prospect that she would find him someday, whoever and wherever he might be, gave her one of those warm sensations in the pit of her stomach. Kristi Lou thought to herself, without words, that this soothing sensation in her stomach felt so much better than the swallowed-an-anvil sensation, mixed with terrifying despair, that incubated in her stomach only about five minutes afore.

Kristi Lou knew she had been sweetly salvaged from the wreckage of quasi-clinical depression by Guinevere and Marsha. Prior to the deliverance provided by her confidantes, the episode of abject despair that had gripped Kristi Lou made her hurt deep inside, attacking her with a deeper awareness of the desolate place where her life currently

ment as in 'we're *only* children,' as if to say 'we're *just* children.' What I meant was that we're only children as in none of us have any brothers or sisters. It's a tad confusing because you often hear the singular 'only child' but the plural 'only children' is sort of a nonstandard phrase. Anyhow, we have no siblings; that's what I meant. But, yes, I get that we're all young adults."

"Darn—somehow I just got that wrong—sorry," said Kristi Lou. "On that note, though, I guess we're all spoiled rotten, as the stereotype goes, huh?"

"No big deal," said Guinevere. "But you're mistaken when you say 'we're all spoiled rotten.' You and I are spoiled; Marsha's not spoiled," said Guinevere.

"I am, too, spoiled."

"No, you're not," disagreed Guinevere. "You're too OCD to be spoiled. Oh, excuse me; I should have said CDO. And, as I recall, we did agree that there should be a fourth letter. What was it, again?"

"We decided on CDOP, for compulsive disorder obsession psycho-quadnutsis. How could you forget? You're the one who came up with it."

"Oh, that's right. So I did. My memory is lucid but not flawless."

"Anyway, maybe it should be CDOM for 'compulsive disorder of Marsha,'" said Marsha, pensively, as she twitched her clitoris four times.

"Did you just…? Never mind," said Kristi Lou.

"Yes, I did."

"You did? Did you…"

"I did a clit twitch."

"Oh my god, is that what you call it? But, but that's…that's about what I thought you did. But, how did I know that? How could I tell that you…uh, did that…down there?"

"Well, I suspect," inferred Guinevere, roguishly, "that your peripheral vision, as did mine, inadvertently caught a glimpse of some irregular vellicative movement near Marsha's pubic zoning, despite being covered by clothing, and your mind made a presumption, what with your being keenly aware of her compulsions since we've discussed them arduously this afternoon. I already knew Marsha did a vaginal ritual; she told me about it a few days ago. I believe your perspicacity rebounded quickly."

"Right—from un-getting 'only children' to getting a clitty-twitchy."

"Plus, vagina-intensive activities are not exactly foreign to you, thus you may have an acute awareness of actions emanating in that area."

"Oh. My. Goodness. You're relentless. You just keep dissing me with your zinger-zappers."

"It's fun."

"Yeah, I know. I like it, too," said Kristi Lou.

"Yes, I know you do. Well, it's getting late. I've been watching the clock; I've been measuring time. There's a word for that, Miss Vocabulary Girl, and you, being a lubricious logophile, should probably know what it is."

"I should?"

"Yes."

"OK, what is it?"

"Horology."

"How do you spell that?" asked Kristi Lou, smirking.

"It's spelled h-o-r-o-l-o-g-y."

"So, it's not w-h-o-r-e-o-l-o-g-y, after all? But, that's what, what you're, uh, intimating, right? Right? Right?"

"What? I would never do that," puckishly contended Guinevere.

"Right."

"Poor Kristi Lou," said Marsha. "Guinevere just won't stop zinging you."

"I know. She keeps nailing me with raillery," said Kristi Lou, who laughed and again stuck her tongue out at Guinevere. "This may go on forever."

"You can count on it," confirmed Guinevere. "Prepare yourself to receive an ongoing barrage of badinage. Nothing says 'I love you' like benign ridicule."

"Bombard me adoringly! Oh, Guinevere, there's this thing I omitted from my anti-atheism, street-side speech your dad heard. So, uh …"

"Go ahead," said Guinevere and Marsha, simultaneously, while smiling.

"OK, I'll delve in. As to accounts stating that Hitler and some of his top-tier executives were promoters of animal welfare, any such Nazi advocacy would constitute a gross anomaly and a bizarre irony. There are conflicting claims as to whether Hitler was a vegetarian. Reputable reports aver that his doctor put him on a vegetarian diet to combat irritable bowel syndrome. But—regardless of whether a few Nazis in high-power positions advocated for kindness to animals while gruesomely murdering people—vegetarians and vegans, long before and after the Nazi regime's rise and demise, have shared a greater commonality with people who are non-cruel to other people than have meat-eaters. Yes, meat-eaters greatly outnumber non-meat-eaters, but look at valid per-capita-percentage data, where available, chronicling conviction records for members of both populaces for crimes against humans. The numbers associated with criminal activity against humans as perpetrated by known vegetarians/vegans are comparatively microscopic. Worldwide, there is zero documented correlation between Nazi-style, violent behavior against humans and persons who compassionately promote kindness to nonhuman animals—other than from a handful of 1930s–1940s Nazis themselves. Such a smear-tactic linkage is asinine. Applying a truth-based, position reversal of that antilogic, we should *not* eat meat because Stalin, Mao, Idi Amin Dada and General Butt Naked *did.* Quite ironically, more members of the population known as meat-eaters are flatly aligned, violent-conduct-against-people-wise, with the alleged animal-protecting Nazis than are non-Nazi, animal-protecting vegetarians/vegans. Animal protectionism as provided by a dozen or so mid-1900s, psychopathic, anomalistic Nazis remains a dramatic exception to who ordinarily achieves said providing. Although most meat-eaters don't commit violent crimes, almost all violent crimes are committed by meat-eaters. Thanks for listening. I feel better now."

"Good points," said Marsha. "100 percent of VEGs are Nazi opposites."

"Any attempt at similitude is idiocy," said Guinevere, as Kristi Lou nodded.

56

"OH MY GOODNESS, GUINEVERE. YOU SAID YOU WERE WATCH-ing the clock, but we're still here," fretted Kristi Lou. "We keep trying to leave but we don't. And I just made it worse by going off excursively about Nazis versus veggie-heads. I don't want you to have a mad dad."

"Nah, he'll be OK. But you're right, as usual; we've gotta go. All right, let's get this covered wagon on the dusty trail," said Guinevere, as she put the Bad Car in gear. The nearly noiseless super-engine compelled the revolutionary vehicle to glide as if on air toward Kristi Lou's apartment. Guinevere had already entered Kristi Lou's address into the GPS navigation.

"Of course, I don't have to actually drive this car. I can just sit here and not step on the pedals and not touch the steering wheel and we'll get safely to where we're going."

"Yeah," said Kristi Lou, "if you can program the car from a remote location to do all those attacking-type things to car criminals, I guess you can get it to stop itself and make its own turns."

"Yes," concurred Guinevere, pridefully, while stretching her arms behind her head. "Ours is not the only drive-itself car, just the best."

"Wow. You and your dad are going to be squalidly nouveau riche someday from from parlaying the technology in these cars into some transcendental coinage. Luddites, you're not. It's hard to conceive of all that could happen, especially if, as you said before, the military wants to use your dad's genius. They'll pay him bodaciously big bucks, I'm sure."

"Yes, that scenario is a virtual certainty. We will likely become involved with the military, as contractors or consultants, and thus become wickedly wealthy. With automotive-tentacle fighting, Dad is a trendsetter, a card-carrying bellwether."

As the avenging machine drove itself and the three young women toward Kristi Lou's apartment, Kristi Lou looked into the backseat at Marsha, anticipating her response to Guinevere's comments plus wanting to visually savor her final remaining moments with her old friends with whom she'd been ephemerally reunited. She was aware of the reality that, after she got out at her apartment, she'd likely not see either of them again until another year of her life had passed.

"Your dad really is a genius, isn't he?" asked Marsha as she quickly slid her fanny sideways for four quarter-inch movements after having had a racing thought about a 444-pound tiger escaping from the Little Rock zoo and trying to eat her mom and Bud.

"Indeed, he is," agreed Guinevere.

Kristi Lou smiled, flashing her odontological-perfection, large, white teeth.

"Hey, Marsha, did you just … never mind."

"Yes, I did," confessed Marsha, who feigned frustration but then grinned broadly. "I had to slide my derrière a bit to save my family. It's kinda my version of Mom's butt-cheek flexing."

"Did you rescue Mr. Battle, too?" asked Kristi Lou with a puckish grin.

"Of course I did. Absolutely. I had to intervene. However, that doesn't mean Bud wasn't defending Mom. He was. I envisioned it all. Bud stood tall, in an allegoric aspect."

"Oh, yes, of course," said Kristi Lou with a quick laugh as she turned back around to look at Guinevere for a second. Guinevere nodded toward Marsha and then looked at Kristi Lou.

"Marsha can be quite clever and witty, and, even better, she can use her mind to prevent bad things from happening—kind of like a superhero with no uniform and about whom nobody knows."

"Right," agreed Kristi Lou. "But since she's a girl, she's a superheroine."

"Yeah, that's true," said Guinevere.

"That's me!" exclaimed Marsha. "From Packrat to Mighty Marsha Mellow! OK, wait, I know that sounded silly—corny, as Bud would say; I shouldn't have said that. I got too carried away."

"No, it was fine; I liked it. I like it when you call yourself Mighty Marsha Mellow, like you did before," said Kristi Lou. "Between you and Guinevere and Pete, you-all may clean up the world."

"I think that's feasible," offered Guinevere.

"Definitely," said Marsha.

"Oh Marsha, I just thought—you don't still have to do your Tar-K and the rest of it—where you have to say 'packrat' backward?" asked Guinevere. "I remember you had to do that in seventh grade."

"No, I don't have to do that, anymore," said Marsha. "Besides, Tar-K-Cap was needed only immediately after I got called packrat in a hateful way, or sometimes later on when I talked about being recently called that name by someone mean like Rudy or Nate—remember them calling me that?—not when I called myself that or would just matter-of-factly say the word around myself."

"You can say words and not be around yourself?"

"Actually, Guinevere," replied Marsha, pausing to ponder, "I don't think I could really do that, so that's a good point. I'm always close enough to myself to hear me when I speak."

"I'm encouraged by your self-awareness," said Guinevere.

"Unless I have an out-of-body experience."

"How many of those have you had?"

"I haven't had any yet, that I'm aware of. I've always had my body with me."

"I'm glad you're keeping yourself together."

"As am I."

****

The trio fell silent for about a dozen seconds as the girls watched the attack car fatefully roll itself near the cluster of two-story structures that comprised Kristi Lou's apartment complex. Guinevere manually, albeit unnecessarily, took over the controls to finalize parking alongside the curb in front of A-207.

"I wanted to park the car, myself, to satisfy my unquenchable craving to have at least some control," said Guinevere, with a smile and a wink.

Arriving home was the inevitable event Kristi Lou had been anticipating with dismay.

"Kristi Lou has to be a groovy girl," said Marsha. "She lives in hippie-ville at the Moon Landing."

"Moonbeam Landing. But that doesn't quite qualify me as being groovy."

"You are groovy."

"Thanks."

"These buildings need two more floors," said Marsha.

"Huh? Why" replied Kristi Lou. "Oh, right—only two floors. OK, I'll have some architects add floors three and especially four for you. I'll get back to you when it's done."

"Oh, tremendous. Thank you."

"You're welcome."

Kristi Lou, strategically trying to delay her friends' departure via proffering any palaver of which she could think, broke about six seconds of silence.

"You both might have wondered why my apartment here at the Moonbeam is called A-207. Well, the property is divided into five sections with three buildings per section. And I live here in section A, in the seventh apartment in building number 2, and they just add a zero in between. Then again, you might not have been wondering about that at all…but…I wish you didn't have to go."

"And we wish we didn't have to go. But, as we've been talking about, this is an emphatically temporary goodbye," said Guinevere, as she lowered both front windows. "I can't wait to see you again next year when you move back to Little Rock. You'll find yourself a tall fellow before long, after you sift through all the many suitors you'll have. I know you've had them here, too—the guys on campus and a different type of, well, male/female relationship thing down at Downtown Secrets. Anyway, we'll all have another reunion next year, and it'll be without these farewells."

"Oh dear God, that's what I want. I'll be looking forward to that day every single, solitary day from now on while I'm still here. But, I'm gonna also look backward each and every day on this day—this day I've spent with the two of you."

"I'll be a looker-backer, too. And yes, Guinevere's right; it's only till next year," said Marsha. "Let me do this."

Marsha took her right forefinger tip and gently tapped Kristi Lou four times on her nasion.

"I read somewhere that some wise man discovered that the central point of anyone's inner being and the gateway to the soul is there—right between the eyes. So that's where I fixed you up. I gave you a really strong four-fix. You should be good to go till next year when we get back together back home. Then, I'll give you another fix."

"Thank you. Although I know I need a lot more fixing, I feel safe now."

Kristi Lou was surprised that, with the car idling and her exit from the presence of her two friends imminent, that she didn't feel quite as morose as she had been sure she would. She grabbed the door handle.

Guinevere spoke toward the dashboard.

"Unlock front passenger door."

"Your super-car does voice-activated commands, too? Well, why should I be surprised? But you didn't use it till now."

"I was trying to not show off too much."

"Oh, and toward that end, you're even letting me manually open the door myself this time."

"Yep."

An elderly couple strolled along on the sidewalk, holding hands while beginning to slowly pass the attack car just as Kristi Lou swung her long legs out over the pavement. The aged gentleman, in his 90s, and his wife, in her 80s, waved simultaneously at Kristi Lou and said, at the exact same moment: "Hi, Kristi Lou."

"Hi, Mr. and Mrs. Smith. How are you?"

"We're just fine," they answered in unison, their voices melodiously amalgamating into a single sound.

"How are you feeling this evening, lovely young lady?" inquired Mr. Smith.

"I'm OK. Thank you, sir."

"You're so pretty today, as always," said Mrs. Smith.

"Oh my goodness. Thank you so much. You both look so wonderful together. I couldn't have any better neighbors than you."

"Thank you so very much for saying those sweet things," said Mr. Smith. "We feel most fortunate to have you as our neighbor."

"Yes," added Mrs. Smith, "we certainly do."

"Bye, now," said Mr. Smith, with Mrs. Smith waving and smiling gently.

"Bye, Mr. and Mrs. Smith. See you later."

They ambled leisurely along, compelling Kristi Lou to alter her moment and think, despite her emotions over the approaching exit of Guinevere and Marsha from the next year of her life, that the ancient couple's destination was their journey.

Mr. Smith used his quad-cane with aplomb as he steadied his steps, with Mrs. Smith tilting her head lovingly toward his shoulder.

"Look. See that?" exclaimed Kristi Lou to her friends in an unnecessarily quietened tone as she sat on the edge of the car's passenger seat with the toe-end of her shoes pressed against the curbside, and the Smiths now about eight yards away. "You see the positions they're in while they're walking? See how they're arranged? Mr. Smith always walks closer to the curb. Mrs. Smith told me one day when he was inside reading and she was outside watering her flowers that he insists on that walking arrangement and has done that for more than 60 years. If a car looks like it's about to come off the road, he'll be closer to it than she is and he'll be more likely to get hit but also be able at the last second to push her out of harm's way. Oh my goodness; I cried right then and there when she told me that. That's chivalry from an old-time movie; he's a true old-fashioned gentleman. That's ancient romance…and it's beautiful.

"They're sweeter than sugar to me. I think they even know what I do. They've been married forever, more than six decades. They know each other so well; it's like they're sort of merged. I envy them. I hope I can do that. This is as mushy as creamed corn, but I hope all three of us can do that—be just like Mr. and Mrs. Smith."

"Yes," said Guinevere, "we can all do that; it's very possible we can. It's doable. We'll need to meet Mr. Right to have a shot at emulating the beauty of Mr. and Mrs. Smith. But yes, I hope we can have what they have."

Guinevere paused.

"I know we can."

"I'll want my man to effuse gushy-mushy baby-talk to our cat—for me, a 24-carat, wet-pussy turn-on," said Kristi Lou, smiling wickedly but tenderly. "On those notes of optimism and salacity, I'm going to go so you two can go. There's Mr. Dooflotcher in the window glaring at me 'cause he's hungry and he wants me to get in there chop-chop and feed him."

Kristi Lou dipped her head under the Bad Car's doorframe and, clutching her purse in her left hand, arose to step onto the sidewalk, shutting the door and pulling her pastel-green cotton summer dress close to her knees lest Mr. or Mrs. Smith looked back, knowing that if one looked back the other would likely look back, too.

Another of her spontaneous thoughts jumped into her head. She spoke inwardly to herself while leaning forward and finger-ironing a few crumply rumples out of her dress.

Here I am a bona fide bawd with my philosophy of being strongly in favor of more openness about sex in society, but I still … I still have this conventional modesty going with ensuring that my dress isn't high by an inch or two. Oh well, who's perfectly consistent all the time? I obviously am not.

"All right." Completing her exit from the sometimes violent vehicle, she unfolded herself upward, erecting the 5'13" hourglass-sylph that comprised Kristi Lou Jones. After obeying an impulse to look down at her now standing-straight-up physique, scanning her body from chest to feet, she, facing the car, bent over curvilinearly, bending her kness and leaning her elbows against the upper doorframe. She lowered her head so her face was just outside the passenger area, into which she gazed.

"Well," said Guinevere, "is that one of your primary poses at Downtown Secrets? You look ready to receive. Any male passersby around here will be most mesmerized by your butt sticking up in the air."

"Let 'em. That's fine by me," replied Kristi Lou, consciously seizing an opportunity to offset her seeming inconsistency of a moment earlier.

"Even if the Smiths turn around and see that pose?" asked Guinevere.

Kristi Lou, losing the defiance in her face, lowered her posterior and leaned sideways against the door.

"Anyway," said Kristi Lou, "we've all got one another's phone numbers and mailing addresses. Golly, I miss you both already and you're still here."

"Golly!" exclaimed Marsha.

"Yes," said Guinevere, "Kristi Lou is a genuine golly-girl—one of the few, rare people alive who'd dare to even think about uttering that word within hearing range of another human being. Golly, golly, golly!"

"Golly again!" chimed Kristi Lou.

"But look—you're going to be fine; I promise," said Marsha. "May the four be with you."

"Yes, thank you for giving me that fortress," said Kristi Lou. "Get it? I said 'for' and 'tress' as in four and then the rest. You probably spell it f-o-u-r-t-r-e-s-s, so …"

"Yes, I got it, instantly," said Marsha. "We all like our plays on words, don't we?"

"Yes, we do," agreed Kristi Lou.

"Yes, you will be fine," said Guinevere. "Regarding the rest of this day, what are you going to do with it? Are you going to work tonight? If you do go in, are you going to do it with anyone? When are you going to quit, uh, I mean tender your resignation?"

"Oh my god! You just sounded like me—with multiple questions. You did me, again," said Kristi Lou.

"You got me! I sure did, but this time not on purpose. Well, don't just stand there personifying the prototypical bombshell blonde who can easily make men walk on all-fours at the end of a leash. Answer them."

"Woof-woof, ha-ha. OK, I just made my decision. Tonight will be my last night at Secrets. No, wait. Cancel that. That wouldn't be fair to Rochelle and Hokey and some of my other coworkers, or to my regulars."

"We did take Davey to Secrets, so he'll likely be there," said Guinevere. "But you'll want to give all members of your fandom a 'goodbye and I'll miss you.'"

"Give them a four-week notice," recommended Marsha Mellow.

"Four weeks! That's too long 'cause I want to … oh, four, of course— with you it has to be four. I hope you don't mind if I shorten it a bit."

"No, of course not," assured Marsha. "You can briefen it some. Did I just say briefen? I did. I said briefen; I might have created a word.

Anyway, I agree with Guinevere that you should make sure to say good-bye to all of your friends there."

"Most assuredly. And I think Rochelle and some of them will want to do something for me, like buy me a present or maybe sign a card or whatever. I really hope they get me a card and sign it. I would cherish their autographs through the years. I'm so nostalgic. As I've talked about before, I'm only twenty-one years old and I love to look back at the past, even if that past is not yet in the past because that past is in the future. Wait…what? Did I just say what I said?"

"Yes," said Guinevere.

"Did it make any sense? Did I sound like an igit?"

"No and yes," said Guinevere.

"Oh, it did, too, make sense," said Marsha. "And she did not sound like an igit."

"I know it made sense—and that she didn't sound like an igit; I was teasing," assured Guinevere with a broad smile. "Sorta …"

"I'm such a dingbat and Guinevere is such a tease," said Kristi Lou as a gust of wind blew a sliver of yellow hair into her mouth.

Kristi Lou knew there was another topic she wanted to tackle but couldn't recall. Then it came to her.

"As far as whether I'll quote do it unquote tonight, I don't have any plans. Then, again, I never do. As to whether I'll do the thing, it'll depend, per my personal policy, on who he is—and how I feel. It's my time-of-the-month time, but that's not a definite dealbreaker. Anyhow, I really don't need the money. I have a seams-bursting exchequer. Look it up, Guinevere."

"Ha-ha. You got me back. Dictionary, here I come," said Guinevere.

"So you're going in tonight?" asked Marsha.

"Yes, even though I'll obviously be very unpunctual, as it's already after 7:30. I'll go in and give them a week's notice. I'll tell them I'll work seven more days and then I'll resign."

Kristi Lou felt Marsha's disapproval before looking at her.

"OK, four days. I'll briefen my remaining tenure to four days."

"That's much better," said Marsha. "And thank you royally for using my newly minted word."

"You're most welcome. And you are so besotted with anything four," said Kristi Lou.

"I'm so be-what-ed?"

"Ooh," said Guinevere. "As with exchequer, I'm afraid I don't know that one, either. What does it mean, Miss wannabe lexicographer?"

"Well, besotted can mean to be very drunk or it can mean to be very obsessed with something. In Marsha's case, I'll let you guess which definition I was applying."

"Oh, when nobody's around, I'm typically drunk—passed-out drunk almost in perpetuum," said Marsha.

"I don't think so," replied Kristi Lou, who quickly felt a crinkle in her eyebrows upon the spontaneous arrival of a self-doubting thought. "I just had an epiphany, it seems."

"And," asked Guinevere, "that epiphanous self-perception is?"

"It's that…it's…I don't know, but…well, it just occurred to me when I was defining besotted that, even though it'd be considered as somewhat of a so-called big word—though it has only eight letters—I haven't used as many … I don't think I have, anyway … used, uh, as many sort of more obscure-type words talking with you two today than I often use when I talk with the girls and guys when I'm at work at Secrets. Both of you are well-educated and…but…most of my Secrets friends—my coworkers and customers—mostly don't have that advantage. So, why am I using bigger words talking with them? When I'm bantering with Rochelle and Hokey, for instance, I'm just joking around, mostly…I think…I hope that's mainly what I'm doing with using words I know they don't know."

"Well, we talked about this earlier and I kinda teased you about being egotistical, but I wasn't seri…"

Kristi Lou was too amped to permit Guinevere to complete her précis.

"But sometimes I catch myself being out-and-out pedantic. As a fervent eristic, I get too carried away sometimes with my dogmatic speeches; I know I do. But even though I'm sincere—I always am—in stating my beliefs, I can be too perfervid. I can also be over-zealous in wanting people to agree with me; I never demand agreement, but I still make little remarks sometimes suggesting that I'd be quite disappointed if they disagree, so at times I'm downright doctrinaire in subtly pressuring people into concurring with my somewhat fanatical concepts, like, about, you know, sexuality discrimination against men and so forth. But, anyhow, the fast thought that sprung into my ditzy, rattlebrained brain was that…that, no, I'm not trying to show off my vocabulary to stroke my ego and espouse my own supposed superiority and say 'I'm *so* superior to you.' I'm not doing that. But I, uh…I think that, that I'm trying to uh, seem…I don't know…trying to seem…"

"Your conscientiousness is unfailingly amazing," intercalated Guinevere, who was now motivated to provide a more comprehensive evaluation than she had originally intended and thus launched herself into a gale-force megillah. "You're trying to maintain psychological space between you and your current work-place colleagues. Although you and some of them have particular qualities in common, such as holding the same opinions on certain topics or being friendly or having a down-to-earth spirit, you sense, correctly, that you're really not one of them. No, you're not doing that in a snobbish, supercilious way; you're subconsciously reinforcing, in your own mind, with frequent repetition, that you are different from them because you realize—although you like them—that you can't be happy long-term with them—not as your primary people with whom you associate."

"Oh my, I…"

"You use the higher-register vernacular to persistently reassure yourself of that divide. With your spur-of-the-moment speeches, I imagine some of your rip-roaring stemwinders around them are characterized by periphrasis. That's one of *my* big words, meaning usage of a needlessly long, circumlocutionary way to express one's thoughts. Yes, I'm engaging in periphrasis right now while talking about your periphrasis. Anyway, you're still probably not seen by them as condescending. And you're not. They just think that that's how you talk. And it is. But you do it more so with them to help lead you, maybe not so *coincidentally,* to making the decision you just made in this conversation—to break away and go back to your true you."

"Oh, oh, oh my goodness. You spilled that analysis out of your face like a perfect word-waterfall; it flowed in total perfection, as if you were reading from one of my psych textbooks. Everything you said is right. I can feel it. That's why I do that—engage in circumbendibus and use whopper words—more pointedly with my Secrets people. Yes, that's it."

"And that's quite all right," reassured Guinevere.

"Yeah," said Marsha. "It *is* all right; it's understandable. You're not being a snob or a jerk-butt or anything—not at all."

"So," said Guinevere, "you and your pretty boobies shouldn't worry about it."

"OK. Thanks. We won't."

"Because," said Guinevere, "you're only temporarily meretricious."

"I am? I'm only temporarily what? Meretricious? I don't…OK…I don't know that one. You stumped me! But, I guess, based on the context in which you used it, plus all your zappers at me, that…"

"I could say 'Look it up,' but I won't say that. The definition of meretricious, as applied to you, is: relevant to or reminiscent of a prosti…prosti…prosti…what's the rest of that word?"

"Oh, well all righty then," said Kristi Lou, laughing. "I'm still gonna look it up, though. And, you know, Guinevere, looking back to our school days at Our Lady, I'm sure it was you with your vast vocabulary who got me going with my obsession about enriching my own lexis and all that. Nearly my earliest memory of you is you getting between me and Nasty Nate Perkins when we were clashing and calling him 'jejune,' ha-ha-ha. You were most inspirational," said Kristi Lou, as Guinevere smiled and then laughed.

"Words, when used valuably, can hold far-reaching value and hence do not exemplify floccinaucinihilipilification," said Guinevere, who, with a mischievous snigger, spelled the mega-word to her eyebrows-raised friends.

"Kazowie!" said Marsha.

"Land sakes alive! That word is a brain-breaker. And a jaw-breaker; you could break your jaw just saying it. The dictionary—king of books—beckons me," said Kristi Lou, as all three ladies chuckled, and then looked down at their midsections.

Kristi Lou, having kept her lengthy physique twisted like a Slinky for several conversational minutes while tilting her head sideways and downward to peer into the car, had developed a slightly sore neck and now also felt the onset of a mild stitch pain arising in her right side. She stood upright, threw her purse strap over her left shoulder and glanced at Mr. Dooflotcher, who had begun to paw aggressively on the living room window. She looked at Guinevere.

"Be careful, Guinevere. You and your dad, I mean Pete—please be careful with your battles against these car criminals in all these cities you're going to. I can still hardly believe that you and he do all that; I mean, it's amazing to just think that you—well, anyway, just be careful."

"OK. We will. Worrieth not, though. Our vehicles are perpetually safeguarding us. When we're in a hotel or at home, the Bad Car and the van are parked outside and they're programmed to auto-activate and blast into action against would-be aggressors who may've found us and want to retaliate against our retaliations. Tentacles will fire hard at anybody who tries to break in or move aggressively toward us anywhere, whether it's me, Mom, Dad, or anyone we want to safeguard, such as Marsha and you."

"My worries are allayed. Thanks for mitigating them."

"Sure. I'll go ahead and tell you quickly right now about a decision we made. I told you that we're going to take our mission out west, to Albuquerque, and then on to California, to Bakersfield, and then continue nailing car criminals throughout the state. I also mentioned L.A. You know—when I compared per capita statistics of L.A.'s car thefts to those of Albuquerque. Well, it occurred to me later that I didn't mention then, specifically, that we're going to L.A. I guess I got sidetracked. But we are going to L.A. Dad and I have special plans for Los Angeles, California. Why? Well, for one thing, because they have a certain glorification of car stealing there based on a certain popular video game and so we think their car criminals—and their victims—deserve a certain accelerated degree of assiduity. It's going to be grand, really grand," pledged Guinevere with an emphasis on the word "grand" along with what Kristi Lou read as a serious glint of anger and determination in her friend's constricting pupils.

"Oh, yeah. You're referring to that violence-filled video game about stealing cars that's sold so many copies. I don't relate to the appeal at all, but, oh well. But, as I said, when you're waging war out there—or anywhere—just please be really-very-super careful, OK?"

"We will. I promise. Remember, Dad's a genius—a real one," reassured Guinevere.

"I know. I can attest to his genius-ness, but still…" said Kristi Lou.

"Bye, Kristi Lou," said Marsha. "I'll call you within the next few days after I get home. Bud's going to be so glad to hear you're OK. And no, I won't tell him about your, uh, occupational endeavors."

"OK, great. Thank you. Tell Mr. Bud Battle hello for me and that I have only fond memories of him and that I can't wait to come over to the house and visit with both of you. Hmm, that might feel a little awkward, at first, but we'll get used to it."

"Of course you will. And that'll be an easily arranged visitation since my apartment is just a hop, skip, and a jump away from Mom's house."

"OK. Cool."

"OK, Kristi Lou. Later! Bye, bye, bye, bye."

"Four bye's back at you!"

Kristi Lou looked at Guinevere, now immutably established as one of the principal forces in her life. Kristi Lou was swept under yet another abrupt, self-arresting revelation.

Oh my goodness. Guinevere and I were together closely for the last half of seventh grade and now, eight years later, for only part of one night and one day, but her impact … She's irreplaceable, nonexchangeable, unfungible.

"Thank you—again," said Kristi Lou.

"I cannot overstate, tall girl, how wonderful it's been to be with you again," said Guinevere, smiling pleasantly and with an air of calmness, as was her way, but this time with an extra sparkle in her eyes, noted easily by her friend of renowned elongation.

"Thanks, again. You're so important to me. I can't find the words. Call me soon, please," besought Kristi Lou.

"Hi, Soon Please. I'm Guinevere."

"Oh, all right. I've never been called Soon Please before."

"That's better than being called Slut, right?"

"Chortle," said Kristi Lou, followed by her chortling. "Anyway, you call me and I'll call you. And we can send email and real mail with our own actual cursively written handwriting, which makes it more personal 'cause someone actually handled a pen and wrote the letters and numbers and punctuation characters and all."

"Aren't we full of mush?" Guinevere gunned the engine, working the controls so it went from silent to sounding akin to a jungle cat's riveting baritone roar.

"Yes, we are. And I love it."

"I love it, too," said Guinevere. "But there is some unfulfilled mushiness that we're somehow omitting. You need to get back in here for that."

"What?"

Guinevere extended her arms.

"Oh my god," said Kristi Lou. "How could I have gotten out of the car without hugging you and Marsha? I don't understand that."

"You were distracted by Mr. and Mrs. Smith and your thoughts were just racing, in general," said Guinevere. "It's OK."

Kristi Lou, after excitedly reopening the door, splashed her naturally contoured, faultless fundament back onto the scientifically perfected contours of the front bucket seat, thus inadvertently seating a picture-perfect match of nature and science, where she and Guinevere hugged one another silently for about five seconds.

Kristi Lou pulled back from embracing Guinevere and then turned to hug Marsha, who had already positioned herself between the two front seats, eagerly awaiting her turn to be scrunched tenderly within what almost seemed to be the toned ropes of Kristi Lou's arms. Marsha and Kristi Lou embraced warmly for four seconds, with Marsha counting audibly but softly into Kristi Lou's right ear. As the two girls disengaged their hugs, Marsha spoke again.

"I can't wait for you to move back home," whispered Marsha. "Maybe when you visit at Mom and Dad and Bud's house, you can already be sitting when Bud walks into the living room."

Upon hearing Marsha's blend of next-year-yesteryear-saturated words, Kristi Lou felt a surge of both remembrance and nexus.

"Oh my goodness Marsha, after eight years I'm still connected with Mr. Battle and it's being manifested literally, right now, through you."

"I know. Believe it or not, I thought that, too—really. I swear I did. And that's cool. It's another coincidence. I suppose."

"Yeah. All right, well, I better go so y'all can go. So, I'm gonna go," said Kristi Lou as she re-exited the car and stepped back onto the sidewalk, where she stood about two yards from the doorframe.

Marsha took her little body and climbed over the console and into the front seat just vacated by Kristi Lou, and then, grinning widely and with her eyes twinkling, looked up at her foot-taller amigo.

"We'll be on the phone talking about everything imaginable before the end of the week. I want to know about the sendoff your coworkers give you as you, er, ahem, retire."

"OK, I'll tell you all about it," said Kristi Lou. As she began to close the front right passenger door, it closed itself, shutting with that muted but solid thunk that Kristi Lou again sensed was a symbol of irreproachable engineering design.

"Well, all righty then, Mr. door."

Guinevere leaned across and above Marsha's lap, earnestly looking at Kristi Lou.

"OK, Kristi Lou. Bye-bye. I'll talk with you in a few days. Dad and I will be in Atlanta setting up shop to prepare for infliction of more adorably poignant, vigilante-style automotive retribution, to commence in early September. And you'll have left Secrets and be back in classes at Wayne State for your senior year to finish what you started and get your degree and then launch the next phase of your life. Right? Let me know if you need help with your homework."

"I might take you up on that offer."

Marsha called out again, almost singing. "Bye-bye, Kristi Lou. See you soon."

"'Soon' has a precise number of letters," said Kristi Lou.

"I know. I now feel that the last word I say to you here has to have them. I'm so glad you picked up on that," said Marsha.

"Obsessive minds think alike."

"Absolutely! All right, Kristi Lou, I'll be seeing you before too long."

"Yes, you truly will."

"Adieu, Kristi Lou," said Guinevere. "Oh! You know what? We can do Skype for video chats, and actually see one another—you, Marsha, and me—while we're talking. Are you set up for that?"

"No, but I wanna do it," replied Kristi Lou.

"Yeah—I do, too," said Marsha. "I don't have it, but I'll get it when I get home."

"I'll install it, pronto," said Kristi Lou. "That's a wonderful idea, Guinevere. You, Marsha, and I can have threesomes!"

"I presume you've become quite comfortable with threesomes."

"Huh? What are you talk—oh no! You won't let it go! Even when we're saying goodbye, you're still persecuting me! You're merciless! For the record, I haven't done *those* kinds of threesomes—and, besides, I don't think we're exactly talking here about ménage à trois!" said Kristi Lou, laughing while housing an un-umpired conflict between amusement and sadness.

"I know. And, yes, I once again proclaim my recycled and obligatory disclaimer: I'm just jocular-vein joking."

"I know you are, and I hope you won't stop."

"I won't."

"Oh, I almost forgot. Please take these little info things I wrote up," said Kristi Lou as she speedily fingered through her purse and then yanked out two of the hand-printed notes she always carried, one of which she had provided to Rochelle two-and-a-half weeks earlier from the same batch, and that bore the addresses of those websites Kristi Lou ardently wished to popularize—www.mercyforanimals.org; www.safehavenfarmsanctuary.org/learn-more/cows; www.nationalreview. com/2013/10/pro-life-pro-animal-matthew-scully; and www.nationalreview.com/2016/12/animal-welfare-standards-animal-cruelty-abolition-morality-factory-farming-animal-use-industries.

"I know you both care sincerely about the welfare of animals and you hate cruelty against them," continued Kristi Lou as she reached into the Bad Car and handed one paper apiece to Marsha and Guinevere before withdrawing completley back onto the sidewalk. "Please visit those sites. And, oh yeah, I'd also like for you to get this book I just learned about that I'm gonna order from Amazon. It's called *Dominion: The Power of Man, the Suffering of Animals, and the Call to Mercy*. I believe you can remember enough of the title to find it."

"Animal welfare—yes! We absolutely will go to these sites," assured Guinevere. "And I'll get that book and read every page. Thanks."

"I definitely will," said Marsha, who added, "and then I'll go to the OCD Foundation site and make myself register."

"Awesome," replied Kristi Lou, with a tired but optimistic smile. "Oh, regarding animals, I've gotta add this: Why would God, if he's compassionate-hearted, create predators who, for their survival, must eat other animals? Why would he allow preyed-upon animals to feel fear and pain while possessing an innate mandate to maintain their lives? An immoral design flaw from a morally flawless being? A more plausible theory is that God, after creating baseline animals who did not require the consumption of meat, chose to withdraw and let nature itself, which he also brought into existence, have its disencumbered way in evolving various species, some of which developed an existential need to consume flesh. I believe that God, after animals perish, sometimes ferociously, probably rewards them with a blissful afterlife, maybe in a kind of animal heaven. I absolutely do not know, but that's my self-comforting belief."

"OK," said Guinevere. "That's an intriguing pro-animal thesis. I'll talk with you about it in a few days, either on the phone or on Skype. We'll all be back together again sooner than it now seems. And, from that moment on, our friendships will be inviolably sempiternal. I promise."

"Dear God, yes, please—inviolable permanence for our relationships, unfading, deathless. No more drifting apart. OK, I can let you go now. Bye, Guinevere. Bye, Marsha. Bye-bye. I love you…uh, hold on, Marsha…I love you much."

"I love you much back," averred Marsha.

"I love you, Guinevere," said Kristi Lou, aquiver with emotion.

"I love *you*, Kristi Lou. Until we meet again, I wish for you unbounded p-r-o-s-t—prost. It's German; look it up!" declared Guinevere, smiling and gazing over her left shoulder at Kristi Lou while rolling slowly away, with their mutual gaze remaining unbroken for several seconds until the automotive gladiator's side windows' separator panel came between their eyes.

The car rolled about 45 yards and stopped. Kristi Lou saw something emerge from the trunk and rise to about 25 feet off the ground. The thing unfolded flawlessly and Kristi Lou beheld a 5-foot-wide electronic sign. Large flaming-red globe lightbulbs formed three giant letters: BFF.

Kristi Lou burst into crying as if she were a six-foot, one-inch baby. She ran about 12 feet toward the vehicle, waving with both hands and yelling "BFF! BFF! BFF!" As she caught her breath, she realized she needed to yell just a bit more. "BFF again. The fourth one's for you, Marsha! I'll see you both next year! Oh God, I'm soppy. I love you both!"

The car began to roll again, with BFF now flashing on and off. After another few seconds, the sign withdrew into the car. But the sign's message had been delivered with the full power of shameless human sentiment.

Kristi Lou looked at Marsha and then at Guinevere, staring back and forth at the backs of their heads, as the self-driving attack car glided quietly onward, winding its way along the anfractuous pathway of egression from Kristi Lou's neighborhood.

Kristi Lou stared helplessly at the rear of Guinevere's departing vehicle of vengeance for almost 10 more seconds, until all she could see of it for one transient moment was a minuscule glimmer of sunlight reflecting off its dorsal bumper. Squinting to drain every quarter-second of opportunity to track the car with her super-sharp vision till it could no longer be seen, Kristi Lou strained in futility to maintain her view of the car while looking through a narrow vista. She squinted, peering torturously through openings between branches of trees, few of which grew along that tortuous stretch of serpentine roadway but just happened to obstructively appear on Guinevere's route of exodus.

As Guinevere's car continued to drive her and Marsha out of Kristi Lou's life, Kristi Lou had seen that final flash of light, which had come and gone in the same instant, slice through serotinal leaves and into her eyes before the car ensconcing her lifeline vanished behind a tattered abandoned house. She realized a moment of déjà vu, but with no illusion, knowing that she now stood watching a vehicle containing Guinevere roll out of sight just as she had watched a vehicle take Guinevere out of sight the day Guinevere moved with her family from Little Rock, in the summer after the seventh grade. But this time, as Kristi Lou witnessed Guinevere being stolen away from her by an automobile, Guinevere, like Kristi Lou, was all grown up, and Guinevere was behind the wheel.

The BFF sign was so wonderful. She remembered. I wonder if Guinevere was trying to look back at me through the rearview mirror till I could no longer be seen, and if Marsha was goose-necking and looking back over her shoulder till I was out of sight. I could see Marsha looking back for about 40 or 50 yards till stuff started getting in my way and the sun's glare got real harsh. I hope they were looking at me. I hope … I hope they were looking at me all they could look at me till they… till… I'll be back with them next year. I will.

Unlike before, so Kristi Lou self-soothingly surmised, because they were grownups, they exerted more control over their lives' destinations, and hence the reassurance of a further, and permanent, homecoming was robust and believable. Thus, the chaotic disillusionment of her first parting as a thirteen-year-old, with life controlled by parental decisions, was replaced by this bitter-but-better farewell, with the fulfillment of an oath to actualize a reunion not just a child's desperate wish, but an adult-driven, platinum-level probability.

57

KRISTI LOU, UPON NO LONGER BEING ABLE TO SEE GUINEVERE'S car, spun around while wiping away tears and directed her lissome body toward her apartment, where awaiting her was the almost insatiably ravenous Mr. Dooflotcher.

After taking a few steps, she saw, in her peripheral vision, Mr. and Mrs. Smith ambling back along the sidewalk, having just turned into view beyond the assemblage of ancient maples reigning gallantly over the street corner of a mostly—but not entirely—rough neighborhood.

Kristi Lou, although having been delirious with seesawing passions while being reunited with her two friends from yesteryear, relished a respite from the emotional vehemence spawned by the reunification. Thus, she turned her protective instincts toward the fragile couple who had been together since just after World War II.

Ancient people walking under ancient trees. In the winter of their lives. They've still got what Mr. Wilmont had till he lost Mary. They deserve nothing but happiness. This can be a rough area, really rough. There better not be anyone who tries to hurt them. Anybody who does will have to answer to me.

Kristi Lou waved again at the Smiths, who were about 45 yards away, with sundown oncoming. Although they appeared to be looking directly at Kristi Lou, they did not wave back.

They're too far away to see me waving. That's all right.

Even though her nearly full bladder was directing her to *urinate now*, she walked up to her doorway but did not immediately go inside. She stood, watching Mr. and Mrs. Smith, ever hand-in-hand while strolling, saunter closer. Kristi Lou sensed that she was now, as she had done many times before for the Smiths without them knowing, keeping an eye on them protectively, the way they probably safeguarded their children, grandchildren, and maybe great-grandchildren.

They move so slowly. They look so vulnerable. One is an octogenarian and one is a nonagenarian. But maybe they're protected by me and Providence. Yeah, I think God watches over them even better than I do.

Kristi Lou, without trying, spontaneously imagined music as she watched Mr. and Mrs. Smith stroll. The two songs that arose by happenstance in her cognizance, with some of the lyrics from both alternating seamlessly as she sang silently to herself, were ballads to which she would occasionally listen on YouTube: "I've Never Been to Me," by Charlene Oliver and "Softly, as I Leave You," by Frank Sinatra.

The lyrics to "I've Never Been to Me"—I think about the meaning of those words applied to me. And with "Softly, as I Leave You"—that tender, heart-wrenching song will soon be for Mr. or Mrs. Smith, after all those years together. But there's "Unchained Melody" by The Righteous Brothers, an upbeat song about saying "wait for me, because against any odds I'll come back to you—if it seems that I can't—oh yes I can, and I will—even death won't stop me from coming home to you." Yeah, that song applies both to me and to the lovely Smiths.

And with me will always be two of my most-cherished songs—The Brooklyn Bridge singing "Welcome Me Love" and Ben E. King singing "Stand By Me."

She was aware of what she considered the likelihood that less than three percent of people her age anyplace in the Western Hemisphere would even know of the existence of these songs, with the possible exception of "Unchained Melody." But she cared not that she might be viewed as uncool for committing the un-millennial gaffe of thinking so anachronistically.

She stood still, continuing to serve as a sentinel for her antediluvian neighbors. She didn't worry about seeming obtrusive, as they could not perceive her scrutinizing observance from their distance on the sidewalk, although they were coming closer to Kristi Lou's apartment entrance. Besides, as she knew full well, they wouldn't mind at all if they did know she was staring at them; she knew they knew she harbored for them a deep-down affection.

Kristi Lou, with Mr. Dooflotcher now frantically pawing the window and her urge to pee having grown to the point of her battling incontinence, felt compelled on this occasion to wait till Mr. and Mrs. Smith were close enough to be able to observe her observing them. She became obsessed with attaining this achievement.

And then she realized that she was, without any intent, closely emulating the predicament of Marsha Mellow in the seventh grade eight-and-a-half years earlier when Marsha gravely needed to relieve herself but required that Mr. Battle release her from the demands of her obsession, the same Marsha Mellow with whom she had been reunited and with whom she had exchanged temporary goodbyes only minutes earlier and the same Mr. Battle to whom Marsha's mother was now married.

Kristi Lou, her thoughts racing within a jumbled entanglement, while thinking of these wonderful reunions and how her old, young friends were probably several miles away on the road and that she'd have to wait another year before seeing them again, felt duty-bound to swap a wave and a greeting of "Have a nice evening" with her venerable friends. She did.

Upon sheltering Mr. and Mrs. Smith with her eyes—as if she were their guardian archangel and her gazing upon them created a shield—for another 12 yards after they had waved, smiled, and spoken inaudibly but warmly to her, Kristi Lou was finally able to release herself to go inside.

She started to insert her key into the doorknob. She was stopped, with her hand reaching out and holding the key, suspended in midair in front of her innie bellybutton, by another thought that barged into her mind. She stepped two feet back from the door.

Oh my god. What if it works out the way I just thought? I just had the thought that … that I'm probably not going to teach high school, what with the way I look and being so close in age to the students. I think maybe I should go for elementary school. But, for some reason, I now feel impelled to teach middle school—in Little Rock. What if … what if I wind up being one of **those** *teachers—a teacher who comes home to roost in her old school where she was a student? What if I go back to Our Lady and what if I wind up teaching with Mr. Bat …? Oh my god. Wow. I can hardly fathom … oh my god. No, I couldn't. But, maybe I could. I don't know, but, well … wouldn't that be something? Talk about going full circle. That would be—what?— weird or amazing? It would be both weird and amazing—that's the long and the short of it. Oh my goodness; I didn't even try to say that as a pun.*

Jeez, I'm on the verge of pee-popping and I'm still standing at my door like some kind of fruitloop. I'm being obsessive like Marsha to whom I just said an only-for-now goodbye and who almost wet herself that day when we were kids at the same school I was merely seconds ago thinking of returning to as a teacher. And, ironically, I myself am about to become incontinent as very old folks sometimes are and how my elderly neighbor friends might be and that incontinence might happen in great part directly because I've been standing here obsessively watching my elderly neighbor friends. So, why don't I stop neurotically stupefying myself and go inside to the toilet that's just a few feet beyond this door and tend to my nature-calling situation 'cause I can obsess while I'm bolting to the bathroom? But, I just wanted to make sure they're OK, but … but-life-is-strange-and-so-am-I.

She lunged at her front door.

58

KRISTI LOU, HAVING AT LONG LAST ENTERED HER HOME, WAS instantly accosted by a frenetic glob of pelage rubbing against her ankles. She spoke to him as she tossed her crossbody purse onto the couch and shed her four green and gold bangles onto a lamp table.

"Hey, sweet baby. I've really gotta go triple-time fast. You can go with me, needless to say. Let's go. I hope I can get there before I have one of your carpet accidents. I may have to use your litter box since it's closer. Let's bolt to the bathroom."

They raced down the hall together and into the bathroom, with Mr. Dooflotcher running ahead and meowing raucously as if to say, "You're going the wrong way; my food is in the kitchen!"

Kristi Lou, after managing to not trip over Mr. Dooflotcher, looked down at him and pleaded with him to be patient. "I'll feed you after I tinkle; I promise."

As soon as she sat on the toilet, he jumped on her, standing on her lap, glaring silently but sternly at her face.

"Oh good grief, Dooflotch! Can't I take a leak without being hounded…or, OK…cat-ed? Why must I be pestered while peeing? Can't I pee in peace and peacefully bung in a Kotex? I guess not. It's not as if you're on the verge of starvation or anything, dagnabbit. I said dagnabbit. No one else on Earth or any other planet still says dagnabbit. Oh well."

About 20 to 25 seconds after speaking her piece scoldingly to her cat, Kristi Lou thought back to when she sat on her slow-closing, no-slam toilet seat. She recaptured the mental snapshot her brain-camera had taken. She then realized that, although Mr. Dooflotcher had indeed glared at her with sternness for the first several moments, his eyes soon began to squint, his face mellowed into a contented-cat expression, and he sat on her right thigh, purring trustingly while kneading gently on her skin.

Kristi Lou flushed and arose from the toilet as Mr. Dooflotcher poured himself gracefully onto the floor.

"OK. I'm sorry I was a bit b-i-itchy with you. You have every right to be mad at me 'cause I'm late feeding you. My bad."

Kristi Lou washed her hands painstakingly, rubbing her palms and fingers together aggressively to create strong, germ-dispatching friction. After generating billowing mounds of white suds, she scrubbed, as always, for 20 seconds, timing her scouring via the second hand on her cyan-colored, round, plastic wall clock for which she remembered paying $8.57 about six years ago in Little Rock. She used lukewarm water and old-fashioned bar soap, which she preferred over liquid soap because rinsing off the saponaceous film yielded by solid soap was more time-consuming. Thence, she had to scrub a few moments longer, probably resulting, she presumed, in the removal of more bacteria and viruses.

"I am the self-described quasi-germaphobe. But, I hardly ever get sick. I haven't been ill with a cough or cold in years. In fact, Dooflotch, you've never seen me sick, have you? And I attribute that to regularly doing this: just the simple act of washing my hands. If more people did it, there would be less miserableness from sickness for those people themselves, plus less contagiousness and thus less spreading of contamination that gets other people sick and there would be fewer job hours missed and better productivity for employees and companies and so on."

She continued to speak audibly to herself and to her cat as she dried her hands on the thick, super-absorbent, forest-green towel dangling from the black plastic towel ring.

"Wow, I think I'm more than kinda like Marsha; I think I am Marsha—except I might be a tad taller, plus her obsessions are so much cooler than mine. Maybe I should get myself a special number by which to be dominated. Yeah, my own number might add some coolness. Oh, what would be a good number for me? How 'bout 0? Or 9, which is what you get when you extract the numbers from 5'13" and add them? Hmm … I shall consult with Marsha and solicit her mastery of numerology."

Exiting the bathroom and then quick-stepping toward the kitchen, Kristi Lou was easily out-paced by her fluffy consort.

She stood with her hands on her hips, looking around the room and feigning fretfulness.

"All right, I'll try to find some appropriate sustenance for the resident furball. Ooh … I don't know if I've got any suitable kitty-cat goodies, though. Uh-oh. How unfortunate. Hmm … I don't think there's anything here he'd like, but I'll keep looking. I just don't know, though. It could be a distressful situation. I'll look some more, but …"

The already annoyed Mr. Dooflotcher was not even remotely amused, as he wailed away and began to stand up straight on his hindquarters, brandishing his forepaws and striking vehemently at his human's legs, albeit while restraining his claws within their sheaths.

"OK, OK, OK! That wasn't funny; I get it. Sorry."

Leaning slightly over the countertop, Kristi Lou began the process of satiating Mr. Dooflotcher's appetite with the super-premium cat food she always served to him, coating the bottom of his greenish-gold ceramic bowl with dry food which she covered with half of a 5.5 ounce can of wet food.

I love buying this stuff because it feeds my sweet Dooflotch. I hate buying this stuff because it's a can full of dead flesh harvested from animals, many of whom doubtless suffered most of their lives through a joyless, anguishing imprisonment, only to be coldly rewarded with a, with a ... yeah ... with a horror-laden omega. Sometimes I cannot not think about it. And so, here I go—cognitively dissonancing once again. Cognitively dissonancing? Yes, cognitively dissonancing.

As always, before lowering his bowl, she held the aluminum lid she'd just peeled off the top of the cat-food can in front of his face so he could lick any juice or gravy clinging to it.

"That lid is yummy!"

After refrigerating the remaining canned food, she chip-clipped his kibble and returned it to its storage place in a high cabinet where Mr. Dooflotcher could not snag the bag and rip it open. She then squatted and placed his food bowl on its spot on the floor next to his water bowl.

Kristi Lou arose and spoke to Mr. Dooflotcher, now eating rapaciously, telling him: "Of course, Dooflotch, after I microwave the other half of that can of kitty-vittles tomorrow morning for your breakfast, you know I will, as always, put the can, with its remaining residue of itty bits of food, under the faucet and serve you one of your favorite things—cat-food-flavored water, always warm, which you and I call cafooflawa. What a word. A silly-dilly word. But it's our word, huh, Dooflotch? Our little neologism. Our own fehumanline meowologism."

She then dropped herself onto one of her inexpensive, metal dinette chairs that sported bronze, hollow tubes and pale, lilac-colored, fraction-of-an-inch cushions. Upon receiving Kristi Lou's rump, the chair's frame twisted and squeaked.

I've gotta tighten the screws on these old, squeaky chairs. Hmm, when I move, I'm just gonna leave these chairs—as well as most of the other inexpensive furniture I brought into this already-mostly-furnished apartment— as a donation to whoever lives here next ... pending Moonbeam approval.

"Hey, you know what I just served you, Dooflotch?" she asked in her earnest way, almost as if she were expecting a reply. "Provender. I just served you provender. That's a new word I found yesterday when I was reading my dictionary. It means animal feed. Do you like your provender? You must, considering how you're virtually inhaling it."

Kristi Lou forgot about everything else and stared at Mr. Dooflotcher with a feeling of deep affection, knowing that, as an indoor cat, he was thoroughly dependent upon her. She saw her cosset as her child.

"That provender is yummy! Yeth, him likes him's yummy provender; yeth him does. It's the most wonderfulest, yummy provender there could ever be; yeth it is. Hims my sweet boy, yeth him is."

Mr. Dooflotcher heard his human but did not look at her, as his meal consumed his full attention.

"Yes, I see you're ignoring me, as if to say 'I don't care what you call what you serve me as long as you continue serving it. What? Do you expect me to look at you now? Can't you see I'm busy eating down here?'

"Yes, I can. I know. I've been practicing my new word on you while you're trying to eat. My apologies for the forced conversation."

Then, to Kristi Lou's amazement, Mr. Dooflotcher interrupted his eating, quick-looked at her and emitted a slight but still audible chirpy meow. Both actions lasted less than a second before he resumed eating. But, for Kristi Lou, the moment jolted her most warmly, compelling her to feel even more bonded with her felid companion.

He acknowledged me. He did. It was as if he were saying 'thank you.' They are smar—they are. They really are. They are smarter—some animals are smarter than some people give them credit for. Oh my goodness, I believe I depend on him just as much as vice versa. If Mr. Dooflotcher got loose and ran away, I'd be lost without him.

59

KRISTI LOU PEERED AROUND THE KITCHEN AIMLESSLY WHILE sprawling there in her cut-rate chair. Deliberately sliding more than halfway off the rickety chair, she unintentionally took a gander at an open magazine that Mr. Dooflotcher had playfully swatted onto the floor. She spotted an advertisement for a bistro, with the image depicting a group of about eight 20-whatevers laughing, toasting drinks, and generally enjoying merriment together. She spoke again to Mr. Dooflotcher.

"Hey Dooflotch, it's just you and I around here, in this apartment. Counterintuitively, other than Guinevere stopping by briefly, I—an easy-on-the-eyes extrovert who is naturally gregarious—haven't had any friends—or anybody—over here in, uh, well…months. Yeah—months. OK, before you say anything, I realize that you, Dooflotch, are not a nobody. Don't go getting your feelings hurt. Sorry. Let me rephrase. I haven't had any people-type bodies over here in months. Anyhow, how can somebody my age go for months without mingling at home with, with…someone…anyone? I could call some Secrets friends such as Davey and invite them to drop by; I got several of their numbers two or three or so days ago. Am I latently in training to be a cloistered nun? This is weird. I am weird. I'm ostrobogulous—wanton and weird."

Mr. Dooflotcher looked up at Kristi Lou.

"Oh, you gave me that look that says 'You're right; you *are* weird.' I know I am. But you didn't have to agree with me."

Mr. Dooflotcher licked his bowl until it shined and then sat catawampus on the floor beside Kristi Lou. After shooting another glance at her, one that seemed to her to say, "You segregate yourself. You're neurotic," he undertook his post-meal feline grooming by licking his forepaws and then wiping them across his face.

Kristi Lou consulted with herself.

OK now. Just relax. It's about 9:30. So, in a little while, even though you'll be quite late, you're going to go to work. And, in a week or two, you're going to reenroll. And then you'll call Mom and Dad and tell them you have reenrolled. And then you'll be on your way to finishing your degree and getting your B.A. in Education. And uh, and then, then you'll get certified to teach. And then you'll move back to Arkansas. No, you've got those last two things backward. After you get your B.A.Ed. here, you'll move home. And then you'll get certified to teach—with a-state-of-Arkansas teacher's certification. Yes—you, I, we will do those things. Can do. Must do. Will do.

Kristi Lou thought about her impending goodbyes to Rochelle, Hokey, Satine, Big Sam, Dan, Davey, Denny, Dopey, Doris, Francois and the other endearing characters, especially Mr. Wilmont, whose paths she'd been privileged to cross, feeling that she would indeed keep her promise to Rochelle to stop in at Secrets to visit now and then while still living in Detroit. But she felt a smidgen of fear that she might allow a fading away of the intensity of her desire to continue visiting; she did not want to fail to miss her workmates and special patrons. They, Kristi Lou surmised, deserved to be missed. And she needed to miss them.

She got up from the creaky chair and got ready to go to work for the first night of her last week as a working girl.

****

Kristi Lou went into Downtown Secrets this night, Saturday, August 18, thinking heavily about how only several hours had elapsed since seeing off Guinevere, Marsha, and Pete. She announced her intentions to her coworkers and gave a verbal four-day notice, including this night, to Doris. As she expected, there was tumult from Rochelle, who, while proclaiming that she "knew it" that Kristi Lou would leave soon and how this was the best thing for Kristi Lou's life, almost shed one tear but quickly wiped it away, needing to maintain her veneer of toughness. Davey was dejected, but knew he would see her again.

Kristi Lou worked uneventful evenings Saturday, Sunday, and Monday, with no sex and—other than Davey on Saturday night—seeing none of her regulars. As she departed Monday, she felt overtaken by her fear that perhaps all of them would fail to be available for her to say her goodbyes. Though she had recently swapped phone numbers with a few of her Secrets customer-friends, including Davey, she wanted to visit with them at least one last time as a worker in the nightclub.

She realized that she felt wounded by the idea that maybe none of them really cared enough about her to show up. *Did they hear that I'm leaving—that Tuesday is my last night? I'd think maybe they'd have heard by now from someone who works here. It could be that maybe they just haven't come in or anything, so maybe they don't know, but…*

****

Upon leaving Secrets on a cloud-covered, moonless Monday night, she looked for Dan but did not see him outside. Wondering where Dan was, she walked home alone with pepper spray ever ready, though it was unneeded. *Where has Dan been? He wasn't at Secrets Saturday, Sunday, or tonight. Does he know that tomorrow night is it for me? Perhaps one of the girls came out and told him. I wanted to tell him, but, I … I hope he, uh … that he knows.*

60

KRISTI LOU SLEPT TILL PAST THE CRACK OF NOON TUESDAY, AUGUST 21, knowing that, after the passing of the upcoming evening, her life would transmute dramatically.

She did not step into Downtown Secrets until almost nine o'clock, having stridden purposely but slowly, meandering and taking her time along her customary pedestrian route. During her quiet stroll on this moonlit night, she encountered no one.

She arrived wearing her most elegant black evening gown, a resplendent décolletage featuring a nearly floor-length, form-fitting, black-velvet dress that kissed the straps of her four-inch, black, high-heel pumps. The top of her curves-hugging gown flashed with gold and black sequins and a semi-modest V-cut that revealed the upper-inner contours of her breasts. The skirt portion of her gown was designed with a slit that rose to just below mid-thigh on both sides. The sensuality advocated by this bewitching raiment, the chicest ensemble in her wardrobe, was not overstated, but, in the case of Kristi Lou's physique and manner of comporting herself, still intense. Her jewelry adornments, while remaining light—no bling-bling girl was she—were more pronounced than usual, and consisted of all gold. Kristi Lou had donned a non-ostentatious thin gold necklace and gold earrings. She had adorned her otherwise bare arms with her gold-colored wristwatch on her left wrist and a gold bracelet on her right wrist.

Kristi Lou spent most of the first hour of her last night as a working girl sitting, drinking ginger ale, talking with coworkers, and mingling casually and briefly with a few clients with whom she was not acquainted. After about 50 minutes, a semi-regular, who came in intermittently, walked into the club. She danced once with him, and then sat quietly by herself at one of her favorite tables. She was momentarily joined by Satine.

At 9:57 p.m., as her foray into professional erotica was coming upon its climaxing capstone, Kristi Lou looked up from her conversation with Satine as she saw Rochelle approach. Rochelle sat next to Kristi Lou as Satine got up and walked toward the bar.

"How's yo finish-line night here goin', babydoll? You banged anybody?"

"Actually," replied Kristi Lou, "I've had nothing but dances these final few nights here."

"In other words, you been struttin' but you ain't been fuckin'," summarized the ever-forthright Dark Rochelle.

"Well," replied Kristi Lou with a quick giggle, "indelicately put, but yes, that's correct."

"I figured dat. So you don't want no bye-bye bang?"

"Uh, apparently not."

"Dat's OK 'cause you ain't hurtin' for no money; I know dat's right. You been savin' most of whatch you been makin'."

"Yes, I have."

"Damn, we goan miss you, girl."

"I know. Same here back at you, Rochelle. I'll really miss confabulating with you."

"Fuck. I don't know if I'll know I'm missin' dat 'cause I kaint know I'm missin' somethin' I didn't know I was doin'. Confab-whatever … we been doin' dat together? I don't remember us doin' anything you called dat."

"Well, we sure did. And we're doing it now. To confabulate means to engage in chitty-chatty chatter; it's lighthearted, informal conversation. Fluff-talk may seem to cynics to be unimportant and purposeless, but when it's sincerely done, nicely and warmly, it's important and purposeful because it fuels shared moments of niceness and warmth. I will miss doing that—confabulating—with you."

"Oh lordy, I knew it was one of yo college-ass big words. Man, I'm goan miss dem words from you. Since you been here, girlfriend, you done pumped up my vocabulary with dem high-ass words. And I learned some fine things from yo crazy-ass sidewalk sermons. And I 'preciate dat shit."

"You're more than welcome. But I want you to know that…that, I, I never, ever meant to talk down to you or Hokey or anyone here. I didn't. I hope I didn't offend you with anything I said—my college words or my harebrained rants."

"No, I was not offended by you, so don't-chu worry none 'bout dat."

"Thanks so much for reassuring me about it. So, I will…I'll be missing all of you more than I can say. But, as I've said before, I'll be back; I promise I'll come back."

"I *heard* dat. And I *know* dat. But, you know what?"

"What?"

"It's ten o'clock."

"Yes, it actually is indeed truly ten o'clock. Are you now serving as my personal clock or something?"

"No, but we gotta little ten-o'clock thang for you 'fore you go."

"Oh my goodness."

As Rochelle stood up and stepped back, Hokey, Satine, and Dopey approached Kristi Lou, with Hokey carefully carrying a 13-inch-high, all-vegan chocolate cake with all-vegan vanilla-crème frosting and one extra-tall candle in the center, along with a Bunyanesque-size, au revoir card, covered outside and inside with dozens of well-wishing inscriptions. DJ YoCrunk abruptly halted the blues music. Most of the other dancers came over. Doris and Big Sam walked up to her together.

Davey Burton, Denny Thomas, and Mr. Winston Wilmont III had been crammed comfortlessly together, hiding in a small, almost-never-used storage room whence forth with gallantry they all debouched, marching lockstep toward Kristi Lou like a freakish conga line.

Oh my goodness! I should've known they'd be here.

Everyone gathered around Kristi Lou, enclosing her within a surreal circle in a dark, smoke-saturated room in the belly of a blues bordello.

DJ YoCrunk had to download an audio file from the Internet with an instrumental version of the old tune "For He's A Jolly Good Fellow." They all sang together:

She's a jolly good woman
She's a jolly good woman
She's a jolly good woman
That nobody can deny.

"Oh my goodness!" exclaimed Kristi Lou, a split moment before a flood of tears cascaded from her eyes.

"I knew it," said Rochelle. "I knew she'd start bawlin' right out da gate."

"She ain't ballin'; she just cryin'. She'd be in da back room if she was ballin'," proclaimed Hokey with a snort.

"Not dat kinda ballin', you dumb shit."

"I know dat; I was doin' what's called makin' a joke, you nappy-haired dummy."

"Well, what-the-fuck-you-ever."

"Oh, I knew you were joking," said the sobbing Kristi Lou, wiping her face with a handkerchief. "This is so sweet. Thank you all so very much."

"You goan sing 'Enchant My Evenin'?" asked Hokey.

"No, Hoke, I'll spare you from another of my amateur renditions of 'Some Enchanted Evening.'"

"You're a humdinger of a singer, Kristi Lou," assured Satine.

"She certainly is, and she's an even greater young lady," added Mr. Wilmont.

"A fuckin'," concurred Davey.

"Oh thank you, Satine. Thank you, Mr. Wilmont, sir. Thank you, Davey. Thank you, all—all of you. You're all so very sweet."

"You sing if you want to, babydoll," reassured Rochelle.

Denny had been waiting his turn to speak.

"You've been very sensitive about my bathroom hang-ups. So, for honoring you, I have, here it comes—poetized a poem—a phrase that offers praise for the type of tautological phraseology you so charmingly use. Here is my Kristi-Lou-istic poetic poetization:

My dearest dear Kristi Lou;

One thing will always be true;

Every time I do a do-do;

I'll always think of you-you."

"Oh Denny, that's so sweet. Yes, when my cognition circuitry gets higgledy-piggledy, I can be quite the tautologist. And, I'm flattered that I'm in your thoughts during these important toiletry moments. I'm glad I could help. I look forward to your, uh, invention about which you told me—so people don't have to go anymore. That'll be a game-changer."

"I'll make sure you get a lifetime discount."

"You're so benefic! Thanks. I'm flush with gratitude."

"Ha-ha," said Denny, with a meek but cordial smile.

Big Sam stepped toward Kristi Lou.

"I've never had anybody better than you working here," said the reticent owner of Secrets, who deemed Kristi Lou's surprise farewell party to be worthy of one of his rare appearances in the club during business hours. "The door is always open for you whenever you want to come back and see us."

"Thank you. You've been a very good boss—stern but fair. Really."

"Yeah, well, I'm glad you feel that way. That means something to me. I…uh…I won't forget."

"I do feel that way."

Kristi Lou commenced hugging everyone who had gathered around the cake in her honor.

After being heartwarmingly regaled with sentimentality-drenched confabulation and eating of cake with her coworkers and regular customers, whom she viewed as also her friends, Kristi Lou decided to leave early. A little after 11 p.m., amidst hugs and kisses, Kristi Lou Jones walked out of Downtown Secrets—staring down at her feet during the first few moments of departure so she could watch them symbolically carry her into her next life-chapter—and onto the sidewalk, culminating what she knew would henceforth be one of the seminal episodes of her life's story.

61

KRISTI LOU TOOK 14 STEPS. SHE TURNED AROUND AND WENT back inside. She remembered something she had meant to do, that she needed to do, that she wanted to do.

Pulling a note from her purse, Kristi Lou marched directly to Mr. Wilmont, who was already reseated at his favorite table, alone again, naturally. Amid the blues music that DJ YoCrunk had already resumed playing, Mr. Wilmont looked palpably sadder than usual, and Kristi Lou knew this was because he was already missing her.

She had often fretted over his sequestration, a feeling of isolation and despair to which she related. But, despite this link of loneliness, she knew she was young and pretty, and that many men would vie for her attention romantically, with Guinevere and Marsha abiding on the horizon platonically. Forming the starkest of contrasts, Mr. Wilmont was an octogenarian with limited time and dwindling hope of recapturing what Kristi Lou believed to be the warmest sanctuary that can be offered by life on Earth, that of guileless, loving companionship.

Kristi Lou stood next to Mr. Wilmont for about three seconds before he noticed her standing beside his chair, towering cordially above him like a fleshly statue of Venus. Knowing that her unexpected return would startle him, she let her presence sink in for a moment.

She gave Mr. Wilmont her biggest smile.

Kristi Lou then leaned over and whispered into his ear just audibly enough for him to hear her voice over the music's din but with such sufficient quietness that he would know she was heard by no one else, thus making her words more personal and special to him.

"Hey, Mr. Wilmont, this is for you. This is my cellphone number. Please call me anytime you need to talk—wherever I might be and whenever that might be, even years from now—seriously. And no, I won't change on this matter with the passage of time, not me."

As he took from Kristi Lou's beauteous hand the quarter-section of white printer paper she had cut neatly with scissors at home for the purpose of presenting Mr. Wilmont with her phone information, he felt a surge of joy that routed and then replaced the sadness that had overcome him since losing his beautiful young confidante just several minutes before. He saw that she had used a pen to write, in aqua-blue ink, her telephone data, and that her cursive handwriting flowed with recherché feminine penmanship that stunningly resembled the lettering his Mary used to form.

"You want me to call you? You mean it? I don't want to … I don't want to crowd your time away from here. I know you've got a life to lead with all that living to do and I'm just an old …"

"Oh, please. Stop that. You're not '*just* an old' anything. I enjoy your company at least as much as you enjoy mine. I like to talk with you, too. I relish talking with you—for my sake as well as yours. I always remember our conversations—each and every never-vapid, always-pungent one of them. But I … I can't stand for you to be lonely. And, as I've told you before, when we talk, you help *me* not feel so lonely. Neither of us needs to be lonely. I'm going to miss you so much. Maybe we can get together sometime—make that sometimes, plural—at the coffee shop or wherever and enjoy colloquies about this and that and whatever."

"Yes, I'd like that. Talking with you is one of the highs of my mostly low life," said Mr. Wilmont while clenching Kristi Lou's phone number firmly but reverently as if it were a passport to heaven.

"You deserve the highest life. Maybe sometimes we can talk just sitting in your car—or someplace like that, that's quiet and private with no interruptions or distractions and we can talk about serious things like loneliness—your loneliness and my loneliness—or jaunty things, too, like the reality of the supposed reality in reality TV or…huh? What did I just…anyway, I really want us to be able to spend time together and stay friends—for both of our sakes."

"I…I really…thank you, Kristi Lou. You still make me feel young and spry, or at least help me remember when I was. You're twenty-one going on one-hundred-twenty-one as far as the maturity of your kindness."

"That's very nice of you to say," said Kristi Lou, continuing to stand beside the seated Mr. Wilmont. "In fact, that's one of the nicest compliments anyone has ever given me. Thank you so much."

"Well, you're welcome. But, you know what I saw a few moments ago when you handed me this—your uh, your contact information?"

"What?"

"You wrote it out. It's enchantingly idiosyncratic like this. It's that— it's that you took a pen, an actual pen, and penned it. I'm not knocking typing on the computer and letting the machine form your letters; it always provisions perfectly formed fonts, most of which—other than those fancy-pantsy-schmancy ones—are very easy to read. But there's something much more personalized about a handwritten note; it's your distinct writing—not identical to what anyone else would write; it comes directly from what your own hand makes happen. And…"

"Oh, Mr. Wilmont, I've gotta tell you about this coincidence because…well, I had friends, old friends, girlfriends, from back in Little Rock, visiting me here just recently. They went back home the other day. But, I was just telling them what you basically just said to me: that when we write to one another—although emails and texts are good for quickness—we should sometimes use real handwriting 'cause it's more personal with the pen strokes that come from our own fingers and all that. And they agreed with me and we're gonna do it. So, yeah—I agree with that—what you were just saying, which is what Guinevere and Marsha and I are going to do. And that's what you and I are going to do, too. So, that's just too cool. And, anyway, I'm really glad you like my writing because…"

"Your writing is not just readable, it's so lovely that it reminds me of…well, I just got through saying a person's writing is distinctly his or hers and different and all, but, but…your handwriting style reminds me of…"

"My handwriting reminds you of how Mary wrote—right? I hope so."

"Yes, it does. It's actually rather amazing. You know, Kristi Lou, I read and hear about how many schools nowadays are de-emphasizing cursive writing, what with all the emphasis on modern communication mediums, mainly keyboards with computers and so forth, and, uh…those fancy mobile-type phones…"

"Smartphones."

"Yeah—smartphones. But, so anyhow, I understand all that, but it's so reassuring to see young people who can write with their own strokes, their own personalities. I think cursive handwriting is somehow good exercise for the brain. But, anyway, your handwriting on this simple note has a true beauty; it's like the calligraphy Mary used to write."

"Oh my goodness," said Kristi Lou. "I was just about to say that I took a calligraphy class. And I wanted to ensure that I effectuated the antipode of griffonage by using my calligraphy to write my phone number to you 'cause I somehow thought—I really did think…I don't know how or why I thought this, but I did—I did think that my best, fanciest handwriting might remind you of your beloved Mary—not that I could ever rise to her level in any way, but, anyway …"

"Oh, I'm so glad you came back in here," said Mr. Wilmont. "Yes, I would like to call and maybe get together some occasional times now and then—but only if you really mean it—I mean really, really mean it; I know you want to be caring, but I'd hate it if I thought I was taking advantage of you because of your kindness. If I was intruding, I would feel very bad, so just be hon …"

"I do care. And you never intrude. And I do mean it. And I am being honest—honestly."

Kristi Lou began sitting down with a powerful, fast motion toward the chair, which she pulled close to Mr. Wilmont during the same moment she lowered her herself onto it. She, on impulse, turned her head right and left quickly to survey her surroundings, and, to her surprise, no one she knew was in sight; all dancers as well as patrons with whom she was acquainted, and with whom she had only minutes earlier exchanged emotional farewells, were nowhere to be seen, leaving her and Mr. Wilmont with strangely unfettered mutual focus upon each other.

"Please call me," implored Kristi Lou, leaning forward and within two inches of the left side of Mr. Wilmont's face. "I've got some things to take care of over the next few days of August, so let's say you start calling me in very early September, OK? Really, though, you can call me anytime you want, even tonight, if you'd like—if you need to—if you want to talk. I want to talk with you some more—and often."

"No, unless I have an emergency, I'll wait till when you just said. I'll call you September 1. How's that?"

"Perfecto. September 1 it is. Really—call me, Mr. Wilmont. Really. If I don't answer leave me a voicemail message and I'll call back. Your number will be on Caller ID. And I'll put your number on my speed dial. I know I could get your number from you now, but I want to get it from when you call me."

"OK."

"I won't let you feel lonely, Mr. Wilmont. I won't. I promise."

"I wish I could find the words. Fifteen years or so from now when you're living with your husband—whoever the lucky guy will be—and your kids, maybe we'll still be friends…if I'm still, uh, still around."

"We'll be friends forever."

"I believe you when you say that. Those words are like soft and gentle easy-listening music to me. I feel like I'm in an elevator."

"I'm not sure if I've ever made anyone feel like he's in an elevator."

"Look, Kristi Lou. I should've already told you. I've gotta tell you that my, you know, my uh, my horrible donkey LSD trip? It's come back only once since we talked—just once! It still scared me, but you know what?"

"What? I was just about to ask you about that, sir, but I wanted to let you, ideally, bring it up, and you just did. So, what happened? I hope it wasn't as bad."

"It wasn't nearly as bad, not as bad at all. It still got to me, but it was manageable because, well, some of those disturbing and gross things I described that night—I won't inflict them on you again now—some of those things, those images—they didn't recur. They didn't—for the first time in a helluva long time—they didn't happen, didn't come at me. And the whole damn thing lasted several fewer minutes. I told that LSD thing while I was in it that you said I'd always wake up and—I'm gonna whip that thing's ass so it leaves me the hell alone for good. I'm doing better, and I've got you to thank."

"That's fantastic, Mr. Wilmont. I'm gladder than I can say. If it continues to come back at all and hurt you, and I mean at all, anything at all, then that'll be one of the things we'll talk about starting in September."

Mr. Wilmont looked down at his knurled hands and then back at Kristi Lou. "This—what you're doing—is wonderful for me. You realize modern cynics would say we are—mostly me—we are being saccharine sweet and too sentimental. But—I don't give a flyin' hoot!"

"I like saccharine sweet and I'm very sentimental and I don't fricking care who knows it," averred Kristi Lou.

"I know. Here you are making an old man feel cared about. Look, you better get on back out that door and go home to whom I'm gonna call your Kristi-Kitty…uh, Mr. Deeflipper. I will call you, my dear, young, good-hearted friend."

"Mr. Dooflotcher. OK, sir, Mr. Wilmont. You *must* call me—and not just once or twice, but often. If you don't, you'll hurt my feelings."

"I would not ever…"

"Oh, by the way, when you see Francois in here—I know he's one of the people you talk with here—please give him my friendly regards and tell him it was nice knowing him and that I always enjoyed listening to his French accent and also…uh, that, uh…"

"I'll tell him—what you said and what you implied."

"Oh. What I was implying, huh? Well, I guess I…never mind…"

Kristi Lou blushed and looked away for a second, sensing he sensed what she let slip partially out.

"His accent—it's so…his accent is so sophisticated-sounding. And please tell him that maybe I'll see him again in here when I'm back here visiting, and that maybe, well, just tell him, you know…"

"Yes, I know. Sure thing—I'll tell ole Frenchy."

Francois had her phone number. But, Kristi Lou would not inform Mr. Wilmont of that reality, protecting him against any dilution of the specialness of her having given it to him.

"You know, I hear tell that Francois would've been here tonight but he couldn't make it because of some situation with having to deal with his girlfriend."

"So, that's why he isn't here. His absence was kinda hurting me. Thanks for telling me."

"Yeah. All right, you need to get started on the—as they say—the, the rest of your life. Now, hit the road. I feel much better now, thanks to you. Talk to you soon."

"Talk *to* me? Don't you mean you'll talk *with* me? Remember, you're the one who schooled me on that."

"You got me. You sure did. Thanks for correcting me and sorta teaching me what I taught you."

"You bet, Mr. Wilmont," said Kristi Lou, before mentioning Davey, whose possession of her phone number she also would not reveal.

"And please remind Davey of what I just told him a few minutes ago—that I'll see him around, though he already knows that."

"OK. I will. Davey's a knucklehead. Inverts his cursing. I'll tell him, though. Bye, Kristi Lou."

"Bye-bye, Mr. Wilmont. Later—but not much later."

"Right—not much later a'tall. I'll call you September 1, per your request."

"It's a date! I'll be eagerly awaiting your call. Bye-bye."

"All right. Now go home and get some sleep. Bye, Kristi Lou."

"Bye-bye, Mr. Wilmont—talk with you soon."

Arising slowly and securing her purse strap over her right shoulder, Kristi Lou wheeled around with the grace of a ballerina and treaded away, twisting to her left after walking about eight feet to glance back, with a teeth-filled smile, at her aging friend. Having seen photographs of herself in Secrets, she knew precisely where to stand so that the bright, glistening whiteness of her salient teeth would slice luminously through the low-light, tobacco-begotten, wispy haze and surge comfortingly beyond the late-efflorescing cataracts threatening to exacerbate the clouding inside Mr. Wilmont's eyes of antiquity.

Upon walking in front of the doorway leading to a large side lounge, she spotted Rochelle and Hokey and exchanged a round of goodbye waves with them as she fast-stepped through the smazy cathouse, cloaked in its Coca-Cola-sin-red-soda ambience, and on toward the door.

Out she went once again—this time looking straight ahead—from the subfuscous but oddly comforting environs of Downtown Secrets and into the humid August night.

62

WAITING FOR HER WAS THE IRREPRESSIBLY RELIABLE
Dan Cobain.

He's here! Someone must've told him. Thank God.

Dan had ensured that he took no other passengers after 9 o'clock, and
had hence sacrificed considerable pay in fares and tips.

"Hey curvy girl, get your gorgeous self in here. I just can't believe this
is your swan-song night. How can it be? It's just not gonna be the same,
not taking you home in the wee hours."

"I know. I just…"

Dan interrupted her as she started to enter the backseat of the taxi.

"Get in the front seat, please. You're riding shotgun tonight."

"Really? Oh my goodness, OK. Thanks for the privilege. I get to sit
right next to the meter—what a special treat."

"Treat? Yeah, right. Sitting next to the meter is your treat, not sitting
next to me, huh?" said Dan, frowning and hunching over the steering wheel.

"Oh, I didn't mean it like that; I'm sorry."

"I know you didn't. And I also knew I could get you to feel guilty about
sayin' that and that you'd apologize and so on. But, I was only kidding."

"I know," said Kristi Lou, who walked around the car and seated herself.

Kristi Lou looked over at Dan as she fastened her seatbelt and they taxied away from Secrets, with Dan driving quite slowly.

"I don't know what I'd have done without you, Dan. You're the best cabbie in the world."

"Yeah, I know that. No, just joking."

"No, you are," insisted Kristi Lou, as she turned around to look at Downtown Secrets, now her former place of work, fade into a smaller sight, "though I might be a bit biased."

They didn't talk over the next few minutes as Dan delivered Kristi Lou to the curb outside her Moonbeam Landing apartment.

"This is a special gift for you, Dan," as she stuffed a C-note in his shirt pocket. "I know you missed out on all that money turning down other riders so you could wait to take me home."

"What? Why would you think I would…? OK, how'd you know? Were you checking out the front of the club to see what my cab was doing or what?"

"No, I didn't check. I just knew."

He pulled the $100 bill from his pocket, expecting to see another 50. "Wow. This is too much."

"No, it's not. And I'm not taking it back so don't try to make me. So there."

Dan immediately sensed Kristi Lou's firmness, sweet but strong.

"Thank you, Kristi Lou. And this is my present to you," as he inserted a $2 bill under her gown and left bra strap. "I hope I don't seem like el cheapo. I know I'm comin' out 98 dollars ahead. But, there's, uh, some symbolic value here plus a little super-silly poetry. I'm not very uh, artistic, you know, but, well, uh…read the bill."

Kristi Lou giggled and pulled the bill from underneath her brassiere and read Dan's note, scribbled in purple ink across the obversely inset image of America's third president, Thomas Jefferson:

"Here's a 2 for Kristi Lou—but she's #1 under the sun."

Kristi Lou cast her baby-blues endearingly upon Dan. Scanning his body from his lap and then up to his face, she slid herself toward him. She leaned over and kissed him on his right cheek, cupping his chin in her hand while holding her kiss for two seconds before withdrawing slowly to her end of the bench seat but stopping so she remained closer to Dan than before.

"This bill is now officially out of circulation; it will never be spent. Its home will be my jewelry-less jewelry box filled with no jewelry but with sentiment and memories. This tender-sweet remembrancer will be part of my future nostalgia as I look back on the warm wonder that is the blessed past."

Dan, at once sexually stimulated and filled with platonic affection, was surprised at how bashful Kristi Lou had made him feel. He felt himself blush, which he was certain he had not done in about 25 years.

"Well," he stuttered, "you can still get rides from me, you know. I mean, you don't have a car, and I work at night and all, but…uh, but…well, if you need a nighttime ride, then you can call me for a ride or just, well, you know, around here is my territory and so on, if, uh…if you need a ride, you know."

"I know. You will forever be one of my all-stars. And, when I need a ride at night you're the one I'll ask for when I call in—the only one."

Kristi Lou broke into song, stunning Dan, as she softly crooned her appassionato rendering of Dolly Parton's "You're the Only One."

Dan's jaw dropped helplessly. As his mouth hung open, within him surged an ephemeral but inspirative revival of his youth.

"As I said, Dan, you're the only one I'll request whenever I call for a nighttime cab. I'll never forget you, my true and real friend. I promise."

Kristi Lou stroked Dan's hair and pulled softly away from him. She stepped gracefully out of his cab. She bent forward to speak, with the tranquil wisdom in her eyes belying the ditziness she at times externalized.

"Bye, Dan. I'll be seeing you."

Dan inhaled deeply to catch his breath.

"Bye, Kristi Lou," replied Dan, momentarily possessed by a high-pitched crackle in his voice and a crumpled face, as he tried without success to stop the liquid in his right eye from spilling onto his cheek.

Kristi Lou closed the passenger-side door, gently and quietly.

After giving Dan one last warmth-drenched smile, Kristi Lou walked to her apartment. She stopped, turned around, and stood at the front entrance. She knew Dan would not leave until he saw that she had arrived safely at her doorway. Kristi Lou waved widely, ensuring her waving hand was visible in front of the porch light. She watched Dan's taxi disappear slowly into the dark. While welcoming the unexpected arrival within her bosom of a soothing sobriety, she calmly absorbed this latest vicissitudinous event, which she saw as symbolizing the vital consequences of her life-amending decisions. Though she did not attempt to self-explain her thoughts in detail—at least on this occasion—Kristi Lou looked up at the full moon and, finding herself enchanted by the lunar light's peaceful invasion of nighttime's darkness, she considered life's paradoxical amalgamation of mutability and constancy.

Something closes; something opens ... sometimes segueing conterminously ... and hence quite gaplessly. Gaplessly? Yes, gaplessly.

She unlocked the front door and waltzed into her living room, where Mr. Dooflotcher greeted her by scurrying in graceful loops around her feet.

63

Over the next six days, through Monday, August 27, Kristi Lou didn't do much else besides consorting with Mr. Dooflotcher, reading, watching the news and her reality shows on TV, listening to music, and dreaming of moving back to Little Rock, where she would permanently reunite with her family, Guinevere, and Marsha. Excepting workouts on her elliptical trainer and washing laundry, she mostly lazed about and vegetated with curative languor, a self-prescribed indolence which accorded precisely with her itinerary to fill most of the duration of the month with a glut of nothing. This luxurious laziness, part of her design to make a clean break from Secrets and to recharge her psychological battery, was that recumbency to which she had alluded when asking Mr. Wilmont to call her soon but to wait till September because she had "some things to take care of" during the succeeding several days.

Kristi Lou consulted Wayne State's online academic calendar and learned that the last day of registration for the fall semester was to be Tuesday, August 28. She studied the curriculum offerings, but she already knew which credits she needed and which electives she wanted. Using the tuition money mailed by her parents, she registered online that Tuesday afternoon. Classes at WSU began the next day.

Wednesday at 10 a.m. found Kristi Lou sitting in a classroom. She had completed the previous spring semester while working nights at Downtown Secrets, and here she was starting the next fall semester perfectly on schedule, as if Downtown Secrets, as far as affecting her education, had not happened. She knew otherwise.

Well, here I am back in the classroom. I haven't taken time off, academically, at all. But, I learned some lessons in another type of classroom.

She did, however, have non-academic plans for the last day of this cardinal August.

Kristi Lou wanted to watch courtroom drama, but not on television. Having kept herself apprised of the Detroit judiciary's trial docket by regularly visiting www.36thdistrictcourt.org, she had a personal interest in the outcome of a real-life judicial proceeding.

I can't not be there.

Knowing what she had to do, Kristi Lou, on Wednesday, informed all professors for her Monday/Wednesday/Friday classes that she would use her first allowed class cut on Friday, August 31 so she could attend a courtroom session. She had never set foot inside a courtroom. Kristi Lou felt she had as good of a reason as any she may ever have to lose her courtroom virginity.

****

Kristi Lou rarely rode the Regional Transit Authority city buses, but she took a seat on an RTA motorbus this Friday morning. She disembarked just outside the courthouse. She walked in and sat quietly in the audience, awaiting the preliminary hearing for Bosco Mason.

After sitting for about 12 minutes, she saw the prisoners led in and seated in their section to await the judge. Kristi Lou, to her mild surprise, upon her first sighting of Bosco since he had knifed her at Downtown Secrets, felt a surge of pity mingled in with the anger and fear she had anticipated. She sat still and watched the arraignment proceedings.

Bosco's was the antepenultimate case presented. Kristi Lou saw what she sensed was surely an argument ensuing between Bosco and his stressed-out public defender.

Unsurprisingly, I think Bosco's insisting his lawyer say, "not guilty," despite the guy's contrary advice. Yeah, that'd be like Bosco; that's what he's doing.

The young attorney, wearing a red tie and beige dress shirt with a tan blazer and black pleated slacks, rose from his chair and spoke, wearily:

"Your honor, my client wishes to enter a plea of not guilty."

A trial date was set for November, as the judge adjusted his timetable by moving up all local car-crime cases.

Kristi Lou could not prevent a fresh upwelling of uneasiness from swirling inside her system.

I hope they put him away someplace with a good rehabilitation program for his sake, but also for mine, because I don't want him to follow through later with that threat he hurled at me. But—I don't know—he may not even remember me after some time has passed. And if I've already moved back to Arkansas when he gets out, I'll be living far away from him. Regardless of where I am, he might not learn my whereabouts. So, maybe you're just being, you know, paranoid… and, of course, obsessional. Maybe you're worrying about zilch. I don't know.

After the inmates were led from the courtroom back to their cells, Kristi Lou sat almost completely still for around five minutes, contemplating her concerns about Bosco, including analyzing herself as fretting too much about what she thought—when she was *in my logical thinking mode*—was the unlikely possibility that Bosco would launch a hunting safari for her.

Oh my. Bosco's hair has gotten really short. They probably made him get a haircut in there. He looked so haggard. But, of course, he's been in jail, so he's probably had a rocky go of it. Anyhow, as you were saying a few minutes ago, there's really no need for your paranoia; perhaps you can instead be just mildly neurotic. Ooh, I saw those reddish streaks on Bosco's face. I made those. We cut each other. He cut me with his knife and I cut him with my fingernail claws. Dooflotch approves, ha-ha. If we both have permanent scarring, his scars will be more prominently displayed than mine. I really shouldn't wish for him to be permanently scarred. I shouldn't, but, well …

A pacifying thought eased its way unannounced into her mind, providing her with a splash of pleasantness she felt in the center of her torso—that demulcent, soothing tingle one can feel when stress is invaded by an awareness of some impending salutary event.

Oh good—something to look forward to. Tomorrow is September 1, when Mr. Wilmont is supposed to call me. He will. I know he will; he's as dependable as all get-out. All get-out? Did I just say 'all get-out,' which resides in the dustbin of desuetude? Really? No one says that these days—except you. I may be single-handedly keeping such patois extant. But why ridicule yourself about it? Sometimes you're like someone who wants to take the wheels off his car and put them on his house. Well OK, but… skip it. Anyway, Mr. Wilmont will make me feel relaxed—and emboldened; he is my lodestar.

Kristi Lou had been passively watching Susanna Willis, who was standing about 15 yards away, converse with two female paralegals. Kristi Lou felt an impulse hurtle into her: suddenly, she needed to go and speak with the D.A.

Rising from her seat at the left end of the right rear pew, she strode up the center corridor toward Ms. Willis. Although Kristi Lou, in order to demonstrate respect for the traditional requirements of courtroom etiquette, was modestly attired in an Amherst-gray, high-neck, non-form-fitting dress that covered the top half of her knees, all male eyes, of which there were about two dozen pairs scattered around the room, instinctively locked in on her as if they were heat-seeking missiles. Kristi Lou, ceaselessly aware of such attention, regardless of environment, felt, as always, flattered and appreciative. She also noticed the long-familiar phenomenon of abruptly hushed men's voices, yielding the paradox of what seemed to be a burst of loud silence.

Kristi Lou stood politely and silently four feet to the side of the three women, waiting for their conversation to reach its natural conclusion.

After about 20 seconds, the two legal aides walked away together. Ms. Willis turned and faced Kristi Lou.

"Can I help you?"

"Hi. I hope so. I think you're Susanna Willis, the district attorney."

"Yes, I am. And you?"

"I'm Kristi Lou Jones. It's nice to meet you."

"Kristi Lou? That's a nice name. Nice meeting you, as well. Wait. That name sounds familiar. Did you testify against Bosco Mason—not on the stand, here, but maybe, uh, with giving evidence to the police?"

"No, I didn't give it to the police; I gave it to this man from your office, over the phone, after he called me. He was quite surprised that I declined to press charges. But, I just didn't want to agitate the situation anymore. Regarding the police, some of my coworkers told me that they said my name to the police when they were questioned about a fight Bosco got into at the club earlier this month. He … he, uh, well, he actually attacked me pretty hardcorely—he cut my stomach with his switchblade. But my friends got him away from me and I wasn't injured all that badly. But later that same night he got arrested. And I actually happened to see his arrest as I was going home in my taxi ride.

"What happened is that, well, I was working in this club, Downtown Secrets, and the management there decided to call 9-1-1 within a few minutes after Bosco had walked a fair distance from the property. They don't want cop cars around the place because that could look bad for business and so forth. But they, meaning my boss and my coworkers, were worried that he might try to track me down so they wanted him behind bars to protect me."

"Yes, now I remember. My assistant, of course, informed me of his telephone interview with you. OK, so you're worried that Mr. Mason believes you helped get him locked up and forced into this courtroom.

You're scared he might aim some revenge your way—that he may want some payback and try to hurt you, again. You had to come here today for an upfront view of his legal circumstances and what his fate might be as far as being free to pursue you and what might be done legally to obviate such pursuit. So, synoptically, is that what's going on, Kristi Lou?"

"Well, yes. Yeah, that's it. In a nutshell, I have a concern about Bosco trying to get me. I was thinking he might want to strike back against me, violently, because he might think I turned him in after he jumped me that night a couple of weeks or so ago. But I didn't turn him in. So … I don't know. But, anyway, thanks for talking to me about it."

"No, it's fine. It's OK. I don't think you'll have to worry about Bosco coming after you. He's recognizably unbalanced. Thus, I understand your worries; they're legitimate. But, he's likely going away for a fairly long while. And, he knows you didn't have anything to do with his getting nailed and jailed for his, well, let's just suffice to say his, uh, other activities. He just got caught. He just … he tried to steal the wrong vehicle."

"Yes, I heard about that," replied Kristi Lou.

"You did? What did you hear?"

"Oh, just some scuttlebutt around the neighborhood about this wild car that grabs car thieves and such. It's been on the news, too, as I'm sure you know. It sounds crazy."

"Yeah, but all sorts of rumors can swirl around a community, so …"

"OK. No. I'll just tell you," said Kristi Lou with a spontaneous interruption. "I'm sorry I interrupted. I know all about the car and the van."

"You do?"

"Yes. I know about how they retaliate against car criminals and catch them and humiliate them with pictures taken quickly at the scene showing them being forced to kiss and wearing girls' underwear and other embarrassing, un-macho things, and then also scattering the pictures, copies of the pictures, around the area."

"How do you, uh …? Who told you all that?"

"Straight from the horse's mouth. My old friend from back in Little Rock and her dad—well, as I know you know—or, at least, I presume you know—they are Guinevere and Pete Lindsay. They told me about it, about what they do. Well, mostly Guinevere told me.

"Umm, OK, just so it'll make more sense to you, I'll tell you that Guinevere was my best friend back in Little Rock in the seventh grade and I hadn't seen her since then but they came up here to get car thieves and they knew before they came that I was here and they looked me up and we got together. They even took me on one of their uh, missions. Mr. Lindsay—Pete—is a genius, really. So, well …"

"Keep going," said Susanna. Kristi Lou had procured her full attention.

"Anyhow, they've been doing their work going after car criminals with these technologically advanced vehicles—the car and the van. And, after they'd done this for a few days here in Detroit, in my area where I live and work, they got together with me and we had a great time reminiscing and all that and I rode with them and they told me all about it and showed me all about it and how they're kinda working with local authorities and so forth.

"So, yes, I know about it. But, Mr. Lindsay told me and also Guinevere told me to please not reveal who they are—and not give out details like going on the Internet and posting on blogs and message boards and such. Of course, I won't do those things; I'll treat their identity as a clandestine matter."

"OK. Well, all that is very interesting," said Susanna, as she was evaluating what she had just been told while sizing up Kristi Lou for integrity and trustworthiness.

"You seem like someone who can be trusted to not say the wrong things to the wrong people. You obviously already know everything. But, it's just that cops can be sorta sensitive about anybody else intruding on what they see as their territory, you know? Some of them don't like—as in they feel a bit psychologically threatened, pride-wise—by someone else coming into their area and doing things better. But, your friends are more than effective, so there's been considerable acceptance and cooperation, both ways—especially when the instructions to be cooperative come all the way down from the mayor's office."

"Yes, I know those things and I understand. And yes, I am trustworthy."

As Ms. Willis shuffled through some papers she was carrying in her manila file folder, the thought occurred to Kristi Lou that this might be an ideal time to inform an official within the legal system about the specific details of Bosco's knife attack against her in Secrets. The wound was healing nicely with the antibacterial gel she had been applying, but sometimes it still hurt, especially when she lay on it in bed.

No, your mouth stays shut about that. You told her he attacked you. She didn't respond with any questions. She already knew about it from when you talked to that guy who works for her. And here's the big thing: you didn't press charges when you first had the chance. And you just finished telling her about how you didn't press charges and why you didn't press charges. Keep quiet.

"All right. Well, anyway, as I was telling another D.A. in a different metro county, the way it unfolded is that the police used the pictures showing Bosco Mason attacking the Caravan before the van counterattacked Bosco. He was arrested. We charged him. We had already done the same thing with Franklin Loper. Then we busted the whole ring, all of them. We also got this contemptible hooligan named Red Roofus, believe it or not. It's not R-u-f-u-s—the regular spelling; it's R-o-o-f-u-s. It's spelled that way on his driver's license."

"Yes, Guinevere told me about the Red Roofus guy—that they were able to nab him and everybody else, too."

"Yeah, we raided all those scummy, skeevy places. That one raid on that Saturday—the day after Bosco Mason tried to get the van outside the gym—that was a very profitable raid—very productive. As I was saying, we got all those delinquents. That particular raid yielded the capture of Doofus Roofus—I just took the liberty of altering his epithet a little bit—and the bust of anyone and everyone associated with that chop shop by late that Saturday afternoon. The police worked fast in securing their arrests, as ole Doofus Roofus was more than willing to talk in exchange for the promise of leniency from my office here during what we accented to him would be a very intense prosecution. And we had that conversation with Doofus Roofus with him in his hospital bed, which is where he was because he got whomped over the head by Bosco Mason with a blunt instrument in the chop shop just after they both heard the raid starting. So, you weren't the only one to get blitzed by Bosco that night. Bosco stole Red's wallet and then went into hiding in the attic and waited till the cops left and then elected to grace you with a visit at your club. Superlative citizens, both of them."

Kristi Lou wondered whether Ms. Willis was revealing too much to a layperson she had just met. *I know she believes I already know a lot, but I didn't know this much detail.*

D.A. Willis checked her watch, and then appeared to try to furtively look up and down at Kristi Lou's body, looking uneasily away and then embarrassedly at the mesmerizing blonde's face but not into her eyes.

*Oh. You may have **those** feelings. If so, thanks for the compliment,* thought Kristi Lou, with a stoic expression, as Susanna resumed her remarks.

"Red wants Bosco dead; we keep 'em apart," said D.A. Willis, veering quick glances randomly around the room while trying to conceal her unease over exteriorizing her unforeknown capacity to feel semi-bi titillation. "Anyway, all these guys've got a chance, just like anybody else who gets busted, gets incarcerated, gets punished, you know? We told them, 'Take your punishment, learn your lesson, walk the straight and narrow, stop stealing cars. After you've done your time, you'll have the rest of your life ahead of you. Don't blow it. Keep bettering yourself.'

"Of course, when they get out, they might have trouble finding a job; getting someone to hire them isn't always easy. Most companies do criminal background checks and convictions are gonna hop onto the screen. But ex-cons do sometimes get hired if they're honest about their crimes and the employer is convinced they've mended their ways."

"I know that having a criminal record has ramifications, but I'm glad when they can get an old-fashioned second chance," said Kristi Lou.

"Yes, I am, too. I prosecute them and get them put away. But, with the exception of some of the more vicious slimebags, I like it when I discover later on that they've upgraded themselves and are doing all right.

"But, I'll tell you this: Detroit-area crimes involving motor vehicles are down everywhere you look. Most of the rings operated out of the Drollman district, but they branched out all around the metro area. Now they've just about been put out of business.

"So, all of them we know about are in jail where they belong, awaiting trial. That'll happen for the whole lot of them in November, just like with Bosco. They're going to lose and they're going to prison. I'm naming this November as 'Detroit-Car-Criminals-Go-to-the-Big-House' month.

"I think they're all worried, though, that one of those cars is going to smash through the walls of the correctional facility and snatch 'em up—makes me laugh every time I think of it."

"I hope they'll all be OK," said Kristi Lou.

"That's quite kind of you. Whether or not they'll be OK is up to them. When they get out, they'll find themselves facing the same bifurcated pathways all ex-cons face. Incorrigible? Reformable? Choose your path."

As she listened to the D.A. speak, Kristi Lou was fascinated by the attitudes expressed by this professional woman wielding lawful authority sufficient to alter lives.

Ms. Willis has a combination of sternness and niceness. I couldn't be that stern, which is necessary for her job. I couldn't do what she does. But that's OK.

Upon the completion of their amicable conversation, Kristi Lou felt reassured regarding Bosco. Smiling as she quick-walked to the exit doors amidst gratitude-engendering multiple male gazes, she decamped from the courthouse in a mirthful mood.

64

DESCENDING FROM THE CONCRETE STAIRS ONTO THE SIDE-
walk and into a sun-filled, warm, but not hot, late-summer day, Kristi
Lou, after noting the time was 12:15, smiled at a group of six eight-
year-old-looking kids who were approaching and running playful circles
around an elderly couple who, waving their hands as if to say, "stay
away from the street," appeared to be grandparents trying to keep up
with a horde of effervescent cousins.

Upon squatting to grab someone else's trash—a candy-bar wrapper and a paper soda cup—that had been hugging the curb, and then
disposing of the debris in a metal trash bin, she felt momentarily irate.
I hate litter. Why not just put trash in a trash can where trash belongs?

But, a moment later, she became sanguinely pensive.

Kristi Lou, realizing that she was about to embark upon talking to
herself—orally and audibly—while sauntering along, was conscious of
how passersby who walked toward her might stare and perhaps surmise
that she's a leggy itinerant schizoid, a misidentification she found inwardly
amusing and which launched her into a buoyant escapade.

*Well, these days, they could speculate that maybe I've got earbuds in my
ears: "Is that girl having a phone conversation or is she a looney-tune about
to accost me for money?" But, psycho vagrants aren't normally dressed as*

well as I am today. Oh, until recently, at Secrets, I was an indoor version of a streetwalker, ha-ha. I can make my ambiguity more convincing by being animated with swinging my arms and gesturing. Yeah—let's talk to ourselves!

"Today is August 31. Let's outline what's next. I'll soon resume waitressing at The Potato Place. Classes began this week. I'm going to graduate next year. And then I'm going home. And I'm going to teach in Little Rock. But, as I was saying the other day, I might wind up at Our Lady and I might be one of Mr. Battle's coworkers and that might be just too…don't worry about that, for now, OK? OK. OK—I won't. Tonight, I'm going to Secrets and visit, plus I want to tell Rochelle and everyone what happened in court with Bosco and those other criminals. They'd like to know about that. Then, tomorrow, I'm going to call Guinevere and Marsha and tell them about Bosco. I'll use Skype if they've got their Skype up and running. Then, Mr. Wilmont is going to call me, and we'll talk about his LSD—and whatever else we want to talk about. Then, I'll pick a Sunday in September to go to Mass at Sweetest Heart of Mary. Then, I'm going to call Mom and Dad and tell them…uh, what? No—of course I won't tell them! I won't tell them too much because they might start asking too many questions about why I was in the courtroom for Bosco's trial and how did I ever meet him? And that could lead to…well, they could want to know, uh, they could want to know this and they could want to know that and…so—no. Anyhow, what I did to make all that money was just for a few months and—and what an experience it was. But I'll, I'll tell them all about it someday…maybe."

She looked forward and then to her rear at the busy thoroughfare to check traffic, which was denser and louder, with numerous blaring horns, than she had anticipated before coming to the courthouse. Still walking, talking, and arm-swinging while enjoying sex-laced stares, she moved farther away from the curbside of the congested street, optimistically re-summarizing—more broadly than during her just-completed, original summarization—what she projected as her long-term future.

"So, I've broken away from the wild-side life at Secrets. I'm going to stay in touch with my friends from there as the years go by, including after I get back to Arkansas, especially Mr. Wilmont; I'm not going to fret about Bosco because he's under control; I'm going to get my degree on time; I flew up here to Detroit on a jumbo jet, and next year I'll enplane and fly home—like a bird flying South for the winter, except I plan on staying there for all of my yet-to-be-lived seasons; I'm going to be reunited with Mom and Dad and Aunt Charlene and Guinevere and Marsha; I'm going to go and put flowers on Buster Brown's grave in the backyard and I'll have Mr. Dooflotcher with me and Dooflotch will walk sweetly upon BB's gravestone; I'm going to drive a car for the first time since 2015; I'm going to get help with abating my obsessiveness; I'm going to keep on thinking that sex is mostly a good thing and I won't cease being unfalteringly obdurate in defending men as not being villains because they're attracted to females' bodies; I'm going to meet—or re-meet—some guy and get married one of these days; I'm going to be thankful for my blessings; and I'm going to be happy."

Brimful of esperance, Kristi Lou understood that with her exultant delineation, she had achieved her own personal dénouement.

She continued to perambulate airily. Realizing that her critical fork-in-the-road plans for the next vital chapters of her life had been formulated, she had no immediate plans for this afternoon; she neither had plans to go back to her apartment nor plans to go anywhere in particular. Invigorated within the warm-fuzzies of her beatitude, she just wanted to go—to traipse merrily along the sidewalks. Burdens lifted and feeling exhilaratingly halcyon, Kristi Lou, for now, would go most exuberantly wherever her long legs happened to take the rest of her; she did not know where she was going and she did not care.

She drifted haphazardly past what at first glance appeared to her to be a '60s-style ice cream parlor, with artwork on the window depicting a chocolate sundae resting atop a pink and purple lava lamp. As she walked by the open front door, she heard the jukebox inside begin to blare "Be My Baby," by the Ronettes. She halted in her tracks.

I love that song. Why do I like so many oldish things? Why am I such an archaism? My anemoia overfloweth. Can I get any weirder? You probably can't. OK, am I now answering myself again? Yes, you are. I bumfuzzle myself.

On a lark, Kristi Lou turned back toward Ye Olde Fashioned CowLess Cream Parlor.

Emerald-green lettering, prominent and bright, was affixed to the middle of the door, declaring: "We are proudly 100% vegan! We harm no cows! Come on in! Enjoy our frozen and creamy CowLess Cream!"

"Oh my. Thank you, God—they're vegan! No cow-tit secretions in a cone! All right, I can go guiltlessly in here.

Kristi Lou entered Ye Olde Fashioned CowLess Cream Parlor.

OK, should I—'cause I'm remembering Guinevere's lesson—should I pronounce that y-e word as "yee" or "thee"? Guinevere said it used to be thee. But, after evolving over the years, yee superseded thee. And it starts with a y, not a t. Since Guinevere prefers yee, that preference is for me. So, yee it shall be.

She sidled to the counter and was greeted cordially by a plump 60-something woman wearing an all-white jumpsuit streaked with multi-colored drips and splashes, and who seemed to be either the manager or the owner. Kristi Lou ordered a lactose-free, super-large, pistachio, almond, peanut-butter-and-dark-chocolate, extra-malt MooLess Milkshake. The shake's base ingredient was the parlor's non-dairy version of ice cream, made with cashew milk and Guar Gum Galore—a thickening agent—and delivered to her booth by a latterly turned-fourteen-year-old boy, 12 days into his first-ever job, who was so awestruck at the sight of Kristi Lou that he almost tripped over his Skechers as he approached about two yards from the table. But the shake was so thick that none of it sloshed from the foot-tall glass.

Kristi Lou contemplated the optional strategies available for devouring her prodigious MooLess Milkshake. She determined that she had to use her spoon to eat it more than her straw to drink it, though she expected to utilize both utensils. She attacked her decadent concoction with intemperate wrath, not worrying about appearing unfeminine because of her uber-fast shoveling of thick confection into her mouth. After about five minutes of voracious consumption, which she timed, she looked at the 40-oz. glass and spoke to what remained of her malted shake.

"You are so savory, so sinfully saporific. In honor of Marsha, I should've eaten you in four minutes. But—oh man, what a delectable sugar rush you are! I dub thee King Sucrose. I suppose I should feel guilty about eating you. But I don't. Yum."

Switching to her straw, Kristi Lou sucked up the last drops of liquid and a few granules of un-dissolved malt powder nestled at the bottom of the glass. She made the slurping sound rather loudly. Embarrassed upon realizing her indelicacy and hoping she hadn't been rude, she looked around the parlor to see if anyone was looking at her.

Oh my goodness, did anybody hear that?

She burped.

I hope nobody heard that, either. No, the other folks in here didn't hear my sucking and burping 'cause the music's too loud. Cool. I always say the old saying that 'it's better to urp a burp and bear the shame than squelch a belch and die of pain.'

Another customer had selected a string of Motown songs, specifically from The Temptations, The Four Tops, and The Supremes.

Motown music in Detroit—perfect.

The cozy parlor, situated about 70 yards from the courthouse, was instantly a newfound comfort zone for Kristi Lou. Having completed the undignified glugging of her MooLess Milkshake, she chose to sit still in her booth and gaze jocundly through the window onto the street.

Amongst the miscellaneous pedestrians meandering on the avenue, there appeared Susanna Willis, who stopped and looked through the pane glass storefront as if she were contemplating whether to indulge her cravings with a cold treat. She pulled herself away and walked out of Kristi Lou's sight.

Oh, she decided to not come in here. She mustered the willpower that I didn't even want to try to muster. Perhaps she's on a diet. She doesn't need to be dieting, though. She could work where I used to work. Something tells me she wouldn't want to work where I used to work. Oh well, she won't know what she's missing; I learned a lot there about … myself.

Kristi Lou, having just devoured with gleeful rapacity the largest and thickest shake she had ever known to exist, became abruptly overtaken by a hypnagogic stupor.

I'm so suddenly so sleepy … so really sleepy. Oh, man. Golly, I didn't see this coming. I'm sooo sleepy. I know there's a cornucopia of tryptophan in dairy stuff like ice cream but it's also found in profusion in nuts like these ones here in my MooLess Milkshake … but I also know that, uh, that tryptophan does not, in fact, cause sleepiness. Well, I … I don't actually know that is a fact, but I do know it's a fact that some scientists claim that that's a fact … that it doesn't … doesn't cause drooziness … uh, drowsiness. But, other science people say tryptophan does cause it. Who's right? I dunno. That's one more thing I don't know, among lots of schlangs … things. Are you babbling and rambling to yourself? Yes, you are. Why? 'Cause that's what you do.

Kristi Lou, after noticing that she had begun to slur the wording of her thoughts, continued unabated to ramble inwardly. While further divesting herself of stress, she felt amused toward herself upon realizing that some of her verbiage during her mental phonations was muddled and imperfectly enunciated. But, despite the blithering, she was aware of a paradoxically heightened sense of probable philosophical verity, which she related in an ontological way to her emergent young-adult life.

OMG. Something just occurred to me, epistemologically. The older I get and the more I know, the more I know there will always be more I don't know than I do know. And, part of being bright is knowing what you're dull at.

Kristi Lou felt compelled to analyze her bodily composition, thinking she was the sum of disparate but interdependent fragments, but that her synergic wholeness was a holistically greater entity than this summation. She sat still. She evaluated her interior mechanisms and her outer body parts, achieving an illusion of being somehow detached from herself, thus enabling herself to objectively observe herself.

She noted that her eyes looked beneath the tabletop to see what her feet were doing. *You eyes are nosy.*

Her shoulders, she thought, allowed her arms to be attached to the sides of her chest. *Way to go, shoulders. You guys—wait, I'm a girl—you gals are both stalwarts.*

She saw that her knees consolidated a union between her thighs and her calves. *Thank you, mighty patella et al. in that region; you hold everything leg-wise together.*

Then, she realized that her brain chose to command her kneecaps to knock together several times in an effort to keep her entire self awake, a ploy that worked well enough to temporarily revive her alertness.

OK, brain, you're in charge. At least I'm normal in that regard; the brain is the boss. The brain is integral to the unified functionality of the other body parts and should be their boss, right? Yeah, right—that's right. But, wait a moment! When the brain—my brain or anyone else's brain—becomes destructive or goes rogue or is somehow treacherously harmful, who or what defies a despotic brain? When a brain says, "Let's rob a bank!" who says, "No!" to brain? I doubt my toenails are going to tell my brain to stop doing anything, such as obsessing like a fruitcake. Do fruitcakes obsess? Don't be so overly literal. Anyhow, how 'bout you, earlobes? Or elbows? Who can step up and get brain to do right? Any organs? Heart? Lungs? Kidneys? What about you, ass? Guys really like you; but—no pun intended and besides that would be b-u-t-t—can you get up off yourself and deal with brain? Such an insurgency performed by any of you could be construed as an attempted coup by corybantic insurrectionists to oust brain from her or his autocracy.

Therefore, all of you ordinarily servile anatomical peons might need to organize and combine forces if you're gonna succeed with usurping the absolute power of almighty Boss Brain. Such insubordination—like in a revolution—might be sometimes justified to... well... not overthrow, but to just get brain to behave. Can y'all do that? No—don't anybody answer—or don't any body part answer. OK. Now I'm somewhat scared, 'cause if I believe I hear even the slightest answer from a body part—like if I think one of my boobs is talking to me—I'll know that I might be completely losing it. But then, what constitutes me? My left boob or my right boob is just as much a part of me as any other part. I think this is my brain coming on again, as in my brain is claiming central headquarters status and... stop, stop, just stop, Kristi Lou! Seek help. When you get back home, see if Dr. Carlisle is still available. He'll remember you. You can tell him you're no longer obsessed with the perils of tallness but you're just obsessed with, with... with things you're obsessed with. Ohhhhhhh, I'm sooooooo ... ferdutzt.

But, on the other hand, golly, it's not really that bad; you're ... lonely. So, you overly interact with yourself and get confused. Guinevere and Marsha are just a year or so away, so chill on it. OK, now I feel good again. Cool.

She was endued with a realization that she was peering not only obsessively but also frenziedly into herself, flitting seamlessly from light-hearted matters to those with solemnity, with no control over where her thoughts stopped. Feeling zestfully safe in her present dessert-haven environment, she was conflicted as to whether to break her free fall.

Realizing that her brain had discontinued its orders for knee-knocking and had not implemented any other strategies to sustain her momentary alertness, Kristi Lou gladly greeted the return of her inertia.

So, I'm really sleepy because of... I'm just sleepy. I'm a sleepyhead. But maybe it's the milkslake ... the milkspake ... say it right, please—the milkshake ... OK, the MooLess Milkshake is perhaps what's so sopo ... sopo ... sopo ... soporific. Maybe the uh, the effect of the nut-filled shake combined with finally getting some, uh, some clarity about, uh, what I'm going to do and…I just feel all that stress draining out of me like a stopper has been pulled from a full bathtub of murky water and it's streaming away all at once and it's replaced by…it caused a vacuum filled by…by this most soothing exhaustion. I'm high. Is this like being high on marijuana? I dunno. If they don't throw me out of here, which I doubt they will, I'm just gonna stay put awhile to rest and digest. I think I'm high on MooLess Milkshake.

She began to feel evermore pleasantly dizzy, almost as if she were experiencing a gentle infusion of clement vertigo.

You're really being a goofy girl; you know that, don't you? What? How dare you say that about you and I and myself and me. We resemble that remark.

Kristi Lou, with a slight grin creasing her lips, looked around to learn whether any people—amidst the loud music and huge barrels of simulated ice cream covered by see-through glass—were observing her, and, if so, whether they might have facial expressions indicating they sensed she was internally conversing with herself.

I don't shink…I don't think anybody's thinking about my thoughts. Nobody's spaying me any attention…wait…spaying me? I hope nobody's spaying me 'cause I'd like to have children someday. Wake up. Nobody is paying me any attention; there aren't any men in here. Well, that boy who brought my shake over here is trying to not let me see him seeing me.

Kristi Lou then looked below her chin at the edge of her booth table, affixing upon it a firm, blissful stare. At that very instant, she unawarely shifted her 44-inch lower limbs—creating a two-seconds-long, unintended four-inch split—toward the CowLess Cream ordering counter, behind which the bewitched boy, with hormones surging, had been sneaking peeks at Kristi Lou's anatomy while wiping down the countertop. Her moderately conservative Amherst gray dress, though not tight, had nonetheless crept up about half a foot above her knees. The unexpected, sudden sight of almost all of Kristi Lou's curvaceously sculpted inner thighs, opening like a long and endless wet-dream tunnel before his eager eyes, illuminated by dessert-parlor festive lighting, was too much for the nether regions of the skeletally underweight, eyeglasses-wearing, red-headed, acne-laden, unworldly lad to manage. His face contorted as he stared downward at the crotch area of his light-colored khakis while trying in vain to not lose his load.

A short and slender, freckle-faced, elfin teenage-girl coworker of the same age had been observing his observations of Kristi Lou and was standing about four feet to his side. She glanced at his pants.

"Yuck! Eww! Gross! YEG! YEG! YEG!" she snickered, followed by a loud giggle as she placed her hands over her face and spun around, laughing through her fingers.

"Shut up!" commanded the bashful boy, with a beneath-his-breath bellow, hoping the Motown music still playing loudly throughout the parlor had boomed out volume sufficient to preclude Kristi Lou from hearing the humiliating exchange between him and his amused, schadenfreude-practicing colleague.

The condolatory 60-whatever manager, who likewise had been aware of the boy's carnal infatuation with Kristi Lou, immediately ascertained the complexities. She walked over to him and spoke with a knowing, supportive smile.

"Hey, it's OK—not a biggie. You're at that time of life. Don't worry; as you get older, you'll get more control. And she's lovelier than a sunset. Just go to the restroom and moisten a few paper towels in the sink and clean yourself up. Dab some water on that spot. It'll dry before you know it."

Mortified to the apogee, off he quickly went, not daring to look at Kristi Lou and hoping she didn't know of his calamitous climax—which she did not.

Kristi Lou, quite drowsy, was entirely oblivious to the occurrence of yet another of her improbable coincidences—she thought of the boy and then a mere moment later inadvertently caused him to explode—and to a right-next-to-her, real-life enactment of the ofttimes dramatic insecurities of adolescence, which she had unwittingly triggered and from which she herself was only a few years removed. During the unbeknownst-to-her hullabaloo incited by her unlatched legs, her interior musings had continued, unabated, shepherding her into a liberating coda.

But, anyhow, as I sometimes tell myself, one of these days I'll conceivably maybe tell Mom and Dad about my goings-on here this year... maybe... when I'm a lot bolder, I mean older... or maybe older and bolder... I just might do it. I shall definitely quite possibly maybe tell them. Am I being dilatorily indecisive? I might be. I'll decide later about my decisiveness... maybe. Que sera sera.

Kristi Lou peeled away one of the neatly folded serviettes from the pewter napkin holder and dabbed up a spill of MooLess Milkshake next to her on the red, vinyl-covered seat. She removed a $10 bill from her purse for the hormonally smitten waiter's tip on a $5.37 tab, securing the greenback under the earthenware saucer.

She felt a surge of semi-sharp alertness, which she sensed was temporal and would soon yield to a return of idyllic wooziness.

Anyway, irrespective of my mixed emotions about coming clean, I indeed perchance will tell Dad and Mom about my walk on the sex side. Maybe I should word that differently. I'll tell my parents when it's time, at the proper time, contingent upon that time arriving. I just might maybe tell them all about it. That's a rock-solid possibility. Yes, I resolutely will perhaps tell them. Oh, I again used different words to say what I'd just finished saying. It's OK.

Something is reminding me of a thing I once read somewhere—one of the kinder wishes you can wish for parents as they grow older is this: "May you forever have the gratitude of your children." My beloved mother and father will always have mine.

Ooh... I feel contentedly snoozy again.

Kristi Lou, now teetering on the threshold of falling asleep in a dairy-cream-less ice cream parlor, gazed through a nebula of enchanting grogginess at her Amazonian, underwear-model legs compacted snugly but loosely underneath the table and spoke aloud, smiling confidently, as if downwardly addressing the supernal firmament.

"I may not always know how to be decisive, but I am grateful to God that I know how to be tall."

Epilogue

Ten Months Later, Sunday, June 30, 2019, Circling for a Landing

"**HEY DOOFLOTCH! LOOK! LITTLE ROCK, HERE WE COME! THERE** she is, looking up at us. Ain't she bootiful? Hallelujah! You've enjoyed flying first class, haven't you? Yep, you got special permission from the airline to ride with me—influenced a weensy mite by my offer to pay a fat fee. I'm holding your cat carrier up so we can look together at the hairline of my hometown—and now your home, too, Dooflotch. You're gonna love it! Mom and Dad and Aunt Charlene and Guinevere and Marsha and—oh my god!—perhaps even Mr. Battle and, and, and I heard tell maybe David Darnell, 'cause Guinevere said on the phone that David might be … David, oh golly. They're all gonna be waiting for us at the airport. And, Dooflotch, we're all set, monetarily. I waitressed again at The Potato Place, plus all that rich-girl cash from, uh, last sum-mer stayed in our Bank of America savings in Detroit, and it'll all be available here since B of A has bunches of branches around Little Rock. Please remind me: I've gotta open a checking account, and, most vitally, I mustn't let Dad and Mom know I might have more money than they have 'cause, er … As you're aware, I chose to not return for Christmas because of the, uh, timeish proximity of 2018 Yuletide to what I'd been, you know, doing and … uh, well … I'm twenty-two and, umm, I've been celibate since last August. Anyway—it's been four years! I'm so excited! I feel like singing the Pointer Sisters' song! I've got my teaching degree and the contact info for the friends I made as a senior at WSU and for my Secrets people, especially Davey and Rochelle and Hokey and Dan and Denny and Francois and Satine and my knight-in-shining-armor mentor, Mr. Winston Wilmont III, who sat next to me every Sunday the past seven months at Sweetest Heart of Mary where he'll keep right on fellowshipping with his churchmates. Thankfully, he now goes to therapy. And … Mr. Wilmont put me in his Will; God bless him. And Dooflotch, there was that night I took you with me on one of my sextillions of visits at the club, from which Dan usually drove me home, and Satine snapped a pic of you with the crew and I came back the next week and they'd enlarged it and framed it and hung it on the main wall beside the great-big cuckoo clock where Big Sam said it'll stay through-out eternity and they put under the bottom of the picture frame that engraved plaque designating you as 'Mr. Dooflotcher, Cathouse Cat.' Ha-ha-ha. Oh my goodness, that's so enduringly cool. I've got a picture of that picturesque tableau as well as pictures of *every*body. Oh, looky there—there's my school! It's Our Lady of Mercy, where I went; I told you about it, remember? I've gotta pause to soak it in. Oh wow, oh wow, oh wow … jeez … and, oh wow again, in honor of quad-girl Marsha. After we get on the ground, I'll tell her I did that fourth wow exclusively for her. I'm so overjoyed my vulva is tingling. What'd you say, Dooflotch? TMI? Sorry. You know what, Dooflotch? As I'm staring down at my old schoolhouse while I'm awash with euphoria, I think that if I could open this window and somehow hang myself safely outside, I possibly might maybe be just about almost longitudinal enough to extend these won-derfully sexualized, elongated legs and toe-touch the roof above my old homeroom. And, I am selfesteemingly fine with that. Selfesteemingly? I adore adverbs, even made-up ones. Yes, selfesteemingly."

About the Author

BLESSED WITH PERFECT PARENTS, MICHAEL P. CAMERON grew up in Georgia, South Carolina, and Alabama. His professional background as a copyeditor/proofreader has provided him with the ego-fulfilling joy of correcting other people's mistakes, a wretched schadenfreude whose existence he has tried to hide. He hates the smell of cooked rutabagas but loves cats and football while embracing other disparate combinations. Michael's personal history includes what were sometimes desperate bouts with clinical depression, low self-esteem, and obsession, particularly OCD. He has, in recent years, significantly subdued these oppressive demons. He believes that life, with its dolor but with its rhapsody, is a fleeting gift and well worth living.